Collected Stories

COLLECTED
STORIES

R. V. Cassill

THE UNIVERSITY OF ARKANSAS PRESS
Fayetteville   1989   London

Copyright © 1989 by R. V. Cassill
All rights reserved
Manufactured in the United States of America

93 92 91 90 89   5 4 3 2 1

Designer: B. J. Zodrow
Typeface: Linotron 202 Palatino
Typesetter: G&S Typesetters, Inc.
Printer: Edwards Brothers, Inc.
Binder: Edwards Brothers, Inc.

The paper used in this publication meets the minimum requirements of the American National Standard for Permanence of Paper for Printed Library Materials Z39.48-1984. ∞

LIBRARY OF CONGRESS CATALOGING-IN-PUBLICATION DATA

Cassill, R. V. (Ronald Verlin), 1919–
  [Short stories. Selections]
  Collected stories / by R. V. Cassill.
    p.   cm.
  ISBN 1-55728-070-3 (alk. paper). ISBN 1-55728-071-1 (pbk. : alk. paper)
  I. Title.
PS3553.A796A6 1989
813'.54—dc19   88-28614
                                                                     CIP

Contents

Acknowledgments

"The Goldfish," from *15x3, Fifteen Short Stories by R. V. Cassill, Herbert Gold, James B. Hall*, published by New Directions, New York. Copyright © 1953, 1985. Reprinted by permission of the author.

"And in My Heart," reprinted by permission of the author. Copyright © 1965. Originally published in *The Paris Review*, #33, Winter-Spring 1965.

"Fragments for Reference," reprinted by permission of the author. Copyright © 1947, 1975. Originally published in *Accent*, Fall 1947.

"The War in the Air," reprinted by permission of the author. Copyright © 1952, 1980. Originally published in *Epoch*, Summer 1952.

"Convoy Sunday Morning," reprinted by permission of the author. Copyright © 1949, 1980. Originally published in *Perspective*, vol. 2, no. 3.

"The Outer Island," reprinted by permission of the author. Copyright © 1949, 1980. Originally published in *Accent*, vol. IX, no. 2.

"The Swimmers at Pallikula," reprinted by permission of the author. Copyright © 1955, 1983. Originally published in *Discovery*, vol. 6, no. 6.

"The Happy Marriage," reprinted by permission of the author. Copyright © 1955, 1983. Originally published in *Kansas Magazine*, Issue 1956.

"Love? Squalor?," from *The Father and Other Stories*, by R. V. Cassill, published by Simon and Schuster, New York. Copyright © 1965. Reprinted by permission of the author.

"When Old Age Shall This Generation Waste," reprinted by permission of the author. Copyright © 1955, 1983. Originally published in *Epoch*, vol. II, no. 1, Fall 1955.

"The Invention of the Airplane," reprinted by permission of the author. Copyright © 1970. Originally published in *Seneca Review*, vol. 1, no. 1, May 1970.

"Fracture," reprinted by permission of the author. Copyright © 1952, 1980. Originally published by *Epoch*, vol. IV, no. 1, Winter 1952.

"The Inland Years," reprinted by permission of the author. Copyright © 1954, 1982. Originally published in *Western Review* vol. 18, no. 3, Spring 1954.

"This Hand, These Talons," reprinted by permission of the author. Copyright © 1951, 1979. Originally published in *Western Review* vol. 16, no. 1, Autumn 1951.

"The Crime of Mary Lynn Yager," from *The Happy Marriage and Other Stories*, by R. V. Cassill, published by Purdue University Press. Copyright © 1966. Reprinted with permission of Purdue Research Foundation, West Lafayette, IN 47907. All rights reserved.

"The Suicide's Cat," reprinted by permission of the author. Copyright © 1981. Originally published in *December*, vol. 23, nos. 1/2, 1981, a double issue of *December* magazine, by December Press.

"The Pursuit of Happiness," reprinted by permission of the author. Copyright © 1957, 1986. Originally published in *Northwest Review*, vol. 1, no. 2.

"The Black Horse," reprinted by permission of the author. Copyright © 1951, 1979. Originally published in *Furioso*, vol. VI, no. 3, Summer 1951.

"A Journey of the Magi," reprinted by permission of the author. Copyright © 1958, 1986. Originally published in *Texas Quarterly*, vol. 1, no. 3, Summer/Autumn 1958.

"The Hot Girl," reprinted by permission of the author. Copyright © 1955, 1983. Originally published in *New Directions* 15.

"My Brother, Wilbur," reprinted by permission of the author. Copyright © 1965. Originally published in *Northwest Review*, vol. 7, no. 1, Spring/Summer 1965.

"Frost and Sun," reprinted by permission of the author. Copyright © 1960, 1988. Originally published in *The Dial* #3.

"The Squeaky Wheel," reprinted by permission of the author. Copyright © 1957, 1985. Originally published in *Epoch*, vol. VIII, no. 3, Fall 1957.

"The Waiting Room," reprinted by permission of the author. Copyright © 1951, 1979. Originally published in *Perspective*, vol. 4, no. 4, Autumn 1951.

"The Winchester Papers," reprinted by permission of the author. Copyright © 1960, 1988. Originally published in *Northwest Review*, vol. 3, no. 2, Spring 1960.

"The First Day of School," reprinted by permission of the author. Copyright © 1958, 1986. Originally published in *Northwest Review*, vol. II, no. 1, Fall/Winter 1958.

"The Romanticizing of Dr. Fless," reprinted by permission of the author. Copyright © 1956, 1984. Originally published in *New World Writing*, 9th Mentor Selection, by The New American Library of World Literature, Inc.

"The Martyr," reprinted by permission of the author. Copyright © 1979. Originally published in *Ploughshares*, vol. 5, no. 4, 1980.

"The Knight and the Hag," reprinted by permission of the author. Copyright © 1958, 1986. Originally published in *Dude*, vol. 2, no. 5, May 1958.

"Shadow of a Magnitude," reprinted by permission of the author. Copyright © 1956, 1984. Originally published in *University of Kansas City Review*, vol. XXIII, no. 2, Winter 1956.

"The Father," reprinted by permission of the author. Copyright © 1962. Originally published in *Esquire*, June 1962.

"Where Saturn Keeps the Years," reprinted by permission of the author. Copyright © 1978. Originally published in *The Missouri Review*, vol. 1, no. 1, Spring 1978.

Collected Stories

Larchmoor
Is Not
the World

In the winter the glassed arcade between Thornton and Gillespie Halls was filled with potted flowers so it smelled and looked like a greenhouse. Last night's storm, blowing in across the athletic fields of the Northwest campus, had left a shape of frozen snow like a white boomerang in the corner of each pane behind the rows of geraniums and ferns.

The first time Dr. Cameron walked through the arcade on this particular day, he stopped to point with his pipestem at the ranked greenery so slightly and perilously separated from the outside cold. "There," he rumbled to Mr. Wilks of History, "is your symbol for this young women's seminary. There is your Larchmoor girl cut off by a pane of glass from the blast of your elements. A visible defiance of the nature of things, made possible by a corrupt technology."

Mr. Wilks grimaced and chuckled, weighed this illustration of their common attitude toward the college in which they taught, finally amended, "The glass is wrong. Glass they could see through. See the world in which they don't live, even though . . ." His thought trailed off in a giggle. At Larchmoor, Mr. Wilks seemed to spend most of his energy looking behind him to see if he had been overheard.

"True," Dr. Cameron said. As they loitered through the arcade the music and the rumble of the student lounge rose to them from the floor below. It rose, mixed inextricably with the smell of baked goods from the dining hall and the moist smell of steam from laboring radiators. Now and then a cry, barbaric, probably happy but otherwise meaningless, punctuated the noise. "The analogy breaks down, true. Listen to them down there. One gets to be like an animal trainer. Sensitive to their noises. If I had no calendar I could tell by their tone that Christmas vacation started this afternoon."

"Then there's an identifying noise that distinguishes Christmas vacation from the beginning of—say—spring vacation?"

"Hmm. Yes, that's right. In seven years my ear has become acutely attuned to it. You'll pick it up eventually. Unhappily, in learning their mass sound you'll become unable to distinguish one of them from the others. Compensation at work. They will seem to you one single enormous female juvenile named Shirley or whatever the name would happen to be of the child movie star ascendant in the year of their birth." Dr. Cameron's baby-pink face grew almost radiant. "Tomorrow," he said, "the sons of bitches will all be gone home and we'll have three weeks of peace. Shantih."

The second time he went through the arcade that day he met Sandra White, dressed for her journey with high heels now and a fur coat, looking like the ads in the fashion magazines with the good sharp empty Nordic shape of her head an appurtenance to the excellent clothes—looking five years older than she had looked that morning in his American Literature class. Her manner, too, had been changed with her clothes, so that she spoke to him as a young matron patronizing an old and crotchety, really lovable duck who had "made his lah-eef out of literature."

"Dr. Cameron. Thank *you* for the list of books," she said. "I don't think I'll give any presents this Christmas except books and I . . ." Yet because this was so obviously a statement coined to please him, both became momentarily embarrassed. It was the girl who first recovered and went on, "I think I'll get Daddy the Dos Passos' *USA*."

"Hmmm." He chewed his pipestem and stared at the glass roof of the arcade, then smiled.

"Well," she said in defense, "Daddy is really searching . . . for . . . *that* kind of Americanism. He's not just a businessman. He's really—"

"Yes," he said. "I understand you to say you wanted this list of books for yourself, not just for presents."

"Oh. I'm going to ask for the Yeats for myself," she said. Her tone, demanding that this would please him, produced from the efficient catalog of his memory the image of her eyes becoming feminine-dramatic in that class hour a week before when he had quoted, "An aged man is but a paltry thing . . . unless soul clap its hands and sing and louder sing for every tatter in its mortal dress." Well, the quotation had been an indulgence for him and not intended for the class at all. It had been a parade before their innocent minds of a conscious expression of his own dilemma. He had spoken the lines to his class with the motives that lead a man to confess to his dog the sentiments for which he has no human confidant. But this little female, Sandra, whatever those words may have meant to her, had caught something of their importance to him and trapped him now into paying for the indulgence with a compliment to her taste.

"Fine," he said, "that's fine."

With a still doubtful look she said, "Merry Christmas," and let him go on to his office.

Here was the sanctuary which he had been seven years in building. A desk barred off one corner of the room. When students came in he sat behind it like a magistrate at the bar. Three walls, excepting door and window spaces, were lined to the ceiling with books. "I bought them," he once told Wilks, "but only for insulation and display. It's fatuous to assume that anybody can own books. I think that President Herman is pleased to find them there when he brings down parents and the prospective customers to exhibit me as a mechanism of the English department."

His swivel chair took most of the space behind the desk. It made of the corner an efficient nest, for he could swing to any of the cabinets and drawers in which he filed themes. Also within reach were the two material items he needed for his intellectual life. One was a bolt tied on a length of wrapping cord that he sometimes swung as a pendulum. The other was a motto that he had lettered painstakingly on colored paper. Originally it had come from an examination paper handed in to him during his first year at Larchmoor. "Shelley's main purpose was to write a lot of poems," it said. "This it came easy for him to do." Sometimes, when he was alone, he would place the inscription before him on his desk and sit laughing crazily at it until all the stains of teaching at Larchmoor were washed away. Then purified, without moving except to throw his shoulders back, he would watch that fraction of the campus where the pendulum of seasons appeared before his window.

This afternoon, the sunlight was a strange and clamorous orange that moved on the black tree trunks and the snow. Here nature dramatized the quality of a Beckmann painting—*Black Cedars over Water*, it might have been, or such a landscape as the horns in Sibelius presented with not so much art as longing, such a landscape as might contain a golden mute princess called out by Death, that central myth that all the Romantics had exploited.

The embroidered, death-bidden, golden will-o'-the-wisp (and Sandra White now drifted on his mind's screen in a role that would have surprised her. Not as an intellect that shared his understanding of poetry but, wrapped in a rich cocoon of fur, wool, and silk that protected her delicacies from the blowing cold, as the image itself which the poets had conceived and desired—the figure on the Grecian urn, the witchlady on the mead, or that which Malraux's Dutchman saw on the Shanghai sidewalks, proud and strutting beyond the reach of the proletariat's desire), like Shelley's Beatrice, must be the fairest, youngest, purest of flesh to satisfy the snowy mouth of the Death the Romantics had imagined.

The peacefulness of snow is pure commercial folklore, he speculated, and in art the cold North always somehow emerges as the symbol of hungry frenzy—like the gelid and perfect tyranny which Plato described as the worst disaster of all that society can manage. The disorder of cold which had wrought the counter disorder of Northern art—the wind-whipped fires in the snowfield—with its load of desire protesting too much.

If Dr. Cameron had moved closer to his window, he would

necessarily have seen more than this private landscape of a few trees, snow, and sun in which his mind pursued the lost girl. He would have seen more than twenty Larchmoor girls standing in the slush in front of the Kampus Kabin while they waited for taxis. They bounced, giggled, sang ("a woman, a woman, a woman without a man, teedlededum, bumph"), chewed gum, shifted packages or suitcases from hand to hand, stamped their fur-topped boots in the muck of the road. He knew they were there, not five degrees outside the arc of vision which the window gave him. "But I have the right not to look."

With the arrival of each Christmas vacation since he had come to Larchmoor, he had discovered himself confronted with a particular crisis of fatigue and depression. The beginning of yet another school year and the first exacting months hollowed him emotionally, and the pleasures of intellect had lost their recreational power. While the girls went off to whatever indulgences the society provided for its most expensive and pampered stock, he went to his bachelor rooms to read and smoke incessantly and consider how he might get a job elsewhere until always, with the passing of the actual and figurative solstice, the change of renewal occurred. What was compounded of hatred and contempt for Larchmoor led him first to review the other places he had taught—the two big universities where the younger assistants whinnied like mares around the head of the department, and the religious college where he had been forbidden to smoke on campus and was required to attend chapel daily— then led through a couple of drinking bouts with some one of his friends, like Mr. Wilks. There had always been younger men like Mr. Wilks coming and going as Larchmoor instructors. Just out of graduate school, they regarded Larchmoor as a stepping stone to bigger schools, but while they stayed—one or two each year succeeding those who had gone—they formed a fit audience though few for such occasions as the Christmas drunks. Those times gave him the chance to elaborate with perverse brilliance on the attractions Larchmoor had for him.

They would be sitting in the easy chairs of his rooms with a litter of crackers and cheese on a card table between them, the black windows frosting over, and in the late hours the monologue would pause only when one or another went unsteadily to the bathroom. "Do you remember reading about that Jap general on Iwo Jima . . . said, 'I will die here' . . . the component of all

the forces of his life . . . so that even the melodrama was right
for the bandy-legged little bastard. Fitting. The answer is a kind
of balance—not balance—but that second in the pendulum's
swing when all the forces are composed so there must be an instant of harmony that the eye isn't quick enough to catch when
one reasons that there must be no motion. Still . . . the effort of
the mind to perpetuate that second by selection out of all the
comic and vicious flux in us and around us is the same as the
slave's impulse to throw off his ropes. . . . Larchmoor locks up
kids that should be out and doing things. Their bad luck is good
for me. There are different ages, and for me freedom doesn't
exist in the world. It's an asylum growth. . . . I've got my office
for asylum like a rat's nest in the corner of a busy house. I
don't huddle there because I'm interested in the house. Nobody
but a damn fool would be concerned with Larchmoor as Larchmoor. . . . It gives me a stable place to sit and watch the 'pis-
mires'"—here he smiled—"'and the stars.' And don't you know,
Wilks, that a man has to actually utter his ideas? Your gloomy
newspapers tell you that. It's such an undeniable premise of
the search for freedom. Here I can say whatever I please to my
classes. Elsewhere, in these days, I might be quickly appre-
hended as a Communist or an atheist, but when I say something
to my girls they put it in their notebooks and there's an end to it.
Oh, I have my disguises here. On another level I can talk to the
vermin Herman"—Larchmoor's president—"the same way. As
far as that goes. When he asked me what I thought of the new
dormitory with the air-conditioned bedsprings, I made some
trivial remark about painting 'our outward walls so costly gay.'
And he thought it was my stamp of approval, yes he did. . . .
And then we mustn't fool ourselves. Where else could I go? I'm
not a scholar in the sense that I've ever felt a mission to get my
name in *PMLA*, or write a book on Chaucer's cook's marmal. I'm
a reader, that's all I amount to. 'Whatever games are played with
us, we must play no games with ourselves, but deal in our privacy with the last honesty and truth.' Larchmoor not only lets
but forces me to be honest with myself. The games it plays with
me are not much bother. To them I'm just an old gaffer that talks
like Bartlett's quotations. I have a place here. They pay me as a
fixture. . . . The girls are pretty. Like old David's, my bones
need the warmth provided by a moderate proximity of young female flesh. My disguises . . . I look too old to notice them. I *am*

too old to letch for any of them, but by God they're pleasant furniture. . . . At Larchmoor I come close to balancing. If it were
any better I'd get involved with it. No doubt I've searched sub-
consciously for Larchmoor all my life. I'm preoccupied with how
I die. Like the Jap general. That isn't morbid at my age. More
natural. I want to die in this moral Iwo Jima . . . and be buried
under the hockey field."

He had put on his overcoat to go home when he passed
through the glassed arcade for the third time that day. This time
a clatter of heels on the tile floor rang behind him. There was a
hand on his arm and Shirley Bridges' face suddenly thrust so
close to his own that he jumped back. At first, the circles of
white around her eyes and the chalky stripes on either side of
her mouth struck him as an antic fashion culled from the pages
of *Vogue* and destined to become a part of the fluctuating uniform of Larchmoor. But even as he began to smile, her hand
clawed down his sleeve until she had hold of his bare wrist and
he understood that her face was marked with some girlish emotion. Her hand on his wrist was wet and cold. He felt pain in the
back of his skull and then a release of anger. "What's the trouble,
Miss Bridges?" He lifted her fingers one at a time from their hysterical grasp. "Are you ill?"

To his exasperation she said, "No. My grade. You—"

"I understand," he said. He cleared his throat the better to
snarl. "In spite of your studious industry, I, I, I have so seriously
misprized you that I reported you to the Dean, who maliciously
put you on academic probation. Now you're going to be forbidden the delights of the jukebox and the downtown dance hall for
the rest of the semester." The tonic of anger had blurred away
any distinctions he might have tried to make between her and
The Larchmoor Girl in a more temperate season. "Every coer-
cion will be applied to force you to the unreasonable humiliation
of reading your books. I am committed to the belief that you will
live through it. Now, if you will excuse me, may I bid you a
Merry Christmas?"

"Please," she said. In the blue expanse of her eyes the pupil
diminished nastily like an insect pulling its wings to its body.

He felt the burning of his face. She'd better not put her hands
on me again, he thought. "Don't take all this so intensely. There
really isn't any reason you can't make up your work. Weren't

you the one last fall who was, well—so sublimely confident of her ability? You sometimes make interesting comments in class. I think you just need to decide to do some work."

"No," she said. "Talk to me." Her mouth hung loose like a bright ribbon, and her tongue arched against her lower teeth.

"You're *not* well."

She nodded. "Talk to me in your office. Please."

One hall on their way led past the president's office and reception rooms. She would not go this way. Without quite knowing why, he let her guide him down a roundabout stairway.

While he lit his pipe and rocked squeaking in his swivel chair, he looked at the girl's hands. The lacquered nails were broader than they were long and the fingers were tapered like a child's from the palm. How do they manage to look like *women?* he asked himself. What corruption and tampering with mortality in the flesh is it that lets them or makes them look generally the same from fifteen to thirty-five, brushed and painted and girdled to a formula that here across his desk was breaking down into its sodden components? He noted that two beads of spittle had stuck in the corners of Shirley's mouth.

What would be the effect, he wondered, if he should announce at once that he had reconsidered her case and had already decided to give her an A for the semester?

"You restore my faith," he said. "In seven years of teaching here I have never seen a Larchmoor girl who spent the day before a vacation even thinking about the college, let alone the grades she might get in one class in Biblical Literature."

"They're going to kick me out," she said.

"Oh nonsense. No final grades go in for six weeks yet."

"They are," she insisted. "They sent for Daddy. He's in President Herman's office now. I know they sent for him to take me out of school."

"Because of your grades? Not because of your grades, surely."

"Oh. I thought if I could get my grades straightened out that would help."

"You mean you've got in some kind of trouble. If your grades were good you might get by with it?"

The note of sarcasm was heavy enough to warn her of a trap. She said, "No. I don't think there would be any trouble if my grades were all right. I could work everything else out, I know."

"If you're in difficulty you ought to have gone to your house-mother, not to me."

"Honest, it's the grades and my classes and things."

Dr. Cameron shook his head. His white mustache dipped at the ends as he made a face. "I'm guilty of many things, but I have never given any grades I didn't think were deserved; so there isn't much use to talk about that. Nevertheless I might tell you something that will reassure you. Among other things Larchmoor is a commercial institution. I have even heard President Herman speak of it as a business. You pay a considerable tuition here which would have to be refunded if you were dropped before the end of the semester. I have no doubt that the administration will find some way to avoid that unpleasant necessity." This will end the interview, he thought. She can understand that better than anything. Coin is the sea that bore them hither and will bear them hence. It is the direct communication, the basis of knowledge on which whatever they might get from the library or classroom would only be fluff. "Does that explain exactly why they aren't going to kick you out?"

"It isn't that way, is it?"

He grinned like a devil. "Undoubtedly." Less because she demanded it than because of the habit of explanation he went on, "There's much more to it than that. I have simply given you a short cut to understanding why you won't be expelled. From your side of the fence everything seems to be an absolute. Every rule, every pronouncement, perhaps. I'm old enough to know there are no absolutes. Everyone here who has anything to do with your case lives in a tangle of confusions and opinions not so different from your own. Out of these will come some compromise that won't be too hard on you. That's the truth. That's the way the world goes. Compromise, compromise. President Herman's decrees and judgments may seem absolute and final to a freshman. They're not, really. He's not God Almighty."

"They're all God Almighty," the girl said. "My father is God Almighty too." He was not sure whether she meant this as a joke or as an attempt at philosophy, but whichever it was it seemed to amuse her. "That's why it's so goofy. They say I destroyed their faith. Didn't you hear about that, Dr. Cameron? It happened in your Biblical Lit class so I guess you knew about it. It's so funny because I think there is God Almighty. Lots of them.

You're another one, because remember at the first of the year you told us to use our minds and question things, and then I was the only one that argued, and you're going to give me an F."

"You haven't handed in any work," he said irrelevantly. He turned the swivel chair sharply sideways so the old bearings screamed. So the other little ones had sat in class all semester being careful to hear nothing, read nothing before their open eyes except what confirmed those memories of Sunday school they liked to call "their faith." All right. He had known that and had remarked on it caustically. But here was the other twist—that they were leagued, each little monster with her shining braids, to smell out differences within the herd which had not been apparent to him. He labored his memory for images of the class from which this one girl would appear standing like a martyr among the Philistian mob. She said that she had "argued." He could remember nothing of the sort. Each day she had seemed as impersonal as a ninepin in a row of her classmates. Her eyes had been as blue as theirs, her hair more blond than some; the courtesy of her bored attention had been the same, though she had not taken notes so assiduously as a few. Somehow, on a level of intuition that he could only guess at, they had found the intolerable difference in her. He remembered the wetness of her hand on his wrist and wondered if it had been fear they smelled.

"I thought you got along all right with the girls," he said.

"I will try. I will get along if they'll let me stay. I think I was just beginning to make some friends." She drew in her upper arms against her breasts and shivered.

"That sort of thing has to happen. I don't suppose it's possible to *make* friends."

The idea, with her own interpretation, had not helped. "I know I could," she said.

"Don't you have any—well, people, girls you run around with here?"

"Oh yes. My roommate. And there's lots of others. I know how to make them like me if I could stay."

If there had been someone impartial with them—Mr. Wilks perhaps—to whom he could have rationalized the abyss he glimpsed, letting orderly words mount like a steel bridge over it, he might still have kept himself from involvement. "One must not seek the contagion of the herd," he would have said. "God knows what conformities they may exact from her once she has kissed the rod. Whatever it may cost to maintain even the fear, if it's only the fear that distinguishes one . . ." If he could have found the words on which he depended.

"'Larchmoor, calm and serene on thy hill,'" he muttered. "Now Miss Bridges, Shirley, maybe we ought to look at this another way. Suppose they . . . suppose you leave Larchmoor now. There are bigger schools you might go to where you'd have a better chance to be yourself."

"Bigger?" she said. "Oh no."

"You mustn't forget that there is time for anything you want to do."

"Not if I go home," she said.

"But you're wrong. There will be fifty years ahead of you," he said, realizing that she could not believe this. "Larchmoor is not the world. Every possibility is open at your age."

"Would you go to the president and tell him I'm a good student? Could you give me any kind of a good grade if I'd work all through vacation?" She rose and came around the desk and stood just in front of him, just beyond arm's length from him. She stood very straight facing him and neither swaying nor looking at him.

"Please," he said. "Sit down. I'm afraid I don't understand at all. I can't understand why it's so important for you to stay here. You have so many years ahead of you. There is plenty of time. Go home for a while."

She sighed like a child, heavily. "I guess I ought to tell you why they sent for Daddy. It was because when the railroad agents came out to sell tickets home I was the only girl in school who wasn't going. I would have stayed here if they would have let me. Then I got scared and rented a hotel room downtown."

He was afraid to ask any further questions. Once again his necessary refuge was not in forty years of the poor scholar's study but only in the pipe which he could chew and smoke and scrape ostentatiously, as he did now. His eyebrows arched as though to admonish her to say no more.

"I can't go home. I'm afraid of Daddy. That was the reason."

"Now, now. You could surely explain to him. . . . Grades aren't that important."

"He fought me last summer with his fists. I'm not quite as strong as he is. He knocked me down and was choking me when Mother came and made him stop." The words were rushing from her throat like a foul torrent heaved up by the convulsions of her body as she writhed from side to side. "Don't know what he'll do to me now. Now. Now."

The revelation of pain, however confused, was not to be doubted.

(So Shelley's Beatrice would have said, "Reach me that hand-kerchief—my brain is hurt.")

Then as though she was rid of it, she quieted. "I hit him first and cut his face with my ring." She held up her right hand, showing the ring, and for the first time that afternoon laughed shortly.

Resentment mixed with his bewilderment and horror. All around them, he thought, on the walls and towers of Larchmoor, on the stubblefields and highways for unimaginable miles, lies the snow. It's as if she's trying to drag me with her into elements that neither of us, teacher nor student, should ever have to face. She's trying to elect me not just her father, but as she said, God Almighty.

"Why?" he asked. His voice seemed to boom.

"I don't know why he did it," she said with crazy slyness, her face weird.

> (Oh, icehearted counselor . . .
> If I could find a word that might make known
> The crime of my destroyer. . . .)

"Are you sure you're well? Have you told anybody else about this?"

She shook her head. "They sent me downtown to see the psychiatrist when they found out I wasn't going home. I told him. He said he'd help me. I think he's the one that told them to send for Daddy to come and get me. I'm in trouble, so they're afraid I'll dirty up their college. But I would be good and everybody would get to like me if I could stay."

The president's secretary knocked on Dr. Cameron's door and put her head in. "Oh, good," she said, seeing them both, and then bobbing her head as though to confirm a suspicion that they were both quite real. "Can I speak to you privately, Dr. Cameron?" She pulled the door tight behind him and whispered, "Wheeeew, what a relief. The whole campus has been upside down looking for Shirley Bridges. Her father wants her upstairs. We couldn't find her in her room and they thought she might have done away with herself."

"Who thought that?" he demanded angrily.

"I don't know. We were all worried."

"But why should anyone think such a thing?"

"We've been having a lot of trouble with her. Her father says she gets in trouble wherever she goes. He just can't seem to do anything with her. He's going to take her home. I guess it's a good thing he came when he did. We had to send her to the psychiatrist last week."

"Oh, that's nonsense. Anyone can go to a psychiatrist."

"Well," she said. "Well, don't pick on me. Will you send her right up to the president's office?"

Instead he went himself. The noise in the halls was faint and infrequent now. Buses and taxis had carried most of the students to the depot. He passed one of the maids locking her mops into a closet and slowed his angry, absorbed march to say Merry Christmas to her.

A little man whose mouth protruded as though he were deciding whether or not to whistle sat in the president's reception room. He looked as sleek and innocent as a little dachshund perched on the edge of an overstuffed lounge. Dr. Cameron nodded stiffly to him. So this is the fistfighter, he thought. The champ.

"Go right in," the secretary said.

The hand in which President Herman held his glasses dangled over a chairback. He gestured with the glasses to indicate that Dr. Cameron should sit down.

"I'm glad you've come, Arthur," he said. "I understand from Miss Lee that Shirley Bridges has been in your office all afternoon. We've been very much concerned with Shirley today."

"As well we might be."

"Yes. Oh, yes."

"She's in a very tight spot. You might call it a kind of snare that tightens the more she struggles."

"She's not well. Upset mentally. There are always the few who can't adjust to Larchmoor. Her father is very much concerned with her, poor fellow." He sighed. His eyes rolled up under their thick lids.

"The girl has a rather different interpretation of him."

"You mean about her father's beating her? That's an unsavory story for her to tell, isn't it?" He looked challengingly across his desk like a lawyer requiring a yes-or-no answer. He's no fool, Cameron thought. This is going to be difficult. The president continued, "Shirley is quite an actress. Her talent should find its outlet on the stage. She's told that story to several people around here. Did she just tell you today? She seems to have fled to you as a last resort. If I'm not mistaken, she told the same story to the housemother before she'd been here two weeks. With different embellishments, I suppose. She'd broken this or that rule and seemed to think the story would be a kind of excuse. Don't you think a less unpleasant story might have served her better?"

"And what if it is true?"

"Do you believe it?"

"Suppose I did not. Why did Miss Lee say to me 'they thought she might have done away with herself'? Whether you believe the story or not, you seem to recognize a terrible situation there."

"I'm sure that I have no idea what Miss Lee may have meant." There was a clock on President Herman's desk with ornate bronze scrolls representing the tails of mermaids. With a lead pencil's point he traced out first one then the other of these scrolls. "I have, just as an assumption, gone so far as to assume that Shirley's story with all its—its morbid implications—might have some foundation. I have a psychiatrist's report in which such possibilities are examined. Inconclusively, anyway. I don't put much stock in psychiatry. It's best not to. But if they had any basis, I would say they were the best of reasons why Shirley—and her father—ought to scamper away from Larchmoor, wouldn't you, Arthur?"

"I would not. She needs something to hang on to. Let her stay, Dr. Herman."

"Mr. Bridges has decided, I think, that he'll take her home. That was all settled before you came up, Arthur."

"Are you going to let him? Whatever else is true, that girl's afraid of him."

"Is she? Maybe she's been up to something that ought to make her afraid of him." He sighed deeply for Larchmoor's sake. "That kind of thing has happened here before. Another good reason she shouldn't be here. Arthur, do you imagine that I am going to tell a parent—a *parent*—that Larchmoor forbids him to take his daughter home?" He chuckled at the impossibility.

("Think of the offender's gold, his dreaded hate,
And the strange horror of the accuser's tale
Baffling belief and overpowering speech.")

"Larchmoor isn't a hospital, Arthur. If Shirley is having mental troubles and her father isn't, ah, just the one to see that she's taken care of properly, some of the family will surely handle it."

"They will? How do we know? 'O that the vain remorse which must chastise crimes done had but as loud a voice to warn—'"

President Herman tapped his pencil impatiently on the desk top. "That's all very well," he said.

"It means, in the language of the Rotary Club, 'Don't expect George to do it.'"

"You think I might understand the language of the Rotary Club?"

"In the situation that's what it means. It's from a play. *The Cenci.* By Shelley. He was an English poet." He had seen the warning glitter in President Herman's eyes but he could not stop his sarcasm.

Yet President Herman maintained the reserve which had helped him greatly in administering a school so old and prosperous as Larchmoor for so many years.

"Arthur, do you realize the scandal we narrowly missed? Seems she had rented a hotel room downtown and told her roommate she was going to stay there and 'get soused.' Can you imagine?"

"So her roommate told you that? My God, my God. Doesn't Larchmoor ever produce anything but little stoolies? I don't understand that girl, but I believe she needs help. And as soon as there is some suspicion that she might, every student and old maid housemother and the administration itself set on her. Did you ever see a flock of chickens go after one with a broken leg?"

Now President Herman's face had grown faintly red. "I must say, Arthur, that I'm considerably interested in hearing your opinion of Larchmoor. You've always seemed rather reticent and noncommittal. All these years. I'm glad to know what you think of us."

The two old men glared at each other. "I apologize," Dr.

Cameron said. "That was an unfortunate outburst. Let me begin again and appeal to you in the name of the Christian principles which guide Larchmoor."

"I resent your sneering when you say 'Christian principles.'"

Both of them stood up. "If I sneered," said Dr. Cameron, "the intonation was superfluous. I told that girl . . ." Compromise, compromise were the words he had in mind. He could see no reason now for saying them.

Blinded by his feeling—the whole compounded hate for Larchmoor, which must gloss over everything—he stumbled against a little mahogany coffee table as he turned to leave. This little and inconsequential piece of reality that had tripped him up was, finally, his undoing. President Herman might have forgiven him or forgotten the hot things he had said. But when he felt the table strike his shins, he stood for just one second watching it, then he kicked it with all his might. It flew against the wall, its glass top tinkling, and lay on its side.

He threw his hands above his head in a terrible gesture. "You dull, criminal, unperceiving bastards!" he shouted and rushed from the room.

If Mr. Bridges had still been outside in the waiting room, he would have struck the man, and seen how good he was with his fists at anything besides beating up his daughter. The little dachshund man had gone. No one was there but Miss Lee, the secretary. She was watching him with terror, and it did him good to see her cringe.

Without beginning to think what he would say to Shirley, only aware that it was now he who must and would protect her, he went to his office with all the speed his old legs could manage.

She was not there. He hunted, ridiculously, in the offices next to his own and in the nearby classrooms, almost dark now. He had a tremendous fear for the girl. His head began to ache as he trotted from room to room.

There is a long hall in the buildings at Larchmoor, beneath the glassed arcade and extending through the principal structures as an evidence that Larchmoor girls not only don't have to go out in the weather as they pass from bedroom to dining room to classroom, but that they need not even veer from a luxuriously straight path. After the classrooms, Dr. Cameron went to the end of this hall. There, far off, down a long perspective of windows and doors, he saw Shirley and her father. They were talking, and as he watched, the dachshund man took her coat from the rack outside the student lounge and held it for her while she put her arms into it and flipped her hair up over the collar. They went out the front door together.

He got his coat and overshoes. He took from his desk the gloves which he had been almost ready to put on two hours ago. He walked down the hall toward the door from which Shirley and her father had left, but slowly, reluctantly. Was it all a lie that she had told him? If he were going to come back at the end of vacation, would he have heard that one of the busy-bodies on the Larchmoor payroll had unearthed the plot? "She just tried to fix it so she could stay in the hotel with her boyfriend. Got caught at it." No, no, it couldn't be just that. Whatever it was, though, however muddled and sordid, the walls of Larchmoor—that were bigger, much bigger than Larchmoor; as big as money and complacency—were going to enclose it gently in indestructible, steam heat. He was the only one who had been projected, tossed, into the cold, where an old scholar had to worry about rent.

The lights along Larchmoor's main walk had a festive air. Each one had been wreathed in red and green for holiday. At the bases of the lampposts and in the trees overhead, driven back only a little, lurked the blue shadows of the absolute snow. It was not Shirley who had lured him out of his warm corner into this, not any real Shirley that he had been protecting or that had determined he would die in the real cold, he thought, defending himself against self-ridicule, self-obloquy. The realer Beatrice, the gold-embroidered princess, the beautiful lady without mercy and without hope had brought him out of the door.

The Biggest
Band

The Corn State Southern Band was a forlorn hope from the beginning, and, like other forlorn hopes, it moved within an aura of enthusiastic propaganda. Perhaps because it had hardly any distinction except size, we had it drummed into our minds that it was "the biggest band in the world." At full strength it numbered about twenty-four hundred souls, and, if we were not literally the most numerous assembly of hornblowers and drummers ever massed in a single field, no one who ever heard us at close range bothered to contest this primary claim. All during the winter I was thirteen, I drank this propaganda of size— and of our destiny—reorganizing it all into the form of personal wishes that I would go with the other members to the Chicago World's Fair.

A dreamer named Lothar Swift had organized the band by combining the available personnel from high school, municipal, club, college, church, and lodge bands from the southern part of our state. The principle of organization was simple. Swift included everyone who had a suitable instrument—there were no kazoos or household implements used, as some of our detractors said later—and who was willing to attend rehearsals of the band's divisions, as they were called. (These divisions rehearsed separately in various county seat towns across the state. The band never rehearsed as a whole before it played in Chicago.)

Later, Swift enlarged the band even further by selling instruments to a great many people who had never played before, and by including them too. He was a partner in an instrument store in the state capital, and by dangling the bait of the band's proposed excursion he greatly expanded their sales in spite of Depression conditions.

Still, since I had shown no musical aptitude whatever up to that year, I might not have been swept into his deal if he had not known my mother from the days when she taught his younger sisters at Germany school. Though he was a big frog in a big puddle that year, he had grown up on a clay farm just as my parents had.

When he came to Davisburg to sell horns and enlist band members he called at our house for old times' sake. Before he left he had sold us the trombone. He had given us a fine reduction on price, since the bell of the horn was dented, and had promised my mother, "If the band goes—and we're going—this lad of yours will go to Chicago with us. Why, by next summer he'll be playing 'Flight of the Bumblebee.' The trombone isn't a hard instrument." He threw in with the horn an instruction book, which my mother and Uncle Lou were to use in teaching me. They both knew a little music, though neither of them knew any more about the trombone than I did. My mother suggested that once I'd advanced a little I could probably practice with the Davisburg High School band as a stepping stone to the CSS Band. Swift generously countered with an invitation for me to come to a division rehearsal "just as soon as he feels ready."

By May, I had learned a few numbers. Miss Sheldahl, who directed the high school band, let me sit in regularly on their rehearsals, though she would not permit me to appear with them in public. And I had been a few times to division rehearsals in our county seat.

But though my mother and I felt that I was fulfilling my part of the bargain all right, Lothar Swift's promise that I would go to Chicago with the band seemed far less reliable. There were rumors going around that he was having plenty of trouble raising money to move his horde so far, let alone to shelter them once he got them to the city.

Presently a form letter came for me. It said that band members had been put on either an *A* list or a *B* list, according to merit. While it was still the band's intention to pay travel and lodging expenses for all its members, it appeared necessary to ask that all *B* members sell two excursion tickets to "band supporters" who might wish to go along to Chicago. The tickets cost $47.50 apiece. Naturally, of course, I was on the *B* list.

I particularly resented the fact that while I had to sell these tickets in order to go, Lard Williams, who was only a couple of years older than I, had been exempted from this condition and put on the *A* list. I would admit that he could play the trumpet a lot better than I could play my trombone, but I still suspected strongly that this discrimination between us had resulted from some kind of malevolence. I thought I might be getting my deserts for the wrong reason.

There had been a brief, bitter time when I thought it might have been Lard who fingered me to Lothar Swift's stooges for playing through a seven-measure rest during a division rehearsal. It had happened in the "Semper Fidelis Overture" when the ninety or more clarinets of this division were supposed to be having things all to themselves. After I'd blasted right along with them through the rest, Swift had rapped for silence, climbed onto his chair at the far end of the gymnasium in which we were practicing, and shouted in my general direction, "One of you trombones—some of you trombones—has lost your place." I sat there with my head down, making business with the spit valve of my horn, thinking he couldn't locate me in that crowd—even after I'd glanced at the nearby stands and discovered that it *was* the "Semper Fidelis" thing the others had been playing, while I'd been tootling along on the "Mission of the Rose Waltz."

"We can't have that happen in Chicago," Swift bellowed.

"The big city critics would be on us like wolves. Now, watch it. Once again . . ."

Riding back to Davisburg later in my parents' car, Lard had whispered to me, so my mother wouldn't hear, "Why don't you just sit there and *pretend* to blow? Hee, hee, hee." So I understood that he knew who had flubbed.

He needled me about it for days afterward, while I tried to defend myself on the grounds that I had been too far from Swift to see his baton or his signal for the rest. But Lard answered me with giggles—like someone who has acted treacherously and wants to make out that there was justification for his act.

So after the letter from the band came, I made some plans for ambushing Lard and fixing his lip so he wouldn't get it into a trumpet mouthpiece for a while. I might have done it, too, if my mother hadn't come through with a timely explanation that she'd seen Lothar's "spies" snooping around in various quarters of the band, "cocking their heads and just listening for any little thing a person might happen to do wrong." I had to admit that one of those monitors might have got me on the *B* list instead of Lard.

Whoever was at fault, I was no longer willing to consider staying home while the band went. Through the winter I'd used the approach of the trip as the vehicle for too many wishes to conceive of giving it up. There were plenty of things I had to see in Chicago—photoelectric cells that opened doors, Bob Ripley's *Believe It or Not*, the Skyride and the Skyride Pylons, and the dirigible *Akron*, which was scheduled to visit the city in the same week as the Band. I meant to see them, come hell or high water. I was going to ride all night on that excursion train and stay in a big city hotel (both for the first time in my life), if I had to rob a filling station to do it.

Most of all, for just this period in the spring, I meant to see Sally Rand. Our Scout leader, who was also the high school coach, had confirmed the necessity of my seeing her. I'd been saving photos of her secretly since about Christmas, but I hadn't mentioned my feeling about her to anyone until one May afternoon at the Scout cabin when the troop came in all pooped from a hike.

Coach Douglas was sprawled out in a downy growth of ferns and Dutchman's-breeches, while I sat against a nearby tree feeling my pulse and wondering if I'd injured my heart from too much exercise in this heat.

"I hear you're going to the Fair next month," he called.

"I hope to." My pulse was over ninety, and I didn't know if that was a danger sign or not.

"Wish I could make it," Coach Douglas said. "I'd really like to see that Sally Rand romp again."

Again! Here was someone who'd seen her with his own eyes. I jumped up and began walking around him in circles, trompling May apples, thyme, and wild fern. "What's she look like?" I asked offhandedly.

"Pretty." Coach Douglas bit through the stem of a flower and spat the fragment toward the blue sky.

"What's she do with the fans?"

"Moves them around."

"Bare?"

"Bare."

Good God. A person could live in Davisburg a hundred years, it seemed to me then, without having the opportunity of seeing a naked woman.

I practiced on my trombone for hours that night. I played all the C sharps that I'd been leaving out because the seventh position was hard for me to reach, and I smoothed out the high passages in "Barcarolle." I was driven by some sort of irrational, superstitious hope that if I suddenly improved enough I might get a letter the next day telling me that it had been a mistake to put me on that *B* list. All the time I knew that it was too late to expect that.

The next day I propositioned my father to buy the two excursion tickets I had to sell. I told him straight out what a crumby life my mother had and how often she'd come close to crying when I talked to her about all the things I expected to see at the Fair. And anyway it would have been pretty funny if they didn't want to come see me playing in the Midwest Concert, given by the biggest band in the world.

"You think I can turn up ninety-five dollars for us to go on?" he said with more solemn concern than my approach deserved. We weren't as awfully poor as we'd been two years ago, but he was just getting back on his feet then from a rough stretch. "Come on, Buddy. I'd have to sell the car. Do you want me to do that? I want you to think about that."

"Couldn't you borrow the money from Uncle Lou?"

"Uncle Lou's helped us too often when we really needed it. No use talking any more. Why don't you go hit up the Packers? That hard old jaybird is the only one in town that I know of who might have that kind of money to throw around."

Wishes gather weight through one's childhood until, mysteriously, they become necessities. I *thought* it was necessary for me to get to Chicago and see Sally Rand. That belief nerved me up to go to the Packers and try to sell them the tickets. It is easy to think now how frivolous was what seemed necessary then. And yet, of course it must have been on the hot afternoon when I went to their house that I began to learn why—really—it was necessary that I make the trip with the Band.

My first call had been pleasant and a lot easier than I had expected, but the trouble was that only Mrs. Packer had been at home. Mr. Packer was a railroad official who spent most of his time at the state capital or in Omaha, seldom coming closer to Davisburg than his big farmhouse just beyond the edge of town. I'd have to look for his car in the drive, his wife told me, if I wanted to catch him, because she really never knew just when his duties would let him come home. And she wasn't going to be the one to decide whether or not they'd buy my tickets.

She'd been so awfully nice to me, though, that I was all keyed up for success. She was a dumpy woman in her fifties, with a fresh-looking pink and white skin and very nice brown eyes. She'd ohed and ahed when I told her about the splendors of science and the glamorous entertainment she was going to see in Chicago. I could tell she wasn't just pretending her interest to be polite. She wanted to go, and I figured that was the point that really counted.

When I came back to clinch my sale I knew that Mr. Packer was home because I'd seen his big black car under the elms of their yard when I went uptown for the mail in the morning, and it was still there. I went up on the shady, wide porch and knocked at their screen door. Their collie came around the corner of the porch, prancing and panting from the heat. He nuzzled bossily at the legs of my overalls.

"Good dog. Good old dog," I said to him in the most salesmanlike way I could manage. I knocked again and the collie whined to be patted.

"Not so loud, boy." It was Mr. Packer who had come to answer the door. I had rather hoped it would be Mrs. Packer, so she could lead me to him and help explain the deal we were working out. "You'll wake Mrs. Packer," he said. "Come on around to the swing and keep your voice down."

It seemed to me that he was hardly more than aware of me as we went to the section of the porch that faced the highway and took seats in the swing. His blue eyes searched among the elms and catalpas of the lawn as though he were looking for some sly, important guest and merely tolerating me until that one arrived. In the midst of my attempt to get my sales talk started he said, "Is that your bike down by the gate? I suppose now that school is out you kids are playing, like kids will. Bikes and all." He yawned in my face and scratched the fishbelly-white fat on his arms.

"No, sir," I said. "I spend nearly all my time practicing music. I'm a member of the biggest band in the world."

If this announcement touched him he failed to show it. It occurred to me that he was looking across the highway at the pure-bred shorthorns in his feed lot and gloating on what they were worth, even at Depression prices. I thought that if he had any sense of justice he ought to consider how much I needed a little bit of that wealth.

"Lothar Swift, the well-known conductor and music teacher, organized it," I said. "We call it the Corn State Southern Band, and it has musicians in it from clear across the state. I play the trombone."

He looked me over then as though I were offering myself for sale. His pale lips showed that he was a little bit amused.

"Can you reach seventh position on that horn? Not quite, I'll bet."

That encouraged me, because at least it showed he knew something about musical instruments. "I can usually reach it," I bragged. Then I struck for the heart of the matter with more language from Swift's circular letters. "You may have heard that the biggest band in the world is going to the World's Fair in Chicago to play its Midwest Concert and make other appearances. Do you know that this band has twenty-four hundred musicians?"

"My God," he said absently. "That's a lot, isn't it?"

"Along with this vast assembly of musicians, music lovers of the state can buy excursion tickets to go along with it to the Fair."

"It must sound like hell," he said.

"Your wife wants to go," I told him. "She asked me to come back and talk to you about buying the tickets."

Now for the first time we had sat in the swing he looked square into my face. There was something so savage and cold in his eyes—a gaze in which I was not a little boy but an equally responsible human—that I considered running for my bike then and there.

I went on recklessly, "I was here a few days ago and she practically promised to buy *one* ticket at least. She said she'd find out if you would go with her."

He kept staring steadily at me while he pulled the collie's head against his knee and began scratching its ears. "She told you that she means to go to the Fair? That she'd go by herself if I wouldn't go? You're lying, boy." He was so calm in his accusation that it seemed he had spent all his life being lied to and had learned finally that all you can do about lies is to sit steady among the trees on your own farm, maybe waiting for the liars to get tired of their business.

I was scared to say anything more to him just then. We sat rocking in the swing for half an hour without a word. I saw Lard Williams and Percy Black ride past on their bikes, headed for the swimming hole in Mitten Creek, and I resented Lard all over again for his freedom from all this trouble I was having.

Mr. Packer said, "I don't think she could have said that to you, boy. Mrs. Packer isn't going anywhere. She's rotten with cancer."

I don't think I quite understood what this meant. Again he had spoken with total calm, and I took the word "rotten" as merely an impolite way of speaking about his wife rather than as a description that might be accurate. "I was sure when I talked to her that she wanted to go," I insisted, perhaps intending to persuade him not to let his meanness interfere with her pleasure.

Of course that appeal meant nothing to him. I had only one line that was not yet exhausted. "Maybe the band can't go at all unless people like me sell enough tickets. And the Midwest Concert will be something no one ever heard before. Since Mrs. Packer was so interested in it, maybe you could buy a couple of tickets and not use them. To help."

"Why should I?" he asked. His big, cracker-white hands trembled in the dog's mane. He stopped rocking the swing. The hot afternoon seemed unbearably still. I listened for the cooing of pigeons or the sound of a car and heard only Mr. Packer's slow, hissing breath.

"Why?" he asked.

"All right, then," I said. I trotted down across the big lawn to pick up my bike. I supposed that this was the end of my chances to go.

My mother arranged for me to go by beating down Lothar Swift, beating him with the flail of righteous anger. I came home one evening soon after my failure with the Packers to find her glaring and muttering to herself. "I don't care how high up in the music business Lothar Swift has gone," she burst out, "nor how many horns he's sold with all his slippery promises. He needn't think he can get away with this with me. Don't you think I remember the time he came mousing around to Germany school in the afternoon, pretending to look for his sisters, though he knew they'd gone with the other pupils, him whimpering and simpering around with his Miss Thurman this and Miss Thurman that, and it all so plain on his face what he'd come for that I finally had to take pity on him for being so dumb and say, 'Yes, if you want me to go to Hopewell box supper with you, can't you just say so?'"

While her fury lasted she called him at his store in the state capital. I stood beside our telephone, watching her face get harder and angrier than I could recall having seen it, ever. "You—told—us—last—fall. What? Why, when we bought that horn you promised he'd go if— What? Well, I suspect he can do about as well as lots of the others that you've put on that old A list. What? Lothar, I—don't—care. You—told—us—last—fall . . ."

In this way she beat him out of my fare to Chicago, sent me there as a musical liability, and as one who had not sold his quota either. But it cost her something to make such an arrangement. Her conscience hurt her. Later that evening she was preoccupied and nervous. She made a big effort to explain to me the kind of person Lothar Swift was. She said he was a fundamentally decent man, though he tried to squeeze too much out of life and this made him careless with the truth. "I don't want to take the bread out of his mouth," she said. "But he promised us. You and Daddy both heard him promise you'd go." Then more of her concern with the band began to come out. "Lothar's ambitious. I've never had a lot of faith he could do all he's undertaken. Your daddy and I have heard that he's borrowed a lot of money and signed a lot of notes he can't hope to pay off unless he has a lot of luck in Chicago. I just don't know how I'd feel now if he had to default his notes and they put him in jail or something."

I was afraid even now that she might weaken under so much worry—that she might pick up the phone again and cancel my trip after all. I clenched my eyes tight shut and thought of Sally Rand. I saw her only as she was in the photographs, with her fans immovably fixed where they shouldn't have been. Somehow I knew I had to see behind them, and if deception was the price, I was willing to pay it.

"But don't you think this excursion is a great opportunity for young people?" I asked her in my oiliest voice. "I mean, to learn music and to see a great American city that they'd never see otherwise?"

That took her in. "Yes. Sure it is. We've got to try things at least, don't we, Buddy?" She hugged me hard against her side. "Lothar's a clever man and maybe he can swing this project better than people think. He's bitten it off. Let's hope he can chew it."

I hoped he would have the courage to go on writing note after note to banks and backers, as careless of what came after Chicago as I was.

He had the courage. By some miracle of paper financing, artful dodging with the railroads, hotels, Fair committees, and terribly inflated promises to the gullible who went as part of the excursion, he took us.

On a rainy, muggy night in June, four hundred of us, constituting the "east-central" division of the band, boarded a special train at the county seat. We knew that some of the western divisions, with whom we had never yet rehearsed and whom we were not even to see for many hours yet, had loaded at dawn—while ahead of us, to the east, other hundreds were boarding a train that would get them to the LaSalle Street Station before us.

My father had bought me a new Brownie "to get some pictures of that Zeppelin," and my mother had packed my clothes with the abstract, enraptured sorrow that you might expect of a Kamikaze's parent dispatching her only son to the Emperor's service.

At the last minute before boarding, quite carried away by the purifying excitement of the moment, I announced to my mother, "I *won't* go to see Sally Rand." I meant it. I had not understood before how holy a thing it was that all this mob was embarking for.

"Well, I should hope not," she said. "Don't forget to get a new bottle of oil for your horn." She had not even seriously considered the possibility that I might court such a depravity. And that, I thought as I swung up, was probably just as well.

"We'll knock them dead," I screeched as the train began to move.

Once the train was really rolling—the one dependable evidence that Lothar Swift would make his promises good, I had felt—I yielded myself to the excitement of departure with a completely simple loyalty. There was a rumor running through our train that Swift had put our movement and the problems of housing us in Chicago under the direction of an Army captain who had moved troops in Flanders during the war. I overheard some smart-alec college boy giggle over this, "Swift might just do better if he'd let the captain conduct the band, too." I thought it would serve such a guy right if he were pushed into the Mississippi River for his ingratitude.

I had never seen that river before this trip, and I kept pinching myself awake until we had crossed it. Lard Williams was as impressed by it as I was. "Did you ever see anything as black as that water?" he shouted in my ear. Then he whipped his trumpet from the case and blew a few notes of "When It's Darkness on the Delta." "Do you realize that river is bigger than the Amazon?" he crowed. "It's the biggest damn river on the planet. I don't suppose you realize it, Buddy, but you ought to be plenty grateful to your parents and Lothar Swift for making this trip possible."

All these things were exactly what I had been thinking, but it spoiled them a little to hear him saying them. I grunted disagreeably and went to sleep.

I was wakened a good deal later by the passage of the sandwich butcher through the car. Careful not to wake up Lard, I bought some coffee and a jelly sandwich and leaned out the window to get the wind on my face while I ate.

We had left the rain behind us. The stars were out, but the roll of the prairie around us was as black as the river had been. I watched us zip through the night with a balancing of joys—glad that the land was so black while our train was so flashing, glad that it was silent so that the chatter of our wheels could print itself on it, like the first footstep you take in new snow.

Lard was snoring beside me. I enjoyed a lot of superior thoughts at his expense. Maybe he's with us for no better purpose than to go see some immoral Chicago woman waggle her stomach, I thought, but I'm going for something else. It seemed to me that in the hour of my success I had promised not only my mother that I would shun Sally Rand—the promise was to all those who had wanted to go where we were going and couldn't. People like Mrs. Packer. I felt terribly sorry for her, all over again, and wanted to tell her that even if her husband misunderstood her and said unpleasant things about her physical condition, I, at least, knew better than he what she had wanted. And in a way, I suppose, I felt that I was going to get it for her. Finally, I felt I knew why I'd absolutely had to make this trip. In that sweet night I imagined all my selfishness to be a kind of altruism.

We woke in a green morning before the train had passed through Joliet. A tired conductor came through and said, "You kids better keep your feet out of the windows. You'll be walking on your stumps."

I looked across the aisle at the French-horn player who sat beside his instrument case. His chin was black with beard stubble, and his skin showed that he'd been seeing some hard work in the fields. This is not a bunch of kids, I thought, telling off the conductor. You know who's in this band? *Everybody.*

Those who watched us pour into the city through the LaSalle Street Station would surely have agreed. There were old German farmers with short cornet cases, housewives with clarinets and tubas, girls with bagpipes, the whole Legion Auxiliary fife and drum corps from Osmatoc, the marching band from a Methodist college, a sect of Amish with beards and black bonnets, high school bands in a flashing variety of uniforms, and among them all the misencouraged young like me who belonged only to the totality. Counting the excursionists, there were more than four thousand people in this horde that Lothar Swift had raised up to follow him east.

All of us rallied for the first time in one of the ballrooms at the Marathon Hotel. It was a wild gathering full of noise, anarchy,

and administrative ineptitude that delayed our assignment to
hotel rooms for many hours. I remember an old lady—she was
one of the excursionists, she said, who had paid her own good
money for the trip—who whimpered ceaselessly after the first
few hours, "I'm tired. I'm hungry. I want to go back." In mid-
afternoon I heard a fat tuba player offer to whip Lothar Swift for
"getting us into all this mess."

But evidently, the logjam was already broken, for a very few
minutes later, the last of us bandsmen were being whisked up to
our rooms briefly before we loaded to move in buses to our first
concert. I had only time enough in the room to look out at the
blue lake, so intimate and so strange that it was like something
that might have grown inside my eye, suddenly striping its color
across my field of vision—and to exult that I hadn't come all this
way to face it in petty company.

There was trouble on the first day in getting us to our desig-
nated area in the middle of the Fairgrounds. Finally, a platoon of
special police had to hold back the normally strolling crowds until we could all pass through into the snow-fenced enclosure that
had been prepared for us.

In the push to the enclosure, I lost the other trombone players
I'd been tagging and found myself in the midst of more bassoon
players than you'd think lived in our state. I had to sit down
there with them when the band started to play. It seemed to
make them uneasy to have me in their midst.

So when the first number was over, I got up with my horn
under my arm and went in search of the trombones. Presently,
as I was wandering, an old man with a flugelhorn grabbed me
and hissed, "Don't you know how bad that looks, romping
around that way during a *performance?*" He took a terrific grip on
my wrist and forced me to the ground. He tried to hold me
down out of sight with one hand and his feet while he played
the next number, but in an allegro passage I twisted free and
crawled along toward a sound like that of trombones.

I got lost again and crawled out of the band to one of the
snow-fence borders. I had no idea what the band was playing—
neither what Lothar Swift was conducting in his faroff center
nor what any of the divisions *thought* he meant for them to play.
I was terribly ashamed of myself for getting lost. I sat there playing "Barcarolle" softly, because at least I could do that better
than anything else.

A kid smaller than I came up outside of the fence and jabbed me with a toy whip.

"Who're all those?" he said.

"Corn State Southern Band."

"Boy," he whistled. "There's sure a lot of them."

"They're the biggest band in the world."

He turned his head in an arc wide enough to take in the nearer and farther edges of the multitude, spat, and admitted, "Could be."

"What's that they're playing?" he asked.

"The 'Corn Song.'"

He began to look slyly skeptical. "Why ain't you in there playing with them? You got a horn."

"I can't find where I belong. I ought to be with the rest of the trombones."

"I saw them ten minutes ago," he said, "when I was around on the other end of you all by the Skyride. *They* was playing the 'Corn Song' then."

If Lothar Swift had been as ambitious as my mother thought, or if he'd counted on the band's creating a sensation that would lead to the redemption of his debts, he was sadly corrected. The Chicago newspapers didn't even bother to comment on our size. There had been some talk that a beer company or a farm implement manufacturer was going to sponsor us, but after our poor showing on that first afternoon no one believed it any more. The crowds on the Fairgrounds walked *around* us, because they had to. That was about the limit of the attention we got.

Our second concert, on the following day, was scheduled for the dinner hour, when the grounds were mostly empty. They put us out behind Machinery Hall, where the ground tapered visibly into the garbage fill on which the Fair had been built. There weren't even enough folding chairs provided us for all the band members to sit down, let alone anyone who might have come to hear us. I wondered where the critics were that Lothar Swift had worried so much about the day I had played through the seven-measure rest.

Most of the band members I was acquainted with were talking cynically. Lard got a letter from his parents with the rumor that the band had barely managed to get out of the state before the sheriff pulled in Swift for his bad debts.

I tried to ignore this general gloom as much as I could. I'd taken some pictures of the *Akron* coming in over the lake. I'd seen the Ripley show, the marionettes, and a lot of other educational things. But I'd let myself be so excited by the idea of the band's triumph that this gloom scared me, like the fog I'd seen edging in over the lake when we played behind Machinery Hall.

There was still the Midwest Concert to play. It was scheduled to be in the Court of Nations. I sent off to my parents a picture postcard of the clean and modern pylons that surrounded this court. The picture was full of flags in bright, primary colors against a sky the color of laundry bluing. "We're going to play HERE," I wrote on the card.

In my stupidity, I had been slow to catch on that the Midwest Concert would only be part of the joke of our coming. We were scheduled to play it at six-fifteen in the morning. No one would be out at that hour to hear us.

When I finally caught the insult implied by this scheduling, I knew I'd taken more than enough. I canceled my promises to be good in Chicago.

That night I let Lard Williams and his older buddies ditch me, as they'd tried to do on the previous night. Sneaking through the Fairgrounds by the less crowded walks, I marched—dry of mouth and trembling—to the Streets of Paris where Sally Rand would turn me into a swine with those adroit fans. I even meant to stand at the side of the pavilion, from which vantage Coach Douglas had said you got a choicer view.

They wouldn't let me in. I ran at the entrance stairs with my quarter steaming in my hand, and the barker dropped his cane across my chest to block the way.

"You came to the wrong place, didn't you, sonny?" he said. He raised quite a laugh from the crowd in turning me back. "I expect you thought this was the puppet show, didn't you? Adults only. A-dults only," he bellowed. "Why boy, you couldn't stand the breeze them fans make when they go into action."

To top off this humiliation, when Lard came back to the hotel room we shared with twelve other bandsmen, he claimed he had seen her. Spiritlessly I asked him what she was like, and he shuddered in a pretense of disgust. "I don't think it's right to permit that kind of indecent show," he said. "Personally, I wish I had my quarter back. I'd rather have a ham sandwich and a bottle of coke."

Most of our roommates were in bed or asleep on the floor. Fortunately the room was too dim for him to see my face plainly, though enough light refracted in from the metropolitan beacons, traffic, and the street lights for me to see him yawn as he started to take off his shirt.

"You fat idiot," I said. I swung with all my strength at his chest and felt the blow glance from one of his moving elbows.

"Here," he said good-naturedly. "Don't run amok just because you've ruined your mind with dirty thoughts. Relax. Sally Rand is probably like any other woman, though not so decent."

"I've never seen any woman," I said.

"You will," Lard comforted me. "Everybody will. There's just as many of them around as there are men. Be logical."

"Sure," I said bitterly. "I'll see one *sometime*. Like when I'm too old to care." But the worst of it all was that I had discovered you couldn't even count on a profit from being bad in a world like this one. I went to sleep on the hotel room floor feeling the misery of those who have tried to sell their souls and have found no taker.

Naturally no audience came to hear the band at six-fifteen the next morning. For our climactic Midwest Concert only about half of the band members showed up at the Court of Nations. And perhaps it is merely a sad irony that we played better that morning than ever before.

In that morning's program was the "Semper Fidelis Overture," and this time even I knew which number we were playing. I was close enough to Lothar Swift to see the sun flash on his swinging baton. During the seven-measure rest, I looked at the nearly empty balconies above us where the crowd might have been and thought how pitiful it was that only a handful of early-rising janitors should hear what we had made such an effort to bring. But when the rest was over I hit the first following note as hard as I could, feeling oddly free to do my best now that it didn't seem to count for anything.

This unattended concert was the end of the band. Naturally, it dissolved without leaving permanent traces when we went back home. Lothar Swift was never publicly charged with any of the frauds he was said to have perpetrated to get us there, but he lost his share in the instrument store in his efforts to appease the band's creditors, and he disappeared from the state not long afterward. My parents were contented to think that I had profited somehow from the excursion, but after I quit practicing on my trombone they were very hard put to explain just what the profit was. Mrs. Packer died in the Mayo Clinic toward the end of that summer, and I might not then have had the courage to discuss the trip with her even if there had been an opportunity.

In all the years since the Fair, I have told the story of our band a number of times, for laughs. This monster that Swift created has come to seem like one of those kindly, vegetarian dinosaurs that once roamed but never ruled the earth—an altogether preposterous blunder committed against nature and a fine art.

But, if in some imaginary circumstance I should tell the story for Mrs. Packer, I would want to emphasize that last dandy morning in the Court of Nations. I would want her to believe that the lake behind us looked broad as any ocean; that the clear sky looked a million times as big as the patch of ground we sat on. The flags of every country were up in the early morning breeze, and on their rippling fields twinkled the mysterious symbols of authority and fidelity—stars, crescents, crests, hammers, sickles, heraldic beasts, and the proud gold lilies of the forgotten wars. From their staffs over the national pavilions the ultramarine and lemon and scarlet pennants streamed out like dyes leaking into an oceanic current. It was only the empty sky that watched us—but my God, my God, how the drums thundered, how we blew!

The Castration of
Harry Bluethorn

This is a story from the time of President Harding. I tell it as I heard it from the older generation:

Ham Snider was harrowing the tough bottom land along the creek when the determination came on him. The harrowing was mean work. This patch of land was of marginal value, not more than three acres with irregular borders of willows and burdocky pasture land. The soil was good but it had never been properly cleared. The harrow kept snagging on roots or vines the coulter had severed and buried, so Ham had to keep halting the team to clear the harrow's teeth. It was unseasonably hot for April. The willows were half leaved out with leaves like gold-green blades, and they choked off whatever breeze might have come down the creek valley. The horses were sweated; they came as near to complaining as horses are likely to do, showing Ham certain signs of disgust that he and they were wasting their strength down here where so little profit was likely to come from it.

Ham was walking beside the harrow in the choking dust it raised. From the corner of his eye he saw the harrow lurch and tilt and begin to pull out a seine of vines from the brown-gray soil. The worst mess of the morning. Instead of clearing it, he unhitched the team and left the harrow tilted at a useless angle and crossed the bridge back toward his barn.

He was going to nut Harry Bluethorn without letting another day pass.

He saw Fay Ellen when he had hung up the harness and turned the team out into the barnlot. She was carrying a pail toward the henhouse. She wore a denim jacket over her housedress because the news hadn't got to her that the morning weather was sultry. Fay Ellen was not contrary like her sister Alice, but she often didn't catch on to obvious things like heat or rain or cold until someone pointed them out to her. Told her to come in out of the rain.

Ham went directly to their bedroom and began to change his clothes. He put on his Sunday pants and shoes, then went down to the kitchen to shave in the wash basin on the shelf beside the range. He stropped his razor a dozen extra licks on the leather before he tested it with his thumb. He worked up a dense lather with the brush and then, as the razor took it cleanly from the tanned pink of his cheeks, he felt a crowing confidence in the blade. In the barn he had considered using the knife ordinarily devoted to yearling pigs, but now he decided on the razor. He wiped it clean and dry and put it in its velvet-lined box and slipped the box in his back pocket.

But unbearable emotions had come over him while shaving. No doubt it was the sight of his dark, honest eyes in the poor little mirror on its nail above the basin that had got to him with a visual reminder of the depth of suffering, humiliation, and shame Harry Bluethorn had laid on him and Fay Ellen. His eyes seemed to be those of Him despised and rejected, and a mockery to the Soap Creek Valley community and the congregation of Bethel Church.

In the grip of such emotion he went into the parlor to ease himself with music. He put a roll in the player piano and began to pump the pedals, his arms dangling straight down beside the piano stool and tears stinging his newly shaven cheeks. The first roll he played was a semi-classical version of a hymn that he and Fay Ellen often sang in church, "He Comes to the Garden Alone." When the perforations of the paper roll had all passed, he pressed the rewind lever and pumped swiftly. He wanted also, before he went, to play "Over There!" It was rousing and seemed military to him. It made him think of his younger brother Pete, who had been killed by machine gun fire in the Argonne.

Fay Ellen was returning from the henhouse when he went out the back door. She was frightened to see him in his Sunday suit on a weekday morning. Her first thought was that something had happened to the children and he had been called to drive over to the schoolhouse to pick up the bodies.

"I didn't think until I was down there plowing that I had promised Vonnie Cramer I would come into the bank today to sign the papers on the seed loan."

"Oh," she said. "Had I known you was driving into town I might of gone along."

"What for?"

"I was thinking I would look for some crepe to make a costume for Allegra when they have the eighth grade graduation. But I suppose I better wait until we go into Ottumwa."

"Yes," he said. "Ottumwa." But they might never go to Ottumwa again.

Alice was even more alarmed than her sister had been to see him dressed up on a weekday, driving the Model T lickety-split into their lane and making the chickens fly squawking to get out of his way. She came running down from the house wiping her hands on her apron.

"Fay Ellen?" she yelled, before she even got to the side of the car. And her eyes asked, What have you done to her? Ham knew what the fear in her face meant. It simply wouldn't register on him for a few hours. He had something too important on his mind to have room for any more complications.

"I need Wayne to help me today," he said.

"He's down in the field with the drill. I guess you can see the dust." She shaded her eyes and looked down past the barn where the ground dipped toward the willows along the creek. They lived just a mile and a quarter from Ham's place and he might have found Wayne quicker by walking up along the creek. "What did you need him for?"

It would take some fancy lying to make a convincing story for her. If he had come in his overalls asking for help that would have been one thing. But a man wearing his Sunday clothes is plainly bound on an errand that does not require a brother-in-law's muscle.

So he didn't answer her at all. He left the car and walked down across the pasture to the field where a little streamer of dust followed the rig on which Wayne was riding peaceably. His Sunday shoes were whitened with dirt after he climbed the fence into the cultivated land. Wayne's dog had followed him down from the house and, glancing back, he saw that Alice was still in the yard watching him.

"I'm going after Harry Bluethorn today," he told Wayne, without any other greeting at all. Wayne wrapped the reins around the brake handle and got down from the steel seat of the corn drill. He put both hands on Ham's shoulders and held him for a minute, looking square into his eyes. Wayne was a slow and placid man, not at all excitable. He had to be that way to live with Alice, who might have stirred up all kinds of fusses with the neighbors unless he kept her calmed down.

"I wouldn't do that," he said.

Ham pulled the box containing his razor from his back pocket and took the top off, letting the razor slide out in his pink palm.

The sight of the razor told Wayne a lot. He took several deep breaths without seeming to exhale at all. "Well," he said, "I guess you've thought it over."

"And I need someone along to help hold the sonofabitch while I do it to him. Or help tie him down."

Wayne shook his head mournfully, continuously. "A thing like this. . . ," he said. He pulled his handkerchief from his hip pocket and mopped his red face. "Doggone, it is sultry, for sure."

"If Pete was alive I wouldn't be asking you."

"Naw now, sure."

"If Pete could give his life for his country, a man ought to be able to take care of things here at home."

"I see that side of it."

"I want that sonofabitch to know he can't just get away scot-free with coming into a fellow's own home."

"Now that's the other part of it," Wayne said. He took one more deep breath, a little deeper than the others had been, then he said what had to be said in the name of justice. "I reckon nothing would of happened if Fay Ellen hadn't been willing. And for that matter, I don't know for a fact that anything did happen."

"I'm telling you."

"And I guess I have to ask how you know. For in these things a man had better be sure."

Ham began to cry. "It came to me," he said. "I put two and two together and then about four more. You know Bluethorn has got a big mouth and you've heard him as well as I have heard him around the elevator or the cream station talking bad about women. I never liked it, and I never liked him, but I kept my peace never thinking it would be sometime about Fay Ellen. She's your sister-in-law."

"Harry's a veteran. I reckon he brought a lot of that back from Flanders' Fields. So he talks dirty, but that's a long way from being proof positive."

"You want me to give you proof? You want to come home with me now and we'll just sit down in the kitchen with Fay Ellen and have a little talk about it?"

"Aw now. Now then, Ham, I'm just trying to get the straight of it. It's no use talking this way unless you got something good and solid to go on."

"I guess that's reasonable," Ham said. But he could not bear what was reasonable now. He ground his teeth to keep from cursing Wayne. The spasm of control was so intense it tightened his neck muscles and drew his head back until his eyelids reddened and paled and he knew if he opened them the sun would burn straight into his brain. Quietly he said, "Then I can do it myself."

Wayne was not going to let him do that. Wayne was going to come along. "I only thought it would be better to wait for nightfall," he said.

So for long, long hours they killed time, driving all over the country, as if on some immense journey, as though Harry Bluethorn lived far away, to be overcome in a distant, foreign place. They refilled the gas tank once in Boda and again, in late afternoon, in Eddyville. They bought bologna and bread and soda pop in Thurman and had a picnic lunch in the cemetery at Wesley Chapel. Wayne did almost all of the talking they did that day, thinking things out with a coherence that Ham was not capable of now. Wayne had explained to Alice that Ham had come to fetch him because he had heard of an old Dutchman on the other side of Boda who had broken his leg and might be going to sell his farm equipment and move into Des Moines. Early birds might find a bargain. "I told her that because if you give Alice reason for suspicion, why, she might get on the phone. And her and Fay Ellen get to talking they'd figure where we were headed and get the sheriff onto us."

Wayne said nothing all day to indicate he would not help castrate Harry Bluethorn that night after dark in some appropriate place. He seemed quite willing to do it. He only wanted to be sure that they had thought it all out before they went ahead. "It would be a little better if we had a gun," he said. "To call him out of his house and put a gun on him. Then we can get him in the car and take him to the country. But if I had taken the shotgun, Alice would have lost her mind. She'd of known it was serious business."

He said, "Now I don't reckon there's much chance of his dying from loss of blood. I sure wouldn't want the rope. If we just cut him and make sure he knows why, he might figure it's not a good idea to go to the sheriff and make it public. He might leave town like Arden Ferris done." Around the turn of the century Arden Ferris had moved to Wyoming after being caught molesting the children of the church janitor. His name was a warning to growing boys about what could come from dirty thoughts.

He said, "I think I know where we can borrow a shotgun. Winter before last I borrowed Alistair Gordon's pump gun, and he knows I have only the single shot twelve gauge."

At the time he came up with this suggestion they were parked in a grove, watching the sun set over the Des Moines River. They were twenty-five miles from home and seventeen miles from the house at the edge of Boda where they meant to capture Harry Bluethorn. They had been to this spot once before when they were boys before the War. They had come with a group of men in spring wagons to camp out for two nights and spend the day handpicking the big catfish spawning under the rocks when the water was low. Now as the crimson sun hit the surface of the river and turned it to a mournful pink, it seemed they had come back to complete an adventure left unfinished when they were boys far from home on a fishing trip, as if their day's travel could have no destination except a return to something purer and braver than what they had known as married men.

"We could get Alistair's gun and some shells and if I know Alistair, he would give us a belt of whiskey," Wayne said. "I think I could use one if we are going to cut Harry Bluethorn."

"I don't hold with drinking," Ham said, both hands gripping the steering wheel so hard he could feel it give. The day of driving around had been either an exhausting dream or an exhausting struggle against being waked from the dream that possessed him in the morning when he knew what had to be done. Then it had seemed to him a straightforward matter of taking his razor and going into town where Harry Bluethorn worked at the cream station, gathering milk and produce from the farms around town and sending it off to the dairy in Ottumwa. Once he got his hands on the man, he had meant simply to nut him and that was as far as he wanted to think about it. And now as he stared straight at the blood color of sun on the muddy water he realized he had been tricked. Wayne had never meant to go through with it.

Realizing that, he finally understood the meaning of Alice's frightened expression when he drove into their yard way back in the morning hours.

"You and Alice have known about it for some time," he said to Wayne with that patient note of betrayal that is beyond bitterness. "You have talked about it. You and Alice know it is true and I suppose she got it from Fay Ellen herself."

Wayne did not try to deny it outright. He just said, "I thought let sleeping dogs lie and it would blow over. I can't say what the women may have passed between them and I don't know if Fay Ellen told Alice that Bluethorn had actually been at her. Just that he would hang around her sometimes when he came with the truck to pick up your cream."

"A man like that," Ham said. "And the children and all. I guess if we didn't get Bluethorn, I would have to do something about her. I have thought about that, too."

"Let's go to Alistair's," Wayne said. He knew there was no way he could back out now.

But even so, they might not have done it if the Lord had not made it so easy for them. Everything worked out very smoothly.

When Wayne went to the Bluethorn's front door to knock, Cora Bluethorn came to answer the knock, peering from lamplight out onto the porch and not recognizing him, even when he told her who he was. She said, "I think you'll find Harry out in the back, in the shed. After supper he said he had some work to do on the truck to get it ready for tomorrow. You go down that path behind the bushes there and you'll see his light in the shed."

Bluethorn was under the truck, lying on his back with only his legs sticking out when they walked in on him. Ham stepped deliberately on one of his ankles where his overall leg was pulled up, showing his blue and white checked socks. "What the hell?" he asked, and then when he writhed around and poked his angry face out, he was looking into the barrel of Alistair Gordon's pump gun.

That calmed him down radically. He seemed to shrivel, as if thinking that the best way to escape what was coming to him was just to shrink until he disappeared. He didn't recognize either of them when he finally got enough muscles working together to wiggle out from under the truck and stand up—or didn't recognize them specifically, but only as farmers with whom he probably dealt from time to time.

"If it's money you're after, it's in my hip pocket here, what I've got, but. . . ." Then Ham told him his name and Harry said, "Oh," for then he knew why they had come on him this way.

"You got anything to say for yourself?" Ham asked. Harry shook his head. Ham took the box with his razor out of his back pocket and showed it to Harry. Harry said, "Oh Jesus, no!" and started to run for it. Wayne, standing behind him, slugged him in the side of the head with Alistair's pump gun, and then it was a cinch.

"Hold his pecker off to the side," Ham said. He did his work with one neat slice.

Harry Bluethorn did not die from his castration. In less than an hour his wife went looking for him and found him sitting on an overturned pail in the back yard. He was, naturally, in a state of shock and it turned out he had lost about as much blood as his system could afford before the whole affair took on an extra dimension.

But, somehow, the main feeling he had from the loss of his

testicles was shame. That night and in the weeks of his recovery the sense of shame overpowered all the other feelings he naturally underwent. He had been fooling around with the wrong man's wife, and this was what came of it.

When they got him into the house, they called the doctor. Old Doctor Glosser, who came in a hurry. It appears that Doctor Glosser was not altogether sympathetic with Harry. No doubt there was more than a trace of old-fashioned bigotry in the doctor's makeup to incline him to the position that anyone castrated by an irate husband must deserve it. And it is possible that he had a small-town doctor's knowledge of some of the other things Harry Bluethorn had been up to—Clarice Baker's pregnancy, to take one example. Poor Clarice may have even made it out to the doctor that it was rape, and how can you tell?

Nevertheless, he said, before he left the Bluethorn house that night, "I think you're going to make it, all right. I'll be back in the morning to check you over again. Now then, a crime's been committed and I ought, by rights, to call the sheriff this very minute. But I'm going to wait until morning unless you and Mrs. Bluethorn think I ought to report it immediately."

"Wait," Harry whispered from the bed. His wife, who already seemed to be having second thoughts and taking a look into the past and future, nodded a grim assent.

On the next day Harry was able to take a little nourishment. When the doctor repeated his question about reporting the matter to the authorities, again Harry said, "Wait." He had learned a lesson.

A major part of the lesson Harry Bluethorn learned was that a man without his testicles does not have the same feelings and principles that the same man, still in possession, would have. The chemistry of the body affects the spirit. With his balls still sending their hot messages of pride and lust to his brain, Harry would have demanded satisfaction for the loss. The loss made him minimize the sense of loss, and his sense of justice dimmed, or he might have made demands of the law or maybe taken a gun after Ham Snider and his brother-in-law.

In the short and long run he did neither. He thought his lesson over. Around town he had taken pride in his covert, rumored reputation as a sporting man with a good score among farmers' wives. If word of his castration got out there would be a lot of snickering—snickering he might have endured or scorned if he still had his balls to support him. Without balls, he could hardly face this derision. In a real sense his decision was made for him. If Doctor Glosser would not report the attack he would not say anything either.

In about a year he moved to another small town across the state to make a new start. His wife Cora stood by him. She was what was known—in the time of President Harding—as a good woman.

Driving home after the castration, Ham and Wayne were speechless, each locked in a sense of awe and horror at what had happened. Literally, they could not believe they had done what they had done. It had happened very fast.

Yet there was a certain dignity of crime that made them seem larger and more solid to themselves than they had ever guessed they could be—like two monuments in granite being carried through the night, rumbling over the planks of little bridges and bumping in the ruts of the country roads, by a ridiculously frail vehicle with a stuttering motor and a canvas top.

For the first two-thirds of their drive back to their farms and their own beds neither remorse nor fear surfaced from the dark ocean into which they had plunged. Then Ham said, "You want to come to my place and wait?" It was understood that he meant wait for the arrival of the sheriff or his deputies.

"I reckon you can let me off at home."

"Are you going to tell Alice?"

"You going to tell Fay Ellen?"

"Yes. I'll tell her."

They said no more for a while. The Ford's headlights caught a very young looking rabbit veering off the road ahead into the weeds springing in the ditch. Wayne said, "Got your razor?"

"Yes." Ham suddenly smacked the steering wheel with the flat of his hand. "Dammit. His balls. I left them on the floor of the shed."

"Oh. What would you. . . ?" The question was impossible to complete, did not need completing.

"It's only I shouldn't have left them lying for some dog to find. I remember sort of tossing them. . . ."

Now he felt remorse. It began as a trickle of anxiety about whether a scavenging dog would eat Harry Bluethorn's testicles, and it burst into an earth-drowning deluge. Remorse for what he had done to Bluethorn, yes, but beyond that remorse for who he was, the whole life of tedium, hard work, and sin he had spent in his nearly forty years, for having begotten children, for having married, for having dragged Wayne into awful trouble, for having been a slacker when his brother went to the War and died over there.

"See you in jail," he croaked as he let Wayne out near the gate of his dark house. Then he sped home.

Fay Ellen was waiting up for him, though the children were all in bed asleep by now. It was not late. It was merely past the routine bedtime for farmers, who had to put in an honest day's work every day the sun shone.

"Where have you been? What did you do?" she asked with a low, piercing dread.

He walked past her into the kitchen without answering. His place was still laid at the table and he saw that she had saved his supper in the warming oven of the range.

She followed him in, whining, "I talked to Alice. She said you'd been there all dressed up and got Wayne. I talked to her again, oh, I guess it was seven o'clock and she said no sign of you. Do you want a bite? You must be hungry."

He shook his head massively. He was so tired he could have fallen right there on the linoleum and slept until the law came for him. But he took hold of her arm and peered fiercely into her eyes until her gaze wavered and she muttered sickly, "What is it?"

"I want you to kneel and pray with me," he said.

"For what?"

"Pray!" he said and with a surge of strength forced her down on her knees.

It was only after he had finished praying—their usual prayer of submission and gratitude for things unspecified—that he told her he had, that day, castrated her fornicator Harry Bluethorn.

"Oh my God," she said. "I knew it! Why'd you have to do that?"

"I had to do something. Now, Fay Ellen, I believe you can straighten up and be a good woman. It seems like I might have to spend some time in the pen for what we done. And I want you to promise me you'll be a faithful wife and a good mother to our children."

She was staring at him with horror and fear, but reluctantly she promised what he demanded.

As far as anyone knows, she kept her promise. Since Ham was never brought to trial, they lived together on the farm for nearly thirty years more. They had three more children, one of whom became a lieutenant commander in the U.S. Navy. Another got into medical school at the University of Iowa but flunked out and became an optometrist.

Was their later life good? Were they happy? Had he done the right thing? They never knew, nor does anyone who told me this part of their story.

Bring on
the Poets

> She's here, installed amid the
> kitchenware.
>
> Whitman: *Song of the Exposition*

I

If there was one thing Janet Welch was sure of, it was that you wouldn't overdress for a summer writers' conference. It wouldn't be exactly a country club crowd she'd be chumming with at Bolling College's second annual rally of poets and fiction writers. The Conference brochure contained photos of students mingling chattily with staff in pine-shaded corners of the campus, and in these pictures everyone seemed to have come from haunts of coot and hern (or, more literally, from a hike in the nearby Berkshires). Bandannas, halters, and jeans were clearly the standard uniform for the younger women at least, but the problem of appropriate costume for Janet was sharpened because most of the pictured females seemed to be either younger or older than herself.

She prepared options. She bought a new pair of pre-faded jeans that made her husband Roger smile knowingly, though she dared him to say aloud what was on his mind. She also packed a couple of top of the line dresses from Nieman-Marcus in Dallas. With them she could go anywhere in the evenings. The brochure stressed the "interaction" of faculty and students, so being asked to parties in faculty homes was definitely in prospect. From her college days Janet had kept the notion that college professors were fairly sophisticated in their life styles. When she was an undergrad at Kansas, she had been too poor to own anything that would pass for smart at a faculty party, just as she had been too poor and hardworking to find time for classes in poetry or painting. Also involved with discriminations in the choice of clothing to pack was her awareness that Bolling College was in the East. Coming up from Kansas, she did not intend to disgrace it. Hence the Nieman-Marcus dresses.

So much for the folly of her anticipations. Conned and self-deceived, here she was steaming with humiliation on a late Sunday afternoon in a soundless dormitory room on the Bolling campus. Her suitcases were open because she was presumably deciding what to wear to the so-called Welcoming Dinner in Maigret Hall. She could neither decide what to wear nor whether or not to hang anything up in the starkly empty dormitory closet. Her best choice might be to close the bags and keep moving, for not only was she alone in the room, but she had the angry, shamed suspicion she was the only soul in the dormitory . . . dear God . . . the only American citizen sucker enough to lay out four hundred dollars (plus transportation) for this so–called writers' conference.

After the flight from Kansas City to Chicago, Chicago to Albany, she had splurged on a taxi all the way down from the Albany airport. As the cab swung down from the freeway under the maples of a residential district and onto the campus drives, the trap of her vain illusions had closed. She had sighed like a homecoming child when they drove past the brick gates and half circled a pond. The ivied walls and the columns of old buildings, the glass and concrete facades of the new were just what she'd imagined an Eastern college would look like. But almost in the breath that took in such loveliness, she had become acutely aware of the absence of human motion. No one on the walks.

No cars in the parking lots, or even at the service entrances to buildings, as far as she could see.

She had made the cabdriver wait while she tried the front door of Maigret Hall. Yes, it was unlocked, and, yes, there was a girl inside sitting dourly at a desk placarded with a sign directing incoming poets and writers to register there for the second annual conference. The skinny, dark-haired girl had an air of poetry and catatonia about her and was offering neither welcome nor explanations. In the upshot she had found Janet's registration card in a filebox suspiciously skimpy and had brought her to her room in the dorm.

"Have most of the others arrived?" Janet ventured to ask.

"Some."

"Are any of the others quartered in this dorm?"

"Some signed up to stay downtown in a motel."

"Will they be at the dinner this evening? And the staff? Will they be there?"

"The dinner's in Maigret Hall. On the floor above where you came to register."

Very fishy, this evasiveness. *Eastern*—in the other sense of that word, Janet thought, as her heart banged on the concrete floor of the dorm. She gave the girl a dollar tip for helping with her bags, though she thought tipping might be a crude thing to do in case the girl turned out to be a fellow poet in one of her classes.

There was a midget concrete balcony opening from Janet's room and when she stepped out on it she still saw no sign of human movement on the whole campus spread before her. There was only the flash and growl of Sunday traffic on the freeway she had traveled from Albany, like something in another universe that went about its business with a blank indifference to her plea that she had gotten off it by mistake.

She decided that for dinner she would wear the clothes she had traveled in. Of course she showered and put on clean underwear, but beyond that she was not prepared to commit herself.

But, after all, the Welcoming Dinner was not as bad as it could have been. Not quite. Folding tables had been set up in an inhospitable hallway. Hangdog boys in white jackets and non-

geometric black ties were their waiters. The meal was of cold
cuts and cole slaw, fruit salad, and a watery pink variant of Kool-
aid. Custard for dessert. Since there were no ashtrays on the
table, Janet would probably not have lit a cigarette between
courses except as protest. She lit another from the butt while
she ate her custard, though the white-haired lady next to her
coughed meaningfully.

Of the twenty odd people who sat at tables laid for fifty, there
were only eleven who could be generally identified from the introduction as paying students. The rest were fulltime staffers of
the English department and one dean who kept counting the
house nervously, whispering to the waiters, rubbing his face
with the gesture of a man scrubbing a blackboard, and probably
totting up the net losses this conference was going to lay on the
college budget.

But among the Bolling professors were the poet W. L. Soren-
son, dreamily smiling as his eyebrows contracted in metric pain,
and Don Collins, the novelist, who was the administrative director of this limping project.

"Are you signed up for W. L.?" Janet's white-haired neighbor
asked. Janet whispered back that she meant to work with Andrew—Andrew Winston, that is—though the dark dandelion of
his facial hair, which had looked so amusing in the brochure,
was not to be seen in this gathering.

"W. L. knew Sylvia," said her neighbor, whose place card
identified her as Robinetta Gleiss. "Sylvia Plath. In the old days.
In London."

Janet's response might have been that her Andrew had
known Jim in his Vanderbilt days and was a good friend of Cal's
and Peter's, going back to the time Cal had been married to
Jean. . . . She was beginning to feel a certain despairing gid-
diness as she realized that, sucker or not, she was going to see
this conference through. Just *see it through,* one way or another,
and get what fun she could for her squandered money. She actually inquired of Mrs. Gleiss whether she knew anything of
Andrew's whereabouts.

"Ssssh," Mrs. Gleiss said, since Don Collins was tapping his
glass with his spoon and standing up from his chair to welcome
them all officially . . . semi-officially . . . with some candor of
embarrassment at what everyone could see was a less than military precision in the opening hours.

Collins was a hulking, honking man around forty with a face often more articulate than his speech. His eyes could flash amusement while his lips were quivering tentatively over a choice of words, and when the words came in a cluster like exploding shrapnel his eyes would retire to watch them bounce around the room in patterns that amazed him.

"Weeelll . . . if we seem like a bunch of refugees, being fed by the Red Cross . . . you think I'm going to tell you tomorrow it will all be straightened out. . . . Those of you who were with us last year can tell the newcomers nothing ever straightens out here . . . newcomers like Janet Welch, who's come all the way from Kansas, so wide has our fame spread, and Robinetta Gleiss, back with us from Florida. Hank's brought his novel back for the final push . . . Mildred tells me she has had no less than seven poems in print since last summer here . . . and if you're wondering where our illustrious and expensive staff of visiting firemen is . . . so am I. I know they're all coming and you'll all get lots of individual attention. I know Andrew Winston is in town because I picked him up off the plane in Albany this morning myself and stashed him in the motel downtown . . . where he's probably either in the bar or asleep or splashing in the pool. But . . . we're gonna have a really successful conference, because all this confusion is the way writing gets done and . . ."

No, it was *not* going to be a successful conference, Janet told herself with a final acceptance of the limp disorder she had, after all, wished on herself through the vanity of picturing it all so differently from the perspectives of Kansas. It's a convention of cripples, her housewifely common sense told her, and the wisdom of her heart said, I came here to find out I am one of them.

Oh hell, she told herself, you can always have peace with surrender. It was the moral of her life and she learned it again at that dinner. She also learned that, contrary to the appearances of her arrival, two other lady poets attending the conference were housed on her floor of the dormitory. Robinetta Gleiss had the room diagonally across the hall and two doors down. Mildred Kern had been assigned a room at the extreme opposite end of the corridor—nearly a hundred yards away, though they would learn that none of the other rooms had present occupants.

"It's not like last summer," Mildred said. "Everything's gone to pieces and I'm already sorry I came back. Last summer seven of us had rooms right next to each other, and we'd order pizza and bring in wine every evening and read our things to each other until just all hours. It did us all a lot of good. I got more from it than anything I heard from the instructors, didn't you Robinetta?"

"There was the problem about smoking," Mrs. Gleiss said.

"Oh, no one took that very seriously. No one was really angry."

"I was," said Mrs. Gleiss. "I'm glad that Andrea didn't come back."

"I think she *is* back. I think she's staying down at the motel. I asked W. L. about her at the dinner. That's where he thinks she is. And if that's where she's staying, that's probably why that hairy Winston fellow didn't show up either. I was convinced there was something fishy between those two when we took our weekend hike in the mountains last year. Her poetry was all sex perversion," Mrs. Gleiss said to Janet. "I loaned my pen to championing women's rights before some of them were born, and now they go too far. Would you write poems about defecation or making fun of a man's penis?" she demanded of Janet.

"I . . ." She was on the point of saying that she hadn't *yet*, but Mildred was a good soul and saved her from declaring on that point.

"Look," Mildred said, "I have a bottle of chablis in my room and if you two would like to bring some of your poetry down we could share it with each other. I'm always less nervous when my stuff is among friends than when it gets torn apart in class. If you're not too tired, Janet? My goodness, you've flown all the way from Kansas today. Why'd you pick a conference so far from home?"

"Mother-in-law and cousins-in-law in Boston. I'm going on there when it's over," she said then, an answer neither wholly true nor untrue, but sufficient for the moment.

"I'll get my poems and be right down," Mrs. Gleiss said. "That Andrea was always tearing poems apart. That Winston fellow encouraged her in it."

II

Within the first days of the conference Janet was excruciatingly aware that the accidents of her arrival had been fateful. A writer, she wrote to her husband her shrewdest perceptions of her place in the picture:

> . . . I am helplessly cast among the little old ladies with tennis shoes. Small and gasping as it is, the conference is divided into factions and cliques. There are—more than half the enrollment—young people who are, during the year, regular students at Bolling or some other nearby colleges. There are the swingers (staff and students) who live in the "motel downtown" (actually a big, ugly Ramada Inn, with a smelly pool and a huge, noisy bar). And there are the three old ladies who live in the dorm—Robinetta Gleiss, Mildred Kern, and your ever-hopeful wife.
>
> These caste distinctions are not painfully evident during the daytime, when I read in the library, play tennis or take walks on the campus, or am involved with classes or conferences about my work. Classes and conferences are good and good for me. At least I haven't disgraced myself, and my adviser Andrew Winston praised my "Supermarket" and "New Year in Wichita" for their "wry factuality" and suggests I send them to his friend who is poetry editor of *The New Yorker.*
>
> But when the sun goes down, the spirit of unity vanishes. The student-age people go out of sight. The swingers go back to the motel to splash in depravity. We three old ladies have a quiet dinner and return to this dormitory, empty as a tomb. We began by reading our poetry to each other. That couldn't last forever. Now we are down to imaginative gossip about the swingers or to recounting family histories.
>
> So I'll have no occasion to wear my best rags until I go over to Boston to your mother's. Of course I'll wear my jeans on the weekend hikes in the mountains, weather permitting.
>
> Love
>
> Janet.

A loving wife, she omitted from this account some factual embellishments that might have distorted her husband's appraisal of her best perceptions. It appeared to be quite true that the poet Winston respected her verse. He *did* go over it with her line by line and almost word for word in the stuffy office provided to him for student conferences. In group sessions he gently and wittily fended off the attempts of Andrea Bagley to put it down as "corn-fed, provincial, sentimental, and lacking in feminine awareness." The drawback seemed to be that in his lifetime Winston had seen too much good poetry. He said to her once, "But why have you come all this way to this rinky-dink conference? You're pretty good. Keep working and you can be better, Janet. But you've got to realize how many hundreds and hundreds and *hundreds* of people are writing pretty good poetry now."

In much the same jaded spirit he had—as Robinetta and Mildred had amply warned her—admired her well-kept body. On Wednesday night he gave a public reading, and when she came forward through the applause to congratulate him, he would not let go of her hand. She had to come along with "the gang" to have a drink in the bar at the motel downtown.

She supposed she knew what she was letting herself in for when she went along, and in the midst of rowdy music while a dozen of them were crowded in a booth she more or less felt that she was in for the game. No great surprise that eventually they were alone in his room drinking from a bottle of Jack Daniels.

But then once, when he rocked sleepily back in his chair, quoting Catullus in boozy Latin, she saw that he had opened his fly to let his short penis dangle in her sight.

It was just too much. She very primly pretended not to notice. At length he sighed and zipped up as secretively as he must have unzipped. He said they must both be tired after a hectic day. He let her find her own cab for the ride back to the dorm.

On Saturday, when they all drove in a fleet of cars into the mountains for an outing, it seemed—for the first time, and for a very short time—that this conference had some kind of cheery unity, whatever might be said of its frazzling shortcomings. Nearly everyone had managed to come along. As they divided up the box lunches prepared by the college dining service and took to the trails, there was some singing, some careless razzing between young and old, professional and duffer, that only gradually faded as they climbed and scattered. The weather was absolutely dazzling, with only a few small, orderly clouds over the Massachusetts line. The breeze that tickled their nostrils in the open died among the pines in an odorous balm of sweetness.

At noon Janet found herself alone with a boy and girl young enough to be her children. They were on a huge boulder that

was like a hog's back stippled with black and gray bristles. They
were eating bologna sandwiches and drinking beer. She found
the boy, whose name was Parker, watching her with embarrassing candor while he chewed. Impulsively she squirted him with
beer and said, "Chew with your mouth shut."

"Naaah," he said with impudent fondness. "You're not as
tough as you make out, Ma."

Startled, she asked, "Is that the impression I give?"

"You're pretty cool," he said. "I know that Mr. Winston
thinks you're better than anyone else at the conference, and he
should know. I've thought about all the analysis he did of your
mythological allusions."

"There aren't any," she said, feeling inexplicably weak and
exposed, here on the rock in the sun with no answers for any
questions they might hook her with—feeling just then as
pitifully and deliciously young as Parker and his Jill.

"Among the cereals she parks her gleaming cart," he quoted
from her poem—a line that had been discussed for fifteen un-
profitable minutes in their class. He was throwing it out now as
an exploratory question, presuming his right to a candid answer
in this guileless environment.

"What about it?" she asked defensively, feeling she was being
nibbled at.

"I thought you'd tell me what it meant. Everything said in
class was bullshit."

Janet gestured feebly from her elbows. "I thought it was sufficiently explained that the poem is a snapshot of me, just myself,
in a moment of time, gathering nourishment for my family the
way you have to gather it. I can't tell you any more than that."

"But who are *you?*" he persisted.

Jill offered, "Cereal suggests Ceres. I agree there is a goddess
in it somewhere."

"Earth mother," Parker said.

Janet scoffed. "Tell that to my two neglected teenagers, stuff-
ing themselves with junk food while Mama gallivants."

But Parker was not to be diverted with flippancy. Janet felt the
flagrant, obscene hunger of his demand, a real panic of bafflement as he stared, staring as far as a Kansas both of them had
lost. He took a big swig of beer. It frothed and ran down his
chin. "You know you're the real mystery woman of this dumb
conference. I've got everyone else figured out, I think. Why

should someone who doesn't have to worry about what to do with her life come so far?"

"It didn't seem strange to me until I got here," she said, rather snappishly. She neither doubted that his curiosity was genuine nor needed to suppose it was intended rudely. But it came close—as close as she would let it—to upsetting her a good deal. Perhaps because she could not satisfy it. As if this greedy boy had tried to suckle from her and found the nipple dry.

"If I was a good poet you wouldn't have to ask me what I mean," she said. But the brain-numbing brightness of the high place and the noon was rather spoiled by the opaqueness of this conversation.

When it was time to drive back to Bolling College, she found she had been assigned to ride with Andrea Bagley. Andrea drove a Fiat that was painted like a circus wagon. For the first half of the trip their conversation was superficial and cautiously amiable. Andrea gave some facts about her former husband, who was an alcoholic, a merchant seaman shipping out of Hoboken and "one helluva stud." She had divorced him because he was getting too dependent on her. She asked about Janet's marriage and her children. She seemed amused that Roger was in real estate in Wichita and doing very well. "You still love the guy?"

"Tolerably. After a long time it's a deep routine."

Andrea said she was getting a headache from being in the sun all day and would Janet drive a while? Then when this switch was made the first thing Janet knew was that the woman had begun to tickle her crotch and was trying to peel down the tops of her jeans. To fight this off Janet had to park the car on the shoulder of the road, and then they had a really ugly tussle. Andrea was the stronger of the two. She kept putting her big, rough tongue in Janet's ear. She accused Janet of screwing Winston the night she had been in his room in the motel. Then she said, "Why else would a cunt like you come halfway across the country to a nickel-dime writers' conference if she wasn't asking for it?"

Janet said, "I'd like to be a good poet." Andrea broke into tears and let her drive the rest of the way in silence and in peace.

Very upsetting. She locked herself in her room early that night and cried a long time. At the core of her distress was the suspicion that the harder she tried to express herself the less comprehensible she became. Probably even to herself.

III

Sunday night Janet was in Mildred's room sharing pizza and wine with her and Mrs. Gleiss when, as suddenly as if someone had spun a volume knob, they heard the blab of men's voices, surely coming from the floor above. It was particularly startling after they had been for a week used to the eerie silence of the building.

Mrs. Gleiss darted to their door to make sure it was locked. Janet stepped out on the balcony to see what might be up. She saw lights blazing in every window on the floor. Here and there on the balconies above were fragmentary human silhouettes against the illumination. Then, just above her, peering down, inverted and staring with a stare both predatory and alarmed, was the close-cropped head of a red-haired man. The face was jerked back behind the rim of the balcony above, and she heard a shout, "Hey men, theah women down there!"

The reverberations of this cry rippled above her head—like the echoes of a gunshot except toned like a locker room chant— "Hey, women down there. Women down there, come on up. It's a PAH-ty. Hey Al, hey Fred, whatta y'know? We're in one of them CO-ed dorms. Hey, women down there! Come up, come up."

The redhead reappeared flanked by two others—one single, vacuous grin linking the three of them like a rope on a line of buoys.

"What's all this racket?" Janet demanded. She had her hands on her hips and, for all the good it might do, was frowning and shaking her head. "If you don't shush right now, I'll have to call security."

From just beside her Mildred muttered, "Robinetta's calling them now." She pointed inside and it was so. Mrs. Gleiss was shaking the phone like a terrier with a rat while she poured her outrage into it.

"All right. We've called security," Janet announced. "You boys better work out a story by the time they get here."

"Yes sir, ma'am," the red-headed fellow said. He did not

seem greatly frightened. He sprang to sit on the balcony railing so he could see a little better the person to whom he was speaking. "You're not students living here, are you? I think we were all given the impression our group would have the building to ourselves."

"We are . . . guests of the college," Janet said. That seemed a touch more authoritative than calling themselves students.

Then—no doubt because she had been jolted askew by genuine fright—Mildred piped up. "We're *poets*."

Janet herself wanted to lie down and howl with laughter when she heard Mildred's absurd and defiant cry—oh, the most ridiculous gauntlet to fling at the hordes and giants abroad in the dark. Fantastic and vain. But at least this much had to be said for it: It was absolutely the most startling identification that could be given to the gentlemen above.

It was the right spark to catch the fuse of their collective high spirits. Along the length of the floor there was the echoing babble as the word was passed along until it came roaring back: "Poets! They say they're poets!" And then the shrill, singular falsetto of the inevitable joker rose like a cheer: "Bring on the poets!"

Into this hail of nonsense came the purposeful wail of a police siren. All the watchers saw the flashing lights of the college security car swing into the street and climb to the dorm.

The newcomers were, in fact, one hundred and twenty farm implement dealers on campus for a crash course in agricultural economics. From her window the next morning Janet watched them march out like a platoon of decency; neatly barbered, neatly dressed in pale summer suits, each one evidently carrying a neat clipboard as the group headed for breakfast and the first lecture.

Of course there had been no great hassle when the security police had come in last night. Mrs. Gleiss insisted that some of the men had shouted obscenities at her and her friends. She was not sure she had not heard threats of rape and the scamper of feet on the stairway that connected their floor with the one above. But while she was telling this story to the officer in charge, Janet had stood behind her shaking her head in violent negation and mouthing silent words: No, no, it wasn't like that. The old lady is piling it on. Don't make a mountain out of a mole hill. The fuss was smoothed over when a spokesman came down from the floor above to apologize most sincerely to the ladies and promise them they were safe as in church.

Then Mildred had to be consoled. The laughter she had provoked by labeling them poets had been a painful scalding. "Did I sound as silly as I think?"

"It was just mass hysteria. Not a bit silly on your part. Anything would have set them off," Janet said and made it stick.

So, like every other episode of these erratic days, the night alarm was tucked back into the banal anarchy of the conference. (Nothing was conclusive, it seemed. Nothing stuck. Janet found a bouquet of roses lying against her door, assumed correctly they were from Andrea, and the two became pointlessly cordial in class discussions. Winston beamed to see them so friendly, for nothing seemed to him worth hostility.)

Then on Wednesday at lunchtime Janet was alone in the student cafeteria when she saw the neat red-haired gentleman from the floor above headed for her table, carrying his loaded tray.

"Hi, poet," he said. "All right if I join you?"

"Poet?" she asked frostily. "What's amusing about that?"

Gosh! The light went out of his face. He was a puppy who had come up wagging his tail, only to get a boot in the snoot. Gosh, how was a farm implement dealer to know that calling a poet a poet was like calling a woman a lady in these times of liberation? Gosh darn.

Faced with the mute eloquence of his hurt, she growled, "Oh sure. Sit down." She had been reading Dickey's "Drinking from a Helmet," but it wasn't in her to stay with any book when the man felt so simply he deserved her conversation.

"Sincerely," he said. "Sincerely, I think it's darn interesting what you're doing here at the College. Heck of a sight more interesting than listening to statistics on median income and comparing charts." He wanted to know just all about what she had written and published and like that, and then when he was told she was not really a professional but was here learning to write poems, he wanted to know how anybody could be taught to write the stuff. "I thought you had to have it born in you, that it was like a gift," he said.

"Yes, like a gift," she said. "What you learn is how to accept it." She didn't try to explain to him that even this wasn't original with her. It was something Winston had said one afternoon in his class, and even as she had heard it from him and seized on it, it seemed to be a principle far older than he, something that had stayed alive generation after generation because it sounded like wisdom, though it could never be quite deciphered.

The redhead thought it sounded like despair. "Hey," he said, "you're not downhearted about what you're doing are you? You're not losing faith?"

"I don't know how to do that, either," she said, "so I suppose not. I guess I've got something out of the time I've been here, but it's about over, and pretty soon I have to draw the bottom line, just like you in your business. If I'd known before I came the things I learned here, I wouldn't have come."

Now he was certain she was blue about herself and—he couldn't help it—his nose, pink with sunburn, began to twitch visibly as the wheels turned in his head. His salesman's mind saw the advantage in cheering her up. "Hey," he said. "I know poets are moody, and I can see I caught up with you on a day when you're contemplating all the grief in the world. But you know what? I don't *buy* it. I just don't buy it. Hey, now that we're getting acquainted you can tell me your name. I want to look forward to the time when I can go in a bookstore and find your book on the counter and say I knew her when."

"It's not going to be that way," she said soberly. "I won't have a book." And as she said it to this agreeable stranger she knew for the first time in her life, really, that it was so. She could still suppose that Winston—who was not a bad guy, either, considered in the Sophoclean light—was sincere and knowledgeable when he said she wrote good poems. She had no reason to doubt that he would show a few of her better things to his friend at *The New Yorker*. But his friend there had a hundred friends like him and they all met students as good or better than she at dozens of conferences like this one, or better, or better known. Because the real gift came to her at moments like this, she knew that the cloud-capped towers of all her vanities would fade, leave not a wrack behind, and all the Janet Welches of this time and this nation would go to an infinite number of summer conferences and back to the husband and the good life, leaving not a book behind. Perhaps it was the high tide of her gift to take that for what it was worth. . . . "Maybe I'll publish a few poems here or there. That's all."

She was getting very heavy for him, and she knew what he

was after as he sat shaking his head in denial because, with her gift, she understood the only thing he would know how to be after from her. But he had not flinched yet, nor stopped listening.

"Well," he thought aloud, "it seems to me if you have a gift and you've gone to school to learn how to perfect it, somebody ought to find it worthwhile."

"I suppose that happens, too. My friends and I—and other students in classes here—read them to each other. They're not entirely lost."

"Hey," he said. "I'd like to hear some of them. I truly would. And there's some other guys on the floor with me that are pretty serious guys, actually. We don't have much to do with our evenings here. I don't care much for movies myself, and it's not much pleasure for me to go down to a noisy bar. I'll tell you what. Why don't you and your friends come up tomorrow night—or tonight if I can arrange it—and read some of your poems to Ernie and Gil and Ben and me, if Ben doesn't have anything better to do. We'll just sit around and listen, and I've got some Jack Daniels, if you and your friends would care for it."

"That's very kind of you."

"Swell, then!"

"All right," she agreed. "I think I'd like that. But I'll tell you what. I don't want to inflict anything on anyone. You're the one who is interested. Why don't I come up alone and just read my poems to you?"

He hadn't flinched before, but now his chin quivered piteously. He would have liked to lift his eyelids and to have met her gaze, but they were far too heavy.

"Why . . . *sure!*" he said. His sunburned nose twitched because he couldn't stop it.

Was she prepared to share with this neat, clean, dumb implement salesman what she'd refused to lay out for that tired singer, Andrew Winston? What she'd fought to keep from Andrea Bagley? What her dear, fine, and tolerant husband Roger did not need of her?

She was prepared for whatever might be . . . appropriate. And as she got dressed up that night, she understood it was for this encounter she had come to this bughouse, rinky-dink conference. All this way.

She dressed in the best of her two dresses from Nieman-

Marcus. Looking at herself in the mirror, she saw that the garment gave her the dignity she had aspired to when she bought it
in May. She was not a college girl now nor a bride but a woman
ripened for purposes that had not been mentioned yet and
maybe did not need mentioning. And the dress was right to
show this.

She took several of her best poems—not too many—from her
briefcase and went solemnly up the stairs to Clint's room. (His
name was Clint. She hardly knew anything more about him
than this, and did not need to know. She liked his name. It had
the right sound. To her Kansas-tuned ear it had the ring of a
horseshoe hitting a steel stake.)

Clint had his bottle of Jack Daniels opened before she got
there. He must have been sipping from it, because his appearance was so grave and thoughtful. He was smoking a good cigar
and there were shadows on his face she had not observed in the
public light of day. It would seem to her later his air was exactly
appropriate for a bridegroom on his wedding night. The austere
impersonality of the room in which he had waited for her made
it seem pure as a snowfield above timberline.

"I got us ice," he said, springing to prepare her drink before
she could sit down in the Naugahyde chair. "There's some mix if
you want it."

"I'll take it neat," she said. "Some ice water to chase it."

He said, "I want you to know that this is a great honor to me."

"Thank you," she said. The whiskey burned her lips like the
touch of fiery metal. As she began to read, her voice was even
and clear as the tone of a bell in a country church.

She read:

> . . . among the cereals she parks her gleaming cart,
> Scanning the price on every package, knowing
> The value of goods not marked for sale. . . .

She read ten poems to him.

When the reading was done, both of them stood up and they
shook hands formally. "A great honor to me," he said. She
blushed a little and nodded affirmatively but made no other
reply.

"Good night," she said after he let go of her hand.

"Good night," Clint said.

Then she went down the chill concrete steps of the dormitory, turned along the corridor to her own room. Entering, she went straight through to the balcony and stood above the campus lights, unseen in her pride. Her body convulsed in a shiver delicious as mirth. The airs of the sultry night paid her the full homage of summer.

It was good that she had come here. Good that she would be leaving soon, for Boston and then her passage west. Good that she paused nowhere very long, sharing, testing here now, the majesty of the gift that was not hers to withhold or refuse to anyone ready to take it.

The Covenant

It was like it had stayed hot on purpose through July of that year, and when Harlan Casey's Uncle Luke was killed in a highway crash the day before the miserable heat wave broke, it seemed to Harlan, who was thirteen, that whatever had been punishing them in Gath and on the farms around should be satisfied now and might let them alone.

On the day of the funeral, a clear north wind bent the poplars around the Methodist church and shook the tasseled corn in an adjoining field. Though the church was packed with Luke Taylor's neighbors and friends, there was no whirring of funeral-parlor fans as there had been during Sunday services since late June. Harlan was comfortable in the jacket his mother had made him wear. He felt better than he'd expected to at the funeral, not even faint except when he had looked down through the white tent of gauze peaked above his uncle's face to keep the flies away.

He had not realized they would seat him this near the coffin, placed with his family on chairs arranged in front of the regular church benches. His father was on one side of him. His mother was on the other side, holding his five-year-old brother, Chris, on her lap. Chris had a red bow tie clipped to his white collar today, and his yellow hair was slicked down with water. His lips were parted solemnly. His eyes, just this summer changing from the dark blue of his babyhood to the brown of his father's and brother's, were fixed on the gauze above the coffin.

Only, even sitting on Mom's lap, he can't see in, Harlan thought. He was glad the kid couldn't see the unacceptable changes on Luke's face. Walking past on the way to his chair, Harlan had seen a funny color of rouge on the cheeks that always used to be so supple and tanned. Around Luke's deep nostrils there was a frosting of powder, like powdered sugar. No wonder the flies want at it, Harlan thought, his own nostrils dilating queasily from the smell of the flowers banked across the front of the church.

Everyone was waiting for the minister to come in now, and he, probably, was waiting for Cousin Edith, who was driving down just today with her big-shot husband from Minneapolis.

Last night at supper Harlan's father had said you'd think that, considering all Luke had done for his girl, she might have come early enough to help clear some of the funeral arrangements with the Gath undertaker, Will Roberts. "She may feel we did it all too cheap. And it's her money we're spending for the funeral."

"It's Luke's money," Mother said. "You know why we haven't heard from her."

But if the parents knew, they certainly hadn't explained. Harlan was pretty sure they'd made a long-distance call after he'd gone to bed. This morning his mother was mad about something special. She kept narrowing her eyes, and a number of her odder remarks implied that *she* wouldn't have *let* her brother die. If what? Who would have if they could've helped it? She wasn't making sense.

Even if some of the new people around Gath—Colliston, the commercial artist who worked in Des Moines, and Miriam Roberts's dad, the undertaker, who just now was in a peculiar relationship to Luke—had treated him as a joke, probably even they would miss seeing him gun his old Chrysler convertible up the blacktop from the farm. To the end, he always came through town waving his hand like a winning politician. He carried his red head tucked over modestly on his shoulder, as if he knew they were all saying, "There goes old Luke, off to another golf tournament. Where's it at this time?"

Uncle Luke had been a "gentleman farmer." Harlan's dad used that term on him with a big variety of inflections and followed it with chuckling spells of various lengths. Last year, for instance, when Harlan had asked for a trumpet and had been told it was too expensive, his mother had soothed his feelings by telling him that she had mentioned his musical interest to Luke. Before Christmas she was pretty sure Luke meant to buy him a horn. After Christmas she was sure Luke had some reason for withholding the present until Harlan's birthday in June. When Luke didn't even stop by their house for a piece of birthday cake, Harlan's father had said, "That's the way gentleman farmers are."

Until his death Luke had stayed on the farm where he was born. The place had gone shabby since Grandpa Taylor had passed away, but in the '20s and '30s it had been one of the showplaces of the county, with its oversized barns, white board fences, and a herd of Shetland ponies besides the Angus cattle Grandpa bred. The roof of the three-story house topped the surrounding maples and catalpas in those days. The garage where Luke kept a rusting tractor and a motorless jeep beside his convertible had been built for a Buick touring car and two runabouts.

Before Cousin Edith had gone away to Stephens College, Luke's infantry buddies and sports from all over southeastern Iowa, state senators and such, used to come in the quail season. After Aunt Madge died, Luke had lived mostly in the kitchen of the big house. Sharecroppers took over most of the actual farming. It was true he still went to the tournaments, but not to play golf anymore.

Luke had placed fourth in the Iowa Open back in '46. He'd never come that close again, though his picture had been in the sports section of the Des Moines *Register* maybe once a year since Harlan could remember.

His mother always seemed to know when those pictures were

to appear. At Sunday breakfast her finger would point Luke out among the tournament officials and whatever sports champion or mayor was there to present the trophies, standing a little back of this year's winners, a little taller than anyone else, with his mop of hair slanting off to the side, like a haystack after a windstorm.

Mrs. Casey had long since convinced her boys that the reason they saw so little of their uncle anymore was that he had so many important friends all over the Midwest. She was sure, too, that these important friends were going to be in town for the funeral, though Harlan had not seen a single out-of-county license plate when he came to the church. Since Uncle Luke had been a Silver Star winner in the war, she was sure that Legion officials from Des Moines and the Quad Cities would be here. Maybe. At least Harlan had seen the rifle squad of the Gath post importantly stashing their Springfields in the back of Mr. Roberts's hearse.

Harlan's father nudged him, and at his left Harlan saw a woman in black with a short black veil between the wings of hair that framed her face. He heard the hammering of her spike heels on the church floor. But even when she went straight in front of him to the coffin and leaned over it, when the minister and a heavy man in black moved up on either side of her and took her arms, Harlan could not understand that this was Luke's daughter, Cousin Edith.

It was not merely that he hadn't seen her for six, nearly seven years, almost half his lifetime, nor that the heel taps were so startling. There was some quality of make-believe in her dress and her gestures that he could not square with his expectations. This was like something he might read about or see on television. It couldn't be happening in the homely old church.

Then, if it really was Cousin Edith, as it was slowly dawning on him it must be, she ought to have said something gentle, at least polite, to his mother. As Edith swayed back from the coffin, he thought his mother was leaning forward to speak to her or touch her. But Edith's veiled eyes were purposely lowered. Her mouth, as she took her place on the other side of her husband from Harlan, was set hard.

Well, all *right*. All right, and let her act how she wants, Harlan thought. The big guy who must be Edith's husband—a college football star and now a mucky-muck lawyer in Minneapolis—smelled of perfume stronger than the smell of funeral flowers. All right, let them do things their own way.

He should have known his mother would not sit still for snubbing. And if he had known, he might have been able to stop what she did now. He would have turned far enough to see her green eyes storm when she put her hands in Chris's armpits and tugged him upright in her lap. Seeing the movement only, Harlan thought she was merely shifting the little boy's weight.

She carried Chris the five steps to the coffin. His legs were still not flexed to take his weight when she put him down, tore aside the gauze, and broke one white rose from a floral star beside the pulpit.

I still could have stopped her. Harlan would repeat this to himself as often as the scene came back later at the frightening edge of sleep, or when he ran by himself under the soundless sky of the following autumn, at cold twilight, as he rushed around his paper route.

"Take it," she said to Chris as she picked the rose. "Put it in his hands."

Chris stiffened in her clutch. His yellow head half swung from one side to another on a neck suddenly too frail and thin to move it. He was trying to say "No." His mouth was round with the effort. Harlan felt his own chest clench with breath—and he would know later it was simply lack of courage that kept him from roaring the word his baby brother was unable to say. Then he actually believed he had yelled his protest, but there was no sound in the church at all, except his mother's crooning moan.

"Put it in his hand," she told her youngest. "There, now, there. In his hand, like that." Her straining hands bent the fingers of the dead man and forced the living ones to leave their gift.

"Now kiss him," she said.

In the funeral procession to the graveyard, whatever was explicable in the scene was explained. From the back seat of their car Harlan listened to his father and mother thresh it out.

"Well now, Mildred. . ." His father seldom got farther than that when his mother was really wound up.

She said, "I ought've slapped that make-up off her face. I'll tell her so, too, before she gets away from here."

"If you're going to make a fuss at the grave. . ." Father

slowed the car and wagged his elbows in a threat to turn out of the procession here and now.

"You keep right on driving. I'm not the one who's going to make any fuss, and you know it. You heard what she said on the phone last night."

"I didn't hear except what *you* said. You told me what she said."

"I'll tell her again I don't believe it was an accident."

"Mildred, he hit an abutment. The highway patrol said he was doing eighty. His neck was broken. And maybe he was dr——"

Their mother glanced furiously into the back seat at the boys and dared her husband to make such an accusation in front of them. "Yes, he was doing eighty. After he'd driven all the way up to Minneapolis to try to make things up with Edith, and they'd shamed him."

"You don't know that."

"I know Edith. After all Luke did for her, the money he spent on that girls' school and when she was chasing after Walker to the Rose Bowl, and all he had to borrow all these years."

"Luke had a few other things to spend it on."

"Don't you say that in front of the boys or I'll get out and walk to his grave. Stop the car. Let me walk."

"Now, Mildred. Now, Mildred. Now. I didn't exactly mean— —You shouldn't have. . ."

"Don't tell *me* I can't guess what's been going on these last few years. Luke was too proud to tell all the things they shamed him about, but I knew what he was thinking. They even borrowed money from him until Walker got his start, and only the lawyers will know if they ever paid it back. You know how he doted on Edith. Edith was all he had, and then for her to ——"

"Well, he had you," their father said.

This time she did not threaten to get out of the car and walk. Harlan saw the scarlet rise from the neckline of her dress up to the roots of her hair. Very quietly she said, "I know you think I've made too much of the way things were when Grandpa Taylor—when Luke and I—when I was a girl. I know you've done your best for your family. I've promised myself never to mention to you again what I grew up expecting. You needn't mention it either. Please. All right. Don't be afraid I'll make even a teeny fuss at the grave. I won't even look at Edith. I won't shame the rest of you anymore."

"Aw, Mildred, you didn't," their father said. "It's only that— you know—Chris——"

"Chris loved him and wanted to say good-bye to him, even if that Edith was so snotty."

"Well, well, hush, it's all over now," their father said.

Without a definite end, the quarrel and the embarrassment faded. The wind that bowed the cemetery pines and loosened the petals of bunched gladioli cooled the shame in Harlan's cheeks. There were two Des Moines cars at the graveyard, full of white-haired men and ladies who called to Mrs. Casey and said she must be Luke Taylor's sister and they wanted her to know what a fine man they thought he was, he really was.

The crowd was considerably bigger than it had seemed in the church. Not only was the Legion rifle squad there in smart, pot-bellied formation; the Stars and Stripes and the Ottumwa post flag were crackling smartly beside the open trench in the earth. Someone had put a flag on the coffin. A high school boy, Buell Grace, was silently trying out the bugle on which he would play *Taps*.

It was easier now, but Chris set his feet in the grass beside their parked car and flatly refused to go into the crowd down toward the grave. Harlan's argument that they ought to be near enough to smell powder when the Legionnaires fired their rifles failed to budge him.

Mr. Casey clicked his tongue and gave his wife a see-what-you've-done look. "Harlan, you take him and walk him around." he said. "Meet us back here afterward."

That was where Harlan's luck for the day took a definite turn. It was a real compensation to walk around and find Miriam Roberts standing beside her father's hearse, parked on a knoll in the high corner of the cemetery. Miriam wasn't his girl, exactly. As a matter of fact, she was two years older and a grade ahead of him. But she was more than just a friend, even if the only dates they'd had had been for Cokes at Jack's Drug Store.

"It's the biggest funeral this year," she said admiringly.

Harlan smiled for the first time that day. "That why you came?" The Robertses were not Methodists, alas. She never came to his Sunday school.

"Daddy likes me to ride along now and then. How come you're not down there with your mother?"

He jerked his head at Chris.

"I don't blame him," Miriam said. She knelt beside the little boy and rubbed his cheek with hers. Her movement was all compassion, but for Harlan it showed how her hair matched the fine, clean color of Chris's.

"From up here it's beautiful," she said. "See the flags, Chris? Oh, see them! But if you get too close . . ." She wrinkled her nose, as if remembering the smells in her father's workroom.

She stood up straight as a Girl Scout and said, "Up here, on a pretty day like this, I feel there is no death." Nothing he had ever heard from a minister on the subject had impressed Harlan half so much.

"Maybe not," he said.

Below them now, on the sun-swept grass, the blue squad of riflemen raised their guns. The crash of exploding cartridges was slighter than Harlan had expected, more like a kind of music. The reports sounded again and a third time. The wind erased the sound briskly, and when the bugle notes came it seemed that there had been nothing before them, and afterward nothing was needed.

"Listen, Chris, just listen," Miriam said exultantly. She took the boy's head in her hands and turned it so he could see Buell Grace leaning into the bugle. "Isn't he fine?" She turned her blue eyes to Harlan and said, "Have you got yourself a trumpet yet?"

Last spring, when he had started to learn on a trumpet belonging to one of his classmates, Miriam had said that he'd soon be good enough to play with her in the school orchestra. "The thing is, Uncle Luke said he'd maybe buy me one," he told her. Then he stopped, unwilling to think how often that man being lowered into his grave had gone back on his promises.

"I am." He spoke faithfully into her asking eyes. "I'm going to get one."

What she had taught him in the few minutes they stood together was that life doesn't pause at all for death. It was funny how everyone had seemed to know that already, except him.

And now, except Chris.

In the remaining weeks of summer, Chris went about his

sandpile games and kitchen chores as if they had never been interrupted by either a blistering July or the funeral. He was to start kindergarten in September, and, as the day approached, his enthusiasm seemed to be growing. He was proud of the new blue jeans and striped sport shirt he was to wear on that first day of school. He practiced playing football with Harlan, so he'd know how to do it at school.

But under his everyday tranquillity something had veered off course. One night, in the room they shared, Harlan caught his brother sneaking a dahlia into the drawer of the table by his bed. It looked like one stolen from Mrs. Ruken's garden across the alley.

"Hey, you don't keep flowers in drawers," Harlan said. "Get a jar from Mom if you want to save it. Don't tell her where you got it." Then, as the drawer slid shut with the flower in it, he skipped across the room. He caught Chris's wrist and forced him to open the drawer again.

The smell of dead flowers engulfed them, the dried and color-less blossoms that must have been accumulated one at a time over the past weeks, softening into one another in a mass of crushed petals—not rotten, exactly, but smelling of misuse and waste, closer to garbage than to bloom.

"They make me *think*," Chris said reproachfully when Harlan dumped the whole drawerful into the wastebasket. "Think about *him*."

Harlan shook his head and had nothing to say. But a few days later he came alone into their room and found a big, motionless lump under the covers of Chris's bed. He supposed he must have known what was hidden there as soon as he saw the bulge under the pink and white stripes of cloth. But he looked to make sure before he went running in panic to fetch their mother.

If she knew why he was so excited, she did not let on at first. "Why, it's only that old doll of mine he used to play with when he was a baby. Poor thing's lost its eyes," she said, lifting it from the stripped-back bedclothes. "Do you suppose he dug it out of the attic?"

Harlan had failed to stop her at the funeral when she had forced Chris to touch and kiss the dead man, but he dared not let her get away with this evasion. "Chris *buried* it," he said.

"Oh, Oh. He——" The tears came in a rush, and she sat down heavily on the little bed. The once-elegant doll hung from her hands as if she had forgotten how to hold one properly. "He misses Luke so much," she said. "We all miss him, and it didn't have to happen if Edith had any human feeling."

"Chris didn't really know Uncle Luke," Harlan said. "How could a little boy know a grown-up man he hardly ever saw except driving past?"

"I know Luke was too busy lately to visit much, but he used to come here lots," she insisted. "You used to like to go out to his farm when you were Chris's age, and he gave you so many nice things to play with. Before he got so discouraged." She put her arm around him and brought his cheek down to a wet contact with hers. "You can't have forgotten how generous Luke was. Why, when I was your age, and then in high school, when Grandpa Taylor was living and we were all on the farm, Luke would do about anything for me. And everyone else would say the same thing in those days. When Grandpa got him his first car . . ."

She was gone in her dream of the old times, of the high school parties they used to have on the farm, when they were "rich" and kids from three counties would gather there for dances and games on the lawn on spring nights, with lights strung between the budding catalpas, and red-haired Luke being chased by all the girls, but never playing favorites, always making sure everyone had a good time, especially his kid sister. She told again how they used to drive through the summer nights in Luke's Model A roadster, over to Fairfield or to the WPA shelter at the lake. And before that . . .

"Have you been talking to Chris about this?" Harlan asked uneasily.

"Chris is too young to understand. You understand these things because you remember more. You know what I mean."

For a second he almost gave in to the temptation in her voice, to the softness of her smile made all the more compelling by her tears.

"No," he said, wrestling out of her embrace. "No. I don't. No."

"Ah. You boys are both unhappy now. I understand. It's still too soon. But you'll get over it. School will be starting soon. You'll have your athletics to think about. And orchestra. I've talked to Daddy and we're going to get you the trumpet Luke meant for you to have."

"I won't have it."

She used her old trick of not hearing. "Chris and you are young and will have oodles of things to think about. You won't really forget your uncle, but everything will be easier after school starts."

When she left him, she took the doll with her, and he believed she had not merely returned it to the cardboard carton in the attic, where it had lain with the other souvenirs of her girlhood for so long; he thought she had locked it in a trunk or wired it up in a crate. At least he didn't find it when he went secretly snooping.

But Chris did. There it was again one day buried under the covers of Chris's bed, motionless and smaller than a child by far and yet the frightening anchor of all their lives. This time Harlan took the doll on his bicycle and carried it four miles out of town, where he threw it in a creek.

Yet, after all the anguish of the summer, Harlan had his new trumpet by the time school began. He had refused again to let his parents buy it for him. He would ask for nothing from them now. But he finally compromised and let them lend him the money, to be paid back from his earnings on his paper route.

The decisive fact was this: The horn represented his chance to keep some contact with Miriam Roberts. She had graduated into high school last spring, out of the upper-grades classroom he would have to occupy for one more endless year. If he couldn't arrange to be involved with her through orchestra practice, he wouldn't have much chance of seeing her at all. With those high school guys rushing her, the competition would be too much.

He had the horn, and he had practiced enough so he thought he could talk Miss Slater into giving him a place in the orchestra, though it was mostly for high school kids. Gath was a small school, and they needed trumpeters, didn't they? In truth, probably not. His earnestness would have to persuade the music teacher to overlook his present lack of skill.

Of course, the horn meant more to him than a chance to see Miriam regularly. At his age a lot of things were tied together by one thin cord, and he was trying to hold them all with it. Besides practicing some simple parts for the orchestra, he had taken the horn to the country a few times to blow it like a bugle and feel again what he had known that day in the cemetery when Buell Grace played *Taps*. He blew against death. Death snuck out of his sight like a yellow dog when the bugle scared it, and the ripening cornfields, the distant farmhouses, and the birds going over were alive, forever alive, alive forever.

So on the first day of school he carried his horn with a mixture of pride and anxiety he had never known before. It was as if it were he himself inside the cheap leatherette case and some kind of boy-machine were carrying him along the sidewalk to where he had to go.

Then—sober and back in reality—he was in the gym, where the orchestra practiced before classes began, showing off the horn to his friends when Miss Slater came down. Buell Grace was hefting it and admitting it had a keen action. Miriam, who played a tenor sax that was gold-plated all over, had said that "a Pan-American is a very good make." With the tip of her little finger she erased a dust spot from the plated bell of his horn and smiled as if her reflection in the polished metal had flattered her. The other kids were tooting their horns and scraping fire-siren sounds from their violins, waiting for Miss Slater to come and assign them their lesson schedules and—maybe—give them a little warm-up practice on this first day.

When she finally appeared on the stairs, her eyes darted busily around the group. "Harlan Casey? Is Harlan here?" she asked.

His spirits sank a little. He had been sure she would at least remember his face from the times he had sat in on practice sessions last spring. "Here," he said.

"They want you in the principal's office," she told him. She seemed a little surprised and not as pleased as she might have been to note that the horn he was holding seemed to be his own. "Just leave it on the edge of the stage," she directed briskly. "Nobody will step on it. I hope." The kids all giggled about that crack.

His heart was drumming and his wind was short by the time he had climbed to the principal's office on the third floor. He couldn't guess what he'd done wrong—already on the first day, when he hadn't even been to his grade's room except to leave his books. It took him a full minute to understand he was wanted on the telephone.

"I'm glad they found you so quick," his mother said. "Now you can get home and back before the bell rings."

"But I'm at the *orchestra*," he shouted desperately. "What's *wrong?"* Maybe he could be back in his room by the time the bell rang. But by then the first gathering of the orchestra would have broken up with no place assigned to him. He had hoped to sit beside Buell Grace and learn from watching Buell, hoped also that when things were tough Buell's playing would keep his own unsounded notes from being noticed. "What's *wrong?"*

"Chris," she said. "You know he was so anxious to go this morning. He had his sack of supplies set all ready by the front door, his new jeans on—just like yours, he said. I thought I'd walk over with him so he wouldn't have to go alone this first time. We got as far as the Reinharts' corner, just at the end of the hedge, and he balked. I just couldn't make him understand. He says he wants to go with you. But if you're already in the midst of ——"

"I'll come," Harlan said angrily.

As he took the hot, damp receiver from his ear, he heard her promise that they would come halfway to meet him.

He knew all he was in for when he saw Chris's smile. It was the kind they painted on angels' faces in the Sunday-school quarterlies—wide, curving, and sweeter than any really honest stretch of the mouth could be. From a block away Harlan saw his mother and Chris lurking partly out of sight at the end of the Reinharts' hedge, waiting for him. As he ran to meet them, he saw hardly anything except that false, bright smile, growing, broadening until it was like a gully into which he had thrown himself by mistake.

The smile scared him, but he kept steady. He skidded to his knees in front of Chris and, after a winded "Gee!" said, "Gosh, Chris, I forgot you and me had planned to go to school together today. Wasn't that dumb? Hey, you didn't forget your fat pencils, did you? Boy, them jeans look neat, and when we come out for recess I'm gonna personally choose you on my team for football. Hey, how about that?"

"How about that?" their mother echoed.

Chris didn't say a word. His hand fumbled upward as if he couldn't see his brother or didn't want to hear him, as if he sought merely a solid touch to get him moving the way they wanted him to go. He was already stepping out from the shelter of the hedge by the time Harlan's hand closed on his.

Behind them as they went, Harlan heard his mother call,

"Harlan, I'm sorry that you had to come all this way back. But see, you won't be late at all."

She was even wrong about that. She had hardly finished speaking when the sound of the school bell spread over their town, through elm leaves hanging perfectly still in the morning air.

That was the way Harlan's life went that year. It just piled up in junk, as his uncle's aging convertible had piled up on a bridge abutment seven miles south of Waterloo, Iowa. The highway patrol had come screeching up to that accident, looking officious while they poked in the wreck, but helpless to do anything about it. All over. Done with. A man with his head broken over against the sod of a ditch. A thirteen-year-old lover and musician ditched before he got started.

Because it wasn't just that first morning he had to get Chris to school and make sure he stayed there. It was every morning, for weeks and weeks—into November, as a matter of fact. The kid simply would not listen to either father or mother if they tried to argue him into going by himself or with other kindergartners from the neighborhood. He smiled and nodded and said no to every inducement they could think of. Yes, he liked his kindergarten teacher. Yes, he liked to cut up construction paper and paste leaves and cotton onto a big yellow sheet representing "Autumn." Yes, the other kids had chosen him leader in a marching game. No, he would not go to school unless Harlan walked there with him and, furthermore, stayed with him until Miss Oakes was ready to start the morning program.

A time or two, even, when Harlan happened to glance out of his classroom window at mid-morning, he had seen a patch of yellow hair streaking along the sidewalk. Then he had to get himself excused, race home, and lie and stomp and threaten and grin until Chris was persuaded to return with him, hand in hand.

One time Harlan's father suggested that maybe it would be just as well to let Chris stay out of school another year. The law didn't require him to attend until he was older. In another year he would be so eager to go you couldn't keep him away. Harlan had no comment on this. He knew what he had to do, and he kept doing it.

Another time, at night when Chris was in bed, their mother

said, "You don't have to keep taking him if it interferes, Harlan. Don't you need to be at orchestra practice half an hour before school begins in the morning?"

"I don't want to go to it."

"Don't fib to me," she said with an attempt at jollity. "Why, you've missed three weeks of it already, and I know how interested you are, how much you keep practicing on that horn. Forget about Chris for a while. He'll be all right."

A boil of long-cherished anger burst in Harlan's mind, and he yelled, "You started it all. By fighting with Cousin Edith in church. Making him kiss Uncle Luke." She jerked back in her chair as though he had slapped her.

His father broke in. "Why—why, now, Harlan, that was just to—to sort of say good-bye to Luke. I don't see what that's got to do with school."

Harlan shook his head, already remorseful. A truth that had seemed very simple was beginning to lose its form and solidity. "You hurt his brain," he said. As soon as he said it, he was unsure that such a thing could have happened.

If he didn't know what was broken deep within his brother's life, surely it was obvious he could not expect to fix it. Attempts to question Chris only wound like corkscrews into his own fears and fantasies of death. Once, in response to a siege of browbeating, Chris said his reason for not wanting to go to school was that "he might come here while I was gone."

"Uncle Luke's not coming back. Never. Never. He's dead in the ground."

Blithely, Chris said, "He's only in heaven. He could come anytime."

Harlan shook him. "You *saw* them put him in the ground."

No. It was Harlan who had seen that—had caught the horror of it, at any rate, and kept it like a patient monster waiting down beneath the edge of his daytime thoughts. When he woke that night with the weight of earth smothering his own breath, he lay in the dark, thinking: Chris would forget what he's scared of if it weren't for me.

He couldn't heal his brother. It had to be enough that he was able to keep Chris going, morning after morning, to school. To make up for what he lost by doing so, Harlan had only those minutes on the school playground before the last bell rang in the morning—minutes when he would be standing at the bottom of the tallest slide and look up to see his brother's eyes catch his, like the hands of an acrobat fastening on a flying ring, ready for the long swoop downward. Ready because Harlan was there. Other times he watched little Chris trail the bigger boys onto the jerking spin of the round swing, eyes always turning to be reassured of his brother's presence. Once he fought a kid in his own grade who called Chris a baby. The blood his fist spilled from the kid's nose was a sign of conquest over something invisible, and he took a wild pride in it.

On the other hand, on many of the mornings he spent with Chris on the frosty playground he would hear the sounds of the orchestra coming through the open windows of the gymnasium. In there Buell Grace was perfecting the trumpet parts. Miriam was fingering her gold-plated saxophone. Day by day they were leaving him farther behind.

After the first two weeks, Harlan had gone to Miss Slater and explained he hadn't given up his intention of joining the orchestra. He guessed she knew he had been keeping up with his lessons and practicing by himself harder than ever. "In a few more days" he could come regularly to practice with the others.

"Oh," Miss Slater said. "Yes, I talked to Mr. Winston." Mr. Winston drove to Gath twice a week from the county seat to give lessons on wind instruments. "He says you're . . . doing all right. Harlan, I think next year we're really going to need you. There'll be a place for you as soon as you're in high school. You can count on it."

Next year! Her promise was as empty as a promise that he could play heavenly music after he died. It was worse than nothing. Still, he never let her see, even by a quiver of the lip, how big his disappointment was. A few months ago he surely would have cried or sassed her. Funny things were happening to him.

I've got hard, he thought. He needed nothing from anybody as long as he was true to Chris's need for him. He was getting Chris to school when no one else could. The bargain satisfied him.

Then he lost that justification too. It went subtly, naturally, by alterations as quiet and treacherous as the passage of seasons. One morning in mid-November he had to stay out with a sore throat. Chris cheerfully got ready to go without him.

"You're not scared to go by yourself?" Harlan asked.

"I was never scared," Chris scoffed.

What kind of brother would have reminded him, "You were too?" Let him go, then, Harlan thought, grinning into the bathroom mirror to show himself he was relieved.

Maybe he *was* relieved, at that. But he was agitated and restless too. The gray day at home seemed endless. When the time came to go deliver his evening papers, his mother suggested he get somebody to substitute. "I heard sleet on the window," she said. "With a sore throat you'd better be careful." He accepted her long wool scarf to wrap around his throat, but he insisted on taking the papers himself.

As he trotted around the little familiar town in the dusk, the pain in his throat was a consolation, like a wound gained honorably. Rifling the papers onto leaf-strewn porches, he exulted in the heroism of his loneliness. Harlan Casey, the Unknown Soldier. Yeah. . . .

He was approaching the Robertses' big house with its jutting wing that served for a funeral parlor. He had their paper already folded, ready to throw, when the porch light went on and Miriam came out.

She was just beautiful in that light. Her yellow hair shone like something left intact from June, some huge and confident flower that couldn't care less about the sleety north wind.

Buell Grace came out with her. He was carrying her instrument case. The bulky black thing bumped on his knees as he helped her down the porch steps and across the sidewalk to his father's car at the curb. His pompadour gleamed. His teeth lit up like a flashlight. When he opened the door to let her in, the case swung to tap the back of her legs so she swayed toward him. It looked almost as if she were falling into his arms, and they were both laughing.

It didn't matter to Harlan that they weren't laughing at him. It mattered that they were off to some orchestra performance at the church or town hall that he hadn't even been told about. It mattered that they didn't even know he was in the same town as they were.

They were going to know. They were going to stop laughing.

From the edge of the street he picked up a stone-studded piece of asphalt and threw. He was already running when he heard the impact on the glass of the windshield.

He came home very late that night. He was ill and woozy. He had run a long way into the country before he could get himself slowed down. He found that he had run clear up to where the road hooked behind the cemetery knoll. When his wind was gone, he climbed the viny fence and went to sit where he had met Miriam on the day of his uncle's funeral.

Now there was nothing but the crunching grass and the barrage of sleet, unbroken by town trees up here. Miriam had said, "There is no death." The wind said different. His uncle had— once upon a time—been some kind of hero. At least, they had brought out the flags for his funeral. There was no flag on the night wind, no volley of honor, no ladder of notes slanting upward from a horn with a golden bell.

They all fooled me, he kept saying to himself. Even Chris fooled me when I thought he needed me so much. But Harlan cried because he had fooled himself.

Only his mother was still up when he came in the kitchen door. She had been reading at the kitchen table. Her glasses were twisted on her nose, as if she had dozed off a time or two before he returned.

She started to speak twice before she said, "Buell Grace was here."

"So?"

"He came with his dad. They say you smashed the windshield of his dad's car."

"Oh."

"They saw you running away."

Harlan didn't say anything.

"It's going to cost about seventy-five dollars to replace it, and I suppose we'll have to pay for it if you did it."

He took a deep, rebellious breath, preparing to say that he would pay it all himself. He had his paper route. He needed no help. But he could not answer her that way. The last coins of his anger were squandered on a silent release of his breath. Silently they faced each other across a web of bewilderment.

She had blundered with her children, and she knew it. She had tried to hold onto the past, and it had turned into lies in her mind. Whoever might be hurt by her stubbornness—Edith, or Chris or Harlan—she had meant stubbornly to deny that things could change.

She had lost expectations she could not stand to lose. So, in his turn, had he, and he had struck back just as foolishly. That was their bond and the tether that would probably always trip them up short of what they had to have.

"We'll talk about it tomorrow," she said, taking off her glasses and folding them. "It's not the end of the world. Be sure you gargle before you go to bed."

They would talk tomorrow about the price of windshields, but would never have language for what counted most. They would never learn how to ask forgiveness of each other or to offer it. That was beyond them and always would be. But through the night, by their sleep and their silence, they would forgive each other for being of the same family.

The Sunday
Painter

Bees were drifting around the hollyhocks by the alley fence
and there was a single incandescent cloud near the sun when
Joe Becker carried his brand-new easel and paintbox out of the
basement. Down the street—probably in front of the Carriers'—
he heard the crickety buzz of a sports car's horn. Joan Carrier's
new boyfriend had a purple Singer, he recalled. The early afternoon flight was coming in from St. Louis. But otherwise, he
thought, squaring off with the backyard poplars, flower beds,
and grass, the afternoon was all his. The kids were in camp and
his wife was making her Sunday circuit to see that they were enjoying themselves.

He put up his easel on the flagstone terrace and set the varnished paintbox on the cocktail table. Then he went to the kitchen
to fetch a bottle of beer for himself and some newspapers to

protect the table. As he settled fatly into his director's chair, mounted the dazzling canvas board on the easel, and watched the fat brown bubbles climb in the neck of the beer bottle he thought, *Only an eye, but what an eye!*

Only an eye—it was what someone had said of Manet, he remembered, belching. He was not sure whether he had carried the phrase from an art-history course, taken almost twenty-five years ago in college, or whether he had got it more recently from the art section of *Time*. But as he drank again from the bottle and watched the organic geometry of bubbles disperse the sunlight, he opined that it was the best of tributes. So who would want to be anything more when the visible world was so good? He noted that he had consumed more than half the beer in two draughts. Only a belly, but what a belly. His senses purred with efficiency like the bass bleat of the Singer bearing Joan Carrier off toward Chicago. He squeezed a finger-sized gout of alizarin onto his new palette and happily waved off the bee that settled toward it. Like the bee, he saw in its sunstruck, oily surface the meaning of ripe berries and all the summer a man could want.

His untroubled eyes accepted the sleekness of the suburban lot that twenty years of luck and work had earned him. Near the perennial bed he saw a gardener's fork stuck in the sod with his wife's blue denim jacket hanging from it. Overhead on the maple there was a shark's-tooth end of a branch from which his son Elliott had plunged two years ago and fractured a collarbone. On the swoop of electric wires between the alley and the house were the stick-and-cord remnants of his daughter's kite. The picture he was preparing to paint would show in its details some touching souvenirs of the family life, but it was the sun on the greenery and the shade cutting diagonally across a flower bed that made the picture he meant to catch. He squeezed out green, intenser than any leaf, finished his beer, and went efficiently to work.

In college Joe had studied for a semester with Grant Wood. Now it was rather hard to remember just why he had swung his energy and faith from his courses in the College of Commerce to art. He had had no previous art training. But he had felt that there lurked in him the capacity to do whatever he set himself at. Near the semester's end his faith was given a swift, humiliating fall when Wood forbade him to register for further work in his class. "You've got more speed and less control than any student I ever had," Wood told him, beaming skeptically from his moon face at the garish cows and chickens on Joe's canvas.

"I'm learning a lot," Joe had pleaded.

"*That* may be so," Wood told him with sad, flat finality.

Joe had thought then that he was being flung back forever into the world of Babbitty businessmen who read nothing, who went to Yellowstone Park for vacations and believed in their hearts that the camera had made hand-painted pictures obsolete.

Well, he had been very wrong in his expectations of the future. The engineers, doctors, lawyers, and young executives who had been his friends since the plant went into war production and he got his first breaks on the managerial level had been at least as devoted to art and culture as he. Take Doctor Wagstaff, or Finaly, or Joe Gross for examples, he thought. They traveled in Europe, bought Picasso prints and pottery, and talked more shrewdly of Marx, Proust, Freud, and Thomas Mann than any of Joe's pink or Bohemian college friends ever had.

The people he lived intimately with now were people of more than provincial experience. They were the kind who could laugh with comprehension when he told them drily of being an art student and of being told he had too much speed and too little control. What had been so painful twenty years ago had mellowed and changed, without being totally lost. As he worked now he felt no regret for the years when he had not touched a brush.

He put the square brushload of ochre-tinted white on the gray beside the tree trunk. With splendid self-control he resisted the tickling impulse to scrub it into the gray. As he rolled back in the director's chair and squinted, he saw that he had given the painting another good lick. He saw that he was painting much more skillfully than he had in college. It was as if some scattered seeds of instruction—or some unconsciously developed way of seeing real things—had been all this time maturing. The way he had learned to live was paying off in the reasonable clarity of his painting.

It was almost frightening that on his first trial he should succeed so well in the modest task of imitating his own back yard on a panel. But there it was, a pristine little diagram of the real thing. He put his initials in small block letters on a lower corner and groped down blindly for the last beer bottle he had opened.

He found it empty, too, and thinking that after all it took fuel to put out an effort such as he had just made, he rose to go to the kitchen for another.

Now he saw the girl who sat on the edge of the terrace watching him. Her sunburned face with its horn-rimmed sunglasses drooped between her shoulders as if she had been there a long time. His sun and beer euphoria gave way abruptly to embarrassment and he took a shy glance back at his painting to see if it was presentable.

"What are you doing here?" he said with annoyance.

She was not in the least budged by his challenge. "I'm baby-sitting next door at the Hendersons'."

"Then why aren't you keeping an eye on them?"

She shrugged, stood up slowly, and dusted off the seat of her shorts. Her eyes were baleful, whitish spots behind the sunglasses. The red line of her mouth was the mere edge of her lip structure. One of her knees was scabbed as children's often are. She did not seem to be more than fifteen, but she had an ancient, withering composure. "I adore to watch artists," she said.

Amusement softened him a little and he said, with a deprecatory wave of the hand, "Then you came to the wrong place. I haven't done much painting for a long time."

Her nod of agreement came without reflection. "It isn't very good. People don't paint like that any more."

"No?" he asked with sarcasm that missed her entirely. "How do they paint then?"

"Pollock dribbled it onto the canvas," she said with an ecstatic shrill of triumph in her voice. "He painted great huge pictures as high as those wires back there." The sweep of her gesture succeeded in making Joe's eighteen-by-twenty canvas board seem trivial as a post card against the scale of the late afternoon. "I mean you don't seem to have anything to express," the girl said decisively.

"It happens that I wasn't trying to express anything. Not myself and not my subconscious," Joe said with grim patience. "You better scoot and see about those Henderson kids. Make sure they haven't locked each other in the icebox or eaten glass."

As soon as he had spoken it, his illustration bothered him with its unexpected morbidity. But it seemed to touch the girl's fancy, and she smiled at him as if he had just revealed his true nature. "I adore artists because they do such crazy things," she said. "Van Gogh cut off his ear, and Gauguin ran off from his wife so he could paint exactly as he pleased. Did you see *Moulin Rouge?*"

Joe's patience broke. It seemed to him that the self-satisfaction of repose in front of his work had been uncannily sapped by the girl's jabber. "Haul out of here," he shouted recklessly and stamped his foot at her. "Go home."

Like a frightened cat the girl streaked for the gap in the hedge that let her into the Hendersons' yard. He saw her broomstick legs twinkle past the hedge roots, then saw her climb the back steps with her pursy little mouth set tight in self-righteousness. To let fly a beer bottle at her head right now might teach her not to trespass, he thought, but with a sigh he realized he hadn't the nerve to do it.

The girl had done her damage effectively. He felt unclean from her intrusion and, presently, depressed by the rage to which he had yielded. When he came back out of the house he brought a tumbler of whiskey instead of another bottle of beer, and as he sat glooming in front of his painting he felt well up in him the competitive urge to show that he knew how to raise hell like Pollock, too. It was true that his wife might like to see how he had painted their back yard, but then it seemed to him that this was one thing he wasn't doing for her.

"When I saw your gear set up, I thought you were painting, Joe," Doctor Carmichael said through the twilight.

Joe rose from his knees and stood with heaving chest and flaring nostrils. At the moment he had exactly nothing to say to his neighbor from across the alley. His deepest wish was to leave the painty imprint of his hands on Carmichael's light suit, but again his nerve failed him.

With the tip of a white shoe, Carmichael indicated the canvas board between Joe's feet and bleated, "Wha-a-a-at?"

"It's a rug," Joe said. "I'm doing it as a surprise for Mama's birthday."

"No, no, no," Carmichael said to placate him. "I *see* now that it's a picture. I only wondered what of. The wife told me you were painting your back yard. I see now that you've done something more abstract." In spite of his neighborly intentions and the probability that he didn't turn a sleek white hair when he came across a patient with hemorrhoids like the grapes of wrath—the expression was his own, Joe had heard him use it at a party—or an old lady with a bean in her nose, he snickered when he said "abstract."

"Churchill paints and all the world wonders. Eisenhower paints and it's good for his health. Becker paints and the whole neighborhood watches to see if he'll assault children next." When he had launched this petulance into the evening air, Joe relaxed. "Sorry," he said. "This painting business takes me out too far. Come in and have a drink to get me over it."

He was listening in an alcoholic fugue to Carmichael detailing the tonic effects consequent to an ileitis operation when he heard his wife return from her daylong circuit and park the car in back.

Susan's face, appearing as a spot of white through the gloom of the kitchen, showed such cartooned anguish that momentarily he thought one of the kids must be hurt—or, in a quick adjustment, he reconsidered, that maybe Janet had been that day disgraced in her specialty of the low hurdles. Susan had worn just such an expression when she told him that Janet had been cashiered out of the Brownies for "rivalry."

"I stepped in it," Susan groaned.

His bellow of laughter soothed her, but still she protested, "I was so excited when I saw your easel I wasn't even expecting the painting to be on the ground. I was galloping in to see what you'd done."

"Probably gave it just the modern touch it needed," Carmichael said with sly malice.

Susan had left her paint-soiled shoe in the kitchen, so now she hobbed touchingly as she ran to hug Joe—to be comforted for what she had done to him and to reward him for pleasing her so much. She kissed his neck and dropped her face on his bare shoulder. And, in this moment of tenderness, his conscience nicked him for having smeared over the painting that she would have liked.

"I was so glad you'd gone back to painting," Susan said. "All I was sorry was I hadn't got you some paints some Christmas when I thought of it. Then bigfoot me. . ."

"I didn't realize old Joe was an ex-painter," Carmichael said.

"I'd loused it up anyhow," Joe comforted her. He was too

proud to boast of how good it had been before he tried the Pollock tricks, but he thought, with a deep, alcoholic vehemence and sense of being cheated, *It would never have been on the ground if that damn baby-sitter hadn't hexed me.*

On soberer days he was sure he could do as well, and better, again. When he went out to paint on following weekends he conscientiously hunted out subjects that he expected Susan to like or remember sentimentally. Now that he had discovered that he could paint, he felt ready to range beyond the back yard and on subsequent Saturdays and Sundays brought back to her small, tidy landscapes of the dunes, the river valley near Peoria, the hills around Galena, and a small town near the Wisconsin Dells.

She liked the paintings almost as much as she liked the fact that he was painting—"again" as she always insisted. She spoke of the canvases as her collection, with just enough irony to keep the curse off. She would have framed the first of his efforts left intact and have put it in place of the Degas reproduction over the TV if he had not kidded her into waiting until he got a little better. Privately he still had the troubling notion that the eternally lost painting of the back yard was the best thing he had done. Until he could come up to it, he didn't want any of them hanging before his eyes to remind him that they weren't exactly what he had once briefly seen.

On the other hand, the temptation to experiment wildly with his style was satisfactorily buried after the misfortune of that first drunken afternoon. His daughter Janet was as skeptical of his results as the baby-sitter had been. He mixed his colors too much, she said. He had to admit that under the guidance of some Miss McKeon at her school she had produced, with showcard colors, works closer to Matisse's than he was likely ever to do. But, "I'm trying to paint what I see," he assured her. "I know people don't paint that way any more, but it's more fun for me this way." Once he explained to Elliott that making a painting was very much like making a piece of furniture or building a house. First you had to shape up the big parts in the rough proportions, then gradually you added touches that smoothed everything together, and you saved the detail work until last. If Elliott seemed only partly satisfied by the analogy, it pleased Joe that he was able to articulate his own method of working. The only problem, as far as he could tell, was to smooth out his technique.

But his second major discovery, with all its troublesome implications, came slowly and inevitably out of the original one that he knew what he was doing in adjusting hand to eye. On a Sunday when he was painting a sand bar in the local river it became unarguably, irrevocably certain to him that he was not painting objects but light itself. He understood very well that such a discovery was no more original than, say, repeating Franklin's experiment with the kite and key to affirm the nature of lightning. It was one thing, though, to have read the proposition, or to have heard it in a college lecture from which he remembered nothing else, and something altogether more impressive to find the truth of it self-evident in a painting he had started to put together like a piece of furniture.

"There I sat, like a frog on a log, painting *light* by God," he said when he showed the picture of the sand bar to Susan.

To which she replied with innocent enthusiasm, "The place hasn't changed much since before the war, has it? Except that there used to be a big tree stump stuck in the sand down at that end, remember?" She saw only the place they had claimed as a family picnic ground for many years.

"I'm going to have this one framed," she insisted. Though he agreed that she could if she wanted to, it seemed to him that a kind of treachery against her was commemorated by the framed painting. It hung over the TV set like a testimonial of her faith in their life together. She had thought he was painting the sand where they had buried hundreds of chicken bones, the water that covered a thousand of their discarded beer cans, and the patch of shade in which they had often listened to Studs Terkel's disc program. So every time his eyes rose to the picture he was reminded of an ominous separateness in their way of seeing things. Light had got between them. Some day he might begin to doubt—or cease to care—that she existed behind the light rays that revealed her to his eyes.

It was a devil of a problem if he bore down hard on it, worse than cheating on her with another woman. He had been technically unfaithful to her nine times during their marriage. None of those infidelities had counted much. But this one could, unless he headed it off.

Joe tried to talk it over with his friend Finaly one evening while they were sitting beside the country-club pool. "It's an insidious notion when you get it," Joe said. "You could find yourself looking at your own kids as light refractors or reflectors instead of the little medical, economic, and social problems you very well know them to be."

"That doesn't rule out love," Finaly said philosophically. His sharp face was angled toward the top of the diving tower where Joan Carrier bounced on her toes and reflected a sleek bit of radiance from her white tank suit. "As a matter of fact, if you couldn't see them, how could you love them? Touch them of course," he answered himself, running his tongue nervously across his lips as Joan Carrier dived through the evening air. "All you're saying, Joe, is that you can *see* your loved ones. Be thankful."

"That's not all I'm saying," Joe protested. "On the contrary, your point is you have to see little Joany to stir you up for the chase—which is not so sporting anyway, considering her age. But anyhow, the way you see her, you can build a plan of what to do about it."

"No I can't," Finaly said. "Not really."

"But if you see what she does to *light*, then there's nothing in the world to do about it except paint it."

Joan Carrier swam the length of the pool beside them with a splendid backstroke and the tic under Finaly's mustache appeared twice. "Why paint it," he asked, "when it's already such a lovely color? You want on it petals?"

"Naturally you don't believe me," Joe said. "But try painting sometime long enough to follow it through. You know what? I'm glad I go down to a nice dull office five days a week and talk to raunchy Babbitts like you most of the time. I can understand exactly how, if someone gets too concentrated on painting, he'd strip his threads. It looks so innocent. There I sit out in the country beside the station wagon with my Big Boy straw hat pulled down so none of my boob friends will spot me and come up for the big haha. And what am I? Just another guy with a fancy hobby. But I tell you, funny things go on in my mind."

"Like what?" Finaly said, turning to him with a swiftly kindled interest.

Joe threw out his hands to convey the hopelessness of attempting an explanation. "Just what the light does. It's kind of haunting."

"Oh." The absence of confessional detail was clearly a disappointment to Finaly. He shifted again to watch Joan Carrier climb out of the pool and flick from her thigh a shower of droplets that modulated the sundown colors. "Haunting," he said with a great laugh of resignation. "Unattainable. You can't deal with it."

The next in Joe's chain of discoveries, then, was that he had waded over his head into trouble. Some time after his talk with Finaly he warned himself solemnly to put the lid on this painting business before it led him to a mental breakdown. If his friends and neighbors wanted to gossip and smirk about his painting, that was one thing. If they got the idea he was losing his marbles, that was something else again.

He pledged himself to stay away from painting as an alcoholic would pledge to stay away from the drink he knew himself unable to handle. One day, when the family drove into Chicago together, Susan suggested that he might like to spend the afternoon looking at paintings in the Art Institute. He laughed haughtily and declared he was getting bored with art. He intended to go with Elliott to the ball game that afternoon.

As soon as he had taken his seat in Wrigley Field he knew that he had made a mistake. He had come here for safety—and in front of him, like Monroe on the office calendar, was the most luscious spread of light he could remember ever having seen. He could not force himself to care about the game. Like a pig he glutted his eyes with the light.

He was hooked and he tried to fight his treacherous addiction by indulgence in the vices that he had learned to manage. Liquor had served him well before at times of crisis—like the time when Susan had discovered he was meeting with Edith Lesseps in Chicago—and up to a point heavy drinking served him now. His family found him somewhat easier to deal with when he was slopping it up. Half-drunk, he could concentrate on anything put immediately in front of him for his amusement. When he was hungover, light was something to jar his sensuousness, rather than excite it—just as Edith had done when he took to liquor to refute his involvement with her.

He gambled more than he had for years and mentally wrote off his losses as the necessary expense of convalescence. He daydreamed of an affair with Joan Carrier or one of her energetic contemporaries. He went so far as to lead Joan out from one of the country-club dances and attempt something halfway between fatherly fondling and assault in the darkness behind the hedges. ("Mr. Becker, this just isn't fair to Mrs. Becker," Joan said to cool him off.)

These diversions helped, he thought, but they were still not enough.

He refused to permit himself any more weekend drives in search of subject matter for his painting. He meant to taper off by messing around "a few more times" with sketches of his back yard—until its familiar forms ceased to have any interest for his eyes and would leave him in peace. As the summer ended it seemed to him that this stratagem was not going to work either.

His back yard, with the purer light of autumn changing it every time he looked, was more than enough to stir him with exciting challenge, and he found himself lusting goatishly to be left alone with it (and his painting gear) for as much time as he could spare each week. And, involuntarily, he found ways to insure that he would be alone. Once he slapped Janet when she peered over his shoulder and told him he hadn't got the top of the Carmichaels' house yellow enough. After this, and some intolerable sarcasm to Elliott, Susan announced that the family would leave the premises entirely while he had his painting fits. Then in spite of himself, Joe felt a sly, sad triumph at this bit of management—as if he had tricked them into parting for the safety of innocence while he dug for a buried corpse that they must never know anything about. It was better to hurt them a little than to expose them to destruction, his bad conscience reasoned.

One November afternoon when he was painting devotedly, he heard behind him a voice that was shockingly more familiar than it had any right to be. "You're still doing the same thing."

It was the Hendersons' baby-sitter, the girl who had interrupted him on his first Sunday of painting. Instead of shorts and blouse she was wearing an ugly fuzzy coat now. All trace of suntan was gone from her little face, and without color there was something especially grisly in her appearance.

"So?" he answered with resignation. As a matter of fact he had just been close to reproducing the success he had achieved almost haphazardly in his first effort. With a mounting, nervous excitement he had felt the growing picture tug him along like a divining rod toward the point at which he would be released into complacency, toward the sense of mastery over his own property and himself.

"I mean, how come?" she demanded. "Don't you get tired of always doing the same thing?"

"I'm trying to learn how to do this one thing right," he said. "It's no skin off you how I waste my time." He remembered that he had slapped his own dear daughter for interrupting him, and he felt his shoulder muscles twitch with the need for anger and action. "I told you before and I tell you again, if you're baby-sitting for the Hendersons, then go back and do your duty. I'll have a word with them if you ever cross over again." He stirred a brushful of cadmium yellow into a pile of viridian and fought down the temptation to throw this gaudiness onto his painting. He was wiser now; he wouldn't let her tempt him into ruining this one.

"Did you see Kirk Douglas in *Lust for Life?* He's Van Guff and he *does* cut off his ear," she said in a purring, recitative voice. "Artists are the most interesting people in the world when they let go. I won't be satisfied until they make movies of all the other ones. Pascin hung himself on a doorknob. Utrillo was a drunk. Modigliani had TB and wouldn't keep his feet dry. Toulouse-Lautrec's legs were no longer than *that.*"

Before Joe's fascinated eyes her hands spread in a truncated measurement. Between the hands her smirking, reckless face leaned toward him as her gaze seemed to probe for his deformity.

For the sake of composure needed to finish his work, Joe kidded her instead of striking. "Not me. I'm no artist. I'm a businessman. Legs normal. Lungs normal. I've got both ears." He lifted his hand to see if he had.

"That's what I *mean,*" she said, snottily minimizing him. "You don't try. You don't let go." She abandoned him then. There was no other way to read her slow, contemptuous retirement through the hedge.

It would have humiliated him to throw a retort after her—though he had one ready—and he turned with desperate concentration to his work. He swept a broad streak of greenish white deftly onto the canvas. It went on like a swipe of cheese on bread, and then the painting was totally successful in what he had wanted for it. Allow for seasonal differences and the fact that he couldn't remember all the brush strokes of his very first painting of it, and then it was the same satisfying image that he had lost under paint squirted straight from the tube on that other afternoon. It was his yard.

In the instant of comprehending his success and lolling back into it, he made his last discovery. It was that painting didn't matter. Just as Finaly had said—and without all the worry of discovering it step by step for himself—you could see without painting, and painting light was only *seeing*. With this fizzling discovery, the dynamics and the worry of his months-long effort failed. He realized the foolishness of adding another dab to this painting or ever starting another one.

With an inordinate sense of relief he slouched into the house. From here on, he knew, he could keep his loving family around him. Janet could have his painting kit if she wanted. It would be useful for a feminine pastime, but he was through with it. What had been annoying his basically healthy system had been explored and rooted out. He had found the buried corpse in the yard and what a fake it had turned out to be. Nothing more than the corpse of his first successful painting. Hah.

His first, second, and third drinks were celebrations of regained satisfaction with himself. At his Sunday ease he expanded a plan for announcing to his long-suffering family the end of his adventure in art. He fetched his paint kit and painted a mustache on the sand bar in the painting so tastefully framed above the TV set. Then nipples. (A little raw for the kids, perhaps, but he counted on their sophistication.) On the TV screen he painted round, idiotic eyes and the motto of his high school class in Latin. He signed Picasso's name in the lower-right-hand corner of the screen. Pollock never went *this far,* he exulted. *None of them ever had,* something whispered in confirmation. He ought to drag that uneducated little baby-sitter over here to show her how far he could outdistance Van Gogh when he wished to.

His bulky arms were trembling when he poured himself the next drink. The outrage he had submitted to from that little witch began to surface as honorable wrath. What did she know about art that gave her the right to talk? Plainly nothing except what she got from the movies and sensational books, but she had the hairy temerity to suggest to his face that his very lack of deformity was a deformity. "Hell of a thing to say to a sincere man," he growled. Hell of a thing to suggest that his very lack of deformity was the buried corpse whose discovery would bring his family to ruin or shame. Hell of a thing to sneak over in his yard—his own yard, as even his painting of it had confirmed— and try to infect him with unanswerable questions, like some dirty metaphysical Typhoid Mary. A person like that would cause trouble in all quarters unless stopped.

If I were her parent, he thought, *I'd know how to deal with her.* Then he realized that, being Joe Becker and having explored art clear down to its sterile origin, he knew anyway. He had learned something of use.

With his paintbox swinging in his hand he ran for the Hendersons'. A wild counterfeit of dedication shone from his rolling eyes.

He was straddling the baby-sitter, painting her green with cadmium yellow highlights, when the Hendersons arrived home and marshaled other neighbors to subdue him.

"I'm not really hurt and I don't think you should persecute him," the baby-sitter said to the intern who came with the ambulance to take him away. "Artists have enough troubles as it is."

The Life
of the
Sleeping Beauty

Her house in the world's eye was 8507 Wickard, a kellystone duplex in Oak Park, but in reality it was among roses and fires that Miranda slept. Within their rings and fragrance she dreamed of a stone angel melted and reduced to its most primitive bulge, like overheated wax. She dreamed that outside the circle of fire waited pale Albert, grim Ernie, the Flier, the luxurious Pimp, Bert the Needle, and Lusty Liverlips the neighborhood degenerate.

The gentlemen have sought Miranda obediently. In the heavy lake of fact they have dredged for the deep jelly of her essence. Ranked in summer they stood once outside the magic of the house in Oak Park and while the trolley bounced flashing on the cable watched the upstairs window light go out behind the curtains of American Miranda—the little ardent boys.

Bert understands that in her life time lies over time like stacked film slides which altogether make one image, but there were

INCIDENTS OF ROSE AND FIRE

The thin branches beside the porch drew back again and again under the wind and then sprang straight, like switches released against the clouds' bottoms. It was almost spring in Oak Park. It was almost time for her to go in from play. Mama would come and ask, "Miranda, getting cold?"

She left the buggy sitting in the middle of the porch. She sat in the corner under a kellystone pillar, watching the branches whip the sky. She sang her own song to them. She encouraged them to whip the white. Billy came out the apartment door and

In a childhood crime she comprehends the populous future.

(Liverlips Sherman caught her arm in the deserted hall at school where her heels clicked on the tile and it smelled of antiseptic from the toilets, and said it to her.

Ernest got so angry he called her a damn PT to her face the night at the beach when only the chilly wind and the gritty moisture of the sand kept her chaste.

Moreen's cousin looked like he would cry and said Oh Damn, why did you come up here if you didn't want to How do you think this makes me feel Shall I take you home now? Then she said miserably, No. All right.)

The boy beast, fretful with jokes, destroys her doll. Through the hollow head of the

put his foot on the axle of the doll buggy. It rolled down the steps and crashed. He said he didn't mean to do it;

(and once only eighteen years later it occurred to her in a moment of hilarious insight They never any of them mean to do it. The cars, the apartments, the drinks they buy for you to get high are just an accident they have. They stumble on your pretty things like they fall over an iron fence What makes them so afraid they call it an accident?)

broken toy she peers toward her salvation by the comic savagery of the male.

he said, shoving her face against the kelly-stone, "Don't you tell your Mommy. I didn't mean to kick it. Wasn't my fault." The stone scratched her face and left red marks that her mother would see. Poor Rosie's head was broken as a cup breaks when she spilled out on the sidewalk. Billy ran away fast.

The boy, by his flight, confirms the dreadful identity of desire and crime—in action enunciates the parallelism of itch and taboo.

(ran away
Sherman ran away when he thought he heard the janitor coming. Ernest didn't run away so fast as he just drifted out of her life more in sorrow than in anger. In June after she had gone with him first to the apartment in March, Moreen's cousin wouldn't answer the telephone, which isn't exactly running away.)

She squatted down, singing magic to herself again, beside poor broken Rosie, then pulled the broken head off. Through the holes in Rosie's neck and the top of her head she looked up at the sky and at the apartment across the street, using the broken head as a telescope. Mama found her then and Mama was mad at her, though it wasn't her fault. Mama said, "Miranda, what happened? Put it down, Miranda. You'll cut your fingers. How could it have happened, Miranda?"

The voices of women supplement the ringed fires of her enchantment.

(I don't know, Miss Wayne. It was there when I came back from recess Thursday.
"You didn't put it in your desk yourself?"
No, Miss Wayne.
"Did he ever—did they ever give you notes like this before?"
Oh no, Miss Wayne.
Miss Wayne's face turned red as lust. She looked

A straightforward invitation from a lad of eleven. Miranda was invited to fornication after the class party held in the gymnasium on a Friday evening in April in her fifth year in school.

Nevertheless, who has more luck than children? There are realities that never happen and reconciliations in innocence.

And the dilemma makes the myth.

at the tinted map of Asia hanging unrolled beside her desk and said, "Do you know what these words mean, Miranda?"

Not that one. Miranda put her fingertip on it on the torn scrap of ruled paper.

"If you know who passed it to you, you ought to tell me. Don't you understand that, Miranda? It's wrong not to tell me."

Yes, Miss Wayne.

"There is a siege and your enemies move day and night and in the health of your own blood, in the flattery of your mirror, in the laundry-smelling white sheets they lie with their ambushes. I am your only friend. Be fearful."

Thank you, Miss Wayne.)

There were Christmas mornings to come creeping down the stairway, the warm flannel of her pajamas holding against her skin, the flannel feet making no sound on the slick wood; to open the door of the room from which she had been kept, the forbidden room, and see—shining over all the years of waiting, the pain of birth among the animals, the expectancy of fear—see the star of pleasure shine brighter and more beckoning than the actual gifts.

(Like the slow March rain on the window, the single lamp—too frilly for a man's apartment, she thought—burning at the far side of the room when she did not care if he was lying when he said he loved her.)

The room at the YW where they had Art on Saturday smelled like the dirty little girls who came there. She sat at a big round table with her brushes in a jar of water beside her. She liked pencil best. It was neater and she almost had her drawing the way she wanted it when thin Mr. Hill, her teacher, saw it. Mr. Hill was from the Art Institute and her mother said he was good and would help her. Anyway he stood there grinning for a minute and said, "Now Miranda, Now Miranda. You're drawing just the same things all the others are. Oh Gee, why do you want to draw a drum majorette all the time?"

The other girls do, she said sulkily.

"Maybe. Sure. I can't keep all of you from doing it, but I expect more from you, Miranda. Can't you think of something else? People at a circus? People in a store? Something *real?*"

A mother and a baby.

"Oh Gee, no. Haven't you seen anything this morning on your way up here that interests you? How about people on a picnic? Or paint something you imagine."

She started with the thin line of roses at the top of the page, one after another across the page. She drew them with her pencil for a long time, until she grew tired. She got one of the big sloppy brushes out of the water jar and opened her orange showcard paint. At the bottom she made a crested smeary line of flames and then another, larger. She saw Mr. Hill coming back toward her, and she tipped the paint jar so she could get it out faster. By the time he got there she had painted the flames to the top of the page.

"Well," he said. "It's abstract, all right."

It's what you told me to do, she said. She went to the cloakroom primly, took her coat and hat and walked out of his class for good.

Art, they say in Oak Park, doesn't necessarily have to be pretty—but it has to be SOMETHING.

THE TRIUMPH OF FIRE

Look where the oak door opens and we pass through darkness to the amphitheater—soft Christians given to our lion friends.

wrought by and in spite of herself by Miranda; completed in January, 1947.

A man like Bert would insist finally on showing you the scar and describing the rate of flow, the sensation of fluidity, the brown bubbles and flotation of his excrement—in torment and, God, should he not be tormented, who from his natal dream had visualized her antagonist who was now his wife.

Feigning and unfeigning, lock and cock, light and spite, are the means of sin.

Shall I expound whore to you? Cold Russian winters that appear so barren, as if nature had forgot the spring.

"The idea," Alison said, "is to get all the wives of graduate assistants to contribute whatever talents . . ."

"Sin?" Bert said from across the room. His voice was hideous in its presumption of suffering. For an instant it seemed that he had joined the conversation she was having with Alison, and then they heard him going on, crying his secret disasters to the pansy in the black coat. "You people talk about it like it was a new subject and you were going to be graded on it. You can't beat the U of Chicago and the fakirs and yogis that apprentice themselves to it. Nor good old Saint Thomas. Oh reverend Sin, protect us from paying our landladies rent, give us a brown nose with the medievalist on the faculty, save us professional students from having to go out with honest men and get a job. Shut all your goddamn mouths about sin. What do you know about it? Ask Miranda. She is one who knows about it. She can smell it out anywhere. Tell them, Miranda."

Fortunately there were only the remains of Alison's party left by this time. Alison and Miranda were in the door of the kitchenette, holding, each of them, a drink in one hand and a cigarette in the other. The grandson of the English Earl was on the floor with the rocking horse that belonged to Alison's boy. Besides these and Bert there were only the three students who had been arguing with Bert for hours on the subject of whether Louis Budenz could be likened to Saul.

"I mean that she has studied it like a woman does," he said.

What did I *do?* she called in a slight, even voice, and he looked at her in anguish.

"Do?" he said. "Do?" He grinned enough to show his teeth. "You didn't do anything."

In the season of sin, refraining is sin.

After that in the hush, he went out and they heard him thumping his feet downstairs, the sound of his steps like a child's who stomps out a reproach when he is sent away.

"Here," Alison said. "Miranda, be wifely and take his coat. A man can't go running around on a night like this without his coat. You can catch him."

But what did he mean? she asked in a shocked voice.

"Oh, honey, he didn't mean anything. He's drunk."

"Do you want us to go with you, Miranda?" the students asked.

No, because he was right and right to run. I understand and you can't. If you came out with me, hexed into the wind and drifts that you misunderstand for cold— you couldn't take it, boys. Thanks.

Carrying Bert's coat she walked exactly as far as the nearest taxi stand on 55th Street, found a cab, and went home. Their apartment was stuffy when she came in. She raised the bedroom window a couple of inches and the snow entered, small flakes that disintegrated over the radiator. She did not wonder where Bert was. She undressed hastily, brushed her teeth, went to bed, and dreamed of nothing at all. Now it had all been fulfilled. After eight months of marriage in which she had tried—in which she had wanted to try—in the emptiness of his grief he had finally shown her to the citizens at Alison's party, lifted the ashen skirt headhigh so they could gape at the curly black souvenir of the chock-full

Isthmus wisdom bides despair.

The smell of Bert is in the room—his pipe tobacco, raincoat that smells like fried fish, toe jam.

You call me ice in the snow city.

mystery of childhood, and there was not going to be any more to this marriage.

If I am not Miranda—she thought once while she was brushing her teeth—then what, what, what, what, what have you made out of me?

Find me a life, she thought, addressing him, and I'll live it for you. But . . .

When did this blaze of snow begin? One other morning when the birds had sung and when she got up earlier than any of the family? She could sniff the rain that had fallen on the bricks during the night. She could see, leaning from her bedroom window, the tree in the yard luminous in the pre-dawn, the black incisions of the wires across the soap-colored sky, the city birds wheeling off over Chicago and the lake. She could hear her sister breathing gently, beautifully in the room behind her. Marjorie was her love, she thought. She saw Marjorie's purse lying on their study desk on a copy of *Vogue* that Mama bought for them both. The catch on the purse was open so it was not wrong to look inside. There might be a snapshot, a letter, a present, in it. The table knife slid out when she touched the purse, tapping the desk top so she thought it might wake Marjorie. Then out fell the fork and spoon—cheap silver from the drugstore on Orlando Avenue. She knew as soon as she saw it that Marjorie had stolen it. She wanted to cry. She wanted to wake Marjorie and ask her why she had done it, but she heard the sweet untroubled exchange of breath, and it seemed all at once, terribly, that it was she, not Marjorie, who had done the awful thing. Waiting, she sat beside the desk. She saw inside the purse the handkerchief with a spot of crimson where Marjorie had

. . . it had begun in multiples. Once more it is necessary to point out that existences proliferate back and forth and diagonally in time.

The sister lies like a mirror wrapped in tissue in maiden luxury of lecherous sleep.

Stolen instruments of gluttony cram the secret purse.

As murderers confess us and thieves bring their loot finally to our hand . . .

wiped off her lipstick before she went to bed, and suddenly it seemed to her that a maggot was creeping through the folds of the cloth. She heard the sparrows on the wires outside. She was chilly now, but she would not go back to bed to lie beside Marjorie.

It was all phrased, the way she would accuse Marjorie when she woke. You did *not* go to the movies last night with Eloise like you told Mama. I know where you stole these.

"Oh foo," Marjorie said, rolled over sleepily. "What you doing up? Don't worry. Just don't worry."

You stole them and your handkerchief . . . (stained bright as blood).

"Just don't tell anybody," Marjorie mumbled. But she did and got the pretty little family of four all fighting over where Marjorie had been and with whom. Daddy wanted Marjorie to take the silver back where she had swiped it and Mama later threw it in the neighbor's garbage can. Marjorie called her names and by that evening she was so sick they had to get the doctor in for her. When she slept, after his cool medicine-smelling hand had rubbed her forehead, the fires licked clear to the top of what she could see and bent their points there like a gasflame under a pan.

(Eloise and Marjorie asked her, "Don't you know? Don't you know what will happen to you?"

No, she said stubbornly.

"Oh yes it does. Hahahahahaha."

Only in the circle of fire I can sleep forever. I don't want to be . . . that.

"When they say wake? When you can't help yourself?" I will not hear.)

At camp coming out of the lake, after she had the shower and rubbed hard and

Relentless reality of Time seeking its own level, eroding the innocence of high valleys and sluggish with pirated earth later.

dried between her toes with the good towels Mama had sent her, then she pulled on the white sterile socks and her sneakers. The thread always seemed starched though it wasn't, and she could feel the firm separate threads pressing into her clean feet. She walked in the powder of dust across the ball diamond to the tent for Handicrafts where she was making a leather and aluminum belt. The sun scoured the whole sky clean overhead and the afternoon was *dry*. She felt a pride in her white shorts and middy with the camp insignia stamped on it in blue—the crisp anonymous uniform that all the other girls crossing the diamond (like echoes of herself) were wearing.

Snow bright.

We are the girls of Sparta. We have played and tired ourselves in the sun.

Been of the same Spartan mind when the family drove next summer to the Point O' Pines for their vacation. In the clear water of the lake the float's shadow across the bottom sand while the sun went over. She swam dogpaddle to the float with Daddy because Mama and Marjorie couldn't swim so far. Daddy lay on his stomach on the float, and she watched the water run down in the creases of his shoulder muscles, making puddles that reflected not the sky only but some memory of the sky as well. They had the float all to themselves for an hour, watching the perch swim under its shade, weightless, rowing themselves delicately with their fins. Then the Beauteous Blonde swam out alone. Daddy sat up, grinned, began to talk to the Blonde. "What kind of birds are those flying?" the Blonde asked, and when she pointed Daddy leaned his cheek against her shoulder to look along the pointing finger.

Intrudes into the idyll the round stamp of womanflesh—the witch of nether heat.

Fears in the lust of her father the fulfillment

Come on, Daddy, I'll race you in. She jumped up and purposely shook water from her bathing suit the way a dog shakes itself, showering those nearby.

Daddy flung up his arm in real annoyance. "Here, look what you're doing," he said. "Swim on in. I'll watch you. I'll lifeguard you." He naturally (abominably) wanted to stay with *her*.

She whined Come on with me. I might get a cramp. I'm afraid.

He shrugged at the Beauteous Blonde, and she smiled, wrinkled her nose to show she understood it all.

It wasn't right for him to be with that woman—so he had to give in and swim with her to the beach where Mama was lying on the blanket reading *Collier's*.

Oh, she had gone far to come back to that old time when the fire scoured everything like the pure sun on the enamel of the sky.

Gone—to hear Bert ask, "Is that all it's going to be?"

I don't know, Bert. Can't you leave me alone?

of the prophecy, the damnation wrought of her own juices.

This like a photo of herself, gangly and long-legged, in the uniform of the camp that she found tucked in a drawer bottom, turning brown and crinkled under the silk things that must have been stacked, restacked over it for years.

it's still me.

Had she come all the way for this . . .

THE KNIGHT'S ATTEMPT

Inside the rings of torment and attraction she lay, bare enough, while in the teeming world they advertised her on the billboards and theater marquees. On December evenings old cripples looked at the frosty signs bearing her portrait and spat seminally into the Northern snow.

In those years she was mentioned by an alias in the perfume ads (Myrna, Gloria, Jehanne, and Lois—sultry as snakes in a fiddlecase, odorous of river-mouth and fish in the nuptial reeds). Her eyes looked

It was a part of the terms of the enchantment that she should be won by the unknown hero, impersonal and existent only insofar as he bodies forth the ritual of the times. Naturally a warrior.

from the covers of periodicals too numerous to mention. They called her the American Girl and sold smuggled postcards of her in the elevated stations. But everywhere they coupled with her the motto

Win her like the champion kewpie. Wear her as a disastrous ornament. Who dares?

WHO DARES?

In the chip from the windowblind and the great loving eye of the mirror she pleased herself alone with what the civilization had built towers of stone to spy out. But, imprisoned, she believed for a long time that no one would dare the fires for her. They would circle and fear.

Why do good girls like athletes? Because they're strong.

Besieged and safe, she grew up the envy of the non-American world, the toast of teams, the image in a calculating eye.

She dreamed of the brown angel stone again and the shoulderblade of a basketball player—and one year had puppy dreams of Ernest May, God bless his boyish heart, who had an old Buick, took her to plays, dancing at Roseland, to the Art Institute (it was the year of the Picasso show), sailing on his grandfather's sloop, on a picnic on a green hill north of Evanston. They were walking along the breakwater, the overlapping waves shiny and phosphorous and the wind feeling her face, ears, hair. Tickling, brushing, pleading, the night won her while fumbling Ernest turned into a repelled shadow, not tall enough, not strong enough, not brave enough. She lost him floating out over Lake Michigan where the other shadows might as well live.

and the granular cold of the sand was his fault.

From Plymouth Rock to the *Reader's Digest* they had put the bel-

There could be only one. He must come armed in steel. It was not as a joke that the enchantment was laid. His face when he broke the flame circle must be a steel plate with slits before the eyes.

(Will there be such a one?

If they need him they will bear him. Wombs work like a potter's fingers to shape the new man.

How shall they know the need?

The women will know.

And this armed one was made?)

They took an ordinary hunk, gave him steel for his hands and feet to control, masked his GI face over with glass, aluminum, and leather. He sent his picture to Miranda, a picture of armor and mask. It did not matter who he was before—she knew him.

She was eighteen the day she saw him last—saw him not as the old type man, but him in one of the tricycle planes rolling and bumping out one after another to the concrete runway, to crouch there, the exhausts blasting terribly while the plane stiffened on its course, straightened, and was airborne.

It seemed, in a brief glimmer of her insight, a lot of trouble to go to just for her in their collective assault—the old lechers paying their taxes and the little boys giving their pennies to bring the ravishing hero flying through the ring of her defenses. But that's the way it had to be it seemed then, when she was eighteen. The stern enchantment would yield to this ordinary one clad in the steel of the big war.

(For him they drew the topographic and aerial maps of her borders, explained in the bachelor relaxation of operations tent the concentrations of defensive fire and the approach to the principal objectives. Owl-eyed G-3 with a long pointer touching the harbor fringe, tracing the line toward the obscene river while the squadron stood there sweating and stamping in

lows to the protecting flames.

Women watch the Sunday morning planes rape the supine island harbor.

What anguish dreamed this monstrous aggregate into the neutral air? Is it still possible that the "invention" of the airplane is not understood in spite of the suggestive testimony of names? Who, indeed, are Kitty Hawk and The Great Artiste?

the tropic morning, the clay of India under their feet for a tent floor.

Rendezvoused in the pyramidal by the beer cooler where he touched her picture and said, "How you guys like my beast?" and rendezvoused again at four thousand over the white contours of the beach, going East. Get the tailwind and keep the nose down all the way in. It's got to be fast.)

His death was quite usual—mark that—and according to the formula of our sentiment. He had her picture in a leather and celluloid case over the instrument panel the day they went in low over Rangoon and the first flak killed the navigator and tore up the right wing. He asked for permission to leave the formation. "We didn't come here to check. Keep your place." Whether this flippancy made him sore—as it probably did—nobody ever had time to find out. The rubber-sheathed tank in the belly was smoldering and exploded.

So, Miranda—who must have had a stake in the adventure too—somewhere inside the myth they had made of her, after that hope was all gone and lousy, got smart enough to deny that the enchantment existed. Am I not Miranda? she asked, challenging. They smirked and let her answer that in

So. The myth-makers really expected success. They laid their money that he would get her, built him the long-nosed airplane to do what they could not accomplish. But the hero burned.

SELF-BETRAYAL

Inside the carapace is rosy whiteness—and the whiteness says Is this not I? The answer is "That's meat."

The jelly at its hideous meal thinks . . .
The child careens through a May evening,
    thinking . . .
The viscera has its southern thoughts . . .
The interior hand is nervous and reaches
    for certainties . . .
The meat thinks . . . is voiceless,
    accommodating.

Something was burning. It smelled like hair or fingernail trimmings in an ashtray. Walking barefoot to the bathroom for a drink of water she smelled it at the head of the stairs and stopped. She had not made a sound she thought, and they wouldn't hear her if she stopped to listen. It was all right for Marjorie to smoke in the house, she was old enough now, and the folks wouldn't care about that when they got home. But either Marjorie or Roger must have let a cigarette burn down and fall on the rug while they were paying no attention to it. Maybe they were kissing. She shouldn't have gone to bed and left them because Mama and Daddy were counting on her to be chaperone. Mama had said, "Miranda can make you kids chocolate and a dessert. Have a nice time. Don't let Roger stay too late."

O, it is monstrous to confuse . . .

The radio had been playing softly and nicely. Roger had danced once with her. She was taller than he and so was Marjorie. "The little squirt" her father called him. Over his shoulder she watched Marjorie roll back against the davenport cushions, cross her legs, reach to turn down the light.

I'm going to bed, Miranda had told them. I have to get up early or something.

"Or something," Roger said, catching on quick as a wink.

Are you objecting?

"No—ooooo," he said. He winked at Marjorie and then at her. "Good girl," he said.

They all three giggled over that and Miranda left them.

Now, half an hour later, she stood at the head of the stairway listening, smelling the burnt smell, listening.

("What do you look like?"
Like a baby doll.
"What do you look like?"
Like a Beauteous Blonde.
"What do you look like?"
You know. Like the ideal beast they cut Joe Christmas for. Like Myrna Loy when she turns around right at the end and looks at Clark Gable. Like Mae West only not so much so. Like the florid gildings and the old-fashioned candelabra and the smooth swish of the elevator at the Sheraton Hotel. Like the waters where the crocodiles dive and hover over the slick mud. Like any night in summer when the moon is a coin or a target in the thick air. Like my first girdle, like a tulip in the April bed in Lincoln Park. Like candy haystacks. Like the highest apple on the branch in the September sky, swinging.

Like the things you will not tell us but talk about alone, letting the marbles lie in the forsaken circle, while you stand on your own side of the playground laughing at the latest, writing it on the brick wall. Like Miss America on the catwalk above the photographers. Like the names you give me in convention. Like a wave. Like a Christmas star, like the sound of the wheels of the ashwagon, like a storm, like a logchain pulled out of you. Like Marjorie and Mama. Like a drum majorette. Like what John Keats saw when he put his mind on the Grecian Urn and shoved it into the downstairs cloakroom and looked at it as long as he could.
"What do you look like?"
Now?)

In the apartment of Moreen's cousin. This blade lived with three fellow-students, all pre-Meds.

The radio was playing sugar and, stopping a minute to listen, half turning back at the top of the stairs, she heard it through another door. Moreen's cousin grinned and pushed lightly on her elbow to urge her on. "It's all right, Miranda. It's just the fellows."

The fellows were getting ready to go out. As he had known.

"It's a sloppy night, huh?"

"It's a sloppy night for this time of year."

"But everything is cozy inside," they said.

The fellows got up like sleek gentlemen to be introduced to her. One of them had been reading *Esquire* and had a cartoon he wanted to show her. In the cartoon a Beauteous Blonde lay on a pile of lacy pillows with a telephone and a toy dog and this was all very funny indeed. "Look," he said. His finger lay on the page as though it were part of the illustration. Funny.

"You go to the University? Chi U?" one of them asked in a careful voice.

Yes.

"First year?"

Yes it is, she asserted. I don't know how I like it. I'm studying Art and Philosophy.

"Oh." He raised his eyebrows as though she had said something ridiculous and a touch discreditable, and that's the way everything seemed. They turned their backs to put on their coats and she was so nervous; she knew they were hiding their smiles. She stubbed out her cigarette after only a couple of puffs. The door had hardly closed and she lifted her arms to welcome Moreen's cousin to the davenport. She giggled nervously because it was as funny as the cartoon lying there on the table.

"We can get you a new doll." Mama said. "Don't cry then."

(in which she appeared Beauteously Blonde with the telephone beside her. She heard him turning the radio up louder. He went to the kitchen. "Do you want a drink?" She saw the rain distorting neon light on the window of the cartoon, the frilly lamp on the table across. Within the borders of the cartoon she relaxed and waited for the joke. When he brought the drinks in and saw her head thrown back, her hair spread

. . . symbol with sub-
stance, the expense of
spirit with its waste
of shame.

on the felt of the davenport her throat
flushed, he gaily pretended surprise. "Who
are you?" Miranda, she said.)

mockingly.

It was then as funny as the cartoon in
the *Esquire* if it was anything at all which
it—while the loud radio produced several songs full of cheap roses which he
liked well enough but which were not her
own—wasn't.

"What do you look like, Miranda? 'The
face you had before the world was made'?"

I *want* to tell you, Bert. If you'll only let
me talk long enough I'll tell you everything. It's so altogether, but some of it was
so long ago. I don't remember some of it
and some of it is still happening. I am
something yet, but . . .

His ardent interrup-
tion chokes hope and
speech.

"What do you look like?"

Like a hollow zero, I guess, Bert. I didn't
ever *know*. I needed you to help me know.
Why weren't you always there when I
needed you? When I was a little girl, why
weren't you the little boy in the block? All I
can give you is an accounting now.

The mirror now is fe-
male to ourselves.

THE TALE OF THE ARTIFICIAL FIRES

You see, Bert, maybe that's what we
keep looking for—not what we're born
with or what they do to us, but what this
all means altogether. Maybe? I can feel
what I ought to have been. It's there, it's
like a little girl walking behind me, standing behind the door, waiting around the
corner. But maybe she was there and is
gone and what's left?

(". . . to become useful, God-fearing citizens," he said and drank as a chicken drinks
from the glass of water on the rostrum beside

him. "Thank you. Thank you, Dr. Evans. I am sure that none of the students who heard you will not profit from your thoughts on Education in Wartime." The assembly clapped and Miranda left to walk down to the streetcar by herself. The streets that afternoon were swept by a cold wind coming in from the lake and almost deserted except for the High kids who had just been let out. All over the world the wind was blowing and pushing itself into the splintered houses wrecked by war. In France a little girl who looked like her was standing by a stone window watching the sleet drift on the cobblestones. In Mukden a line of little girls stood with bowls in their hands and the door of the kitchen wasn't opened yet. Their noses ran while they waited in the wind from Siberia. The wind off Lake Michigan stung her silk-clad legs and she was going to talk to Daddy and Mother about it at dinner. They would plan to give some money to the little foreign girls in the cold. And there must never be a war in which so many of them were cold so long again.)

"Nie wieder Krieg," Bert said. "How pretty! But there's always war."

Some kinds don't hurt as much as others, she said.

"Yes they do," he said. "It's stupid to think the amount of war that resides in people can ever be increased or cut down one jot or iota." (Stupid—if he had not used the word so much she might never have needed him enough to marry him.) "You talk about bombs," he said sourly, "and you know in your heart what you really mean. The imaginary planes overhead are the symbol of the Seignorial rapist, refined with the skill of three hundred years of scientific obscurantism until a simple girl can hardly recognize them. Knights in Armor. Exactly. Don't you see what they are?" In his shrill, pompous, lonely voice, loud enough so most of the students and rummies in the U Tap could

What fear is this, that we can come upon ourselves only as strangers?—only *in the world* and never in the street or familiar room?

She sees the world shrink like a child huddling against a kellystone wall on a spring day, welcoming the educational fracture of death.

Pedals his tricycle mind where the other flew mindless.

hear him, he announced, "There is war at this table, in this room. It does not get bigger or smaller when you move it onto a map and use figures with billions. Billions, ha ha." He laughed in contempt of the world's size.

Another Jewish boy who had been sitting behind them recognized Bert's voice and pulled up a chair with them and wanted to get in the argument.

(But once good Mr. Ellington had looked at her respectfully, run his hand through his gray hair, blown a plume of smoke upward so it rose into the dark in the upper reaches of his office. "You have a good mind, Miranda," His smile was fatherly. "Something there all right." He tapped his forehead to illustrate what he meant. "When you awaken from the dream of childhood—my dear, there are tremendous *problems* your generation must face—social, ethical . . ." He was saying this because he knew she meant to marry Bert? "Stand firm, girl. Be true. Be true.")

Bert finished his glass of beer, leaned forward with his drawn face accusing her. "You lament this sweetheart"—he slurred the word harshly—"that was killed in the war. Then you let it slip out that you feel guilty about his death. Well, why shouldn't you? Do you understand what I'm getting at?"

"Let me get this straight," the newcomer said. "I doubt if I agree with you."

("It isn't that Bert isn't *all right*," her mother said. "I'm sure he's just as brilliant as you say he is. He might even snap out of it and be able to support you some time. And it is *not* that he is a Jew . . ." And Miranda thought, No, it's because she thinks I will be the little puppet she imagines me. I will not be a cutout from a family magazine. I am not her daughter to dress cute any more than I am someone else's joke to undress. I am not. I'm going to be Miranda and Bert will help me.

She pressed her nose and lips against the windowpane and listened to the sound of her mother's sewing machine. In anger she thought, Shall I tell her what I was last spring? How I dressed like any good Oak Park bitch just to go downtown to sleep with a junior pill salesman? And it occurred to her, almost without bitterness, that her mother must know that—oh, in a general way.

"He is so . . ."

Absolute, Miranda said.

"Absolute? I'm not sure what that means. Maybe stubborn. He would never see your side of things, dear."

Do I have a side? Does it have to be a battle?

"You know what I mean."

Not any more. But Bert knows me.)

Bert stood with her on the beach while she told him about the talk with her mother. He said her account gave him an idea for a painting. He would call it *Pragma and Enigma in the Desert.*

The scene—the black waves returning like iron ducks in a shooting gallery.

The light faded more and more. They started singing "Pragma and Enigma were sweethearts" and then went to the Loop to get spaghetti.

THE REALISTIC ACCOUNTING

SO I BELONG TO YOU, BERT, BECAUSE I'M . . . . . .

(Dr. Whiteside sat jovial on the bed while Mama and Daddy edging into the shadows as in a picture watched anxiously until he said, "There's nothing wrong with her." He poked his finger into her tummy to tickle her. "You rascal," he said to her. His teeth shone like white cups on a shelf. And she knew, she could not tell them, There's nothing right either. When will I be a woman?)

My God—marriage just gives them the chance to confess in security so that the sin of worldliness becomes the sin of emptiness and they live in a weedy hollow between two ramshackle conditions.

When will I be a woman? When the game boy with the mask takes both my fires and roses in a fierce year of destruction. When the raider swings over the white sea-rimmed beach, the motors pound immensely out of the open sky.

When shall I live?

Bert sat beside the bed. It was August and she had been sleeping a long time with only a sheet over her. She could see nothing but his shoulder bent in a line of anguish, sharpened in her sight when the IC trains passed outside and clamored to a stop at the 55th Street station. He smelled of wind and vomit. "Why didn't you tell me the way you felt, girl?" he said.

Because you knew everything but that.

"It's my fault," he said. "Only you ought to have told me."

Yes, she thought, I did know.

Her voice answered him, It was what you wanted. I'm your bargain. We can't live now. We can only sin—if you wish. She pushed the sheet off her body and lay there looking exactly the way Miranda would have looked, except she was crying. It's because you were too much like the others. You don't love, you wish. I found that out.

(the time of the Winter Dance when I went with Ernie May and Albert Blake followed in his brother's Chevie. I had my mother's fur coat, my second and nicest formal, and Ernie kissed my hand he said I looked so much like a lady, and when we came out afterward into the frosty air on the stone steps of Memorial Hall there was Albie waiting for us in his cheap overcoat and broken shoes, jumping from one foot to the other to keep warm. He had waited for hours there so he could call me a whore and run away. He was a poor boy and thought that Ernie's tuxedo and flask and Buick were part of what I was. I had become something both bad and impossible that he could only glorify with the name whore. That wonderful I was not. Did I have to be? But you believed and your believ-

---

That if anything escapes the foolishness of experience, it's eaten up by the acid of knowledge which experience produces.

. . . to part at last without a kiss?

ing fingers have got me now. You all of you
have what you want.)
 . . . . NOTHING ANY MORE.

LAST MORNING

   She woke early and wondered if he had
found his way back from Alison's party.
She knew she didn't care, but there would
be an awful lot of trouble if he had fallen in
the snow somewhere and just died.

   This was Sunday morning and there
was no light yet in the alley outside their
apartment.

   The storm of the previous night had
stopped perfectly. The city was like the
interior of a piece of lead. The snow had
fallen patiently on it and on top of the
snow a cold fog had come so that the traffic
lights on the elevated were set like enamels
in a gray stone.

   She went to the door and unlocked it
and there he was, all right. He had come
back because he wouldn't accept death like
the rest, like the other one. The bravery of
his return moved her, though it was not
enough. It happened that he was sitting in
the frame of the door and he lost his balance when she opened it.

   Bert, she said. Oh Bert, Happy New
Year or something. Come in, my darling.

   His dark, bloodshot, lifehunting eyes
were suspicious. No, come in, she said.
I can't hurt you any more. It's time for
breakfast. He got up. His clothes were in a
terrible mess.

   Were you awfully cold? she asked.

   He slept until three o'clock in the afternoon while she read, first the Sunday paper and then, when she felt more up to

*and the case of bootleg
reality and black-
market Time.*

*There are no second
acts in American lives,
said Fitzgerald.*

it, *Ape and Essence,* and then woke him. She scrambled eggs and made toast in the toaster her mother had given them for a wedding present.

"I do love you, Miranda, damn it," he said. "It can work. It's got to work," he said. As though she were a machine that thwarted him because he still did not understand it. Looking at her, searching all he knew about her with his eyes that should have had tongues and teeth in them. "Maybe we ought to have a child. I thought about that last night. I couldn't get it out of my head."

Can we? Her eyes met his in hope. Then she laughed insanely. I can't get it out of my head either.

The Goldfish

Probably it was the light of the intensely summery afternoon which exhausted me initially, for, after a shower and a shave, I had felt very fit when I left my hotel room in the Loop. Sometimes I develop headaches or dizziness on days as stunningly blue and luminous as this one was, even when I am strolling on the campus or in the countryside close to home. I am sure that there is some unusual type of photophobia—a recognized disease—which inclines me to these symptoms, but neither doctors nor optometrists have been quite able to pin the condition down for me, though they admit that it must have an organic basis.

It could hardly have been any anxiety about seeing Linda that was playing hob with the way I felt. I had not the slightest reason to doubt that she would be glad to see me. I knew from recent letters that she was happy and well. Perhaps I was responding, in some delay of reaction, to the outdated fears I had once had for her and had fought down too brutally for my own good. Perhaps—But I was truly bothered by that sunlight coming in among the increasingly rotted buildings that lined the street, and I had been hanging for thirty blocks on a porcelain strap that was positively mucilaginous with a deposit of sweat before I gave in and asked one of the Negro boys beside me for his seat. Without any questions, with a perfectly natural politeness, he rose and nodded for me to sit down. Before I could make it, a fat white woman had slopped herself into it. Well. The eyes of the Negro boy met mine; he lifted his shoulders in an amusing way and thrust out his lower lip in an expression that spoke volumes. I smiled back to show I understood perfectly what he meant, clenched my teeth and hung on. It was only a few more blocks to my stop then, and I made it all right—covered with chilly sweat, though.

It occurred to me that perhaps I shouldn't rush on to Linda's feeling as shaky as I did. Wouldn't it have been silly to knock at her door for our first encounter in more than two years and then practically collapse into her apartment calling for water or smelling salts? Worse than silly in the circumstances; it would have been a downright disaster. That's why I permitted myself to go into the bar on the corner, where I quickly had a shot of whiskey.

Of course, it was a Negro bar and not at all well kept, but I must say that I felt more at home there *at once* than I had on the streetcar among members of my so-called race. If they'd like to know, their blue eyes had made me distinctly nervous, or perhaps defiant is a better word. I'd felt if any of them wanted to question my leaving the car in this colored neighborhood I might have said quite rude things to them.

Leaving the bar, I passed two incredible blocks. It would be good to have photographs of such places to show my rather easygoing liberal friends at the college, who admit, of course, the plight of the Negro, but who do not seem to be able to keep the image of actual conditions before their eyes. If they could have seen this neighborhood . . . well, it looked certainly as if these blocks had been bombed from the air.

Right in Linda's front yard, as you might call it, there were tottering brick walls and open foundations and basements. There was untouched grass growing over and through the ruins, with paths cutting it that could have been made by either animals or neglected children. At the entrance to one path I saw a discarded diaper and a candy-bar wrapper, meaning nothing perhaps, but shocking to find under your feet.

Happily, the apartment building where Linda actually lived was a sturdy old place. It looked bourgeois and homely at the far side of the ruins and grass, and if it hadn't, I might still have lacked the nerve to go in.

It was like coming to shore to find her card and doorbell button in a row of others beneath polished mail boxes. The instant I rang I heard a door open above me. Probably she'd been waiting nervously since I called her from my hotel.

Her face, in my first glimpse, appeared both whiter and more mature than I had expected. Worn a little, yes, but finer.

"Hello, friend, come up," she said and gave me the precise, square smile which I remembered from the time she first walked into my class one September day four years previously, and I wanted to bless her for appearing so—thank her, that is.

A great deal had happened in these four years. That is, a great deal had happened to Linda. To me, nothing at all. Nothing. There's the ultimate grief of being a teacher. One sees his students come in from a past which lies behind them straight as a string, watches them change and grow for a time, then go straight away into their lives while their teachers must slip back year by year to begin the process which comes to seem—and I shouldn't say this—like a misconceived attempt to go somewhere oneself. Sometimes one feels like calling out to a departing student, "For heaven's sake, take me with you. Help." Perhaps I was not meant to be a teacher, and made a foolish choice of profession somewhere a long way back. At any rate, if it were not for my wife's example and steadying influence, I've no doubt I would have bolted before now—my wife's health has always been uncertain, just as her courage and cheerfulness have always been completely certain. Maybe I've remained a teacher because that's one way I could pay the doctor bills. I am not—at least no longer—suited to earning a living outside teaching. It could be put that way.

Perhaps with Linda more than with any of my other students, I had felt a real compensation for being caged in my profession.

It was as though I *had* gone with her in some way, I had been so close in sympathy with all her struggles.

She left college after her sophomore year to marry, and you can readily imagine the fireworks it caused in a staid school like ours when the word went around that she had married a Negro. "Not Linda Harris!" they said. Just that way, "Not Linda Harris!"—as though they knew anything about her beyond the superficial facts that she was a beautiful girl and a more than usually popular one. The idiots had known nothing at all of her inner self, and hearing them rant and take on as they did always gave me a tiny thrill of satisfaction—of satisfactory complicity perhaps, because it was I alone of anyone at the college who knew her well enough to understand what she had done and appreciate the nobility of it. I just could have said plenty to them on the subject of their bigotry, but it contented me to keep quiet and exult with the notion that Linda Harris had shaken them up in a way they weren't likely ever to forget—and that I perhaps had been the catalytic agent, so to speak, which had precipitated from her the essentials of character that permitted her to leap over the false boundaries of race in fidelity to her true feelings.

I was Linda's adviser as well as the instructor of her freshman composition class. I remember—like touchstones representing all our association at the college—two conferences with her which seem to justify me in feeling as I did about my influence on her. Once she'd gleaned some academic prize or other and while I was congratulating her on her intellectual growth she suddenly broke in with that sudden and startling frankness of hers, "Why is it, though, Mr. Mansfield, that the more I think I'm learning, the more I feel like breaking and running for it?" Well, that was a devastating question to come from a girl who seemed to have everything in the world to give her confidence and assurance of the future. I didn't bat an eye. I understood what she was trying to get at, and starting with the concept of *delaissement*, I tried to explain that this was perhaps the condition of mortals who attain a certain degree of self-consciousness. I insisted—what I've always clung to for myself—that courage alone was an adequate response to what everyone must finally discover himself to be. I gave her something to read then which could explain this better and more poetically than I could hope to.

The other occasion of importance commenced with her bringing me a paper which she had handed in to her political science professor—a Mr. Wiley and an old goose if I ever saw one. Her subject was intermarriage, and she'd made some comments which evidently had upset him. Perhaps he was afraid someone might think she'd got such courageous ideas from *him!* Well, not in a million years, but then one should never underestimate the timidity of a teacher at such a college as ours, which might be considered way down the academic ladder, but where some people cling to their jobs like living death. Linda was really hurt by some of the catty little reactionary comments he'd penciled in the margins, and she was so innocent of pedantic cowardice that she couldn't see what had motivated them.

I explained the vicious mechanism to her, straining to do it in such a way that her still-fresh confidence wouldn't be replaced by cynicism, of course. I can congratulate myself on a good job of expression that time. It hit and we ended our conference—it probably lasted a good two hours—laughing hilariously and eagerly like a couple of kids in the pantry. That was one of the most rewarding moments of my life. We achieved a moment of shared insight, I have felt, that nothing could ever take away from us. Altogether good. It was a spring evening, the first day of that season when I'd been able to open my office window, and I remember glancing out with surprise when we were through talking to discover that it was almost dark outside. There was a dead, mellow calm in the air. The campus lights were coming on. With all this it seemed to me that Linda and I—a little like Swift and Stella, a little—had escaped from what people think—and they're right—is inevitably a characteristic of colleges, into a knowledge that was half sympathy, half rational comprehension, and altogether lively, a living thing. We stopped even laughing and sat there awhile without needing to laugh or talk. I sometimes thought that just then in some unplaceable moment before I grabbed my briefcase to go home I gave Linda some supplement of assurance that enabled her to go courageously to what she did later. And by being just what she was, a student willing to receive the best I had to give and carry it out into life, she gave me something that has made my own problems endurable.

While the substantial look of the apartment building where Linda lived had quieted my anxieties about her, my minimum of complacency was quickly enough stripped away by the quality of the apartment itself.

The rooms were large but grossly misproportioned; very narrow, as though they might be only half of what they were originally built for, divided quite ruthlessly after the design was finished. There was layer over layer of poverty, like layers of wallpaper, and I tried in vain to find on top of this something that Linda might have brought to it that would have redeemed the whole thing.

She used to paint very nicely when she was in college. Perhaps I had set myself to expect that her talent for colors could have touched up anything—with drapes, or paintings, or something.

What actually caught my eye, though, was a pile of laundry in the seat of an old green sofa. From it the arm of a man's shirt hung into a puddle of sunlight coming from a window up behind me. There was an odor of cookery and staleness that I had not noticed in the hallway. I must report the truth that, finding Linda in the midst of this, still looking and seeming as beautiful as ever, I could almost hear myself saying, as the college people had, "Not Linda Harris."

She was from the first instant flexible, lively, and full of chatter. "Ralph's not home yet," she explained. "He won't be for a while, but you've got to stay till he comes. He wants to meet you so much. I've told him you were God." She was mocking me with a freedom and friendliness which was new, and which I found quite attractive. I had thought of her as being, perhaps, a trifle oversolemn except on rare occasions.

"He's going to school now," she said. "He's a talented guy. You know, he is, honestly. I'm glad he's getting his chance. You know you got here a little faster than I expected." I took this to be a carefully shaded apology for the condition of the apartment, but if it was an apology it was in no sense a lowering of her banners.

"Don't you think we have a cozy place here?" she asked. "It's pretty ratty, huh? We think we have something lined up on the South Side, come fall. It's a better neighborhood."

"I'm glad of that," I said. "This is spacious." She had led me by this time through the first room into their parlor, which was not quite so bad as the other, though furnished like it with heavy and worn-out pieces representing the taste of Sears-Roebuck customers of the twenties. There was even a huge, very

old-fashioned aquarium—a square glass box sitting in its own
wrought-iron frame—which I took to be one of those inescap-
able monstrosities dear to the hearts of landlords. Really an
atrocity, besides obstructing any rational distribution of the rest
of the furniture.

"You're right," she said. "It's eighty feet long, stem to stern,
and that's all one ought to claim for it. Don't be falsely hearty,
huh?"

"I hope not," I said.

"Not you, Wilson." She shook her long hair in a suddenly
vigorous gesture, as a small girl might to rid herself of an annoyance. "I get heartiness in gobs from the family," she said.
"That's the new phase. They've long since stopped threatening
or praying, or weeping or fasting maybe. I'm not sure it's an improvement. I'm not sure. At least it's easier on my nerves."

I held her hand a minute. "It's been a long war, hasn't it?"

"You don't know," she said. "Yes, you do, don't you? I wrote
you so damn much about it all you must have felt that you were
right here in the middle of it. Poor old Wilson. I pictured you
sometimes as being all soppy with Papa's tears and—I don't
know—squeezed bloody with Mother's embracing me. I tell you
it was just the funniest thing I've ever seen in my life. That
woman embraces like a python. They'd come in our place over
on Harmony—that was even rattier than this—and be polite to
Ralph for about ten minutes and then he'd leave. So they'd start
talking annulment and pretty soon Pop would have used up his
arguments and would pound his knees. Mother would be more
ladylike than you can imagine except that every three minutes
she'd be up hugging me. Ooooh. But I wrote you all that."

"Not quite."

"Not about Mother's hugging. It didn't seem as funny then as
it does now."

"But they're finally reconciled to your marriage."

"They're hearty. Can you imagine another phase after that? I
don't know. I wait and marvel. It's kind of funny the way they
run their heartiness. They *ignore* me practically. Everything's
Ralph. 'Isn't it wonderful Ralph's putting on weight? Isn't he
looking well? Wasn't that a witty thing he said the other day?'
And he kind of likes it. Why don't they just stay away?"

"Now, now." I felt very cautious about commenting at such a
delicate point. I tried to make my expression count for the things

I couldn't risk in words, and I think it did, for she replied, "I know, Wilson. I know, I know. The trouble is they can never do anything right together. Pop would be all right by himself, I know he would. He's kind of like you, Wilson, in a lot of ways, really. That woman always manages to cross things up. What a talent."

"At least the big battle's over, and you've won."

"There's a fact," she said. "Oh, look at us—right off the bat gabbing so fast I haven't even asked you to sit down. Sit down? And you do drink, don't you? We'll have one and get down to serious gabble. I'll only be a second. Relax, and think of dozens of things to tell me about school. I'm tired of talking about Ralph and me. Or you can sit peaceably and watch the goldfish."

I wasn't quite sure whether to laugh at that remark, and she gave me no clue. I looked at the big old aquarium with a faint smile that could be interpreted as she wished.

"The fish are Ralph's," she explained. "I'm not a great friend of fish. I have been meaning to do a watercolor of them, though— been going to for about a year—the way they move like flags in a jungle. See, they're just blocks of color against those green plants. Be right with you, sir."

So I sat staring at the aquarium and seeing the gold banners Linda had set in motion for me—the brave banners of her vision and courage, if you like, or her youth. Those had never gone down, I understood, and it seemed to me very clear that I had not come on this visit to bring encouragement to her, but to get it for myself, however I might have thought of things previously.

I thought those gold blocks of color were the banners of an exiled queen and, paradoxically, of a girl who could only become a queen by accepting her exile. Actual tears came to my eyes just then, and I caught myself whispering, "I'm so proud of you, Linda. You've won." Well, that's just the sort of thing I might have wished to whisper to a daughter if I had been a person destined to have one. And she had said I was something like her father. Maybe—I toyed with the idea, turning it to the light—her words meant more than she knew. I allowed myself to think that in the world beyond appearances I was her father. Why should it not be so? With my soul I took her for my wished-for own.

In that sentimental relaxation I also recalled that she had been calling me Wilson. This was new, and a symbol, I thought, of the fashion in which our relationship had grown closer since we had last seen each other. While she was in school we had always been Miss Harris and Mr. Mansfield to each other, and though I had signed the many letters which I sent her during her hardest trials "Wilson," her replies had always come back to "Mr. Mansfield." I had wondered why, but had attributed it to a delicacy of feeling in her. Perhaps Linda had felt that my wife would not have understood the familiarity, though I am sure she would have, if I had felt justified in burdening her with the really shattering problems of which Linda wrote. My wife suffered a great deal during the war with the general sufferings of humanity. I did not believe that was entirely necessary and perhaps have more and more sheltered her from news or knowledge of suffering.

Sitting there, letting so much flow through my mind undammed, I realized how tired I had been for a long time. From far at the other end of the apartment came the sound of Linda's movements in the kitchen and the sound of water gushing into the sink. I *let* myself realize how tired I was, for in this moment it seemed to me that finally I could afford to. It's all right, I thought, *she's* all right. I can testify that I'd had some grim visions of what might have happened to Linda—the crime rate is high in the submarginal districts to which she had been forced—and I could let these go now, forever. The worn and tasteless parlor seemed more like home than home was. Linda might have found me asleep if she'd taken two more minutes with the drinks.

Too soon I heard the agitated tinkle of ice in glasses and turned to see that Linda had been stopped at the parlor door by an enormous black cat, which was entangling her steps and forcing her to pay it attention. She kicked it lovingly and tried to step around. "This is my old Lucifer," she explained. "Let go, you dumb old goof. Ignorant wretch."

In spite of her gentle kicks the cat wouldn't let her pass. Its claws were in her stockings, and with slick, strong movements it clutched around her ankle with a foreleg. I never have liked animals much. It has always annoyed me terribly to see them occupy the attention of people as though they had a valid claim to our precious time. So the note of affection in Linda's voice as she spoke to the cat came to me as a minor annoyance—it was almost as though I were annoyed with her—but I caught myself up with the reflection that the kind of isolation to which society has subjected Linda might well force anyone to turn some of his affection away from the human species. I have no difficulty understanding why Swift found horses more virtuous.

"Here," Linda said, "take the drinks a minute, Wilson, please." As I did so she picked up the cat, lifted it over her head with both hands as I have sometimes seen people lift babies, then lowered it to her shoulder, and rocked it a moment before she tossed it to the couch beside me. "Sleep, you old mutt," she said softly. "He's Lucifer because he's the proudest of the angels. What arrogance, but I love him. He's convinced Ralph and I belong to him. On top of that we've discovered that he eats Ralph's goldfish. I don't know what we're going to do about him. Anyhow, I'm afraid to plot against him."

"You could throw him out of heaven," I said. "That neat solution once occurred to the Supreme Intelligence." She was momentarily more concerned with watching the cat settle than with my joke, then she wanted all the news.

Was Charley Watson still teaching painting at the college? She'd read that a picture of his had taken some prize in a show at the Art Institute and had meant to get downtown to see it. Did I know that Joan Wiley had married a forest ranger and that they were living in Wyoming? Imagine Joan on a horse. Kevin Rice was living in town and had called her once. He was an interviewer for some company that surveyed public opinion. She told me about her own employment—occasionally as a salesgirl, now and then as a model for one of the big stores; right now she was making out bills for the gas company. I kept nodding approvingly and hating more the drudgery that confined her.

Her best friend at school, a girl named Evelyn Wright, had passed through town not so long before on her way to Baltimore with her husband, her new husband. "Evelyn came to see me *alone*," Linda said. "So that's fine, if she wanted to; why not? But we never really got beyond that point. She kept sneaking in apologies for not having brought her husband. Isn't it funny? You know it was through Evelyn that I met Ralph in the first place, and she wouldn't stay long enough to see him. I guess that comes under the heading of ho hum, doesn't it?—or 'Should a wife be jealous of her husband's past?'"

Hastily I inquired if Evelyn was still painting.

"Oh, sure. She brought along a portfolio of little things to show me. She's good, you know. She was at Cranbrook last summer and they're going to Mexico this winter. Her husband has work there and she can study." I want to make it perfectly clear that there was no tone of envy in Linda's voice as she spoke of the good fortune of others. Of the two of us, it was I who was having the difficult going.

Trying my best, I said, "That's fine and I certainly hope she goes far, but I hope you do too, you know. I hope you're still finding time for work—your painting—in spite of all your work."

"No. I mean I do a little. Not much," she said. "Ralph's been doing quite a little."

"I didn't know he was a painter too."

"He isn't. That's his watercolor over there against the baseboard, poor thing."

"It's quite good."

"It's not. Painting makes him happy, though. It's another thing he's taken away from me, and that's why he likes it." She set her jaw stubbornly and almost seemed to dare me to argue with that interpretation.

I couldn't have argued. I was too much bound by loyalty to her for that. I thought round and round to find an oblique way of reply, some way that might turn away the unhappy implications she had spoken without striking at them.

I said after a while, "Let's agree that I can't guess what all your troubles have been. Perhaps I was dull enough to think they all came from the outside and the things people put in your way. Forgive me, but let me tell you something. Perhaps you don't know how much it did for me—really did for me—to get your letters and see the courage you displayed all the way along. There have been times when I don't think I could have gone on if it hadn't been for your example. What you proved for me was that love was possible, by you and Ralph finding your way through. So you've given something crucial to at least one poor mortal. That's bigger, isn't it, than . . ."

And all the while I was talking I felt that things were twisting farther from what I wanted them to be. All our sympathy for each other seemed to be blunted. It was almost as though there were an active, evil presence in the room twisting what I meant and what I hope she meant.

"Why did you have to make that speech?" she asked.

I sat stiff and looked at her until she went on, her voice a kind of hiss, "Wilson, were you in love with me that spring you encouraged me to marry Ralph, and didn't have the nerve to say

so? Was that what it was all about? Because I was in love with
you. I know because my psychiatrist told me. I *was*, I mean, and
it was pretty silly both ways, wasn't it?"

It's hard for me to recollect what we said next afterward. I've
honestly made an effort to piece it together. However painful it
may be for me, I couldn't live with myself if I didn't make the
effort to see things exactly as they are and face them that way.

I think I convinced Linda that I had never felt anything for her
except the deepest kind of admiration and respect, that there
had never been any question in my mind of loving her as a man
loves a woman. I tried to give her terms to see how a young,
beautiful girl with a passion for what is good and right and possible in this world of ours can seem to a teacher—a rather discouraged one—the most valuable creature the world can produce. Yes, in that way I loved her, of course.

I don't know if my means of expressing myself then were as
good as they might have been. I cried a little and that may have
discredited some of the things I meant. I might have done better
if her husband had not arrived when he did.

He came in all handsome and jovial, carrying a white cardboard carton of the sort that ice cream is packaged in. It was, as a
matter of fact, impossible not to notice he'd brought it, because
he held it with that kind of ostentation that goes with a slight
pretense that something is or should be concealed. After kissing
Linda perfunctorily he placed it on an end table beside the
couch, chuckling, half-embarrassed.

He removed the cat and placed himself next to me on the
sofa, leaned his forearms on his knees so that he addressed me
over his shoulder, though with a great deal of affability and
respect.

"Why don't you get us all a drink, Linda?" he asked. "I, for
one, have a real thirst, and I suspect that Mr. Mansfield wouldn't
be averse to having a refill, would you, sir? For myself, I've been
in the academic mill today and nothing exacerbates my thirst
like the application of the old brain."

"Linda told me—"

"Yes, I'm enrolled in Northwestern University this summer,"
he said. "Law is my field. That is to say, law may be my field.
I'm, you might say, exploring my capacities this semester."

I was trying to like him. It's not hard to see that I had a great deal staked on being able to like him. I never expected to have so much staked in such a way. He was, too, in many ways more charming and impressive than I'd dared, in the years just past, to expect. And I hated him.

The worst of the remainder of the afternoon was the line of talk we fell into when that ugly black cat began pestering us again. It ran across in front of Ralph and me while Linda was in the kitchen, then began playing with us, attacking our feet with arrogant stupid leaps. Ralph dragged it by its tail from under the end table. He began to caress it and slap it playfully, mastering it, one might say, by paying it this undue amount of attention. "Are you fond of these beasts, sir?" he asked. "I don't care much for a cat, but my wife has an obsessive attachment for them. I point out to her that this one goes so far as to eat my goldfish"— he gestured toward that horrid, jungly aquarium—"but this only amuses her. That's quite true. I've formed the theory that women are fond of certain animals and men of others and that's all there is to it. Does your wife like cats, sir?"

"I suppose she hasn't much time for pets," I said stiffly. I heard Linda come back into the room with the drinks, but even when she offered me mine I couldn't meet her eyes, feeling, as I did, embarrassed for her. "My wife is not very well."

"That's right," he said patronizingly. "Linda explained that to me, too. But other women, women ordinarily, I've found that most women like cats, and I'm almost tempted to the study of psychology to determine why. Can it be for aesthetic reasons?"

"He *is* beautiful," Linda said from across the room, speaking with a strong voice. "Furthermore, he keeps the rats away. That's necessary in most of the places we've lived."

Ralph chuckled. "You see, sir?" He dropped the cat between us on the sofa and turned his attention dramatically toward Linda. "But he eats my goldfish," he shouted at her. Then he spoke to me in a sycophantic tone. *"They're* beautiful too, wouldn't you say, sir?"

"Well . . ."

With a queer nervous excitement he stretched himself upright, and, as though the dramatically appropriate moment had arrived and been recognized, he took up the cardboard carton and opened it for my inspection. "I thought I'd better pick one up to replace the one he got last night," he said to Linda.

"Sure," she said. "They only cost a quarter."

"You begrudge me that quarter?" Ralph demanded in a hard voice. "You don't want me to have my fish?"

She tried to laugh away the foolish insistence of his challenge, but he was not going to let himself be distracted. It was as if he felt some clear necessity to show me how she could yield. "Aren't you glad I got the fish?"

"If that's what you wanted," she said, reddening and turning her face away.

"Yes?"

"Yes."

Ralph suddenly thrust the carton in front of me so I couldn't avoid looking down at his goldfish hanging in exquisite detachment between the white cardboard walls. As I stared I felt the cat crawl familiarly against my leg. I can't explain what possessed me just then—it was as though I knew what the cat was thinking better than I knew my own thoughts. The cat understood what was in the carton and was moving toward it hungrily. In a kind of premonitory horror I sensed the fishy taste and the crunching of spindly bones.

I laughed sociably. Both Linda and Ralph swung to stare at me and then I *heard* myself. It was the ugliest laugh I had ever heard.

"I'm not feeling at all well," I said. I did not know how much longer I could be responsible for what I said or did. "For pity's sake, help me downstairs and get me a cab. Meow. Ha ha. I'm sorry."

And in
My Heart

They came across like a flood when the traffic light changed, the girls in sweaters with books shelved in their folded arms and the wind fiddling with their hair, the young men in shirtsleeves or field jackets, bareheaded or wearing canvas hats. Toward the time when the campanile bell would ring two o'clock they had loitered out as couples or little groups from restaurants and rooming houses until they jammed the corner opposite the campus with a nearly amorphous concentration of movement. Except for linked arms here and there and a few couples holding hands, the bodies in the crowd did not quite touch. Nevertheless, when the light turned green, they moved as a single mass and carried Orin Corrigan with them over to the diverging campus walks.

A girl in a plaid skirt shouldered into him, looked up with in-nocent, hard eyes. After she had reasoned that such an old man must be a professor, she said, "Par me." Then she trotted ahead of him as if she counted on pure hurry to bring her up with friends sooner or later.

Corrigan took the same walk as she and watched the distance between them increasing. He saw her fat little hips work comi-cally under the plaid until she was screened from sight by a crossing flow of students. I wasn't really laughing at her, he thought, turning right to avoid the crowd—nor at any of their genitive fashions. He was laughing because to his eye all this had never changed.

Once again the drying elm leaves and the autumnal brassi-ness of the sky kept a silence for him over the babble of the stu-dents surging toward their first classes. Under the changeless sky their rhythm and tone seemed exactly what it had been when he first came along this walk in 1921. He was a student himself then, but had been no more a part of them than he was now. Then he was, if you please, a cowboy from western Ne-braska who had never been farther from home than Fort Riley, where he served a short hitch in the cavalry. He had come to the university with a new black suit from Denver wrapped in paper at the bottom of his suitcase, wearing that same black suit nearly every day through his first three years. He had worn it on this very sidewalk, his hands hanging raw and big and awkward from the sleeves like the token burdens of his separation from the others. He was older than they, even then, almost thirty when he enrolled as a freshman here. He was also taller than most and had the habit of walking with his head thrown back a little—partly from shyness, partly to catch the air and the over-head sights, and partly because it had seemed a poetic stance.

His unaltered habit of alertness let him hear and see—no clearer after all these years of expectancy—the murmured har-mony the unknown students made with such a day. The emo-tional part of his imagination transposed it to an entity crowded with wings and horns that blew the failing seasonal magic, the dignity of youth, and the dignity of their faithful ignorance as it clattered on under such a sky.

Well, well, well—he had caught this much of meaning before, many times. He had come to the university first because he caught—like a tall snowman catching snowballs in the face—

many things which beat up his emotions and which he meant to write out as poetry. And when you came right down to it, he had stayed too long because he had never quite managed to find the verbal shapes for what he knew. There had been no failure of initial vision, he thought soberly, but a failure of language, a failure to convert. The passage of thirty-odd years had clarified and then accommodated that failure.

Quite a lot of years ago he had published two volumes of verse—*Ranger Ballads* and *Days West*. Nice things had been said about the books when they were new. For a little while in the late twenties he had been a figure on the national literary scene. He was one of the "younger poets" compared rather favorably with Sandburg, Masters, and Lindsay. That was fine—worth what it was worth. His wife had been proud of his position, though by the time he had married Gail, his little bit of fame was already fading into the past. To the end of her life Gail believed that he had "contributed something" to American poetry, and he was glad she thought so. But for him the illusion that his published work mattered went with everything else.

It was not in his nature to be bitter about his failure. The effort to write had carried him high enough to see life better than if he had not tried. If there were no words of his own for *all this*, there was, like an armory open to him, poetry to borrow for the expression of his reverence. He might have "gone farther," as some of his colleagues said, if he had not learned here so awfully much of the poetry on the library shelves. He thought what he had learned worth the price of ambition. He had got what he needed most.

For two steps he limped as the shock of remembered words met the shock of his straining senses. "And in my heart how deep, unending ache of love . . ." For every detail of it all, he thought—for these kids, the weather, the disastrous neoclassic buildings of the main campus, the postprandial mellowness of his bowels. Armed with verse he could confront the mystery of the day without a shadow of dread.

A workman on top of Sedley Hall threw down a handful of leaves from a choked rain gutter. They fell separating and flashing yellow from the height of the building. A few struck among the vines on the wall and then tumbled after the others like a shower of notes from stringed instruments. "Beauty is momentary in the mind . . . but in the flesh it is immortal." Stevens's paradox might be a game of wit for some of his younger colleagues. As for himself, he believed it. Leaves fell and his good young wife was dead and their beauty for having been was immortal. What had been was the unchangeable and everlasting.

In truth—through the truth of poetry—what *had been* was enough for a man and left no room for anguish. He had lived close to despair when Gail died two years before. She had so much wanted not to die, and she had gone before he had taught her that neither of them quite needed to be what she had always wanted and sometimes imagined them to be. "A little too soon," he had thought in a terrible sacrilegious rebellion against her death.

But finally he knew better. In the very incompleteness of life was its immortality—a tricky and worthless enough immortality without poetry to illuminate it, he supposed. But there *was* poetry, and in it the whole story was told, finished, rounded to completeness. The true aspiration was not to alter or add to it, but to rise through emulation to the point at which it could be grasped. That was all he must slyly teach his students. He must nudge them on to accept gladly the loss of the world.

His beginning class in writing was waiting for him in the room directly above his office. He knew two of the boys from the spring semester of his Chaucer class. Good boys, and he had seen some—well, uh—*promising* verse that each of them had done. The others were all strangers to him. The leavings from Moore Tyburn's class, he supposed. He had not gone to registration this year, but it did not require bitterness for him to believe that most of these—provided they were really serious about their work—would have preferred to leap right into Tyburn's advanced class and probably would be there if Tyburn had accepted them.

The girl sitting next to the door had the library's ancient red copy of *Days West* on the arm of her chair where he could not help seeing it. She bit decisively at her nails as he walked past her to his chair.

"Now then," he said, swinging his chair to face them and crossing his long legs. "I want to tell you how glad I am to have you with me this semester. I'm a little surprised, though, on a day like this that you would come to class. Perhaps I'm a little disappointed. Independent spirits ought to spend a day like this inviting their souls and confounding academic conformities."

The nail biter giggled and nodded to show that she was going to be fast on the uptake for his humor.

"Bu-ut, since you have accepted the yoke, here we are in what I want to be a very, very informal circle. We're here because we want to learn what we can about writing. Naturally I include myself when I say that. The university says I am your teacher. But you know how universities are. They like to set up chains of command, like the army, while literature is maybe not even a republic but an anarchy . . ."

The boy to his left, the Jewish boy in a field jacket and suntan pants, was watching him cynically through the fingers on which he rested his face. Obviously he was thinking, What a lot of horsehockey. Clearly this boy was one of Tyburn's rejects, doomed to miss—and to resent missing—Tyburn's incisive explications. Noting the boy's disrespect for what he had said, Corrigan liked him at once.

But he went on evenly with his familiar banalities. ". . . only eleven of us altogether, and we want to speak with perfect frankness with each other about our work. We'll take turns reading our work aloud in class. I've been working on some verses that I'd like to expose. And I hope we'll all put aside any feeling that an honest criticism of what we write is, ah, an equivalent of an assault on anyone's chastity."

Again the nail biter giggled helpfully. From under his lids Corrigan glanced at the other three girls. Two of them were smiling with ordinary tolerance. The beautiful girl in the corner sat as though she had not heard—in fact, as though she were not listening to anything he said. Her face was as perfect and lustrous as china, and except for its excellent shapes seemed just as expressionless. Her pale hair was drawn back with a lavender ribbon so that her ears were exposed, and these, Corrigan saw, had an extraordinary translucence. Glass ears and glass eyes, he thought, wondering why she had come to his class. It was part of his belief that beautiful women never wrote much or well, nor wanted to.

". . . I have no lectures for you. Rather than ramble on like this through the period, I'd like to make a game of having each of you write a description of—well, of a tree. That sounds trivial for your talents, but it will serve for a beginning. Write about any tree you've seen or imagined. We don't want to admit that only God can make a tree. Everyone shall put forth his own leaves in this class. With hints from nature, of course." He waved his hands in a coaxing signal for them to get ready, set, and go.

He gave them a quarter of an hour, and when they were finished the papers were passed around the circle of chairs to him. He leafed quickly down through the pile, his eyes alert for something that might set them arguing. The top paper began, "My tree is a friend . . ." Oh, oh. From the nail biter, he guessed. Perhaps when she felt more at ease in the class she would do better.

"Here's something interesting," he said. He extracted the paper and held it up. "Whose prose?"

"Mine." The boy in the field jacket flipped up one finger from his chair arm to identify himself.

"Mr. Forest. Steve Forest," Corrigan read. "I'll read Mr. Forest's description of a tree to the class and the rest of you will be preparing to criticize it as I read. Now," he said, hitching his feet back under his chair, readying himself for the sport.

" 'The tree looked like a broken hand. Every branch had been cut by shrapnel. Some of the branches were ripped off clean, but most of them hung by fibers like tendons sticking through skin. The stripped trunk looked like a patient idiot who had been beaten a long time and doesn't understand why. There were ax marks on the trunk which were still bleeding a clotted sap. The ocean clouds behind it looked like scabs floating in a bucket of mucus.' " As he read the last simile, Corrigan let his voice rise up theatrically. "There!" he said. "There we have something to talk about. What do you think of this bit of writing . . . Miss Emery?" He had picked a name at random from the class roll.

The nail biter answered. "Why—why—*goodness!*" She had expressed herself so adequately that all of them laughed. "It doesn't sound like just a tree, I mean," she said, and the laugh went around again.

"Mr. Kelsey."

"Mmm. I liked it. It's kind of Wastelandish."

"Mr. Jost."

"I think it has its *own kind* of power. I think you *see* this. I think he gets you to sort of *know* what kind of tree it is he means."

"I don't *see* it," Miss Emery said, bold from her previous success. "Is it an elm or a maple? Ha. *What* kind?"

Corrigan saw the blaze of Forest's contempt leap toward the

girl and diverted it by saying, "Mr. Forest, you might like to tell us—"

"I think *this girl* simply doesn't want to see it."

"I certainly don't," Miss Emery snapped. "There's nothing objective about it."

"Let's have another opinion," Corrigan said. He swung his glance around the circle and picked out the beautiful girl. He indicated that she was to speak.

"I . . . I . . . I don't feel well," she said. The class roared its delighted approval.

But the girl got up and raced for the door. She was barely past it when Forest jumped up and followed her out. The others watched with various shades of amusement and sympathy.

Corrigan dismissed them all soon afterward, diverting their thought from the little episode as well as he could. He anticipated the problem the girl might have in forcing herself to come back. Like an animal trainer quieting his beasts, he called up the tricks learned from many years of teaching to blur down and unfocus their curiosity. By the time they all left, he felt that he had been successful in his attempt.

But his own curiosity was caught on the spike of a single question—why it had been Forest who had followed her. Forest and the girl had been sitting on opposite sides of the room. He had caught no sign of familiarity between them, and, granting that Forest might be the kind of rambunctious boy who would try to shoot all the quail in the class, still following a girl when she is about to throw up is an unpromising approach. Maybe it was pure compassion or even guilt on Forest's part.

Half amused, he thought of Forest following the girl with remorse and saying to her, "I'm sorry I wrote that tree for you. Look, I'll write you another, with unspoiled green leaves and a little toy wind monkeying around in it . . ." He had liked Forest, and he rather hoped this was the way it might turn out.

As he dawdled in the classroom then, Forest came back. The boy seemed to want to say something, and Corrigan waited. Forest gathered up his books and crossed the room to gather those the girl had left.

"We must grant a certain *power* to your prose," Corrigan said gently. "Is the young lady all right? Or did she vanish? She seems a very ethereal creature. Not quite of this world."

"Of this world, all right," Forest said bitterly. "I told her not to come in this class. But I'll be damned if her being here is going to keep me from writing the way I please. And to hell with all the other bastards, too."

"Why—why—"

Corrigan saw the boy's brown eyes fixed on him with reckless begging. "Why, they all mean well," he assured Forest. "They may be sort of amateur in their standards, but they mean well. They—I take it you know this young lady?"

"My wife," Forest said, his beggarly eyes shifting now as if he could not meet even Corrigan's gentle gaze.

"Wife? I didn't see any Mrs. Forest on the roll," Corrigan said. "But then I miss things."

"Elaine Biddle," Forest said. "The two-day bride. We're not living together. She only came into this class because she's damn sure she's going to get at me. If I could've got in—"

Forest stopped with clumsy abruptness, but Corrigan finished the sentence for him. If Forest could have got in Tyburn's class, the wife, parasite, nemesis—what was she, then?—would have been kept out where she belonged by Tyburn's standards. Kept out of the realm of art where this boy was scrabbling for a foothold. But in Corrigan's catchall class, open to all comers, she was very much a presence to be reckoned with.

"I'll be glad to hear more about all this," Corrigan said encouragingly. "But I don't feel we can exclude her from the rolls—if that's the problem."

"It isn't that," Forest said. "It isn't that. It's so goddam much more than that."

"If I can help—"

"You can't help," Forest said. "Only I may drop your class, too. Nobody can help." Abruptly he turned and stalked out.

But he's taking her books to her, Corrigan noted. He sighed as he started back to his office. He felt a faint, undefinable disappointment at Forest's outburst. He liked the boy so well that he wished him beyond self-pity.

Moore Tyburn was doing the talking. It seemed that from his strategically placed easy chair in the corner of the Franklins' living room he had been talking for a very long time; his speech had the quality of a monologue that must have had its true beginning not only hours or days but years before this little gathering of professors and their wives had assembled in the house of the head of the English department.

He sat under a modish floor lamp, drinking from time to time from a glass of milk that the wife of Professor Peltus kept constantly refilled for him. He finished a story about Dylan Thomas and the old days "at the Horse" with a contemptuous, final remark about the degeneration of this tavern in the Village since Thomas's death. "No one goes there any more," he said.

"We were there just two weeks ago," Mrs. Peltus said, with a half-defiant, half-apologetic snicker. "Just to *see* it. It seemed to be quite full of tourists and phonies."

"Oh?" Tyburn asked her coldly, pondering her qualifications for distinguishing phonies from genuines.

This was Tyburn's first year on the faculty. He had lectured here at the university once during the past winter, had thereafter been considered as a possible colleague.

When it came to hiring him, the executive committee of the department had gone along enthusiastically with Corrigan's recommendation. "We need somebody who's in touch with the new things. A writer from New York, preferably," he had said. Among Tyburn's qualifications was the fact that he had been on the staff of a famous literary review and appeared ready, like some of its other editors, to move up to *Life* or *Time*. He was a real catch for the department. Their formula for accommodating him was that he was hired not so much to supplant as to extend the writing program that Corrigan had run for so long. But they had greeted him with lively expectations and no little awe.

Physically he was a fascinating little figure, with an aggressive, blue-stubbed chin that flashed metallically when he spoke. His slightly protruding eyes never met those of the person to whom he was talking but swung with quick anxiety to that person's face as soon as his gaze was distracted. His wide, curving brow was in constant perspiration this evening.

He repeatedly "denied intellectual responsibility" to this or that writer of national reputation and had several times referred knowingly to Trotsky as "the old man." An air of barely suppressed wrath charged nearly every one of his sentences. And these mannerisms of his speech exerted a hypnotic fascination on the listening faculty wives.

Corrigan sat there almost as rapt as they. For several years he had admired Tyburn's poetry and his critical articles on Joyce, Thomas, and Lowell. He was happy to see the young wizard in action, to note with sleepy irony the adroit corrections he was administering to Mrs. Peltus and the liberal Mrs. Thorne, whom Tyburn quickly exposed as "Stalinoid," denying her intellectual responsibility between two sips of milk.

But before long Corrigan began to sense his error in coming to sit at the young man's feet. (Figuratively at his feet; actually he was clear across the room, in shadow, being as quiet as an old man can who has taken enough good Scotch whiskey to scramble his senses.) In his earlier talks with Tyburn there had been a tacit fraternal ease, the complicity of two practitioners isolated, as Tyburn seemed to see it, among the mere merchants or middlemen of literature constituting the rest of the staff. But as this evening progressed Corrigan began to hear in the passion of Tyburn's monologue a probing scorn that he could only take as personally directed at him, whatever the others made of it.

"Our great curse at the *Review*," Tyburn was saying, "was that absolute legions of contributors failed to realize that Whitman is dead. The old beard is gone. For my money he's back at Paumanok where he started. And yet, though it's past mid-century, there are still these highly emotional sodbusters and sodbustresses who go on trying to extend the Whitman catalogue of American goodies, busters who feel that coming from west of Chicago is, in itself, qualification as a poet. You can't imagine how many man-hours the staff wastes reading poems in praise of Lake Michigan and Abraham Lincoln. It's perfectly true—so what?—that every American hamlet is a Spoon River. Go read the gravestones, feel deeply, send the results to the *Review* with—by all means—return postage included. Maybe it is Edgar Masters they don't know is dead.

"Maybe the new leisure is going to continue the explosion of yokel poets, but it's the duty of responsible local and state officials to head the stampede off, stamp it out wherever it shows its dowdy head. I've seriously weighed the possibility of putting poets on reservations like Indians and prohibiting the reading of Whitman and Masters in the same spirit that firewater is prohibited our red brethren. The sheer increment of defiled paper coming from the hinterland is enough in itself to delay the building of a literature. And Europe's gaining on us again. We've got to clear away the crud. Obliterate." For a moment he dropped his face into his spread hands as if to weep. Then he shook himself and hissed, "I do blame it on Masters more than poor old Whitman. If the sonofabitch were here I'd hit him in the face. *I'd hit him in the face.*" He struck his knee with his clenched fist. "Once I went to the trouble of finding out where Masters was buried, and I made the pilgrimage there to spit on his grave. Pork-barrel poetry is killing us."

Mrs. Peltus, her face aglow, poured him another glass of milk. "Masters was one of my favorite poets—*when I was in high school,*" she confided naughtily.

In the center of the room Professor Peltus shuffled his feet and coughed. "That's very interesting. You would agree with James's remark in, I believe, *The Art of the Novel,* in which he says he sees no reason why the acceptance or rejection of a duke shouldn't be more interesting than, say, a lady with a cicatrice or, say, the adventures of Jeeter Lester's daughter. Not of course that James had read Caldwell. In merely using that as an illus—"

"People aren't talking so much about James now," Tyburn said ominously. "But exactly. The smell of horse dung does not automatically make it literature. But what a long time that theory rode in the saddle. Hey. You see I'm using the regionalist lingo myself. Help. I'm drowning."

Belatedly sensing that the stage had been set for a debate between Tyburn and Corrigan, Peltus said, "What do you think of that, Orin? Your interests have always been more or less regional. Not that Professor Corrigan as a poet *was* a Regionalist," he said with a castrated chuckle.

"I've read his books," Tyburn said sharply. He was not going to allow quarter.

"Bu-u-ut," Peltus said, oblivious, "he was something of a forerunner of the Regionalism that developed here—in the thirties. Never a part of it, but—"

"I think . . ." Orin Corrigan said slowly, setting his empty glass on the rug and pulling his legs under him—then, in a moment of terror, he did not know what he thought. There was an absence, as if the growing nausea and resentment with which he had been listening to Tyburn had brought him to the edge of a precipice and pushed him over. Recovering with a burst of anger as if adrenalin had been spilled into his bloodstream, he thought, This tormented little bastard has always from grade school up had to assert his superiority by running something else down, and doesn't even know he's doing it. He's got his little yellow teeth in the butt of something marching to power and he doesn't mean to let go. He'll hang on for the ride the way ten years ago he would have held onto Henry James and twenty years ago to Regionalism. And he's got enough teeth to hang on tight. More than enough. If you heard—*heard* what he said about Masters and still think he's a fit person to discuss things with, then nothing I can say or have ever said in the years you've been my students and been on the staff with me will make any difference.

He said, breaking with his thought as the thought had broken angrily with the darkness beyond the precipice of surrender, "Will you pass me—or, no, would you fill my glass, Mrs. Dillon? Scotch and water. Thank you. I think that Regionalism had its weaknesses."

Did they—did any of them—realize how baldly Tyburn's remarks about Masters had been meant as a thrust at him? Evidently not. And in a smeared moment of self-pity he stared at Tyburn and asked, silently, Why? Because he had written and published a few poor poems a long time ago? If they were so bad—and no doubt they were—then they might be allowed to die out gently, as such things always would. But he knew, intuitively and with a fear he could not wholly understand, that Tyburn did not mean to let them die quietly. They would have to be ridiculed and hounded from the minds of men. He did not, just then, hate Tyburn, but with despair he recognized Tyburn as a pattern of things to come. He would be the new power on the English staff here. His sharp tongue and his hate would mold these opinionless men and women—these Peltuses.

Blind among enemies. Orin Corrigan thought as he drank his Scotch and water down swiftly. Then the corrective intelligence in him changed this modestly so he thought, Only, I am the one that wrote *Sweet Grass Bend* and *Crazy Horse Is Dead*—not either *Lycidas* or *Paradise Lost*. That's not my line. I didn't write it, so it's not my line. Great Jesus, men who were not poets (practicing) could claim, in their anguish, the great things Milton said. But once you went in the ring, you had to fight there with your own.

"Now in your class in writing . . ." Tyburn said challengingly, sensing his advantage, meaning to pin the old man to the wall. His voice was exultant, triumphant as a steel rasp hitting pith.

"It hasn't been awfully successful," Corrigan said. "None of my students ever published much." He groped his way to his feet, nodding and smiling and thinking that he might have acquitted himself better if he had not had that last Scotch.

Outside the maudlin, red moon shone on the streets and through the frames of branches. There was an extravagance of longing and of inhuman loneliness in its color.

But don't write about that, Corrigan thought. He felt giddily drunk and tired and ashamed of both these things. Don't write about that moon, or the seventeen miles of grass that lie between Emerald and Dumont or the way young men used to ride it (before that war, before that Strange Thing, Phelps Putnam called it, when the talking rats of Europe came and carried us all off from what we were), singing and passing back and forth a bottle of corn whiskey on a night like this, or how one of those got killed the next day in a Regionalistic manner (by the brother of the girl he fooled. Who said they would marry in a month and a day?). Don't write about such things or some sonofabitch from New York will ridicule you for it sooner or later. Maybe he ought to pass that bit of wisdom on to his writing class.

I could go back and sock the little bastard, he thought, bumping against the wall of a building and recovering himself.

Without knowing how he had come there, he was downtown in the traffic of the little city that lived off the college. He saw the door of a bar which was as purely anonymous to him as any could possibly be. A platonic bar. He went inside and had two more drinks while his suppressed rage against Tyburn swung tormentingly against himself. It was no one else's strength but merely his own weakness that was hard to face. It was hard to endure the change of things where the best that you had known and done became, in the metamorphosis of time, the unmistakable sign of what you had missed. Some devilish spirit of justice impelled him to think that Tyburn must be right. What had been the truth was changed. Then it was but now it wasn't. . . .

Suddenly he realized with shame that he had slid off the seat of the booth and was sitting on the floor without strength to raise himself. The waiter was supporting him so that he would not fall flat.

"You got to watch that forty rod," the waiter said. "Work up on it more easy, Professor."

He knows me and I ought to know him, Corrigan thought.

But as far as he could tell he had never seen the waiter before in his life. When the man helped him shakily to his feet, he managed a small laugh and said, "I'd appreciate it if you'd call me a cab."

Looking around now, as he had not when he came into the bar, he saw that two of the young men from his class, Forest and Kelsey, were watching him with a sort of skeptical compassion. He grimaced and waved to them before he waddled out. He did not think they had been laughing at him, but that made very little difference. They had seen. He had lost something to them that he could probably not afford to give up.

At the door of his apartment he thought miserably, If Gail were here the whole smeared evening could still be made all right and its misfortunes be given the quality of an ultimately joyful farce. I'd go reeling in to tell her how beautiful the night is, he thought, and that all the sonsofbitches in the world don't count. But she wasn't there and they did.

For the first two months of the fall semester, the beautiful girl, Elaine Biddle, handed in exactly nothing to Corrigan. He made no formal demands on any of his students for any particular volume of work, preferring to let them go at their own speed, concentrating his critical assistance on the best of what was brought to him. He hoped the encouragement and examination of excellence would do all that could be done to lead the stragglers.

But the Biddle girl—or Mrs. Forest, whichever might be the truer name for her—gave no sign that she ever meant to hand anything in. She came regularly to class and sat always in the same chair. Once she had found her place she sank into a beautiful remoteness which isolated her like a bell glass from the rest. It was not that she was utterly speechless or expressionless—when one of the other students had read aloud his production, a poem or a short story, and Corrigan called on her for comment, she would open her pink lips to deliver a brief cliché of praise. When the rest of the class laughed or grew excited in argument, an extremely faint smile or furrowing of her sleek brow indicated that she heard and was acknowledging from far away the concerns that the others met so frankly.

It was clear by now that Forest—her husband, in a legal sense at least—was a storm center of the class. When Miss Emery read a story of her own about the adventures of two girls on a bus, Forest announced immediately that it was "crap." Whereupon Miss Emery fled the classroom in tears and Forest tried to cover his real consternation over this result by an impassioned attack on all stories that had surprise endings. When Forest read his own work—he had read two stories thus far—Miss Emery got her own back by saying they were certainly very much like the stories of James Farrell, if *that* was what he had been aiming at. Scabs in a bucket of mucus, *indeed!*

Well, it certainly was what he was aiming at, Forest told her, only he meant to write a better prose than Farrell's. And the whole class—except his wife—slam-banged into an argument about realism, naturalism, and the happiness of most human beings.

She only watched from her china-blue eyes, as though she were looking in at the rest of them through the bars of a cage. She had no opinion to offer.

And finally Corrigan concluded that she was not in the class because she wanted to write—whatever her motive for being there might be. It was largely curiosity that moved him to keep her after class one day when the others had left.

"You haven't handed anything in to me yet, Miss Biddle," he said gently.

A quizzical expression showed on her face, as though he were giving her some odd bit of news. Then she nodded in agreement, but she said nothing.

"Well, when can I expect to see your work?" he prodded.

"You mean," she asked slowly, "that I'm supposed to write something?"

"That's the general purpose of this class," he said. As he watched her, trying to see through the mask of her withdrawal to the real person within, it suddenly occurred to him that maybe there wasn't any. This manner of hers might cover an incredible vacuity, an absolutely interstellar emptiness onto which most observers might project an image of themselves. As on the first day she had come to his class, he was struck by the inexplicable peculiarity of her beautiful head. Now, as then, her hair was held back by a lavendar ribbon. She wore a lavendar cashmere sweater on which he saw a pearl-rimmed sorority pin. She seemed to shrink inside the sleek, furry black coat that she had thrown over her shoulders.

"All right," she said faintly. "I'll write one." With the faint grimace of one who tries to remember something, she turned and left him.

The next morning he found her story on his desk when he came to his office. It was on ten faultlessly typed pages, the pages themselves conveying some of the quality he had sensed in her person—aloofness, a sort of nonpresence that still left a physical track to dissemble its lack of reality. And the story—the story was wonderfully, or horribly, more of the same. As he began to read it he had no sense of its quality. In terms of language it had none of the awkwardness or straining for effect that he was so familiar with in the attempts of his students.

On the other hand, he had the sense that it might have been written at top speed in this single, perfect draft, with no pauses at all for reflection and no conscious concern except for an awe-inspiring neatness. He was not sure that her story meant anything at all.

"It's not a realistic story," he ventured as an exploratory beginning on the afternoon when he called her in for a conference.

"No," she said. Her pretty head was inclined over the pages laid on his desk top, and it seemed to him that there was an unusual flush to her skin, as if she were afraid.

"But it's interesting," Corrigan said. "It *seems* interesting, though I have to admit I found it opaque. I read about the old woman and the girl and her doll, and I know that the old woman breaks the girl's doll. But I don't know what this all means, what I'm supposed to understand by these events."

He saw the coral-colored tongue touch the girl's lips, and she said in a small, thrilling voice, "My theme is the death of beauty."

The precise little sentence stung something in Corrigan's mind. His first—defensive—reaction was that such precision was comic. He was glad she had not declared herself with such patness in front of the class. He could imagine their nervous intolerant response. But as his mind repeated the silvery tone in which she had spoken he heard in it an unbearable candor—as if, he thought, a sibyl had spoken directly to him. It was at some deep level terrifying to admit what he had heard.

"Yaaaas," he said in his encouraging classroom voice, urging her to go on, to expand her explanation of this theme. But she sat as if she had told him all he needed to know.

He dropped his attention to the baffling pages. As he turned through them he began his own paraphrase, in the hope that his interpretation might unlock the frozen structure of it. "Yaaas, I see. The doll is the symbol of beauty, then. Something that the living little girl holds and loves in her naïve childish belief that because it is beautiful to her it is also eternal—or we might say indestructible. Then when the old woman wantonly takes the doll from her and destroys it, the girl learns that beauty is transitory. That's the main line of the story, isn't it? *Now*, what does this discovery mean to the girl? What does she do with it, for the rest of her life?"

"Nothing."

He laughed at the abruptness of her answer—hearing in his own laughter the bray of insensitivity, but puzzled as to how else he might proceed. "I mean, suppose that in life someone perceives things as this little girl has. Now, as we go on living this perception somehow gets carried into our lives. How would it affect her relations with other people? What's the human consequence of this rather abstract perception? Does this girl go on through life making her protest against the death of beauty? Is that her problem? I don't mean you have to write all this down in the pages of your story. I'd like to help you think around it, to see if we can't bring its meaning more out in the open—"

Now Miss Biddle was shaking her head. "The girl doesn't protest. She's glad the doll is broken. Here . . ." She reached for the manuscript, opened it with precision and put a sharp fingernail on a line near the bottom of the page. "She laughs because the old woman does what she wants in breaking the doll. See?"

"Go on," Corrigan encouraged. He had read the line she indicated. It said the little girl laughed—but there was a total omission of motive for the laugh.

"That's all," Miss Biddle said. "She's glad it's broken." She swayed back from his desk and the manuscript into a ramrod stiffness in her chair. Her exquisitely painted lips were open just enough to show the glitter of her teeth. "If it's broken no one else can have it," she said slowly.

Again it seemed to Corrigan that he heard a sibylline finality and inclusiveness in her interpretation—if that was what it could be called. Beyond any psychological interpretation that might be made of either her story or her comprehension of its meaning there seemed to ring a metaphysical knowledge. It was as if she said that beauty might act on men but had no intention of rewarding them, that it did not intend itself for life, but was a mischief there.

She knew that? Slowly, and with a certain fatigued resignation, he assured himself that she *knew* nothing of the kind. Any attempt to question her in the words at his command would only baffle her, he believed, would break like ocean froth against the stone limits of her vocabulary. And yet it seemed to him that the knowledge was with her, and he felt something of the ancient terror that might impel a man to lay his hands on an immortal and hold on for an answer that he must have.

He brushed the manuscript aside decisively. "Well, it's *interesting* work," he said in ironic bafflement. "Now there's one other matter I've been a little curious about. Sometimes I've wondered *why* you were in my class. I've had a chance to discuss their intents and aspirations with other members of the class, but you and I have never talked much. Now just what—"

Her eyes blazed fiercely. "*He's* been complaining to you about me. He thinks I'm just here to spy on him. But he needs someone to look out for him. He's got to be careful." There was no doubt in Corrigan's mind that she was talking about her husband, but the emotional outburst was thus far as opaque and inscrutable to him as her manuscript had been.

"Now, now," he said, trying to placate her. "No one's complained to me. Maybe if you'd tell me a little more what this is all about, I could—"

"It's none of your business," she said in anguish so unmistakable that he was stung to the heart by it. "It's none of your business." She snatched her manuscript and dashed from the office. She left behind a faint odor of perfume and scented soap. Corrigan heard the sleet rattle on the window of his office. Outside he saw the black trees motionless in the icy downpour, and like a child terrified to learn that others, too, are lonely, he suffered from the ache of mystery she had left.

"She didn't write that, you know," Forest said. "She got scared when you asked her why she hadn't handed in anything and went to the sorority files and found something, copied it, and handed it in." He ended his charge with a low-toned but almost hysterical intensity. Corrigan saw that his hand was trembling.

He had been walking along the street when Forest called to

him—from the door of the bar in which he had collapsed that night at the beginning of the fall. There was something very important that he needed to know, Forest said, inviting him into the bar for a drink. And as soon as they sat down he began an impassioned revelation of how his wife had cheated by handing in a story she had not composed herself.

"It was quite an extraordinary piece of work," Corrigan objected. He squinted into the fog of pipe smoke that he was laying between himself and the boy. Since his interview with Miss Biddle he had permitted his imagination to wind around the meaningless—or uninterpretable—elements of her story until they had closed into a coherent structure. Her offering had struck its needling roots into his thought and his thought had nourished it, until by now it had become more a story *about* the sibylline Miss Biddle than a product by her—or by someone else, if he were to credit her husband's information.

He did not want to credit it. The story of the child and doll, the old woman and Miss Biddle, was now, in its growing, his property. "It's an especially unusual piece for her to find in the sorority files. I thought they were more given to storing successful freshman essays than this sort of thing."

"Maybe they clip literary magazines from other colleges," Forest said. "They're resourceful. They'll do anything. I don't know where *they* got it, but I know where she got it, because she told me."

"And you're telling me," Corrigan muttered into the cloud of pipe smoke. With his usual moderation of tone he added, "I'd have preferred to find this out—if I found it out—by myself."

Forest nodded somberly, "So I'm an informer. I don't care. I've got to do things the only way I can. With her it's kill or be killed."

"Oh, now," Corrigan cautioned. "It can't be that desperate."

Forest spread his hands in suffering exasperation. "For me it is. If she'd give me a little time, then it might not be. A few years. I know if I'm going to make anything as a writer I'd better concentrate all I've got on it now. I'm not so strong that I can afford not to." He peered down in dismay at his quivering hand on the table top between them. "I think if I can have as much time as Dostoevsky, and nobody gets in my road, then I'll be as great as Dostoevsky, because I see what he's talking about. You know what I mean."

"Yes."

"But she doesn't want to give me any time. It's *now, now, now* with her. Like her getting in your class and pretending to be a writer. Ha. *That's* why I have to stoop to informing on her."

"Mmmmmm." Corrigan was not, by any means, sure that he understood what he was hearing. Hints of a pattern from Forest's rambling seemed to spread sensibly across his mind, but it was such a pattern as only the imagination can credit, and not the sort which could provide a credibility sufficient for action or even advice. "How did you happen to marry this—this virago?" he asked.

"I hashed at her sorority house last year," Forest said toughly. He took a savage gulping drink and then, while his eyes met Corrigan's with beggarly frankness, the left side of his mouth sagged as if it were being pulled down by a hook. "I fell in love with her, with *them*," he said, and with a resumption of his tough affectations went on. "That sorority was a heady brew for somebody who comes from PS 214. And the year before I'd been in Korea. No hero stuff. I was a clerk in Pusan. But it *was* Korea. And then you know how the girls smell when they come down for breakfast."

"I expect they must perfume themselves."

"Whether they bathe or not," Forest said, writhing with the memory of his temptation. "Every one of them smells like the big thing asleep upstairs."

"Thing?" Forest had made it sound like a hibernating female mastodon, drowsing in some gilded twilight where all mastodons are gray.

"The girl thing," Forest said impatiently. "The real thing. The most important of all. So you get to telling yourself if you could just get into one of them once it would be the moon. You'd have it. You get desperate enough you'd even marry one of them for it."

"Desperation indeed!" Corrigan said, but he was no more amused than impressed by this passion.

"Well, maybe it wasn't just as crude as that," Forest conceded. "Maybe I even loved her. I don't know any more. I really don't know why I married her or why she married me. But I know that even if it was made in heaven, now—this year— wouldn't be the right time for it. Do you see? And she doesn't want anything any more except to ruin me."

"I doubt that. I really doubt it," Corrigan said. It was his public duty to doubt, and his private, poetic and illicit pleasure to believe that he was listening to the simple truth. On Forest's hints he was visualizing the girl not as an object of love but as Love herself, an emanation of intolerable perfumes from tabooed regions that Forest called "upstairs." An implacable spirit whose purposes were no more charitable than those of a dynamo or a forge.

And in the core of his being he could believe that Forest was the chosen victim of divinity pursuing its own ends, the crass youth who ignored all warnings of normalcy, who might have peeked on Diana herself and was now torn by his own hounds.

Against such belief, of course, his duty as a teacher stood foursquare. At the command of duty he must categorize the Forests as a fairly ordinary young couple agitated by the ordinary discords of those who marry in college. It was his duty to submit as a listener while they needed one, to let them use his ear as a poultice drawing out the poisonous extravagance a literary temperament would stir up from the commonplace.

"One of her tricks was to be at me every minute," Forest was saying. "Sexually. She may look cold. Before we were married I thought she would be," he confided, only refraining from the probable truth that he had hoped she might be. "But when I got a lousy bronchial condition I didn't feel like doing it, and even then she wouldn't leave me alone. Not that she liked it—"

Corrigan gestured for him to stop such revelations. Of course it was for Forest's own sake that he wanted him to desist. Nevertheless, his old nerves had tingled as if in the presence of a sacrilege. Superstitiously he felt that *She* was overhearing them and would be revenged.

"Now, now, now," he said in a cautionary tone. He increased the density of the smoke cloud into which they were peering so profanely. "Now we needn't transgress certain secrets."

"I don't give a damn about proprieties," Forest said. As if he had not already made that plain, and made plain that a blindness to the real nature of his antagonist was part of the means by which She was destroying him. "Christ, I've talked about it to other people—"

"And they all laughed," Corrigan said, laughing gently, feeling a superstitious shudder threaten his control, threaten to crescendo the laugh louder into an obscene hysteria. "She's a very attractive woman, and it's easy to see you wouldn't get much sympathy as long as she's pursuing you. No."

"They all laughed," Forest said. "Nobody else realizes what a bitch she is. Nobody can tell—like in class when I try to say something. She's there hanging on every word I say, so that I always mess it all up and sound *stupid*."

"She delivers you to your enemies," Corrigan mused. And it seemed to him that the other members of the class, who did not think of themselves as Forest's enemies, who in general admired him at least for his stubborn, headlong ferocity and probably for the glow of real promise they saw in his work (he the one they would most probably think of as an artist)—they were indeed the enemies of the biding, still-imperfect self that Forest staked everything on becoming.

"Perhaps because she loves you," Corrigan went on tentatively.

"I don't ask her for that," Forest said bitterly. "That's the last thing I'd ask her for."

"But more likely because you love her," Corrigan said, feeling with a certain relief that the clichés of verbal communication tempered and controlled the very paradoxes they might create. "You don't want her to see anything but the best. Yaaaas. It may be that I understand. I see it might be better if you weren't both in the same class."

"If she was only willing to *wait*," Forest said. As if the arrow flying at the heart could listen to the merely human cry that protests its flight. "See, I want to be generous with her—or anybody. I don't like what I'm doing to her. But before I could ever get quite set to give her something, she'd already asked for it and tried to get it."

"Well now, well now," Corrigan said. "I can't do a miracle for you. Alas. But now I wonder if I can't do something to relieve your situation. Let me try."

Because he would not and could not—given what he had glimpsed, being transformed thereby into a less than innocent bystander—expel Miss Biddle from his class for cheating, he chose another method of separating her and her husband. He went rather humbly to Moore Tyburn and asked him to take Forest into the advanced class.

"Why not?" Tyburn asked. His hurtling, insatiable appetite for fodder to hurl into the mill of literature had brought him past the point of setting standards for admission into his class. He would welcome new recruits.

"Actually this boy does pretty well," Corrigan said. "Most of his stuff has been fairly autobiographical, but melodramatic, accounts of his war experience in Korea. He hasn't much sense of organization, but if you'll read these things of his I've brought, I think you'll find a certain power."

"I don't need to read them," Tyburn said. "If you found merit in them, that's good enough for me. I'll be glad to get him. Sure, send him to my class. Do you want to handle the red tape of transferring him or shall I?"

Corrigan said, "There's possibly just one thing I ought to tell you, and that is you'll find Forest . . . fragile. No, that's not the word, but he's more advanced in his opinion of himself than his work will show. *He's* out ahead of his obvious limitations. He's the 'artist as a young man,'" he concluded awkwardly.

And admitting the awkwardness of his statement, he could not exactly blame Tyburn for laughing in response, "Oh. *That* bullshit. I've pretty well got my people over that so they look at the *work*. I've convinced them they're all Midwestern bourgeois anyway, who've been laved by the horn of plenty since the war, so there's no bloody use in them going around like the *poets maudits* or sobbing about themselves as if they came out of the thirties."

Corrigan waved a big, soft, freckled hand as if to erase an error written on a blackboard. He said, "I don't mean that Forest is full of self-pity. It's hard to state, but he sees himself as—well, as he said to me, as an incomplete Dostoevsky." He put one sausage-sized finger at one end of Tyburn's desk and one at the opposite end and said, "*Here's* what he actually is and *here's* what he *knows* he is."

Tyburn nodded in smiling complicity, closing his eyes. One staff man to another. "I already had one of those," he said. "I beat that bullshit out of him and now he's doing some pretty fair things."

"Well," Corrigan said. "Maybe you can beat it out of Forest. There's another thing. He's having a lot of trouble with his wife and—"

"Who hasn't had?" Tyburn said gaily. "Anguish and agony. We all get it. There'd be nothing to write about if we didn't. Good," he said, like a colonel accepting a junior officer from another colonel. "I'll be glad to get your boy. Look, Corrigan, I was going to call you. You know Randolph Markwell is coming here

Tuesday. We're going to have a few drinks with him and eat at the hotel before he goes up to Old Main for his lecture. I wondered if you'd go with me to his train to meet him. And I *also* wondered if you'd introduce him instead of me. Franklin thought I should introduce him, but I have the strong feeling that since we *made* him at the *Review*, it would be fresher all the way around if you or someone else from the outside sort of summed up his work for the audience."

The direct consequence of Corrigan's meddling was that Forest's wife quit his class. She came to him in a quite unexpected burst of passion. Her translucent ears glowed like pink neon from a suffusion of blood. (Was it from the cold, which by then had gripped the campus in a pre-Christmas chill, he wondered when she came into his office? It was not. It was from sheer female rage.)

"I know all about it," she said in a shrill, simple voice. "I know you listened to him and believed everything he said to you about me."

"Now, now," Corrigan said in a fumbling, pipe-stoking embarrassment. "You surely don't think I'd listen to anything too personal in nature. Or that he would divulge so much of your personal affairs as you seem to think." As he spoke he remembered Forest's telling how she would not leave him alone even when he had a bad cold—and her ice-absolute blue eyes seemed to be reading now the exact content of Forest's confidences to him. "He wanted to get into the advanced class. I felt it justified—oh, for a number of reasons. I have great hopes for your husband, Mrs. Forest."

"Don't you think he told me how he'd tricked you?" she said. "He's a lot more neurotic than you think. He's told me that you fell for a big old sob story he gave you."

Corrigan took the implications of this as calmly as he could. "You'll—both of you will—have to forgive me for not keeping your peace. I've never quite encountered a similar situation before. I wasn't aware that you and he were still in such close communication. Evidently I misjudged."

"Oh, he comes around to tell me when he thinks he's put something over on me," she said. Then in the exhaustion of her anger she said with a grave mellowness which in its commonplaceness might have been that of any girl, "I only try to do what I can to take care of him. I don't want him to hurt himself. He is a strange one. I knew that and Mother and Daddy knew it and everyone at the sorority house knew it. But everyone wanted to help him. If he could just accept anything. If he could just accept for me to be with him. At least I could keep him from killing himself. He's not such a genius as he thinks. But you encourage him."

"Do I?" Corrigan asked. Then, smiling and with half-closed eyes, he said, "I don't know that I do anything at all. You two seem to be using me for purposes I don't understand. I feel like the hall carpet. I sense a great deal of running back and forth over me."

Finally, more in sorrow than in anger, she announced that she would not be coming back to his class. Tacitly they both agreed there would be no point in her continuing now.

The visit of the poet Randolph Markwell went off rather successfully. To begin with, his appearance brought the welcome necessity for Corrigan to read all three volumes of the young man's poetry, where he found, as he was prepared to do, an excellence and a power that moved him greatly. One night as he read late in his study at home, he let Markwell's book fall from his hands and smilingly remembered the evening at Franklin's when Tyburn had spoken of going to spit on Masters's grave. Yes, Corrigan thought, what these young fellows of Tyburn's and Markwell's generation had done justified all the fury they might feel toward their predecessors. "Drive your plow and your cart over the bones of the dead," he thought. *They* had obeyed Blake's injunction in these last twenty-five years, and if they had ridden over many things that had been precious to him (even Whitman, he thought, they had to grind into the earth to get their foothold), here, in this book he had been reading, was the warranty for their ruthlessness. It *was* better than the poetry produced by Masters's generation; at least it was alive now with that keening thrum of work that has matched its hour, while the verses of Sandburg, Masters, Robinson, Lindsay, Jeffers—even Frost—remained alive in another sense altogether, like memories of joy or honor outlived.

He had been reading Markwell's long poem on Orpheus and Eurydice, marveling at the rich progression of the structure— the first section, in which themes, rhythms, allusive names, hieratic words were strewn down with a profligacy approaching disorder, to be caught up again, expanded, connected with each other, inflected by their new place in the constellation of images, brought to an ironic halt, destroyed, and then resurrected in a final choral harmony where each held its properly subordinated place so that what was partly a narrative of the search through hell for the loved one moved not merely in a narrative line but on a broad, devastating front. There was something of Rilke's treatment of the myth in Markwell's poem—none of the good young ones since Eliot were ashamed of confiscating what they needed—but there was in the poem as a whole the honk and gibber of an emotion that exceeded the form. The hell where Eurydice was sought was real and no less mythic for being the contemporary scene and culture, Eurydice no less fabulous for being—as the literary gossips were well aware—the poet's first wife, now in an asylum in Massachusetts.

The poem lit up many darknesses, Corrigan thought, half-drowsing in his chair. It was in the glow of the poem, after all, that he had seen the propriety of hatred between a generation and its predecessors, a rigid necessity of rejection that was not without its beauty. And then—perhaps more important, perhaps less—there was a kind of morality in the very structuring of the anguish and separation that were the subject matter of the poem. If it did not, by its argument, justify God's ways to man, it did justify again his belief that art was not helpless before the sweep of time. It was strange how that knowledge satisfied a need primitive as hunger.

Of itself the story of Orpheus and Eurydice was unbearable. Not only the loss of the wife, but the mocking condition of the God—the *Thou shalt not look back* which demanded a faith that uncertain humanity could not bear. But the bargain was otherwise with art added. The loss was irreparable, but the looking back was not a hopeless glance into the void. Out of memory a song could be made, and the celebration of what had been defied the mockery of gods or things. She *was*, the poet said. I *loved*. And loss was not the void.

Why, I've moralized Mr. Markwell's very modern poem, Corrigan thought slyly, and I don't think he'd like it if he caught me pinning a tail like this on it.

But in the comfort of his study and his solitude, he did not care much what Markwell's response might be. The poem was his tonight, and he could dandle it on his knee and spoil it like a sentimental grandfather if he chose.

He looked out through the wide windows to where the street lights were shining on thick snow. He knew well enough that that denying whiteness was hell, and he knew with a sort of total clarity how sick with love he had been for his wife and others who were lost in it. I can watch them go without howling, he thought, because I can look back and know that if we go, we have been.

Carefully withholding the private reflections that had come from reading Markwell, he shaped his other thoughts of that night into an introduction for Markwell's lecture in the Old Main auditorium. To which Markwell responded, as soon as he rose to speak, by saying, Goodness, he hadn't known there was *all that* in his l'il old poem about Orpheus and Eurydice—a tongue-in-cheek disclaimer which satisfied the entire, diverse audience of librarians, English faculty, graduate English students, writing students, and a scattering of out-of-towners who had driven in through a growing blizzard to get the Markwell word. It produced a yak, and, as a lecturer, Markwell was in business for yaks. His enthusiastic approach to modern poetry was of the golly, gee whiz, lookee how old Eliot juggles so many balls at the same time school. He was not going to be caught *solemn* by any quick throw rifled down the third-base line, he let it be known.

His talk was unflaggingly entertaining, Corrigan thought, and foolish. To which he had no objection at all. It seemed to him that anyone who had written *Orpheus and Eurydice* had every right to masquerade in public as a clown and a trifler. There was no safe audience for a poet to meet face to face. And yet he felt a qualm lest some of those he saw down there in the audience should think the stream of sparkling inanities from Markwell was the business of a poet. Loafing in his chair beside Markwell and screened from the room's attention by Markwell's pyrotechnics, Corrigan could watch the faces of his students lifted in the bright hypnotism of belief that the end of their efforts was to be, somewhere and sometime, as entertaining as Markwell was tonight. Of course, he supposed, it was part of the department's purpose in bringing "name writers" here to the campus to foster the illusion that a writer's career might come approximately to the same kind of success as that available to an actor or an automobile salesman. Given the hostile pressures of the world they would have to find their lives in, it was, perhaps, an illusion they deserved.

He saw Elaine Biddle in one of the front rows. She was watching Markwell's every move with a coldly carnivorous stare as if she meant to find, then and there, the secret of his success and appropriate it. At least so it seemed to Corrigan, sensing her ruthlessness, though he could hardly have said why she might want the secret. Surely not for her own use, unless she meant to make a career out of plagiarizing manners as well as manuscripts.

He was still wondering about her motives for venturing out on such a cold night when he saw her at the reception for Markwell that Tyburn had arranged to follow the lecture. "I'm not asking any of the old goats like Peltus and Franklin," Tyburn had confided to him, marking him sheep with the same opportunistic recklessness that had marked him goat on another occasion. "I plan to lay in a little booze and give the writers on the campus—maybe some of the younger people from the art department—a chance to take down their hair with Mark. He'll like that." For this proposed intimacy, Tyburn had rented a private dining room above one of the town restaurants.

The room was filled, an hour after the lecture, with the happily drinking young sheep from the writing classes and faculty. A bar had been improvised at one side of the room. Opposite it, on a couch that seemed to date from pioneer days, Markwell continued to play his role of Poet as Success. Corrigan made no immediate effort to join the group around him, but paused on its outskirts long enough to hear that the topic was basketball and the university's prospects during the current season. He saw that Elaine Biddle had found a place beside Markwell on the couch and was watching his face with that unwavering intentness that a careless man might mistake for an interest in what he was saying.

At the bar Forest was haranguing Kelsey and Jost. He had not taken off his green GI coat. His face was red and sweating and he was drinking very fast. "No," he was saying as Corrigan came up to them, "no, that's not my point at all. I'm not saying Markwell is no good. I haven't read his stuff, so how could I say that?"

"If you haven't read his work . . ." Jost said, shrugging and laughing.

"I have read *some* of it," Forest insisted. "Not bad. He's got some good lines. What I'm talking about, for Christ's sake, is why he's doing the kind of thing he's doing and how he's got where he is. I mean, what's the good of writing that kind of thing any more? So he does it very well. So he's learned *how* to do it very well and he knows all the tricks, and how to make it sound like it said something on three levels, and so maybe the quince is the emblem of love and happiness to the ancients *and* the symbol of European civilization. What difference does all that make? Who cares? Do you care?"

The rhetoric was addressed to Jost, who, more nimble socially than Forest, ducked it by stepping back to acknowledge Corrigan's arrival, at the same time passing the question to him as if it were a plate of cookies. Noting that Corrigan must have overheard the substance of Forest's question, he asked, laughing, "Do *you* care, Professor Corrigan?"

With Forest watching him from furious eyes (though he was laughing too), Corrigan considered the question with hmms and ahhhs until they had put a drink in his hand. Then he said, "Do I care about the symbols of European civilization? I hope I do."

The young men, Forest included, took his answer as a joke and respectfully ignored its feebleness.

"I don't care about them," Forest said. "I don't feel anything for them at all. They're a lot of junk jewelry as far as I'm concerned. One thing I have read of Markwell's is this long-winded pretentious business about Orpheus and Eurydice. No doubt it's a pretty story, but it's not important to us."

"Important as what?" Corrigan asked.

Forest seemed annoyed by the pedagogic demand for an illustration. "Well, as important as the things Dostoevsky wrote about, for example. Or the things that Lawrence wrote about. You see what I mean." His tone added the impatient postscript "If you seriously want to and aren't just wasting our time."

Corrigan said, "A colleague of mine consistently finds Shakespeare superior to all modern poets. Maybe that's not all there is to be said, though."

"I mean there isn't any point in second-rate work," Forest said. "Anything that there's something of it better than just clutters up—"

"'Something of it better than . . .'?" Jost giggled. But Forest was above any mere sniping at his syntax. He was plainly in the grip of his vision, which happened, as it had with more than a few from the literary pantheon, to be a vision in which he did not distinguish between himself and greatness, between the plant that does not grow on mortal soil and the imperious need for recognition he felt within himself. At this point he plunged on to another incoherent fragment from his reflections. "You read about Van Gogh at the time he and some of the others, Impressionists, had a show of their paintings, and you can see Van Gogh standing in front of his, waiting for people to come and look at it. How embarrassing he'd be to everyone else who'd kind of stand back and say, 'My little daub doesn't amount to anything,' when Van Gogh knew his did and no one else could see it." It was shockingly clear—to Corrigan at least—that Forest was talking about himself, that he saw himself here, among this crowd of dilettantes and poseurs, as the lonely and furious Van Gogh.

And would it not be, Corrigan wondered, an impertinence to ask, Where is your work? Van Gogh, Rimbaud, Joyce, or any other of the furious egoists must indeed have seemed as intolerably vain as Forest now, but couldn't Forest realize that everyone else looked at that vanity through the justifying frame of hallowed works, while only he presumed to look at it nakedly and share it with no visible sign of justification? To feel oneself not only an artist but a great artist was a recklessness that approached insanity—and he could believe that was exactly what Forest felt of himself. He did not want to deny what Forest felt, but by his whole temperament and from the mellowing that age had given him, he wanted to interpose a *maybe* between Forest's reckless *I am* and the certain denial he would encounter if he exposed himself too far.

"I have the weakness of liking all art," he said, seriously wishing to take up Forest's argument. "For me the libraries and museums aren't big enough. I like whatever is done in the right spirit, and I don't always know how to put it in ranks—first, second, and so on." It seemed to him at that moment he knew what it was he had to teach Forest, if there were time and opportunity for it—the way to accept a scaling down from the vision to the accomplishment. He knew what it meant, and the boy needed to know, and there was the true valence of pedagogy. But as they were met here, he could not even find a way of assuring Forest. While he was composing a way to lure on Forest's argument, Forest's wife slipped between them and took her husband's arm.

"Come on over and talk to *him*," she said to Forest. "He said to bring you over."

"Go on," Corrigan urged. "It's not every day you have the opportunity." He was lightly disappointed by her intrusion at that moment, but ironically pleased, too, that she should be demonstrating her usefulness as a wife. So now he knew why she had braved the blizzard to come out tonight. The little pirate wanted Markwell for her husband—not his scalp or his money, but the Success of him, softened up and in a mood to talk to Forest as an equal. She knew, he thought, what kind of gifts were likely to touch this strange husband of hers, and if she could not offer him her physical charms directly, at least she knew how to use them in barter for something he wanted.

He had fallen into a banal, edgeless talk with Jost when he heard the shouting from the couch. It was Markwell's voice.

"Everyone's a writer," Markwell was shouting bitterly. "Paper's cheap, so you're a writer too." It was Forest at whom he was shouting, Forest planted on a chair in front of him, staring at the poet with the knowing smile of an inquisitor who has just exposed a phony. "Jesus Christ," Markwell shouted, "I know your type. The Village is full of them. Find them in every college, little sonofabitching pipsqueaks who have to bolster their ego by attacking someone. How I *pity* you. I didn't come here to be attacked. I thought I was among friends." He swung, as if desperately, toward Forest's wife, and, seeing in her eyes the sympathy of a mother cobra, twisted toward Tyburn as if Tyburn could exorcise these nightmare figures which had appeared to disturb his peace. "I'm leaving. Moore, I'm going back to my hotel. When's the first plane out of this goddam hick town? All I asked for was a reasonable amount of manners. Did I ask for anything more?" he demanded of the hushed group gathered around him.

"Take it easy, Mark," Tyburn advised. "Get him another drink, you. I don't know where this one crept in from," he told Markwell, pointing his elbow at Forest.

Then the voice of Forest's wife, piercing and memorable as the shriek of a seabird, cut its ice edge through the racket. "Well, it was stupid," she said. "Everything you said all evening was stupid. Did you think you were talking to a kindergarten?" she said to Markwell. She dragged at Forest's shoulder. "Come on, Steve," she said. "Let's go out of here."

As if he were intoxicated, or rapt in the continuation of the dialogue that Markwell had cut off, Forest, still smiling his fixed, catatonic smile, let her lead him from the room.

"My God," Corrigan said to Tyburn a while later. "What happened over there?" He held one hand over his eyes as if it were his own embarrassment he was hiding. "What brought on the fuss?"

"This kid attacked him," Tyburn said. "Mark was just talking about the Dodgers—perfectly innocent—and what's-his-name butted in and asked 'Who do you think you're talking to?' and Mark ignored that. But he butted in again with something about Mark sounding more like a traveling salesman than a poet. Wow. Where do you dig up characters like that? It's unbelievable. It was like some silly thing out of Dostoevsky. And then that girl with him, who'd been making big eyes at Mark, turned on him too. Christ, I don't want this to get back to New York. Now I'm going to have to get Mark good and drunk."

As he filled Markwell's glass again with shaking hands he demanded of Corrigan. "That's the boy you peddled to me, isn't it?" With a semi-tolerant laugh he accused, "You didn't tell me he was crazy."

"Ah, well now," Corrigan comforted, "the boy's just awkward. I don't suppose he meant to offend anyone."

"These bleeding little egos," Tyburn said. " 'Exterminate the brutes.' " There was a momentary flash of puzzlement across his face, a frightened wonder, as if some perversion of the optic nerves had given him a short glimpse of a chimera. But then he said, "*Otherwise* it's not a bad party. Mark's seen students before. He'll just have to lump it. But the kid must be a clinical case."

Corrigan bowed his head to this judgment.

It must have been that night when he caught the bug. When he left the party not long after Forest's bombshell, the snow was falling with soundless emphasis, as if it meant to finish things off here and now. It was falling on top of other snow and already had hidden the hubs of cars parked along the street. Under the street lights and the shop lights it glittered with a fluffy, malign purity, and its delicate texture muffled the sound of the few cars still passing on the street.

The air was not cold. After the wind that had blown all day had died, there was a sort of neutrality in the temperature. Corrigan was sweating under his overcoat as he came into the district where no tracks broke the snow along the sidewalk. He had to wade with high prancing steps for the last few blocks before he came to his apartment building. He was panting when he came onto the steps, which the janitor had shoveled clear.

Then as he stood there looking back on the formless white that was already filling in even his own tracks, it occurred to him that he did not want to go in. Some rollicking impulse to go flounder in the inundation of snow held him awhile, staring back. Childish, he thought. Then he thought, Children hear it—the siren appeal of the snow that dissolves away the familiar forms and outlines of things so they know the intimate attraction of nothingness. Like a memory older than any memory of love he knew how falling snow and the night posed the question, "Do you care?" and what drunken delight it was for the child to answer, "No." Nothing in life was quite so keen as that presexual thrill of abandonment back to nothingness, the white center.

He heard the temptress's voice, oddly like Elaine Biddle's, and he thought, No one else I know would guess what lasciviousness it will be to yield. And then, as if he needed a conventional reason for staying out, he thought, I won't go far, and it is beautiful. To watch it awhile longer can't hurt. But the legs of his trousers were damp above the tops of the four-buckle overshoes his wife had bought him. All right, not tonight, he thought sadly, and went in to the comfort of his apartment and the precaution of his cold pills.

Nevertheless, in spite of caution, he had caught the bug. His first sign of it was an extremely nasty and literary waking dream of Forest's wife, in which she took the double role of the child and old woman in her story. It was nasty in its gross sexuality, and it was literary in its fantastic resemblance to the hunting days in *Sir Gawain and the Green Knight* when the Green Knight's wife comes to Sir Gawain's bed. Mrs. Forest had been to Corrigan's bed in a wintry castle and he had accepted her—if that was the word for the ugly connections they had made—both as prepubescent child and dripping grandmother.

He woke with a heavy sense of self-repugnance, found that his eyes and all his muscles ached, as if from immense effort, and that his throat was painfully sore. Some strain of ancient

Calvinism made him glad of the pain. It was a specific and merited punishment for having dreamed as he had—though at the same time, at a remoter level of awareness, he understood that the dream itself was a graver rebuke than the pain. He gargled and tried to stretch his muscles with some bending exercises. Finally he got himself in shape to go to his office long enough for conferences with Miss Emery and a doctoral candidate preparing a thesis on Chaucer.

By afternoon he had to admit that he needed medical attention. He took a cab to the dispensary at the university hospital, and there, after an examination, the doctor ordered him into the hospital "for a few days."

"Bronchial pneumonia," the doctor said. "I don't think it's going to be serious, but we want to keep an eye on you."

"Sounds as if the police were taking me in," Corrigan said, his little pleasantry reflecting a deep-lying guilty sense that it was not for his illness that he was being taken in but for the improper dream that had accompanied it.

"Yes, protective custody," the doctor agreed absently, already occupying himself with the formalities of ordering Corrigan's admission. "I'm not expecting anything serious to happen. But we have to think of your age."

The pain was still slight, and that afternoon began like a holiday for Corrigan. Lightly intoxicated with the fever, he submitted contentedly to the attentions of the orderlies helping him into bed. The neutral whiteness of the bed in which he lay seemed a wonderfully privileged substitute for the snow that had called to him the night before. This was like a child's pretense of dying.

He felt fine in the bed; he felt wonderful. He had needed, he told himself, this stage setting for his thought more than he needed medical attention. After submitting to having his temperature and pulse taken he let himself slide swiftly back into a rehash of his morning's dream. Let the doctor believe he had pneumonia; he knew he had caught the Forests—they were in his psychic stream like the cocci in his blood. When he was prepared to deal with them—lying flat on his back seemed the position of choice for doing so—then his blood would expel the hostile bugs quickly enough.

In the meantime he was close to enjoying the spectacle of his fight against the contagions. His hospitalization was like a warrant for digging back through the unconscious panorama of the dream to the conscious preparation for it. (Only enforced leisure could warrant the impracticality of such speculation. It could produce no valuable return.) Here he would speculate on the way his dream of Forest's wife had grown like a wild vine from his perfectly conscious interpretation of her story, the way that little stolen seed had gestated within his life as within a natural womb.

As he lay there looking out from his windows onto the white campus and the white hills beyond the edge of town, it seemed to him that he could see through arch beyond arch beyond arch and behold, almost diagrammatically, how the process of imagination worked. And it seemed to him, with an exuberance he had not felt since he was a young man, that he was about to begin a tremendous imaginative work. Little Miss Biddle had stolen a story, and that was a crude illustration of how the process worked. But he—well, he was going to steal Miss Biddle and her story, and the story of her stealing the story, and the story of his stealing and, . . . Contentedly he fell asleep.

Within a few days he saw how he had been tricked into this euphoria by his fever. *Something* strange was happening in his mental life, but it was not the beginning of a new phase of creativity. All over again he had to admit what he had long ago humbly concluded—that his ability to write had been exhausted. The lifelong accumulation of experience and insight from reading had been somehow tipped loose and was avalanching *as if* toward some point of concentration where it might be transformed into a work of his own. But it never quite arrived. Instead it seemed to exhaust itself in the fireworks of literary dreams about Forest's wife and—sometimes—Forest. He had tried imaginatively (using the same heavily equipped critical probes that he might have brought to a poem) to pierce their lives. And he had gone too far. He no longer had any defense against them. Whenever he slept he would find himself dreaming about them in one literary situation or another. They were everyone, from Popeye and Temple Drake to Dante and Beatrice, Gatsby and Daisy, Heathcliffe and Cathy, Paul Morel and Miriam, Raskolnikov and Sonia, Paolo and Francesca, Maggie and Jiggs. Sometimes he was involved in their relationship carnally, sometimes spiritually, but after a time these dreams became his chief source of discomfort. Then they began to frighten him as he recognized them not as promises of new insights but as signs of dissolution.

After a few days he complained of them to the doctor. "They're embarrassing," he said.

The doctor listened but was not greatly impressed. "They'll go away when we get your fever down. You're clear enough when you're awake, aren't you?"

Yes, Corrigan admitted, he was, but wakefulness had become increasingly boring. Now his days seemed to pass in an uneasy suspension between the boring winter whiteness that his consciousness perceived and the unholy medley of his dreams.

It was as if he had abandoned that familiar vantage point from which he could turn safely toward either reason or fantasy. He felt a great fragility in himself and a bitter impatience with it.

The upshot of it was that he stayed in the hospital longer than his doctor had expected. As the doctor had promised, the disease had taken no serious turn, but his convalescence was slow. After the fever ended, his horrid literary dreams disappeared, and that was a testimony to the doctor's acumen, but Corrigan believed they were still going on inside him, more and more identified with the secret processes of dissolution that his bout of disease had accentuated. It was a humiliation that his last spark of creativity had turned to ashes so quickly.

The Christmas vacation passed while he was still in the hospital and he remained as the first semester drew to an end. It was late in January when, one day, Tyburn came to call on him, bringing a bottle of whiskey and an issue of *Botteghe Oscure* in which some of Tyburn's poems had been published.

At first Corrigan thought irritably that the younger man had come simply because it was the season when promotions and salaries for the following year were about to be decided, and that Tyburn might be simply angling for his support and a good word to the head of the department. That support wasn't needed. This was Tyburn's time. He was on top. He could ride. His generation had secured their reputations, and the head of the department could count up the number of publications credited to Tyburn without any help from Corrigan. (The departmental secretary kept a chart of publications by members of the staff, a chart which had always reminded Corrigan of the stack of an aircraft carrier with its painted emblems of the kills to be credited to each pilot.) Tyburn would rise.

But evidently Tyburn knew that too, and something else was bothering him. In the little time since last fall he had passed from worrying about his security on the staff to a deeper concern. When he had drunk a couple of drinks from his present to Corrigan, he slapped the *Botteghe Oscure* against the bedside table and cried, "The poems I've got in here are *wonderful*. But as soon as I read them I tore up everything I've written since last fall. I've lost my ladder."

"That can happen," Corrigan said drily.

"You've been through it," Tyburn said. "You should have a perspective on it. You were doing wonderful stuff before you settled down to teaching. So tell me, is it worth it?"

"I don't know."

"I've got to decide. It's not going to hurt me to stay here another year, and Franklin knows the people at the Guggenheim foundation, so there's a good reason for staying next year at least. But I've got to make up my mind. I've got to decide whether what I can do for my students is more valuable than what I can do for myself."

"Well?"

"I don't know," Tyburn said somberly. "I can't get the score. Look, that kid you sent to my class. The nutty one. Forest. You were there the night he took off on Markwell. All right. It was a thing that happened, and I made up my mind that it wasn't a capital offense. So, I called the kid in and had a long talk with him and thought we had everything straightened out, really. It seems there was more to it than met the eye. Markwell had been pinching his wife, this girl Markwell had been pinching was his wife, and *that* is what riled him up to call Mark down. Which makes *sense*. Those things happen, and I've seen Mark in trouble before, but I didn't know it at the time. So Forest and I had this good talk and I thought we were seeing eye to eye. Then about a week ago the kid gave me part of a novel he's been working on."

He paused and shook his head ponderously and poured himself another drink.

"Did it show merit?" Corrigan asked.

"*None,*" Tyburn said briskly. "Or I shouldn't say none, but it wasn't good."

Corrigan nodded slowly. "I'm afraid that Forest, after all, is a mute inglorious Dostoevsky. The fascinating question is whether or not that is a contradiction in terms. If mute, then Dostoevsky?"

"He *thought* he'd put so much into it," Tyburn said. "He thought it was the history of all the anguish he's had with this nympho wife of his, and there are some moving touches—uh, *moving*—when he describes how she made insatiable demands on him while he was suffering from the common cold and a big dream sequence where he has her raped by a gang of hoodlums in Chicago, but it's pornography at best."

"Oh my," Corrigan said, clicking his tongue.

"But when I tried to tell him this—"

"You didn't," Corrigan gasped. He could feel the spastic twisting in his stomach now, fierce and undeniable and hot and passionate as belief itself. "You didn't tell him it was pornography?"

"What's the point in criticism if it isn't honest?" Tyburn said. "So I told him. So—"

Through the muffled, bombing bursts of his breath, Corrigan gasped, "He swung on you." He saw Tyburn's eyes round out in solemn saucers as he nodded.

"Thank God I didn't lose my head," Tyburn said. "I ran down to the departmental office and the secretary and I held the door on him while Peltus called the campus police to come and take him away."

"Hooooo-ooooo," Corrigan shouted, the breath exploding now from his cramped lungs, "Hooooo-ooooo, hah." Like a leaping trout he flung himself up, scattering bedclothes wildly as he turned in midair. When he landed, with his face half-buried in the pillow, he was sobbing with helpless laughter.

"Tell me again," he gasped. "How you-ooo-ooo held the door on him."

Happily—it might have gone otherwise—Tyburn began to laugh too. When he could control himself Corrigan sat up and grasped the whiskey bottle by the neck. Between fiery gulps he said, "Don't talk any more about leaving, Tyburn. Where else would you find it like this? Where else on earth?"

"It is pretty funny," Tyburn said.

When they had finished the bottle between them, Corrigan was shouting for the nurse, demanding his clothes, swearing that he was going home.

He thought after this that the Forests were through with him. Just as the embarrassing dreams vanished—or went underground—after the fever, the young people moved in the course of time beyond his purview. When the second semester began, he learned from gossiping with some members of his class that Forest had not registered. He had left the campus, and Corrigan's informants did not know where he had gone. And his wife? Oh, still around, still living at the sorority house where she had been all winter.

Corrigan saw her one evening when an unseasonable warmth had turned early March for a few days into May. He had taken a long walk in the afternoon and was coming home feeling hungry and fit. He had entered Fraternity Row a few blocks above the campus. The imitations of English country houses spread a theatrical setting down the street ahead of him, and into this setting, like a swan boat, came the largest and most chrome-laden convertible he had ever seen. Softly, swishingly, ponderously it glided to the curb a few dozen yards ahead of him and stopped. From a door wide and massy as a church portal, Elaine Biddle Forest descended. She was in a white evening dress and on her shoulders was mink.

At the instant of her descent a gold bar of sunlight flashed through the thicket of elms and fraternity plantings across the street to illuminate her almost to incandescence. As if she had been expecting it, she paused momentarily in the light and with mannequin grace, mannequin blankness wheeled slowly for all the world (or all the universe, Corrigan thought breathlessly) to see.

Then her equerry—tall, broad-shouldered, short of hair and clean of feature, dinner-jacketed and most evidently odorless as the stratosphere—leaped out behind her and with an athletic step led her up the front steps and into the fraternity.

That tableau was staged to mean something, Corrigan thought. No part of it was accidental—but where in the universe of accident was the origin of this theatrical purpose, and *whose* exactly was the discrimination that chose the details of costuming and light and arranged the tempo of this visionary scene so that fleeting as it was it should continue to vibrate like the persisting hum of a tuning fork? Mine, he thought with ironic arrogance. It was my little eye that saw it all. But whose eye was his? The wind blew acidly from the northwest as if to remind him that the false-spring blandness of the afternoon was an illusion made by powers who need not recognize his claims as a stockholder.

As the tuning-fork hum of beauty died out and he walked on toward his dinner he fell into a depression, as if it should be an automatic hangover from the exultation he had felt in the instant of seeing her. The depression moved through phases as distinct as spectrum bands. He felt a kind of groaning compassion for Forest that he had lost this girl, that he had let her beauty go by default into the hands of—of that Philistine, that embryonic hotel manager or corporation lawyer. It was one up again for the enemy. In this vein of thought the convertible, which had seemed a swan boat to his eye, became a vulgar bit of ostentation, a commercial virility symbol by whose authority (*in hoc signo*) the collectivized male should ravish away the Queen of Love herself. Not that Elaine Biddle was, in this discounting phase, worth likening to the Queen of Love in any way, shape, or form. He had it from Tyburn's instructed epithet as well as hints that Forest had given him that the girl was a "nympho." Probably very little ravishing was required. But at the basest level she was valuable poetic property, and recruit writers should learn to cling to their beautiful women, just as recruit soldiers should learn to hang onto their weapons.

In the violet gloom of his depression he realized with a nauseated shock that it was not exactly for Forest's sake that he regretted the loss of Elaine Biddle to the others. Remembering those desperate dreams he had had of her while he was sick he admitted with savage frankness that in his decrepitude *he* was the desolated lover. It was his abandonment and jealousy he lamented now that she had been carried away by that gloomy chariot. He thought, raging, If I had it to do over again, all my life, I'm damned if I'd be a poet. I'd have her. Like a sign of the imminence of his death he felt a swift resentment against his dead wife—that good, warm, encouraging, wise, and loving companion, whose very goodness had tricked him away from the absolute abandonment to a single need which had been—he saw it now—required of him. Insanely, he hated her.

And then, of course, he neutralized the insane revelation with countervailing admonitions to himself. He had had a fit and was over it again, luckily, and able as he had almost always been to see things in proportion. He would go on to the end as himself—a limited man trying to make at least the holy counterfeit of salvation out of his very limitations. With his mouth he would not willingly or overtly deny the woman who had been so faithful and precious to him. But in his heart, in its despicable slime and fear . . .

To the end now, he supposed, that heart would be telling him that he did not care about the past with its measured successes and its limited failures. It was only the monstrous and chimerical future that he loved, the future in which he had so little stake, the true hell of exclusion from which no singer could bring back a credible image of love.

She came to him within three days after this, arriving at his office so demurely and so dully earnest that he would not identify her with the girl he had seen getting out of the convertible.

She had brought a package for him. She wanted him to read the manuscript of her husband's novel.

"Well, but if he'd wanted me to read it . . ." Corrigan began protestingly. "Mr. Tyburn's already read it, I think, and discussed it with your husband."

"Read it," she pleaded. "I want to know for sure if it's any good or not." Her pale eyes looked more guileless than she could possibly be. She had laid the swollen bundle of manuscript between them on the desk and, while he had not yet picked it up, his wariness conceived it as a bait that he still had the chance of refusing.

"Why?"

"Because as far as he's concerned he's thrown it away," she said. "He wouldn't even take it with him when he left. He would have burned it if I'd let him."

"I heard he was gone. Where?"

With a frown and small shrug of repugnance she said, "Back to New York. His brother-in-law edits comic books. He's going to work for him, writing stories or dialogue or something like that."

"Too bad."

"He had such high ideals."

"Too bad," Corrigan said, "but this isn't the end of his life. I have the hunch we're going to hear a good deal from that young man before it's through."

She, with that air of not seeming to hear anything she did not want to—rather, of testing with her need whatever was said to her and accepting into the realm of her concern only the useful—said, "I want him to come back here. I want him to finish this book."

"Why? A good many times it's wiser to put aside something that's badly begun and make a fresh start. I think you want me to advise him—encourage him—to go on with this, and I suspect Mr. Tyburn may have discouraged him rather sharply. But isn't it likely that I might have the same reservations about it that Mr. Tyburn had?"

She did not hear him. She merely waited for him to admit the folly of his evasiveness.

"Why?" he asked again, and because she did not answer he answered the question himself with a sigh of resignation. "Because it's about you."

"It's about both of us," she said in a high, silvery voice. "And he doesn't need to think he can leave it like this. I know him. He won't ever do anything without me. He's got to understand that. He's got to face it."

It was no outward display of force that lent her speech its absolute certainty. She was not the kind to clench her lovely jaw or even to lean forward for emphasis. The certainty came rather from that tantalizing, centripetal glow of frailty toward which she expected force to flow as the normal pressure of air breaks in toward a vacuum.

"You mean I've got to face it," Corrigan joked oddly, picking up the manuscript and hefting it. "I'll read this. I want to read it. But I don't know if anything you want will come from my reading it. I couldn't possibly use it as a basis for intervening in your personal life—even supposing that I had means for doing so effectively. I feel that you've brought me this as if I were a lawyer and this was a document—"

"Just read it," she said. "You'll see."

All through that night he sat at home reading the story of the Forests. It was not the "true" story of what they were and how they had come, so strangely matched, together—for, as he had often admonished his class, truth requires form, and the intent to tell the truth is no guarantee that it will be uttered. After the glimpses and conjectures by which he had known the Forests during the past winter, here was only another glimpse and conjecture. The manuscript was—as Tyburn must have pointed out—formless to an extreme. Sometimes it was confessional in form and reduced painful scenes to comedy, and at other points it was so ponderously stylized and rhetorical that the tissue of dialogue and scene was squeezed to death by the language. It was a big manuscript, and it was tedious. As a literary effort it was quite unmistakably inferior to the Korean war stories that Forest had shown him (and Corrigan realized with a pang that this was the precious work going on behind the scenes, saved until it could be shown to Tyburn's more fastidious gaze, while the pieces on which Forest had staked less were being shown to him). If he were to answer as a responsible critic, he could only say that the work was a complete failure.

And yet as he read toward midnight he knew that there were images rising from the turgid brew and begging for completeness that were of more than ordinary power. Mangled giants struggling through a swamp, he thought, and it seemed to him that what the work needed—all that it needed, but that which a literary work must never need—was to be considered an amputated chunk of the reality which should have been its subject.

He read of the spring night in the sorority house when Steve Forest (called Sid Fleischer in the manuscript, with a transparency so futile that Corrigan ignored it) had been washing dishes alone in the kitchen. As the young man worked at the sink he suddenly began throwing pieces of china out through the open window beside him, at first fearfully and then, when no one appeared to stop him, in an increasing rhythm, hearing them tinkle in the lonely dark outside. If he had stopped to think he might have rationalized this gesture as an appropriately defiant resignation of his job as hasher at the house. But he was not even thinking of it as defiance yet—only as something he must do because he was young and it was spring.

Then he heard behind him, without having heard her footsteps as she came into the kitchen, the trusting, uninflected voice asking, "Why are you doing that?"

Not knowing yet and never to know, Corrigan thought, how she had heard the tinkle of destruction and had come down from her second-floor room because it was destruction she loved, needed, or chose. Because she would have recognized any splintering of windshield, crash of falling walls, smash of bottles as a call to which she must respond, faithfully hound-dogging the sign of destruction because it would have been for her the sound of her prison door opening.

"That's a stupid question," he had answered. Frightened, Corrigan thought, because he had been caught, expressing his fright in aggression, ready to "walk out" then as always later with his thumb to his nose, but tolerating her there, waiting, because she had come down smelling of them, all her sisters, because in her person *they* all stood there obediently waiting to be snowed with any silly explanation he might make up.

Then under her non-accusing stare Forest had panicked. He did not want to be fired for breaking dishes, but most of all he did not want to be fired for having done something that he could not explain with dignity to the housemother when she got around to firing him. So he had gone out into the back lawn of the sorority house and begun to gather the broken pieces of china up in his bare hands and carry them down the slope to the trash barrels. The girl, still in stocking feet as she had come downstairs, tried to help him and (with what meaning, purpose, cunning?) stepped on a shark-tooth fragment of a cup. She sat there with the faint light slanting down on her from the kitchen window above, holding her foot while they both watched the blood ooze out through the dirty nylon. She said tranquilly, "It doesn't hurt. I can't feel it."

This was the image of their recognition. Its felt load of significance was grossly disproportionate to the scene in which Forest laid her for the first time some weeks later. Perhaps the one moving statement about their mating in the basement smoking room of the sorority was the sentence, "She cried." Only that in twenty pages of prose that Forest might have memorized from the reading of spicy magazines during his lonely nights in Korea.

There was little enough to be made from Forest's report of the long-drawn-out conversations they had during the time they decided they were engaged. Except even then Forest seemed to have suspected—what never became more than a suspicion—that she wanted him because she believed that he was "lower" than she. Her father was a lumber dealer in a middle-sized Illinois town—Anglo-Saxon, Methodist, the owner of a Cadillac and a twelve-room house, member of the country club, father of two boys in the insurance game, and a Republican. It never occurred to his daughter that these attributes were not marks of superiority. It was merely that she did not want them. Forest was a Jew, a houseboy in her sorority, and—in his own admission to her—an artist. By these signs she recognized him as beneath her, and she wanted him.

Already by the time she had gone home to Illinois for the summer vacation the horrid comedy in which she pursued and he tried to evade had begun.

If it had not been for their separation, Forest might have escaped her. He went with a friend in a battered car to Oregon for the summer. He hocked everything and borrowed money from his parents, intending in his own phrase "to jump off a cliff and live." If he went too dangerously far in his self-abandonment he would "knock himself off. A nice cool bullet through the head didn't seem like such a bad idea sometimes." But in Portland he got mixed up with a crowd of painters at a beer party and had an affair with a coed from UCLA "whose equipment was phenomenal." He could, or would, or should have been content with her and have transferred to UCLA for the fall term if it had not been for the letters from Elaine in Illinois.

He quoted one of the letters. It was an utterly flat and dull account of a weekend in which she had swum three afternoons at the country club and danced three evenings with some boys her cousin knew at Northwestern. She had been bored by it all, she said.

But the point was that Forest didn't believe the letters.

Precisely because they were so void of content, he had believed in anguish that there was something glamorous going on that she was not telling him. The hot prairie nights, the band playing under the stars, the colored lanterns quivering like live things in the palpitation of the air—Forest could imagine this and in the grip of his imagination could not conceive that in such a setting there was nothing going on that he needed to know about.

But you should have believed her, Corrigan thought, involved like the ever-passionate hick who yells warnings from the theater balcony, the sympathetic freshman who wants to tell Othello not to believe Iago and doesn't give a wandering damn whether Shakespeare made a work of art or not. You had to believe that it was dull there because—well, because if you or I or anyone else following us could just hang on to the literal truth of things we'd save ourselves this awful bother of fiction, poetry, pursuit of phantoms.

In the moment of his excitement, something banged Corrigan's chest like a stocking filled with sand. Palpitations, he thought. He poured himself a large glass of whiskey for a cure. It was not late yet. Not midnight. He was going to see this manuscript *through* before he went to bed, he told himself.

The memorable image of Forest's wedding was the present given him by his wife's parents. Because he was a writer—he took no pains to hide this from them when he suddenly appeared in their Illinois town and, with Elaine, announced what was about to happen—they gave him a Webster's unabridged dictionary.

But aside from the presentation of this ambiguous symbol the bride's parents seemed to have acquitted themselves rather decently under the shock of the marriage. In his manuscript Forest took pains to mock their staid Republicanism, and he had "bit his lip" to keep from laughing at the marriage ceremony performed in the Methodist parsonage. But the sheer fact that they had permitted it to take place at all stood mutely to their credit, as well as the clumsy attempts of the parents to make him (the dark, exotic stranger come into town hitchhiking and carrying only one cardboard suitcase) feel that now he must look to them for help "if things ever didn't go quite right."

Justifiably, Forest contrasted the price of the dictionary to that of the Packard Sixes which the family had given his wife's brothers on the occasions of *their* marriages. Truly it was as if good common sense had told them not to spend too much for a marriage that wouldn't last. But again they had acted decently against this wariness in loaning the newlyweds the family Cadillac to drive to Chicago for a honeymoon.

The honeymoon was a horror. On the one hand he expected her to bring to the marriage bed in a cheap Northside hotel that glamour which she had so tantalizingly left out of her letters, that glamour of the upstairs in the sorority house—to bring him *the others* with whom he had so hopefully identified her. And she had lain there in his arms a single, naked, demanding self— not even as "phenomenally equipped" as the girl he had left in Oregon. He was too close to her, suddenly, to see that she was beautiful.

On the other hand, as soon as their first hasty bout on the rented bed was finished and even before she had commanded in that unworldly voice, "Do it again," he had glimpsed the immensity of her demand on him, the motive that had overridden parental objections and sorority platitudes about love and marriage as if they didn't exist. It was, Corrigan sensed, the depth of nothingness in her which had on the one hand permitted Forest to see whatever his desire could paint in her and conversely established her need for him. She must have someone whose imagination, whose occupation with her, would give her the reality she did not feel. From that first night when she had stepped on the glass and reported that she felt nothing, she had recognized Forest as the fabricator of her reality. She had watched him read *pain* when he saw the blood flowing. And if he had, in the proof, turned out to be an insufficient artist to turn her nothingness into existence, at least he was the only artist she had ever known. And she was determined that he must suffice.

Her demand emerged as a metaphysical one, and to call its expression nymphomania was at best a clumsy metaphor. In the same way it was clear what her ultimate motive had been in requiring Corrigan to read the manuscript about her. On the paradoxical bed in Chicago the Forests had failed the test wherein illusions and the need to be created might have fused in reality. Deserted, and as if feeling herself fading back to the nothing she had been, she had called out one more time, and this time not to Forest, but through Forest's work to him, "See me. Make me real."

The cursed honeymoon had lasted just two days before Elaine drove the Cadillac south out of Chicago by herself. And there was only one happy memory of it which Forest, with "Dostoevskian" self-abasement, had put down. During an hour when his new wife was out of the room he rifled her suitcase. It was full of such splendid underwear as he had seen only in store windows and advertisements before—a foundation garment of orchid-colored silk, a black half-bra and panties, a cloud of white lace, and a crisscrossing of white elastic straps with gleaming buckles—all that modern heraldry of romance and woman cult suddenly, as he said, "his." Staring down into this treasury, Forest confessed, he felt the one moment of generous lust that he would know on the entire honeymoon. This, and not the dangerous void of the woman, was what he wanted. He had plunged his hands recklessly into the yielding stuff.

(". . . arms closing on wind, lips speaking a name which must be her name . . ." Corrigan incorporated this fragment from Markwell's Orpheus poem to piece out the prose with which Forest had described the episode. But he sensed, in an uncontrolled impulse of compassion and humility, that he was being called on for a belief greater than his belief in poetry. He must not lament—and poetry was lamentation—on pain of losing her. *Do not look back. Believe she is with you.*)

The Forests, he read, had made another effort to live together when they came back to school at the beginning of the fall semester. They rented a tiny apartment, installed in it the cloth of gold of her underwear, and his Webster's unabridged dictionary, and within a very few days it had become untenable for the two of them together. ("It was like having a body in the house with him," Forest had written with unintentional comedy.) She wanted to cook for him, and he was used to cooking for himself, a much better cook than she. She wanted him to stay home in the evenings and read his work aloud to her. (Since he was already deeply involved with this present manuscript in which he had so many derogatory things to say about her—its composition seemed to have progressed like that of a journal—he felt trapped by her request, dreading at the same time that he might hurt her and that she was stifling his "honesty.") When he did read to her he had the feeling that she was not listening "critically." She seemed to bathe in the sound of his voice with no interest in its meaning. When he tried explaining to her that he wanted to be like Dostoevsky, she smiled a catlike smile of satisfaction with him, as though he were *announcing* to her that he already was Dostoevsky. This made him wild. Couldn't she understand how goddam lousy and imperfect his work was *now*, while he was learning his craft? To which she would reply maddeningly that she could understand that *too* and at the same time. In her oceanic emptiness she drowned his attempts to organize his life and his work logically. She cared nothing if he choked on his own inconsistencies as long as she could have him with her—"In there with her," he wrote, referring to the hated apartment.

(" 'You're trying to make a doll's house out of this,' Sid Fleischer yelled as he walked out. He was going downtown to get drunk. He was going to get damn good and drunk. Let her fester there in the festoons of the bourgeois respectability she had brought with her. He thought of how she would be in bed waiting for him when he got home. The covers would be pulled up to her eyes. Her catlike eyes would be watching him when he came in reeling drunk. She never seemed to sleep. If he woke during the night, she always seemed to be awake before him. Let her stay awake tonight. He was going to get drunk and he was not coming home.")

This must have been about the time I first saw them, Corrigan thought. He wondered with a sort of tense fascination if he would presently appear as a character. He thought not. He would have seemed too unimportant, too neutral, to Forest. (And now he felt a queer, repentant impulse to accept Forest's judgment in the matter.)

It's only now, this way, as a reader, that I can belong in the story at all, he thought. Then he thought, They need me. If I weren't here, what Forest thinks of himself and her would be true, and if it is, he's already lost her. Or what the world thought of them would be true. And if it were, Forest had never loved her at all. It *must not* be true that the boy was a spoiled piece of slag from the Age of the Wars, an egomaniacal piece of waste who had blundered into marriage with a nymphomaniac. But if I am not real in this story by reading it and holding it all in my heart, then whatever game we've all started to play when we play at writing is lost, he thought. He was very tired now from the effort to compose the Forest story, but for the most important of reasons he would not let himself quit and go to bed.

He read on into the dream sequence that Tyburn had mentioned to him and discovered what Tyburn, with his psychological insight, must have discerned—that it was a wish-fulfillment fantasy, in which the imagined rape of the wife was a hope of diverting her frightening attentions from himself. But it had another correlation, too, which opened out like an exploding fireworks bomb. Placed against it with a perhaps unconscious cunning was a passage describing her confession of her first sexual experiences. Forest had overcome her reluctance to speak of them by making love to her, and in the very tempest of their embrace had paused to whisper, "Tell me all about it"—delighting to learn that it had been "a fraternity man, a real Joe College" who had deflowered her after a homecoming game.

Voyeur too, Corrigan thought with a groan, recognizing the dream as a means by which Forest saw through his wife to the

multiplicity of experience that could never be his. Voyeur . . .
that term must be justly added to the long list of other truths
about this—this *writer.*

Yet, conceding impatiently the depravity involved, he relived
in an overlapping revery his own recent glimpse of the girl. She
was again in front of the fraternity house, descending once
again from the swan boat with the twentieth-century trim. The
sun struck her gold. She turned with a hungry smile toward the
light. Then, between submission and rapture, took the arm of
her escort to let Joe College lead her up the stairs and in through
the secret door of the fraternity house to her destiny among the
lives of strangers. As she disappeared—out of memory, out of
conception—Corrigan felt his own lips shape to the begging
question, "Tell me."

But the door was closed behind her. She had come to them—
not reluctantly, but pleading to be made alive. They had lost her
and this was the way the story ended.

He finished the last pages of the manuscript. There were no
surprises left to come. He looked up at the mantelpiece clock. It
was almost three now. Of what night? Of what reality? He was
an old man fondly wishing—and not for the first time, of
course—that experience could be as coherent as desire. Then
would I have held her—held them—in my heart.

But time was again the clock's time, and the story would end
there as it must end. "Arms closing on air . . ." and "lips that
would kiss form prayers . . ." while "love that robbed us of immortal things" gave nothing, gave nothing that time could not
take back.

How could the Forests' story—which was his, now—end in
time except with Forest going off to forge in the smithy of the
comic-book trade the uncreated conscience of his race? While
little Biddle, Eurydice of the expensive underwear, dropped
back into the social millpond from which she had so maladroitly
and with such wasted expense tried to raise herself.

In time the story ended with time's ending, and there would
be neither occasion nor need for him to say the one thing that
mattered. Precisely there was the unavoidable terror—that he
could never say to her with the imperial emphasis required to
establish all it meant, "I saw you."

In defeat he rose from his chair and started toward the bedroom. Tomorrow he would return the manuscript to Biddle

(half-regained, lost on the instant of discovery), and he would try to be socially kinder than Tyburn when he discussed its weakness and its merits.

It is a terrible thing to be kind when you want to love.

He would, out of kindness, refuse her any encouragement she could pass on to her errant husband. What could he say except that time would have its way with them and their stories, fictionalized or real; that on either side of its narrow course remains the same primitive wall of darkness that has rimmed it from the beginning?

We cannot speak the living truth to each other. That was *so,* he thought furiously. But must not be. In the middle of the living room he stopped, feeling all his limbs tremble.

Suddenly—involuntarily, he thought—he spun on the toe of his right foot, kicking his left heel in the air. His left foot crashed down on the hardwood and he whirled on it. Around and around the room he went in a dizzying circle. Beyond all reason (but also beyond all wish to stop) he yielded to the necessity of the dance. Bones creaking and muscles twinging he rioted on his way, an old man refusing to die until he heard the Forests' story come out right and clear, dancing in the face of its tragic fragmentation, dancing because in the circumstances it was the common-sense thing to do.

Fragments
for Reference

Lust and forgetfulness have been among us . . .

FORMULAS OF BIRTH

To be born is no different than they say it is, only this time it's you.

The prints your fingers make. They say nobody else has that pattern or if they had there wouldn't be that scar across the second finger (which the barbed wire tore one December day when you were hunting). There wouldn't be that lead-colored sky and the white flakes that drifted over the stubble. There wouldn't be the fence creaking and springing out from under your boot. There wouldn't be that day.

Repeatedly spring delivers you in the same harsh way it delivers buds or the first grass. Time after time you have to find out how cold the glitter of mud in March is.

The repetitive process, when you are young, keeps bearing

you into a world that has centers and no edges (remember the embarrassments of childhood, your hand lifted expectantly to the center of the loaded tree, the laughter of the adults. Or watching your own fat belly. Thinking how sweet it is.) and if you make it, to be born again old is to live with the edges. The days gone, the nights gone, the land of memory where the edge-eaters live.

The shape of a birth can be cut out of the muckiest stuff. When the months of the war of nerves are run through, the border is crossed, the pretense of decency and the scruples are cut, the loyalty forsworn, the red, loving past surely behind you. And damn them then. You're your own little man. No blood pumps into you that's not your own. After nine months waiting you need neither cord nor the shape of the sack to hold you. You can remember from that pre-world the voices of a dreaming order telling you (you not-yet child) that Lincoln freed the slaves and loved his mother, that Washington didn't lie, that boiling in oil took place in olden times, that Columbus discovered a New World (you thought the sails swelled out on big sweet winds blowing into the future), that Daniel Boone found a country that shone as green as green moss in the snow.

HOW, BEING BORN, TO GET WHAT YOU WANT

Listen to the big boys, the boys who've been around. They'll tell you it's sure fire. Just reach out, they'll say. There, there it is. Take it.

If your eyes are as sharp as your teeth are, remember this bit of the sharpie's remark, "I'd like to sink my long yellow teeth into that and let it drag me to death."

If your heart has to be as stubborn as an iron lock, remember hearing, "I have his picture yet. It isn't a very good picture. Sometimes I go to the places we used to go. There isn't anybody I know there. But—I don't know how to tell you—I don't forget him."

Or

"It doesn't matter what she does or anything. We were happy for a while and I know she'll never be that happy again."

(In the middle of summer, this one Sunday, I felt the Dakota wind run over my body like warm water in a current. After dinner we had had a fight with corn cobs in the barnyard, and when we were all worn out, we lay on top of a shed in the sun. The little girls came walking by in a row abreast, five of them holding hands. When they saw us up there watching them, the lot of them wavered like a five-leaved vine that swings loose from a wall in a light breeze. My cousin Walter yelled at them, and they began to giggle and shiver. They muttered and mumbled, then all at once gave a laughing screech and turned and ran. A little cloud of dust followed each one, a delicate cloud floating off through the pasture fence.

Once we fished a garter snake out of the cistern. Walter fastened a wire snare on the end of a pole to catch it. Four of us crouched around with our heads down in the water-smelling dark hole. We saw our faces reflected around the reflection of the clouds up behind us. The snake swam about slowly and aimlessly as though he did not mean to notice the wire slide under his belly and draw tight. A little afraid of him, we tramped and kicked him until his green hide broke and the red of him was smeared with dirt.)

(I rode one night in a coal car down across the Utah desert and when the sun came up like steel on fire, the little man with me took some bread and onions out of his shirt and we ate them. "Wunt you rather eat out like this than in some damn restrunt?" he said.)

In public parks there are shady spots where you can lie and watch the girls strutting around the pool, watch their tense bodies balancing when they go up to dive; or if you haven't anywhere else to remember

the old men with cheesy eyelids in the libraries, behind piles of books, the white-skinned hands busy on letters to the editor. The words that go on the page bitter and young, "My dear sir: The presumptions of your ignorance . . ." The minds hunting like a hawk hunting over a grassy field.

(We marched in toward the hills that afternoon, coming to the edge of them, filing in among the boulders just before dark. When we sat down for ten, I saw Martin leaning back on a rock just to my right. There was brown dust all over his face except where the sweat had run down through it. "My feet," he said, "they're throbbing like a mockingbird's ass." The taste of water washing the sand out of my mouth. I remember the flocks of sparrows sweeping over while we made our camp. In the gray light.)

OR HOW TO EVADE REALITY

Reach for clouds, roads, sky, apples; imagine arms which are strong enough to hold anything that time wants. Reach your hand out of a train window into the dark, and if your hand touches a hand out there (it will seem real) get off the train and look and look and look for whom you touched.

There should be caves in reality. There should be a thicket. There should be a station along the way. Sure, Jack. But come on. Hurry.

(In the fall evenings, above the oak trees big V's of geese came over. If I pointed a stick at them, or the handlebars of a junked bicycle, they were formations of enemy aircraft. And over the mountains, when the light remained only in the top of the sky, the bombers with the orange color of the sun streaked on them were geese following an old river. The *American Boy* and *The Wonder of the War in the Air*, which had led me by the hand through imagination to the season of reality, could not lead me back.

The hills rising up sharply out of the desert at Kasserine reminded me of the river hills I'd once imagined full of battles— and seen lightning as artillery fire a long way off.)

To lie in summer looking up the trunk of a box elder tree, to watch the leaves open a soft door and to see the deep sky through it isn't

the same thing as the New Empire Hotel (walk up one flight and register as Mr. and Mrs. Jack Chance from Reno, Nevada— the clerk is an old acquaintance of the Chances) or the cold awakening and the return down a street crackling with rain.

And finding at the edge of your own town an old house with the roof fallen in and draped over the walls as softly as wet burlap, newspapers stacked in its cellar telling of the inauguration of Grover Cleveland, a coin and an old tin can on the damp stairway is not quite the same

as climbing into the house in the village, the one house that looks undamaged after the bombardment, and seeing the black wall and the chairs scorched hastily with a flame-thrower and expecting to see the faces suddenly come back, the children reappearing at the door. When you tell yourself the faces of the dead won't hurt you if you don't see them. When you wonder if someone is just outside. Are there footsteps coming up the alley?

In the movie you see certain strangers (but their caps look familiar, their coats, too) walk through the Newsreel as though they had their minds on the blonde in the Main Feature until the planes come up the street behind them and they run for doorways and some of them fall, Jesus, you're safe and indignant all at the same time, and while the feature is on you don't have to think that if the blonde's real then safe isn't, or if safe is

the blonde isn't and isn't anybody you know in high school and has never claimed to be

any particular friend of Jack's

who you aren't anyway.

(The causes of war are economic, you will learn. But what if I said maybe that's a dollar you're giving me and maybe it isn't a dollar and he let me bite it to see and I said maybe it's a dollar and maybe it won't ever be a dollar. Would his surprise be real?

Or if I took the dollar without question and in good faith and held it really there in my hand would Mrs. Chance with her best dress on, wagging her hips in just that way that makes you cry to watch it, come down the street and stop to say, "Hello Jack. You've been a long time gone"?)

HOW TO ANSWER A LETTER
READ IN A BAR IN 1940

Begin at once to compose a reply. Make it exact and calm but fairly representative of your feelings. Say this is winter. The sun looks more like a reminder than a sun. The street outside is mostly covered with snow. In this bar there are no individual or separate shadows.

Refer to a parenthesis of her letter (when I come in the spring).

Pause for the necessary interruptions, or rather, those you

can expect in so public a place. While the clock hand swings back and forth across five o'clock, seeking eternity, learn that the road to life leads back and forth past these epitaphs:

"I done every dirty thing you ever heard of, and I never got anything out of life either."

"I said, 'Don't tell your ma I give it to you, but here, take this money to buy the stuff for supper. Get us some nice boloney. I ain't no bum.'"

"He came home drunk and fell on the floor. His wife was pregnant and couldn't bend down to hit him. So she started kicking him."

"I wrecked his car for him and damn near killed him, and I wish it would of been me and done a good job."

"I wish to Christ they had just sewed up everything when they did that and left me open on only one end."

Resume: This place in winter is a concave monument. As for myself (what am I thinking these days?) I'll try to explain. I have imagined a mirror in which I am not yet walking. In it a figure appears burdened with talk. The talk concludes, "Maybe what I always figured, thinking I was someone special, that I could do anything I made up my mind to do, was that I'd be the American Lenin or something like that. Aaah. Boo. I've lied to myself for twenty years. Or is that true, even? Anyway, as long as I've known how to. But still, what I wanted to see you for . . . You're a writer, or you say you are, and I didn't want to do this unless everything about me, all this I've told you, could be written down. I've made up my mind, but I can't get rid of the idea that my life ought to be understood. I don't think it's worth living, but maybe someday somebody will live better and it will do them good if they know about me. Just on paper it might look better than it feels. There's too many things that can be done to you while you're really alive. Your nerves are too near the skin. Think about all the clubs and whips and fire they apply to these guys in these skillful, persistent ways. And I'm as happy now as I'll ever be, so why stretch it out? Only you write it all down, everything I've told you, because just in that one way I don't want to ever die."

The imagined figure points forefinger to forehead and pretends to snap the thumb down like a gun hammer. The figure falls half out of the mirror. People I know gather before the mirror and look at the sideless head. Their voices explain that this was I. The things that persist of him, like ghosts in their minds, are the realities of my life, stripped from me and given to this one.

If I resist this robbery, other figures appear in the mirror—soldiers and partisans—and describing voices give them my realities. They die by millions and pass out of the mirror wearing my guises. I keep the breathing of my own life, but it too becomes caught in that mirror as in childhood we are caught in a constricting dream. You know, the dream in which tigers leap and the finger can not pull the trigger in defense.

Conclude: I have read your letter over and over. All you say is Wait. You will come in the spring. I cannot understand this, this attitude. I believe this winter is real. It will never be over just because this spring you talk about comes.

IN THE WORLD YOU MEET
THE STUBBORN ONES

There was the story about her, never becoming quite clear, that she had been in love once with a fellow who moved out West and never wrote back to her. Whatever it was, when she married she wasn't happy, and the children she bore did not make up for what she thought she had once seen in the world. She was always planting flowers and kept the house full of potted plants all winter. In 1927 she joined the small town's branch of the foreign missionary society. At night when she thought about it, lying awake, she told herself that the Good Lord did not intend his children in China to eat grass and mud. She could imagine then the taste of grass and mud, and it helped to believe she belonged to a society that was doing something to distribute God's Daily Bread. It helped her not to think about herself so much.

In the years when the Japanese planes flew unmolested over China and bombed unmolested, it seemed to her the bombs were destroying something very important to her, some vague imagined substance (not quite people) of her love. And it's easy to understand the devils in the planes when they blast the image you had felt secure within you. She did not ask whom she should hate.

She understood the war without the help of the columnists. It seemed very simple to her. On one side were the guns and those who owned them. On the other side she counted those whom she believed counted on her. When the war was over, she still understood those who still had guns.

AND THOSE WHO DIE YOUNG

He was nineteen when the war was over and had been knocking around the infantry camps in the States for a year. In the fall of 1945 he was sent to Japan. He arrived too late to see the Little Yellow Bastards, but he saw men and boys still walking in the cold streets in the remnants of uniform, and the women with bony, expressionless faces, with children slung on their backs, kneeling gracefully before an overturned garbage can from which they took egg shells and sucked them.

He made a sight-seeing trip to Nagasaki and wrote a letter home saying, "It doesn't look any different from the other cities they bombed. It's only when you think that it all happened at once and more people were as a result of this killed that it seems different." He didn't know what to think of the Jap who told him, "It's a good thing you have bombed our cities. Now we can rebuild them with wider streets." It didn't seem quite right to say that.

He had no regular job in the outfit and one day they sent him with another GI to Sasebo to pick up a freight-car load of beer. On the way back with the load the two of them went to sleep in the freight car. The cases of beer shifted, pinned them both down, but pinning his blanket tight across his face. He could still yell for a while, but the other man couldn't get free to help him. Before the train had passed through the tunnel into Honshu, he was dead.

And another one who didn't see the end of the war. He had the name of a famous general except that his middle initial was different. He was standing in front of a plane that had just come in when one of the 50's, for no reason, not quite cold yet, blew his head into a pulp full of bone splinters.

AND THE OTHERS

He was Master Sergeant in the Headquarters Company at the time they landed on Bougainville. One night after supper—they had just come back from the mess tent near the beach, he said—while they were shooting the breeze a Jap came running out of the palm trees. The little rat must of been out of his head, like, because's just running up to us screeching Kill me, kill me. His Tommy gun was where he could reach it easy. "OK," he said. "OK." Damn near cut him in two.

They shoot a .45 slug, don't they—a Thompson?

APPROACH THE PRESENT

The world is always turning into now. In childhood now whips by with a whistle like a green switch in the air.

Then it slows down and as things end the ends get fuzzier and slower. The last end is a pile of the unraveled, fit for cobwebs which might as well be public property if they were property.

(When Roger came to play with my brother they hauled sand in toy dump trucks, but I wasn't old enough to play with them. I tried to kick over their trucks. They took me down, poured sand over my face, and ran away. I waited behind the front door with a club and hit them both when they came back. I made them cry and got whipped for it. When I was sent to bed, I knew I'd done wrong. Giant frogs and yellow lights from hell threatened me.)

"Never, never. Not until you're grown up."

When you're grown up some there is another voice,

"Full many a rose is born to blush . . ." the fat-rimmed eyes crinkling with amusement. "How does that go, the rest of it? Anyway, I'm sorry there's nothing we can do for you." I got what I wanted but so late I'd forgotten why

I wanted it. "No sir. I don't imagine and I didn't expect."

A parenthesis of words—the first end and the second end: "Darling, let's watch ourselves so nothing don't happen." and "Hello, I thought I recognized you when you came in, but . . ."

As a parenthesis for:

Her arms around your neck while somebody else's radio is

saying (on a fine warm night) "Reichschancellor Hitler has ordered his legions to meet force with force."

We had a twelve-day passage on the troopship coming back. In our cabin nobody talked much but one Lieutenant Smith. He'd been with an outfit of niggers—"more —— trouble, but me and the old man fixed their —— wagon." "You hear the news? They want to send food to them —— —— in Europe." "One officer we had was smart in books, but he didn't know a —— thing about the army. The mens, they called themselves the mens, were asking me about him, and the old man and me snuck down to see if we could catch him at it, but it turned out there was nothing to it." "These —— —— Jews. Aren't any of you Jews, are you?" "By God, if I was commanding general there wouldn't be no mass meetings." "I'd take the —— atom bomb over there and clean them all up." In twelve days we learned he hated niggers, foreigners, politicians, enlisted men, Jews, women. Andrews said he was a radical, but nobody told him to shut up.

BUT DON'T WORRY

Stop the subscription, sell the radio, pull the blind on the window facing the street. Come and kiss and let's get acquainted. How can the world end twice when it's always ending?

CONTEMPORARY METAPHORS OF BIRTH

Toward the day and the hour, when the divisions were bulging the border and the ships lay fat with troops (while the last pretense was asking, "Do you want me? Do you need me for anything, sir?"), the blood-stream thoughts split as the eyes became aware of light. The ships opened and the border broke.

When the period swelled through its last month, the only questions left were: How can we cling? How can we hide in this sweet dark?

The red expulsion into the new, new world. Through the mirrors of the rosy walls. The reflection of our frightened eyes no longer sheltering around us.

REVIEW THE WORKABLE FORMULAS

In the Blood. In blood.

In concocted faith or hope that needs no object—waking on a train when the morning whistles cry out a new city, climbing ladders of a ship to see the newest harbor, sitting in a house when a new voice speaks—it may happen to you,

Or the tyranny of those who become as little children.

The War
in the Air

Even when Jimmy Stark was dead his parents had no idea of what he had been doing that could kill him like this. They went to City Hospital when they were summoned, after the police who had found him in the park had traced his address, and saw his unmarked body lying loose on the bed as though inside him the bones might have all been broken into dozens of pieces or been softened by the impact of death into a substance softer than his ten year old muscles.

With awed, servile curiosity they asked the doctor what had happened to their son and got only a kind shrug for an answer. There could be an autopsy if they wished. Perhaps it was a stroke, the doctor said. Perhaps Jimmy had overexerted himself in play. That happened sometimes. Not very often of course. Was Jimmy inclined to overdo things?

"Yes, he was," his mother said. "Oh yes. He was an eager little fellow."

The parents trembled in the shock of seeing the boy dead and went home by taxi to sleep in the mediocre suburb where the need for victory is born but where it becomes acute infrequently, where its imaginative forms are invented but not understood.

Jimmy had taken his first air victory in June of 1951, at a time when it was critically necessary to him as a matter of morale. His world, which was pretty much composed of his mother and father, had come to depend on him with a weight that could only be relieved by that swift successful pass of combat more intense than love and more impersonal than murder. Through the preceding winter and spring there had been reason to worry—if there had been anyone able to understand and willing to worry—about the tension building up in him as he waited for action. The tension had led him frequently to melancholy and crazy fits of temper at home or at school, the sort that would have been familiar to anyone who had spent some time in an Air Corps Junior Officer's Mess, but that were merely puzzling to his folks.

The first combat took place in the southwestern corner of Lincoln Park while he was on his way home from swimming. He was thoroughly miserable. On top of other things his nose was stopped up from the irritation of the water so that he could scarcely breathe. He disliked very much having to go home. His father would be testing the lawnmower in the back yard or working on it in his shop in the garage. Probably his mother would be next door at the Vicos', perhaps sitting in the porch swing behind the vines with Harlan Vico and Harlan's mother, the clink of ice in their three glasses and the hard murmur of their laughter coming from the shadow of the porch like pellets flung from ambush.

If that turned out to be the way it was, Jimmy would go in through his own front room, the dining room, and to the kitchen, and the twilit rooms would whisper a little to him until he found the cord to turn on the kitchen light. They would whisper "your own mother" as he passed the soft shapes of furniture and the lecherous open spaces of the floor and remembered the doggone things Billy Cornwall had told him. He would stand in the kitchen with the light from overhead glinting on the unclean porcelain of the sink and the dishes, wishing awfully that his mother would keep things clean, wanting to break something but with nothing in sight that he dared to break.

So, because he had to go home to that and didn't want to, he took the long way through the park to the streetcar instead of the short way. This journey brought him to the clearing where the older boys were flying their model of a jet plane.

The model was attached to long cords that held it in a circle and at the same time controlled it. When he saw it first it was swinging in high, fast circles. It was nearly as high as the tree tops, he thought; at any rate he could see it move above the dark green of the trees beyond the clearing before he had time to see the boys controlling it from below. For a stunning second it seemed to be a real plane and to be his.

Seeing it, he stopped in the thrill of recognition. He stood a hundred feet from the boys and the plane passed directly over him at one extreme of its orbit. Time after time he watched it go over. Each time it passed him was like a touch and he grew dizzy with the excitement and with keeping his eyes on its fast circle. He could feel his hands tighten like claws and all the muscles in his trunk contract. It hurt. He crouched a little and let the pure spasm of hate possess him. "Vico," he whispered. The plane swung in two more intense circles. "Vico," he whispered again through his bared teeth.

The model, controlled by an ingenious rigging of cord, was built to perform a number of maneuvers besides level flight. As he kept repeating the name like an incantation, some unseen tug of the controls sent it diving, and like a real plane, the sound of its motor changed pitch, and in the rising whistle all at once Jimmy felt himself confirmed, safe, as though a door behind him, opening formerly on danger, had been swung to and bolted.

As though he could breathe now—only now—he threw back his head and drew in the damp lakeshore air in big gasps. It was like coming up from swimming underwater, he thought, and the images of his afternoon at the beach blent with the present moment. Holding his breath under water he might have felt like saying, "Vico." Then the air could have come miraculously into his lungs.

"Vico," he said quietly now, and the name was both relief and requiem, the amazed acknowledgment of intimacy so fierce that it could never be glimpsed except in its own light, like a welder's work, illumined by his working torch beyond the dark glass of his mask.

"Vico," he said to himself in wonder as he walked on across the park to the streetcar stop. He began to laugh and raced on, ripping leaves from the bushes and tossing them over his head.

So he was not surprised when he found at home a scene that was different from the one to which he usually returned, something festive and vaguely scorching. His mother and father were at the table together in the kitchen and they had just finished eating. His mother was sitting stiffly in her chair. She had on a pretty blue and white dress, a cool dress for summer, and her face was pale but very pretty he thought.

His father was leaning across the table toward her, and he had heard his father's voice rising fast and unusually confident when he came in through the front rooms. His father was bare to the waist and hair on his chest was spotted with bread crumbs.

When he drew his own chair to the table and his mother had passed him food, his father turned to him and said, grinning, "We're having a little old celebration tonight, Jimmy."

"Uh huh."

"Don't get him in this," his mother said. "Please, Stuart."

"We're having a few drinks to celebrate," his father said. He raised his water glass and Jimmy saw that it was full of whiskey. "Yes, sir, things like this don't happen every day."

"No, sir," Jimmy said and his father looked at him owl-eyed as though he had expected a question and was thrown off track by his complacent agreement.

"You know what we're celebrating? We're going to have some new neighbors on the other side of the goddam fence. Old Harlan Vico has decided to move back home—back down Saouth where folks are *friendlier,* I hear, but I expect he thought they were pretty goddam friendly here, some of them."

"Stuart, that's enough, that's enough," his mother said. She dabbed her eyes with her knuckles and left the table. Jimmy heard her go into the bedroom and shut the door.

After a while his father said to him in a gentler voice, "It's true. The Vicos are moving."

"I know," Jimmy said.

"Wasn't he a slimy little mink, though? I knew what he was from the time they moved in. You have to hate a guy like that."

"I hated him," Jimmy said. He helped himself to the pudding which was still cool from the icebox and had large slices of banana, still partly crisp, in it. It was his favorite and he thought his mother must have made it especially for him, as if she had known he would deserve a treat this evening.

His father stared hopefully at him. Between the man and boy there seemed a strand of hope that the events of this day might have awakened something slumbering a long time, some demand that had month by month and year by year been buried under the routine of work and home until it was conceivably dead forever. He put out his hand and rumpled Jimmy's hair. He said, "Things are going to be better, kid. Whadda you say? Whadda you *say?*" . . .

"Sure, Dad." The pudding was good, and Jimmy helped himself to another bowl of it.

His father went in the bedroom and presently came back carrying a large stack of movie magazines, confessions, and religious periodicals. "Burn these, will you, kid?" Then in embarrassment, as though he must momentarily play a role effeminate and formal—effeminate in its very formality, perhaps—he said quickly, "I think these were a lot of her trouble. You know she would read them so much. Burn them tonight, huh, kid?" Then his father turned, went to the bedroom, and shut the door firmly behind him.

Dreamily, lazily, almost as though something inside himself were trying to laugh but he was too lazy to let it, Jimmy finished eating. He drummed lightly with his spoon on the edge of the empty bowl, listening to the silver and clear sound of its ringing.

But when he carried the magazines through the back yard to the incinerator in the alley he noticed how *feathery* his legs felt, and a headache had begun, a small pain above his eyes.

He ripped the magazines apart so they would burn. In a minute or two the flames were rising higher than the rusty top of the incinerator. On the blast of hot air, sparks rose and floated between him and the pale stars. It was like watching a Mig burn, he thought, remembering the name Mig without giving it any particular association, not wondering even from where he remembered it. There goes the fuel tank, he thought, as more pages caught and the fire came up. He felt a proud, melancholy identification with the man he had shot down—not bothering to name the man Vico any longer—and this seemed to justify the pain in his head. He felt that what had happened separated him from other people. He *remembered* that this uprush of fire into the night was the token sigh of his manhood and mortality and that properly the sign confirmed his aloneness.

Behind him he heard bicycle wheels on the cinders of the

alley, but he did not turn to look until he heard the whisper, "Hey, Jimmy? That you?"

It was Billy Cornwall, the fat kid who lived on the other side of the alley. Billy was thirteen, three years older than he, and he never knew whether Billy was going to pick on him or not. Billy was apt to if he said a word that questioned Billy's opinions or actions. He hated having Billy come up and catch him looking at the fire.

"What are you burning?" Billy asked.

"Nothing."

"OK," Billy said. He pushed his bicycle closer so the front wheel was almost against the wires of the incinerator. He kept one fat leg over the frame of the bicycle and leaned on the handlebars. "Where were you this afternoon, Jimmy? You know what happened at your house?"

"I went swimming," Jimmy said. "I went to Lincoln Park like I always do."

"Wow," Billy said. "Things were really humming for a while. Your dad and my dad and Tom Simms beat hell out of this old Vico. Your dad come home early and found him and his old woman at your place, so he got these two and they went back for him. Boy."

The light of the flames in the incinerator was going; only a few black and weightless fragments, rimmed with sparks, came up now from the pile of ashes within the fire-rusted wire frame.

"Your dad tell you about it?" Billy asked. "Jeez, when I got there old Mrs. Vico came running out of your house in them shorts she wears, yelling for the police—'Poh-leeez'—and Tom Simms caught her right by the fence and twisted her arm up behind her and he said, 'You want to call the police, lady?' What they did to Vico! I guess it wasn't what they ought to have done for what he did, I don't think."

Jimmy glanced toward the Vico house and saw it was without lights. He wondered, though, if the Vicos might not be in there anyway, really, moving about in the dark where they no longer could move in either lamplight or daylight.

He smelled the horseweeds around his gate. He started for the gate but Billy quickly ran the bicycle across his way. "What did your dad do to your old lady? I bet he slapped her around, didn't he?"

"No, he didn't do that at all," Jimmy said. He tugged at the gate, but Billy wouldn't let him open it.

"I would've, or any real man would've," Billy said. "For what she did? She had it coming to her all right. I told you what I saw that time I hid in the bushes by your porch and Vico went in the kitchen with her."

"Shut up. Shut your mouth." Jimmy said.

Billy let the bicycle drop and grabbed his shoulders. "Who you telling to shut up? Do you mean it? You mean you want me to shut up?"

Jimmy clawed at Billy's face as he half lost his balance. He felt his fingernails hit the fat cheek, but then, almost before he realized that he was going to fall, he was down and Billy was astraddle his chest. He felt Billy's knees grinding into his arms.

He said, "Get off, you fat dumbbell. Get off."

"Take it back," Billy said and slapped him.

"You stinking fat dumb. . . ."

"All right then," Billy said. "Don't think I didn't hear that." He fumbled for Jimmy's ears and twisted them. "Now tell me what your mom did with old Vico. Say it."

"Nothing," Jimmy said. "Get off me. I won't." Then with a wild pain in his ears rising to a climax, he felt a calm begin, as though the pain itself were opening another door and closing it solidly behind him when he had passed. Strangely he let himself lie inert and the frightening inertness communicated itself to Billy, who let go his ears.

"Do you want me to say it?" Billy asked. "All right." He leaned forward and spoke repetitiously into Jimmy's face. Then he took down Jimmy's trousers, spit on him, got on his bicycle, and rode away.

Jimmy felt the cinders through his thin shirt, cutting him, but his knowledge of them was remote and actually trivial. He looked up at the black, mastered sky and knew himself borne steadily at the airy center of things. "Billy," he whispered and was able to laugh.

II

He was awake before light, before the hour of dawn patrols, and he lay there for half an hour toying with his illness. There was still a pain in the back of his head, and if he stirred he felt nausea and a cramping in his bowels. If he lay absolutely quiet, both these disturbances, having something feverish about them, were comforting, like a hot towel or like lying in a hot bath.

As the light came on among the trees and telephone wires that he could see from where he lay, he played a game with the cord ring hung from the curtain. It was a ring sight, and through it he searched the sky for a passing bird or anything alive that would give him practice in killing. He aimed at leaves, and there was a fly that crawled up the screen and directly through the cross-hair center of the ring. That fly was a deader, he thought.

At six-thirty he had to go to the bathroom to throw up. He was as quiet as he could be, but his mother must have been awake, for she came in as he was squatted on the floor with his cheek leaned against the soothing porcelain of the stool.

"Jimmy," she whispered. "What's the matter, honey? Hey, can you stand up? Let's get you back in bed. Why, you're burning up, honey." Her hand lay wonderfully cool and limp on his forehead, and he began to whimper in a mixture of pleasure and solicitation. He stood up and leaned against her hip as they walked back to his room.

She brought him a poached egg on toast for his breakfast and sat beside him, stroking his head while he ate. His father came in before leaving for work and asked if they shouldn't call a doctor.

"I'll take care of him," his mother said shortly.

"Well then, see that you do for a change," his father said. His father seemed, this morning, to have fallen back into the old helpless surliness which for a while last evening he had broken free of. It was pitiful that he had not known how to hold his victory, had given it back.

"All right, all right, all right," Jimmy's mother said arrogantly.

When his father had gone out and the room was hushed except for the endless remote noise of traffic spreading away like a battle front on an indecisive day of combat, Jimmy turned his face against the pillow and closed his eyes. His mother must have thought he was sleeping, because she left him and tiptoed toward the door.

He said, without opening his eyes, having something to hide from her, "The only thing is, Mom, I've got to be well enough to go swimming this afternoon."

"Oh no you don't," she said. "I'll say you don't, honey. That's what made you sick today."

"But if I feel good. I may feel swell by then," he said. He

knew he would not and the effort of lying when he didn't want to entirely forced tears up to burn in his eyes.

"Well, you won't," she said. "You can go another day. The lake will still be there."

During the endless morning he heard her playing the radio, then singing, then crying. When he heard her crying he went back to his killer game with the curtain ring.

Shortly before noon he caught Billy in the ring and held him there for a full minute, sliding down the bed to keep the fat boy centered until he disappeared past the end of the block. He had heard Billy's loud, happy voice and had come to immediate cramping attention. Then he'd caught him all right. Nothing happened. He whispered, "Billybillybillybilly," and waited for him to fall, but Billy rode his bike right on past the corner, dodging the trucks on Elm Street in the smart alec way he did.

Reflecting on this, Jimmy understood how truly necessary it was for him to get to the park. He spoke about it again to his mother when she came in, but she was wrapped in her own misery by now and answered sarcastically. "From now on no one goes out of this house," she said. "Our happy home. I guess that's how it will be. No one will have any fun or talk to anybody that is any fun. That's the way he wants it." Her eyes glittered hatefully. "Listen, will he ever take us anywhere on Sunday? Will he ever talk? In the spring I wanted him to take you out in the country so you could get some air and sun, but did he? He won't even take us fishing—goes with those mutt friends of his. What will he ever do but go out in that workshop and fiddle with that lawnmower? Does he think he's an inventor like Thomas Edison? Don't you think he could be a little human sometimes if he wanted? You don't know all about how he is either, Jimmy." She threw herself flat on the bed with a grotesque squawk. "Listen," she said with excitement, "what did he tell you about me last night?"

"Nothing," Jimmy said.

She watched him suspiciously. Enduring her stare, knowing that she was getting ready to lie to him, Jimmy wanted to bury his head under the pillow. He held himself quiet and said, "Nothing," and that seemed to convince her.

"He said ugly things to me and said a lot of things I never even thought about doing."

"He didn't tell me anything," Jimmy said, and his mind raced like a steel hammer falling on a pin, "billybillybillybilly." "I want to go to sleep," he said.

She kissed his brow. "You sure sizzle," she said. "Try to sleep now, honey." Then she added before she left. "Those magazines. Did he make you burn them all?" Getting no answer, she left him.

Jimmy waited motionless and without patience. He counted to sixty several times—he could not keep count of how many times. He could not hear her when he quit. He dressed, pushed the screen from his window, and dropped to the ground. He went around the yard to the back gate, past the incinerator and down the alley to Elm Street, where he caught the streetcar that would take him to the park.

The ride was a nightmare. It was like riding a dull ship in convoy, annoyance without interest. But in the park itself, among the still flowers and the trees swaying gently up to the point where the highest leaf gave way to the shapeless sky, he became serene. It was then as if he had separated successfully from the other world.

He had a long wait still. Four o'clock passed and the boys with the model plane had not yet appeared where they had been yesterday, but he waited now with certainty.

He sat on a bench a little removed from the clearing. A policeman who had circled past him several times looked as though he wanted to question him but never did.

A dog came and sniffed at his shoes. He patted the dog and made friends with him. Carefully saying nothing, he developed a language of gestures that the dog understood. He would pretend to throw a stick and the dog would race a few steps after the imaginary stick and then return to him with its bright eyes puzzled. A little more urging and the dog would retrieve it, he was sure. He laughed at the dog and the dog cocked its head cutely in a sort of reply.

At five the boys came carrying the model plane and the apparatus for its control, and he was ready. He watched them lay the cords out on the ground and pace off the orbit to be sure there was plenty of clearance within the trees. He saw one crouch with it to get it airborne. Then he walked closer when it began to circle until he was again standing under its path, and presently he felt the second approach when it would be made to stoop in its killing dive.

Afterward he walked with difficulty to the streetcar. He had left the house without bothering to get money for fare, and it was his luck that he found three tokens in his pants pockets. Just his luck. He gave the next to last token to the conductor for this ride home.

When the car turned onto Elm Street, from a long way off he could hear the purr of a siren running at low speed, and as he approached closer to his own corner he saw the crowd on the curb and the red light turning and flashing in the sunshine on top of the ambulance. He saw the truck slanting up onto the curb, its double wheels resting on the bicycle frame. The frame was bent curiously, like the soft shapes of spaghetti. Jimmy felt a lonely smile shape his lips.

III

Then he was really sick. For two weeks he stayed in bed with a fever and a dark half-awareness of his mother and father coming into his room, and the doctor. It was not time in which he lay, but an uncomfortable timelessness in which he heard things and then lost them so that he did not know any sequence. Once his mother told him about poor Billy Cornwall's accident. Once she asked him if he had burned all the magazines. Once she said, probably to the doctor, maybe to his father, "It's this summer. He hasn't been real well since school was out. Maybe when he goes back in the fall he'll be himself." Then he had drifted down into the red-threaded blackness which was sleep, amused because he knew there was little chance of his returning to where school was, in some country oceanic distances away.

Once again Billy Cornwall came with a red star on his forehead, the star shining like blood on his fatty skin, and told him again what he had seen from behind the bush in the back yard— the thing that couldn't be true because Billy was a liar—and his mother whined, "He hurt me." Or his father was welding in the shop in the garage and the fire came from his torch like tracers from the guns in movies.

Then in the week when it seemed he was getting better, his mother told him how he had crumpled up on the porch that evening when he got home from wherever he had been.

"Where were you anyway that afternoon?" she asked him. "Boy, was I scared." The question seemed to touch her curiosity sharply. She asked him several times as though she had forgotten his answer.

"In the park," he usually told her. She looked at him skeptically, rumpled his hair and said, "Aw, you don't know where you were. You were delirious or something." She added with passion, "It was his fault, the things he told you."

Once, to his terror, he slipped and told her, "Flying."

"Flying? Judas Priest. Well, I guess you're not going to tell me. If you know, I mean, and I'll bet you don't. What do you mean, flying?"

"I don't know," he said, carefully now. "I don't remember so good."

"We'll get you out in the sun today," she said, "where you can see some sky. You don't have any tan at all. Fishbelly. If your father would get a car and take us somewhere—I guess I could forgive him some other things."

She went on absently arranging things in the chest of drawers and organizing her wishes like plans. "We could have a vacation," she said. "Lots of people with no more money than us have vacations every year."

"All right, Mom," he said. "Don't talk about it." He could not stand the note of complaint crying through her voice, though he felt guilty not to listen to it, for not being strong enough to listen and console her. "I have to sleep," he said. When he slept after a session of her complaints, Billy Cornwall would come with the red spot of death on his flesh and in the remote alleys of the sky he would have to kill again.

For the next week he spent most of his time sitting under a tree in the back yard. His father had once built an arm chair for the yard, and he sat there through the long afternoon, reading sometimes and sometimes drowsing. His mother bought him a lot of comic books. Most of them were about air battles, because those were the ones he asked for, but she got Jungle Queen and Superman because she liked them herself and thought he would like them too.

It tired him to read. Up to a point he could get interested in these books, but they were full of Spads, Nieuports, Fokkers, and Camels—old-fashioned junk that didn't seem real except for the queer excited feeling they gave him of a familiar anxiety. He wondered if a German had ever spit on Lt. Frank Luke or Capt. Eddie Rickenbacker. He thought this might have happened and that's why they were good aces too. Finally he would let the books fall from his lap and sit looking at the clouds or the leaves against the summer sky.

The doctor came once more and said there was nothing wrong with him now except that he was run down, needed vitamins perhaps to tone him up. His parents talked a little of what might tone him up, but ended in making the discussion their personal battlefield. The argument was nothing new, only more vocal than it ever had been. He for one had work, the father said, and she wanted to cat around for her own sake, not the kid's. Work? What was he doing with the lawnmower he spent his time on? Did he think that was the way things were invented? They had factories with lots of people working in them to invent things nowadays. Why didn't he catch up with the times?

It seemed to Jimmy, listening, that their argument would never be settled. It was somehow up to him to settle it for them. As long as they lived they would fight this way unless he could tip the balance. He didn't know how. He had got rid of the Vicos for them and got rid of Billy, but nothing was any better, and he felt no longer responsible for them except as a judge feels, waiting to utter a judgment that will not be his own but the Law's, a judgment superior to himself.

In the evenings he would sometimes go sit on a stool in the garage workshop where his father was building the lawnmower. There were two masks in the shop, and his father let him watch the welding through one of them. His father was rather pleased to have the boy sit there fascinated beside him.

And Jimmy liked this watching. At such times his sluggish heart would beat faster against his ribs. The tracery of flames, appearing through the complete darkness of the mask, was somehow the real thing. He could breathe easily as he watched, and usually he had to make a tiresome effort to breathe.

Nevertheless, the watching frightened him. He recognized his fear initially in the form of an anxiety that his father's hand would slip and let the torch swing against himself. Be careful, Dad, he thought angrily.

He began to feel that an injury to his father would be no accident; it would be the work of the power he had discovered that day in the park, and he was not ready for that.

While he watched the dangerous flames, he remembered his

father on the night of the Vicos' departure, marching with shabby arrogance to the bedroom where his mother lay, and this memory frightened him, because then he almost felt triggers ready under his fingers, and he believed there was no reason to use them yet, not against his father who was going to make a lawnmower that would make them rich, maybe.

An occasion had come when he was so close to opening up, though, that in panic he jumped from the stool on which he was sitting, threw the mask off, stared a second at the naked torch and then ran for the house.

He heard his father following him, asking what was the trouble. Having temporarily blinded himself he stumbled on the doorsill and wailed as he dropped to the kitchen floor. His mother jumped to pick him up and before he could explain, both his parents were fighting across him. "Well, did you burn him?" "Can't you see if he's all right before you start shooting your mouth off?" Their voices rang with self-pity and hatred so stupid that they could find no instrument to execute it except their son.

Weighing this, sensing the suffocation to which the three of them were committed, grasping it not in langauge but in the warlike images of his education transposed to fit the personal situation, as a dull preacher might use the myth of Genesis to illustrate the planting of crops, that night in his bed Jimmy made a decision.

Lying in his bed stiffly, staring toward where no ceiling appeared, almost without passion, in the interests of justice, he thought his father would have to go. He could feel his throat and lips getting ready to whisper. He still held back, hating to whisper the name—then he let go, "Dad," diving past into the security of sleep without troublesome dreams.

In the anxiety of the next morning he wanted to take it back, but he was not at all sure that he could. Of course it was possible to stay away from the park and the model airplane—if he wanted to. But like a hypnosis an impulse thrust him toward them. It might be that he would *have* to go after such a commitment. He wished for more reasons, though, if it had to be that way.

He went to the workshop in the garage and played thoughtfully with the masks he and his father had worn. He slipped on his father's mask and shuddered at the smell inside and at the sweated headband touching the skin of his forehead. He discovered the dimensions of the darkness inside the mask. It was as large as the darkness of a whole night, of his room when it was utterly black, big enough for anything. And this darkness was filled with the hateful smell of his father. "Let him do one more thing to her," Jimmy thought, "and I'll go." He sat there imagining his father's hand lifted to strike, but frozen yet in the gesture for which he waited.

And then one morning he knew why he had waited, why that abstract and superior justice whose servant he had become had obliged him to wait. That morning when he returned from an errand to the corner store carrying a sack of groceries, entering the kitchen he heard his mother's voice from the back porch and a man's voice, unfamiliar and familiar at the same time, answering her.

Jimmy set the groceries on the table to free his hands. The voices from the porch fumbled viciously, as though on purpose, with the lightly balanced mechanism of his consciousness, and he stood there, taking the shock of their violation and accepting his responsibility for what he heard in those careless, awful, summery voices. He listened to his mother's laughter, and then, surprised but certain of what he thought, he whispered to himself, "They've all got to go."

His mother came into the kitchen for a dishpan. "A man's here selling sweetcorn," she explained. "Won't that be good? That will taste good."

To Jimmy the flush in her cheeks was a sign of her guilt, and, more than that, as he looked down from a peak of agelessness, it seemed a sign of some corruption of youth that was intolerable. "Aren't you feeling well again?" she asked jauntily. "Maybe you'd better go to your room and lie down. Go on now."

"No."

"Jimmy . . . Go on."

He stood fixed and then watched from the rear window while she went out with the vendor to his truck parked in the alley. He felt the pity of her going, because in this moment of discovery he knew that he must kill her, along with his father, and that afterward there must be an accelerated pattern of killing to which there was no imaginable limit. He felt also the pity of her sacrificing him to be the agent of this necessity by failing to be good. At the same time he made no attempt to argue the consequences of what he believed to be the truth. Now he could see the steps of a great wrong reaching back to what he did not need to bother to think of as Eden.

Where was it the family had lived before they moved here? he asked himself. He had no exact memory of another city, but he felt it. Caught in the vision, it was as though he might have been circling at a great height and seen in the haze which for airmen replaces a horizon some kind of dimple—not quite a form but a potentiality of form—that he recognized as home.

In the moment of his submission to the necessity, as though clutching at one more last human reason for what he had to do, he remembered Billy Cornwall's words about his mother. He imagined Billy waiting behind the door of the next room, ready to knock him down and spit on him. He squared his shoulders and forced himself to walk through the door to see.

Going to the park that afternoon, watching from the streetcar window the blue wink of the sky, he kept thinking to himself, "If she just hadn't of laughed with that man. . . ." The improper laughter hissed toward him from the anonymous crowd with whom he rode—all of them condemned now by what he meant to do. Every one of them had to die in his turn.

On the park bench he recaptured the vision and certainty he had known in the kitchen. The streetcar had dimmed it, like a flashback of memory where all sorts of trivia creep in—sentimental sounds of voice, promise of storewindows, weather compositions, faces reminiscent of jollier times and places back on the other side of the ocean, maybe—but triumphing over these he rose easily again and began circling. The dimple of home appeared first over one wingtip and then the other.

He saw, between home and himself, little black shapes swift as insects rise toward him from the checkered landscape. He recognized their number and their hostility without panicking. It was part of the compact that whatever he needed enough would be provided. There would be time enough.

As on the earlier occasion when he had shot down Billy he had to wait a long time. The black planes hovered in remote perspectives, waiting with him. Then, as the boys appeared carrying their model, the black planes moved in to intercept him.

The model raced on the end of the cords and Jimmy walked toward its orbit. He felt himself go with it, and in the moment of climbing for an attack position was happy enough. This time, better than on any of the earlier occasions, he sensed the moment for his diving pass. "Now," he cried to himself, without hate, without love.

It was a long way down and something seemed to thrust against his cheek and stomach and drag his breath away. Then, like a blackout from the strain of diving, dark replaced the light and the shapes beyond the cockpit bubble. All together the ground beneath, the insidious planes, the imaginary haze of the horizon, the actual grass, the boys in their T-shirts, vanished.

He did not see the model crash splintering in the grass of the park, nor the boys, its owners, rushing toward it with varied expressions of chagrin and repressed pleasure on their faces.

Convoy Sunday Morning

McGarrity had his shelter half hung up between the winch and the foremast and there were three of them in its shade, crouched away from the hot plane of the deck that advanced on them very slowly as the morning passed—seeming, in the way the ship rolled, to be wound slowly closer on an enormously inefficient spindle. McGarrity had his carbine apart. He was rubbing each piece with an oiled rag. When he had finished all the rest, he spent a long time polishing the stock.

Quist and Reed were lying on the deck close to his knees. Quist was dealing blackjack hands for himself. From time to time Reed tried to talk to the other two, without much luck. He was trying to tell them a story about the famous murderer the FBI had caught in his home city a few years ago, but he could not remember the murderer's name. He asked McGarrity and

Quist if they didn't remember the man he was talking about. "Sure you remember," he said. "The guy all the cops in New York and the East were looking for and couldn't find? Don't you ever read the papers?"

"What do you try to tell me a story for when you don't even remember who you're talking about?" McGarrity asked.

"Christ, I do remember. His name just slipped my mind," Reed said. He stopped talking and looked out at the other ships on their port, still trying to remember the murderer's name. Dolan? or Fagan? No, Fagan was in the funny papers.

It was nine o'clock and every part of the sky seemed to shine like a focusing mirror on the ships. The sea was rolling in swells stippled with thousands of small, sharp peaks, but there were no whitecaps today. On the wing of the convoy the DE seemed to be pitching a lot. The bigger ships moved as steadily as box cars crossing a prairie.

The PA system came on with a buzz and there was an announcement that Catholic Mass would be held in thirty minutes on the rear hatch.

"Aren't you a Catholic, McGarrity, with a name like yours?" Reed asked.

McGarrity went on polishing his gun. "What makes you talk so much, Reed? I never saw such a boy that was nothing but lip."

"I like to improve my mind. I like to ask questions and hear what all kinds of people have to say."

"He's going back to Des Moines and be the congressman," Quist said.

"Des Moines, the city of certainties. Yes sir," Reed said. "How do you like that? That's what they used to call it or still do because of all the insurance companies there."

McGarrity wiped his hands on his pants. He took out his handkerchief, knotted its corners, and pulled it down on his head. He began to chuckle to himself and after a while said, "Your Des Moines girl quit you, didn't she? What's a certainty about that?"

"It was certain she wouldn't wait for me. That's Des Moines for you."

"Tell us about it again, Reed," McGarrity said. "Or go get the letter where she tells you how this guy made her. I get tickled every time I hear how nice she put it."

"Why don't you memorize it?" Reed asked.

"Quit kidding."

"I memorized it. I could say it to you. But that took all the kick out of it so it wasn't like reading it," Reed said. "What makes me mad is I never knew how easy it was until I got away from them. I knew a lot of girls I'd grown up with and gone to high school with and I never got around to really going out with any of them much. This Laura wasn't really very much my girl. Now they're all getting married and running around and all that while I spend my damn life on ships it seems like."

"You'll be back among them in forty-eight," Quist said. "The little ones will be big then."

"Damn it. I don't know any little girls."

"I thought you did," McGarrity said.

"All I wish is I'd never left. I got that letter right here, boy. You want to see it?"

He was just lifting his hip off the deck to reach in his back pocket when they heard the whistles all over the convoy, beginning up ahead and roaring louder and faster as all the ships joined in.

Reed jumped up. He climbed onto the winch so he could see on both sides of the ship. Other men were scrambling to their feet around him and there was a movement toward the starboard rail.

The destroyer that led the convoy was coming around in a fast turn on that side. The curl at its bow rose from the black water like the hard shaving a planer cuts from a piece of steel. At full speed it steamed back through the convoy, moving with a kind of vicious ease.

The men on deck were massing on one side to see what was going on. The PA buzzed again and a mechanical sounding voice from it said, "Clear that starboard rail. Guards, all guards, clear that starboard rail or we'll put the army personnel below." And nothing else happened. No more whistles blew. There was no call for battle stations or abandon ship stations. The immense silence of the day reasserted itself over the brief clamor.

"That's a funny business," Reed said. "That damn destroyer is clear out behind us all and still going."

When a friend of Quist's came around from starboard they asked him if he'd seen what was going on. He squatted down with them, bowing his head to get it in the shade of the shelter half. "I don't know for sure," he said. "I didn't see them depth bombing anything. You know last evening? Somebody tells me it was a whale that got them all scared when the destroyers was over to that side." In a few minutes another pal stopped to tell them he'd been standing beside an officer with binoculars who had seen a man go overboard from one of the transports just behind them.

Quist said, "They won't turn back for anybody that goes overboard."

"That's a hell of a thing," Reed said.

"Well, you heard them say that yourself."

McGarrity picked up his carbine again. "Sounds like a lot of rumors to me. Everybody'll talk it up a while and then somebody'll come along and say there's nothing to it. We never will know. I'll just worry about this one ship. Hell, they won't even tell us what goes on here. I don't even know what time I eat until I hear them call my section and that's a hell of a thing to get used to."

"I guess the ship officers ought to know if it was a man," Reed said.

A little later as he was lying on his back with his arm flung over his eyes he began thinking about that man. He started out thinking of the way the big ships of the convoy had kept going straight ahead like there wasn't anything they'd turn back for. Their engines kept pounding away, pushing them on like they were the important things and not anybody that might fall off. So they wouldn't turn back for anybody? Well, what if a lot of guys fell off? he thought belligerently.

Thinking about falling off while he had his eyes closed gave him the chills. He sat up and blew secretively into the mouthpiece of his lifebelt to test it; but as he did so First Sergeant Swaner spoke dourly from somewhere up behind him on the hatch cover. "Don't want to catch you again using that for a pillow, Reed."

He sank down again, wondering if the man who had fallen off had a chance to get his life belt blown up and if he was still floating. Maybe the destroyer had picked him up by now. It must feel pretty wonderful, he thought, to get rescued that way after you think you're a goner. But if the destroyer hadn't found him, think how it would be to bob around there by himself with only that cheap little belt of air holding him up and his feet swinging under it and watch the convoy go out of sight and see the destroyer quit hunting for him and run back to catch up with the other ships. Reed found himself thinking how it would be to float there all day, watching the sun get higher and higher and there wouldn't even be anything as solid as the shape of a cloud to watch. That was the worst, everything moving with you hanging there five miles above the bottom. In the evening there would be those long shadows of the waves on other waves all flickering around you and when it got dark there wouldn't be anything to feel but the bobbing and nothing to hear but the swishing.

He wondered if the guy would yell then just to hear his own voice. He remembered reading somewhere about a guy who had been lost like that writing a letter to his loved ones and putting it in a bottle or something. He had his letter from Laura in his pocket. If he went overboard he could pull that out and read it, but it wouldn't be much fun if there wasn't somebody to hear it and laugh about it. He imagined writing an answer to it while he was floating and putting it in a bottle for Laura.

Lying there thinking about it upset him so much that he sat up and started trying to talk to McGarrity and Quist again. He pulled out a cigarette, but as he started to light it the PA came on to say, "The smoking lamp is out. Knock off all games on deck. Divine services being held on the rear hatch."

"That's a funny thing, too," he said to McGarrity. McGarrity looked at him with an expression of ill-tempered amusement and asked what was funny.

"I was thinking about this guy that fell off that ship. What gets me is they don't turn around or slow down the least bit and now they run church services just the same as any Sunday. Knock off all games and so on. And here this poor bastard is floating around by himself out there. I wonder if he thinks it's Sunday."

"What guy? Where? That's what comes of you listening to scuttlebutt," McGarrity said. "You don't know but what they was dumping the garbage and somebody seen it. Nobody you can believe is ever going to tell you about it."

"I know it," Reed said. "That's what's so funny about it. See, maybe it's silly but I can't help wanting to know about that guy. Maybe it's just like a dog goes out and sniffs at it when another one gets run over. He's curious. But it makes me want to know.

When we land so I can ask somebody I'll have forgot about it, see? That's what's funny."

"OK. So you'll have forgot about it. You won't have to worry about it."

"But I'm thinking about it now. I don't want to forget it, but I'm afraid I will."

"Jesus. Oh Jesus, Reed. You're a comic."

"Hell with you McGarrity. You don't see what I mean. I mean it makes me feel funny now to think I have to keep riding this ship until I forget this guy. Or like you say, maybe there wasn't anybody fell off this morning. Then I just keep going so long I quit wondering whether there was or not."

McGarrity laughed at him. "Hell with *you*. You don't know what you mean either. Why don't you worry about this ship? Go up and tell the captain you're worried about it. Go tell the chaplain you're worried about me. How do you know what's going to happen to me?"

"All the same, I can't think of any worse way to die than get left out there."

Quist said, "Did I ever tell you what happened at this field I was at in forty-two? That was something for you, Reed. There was a C-47 got lost in a snowstorm and they all had to bail out and this one guy gets scared and pulls his chute in the plane and got it all fouled up. So he didn't have one and he was going to ride down on somebody else's back. They was too heavy for it or waited too long and when the chute opened it broke the guy's neck that was wearing it. So here he was, see, on a dead man's back and then he started slipping. Must have slipped real slow all the way down him. Then when he was just hanging by this guy's boots his bootlaces bust. They found the guy with the parachute without any boots and the other guy still had a hold on one of them. How'd you like that?"

McGarrity said, "Did I ever tell you about the guy I knew that was killed falling out of bed in a psycho ward? Three feet straight down. He never knew what hit him?

"What's psycho about this?" Reed asked. "These things happen."

The sun was coming over the top of the shelter half by this time. The orange-flecked paint of the deck was getting hotter. Reed got up restlessly to take a walk as far as Officer's Country.

He stopped by the rail at one shady place to lean on it while he looked out over the ocean. He tried to make his eyes fix on one of the other ships of the convoy, but somehow he kept looking at the spaces between the ships, where he could see to the little fringe of waves at the horizon.

When he came forward again, McGarrity had finished his gun. He was reading a small brown rectangle of paper.

"What in hell is that?" Reed asked him.

"It's a candy bar wrapper. I never knew what they put in a candy bar before."

As Reed sat there he remained unusually silent. He had a rash on the inside of his leg and he pulled up his pants to keep it from getting sweaty.

"You still thinking about that man overboard?" McGarrity asked him.

"Yeah."

"You're emotional," McGarrity said. "You got emotional because your girl quit you."

"The thing that gets me is the way all these ships looked just steaming straight on after this guy had fallen off."

"Puff, puff, puff."

"They never budged an inch one way or the other."

"Puff, puff," McGarrity said.

The Outer Island

"I've got all the testimony," the major said. "There won't be much for you to do, I should think. I've been over it all with everyone who'd know anything about it." It was the second time he had said this since the lighter had left the main island an hour ago. It concerned the business of their voyage across the channel, and also, as though by mutual accord, seemed accepted as the only matter of common interest to the major and the little Jewish captain from the Island Surgeon's office.

Actually, Captain Stern was too seasick and generally uncomfortable even to pay much attention to what the major was telling him. They were driving now straight against the waves coming in with the channel current. His right hand, tight on an upright of the rail around the pilot's deck, was stung by the jar of the waves as though someone were irregularly beating the rail with an iron club. Since the submarine net had been passed a mile or so back, he had watched steadily and with sick fascination the dark water which alternately rose to the gunwale beside him, then slid down and away with a hiss.

Everywhere on the waves and on the spray beaten upward by the prow of the boat the sunlight glittered and flashed points of light that hurt his eyes. He was obliged to pull his sun helmet down to a ridiculous angle over his eyes. Whenever the major spoke, he hastily smiled without separating his jaws and muttered back, "Yes, I see."

"I think that's the whole picture," the major said. "The IG has seen my report, and he said he'd approve it but I'd have to get a psychiatrist's testimony to clinch it. It isn't as though you had any big job to do and I'm sorry we had to bother to take you over there. Just a formality, but the army likes to have things done up the right way. The main thing I'd say there was left for you to do is go over it with these men and draw up your conclusions. You know the regulations say it has to be done when a fellow is out of his mind or crazy or they won't pay the insurance. There isn't much doubt in my mind that he was temporarily insane. Maybe just that one night, or maybe just for a little while. Would you use a phrase like 'temporary insanity?'"

"I could," Stern said.

"That's all it takes to settle it."

The major was wearing only shorts, cut down from issue pants, and a fatigue cap and tennis shoes. His big legs and chest were burned dark from the sun. All morning he had been brusque and cheerful, and even now the good-natured expression of his face was not quite spoiled by his squinting at the bright light on the water.

Meeting him for the first time at the small-boat pier, Stern had begun to like him at once. He said to himself that this major had what you expected of a good C.O. You wanted an even temper and decisiveness and some intelligence, and if these things could be wrapped up in a football player's body, there was your working combination. Before this man, Stern was ashamed of his queasiness and the fright the ride was giving him, but he could not help himself. The slight, compulsive fear kept him watching the onrush of water, and he huddled down miserably when the spray was thrown over him.

The major apparently had chosen not to notice his humiliating condition and went on talking as he watched the little island ahead. "Another thing I want to make plain is this Cramer was a damn good man. A good officer all the way, see. Hadn't been with the outfit very long—over here about six months I guess; on New Caledonia a while—but we got so we knew we could give him a job and he'd do it. Normally he just wasn't the kind to get himself all worked up and emotional. When you read my investigation, you'll notice one thing I wrote down. I don't know just why I put it in except to make him look as good as I could in the report by making him look really GI. Our Corporal Miller, out here at the post, told me, 'He's the best officer we ever had. When he wants something done he tells the sergeants and the sergeants tell the corporals.' Maybe they're just saying that because he's dead. I don't know. But these colored men like to have everything run GI. They like to know where they stand, so they want an officer who will keep his place and not be making friends with them one day and eating them out five minutes later."

"You thought he was all right?" Stern asked absently. Until they got in quieter water and out of this sun, he wanted at least to pretend to follow the conversation, wanted not to seem a complete fool. When they were ashore he would try to straighten out these parts of the story which the major had been telling, these phrases which floated in such odd patterns now on his sunfilled consciousness.

But he seemed to have said the wrong thing. The major looked at him sharply. "Sure. Certainly. Naturally I wouldn't have left him out here by himself if I had any idea he would shoot himself. It would put me in a spot any way you look at it. See, we have a system; we've always worked it the same way ever since we put the battery out here. The officers only stay out here a month because there is only one of them at a time. Then I come around once a week to inspect the lights and camp, and I talked to him a few days before he did it. That's one reason I was telling you I thought your verdict would probably be temporary insanity. I wouldn't say he was just, oh, say overjoyed or kidding me all the time when I saw him last, but he never was that way. But he was OK when I left him and he only had a couple of days to go before he came back to the battalion."

Their boat was close to the little island, and now its cover of jungle looked greasy in this light, impenetrable and as smooth on top as a prairie hill. There was no break in its green shape except for the little beach a mile farther down, where they would land. The pilot swung them in to follow the shore. They passed into quieter water, sometimes passing over flat gardens of coral full of the glimmering colors which the sun seemed to have driven out of everything above the surface of the water. Soon the general color of the water under them changed from black to lightening shades of blue and farther in to a clear green. Near the beach and the outpost landing the bottom sand looked as clean as frost ten feet under the keel.

Four or five men of the searchlight crew lay on the planks of the pier. They lay motionless on their bellies, and their black skins sparkled with sweat. The man at the end of the pier lay with his arm over the edge; and when they came near, they saw that he was holding a line and watching, without either interest or patience, the little fish that swarmed around his bait.

The men raised their heads when the boat swung in and sat up drowsily when it bumped the pier and the two officers stepped out. None of them spoke, nor did the major speak to them. A thin boy in khakis without insignia walked down the beach to meet them. He saluted when he came up, his hand touching his cap once for each of them in a loose, polite way.

"Hello, sergeant," the major said. "You want to run and find the lieutenant for us?" To Stern he explained, as though caught in some error but still expecting Stern to be a good fellow and understand, "I guess he wasn't expecting us. Could even be in his sack. There's not much to do here, and I try not to give them as far as I'm concerned myself too damn much GI formalities."

Stern stood dazed, looking at the camp. He could still feel the roll of the channel, the strange hypnosis, which even in a short crossing, in these few miles, seemed to have taken entire possession of him. Out in the boat he had comforted himself with the notion that he'd quickly find a place to sit in the cool blue shade when they reached shore. But this beach at noon, flinging up a heat and light as sterile as the sand, and the little camp above it, denied the promise of ease which had seemed so definite from a distance out. On three sides of the clearing there were trees matted from ground to top with vines; so the whole space was like a green quarry pit open to the sun. The floor of the pit, an area grown with brush and irregular formations of banana trees, held the tents and two buildings. A few trunks of girdled trees pointed up into the glaring sky.

"Pretty sad place, huh?" the major asked, grinning. "Gets even better here in December. It's pleasant sometimes, though, when the sun gets down a little. Come on up to the mess hall and we'll get some lemonade anyway while the sergeant rounds up Lieutenant Singer."

The mess hall was a frame building, completely unshaded. The tarpaper on the roof and walls shone like the skins of the black men who had been on the pier.

One more structure stood in crude isolation on a mound of coral at the center of the clearing. It was a little wooden shack with a tent roof, so narrow that it looked from the front like a country privy. "Officers quarters," the major said.

"That's where . . ."

"Yeah. We'll look in there after a bit. Singer hasn't moved into it yet. I didn't want anything touched until I finished up my investigation. Had a guard on it until three days ago when I cleared it with the IG that it couldn't have been a murder. Then I figured I'd leave it for you to look at if you wanted to."

"I don't know if that was necessary," Stern said.

"I wanted to be thorough about it. Thought you'd like to look at his letters and all just the way we found them." As they sat down in the mess hall, he went on, "You won't find anything from the letters, though, unless you can read minds. I brought him some mail the last time I was out before he did it, and so I thought right away there might have been something in that. You know, some bad news. Nothing. Wait a minute, I know what you're going to ask about that—if he might not have got some bad news and thrown the letter away. Well, I happened to remember what I'd brought him, and when I checked up, he had those letters all there."

"I wasn't thinking of that," Stern said and smiled. "You're a better detective than I. That hadn't occurred to me. I can see you've covered everything pretty thoroughly."

"Ah. Well, I tried to . . ." The major made a self-deprecatory gesture, half a shrug.

"I don't suppose you need me in on this, really, to get what you wanted," Stern said.

"Oh," the major said, "you'll be able to point out probably a lot of things that we never even thought of."

While they were eating—some corned-beef hash that the cook had opened for them—Lieutenant Singer came in. He was a tall young man, dressed no more completely than the major and burned almost as dark a red. He sat across the mess table from them and leaned forward on his elbows. "Hi, major. Good trip?" To Stern he said derisively, not quite impolitely, "This isn't the kind of chow you get over at headquarters on the island is it, Captain?"

Stern said quickly, "We eat hash, too."

"Yeah? I was up there a while back for a steak dinner. Tablecloth on the table. Nice cool mess hall."

"We do have it better, all right," Stern laughed. "You and the major will have to come up sometime and have a meal with me."

"Right; thanks." Singer still sounded a little derisive, as though he wanted to make it clear that he was a field soldier by nature.

The major had lit a cigarette and was staring at the smoke that rose from it like a tall feather in the heat. "See," he said. "That right there illustrates something else I pointed out to you while we were coming over, Captain. These young guys get a month's duty here at the outpost, and by the end of the month they're damn eager to get back to the main island, dress up a little, get a little liquor and some better food—we've got a pretty good mess and club of our own at battalion, you know. Put on a necktie and date up a nurse. Anyway they've got something to look forward to. And the damn men have to stay out here for six months. Have to, nothing I can do about that. It's not too bad a break for the officer, and Cramer only had a day or two more to go before he was relieved."

"I suppose the attractions of the main island aren't very great, after all," Stern said.

The major frowned, "No. Hell no, when you come right down to it. But comparatively. Look at it comparative to this place. And that's the only way you can look at it that makes sense, it seems to me. Anything looks good after you've been here a month. Right, Singer? Right. And then the day before he gets relieved."

"I don't know," Stern said. "When you're in a bad spot whether you compare it to anything else. Maybe. I don't know whether I do or not."

Singer said, "I reckon if you'd been in any tough spot you'd have that figured out. Wouldn't he, Major?"

Looking at him when he said this, a little surprised at first, then recognizing some barely apparent but old familiar voice speaking through the man's emotion, Stern thought. And if I would ask him now what tough spots he's been in in this war, he'd ask me what my name was. He sat for a little while turning his plate idly with his forefinger. "I was wondering about the men," he said. "You say they have to stay here six months . . ."

"Well," the major said, "that's one of those things that's a question everybody that has colored troops has to answer for himself. I've got a short answer for it for myself, and I never worry whether it will explain anything to anybody else. See, I think I've got as good a record as anybody for handling colored men, and the way I do it is never question what my higher-ups say to do with them. Take the situation they give you and work from that; make it as good as you can, but don't squawk. OK, you'd say the black boys get the worst of the deal in the army. If I was going to argue, I'd admit that right off. But maybe it's as good as you can expect, the way things just naturally are. Anyway, I've seen a guy or two on this base who had colored men and tried to bull his way through what headquarters told him to do and really got himself and his outfit in a royal mess. These guys would have been good officers, too. Both ways, they could have done a good job for their men if they hadn't tried to buck the set-up."

"Yes," said Stern.

"These guys have got in trouble and come to talk to me to see if I'll back them up, and they say, 'Look, such and such is wrong. Such a deal my boys got was wrong.' They want me to back them up because I've got a good record at headquarters for one thing, and they know I like my men. But I'd say to them, 'Don't tell me it was right or wrong. Maybe it was wrong. But you had a simple damn situation and you knew where you stood. You could have made something decent out of it and what have you got now except that thing in your eye?'"

Singer laughed.

The major had been stressing nearly every word he said, intently, almost with passion. Because it's a matter of faith by which you take a position like that, Stern thought, just as I have said to myself there's no other way to stay steady in the world. . . . He said, "We do about the same thing in psychiatry. I never believe any conviction a patient has is right or wrong. I try to find some simple way this helter-skelter of his thoughts can be channeled to do him some good instead of hurting him.

But you know, the funny thing is that even if I won't let them hang on to their arguments, I find myself turning them over and over in my own mind. I suppose everybody keeps the question of his own principles always open."

"Not while you're in the army," the major laughed. "I'm glad we agree though. I was a little on edge about having you out here. I can see we're going to work this out right, though. I haven't really asked you yet—I thought it wouldn't be ethical, or something—but do you see any reason why we can't call this thing suicide during temporary insanity?"

Diffidently Stern said, "It seems impossible to me, after a man's dead, to know without pretty good circumstantial evidence whether he was what we can legally call sane or not. I guess there isn't any reason for not calling it what you say."

"The main thing I'm after is to get it through properly and see that his folks get the insurance."

"It's good to have a feeling of personal responsibility about your men's affairs," Stern said, nodding and smiling.

"Sure. I take care of my guys. Isn't that right, Singer?" Stern thought he meant this clumsy question for a joke, but Singer said earnestly, "It really is, Captain." Stern wondered how he could say it just like that, but he saw it was meant for the truth and not for flattery. Surely there was a kind of innocence in these men. "I'm sure I'll be able to help you," Stern said. "Can I talk to some of the men?"

He studied a copy of the major's investigation until the men were gathered on the shadier side of the building. They came in then, one at a time, answering his questions politely, telling him, just as the major had it written down, how Lieutenant Cramer had come to supper that last night, what he had said to the sergeant—something about the crew roster for one of the lights—how he had played the radio in his little shack until after most of them were asleep, how they heard the shot and someone had run to his shack and found him.

Once in the course of the testimony, he heard an echo of thought so clearly stated as to be startling in its correspondence. One of the men said, "Sir, I believe he was about the best officer we ever had out here. When he wanted something done he didn't speak to the private about it." As he recognized this remark, Stern thought at first how strange the repetition was—as though the whole story might have been rehearsed among them.

But in a minute it struck him this must seem so because no one had much to say, none knew much, about the dead man. From their point of view the story was short and very simple. It could do no good, he thought, to pry at their knowledge. From it he could learn no clues or motives better than those he had sensed when he first saw the isolation of this camp or when he found that the shore offered no haven from the heat and malaise he had felt in the boat.

Before he quit his examination, he asked the sergeant how the men spent their days here.

"To tell the truth, Captain, there isn't hardly anything to do now. We work around the camp a little and sometimes we have a practice on the lights. Somebody has to be the CQ on the phone and there's a little work in the kitchen."

"Most of your time is free?" Stern asked.

"I suppose you could call it free. We just sweat it out."

"Do you get pretty anxious to get back to the main island?"

"Oh no sir, we don't. We want to go home. That's about all."

"You swim and fish a little?"

"Yes sir."

"Did Lieutenant Cramer swim and fish with you?"

"No sir. He never appeared to care for that."

Throughout Stern's examinations the major sat close. He explained some references from time to time, smoked a good deal, paid close attention, sometimes nodding in agreement with the testimony. Stern said to him, "I don't see any use in talking to any more of them."

"You made up your mind?"

Stern shrugged, "I don't find out much one way or the other. A psychotic state isn't something you can just guess at after a man is dead. It's something you have to see, in one way or another, to describe. I don't know as much about Cramer as you do."

"Yeah, but you can write it down can't you?" the major asked. "You know, in medical terms just for the record. You know how the army is. It's got to be written up that way."

"I know the terms, yes," Stern said, "but what shall I write?"

In the major's eyes he saw the flickering of amazement, the unbelief of a man walking on solid ground who suddenly finds himself flung into a hidden snare—the unbelief which hangs a minute behind hostility.

"Why, that he did it while he was insane. You said . . ."

"That's just the thing I don't believe we can find out now, Major. You see, diagnosis is sometimes a more complex matter than an outsider would think. You've probably heard jokes about how long we talk to our patients. There's a reason for it." He sensed that the major was paying little attention to what he said, was only listening while he gathered himself for further argument. Stern concluded abruptly, trying to lighten the matter, "We ask them about their sex life. You've heard jokes about that."

"Well, he didn't have any sex life; that's for sure," the major said.

"What do you mean?"

"Why on this little island . . ."

"Oh yes," Stern said. "I misunderstood. Of course. But even there, Major, it isn't really correct to say a man has no sex life just because he has no contacts with women. It goes on continually in one way or another."

The major interrupted him by drumming his fingers on the table top angrily. "I don't think so. If I know what you're getting at. He was a nice sort of fellow. He was a grownup man."

"I was thinking in terms of fantasies and anxieties," Stern said.

The major looked at him with clear suspicion now. "I wouldn't know about that," he said.

"Those are the things I'd have to know."

"Look"—if the major was exasperated he controlled his feelings, spoke as though he were giving an order and wanted each word of it clearly understood. "You'll never know and I'll never know and the godalmighty war department will never know what was on that boy's mind. So what's the answer? For my part it's pretty plain, if we want to be decent about it: give the kid a break. Let his family put a gold star in the window and collect his insurance."

Stern opened his mouth to speak but let the moment pass. He noticed Singer watching him through narrowed lids and gave up the thought of further explanation. "I suppose I haven't any way to oppose that line of reasoning, Major. It sounds humane and practical."

"But you don't agree, huh?"

"I don't know," Stern said. He glanced again toward Singer and saw that young man make a disgusted face.

The major said, "I'll tell you what. You can make up your

mind in a little while can't you? I'm anxious, damn it, to get this whole thing all straightened up. I've got plenty to do besides this investigation. You could write it up this afternoon, right now, couldn't you?"

"I'll do it if you want," said Stern.

"You can go over to the officer's shack if you want to. Matter of fact you'd probably like to look it over by yourself. Make up your own mind about it, see, without me influencing you. Singer and I will go down and take a swim off the landing. If you want me for anything, anything you want to know, just yell down."

The major and Lieutenant Singer walked out while Stern was gathering up the investigation report and the few notes he had made. Once out of his hearing, Singer said to the major, "What in hell is wrong with that guy?"

The major laughed, "He's just an odd character. I guess he'll do all right, though. Wants a little time to make up his mind."

"Damn stubborn wrong-headed Jew. Would anybody else take that attitude? Huh?"

"Now, Singer," the major said as he hurried down the sand. "Take a swim now and cool off."

"You'd think it was going to cost him money to get that insurance for Cramer," Singer said.

"No," the major said. "He's probably not used to making up his mind fast, I guess."

Singer said, "Well, if I blow my brains out, don't get that bastard out here on me, will you? You don't suppose he's going to louse things up for poor Cramer, do you?"

"If he does," the major said, "I'll get another psychiatrist to write it up. The IG is pretty well sold on the way I wrote up this investigation and he's going to let me get it through one way or another."

There was still no sliver of shade on the privy-like hut where Cramer had died. It was screened on four sides so a breeze could have come through it. But there was no breeze. When Stern sat at the desk inside, he could look down on the beach and on the nibbling tremor of the water at its bone-white edge. All around him—among the tents under the banana trees where lustrous weeds sprang into tangles too thick to walk through—there was no other movement to be seen. Everywhere was the unnatural stillness and the sun.

He knew that he must write what the major had so bluntly

asked for. But in the moment of realizing this, he knew that he did not want to. Because he thought we agreed, he thought we looked at it the same? he asked himself. Why should I write what he wants instead of what Cramer wants? Then, amending the thought, no, instead of what I want?

On the surface we do agree, Stern thought. He considered how his two years in the Pacific had emphasized for him the beliefs which by training, and, as he thought, by temperament he held—that the choice which offers a practical course of action is the proper choice. "Don't tell me it was right or wrong"—the major's sentence was no less than the principle which he had followed in practice and in the army. Where, then, was his objection? Was the heat making him quarrelsome and petty? Was this the shadow of contagious emotions which he sometimes picked up from his patients, an emotional identification with Cramer which bordered on self-pity? An urge to contrariety because he felt the major overshadowed him? A desire to assert his ego by allying himself with the dramatic force of Cramer's suicide?

He thought again how little he could ever know of the dead man. His possessions, still as he had left them, showed nothing of any consequence—the uniforms hung neatly in the corner, the pipe and half-empty pack of cigarettes on the desk, the little stack of technical manuals, a comic book on the floor, the line of shoes under the bed. There was a picture of Cramer and a rather nice-looking girl standing in front of some civic building somewhere and another of Cramer with an older man and woman. There were a few letters with no particular individuality. There was a story in them, maybe, but no way to know it now. Only Cramer himself provided any continuity among these diverse scraps and shreds. Any of a million men might have lived in this hut a while and left identical traces.

He could not know the man's mind now—then why not smooth over the circumstances of his death, salvage fragments of some sort from the wreck? In one way it seemed sheer perversity to write an opinion which would not help save the slight things left.

Yet it was toward that perversity that his conception of the truth inclined him. In the absence of any findings, the really honest thing to do would be to report no findings.

Beyond that, less scrupulous but more urgent in its insistence, was the notion which he had got that this island and the broad approaches of the sea were like a contrived monument of isolation. If you stayed here, he thought, every day it would remind you of the absence and isolation you've known in your life. To live with these men, whose color and your rank made alien, not even to have the necessity of fixing your own food to keep you from thinking—with only two more days to wait here you might have looked so clearly into the emptiness of things that you would understand that you could not go back. It might be like freezing to death. After you give in to the cold, which has been there waiting for you always, you don't want to move. You get drowsy with it.

Even as he thought of this, Stern could imagine the major replying, "Freezing to death here?" and laughing as he rubbed the sweat out of his eyes.

Or memorizing the whole catechism of loneliness while you were shut on this worthless acre and knowing that you would always have it at the tip of your mind wherever you went after this. However deep the loneliness might have been, though, it was not the same thing as insanity.

It wasn't comforting to think of this unknown man swimming down into the loneliness he was finally too weak to stand. But all over the world now the bodies of men were going into holes and pits, into the flat dirt and taking with them unanswered questions, hatred and anger and disgust which nobody would ever speak, a bitterness that could never be paid back to them. And would you wipe this bitterness out of your sight because it was not comforting? You had shared their times and the world with them. What they thought and wanted, you in some measure had wanted with them. How should death split this sharing? Or could you bring the truth, like a led horse, only to the edge of that pit, so if you went on across you had to go without it?

The ordinary slights and contempt that came to him in the army never made Stern intensely aware of his race; but in the presence of tragedy it was natural for him to assess it in terms of his own people—not his family, but many he had lived among not many years ago he knew had been starved and butchered in Poland. And how had their deaths been recorded, what empty, contemptuous phrases had gone into the archives to mask the bitterness of their death and the fact that they had been more than digits or names? Maybe worse than the guilt of their death was the denial that they had lived—diverse and intricate men and women. If he now wrote an opinion to explain away this man, in kindness though it might seem, he would make the same denial.

He could imagine himself trying to explain this to the major and saw the major shaking his head and saying, "Cramer wasn't a Jew." This thought came first to him as a sardonic commentary on the limits of the major's mind. And then the reply to it came— not comic now, but furious and furiously illuminating his growing dislike for the major. Because he was the same as them to me, Stern thought, the same as everybody killed in these bad years, and because you can keep your principles in question just so long and then if you haven't decided what's right and what's not the decision is made for you.

That's what the major did for me, he thought. Bringing me to this trap of an island and making me see it. And now I'm like him, because I didn't make up my mind in time and it's made up for me. There isn't any question any more. But there isn't anything I can say about it, either.

"He wants to get this straightened up," he thought. It seemed to him that if he could only get the major to see this death as something more than a milestone for those still alive, he might save something from the wreck of his own conscience.

Even so much was much more than he could expect. So he wrote a number of points which served to indicate that Cramer had killed himself while temporarily insane and then walked down the slope of coral and the beach to find the major. To get in the boat, to cross back again, fleeing the island.

The Swimmers
at Pallikula

In the middle months of the war our Marine Quartermaster unit was set up on an island south of Guadalcanal to repair trucks; but our main effort, we said then and remembered later, was to sweat through our time in the heat and wet, where time turned into something very tricky and demoralizing. Remembering this, I realize how much I owe to the Gunner for nudging me through those months without a crack-up.

Almost every afternoon he bullied me—because I was the junior lieutenant and senior goldbrick in the outfit and quartered with him and bullied by him in everything else, too—into going down back of camp to the Seabees' beach for a swim. Usually I was glad enough to go, once we were started, though the water was not nearly as much of an attraction for me as it seemed to be for him.

I am sure the daily swimming made up to him for a lot of challenges and pleasures the island didn't have to offer. I came to see that the swimming was more than a sport for him; it was a duel and in some ways he made it take the place of the combat he had never seen after all his twenty years of service. Off the coral pier at the beach a barge was anchored and a couple of hundred yards out there was a red steel buoy. When the blur and mist of the rainy season almost hid the buoy, and when he and I were the only ones who ventured to the beach, he'd stalk around the barge peering grimly out at the buoy and muttering that if we didn't make our daily turn around it we'd better stop calling ourselves marines. He talked up all the risks, and I suppose that each time he threw his body—flying like a bull calf shoved from a truck—into the water he had a sense that the ocean was paying him personal attention and had, you might say, drawn a sword to repel him. And he would crawl out, after we'd gone around the buoy, grinning contentedly at the way he'd parried its secret blows.

It was on one of the first bright days at the end of the rainy season that we crashed down the frond-crossed and spider-webbed path among the coconut trees to find a jeep parked briskly at the end of the pier.

On the barge sat a woman in a yellow bathing suit, leaning back on the support of her arms; her head sagged forward as she stared out to sea. When we climbed the side of the barge she turned, half-frightened—then decided we were not rapists, showed her big, pretty teeth, and said, "Hi, fellas."

The Gunner took a quick look on the seaward side of the barge and frowned in a pleased, fatherly way at her. "What are you doing out here alone, young woman?"

"I'm not alone," she said. "Out there." She nodded toward the expanse of green, bouncing waves. We looked in the direction of her nod, then farther, and got our first glimpse of the Boy Major's blond head. He must have been nearly a half mile beyond the buoy.

The Gunner began pacing nervously across the barge deck and back. "Shouldn't be out there," he said meanly. "A person shouldn't swim that far by himself."

"Oh." The woman shrugged. "He's all right. He's a champion of something. I forget what, but he can swim." She smiled when she said that, and it seemed to me that I caught the suggestion of a wink, some indication that she was not going to concern herself with the useless prowesses of that one or any other man.

"Then he ought to know better," the Gunner said. "It's an elementary precaution not to go beyond the reach of help. Endangers not only yourself but the rescuer." He slapped at his biceps as though he had caught them stealing. "Suppose that fellow got in trouble right now?"

"You'd go after him," the woman said. "Wouldn't you?" She gave him a flattering smile.

"I'll be damned if I would," the Gunner said. "Anybody who is foolish enough to show off that way deserves what he gets."

"Then we'll have to hope he can take care of himself after all," she said.

"He's a champion," I said, and she turned to approve me for not being quite so solemn about the matter as the Gunner. "Let's go around the buoy," I suggested to him.

"That's all right too, but I just want to say there are a lot of statistics on people who've drowned showing off in front of women." He glared down to show her what her responsibility was, set himself to crash the next wave, and pounded away in a heavy, self-taught version of the crawl along the course that he and I had swum so often.

Past the red buoy he treaded water, bubbled, spat phlegm. "Want to go out?" He jerked his head seaward.

"You worried about that guy?" I asked. "Let him take care of himself."

Without answering, the Gunner started to swim out. The water was choppy and rolling enough so that from time to time I lost track of him in the bright wave slopes. Following him as best I could I began to worry that what he really meant to do was swim out farther than the other fellow had, just to show—somebody. I yelled when I couldn't see him, saying I was going back. I heard his voice and felt a great relief when I realized it was coming from behind me. He'd been holding back. "Great sea," he was shouting. "Great day. Great sport. Great sea." I knew he was so scared he didn't actually know what he was saying; and I was glad of that—it was like being given permission to turn back from my own fright, without prejudice.

Somewhere among the waves the other swimmer had passed us. He was dripping and panting beside the woman as we returned to the barge. He watched us with a kind of eager attention, wanting to be friendly, I thought, but wanting to be friendly on his own terms. It was as though he were trying to figure out if we were officers or enlisted men and hoping we were enlisted.

"Damned invigorating today," he greeted us. He bit off the words like cigar ends. "Nice though."

"Too rough," I said.

"You fellas swim here much?" the woman asked. She was leaning one hand carelessly on the guy's kneecap and her lacquered nails were busy with it.

"Daily. The Gunner likes it and I have to watch him so he doesn't drown." Then I introduced the Gunner and the Major introduced his nurse and himself. Major Walker and Miss Hay. The Major asked a question or two about the Gunner's rank and looked smug when he learned that a Gunner was something between an enlisted man and commissioned officer.

"Ever cross over?" the Major asked. He nodded to the string of little barrier islands. They looked like a pale arm, submerged except for certain bumps of muscle. A green fuzz showed on some of them and beyond them was the surf.

"Too far," I said. "Out and around the buoy is far enough for amateurs like us."

The Major squinted his blue eyes at them and his nostrils jumped. "They're not far," he said. "Two miles? I've swum farther than that. I'd be more concerned about barracuda or sharks than the distance."

The Gunner said, "Barracuda won't attack a man swimming. They're cowards."

"Maybe they don't," Miss Hay said, "but do they know they don't? Isn't it a little silly to take a chance, Gunner?" She laughed milkily and punched the Major's calf with a small fist.

"Ha, ha," he said. He turned a commanding eye on the Gunner and me. "Why don't we all three swim over some afternoon? Simply to keep in trim."

"No," I said.

"A man doesn't dare let himself go slack," the Major said.

"Why nawt? Why nawt, Billy?" Miss Hay teased him.

"We're not in that class of swimmer," I said stubbornly.

I heard the Gunner jump to his feet. "Chow time, Lieutenant," he said shortly to me. He jumped halfway in to the pier in his dive.

"See you fellas again," the Major called in his cheerful tenor when I followed the Gunner. "Someday we'll go over."

That night the smoldering Gunner blasted into the middle of some chitchat with me to say that he'd *never* heard of barracudas attacking a swimmer, especially out here.

"That pokey little fag merely likes to sound off. I know the type. He'd never swim out to those islands. Not this year, not ever. So he's got to have some excuse—some *reason*—why he wouldn't go. That's where he got this error about the barracudas."

"It's two miles too far," I said. "That's my reason. So I forgot about it."

The Gunner's face knotted up. "It's not all that far," he said. "Of course I grant it would be criminal foolishness for anyone to try it alone, but . . ."

"Not me," I said. "No. Absolutely no. I won't. I'll turn in psycho at the hospital. I'll blow off my toe. I will not swim across to those islands."

"It's a matter of pace," he said. "Swim, then rest. Swim, rest."

"No."

He studied the problem tolerantly and came out with this: "I agree. I don't approve of talking about something instead of having the guts to do it."

"I don't even have the guts to talk about it," I said. "Let's go see what's on at the movie."

The Gunner disapproved of movies on the grounds that they had happy endings, but this time he said, "Why not?" and came along meekly. The movie was a musical. I sat through it hardly listening to a song, already thinking, He's tricking me. He'll say he came to a movie he didn't want to see so I've got to . . . No.

After that we ran into the Boy Major and Miss Hay—Alice— two or three times a week at the beach. Whenever we saw the jeep parked at the pier end, the Gunner would get sullen, and the sight of Alice's yellow bathing suit, like a victorious college's pennant against the blue water, would shut him up entirely.

During such time as I spent talking with her and the Major, the Gunner dived for shells and coral down the anchor cables of the barge. He would bring up a find, examine it in the air with disgust, and throw it back. "He's bashful," Alice said once, and she was exactly right.

Now when the Gunner and I took our daily turn around the buoy he would insist on going a long way beyond it. Training. If I accused him of trying to impress Alice by taking us out farther than the Major had been he would shout across the water, "Bull.

You've got to get over the idea it makes any difference what they think. If I wasn't married I'd show you she's got no more prejudice than the next one."

Whatever he really thought, the longer swims were making him happy. In that dry season sometimes we got a breeze. The whole camp and our work and the general sweating out of the war were lighter. The Gunner muttered less about his enemies and the disaster of having been born.

Then one day, coming down through the coconut grove, we saw the jeep parked on the pier but no sign of Alice either on the barge or in the shallow water where she sometimes swam. We didn't see the Major until we'd climbed the barge and looked out. There he was—about the same god-awful distance as he'd been that first time. Pretty soon we made out that he was headed for us rather than for the barrier islands and I breathed a lot easier, but even so we stayed out of the water to wait for him as if by agreement, as though he were bringing some decision to us like a man carrying mail.

When the Major stopped to float alongside the buoy, the Gunner could hardly stand it. I saw his fingers reading an old scar on his arm like Braille, and I hoped it said the right thing to him.

The Major came in perfectly relaxed. I guessed that he'd rested by the buoy on purpose to affirm the impression that whatever he'd done had been easy.

"It *was* a good stretch," he called from twenty feet out.

"You went over?" I asked.

"Yup."

"Nice going. Barracuda chase you?"

He laughed falsely. "Not a one. I had to outrun some sharks, though."

"That ought to have been easy for you. Alice tells me you're a swim champ, medalist, prize winner." Now *there* was a desperate thing for me to say because, for one reason, he'd never mentioned it to us to build himself up. For another it was bad because I was using it to keep up a distinction—for *you* it's nothing, for *us* it would be too much—to hide behind, and that was wrong because all three of us knew, each in his own way, that it was not skill being measured here but courage.

"Nothing much," the Major said. "I've never swum distance in competition."

"I'll swim over with you," I heard the Gunner say. "I've been wanting to go over."

The Major swung to him with a hint of panic on his face. "Now?"

"We've got three hours before dark."

"My God," the Major laughed, "I couldn't go now. Alice is expecting me to call at the hosp—No, I'm tuckered, man. We'll do it another day."

"Yes," the Gunner said.

"One day soon," the Major said.

"Yes."

While we sat on the barge watching him towel off beside the jeep on the pier, the Gunner said grimly, "I called his bluff. I wouldn't wonder that we'd seen the last of him."

"What?"

"You don't believe for a minute he was telling the truth, do you? What reason would he have to try it, even, except to show off for this ginch? And where is she? Huh? A type like that has to have a *reason* for doing things. Use your logic, that's all."

"He was pretty far out when we saw him."

"No farther than we've been," the Gunner said. "Maybe not as far. I'll just take a bet that the boy won't be around any more."

I wanted to believe that he was right, though I would miss seeing Alice. At the same time my own brand of logic wasn't quite the same as the Gunner's and I was still afraid that someday we were going to look mighty silly or do something even sillier. So to put my mind at ease, one morning while the Gunner was out of camp I got Sergeant Weber to bring a rubber boat to the beach and row alongside me while I swam to one of the barrier islands. I made it. Afterward I felt a lot safer and as if I had settled a problem that foolish talk had called up to plague me. The beach was secure again.

My worst mistake was right there. If I hadn't known I could do it, I'd never have gone over with the Major and the Gunner the day we heard his tenor voice sing, "Hi men," and looked back through wave froth at our shoulders to see him crashing on like a side-wheeler toward us.

I hadn't heard the jeep wheels skid on coral as he braked to a stop back there on the pier, and I wanted to believe he was unreal. But there was Alice tanning on the barge in a posture of sweet patience.

"Fine day," the Major said suggestively. "Fine day for it."

The Gunner's eyes suddenly looked like two pistol targets. Then he closed them and it seemed to me he shuddered.

"How about your girl?" I called to the Major. I tried to make it sound like a shame to make a nice girl wait while we swam any great distance.

"She won't mind. How about it, Gunner?"

Instead of answering, the Gunner threw himself straight up half out of the water like a leaping seal. Once more his eyes were absolute circles while he looked at the water and the islands. This time when he closed them he started swimming as though he meant to go all the way without a break. The Major followed with an easy breast stroke. Something that sounded reasonable and deadly said to me, *you've done it before.* So I followed them.

The water had a soft roll, completely without any sharp waves. The confident half of my mind said it was beautiful, and the other half said nothing yet. With a new awareness of them, I could feel my bone joints and muscles working as though I were roaming my body inspecting each one of them and finding them all right. I knew beyond any kidding that this swim was dangerous, and the knowledge sharpened me. Too much.

Halfway over I knew I was swimming against something tight as a harness, and I knew it was the fact that every stroke I made would have to be duplicated on the way back. I speeded up a little to catch the others. It seemed less lonely if they were within shouting distance.

The extra effort of catching up tired me. I saw that the Gunner still—or again—had his eyes closed, and I closed mine. I wondered such nonsense things as how deep the water was and whether certain surface conditions could make you seasick while you swam. I wondered if there might not be sandbars on our side of the islands that would cut our distance by, maybe, a hundred yards. It seemed reasonable that there should be. If I could have believed that just one hundred yards had been subtracted from the distance I thought that this would make all the difference in my confidence.

The Gunner yelled a great blubbery sound. I was surprised that it came from behind me. I opened my eyes to see his green face go under the green lick of water.

"Get him," the Major called. Automatically, hating the loss of distance, I went back. I reached him just about as the Major did.

He was like a soft, enormous child in our hands. He couldn't or wouldn't move to help himself, and he couldn't seem to understand when we asked him what was the matter.

"Pull'm," the Major said. "Not so far."

It looked mighty far to me, but it was really better to go along pulling at one of the Gunner's armpits than it had been swimming alone. The contact had a kind of social value. Still when I put my foot down for the tenth time and finally felt sand I thought I was going to cry.

The Gunner floundered a minute as we let him go. He found his footing, looked up at the tiny island as though he'd just discovered America. Rubbing his scarred arm he said, "I don't know what happened to me. The old heart got to pounding, you know. Nothing would work. I couldn't reach out ahead of me. The arms." He lifted them now to show us how wonderful it was that they would work again, then he vomited into the water frothing around his knees. "Wheew," he said. "That ought to help."

The Major watched us with an expression that wobbled between a Boy Scout pride for having taken care of us and a kind of scared disgust at the trouble we'd got him into. I guess he wouldn't have been really surprised if we'd hollowed him out and rowed him back—probably figuring by then we were capable of something like that.

He went to the six-foot rise that was the highest part of the island and waved back in Alice's direction. He smiled for her just as if she could see his face across two miles of water.

Then for quite a while the three of us lay dead silent close to the water, and I suppose we were all thinking exactly the same thing. It was I who had to say it. "How do we get back?"

"Swim," the Major said.

"Can't." I jerked my thumb at the Gunner, who lay on his back, breathing through his mouth. "If we wait long enough Alice may get the idea of sending someone with a boat."

The Major's jaw tightened. "Alice? I'm going to swim back. I'll send a boat for you if you want."

"No," the Gunner said. "To hell with the boat. We came here swimming and that's how we'll go back."

"You couldn't make it," I said.

The Major swirled the sand thoughtfully with his forefinger. "I made you fellas an offer. I suppose I ought to make it an order. Wait here."

The Gunner said, "You can't order us, sir. We're marines and no army . . ."

"Oh Jesus," the Major said. "Not that. Not that. I don't have to take that. All right, let me tell you—I'm swimming back by myself. If you try to swim back it is obvious that you're going to drown, and I want to make it just as clear that I won't lift a finger to save you. Either of you."

"Yes sir," the Gunner said. "Yes sir."

The Major hopped up in a flurry of sand. Hitching his red trunks he walked with great determination to the water and swam toward the barge, his jeep, and his girl.

"Well," I said to the Gunner after a while, "shall we wait for a patrol plane to spot us? Maybe tomorrow? Maybe the day after?"

"Hell, I feel a lot better now. I'll know how to pace myself better on the way back. I didn't want to admit it in front of that little blowhard, but what happened to me was I lost my nerve and pushed myself too hard. Wore myself out. But I've got the idea of the pace now."

"*You've* got it? How about me?" I said. "Gunner, you can go to bloody hell and what the Major told you goes for me too. You're on your own. *Pace.*" I hitched my trunks and went back into the water that seemed now almost of body temperature.

My knees were wobbling as I waded in, and noticing this made me madder yet. It wasn't enough that I was in some danger—I had to be humiliated by it too. Pretty soon every bit of my feeling had melted into a plain, blistering anger, and I think that helped. The sheer energy I generated from being angry made the trip back easier than coming over. I swam hard for a while and then lay bitterly in the roll of the water with nothing but a cloudless sky in the range of my eyes, and the sky actually looked red. I was sure for most of the way that I wouldn't make shore, and I was so angry I didn't care. Partly I was thinking and partly I was simply aware of the absurdity that had brought me to this present instant. It was absurd that I should have been caught in the boys' game of dare between the Gunner and Major. It was absurd that I should have spent all these months in the Pacific out of respect for my countrymen's judgment of me if I was going to drown this pointlessly. It was possibly even more absurd that a nice consideration of what the Gunner might think of me had euchred me into a position of disclaiming any concern for his safety and then drowning here *anyway*. It came to me very clearly that every judgment I had ever made had been accumulating to herd me along to this moment of nonsense. As I bobbed up and down like a polyp, I was—no use putting it another way—totally insane with my raging rejection of the self I'd been for twenty-one years.

I swallowed myself like those animals in the pseudo-folklore stories, and when I put out my right hand for another stroke at the damned water I did it because my whole life and its possible end there was so silly I wanted to swim away from them in disgust.

The next time I rested I taunted myself with having made this silly swim because I wanted to show off in front of Alice, though this was just a lying accusation I'd picked up from the Gunner's random discard. I was so peeved with myself that anything which hurt was welcome. Actually, I felt in my new wisdom, I'd spit on Alice for being of the gender that sends men to absurd deaths.

I saw that innocent shore all covered with coconut trees and jungle and bright as metal-woven cloth in the sun. It occurred to me that before I could never admit openly that I loved the way things looked, but now to confess that I had done so made me viciously happy. I swallowed a batch of salt water laughing at the folly of getting caught by an appetite for green and pleasant surroundings, but even that didn't slow me down. I must have had a pint of c.p. adrenalin in my bloodstream by then. It's heady stuff.

I passed the red buoy, thinking it would have been a good thing for me to have got a cramp and drowned one day while the Gunner and I were still doing our constitutional turns tight around it, because that would have saved me from the scald of this new knowledge. I went in from there like a champion—six measured kicks to an overhand stroke and every breath regular as a flywheel. I had never swum that well before while I had any respect for my fear of the water.

As I pulled alongside the barge the Berserk Major and his floozie looked down their long noses at me from the deck.

"Leave your buddy to drown?" the Major asked, with just the loathsome sarcasm I wanted him to intone.

"Yezzur," I said. "You're not the only peckerhead on this beach."

"Gunner's coming," Alice said in her professional bedside manner. "Don't you worry about him."

"If he was drowning in a bathtub I wouldn't pull the plug," I said.

She said, "Oh oh!"

As soon as I pulled my khakis on over my wet trunks and worked my salt-swollen feet into my oxfords I took off up the hill for camp, still not looking back to see if the Gunner had made it, if the Bold Major had gone in to help him, or if he had sunk.

On my way I ran into one of those tough spider webs that here and there laced the coconut fronds together, tough and broad as a bedsheet, and this made me angrier yet. Everything ran the same way for a while. I stood there crouched with the web sticky on my face and throat, daring that damn spider to come at me. That instinct should have made the spider evacuate his web and climb the tree to find a safer spot for his next try seemed only another example of the way nature conspired to make human impulses appear ridiculous and despicable.

From camp I took a jeep straight to the Junior Officers' Club at Base Command. I won eighteen dollars there on the nickel slot machine while I was getting drunk and lost the same plus twelve on the quarter machine before I got sick and went to the movie to sober up. The movie ended with a grinning clinch for the villain's daughter and the fag detective who'd just put a slug between her old man's eyes, and I cheered it so much that the gray-haired commander behind me tapped my shoulder and said, "Young man, some of us are here to enjoy the picture."

The adrenalin was gone then and just the surprising touch of his hand reminded me of all the fear I'd had a few hours before in the water. It was admirably clear to me that I'd been loading alcohol to cover the dissipation of the anger that had saved me. I was trembling like the soldier hero in a thirties peace movie. I drove home at eight miles an hour thinking a jeep was built too high off the road for genuine safety.

In our hut I found the Gunner loading himself with his evening whiskey. The glass he had was fuller than usual and it was obvious that he was not on his first glass.

Neither of us would speak to the other for a while. I put my shirt in the wardrobe and pretended to read a couple of paragraphs before I would even exchange guilty looks with him.

Then we each grinned like small-town bankers caught absconding with the church building fund. The Gunner sniffed his loaded glass and said, "You know, I guess I was wrong to think the Major had never swum that stretch before."

"I guess you were," I said nastily.

"What the hell? We've done it too. They can't take that away from us. We've been there, Bob. You know what I think? It's not what the public gives you credit for that counts. It's what you know you've done. We've been there and we don't have to talk about it like some would."

"Yup."

"You looked good out there," he said. "You saved my life and you'll remember that."

"Listen," I said. "Maybe nobody *has* to take it away from us. You know what? I hated saving your life. I *wouldn't* have gone back for you on the way in if I'd known you were drowning."

"Nobody asked you to," he said with an old man's dignity. "Did *I?*"

"I don't particularly enjoy knowing that about myself," I said. I felt sick and weepy and I really knew there was nowhere to turn to unload that.

"Yeah," the Gunner said sadly. "I didn't look so good out there either. Next time we'll stick closer to the buoy."

"Do so if you want," I said, "I'm staying away from water for awhile. I found out all I want to know." I shucked off the rest of my clothes, sprayed my mosquito bar, and rolled into bed.

After the Gunner turned the light out I rolled toward the hut wall to find a total shelter from the play of the area lights. It was as though I expected to douse out the clarity with which I was seeing the months ahead. We had the skinny then that there would be a landing in the Philippines in a few months and maybe within the year they would close this base out. But it was going to be a long time yet. Long until we moved, but a short time before the next rainy season came on us with the days counting themselves out in the dripping slop from the eaves. However pitying we felt toward each other, the time would come in that season when the Gunner and I couldn't stand each other any more and we would have to change quarters. I could wish to make the day come sooner but still I hated its coming. I expected that after we broke up altogether I would be seeing a lot of movies from home with their sour, happy endings—all those frigid Cinderellas and Jacks that kill the wrong giant and the rest of that crud that kills your soul by being too much like life.

The Happy
Marriage

I

The skinny was always:

You married specifically against death. Young enough I had said "Better marry" and "I will not die here," when *here* was the attic in Chesterfield where I found the arrowheads in the trunk under dust-smelling calico, the letters of Genevieve Wren to Morton Wren, and the old book with angel pictures (really cupids, their bare butts square in my face when I opened the pages). I knew at once that love's chemistry burned such fat.

Outside, the grass was browning in the degeneration of August, the sore-pocked shepherd dog chased chickens, the fishpool scummed, and the wind turned high and blue on a wheel's paradigm, turning on the dear axle of my body. I shouldn't die here, I thought. I love this dark attic too well and myself bare like these angels.

Once I found a pine cone in the dark woods. Put it in a milk bottle filled with water and hid it away. Later the water had turned purple. Thus God instructed me.

And once we went to the cabin on Crow Island in May when the river was low enough to ford. Behind Clayton on his pony the rest of the troop rode bikes or went scout's pace. The ranked cottonwoods of the island were to be our fort against the Nebraska sky. The undersides of logs drifted on the island were still wet from the floods in April, and we found mushrooms warm as our hands in the sticky shadows. Rhubarb and dutchman's britches lined the path to the abandoned Scout cabin. The path was velvet with fine grass like the fuzz that grows on a burn scar. The insignia of the Eagle troop hung on a rusting nail beside the door.

In the afternoon we stripped and lay belly down on the sandbar and talked about Clayton's cousin—who was eleven and that was the sweetest age for girls—and how she ought to be there with us. I looked up and saw her coming in over the cottonwoods like a highjumper or a monoplane, naked as a cloud and about eighty feet tall. Judas, I yelled. I had to run and throw myself in the cold water while the sports laughed at my trouble and flung sand.

At night all the girls we knew were among us when we jabbered and tightclosed our eyes. I saw them all parade hot white and featureless as mushrooms. Reasoning toward midnight, I knew clearly that never in this world of dark in the trees and wind and river sweeping our island was Clayton's cousin going to wrap me with her candy arms. I turned my face to the logs and in loneliness asserted the possibility realized on the mainland of June, in a more sober year, in an apartment we were lucky to find for $22 a month. We had two rooms and the kitchen window looked out on a slate roof, more sky, and more noon than God bargained for when he made my world. Pure luck.

Mr. Nixon, when I told him I would marry without it if I had to, gave me a raise to $105 and fixed things so I'd have time at noon to walk home to her and that great window. Who do you love? she said in jealousy of my staring out. You, I said.

One of our first days there she was cleaning the apartment and found in the cupboard under the sink a mouse's skull. Our insects had eaten it clean. It was so fresh it still looked pink and white as a flower, or the fresh bone on a butcher's table. She shivered and tried loyally to hide it from me. Put it back and leave it, I said. It's the totem to bless this house. She laughed and that afternoon while I was at work took it out with the trash.

When I knew it was lost I was afraid. Where do I have to go to find it? I said.

Then there was the war and I came back from it to a different apartment. The first winter home I was sick, and one night in a fever dream I told her where the skull had gone.

You found it there, she said. Cheat.

I said, That's right. In the amphitheater of water fear I crushed it. It was more fragile than I had thought.

You won't die out there, she said. Look, I've put yellow curtains at the window, as I wrote you. Come home and cry.

I awoke crying all right, and there she was in the kitchenette as big and pretty as life, breaking an egg into water and saying, Do you want it on toast, my lad? You'll feel better if you eat.

Not yet, I said. Wait a while. Come listen.

To what?

To me.

II

I have a twin named Lynch, I said. His soles walk on the soles of my feet.

That's chummy, she said.

He is in death. He braces against me on the edge between life and death. You have no business knowing him, since you threw the skull away, but I know him. I was down there with him.

I thought you were in the army.

Listen, I said. I *went* to that island. I know what it's like. You don't.

Is his name really Lynch? Or is that a joke?

Lynch by name, Lynch by character. He was absolutely no good. Liar, lazy, cheat, half-wit, Regular Army chicken and the Captain's suck. Face like an old man's except no calm in it. Simultaneously sleepy and tormented. Didn't know a soul in the outfit except by name and didn't want to. Wanted to "get up North" and get him a Jap's ears. Wrote no letters, got no mail. Never played softball in the evenings with the rest of us. Played poker only to win. So he was in my work crew for two weeks while we were building the airstrip at Pallikula. I had trouble with him every day. So one day we were blasting coral. I had lit all fuses and started to run. He was there beside me, grabbing my arm, saying, What's the matter, Sergeant, you scared? I hadn't been, but he scared me. What's the use of running? he said and showed his teeth. I jerked away like an animal that pulls its leg off to get out of a trap, and sprinted to flop behind a coconut log. Real flat on my belly, real flat, like I was holding onto you. Waited. I wouldn't look up to see if the bastard had taken cover. Then all three of the charges I set went at once, and it seems he hadn't.

Dead? She asked. I could feel the jerk go through her when I answered and then the terrible unstiffening of her arm. We were sitting among pillows in our Dearborn Street apartment, God's safest children, but something hit us. Flying coral.

It wasn't your fault, she said.

No; my death, I said. I had it in my hand to save but I squeezed too hard. When I looked over the log and saw the black blood coming from his mouth I knew I had nothing to hang onto but love. I think I let him go for your sake.

That's enough, she said.

No, I'll tip. You don't understand, I said.

If I don't, help me, she said. Help me.

When the finger touches the hollow in the elbow and the wiggle of the ordinarily hidden vein, touches skin running from oil smooth to dusty rough on the circumference of the thigh, the stubble in the armpit, the loaded velvet of the lip, the humorous wobble of the kneecap, the hard curve of rib, the rebounding curve of the breast and the frantic nipple—there is no understanding.

Or when the body settles like a rigid numeral paired with a nubile zero, what understands us is not ourselves.

Understanding is afterward, the long afterward and the falling apart. As decay is a vegetable.

What *doth* man of woman require?

The spangled lineaments which represent desire? Or only the sea-brine reminiscent harbor of the sea's disaster?

Within the shell of happiness the kernel of repudiation. In the timbre of the sexcry, wailing. In the after-fondness (counterfeited) the true coin of innocence. In promise, denial. In wholeness the explanatory shape of division.

Is all that possible, darling, my darling?
No.

III

Whom do you love? some others said, conventionally.
"Qu'est-ce-que tu aime?" the whore said. What do you love?
Thee, when I came in from the snow-bewildered street, moist
snow dripping from my hat brim; when I ordered a cognac from
fat Margot, the barmaid with the biggest radio—six bands and
enough dials to tune in clear any station in Europe.
"Une femme cruelle? Les garcons?"
Thou—when you bumped plumply against my knee without
taking your eyes from the red-headed soldier in the corner;
when you said—as if the pity of it might brim over the cup and
anoint me with its excess—"Lousy night. It's always slow the
week before you pay your GIs." Then did I wish to make the
house, to lay down in a joke the aspiration with its strange device, the image of man, instructed and moralized. I offered her
the watching skull. I said to her, As Pascal cried in anguish, *Who
watched with Lynch?*
"You have fear?" she said, who knew I had.
I bought that out, I said. Am buying.
"It costs dearly."
Dearly.
In lieu of action, for 1500 francs I recounted my triumphs in
the erotic field, the time I went down on a nightingale at Dover
Beach, frolicked with the blue china poor Rupert loved, made
out with a sonnet, got to the Hegelian dialectic, exposed myself
to bullfights, Mahler, and the sea.
I love plain living and high thinking.
Excellence.
Airplanes.
Samson Agonistes.
I will not let you go until you bless me, I said.
The loathing and contempt of her eyes made me think of a
mongoose examining a garter snake. "Qu'est-ce-que tu aime?"
she said.
Everything.

She grunted. "Some other night, then, cheri?"
In the springtime.

But in the springtime, the season sweet and colored in lofty blossoms like the skulls of mice, what was there to do but act out the mysteries with two Danish girls? Their eyes were all four blue as that original window opening North. They were sixteen and seventeen and hitch-hiking around Europe. For culture.

"My name is meaning the night," the sixteen-year-old explained. I had bought her peppermint candy and her tongue was red as macaw feathers. She bobbed like an earnest daisy when she insisted, "I is always loving dezz."

I laughed and lightly told her what Rimbaud, dying, said to his sister, "Tomorrow you will be in the sun and I will be in the dark."

She licked her candy and seemed pleased, as though I had paid her a personal compliment. But the next morning, lying in her friend's arms, she called across the hotel room to me, "No, *you* will be in the sun and I will be in Hell wiz my sisser here."

Their Danish wrists were laced delicately with the scars of old razor cuts. I had never pondered that Gillette had undone so many.

"We has found somezing beyond the ee roh teek," she called. From her tone, that something could have been faith, wisdom, or charity. Turned out to be ether.

We lay in the Parisian spring, three cotton pads to our faces, dreaming that outside the room bells rang a chivalry of disaster. Under chestnut trees the dead girls paraded, those whom Paris loved, and in spacious evenings they rumored the infidelity of life as if they might be gossiping the anxieties of fashionable love.

The spike of her bird-feather tongue was bitter with the taste of ether. We lay two days conversing in our respective languages. She told me how the razors tickled her wrists like shy schoolboys, driven to horror that so much beauty was abroad in the uncertainty of a temporal world, unsaved among war, lechery, or the fluctuations of paper currency. Like a painter's brushes the razors had stroked to fix that beauty—a fresco in a lightless corridor. Her father, she said once, in the children's hour when we had all three sobered enough to use common words, when we looked down together from the hotel windows into the damning illusion of the street—her father was literally a painter, had known Munch and Ensor many years ago. Her mother was younger and danced the Charleston. She must send them a post card so they would not worry about her.

They must not worry, she said, slopping the virgin handful of cotton from a newly opened liter. There was nothing to worry about. In the gently downward planes of these dimensions neither she nor her sister-friend and I must worry that sometime in a Marseilles canal her dancer's body would float headless, with an illiterate love note stuffed into her brassiere.

I should not worry, the ether and the razors said, that I had been unfaithful to living friends and wives. You never wanted any more, they whispered to me, than just to eat your cake and have the eating of it, than praise for the bashfulness with which you sinned, than immortality, than to bury the dead in another chance and time to come.

There were no razors but I felt them crawl like instructive maggots on the wrists to which I held a claim. Little brothers beyond the ee roh teek. By the second night I had learned everything from them.

I can tell you that Ee Roh Teek is a mountain in Central Africa and not everyone knows why there should be leopards on it. It is the yellow sugar gate to Hell and beyond it are all the eyes. Beyond it everyone may call for Lynch and anyone may answer. He will approach you like a child and whisper, "Lead me back."

Come on, I said.

"Is it far?"

Not very *far*, but there isn't any *way*.

IV

Out of sheer habit I came back.

With the damnedest hangover, an oceanic, sloshing void in which floated everything. A hangover as big and hollow as a cosmos in which a filament suspended me at the center of appearances.

I was in my room behind the Sorbonne and had no idea how I'd come there, except that my ragged pulse suggested I might have galloped on all fours. I closed my eyes and tried to imagine what a fish would do if it wanted to evolve into a man. There must be something it could take, I thought. I expected to die unless I could damn soon discover why to live. I tried to remember back to Crow Island. If I could lie by the muddy edge of the water in a growing season and count new pubic hairs, if I could climb to a blue window or the attic in August to feel the sweat pour out of me like evil going home, if I could remember why Morton Wren loved Genevieve then I could instruct my body how it must endure.

Looking at my unmarked wrists I could not even remember for a while whose were scarred. Who is in the sun and who is in the dark? It seemed to me I had left her, too, beyond the mountain, but the her I left had no identity. Something I had done, as with a razor, had fragmented the person with whom I had talked and lain. I knew I wasn't winning and then my only chance was trying to make it to a bar.

In the blue morning the tower of Ste. Chapelle trembled like a flower stem. Now I'm all right, I thought; since it was real I could put my hand out to steady it. But then I passed a news stand and saw the headlines about an English murderer. He had slashed the wrists of innumerable girls and they, poor things, these moorings cut, had gone drifting down the streams of summer. The killer, I read, was still at large.

Still at large. I took a deep breath. The medium I breathed was horror, and all its aspects were fair to the eye. The shade that fingered the sunny pavements was horrible and lovely and I was still, horribly, at large.

I sat outside the *Old Navy* Bar-Tabac fingering a glass of wine the color of the Danish girls' hair. They were my guides, I thought. I needed the right girls to lead me past the meridian, where I could admit in the presence of judges that I had renounced my rebellion against death. Through the luxury of their doomed flesh I had come to where the ideal Lynch had meant that I must. Now I would leave him where he was nothing. The negative twin no longer had to exist. I had bought out the title of my fear.

Now, in the noonward tending light, and a hangover imitation of the Passion, it seemed permissible to remember Lynch and the other dead. Now, I could fix the place in time—far back, far back—when I had seen the naked bone like a flagstaff in the glutted foxhole, when I had tried to swear *I will come back one more time to give you a decent burial, O denied*. Now, like an animal of the afternoon which does not remember the morning in which the bones lived, I could enter in the body of the abstract woman and hive in the moisture of time to come. That spot of blood in my eye was a ruptured capillary. Only from drunkenness.

In my jacket pocket was a card with the names of the girls. *De votre malheur il ne reste que les noms.* Good-bye, I said. O, good-bye.

Then it was the sun's noon, and under every morsel and scrap on the pavement the shape of shadows changed. The jerk of my healing finger tapped the wine glass on the table top. In the yellow-white ripples I saw all timeless constancy twitch and quiver to the disturbance of my inconstant caress. I believed this city was mine.

Love?
Squalor?

Just recently, by the Village grapevine, I heard about a wedding that's supposed to take place in my neighborhood during what my landlady refers to as "the cruelest month." It's a wedding I probably won't get to, though when I first heard about it I lay around my pad, deep in thought, trying to compose what I call a *stance* to take during the services. "Something incomparably light and deft," as my landlady says—an attitude and a grimace that would contribute to the occasion. Personal judgments be hanged, I'd like to be able to go there and smile. However, to keep from thinking too deeply about all this, I talked it over with my landlady, a remarkably demoralized harridan, and decided against it.

For one thing, as she pointed out, I hadn't been invited. And moreover my presence there might cause the groom an uneasy

minute or two, because as I'm given to understand, Nathan has
spent a lot of time refining the bride—like, her language and the
things she's apt to talk about spontaneously.

As my informant, who's known Mesmé at closer range than I
have in the last several months, says, "It was an apotheotic moment for Nathan when she walked into his office from the *street*
and said she 'couldn't cope,' she simply 'couldn't any longer
cope,' with the horror of looking through the Village for an
apartment.

"Of course first of all she reminded him of all his years in England during the war—he wasn't even in London, for Gawd's
sake, but *Bristol*—while he was waiting to come to the States;
waiting loyally enough, but at the same time wishing he could
have been *there*, in the ideal Britain, when there wasn't the war
and the Empire wasn't dissolving, and if he could have spoken
English then. And, fifteen years later, there *she* is, the reasonable facsimile of Unity Mitford herself, with her gargoyle voice,
wiping the sweat of August off her lip and asking him couldn't
he please help her find something with bawth inside that wasn't
for a working girl—and part-time at that—'too deah.'

"And it was a great thing for Nathan to be able to say and believe that he *was* helping her then 'because she had suffered
so much she deserved a good time' even, or especially, when
he followed her into the apartment he showed her—and subsequently didn't even bother to rent to her—on Barrow Street,
and in the same August sweat and heat tasted the facsimile of
Mitford-flesh on the Salvation Army couch that she pronounced
'not posh but homely.' And because for any man the occasions
of lechery and charity are rarely simultaneous, Nathan was already, in that first down-sinking, reassured and reassuring embrace, wound and knotted not only in the tentacles of his exile
dream come true, but was grasping the opportunity to atone for
gouging his myriad other tenants.

"One fly alone sullied his ointment. Before they even got back
to his fern-filled office to sign the lease, she said in that voice of
jaded Empire, 'Now that you've ———— me . . .' and the next
day, while he was explaining in his inimitable confusion of
senses that she needn't really make a payment until she was on
her feet again, she said, 'I anticipated such an offer now that
we've ———— each other ———— . . .' At which Nathan, like any
man, felt his charity lose its bloom, and, being a practical man,

he set about with carrot and stick to clean up not only her language but her memory as well, restoring, if not virginity, at least the paradigmatic *tabula* on which only the future may inscribe."

Yes. And since I knew the bride before purification and the obliteration, the *rasa*, I have the feeling that her history might break out on me like a childhood contagion, and right there at the service while I stared at the well-scrubbed and rosy groom, my lips might whisper that language once so familiar—"Mesmé, do you really ———— ———— ———— when he ———— you? Though you are even more fastidious than when I knew you in your emigration, do you really like for him to ———— in your hair?"

Nevertheless, I'm setting down these notes in payment of a debt to Muse Clio, her of the sardonic silences, the lady of the white lies and gaudy ellipses, *mater narcissus* herself. I don't want to make any public opposition to charity, or even to its side effects, or even want to doubt that it endureth forever. For the sake of the bride's multitude of former friends I'll shore these fragments against their ruin.

A few years back, in April, I was traveling home from France on a British ship. For the voyage I shared a cabin, forward and low beneath the water line, with two Britishers on their way to Canada, and with a dark, discreet gentleman from one of their recently liberated colonies.

The Englishmen, called Dexter and Billy, had been hired to work for an American contractor on some Thulean defense project. The bigger one, Dexter, never left his bunk, as far as I saw, for the entire trip, and I remember him as permanently propped on one elbow, his huge, tattooed bicep glowing like a fish belly under the gray short sleeve of the underwear he slept in. He was handsome in what I was to have explained later was a lower-class style, and except for the cowardice that kept him permanently in bed from dock to dock, might have effectively bullied all of us cabinmates throughout the ship. As things were, he could only work his tyranny while we were in the cabin. It seemed to me that every time I was preparing to leave it he would call down from his perch, "'i, mite, if you see the steward in the hall, ask 'im if he's got a bit of chicken or a chop, wot? Gives a man an appetite, this sea air." The air was musty and ammonic in his corner of the cabin, and, after the second day out of LeHavre, there was usually a semicircle of chicken bones beneath him, like refuse beneath the nest of a loyal mother vulture on her eggs.

Since I was out of the cabin as much as I could be, I know the duty of attendance fell mostly on little Billy. The two of them owned a gramophone without a changer, and Dexter never tired of listening to *The King and I* and *My Fair Lady*. Not only was it incumbent on Billy to keep changing the records, in rough weather he had to hold the tinny machine in his lap to keep the needle from skidding. He rolled on his bony little hips against the roll of the sea and hugged the machine as if, in the event of shipwreck, he and it would gurgle down together, emitting, "The chillll-druhn, the chillllll-duh-runnnn," or "Why can't the English teach their children how to speak?" which Dexter, broadening his accent, would take off as "oh-ah-ee cawnt thee Inklish tich theh chi-ow-druhn a-ow tee-oo spih-eek?" Then he would comment, "True. You Yanks have got everything now. Even our bloody language; we can't speak it no more." Accusingly he would ask, "You know how much I'm going to make up there north? Bloody more in a month than I'd make in six, home in Yorkshire."

"England is done for," I said agreeably.

"Bloody well right it's done for," he said. "*I* never want to go back, 'ow about you, Billy?"

"Not me," Billy said. "You know, mite, London's filling up with niggers. You chaps know how to handle your niggers. More'n what we know any more."

Fleeing Dexter and Billy, the chicken bones, and the death of Empire one rough morning, I took my reading to the salon forward on A deck. And that, of course, is where I met Mesmé.

I didn't right away see that straight, upper-class, ash-blond hair, her exquisite forehead, or even her hazel, sated eyes, for the simple reason that she was huddled—almost enveloped—in a huge, furry coat. The coat seemed to cover the green lounge chair and occupant entirely except for one protruding, shoeless foot. Her chair was near one of the front windows, and with a cold, blasting rhythm the sea banged those windows with black and white explosions of foam.

Seated fifteen feet from her, I caught her as a forlorn detail, an undigested lump in the attention I was unavoidably paying to the threatening clamor of the water. I've been on ships enough to know they're all unsinkable these days. I always say so, but

on mornings of bad weather my eye and ear go on responding as
if seafaring were still hazardous. And it was my anxious, un-
educable eye, scared of the sea, that began, all of itself, to marvel
at my swaddled companion.

She and I were practically the only occupants of the salon that
morning, though a few hardy old ladies were spaced unsociably
across its rear wall. I brooded and watched, and presently it occurred to me that the girl looked somehow like a caterpillar on a
drifting shingle—so forlorn—but nevertheless like a caterpillar
which had already had its chance as a butterfly and was revert-
ing back to a condition safer and cosier in these mid-Atlantic circumstances. She looked, for the moment at least, safe against
the morning wrath of water, and, if it hadn't been for the butterfly foot exposed, perfectly invulnerable.

Maybe the fortieth time my gaze gyroscoped in her direction I
saw a ruptured eye staring back at me out of the swirling coat.
When it was steadfast through the fiftieth, on that hint I spake.

"I suppose you're wondering where I got this military-looking
wrist watch which tells at which velocity one is walking if one
wishes," I said, approaching her chair in a series of lurches and
clutchings. She pulled even her foot inside the coat to make
room for me to sit on the footstool anchored against her chair. "I
got it from a chap in the army. Writing fellow who called himself
Corporal X and was medically discharged for that and other reasons. I understand he is now profitably employed repeating the
Jesus prayer without cease and flattering fat lady readers; but
wherever he is—I might say *who*ever he is—he don't need this
watch any more, for Gawd's sake."

The rapt eye looked at the watch—which I held right up at
the opening of the coat—and blinked. Then the impeccably
Aryan face was exposed while she said, "Have the bitches been
around with tea yet? Do you suppose the chemists would have
some aspirin?"

I explained to her how bloody *awful* aspirin was if—as I suspected—she was seasick. I offered Dramamine, which I just
happened to have a little vial of in my jacket pocket. She asked
what on earth that was and while I was explaining, I could see
her purposely, regally cast away the thread of my lay discourse
in favor of what it sounded like.

"An intellectual?" she asked. I showed her the heavy book I
was reading, but that didn't seem to pertain. "I know hundreds

of intellectuals in London, but no American intellectuals, though I know dozens of Americans."

I persisted in offering her the Dramamine, and she took it, at length, rather suspiciously, as if it were some miracle poison that could change her on the spot into a conformist or McCarthyite and spoil her taste for the Third Program. She set it just on the tip of her pale spiky tongue and tossed it backward like a musclebound child throwing a rock over his shoulder. Her eyes seemed to follow the pill back on its inner trajectory and fix on it when it landed—the first time I noticed her talent for absolute withdrawal when a memory or a visceral sensation claimed her.

It was weird enough to see this reaction, and momentarily she convinced me I had got the wrong vial somehow and had poisoned her. Her grip on that rug of a coat relaxed and it gaped in front.

"Is that a Campbell tartan?" I asked excitedly.

"Fortune and Beasly," she said. "It is rather *like* the Campbell tartan. I couldn't say what it is, really. I know the Duke of Argyll through H. E. Martin Pummer's daughter who was a deb three winters ago and knew his grandniece."

I said that London seemed to be a very small place where everybody knew everyone else, and she said Oh, it *was*. She peeked back at the pill again and said with conviction, "Most debs absolutely wear themselves out in their first season. They sleep with everybody, because it's the thing. I wouldn't sleep with everybody. They've lost their figgers and their complexions and look ancient. How old do you think I am?"

I told her not to be silly, that I knew very well she was twenty-eight, had a title that she preferred not to use—par*ti*cularly while traveling third class—that her father had been killed in the North African campaign, that she had a real boy's boy of a brother, and that she had been raised, after her untimely orphaning, by a noble aunt.

"That's not *quite* right," she said. "How did you know?"

I explained to her that she had once and for all been definitively described as one of the two kinds of English girl encountered by our forces during the war, and that the other kind had been somewhat older than she at that period, had had husbands overseas, and believed that if they remained standing they would remain guiltless.

"Knee-tremblers," she said with an explosive, extroverted

laugh. "You're entirely right, except, of course, I don't have a title, though Mother's great-great-great was noble in the eighteenth century and my father's great-uncle, who was in the forces, should have been knighted after Mafeking. Jealousy, you know. It's all politics there. My brother's not so boy any more. He's married a Bonstacker and opened a shop in Kent. Scabby girl, but no character, and they've produced an *enfant*. No future."

"Out of Harrow to a Kentish shop," I said, clicking my tongue with dishonest sympathy. I was braced against any I-knew-the-juke-in-London snobbery—braced a little too hard, like being braced for a pitch of the ship that didn't come.

"He would so have gone if the RAF pensions weren't so mean. It's rotten not to have a parent. Mother's gone out to Canada, you know, and *she's* all right, but Charles and I haven't et very high on the hog."

"You're going to join your mother?"

"Jesus H. Christ, no! I'm going to New York. All my friends said I wouldn't do it and here I am."

"High on the—? Jesus H. —?"

"Texas," Mesmé said. "One meets lots of Americans, though intellectuals very few."

I ventured that most of them had been cleaned out of the services at the same time as Corporal X, and she agreed, but said she knew a lot of Americans besides those in uniform—journalists, barristers, and movie people—and that none of them were intellectuals either. "I like Americans because they're so demonstrative, though. The English men—well, most of them—don't marry until fairly late, because they can't afford it or don't want to and in the meantime they develop a most in*diff*erent attitude. They don't *try*."

"Texas tried?"

"Oh," she said. She got to her feet and stood there, very tall, her ash-blond hair bordering those crazy eyes with a straight severity. "Tex came into the bar where I worked and, as he told my best friend, before he even saw my face, the moment he saw my hips, he said to himself, 'That's my girl.' He used to call me Slim." She flashed a sick smile, hummed a few bars of "Deep in the Heart of Texas," kicked her feet—I thought she had lost her balance from the pitching of the ship—and said, "See? The

English can still dance. That Dramamine of yours is no bloody good. I have to go to my cabin for some aspirin."

And with that she left me. I thought I might not see her again, except as one sees everybody again on a seven-day passage— going to meals, playing horse races, in the bar, the writing room, or on the deck if there is good weather.

But that same afternoon she descended on me in the smoking lounge, towing a young man whom I might as well call Corporal Y, since he is going to be the straight man of this narrative—the crude, uncouth, unquiet American. I'd had some talk with Corporal Y, since we sat together at a large table in the dining room, and so I knew that he had spent some months in Germany as an agent for a company that supplied local products for army PXs. Corporal Y hated Germans and was constantly pressing me to read a book called *The Scourge of the Swastika* which he said "finally" told the truth about Hitler's Germany. I said I had hated Germans for twenty years, but since I wouldn't read the book, he remained a little suspicious of my politics, and I was a bit sur*prised* to see him allow Mesmé to come to my table.

"Meet Lady Brett," he said, "for Chrissake. Hey, OK if me and Lady Brett *Ashley* proceed to forget the terrible wound I got in the goddam war by joining you for a goddam *pernod* or something?"

"He's an intellectual, too," I said to Mesmé, rising and bowing slightly as I pulled out a chair for her. "You got the wrong goddam war," I told Corporal Y. "Mesmé's nothing like the Lost Generation. She's more the detritus of Their Finest Hour."

"'Their Finest Hour.' Will lovable, crotchety Uncle Winston bow to the Loot Waffy? Will Paddy Funyoucame get his baling-wire and orange-crate Spitfire airborne in time to meet the dread Stukas?" Y demanded of his audience. "You know what Hitler planned to do to every potent male in England if he conquered?"

Mesmé said, "Aunt Cecile used to wear a pistol around the garden. She was going to shoot me if the Germans landed. We were just playing a guessing game of the capitals of your states and we couldn't agree on the capital of South Carolina. I said *you'd* surely know. So we've come in search."

"Charleston," I said. Corporal Y guffawed loudly and offered to bet me ten goddam dollars that it was either Columbia *or* Sumter, while Mesmé, he said, was holding strongly for Columbia.

"Do you know this other guessing game?" she asked, chewing off the tip of her left little fingernail. "The one in which it is the object to guess whose is a certain quotation? Who said, 'Kiss me, Hardy'?"

"Mrs. Hardy," Corporal Y said. He emitted an artificial yak and slapped my shoulder and Mesmé's knee.

"Lord Nelson," she said. "He had been struck at Trafalgar. He knew he was dying."

"But who was Hardy?" Y said. And in this pleasant way the three of us fell into the infinitely slow-paced comradeship which means so much on ocean voyages. In fact, by the time we'd had our third bourbon—a drink suggested by Mesmé, who 'lowed as how that was what they drank in Texas—we were all three sure we were fond of each other.

Y had begun to recite many limericks from a collection he had bought in Paris and memorized. Mesmé laughed at them so hard that our sheep-nosed waiter was lurking near the table to get the overflow of jollity. She asked, "What's that one again about the girls at Fortune and Beasly? Really I must learn that one. I've worked at Fortune and Beasly in the holiday season, you know. Tell!"

It came to me with one of those little jogs that show the pattern in which you've been hearing awhile that I hadn't, before the limericks, heard Mesmé *con*centrate on a single topic. I mean, now that it was dirty, she re*sis*ted the impulse to tell us who came into the store and what they said to her while she was on duty at Fortune and Beasly. ("Fulke-Binsmith, who used to live with Molly Proudflesh, has done certain art criticism for two or three of your better journals, *he* came in one day to buy Sally Gunn-Tewksbury a *souvenir sentimental* and saw me at the cosmetics counter and said . . .") Well, there was *none* of that now. She was listening to gospel.

I mean I already saw what would be confirmed later, that she was reverently listening for the single theme that could make both her memory and attention cohere enough to convince her that she *was* a survivor amid the English ruins. This story is going to have a numinous moment and a moment of illumination that I trust will make clear why Mesmé would lay off nail biting and stop reversing her eyes when the talk was sex. But for the time being, since what I knew of her was known because of certain unprovable intuitions I got that afternoon, it's got to be a kind of *pas de deux* for a while. On certain points you'll just have to take my word that I knew them until I get around to explaining why I was sure.

Through that afternoon and in the evening when the three of us got together after dinner, I kept watching and listening. When Mesmé egged Corporal Y on to tell about the time he played doctor with his little cousin in full view of the IC trains, I thought she had a goal in mind. She was like a tomboy daring her guileless buddy to leap off a bridge so she'll have nerve or at least justification to do the same. And as soon as he had ended with a self-amazed, Philistine chortle, she said, "I believe we haven't such a game in England, but I am reminded that when I was visiting the Earl of D——'s daughters, the eldest sat on my head while her sisters stuck straws up my arse. It was three to one. Most unfair. Though I suppose I didn't really mind. If it's one's natural bent. . . . One takes to that sort of thing like a duck to water and from an early age."

"How early?" I had to know.

"Nine. Well, not really, though an aggressive boy my age attempted to have at me. I suppose nothing really happened. Eleven. We'd been evacuated to my aunt's. George and I were put to sleep in the summer house because we were the children, though George could hardly be called a child. He was about to be called up. George was a sort of cousin, though the Bevilles——"

"No genealogy," I said. "Leave me with pity and terror." As a matter of fact, she had struck for the heart and nailed me. I saw the child in flight, the old evil confusions of the blitz. "Bad George." I could have shot him with Aunt Cecile's pistol.

"He had to go in service," Mesmé justified sulkily. "And it was pleasant. We didn't do anything really, anyway. I put my hand under the sheet as directed."

"My Cousin Imogene——" Corporal Y began. But by this time Mesmé was talking only to me. In implying a moral judgment, I had stirred up a bristling response.

"I did nothing definitive until I was twenty and had gone to London," she said. "I startled the physician who examined me in my first pregnancy by being *intacto*. '*Intacto*,' he said. I hadn't really done anything and it was most unfair that I should have got caught. Marriage was absolutely out of the question because he was colored. Not terribly. Merely a lovely, lovely shade of pale chocolate. Yum. At any rate, his father was a prince and it was out of the question his marrying *me*."

"Well, this here ticktacktoe—how could you get in trouble without . . .?" Corporal Y asked.

He tried to kick me under the table, but since Mesmé had her foot up my pants cuff, he kicked her instead. I'm not sure he realized that, but she interpreted his move correctly and, turning to him, blushing and defiant, said, "I suppose we were petting. What you Americans call necking."

"*I* call that *necking*? Wheeew. Taken this reader up too high. Need oxygen. Not *necking*. No, no, no, we neck them all," Y said. He began to twitch in his seat and turned, now and then, to make commanding gestures at the waiter, who ignored him. In a moment, assisted by a roll of the ship, he lunged up from his chair, and in a half crouch went lurching toward the bar to serve himself. He called back, "Hold it, hold it. I want to hear about this. I don't wanna miss a word. I mean, I need *instruct*ion."

"Was I that funny?" Mesmé asked.

"Very funny."

Both of us bent our attention to some matchbooks that just happened to be lying on the table among some soggy paper napkins, and I, at least, began to read mine. I mean, I didn't want her to think I was goading her to go on with any tales that might be painful to her. We were only strangers on the same boat. We weren't the goddam Canterbury Pilgrims.

I glanced up to see Y fighting and elbowing his way through the pile-up of after-dinner drinkers around the bar. I glanced at Mesmé's face and saw her skin glowing bright rose. "Take me somewhere and ——— me," she said.

I fitted the cover of my matchbook carefully under the striking strip and dropped the thing an inch and a half to the table top. I reread it carefully. It could have had the Ten Commandments on it. "Get a high school education at home," it said. I thought of Dexter, who never left our cabin—then of Billy and the King of Siam—all of the detriti of the humpty-dumpty empires.

"There isn't any place to go," I said. "'There's no upstairs to go to,'" I said.

But there always is. I mean, if you've really got through the wars with all your faculties intact except those that might save

you from peeking over the rosebush edge of the pit and discovering the female damned writhing below you, then you're capable of wandering around the windy and half-lit decks of a
goddam ship until you discover the cranny where the deck
chairs are stacked, tarpaulined, and roped down. You're capable
of anything, even coupling while you lean against the stacked
rungs of the deck chairs, both of you as much inside that monstrous coat as possible. I said, "Kiss me, Hardy."

And I gathered even then that it wasn't any friction or contact
of our goddamned epi*thel*iums that counted as much as the
moral fact of having done. It was to be a fact that won her certain
privileges of frankness and even *lèse-majesté* with American me.
She was paying in advance for an intellectual confessor to hear
the brag of herself, the pitiful brag that was all she had to set
against the terrors of emigration. She wasn't bringing very much
with her, she would confide later. Oh, she had been traveling
light since Cousin George was called up—lighter than ever now.

We didn't have to stay on deck very long for the moral accomplishment. Less than an hour, certainly. It was cold and we
would have got moody, and there was no point in *that*.

Apparently we were even looking to rejoin Corporal Y when
we climbed back down and went into the bar. He wasn't around.
Whatever he made of what he'd heard, he wasn't around much
for the rest of the voyage, though we saw him once a day, here
or there, with a homeward-bound girl from Barnard. He and I
would have a little talk—about Mesmé, of course—before we
reached New York, and I'll come to that later.

The bar had filled with people while we were gone. The only
point of relative isolation we could find was a long couch by the
window that looked onto the rear deck. We flopped onto it like
athletes returned from the games. Mesmé's cheeks—only her
cheeks now—were shining like spots of health paint.

"Now you've had a Limey," she said gravely.

"What were you telling me when we were interrupted?" I
said. "Pale, yummy chocolate prince, whose hand was ever at
his lips, bidding adieu . . . ?"

Now that she had earned the right, she didn't tell me everything. Only as much as there was time for and she could remember. And now that we have finished the squalid part of the story
and are ready for the love part, I will remove myself, insofar as
possible, and tell it as I heard it. I heard it in a voice which,

though it may never have breathed over Eden, has certainly breathed through our commercial dreams of what a lady *ought* to sound like; and even I, who probably heard more than anyone else has ever had time for, kept to the end doing double takes when she said things like "I'm very fastidious, but I let him —— in my hair" or "Donald and Esther ate each other's excrement. I shouldn't do so in any circumstances." I would think for a minute she'd said, "I'm very fastijjous, therefore only Yardley's Old Yeoman Downyflakes ever touch my dainty things," or, "Donald and Esther use tea bags; I demawnd Lipton's prime leaf, properly brewed." Now what I'm not trying to say is that the elegance and the apposite trenchancy of her phrasing redeemed the grossness of her goddam subject. I mean, redemption doesn't grow on any goddam trees, and you have to muster a lot of faculties to extract it. Just think, for the time being, that I heard a curious tension of opposites between manner and material of what she had to declare.

Our girl had gone down to London, then, after that first operation, which to the confounding of all expectations had to remove not only the royal chocolate polyp in the womb but nature's Aryan-pink demishield. Had gone down to seek her way because RAF pensions are mean and the money once set aside for her schooling had been badly dimished to pay for something the Health Plan didn't cover. Had gone (I mean to follow the straight road of how she told things, not yet involved with the deviousness of mere chronology, since I suspected all the while I listened to her that Time was the gray lecher she sweated under on those innumerable cots, beds, swards, tables, benches, and blankets where she, taken to water, had no more questioned her element than old Drake himself. I more than lightly toyed with the idea that it was really she who had tried to break this goddam wrist watch I got from Corporal X, and you know what *that* means)—had gone to the second abortion that both the frustration and the demoralization of the first had rendered as inevitable as the abortion of peace in our time. I mean the climax—the culminative disaster which or whose consequences she was running from now on her way to America—was the natural point for her to begin.

This second time she "'lowed as how" it had been the Texan done it, he who had called her Slim after he found her in the bar where she was working to support Jerry. (Jerry? Later. . . .) She was carrying a picture of Tex in her purse the morning she told me about *him*, not an ordinary snapshot, but a clipping from the *Express* that showed him with a slanting cartridge belt, low-slung holster tied above his knee with a bootlace, and wearing on his head what might have been either a cowboy hat or an Aussie bonnet. Since restrictions against killing niggers had tightened up in his home state, he had been off in Kenya scoring against the Mau Mau. The caption said he claimed ninety-two.

At the time she knew him he still seemed to have some hush-hush connections with either the CIA (for whom he had probably run guns into Cuba and Vietnam) or British Intelligence. He seemed to have plenty of money from somewhere and used to drop out of her sight for days on end with no explanations to her, and this at a time when they had become so firmly engaged he was able to persuade her that dutch cap and french letter were as abhorrent as bob-wire to a freeborn puncher from Texas. "Bastard even went up with me to call on Aunty and the Vicar," Mesmé said. "He charmed them, of course. So frank and open. Honestly, you Americans all tend toward candor and liberty. We do find you so."

Happy-go-lucky Tex didn't turn a hair when she gave him the big glad news. He just *disappeared*, as if the Commies were rampaging again and his fast gun was needed in the jungles or on the beaches. She was two and a half months along when Scotland Yard called to ask if she knew him and could account for his presence in London on a certain day in July. She could indeed, since she had marked all his "visits" in her diary, cross-referenced to her menstrual cycle. In exchange for her information she was finally told by Yardsmen that Tex was in jail. Whether or not she would be called as a witness depended on the Foreign Office. But, whether or not, he would undoubtedly have to serve time for passing bad checks, defrauding a landlord, and violating currency regulations.

Could she see him at his place of incarceration? Inadvisable, since that might upset his wife, she was told.

From the purse that had yielded Tex's picture, Mesmé produced another clipping, notably less worn than the first. This one was from the *Mirror*. Smiling staunchly into the camera was a wee, pretty Indonesian woman embracing two cold-eyed, double-holstered, booted and lank boys of about three and five years. Beneath this family grouping the caption read, "I Married a Cad."

"And to think, so might I have done," Mesmé said. "He was a

Libra and I was a Taurus. I should have known better from the beginning."

Plainly she could not go again with her trouble to her mother, who had once arranged "the best Harley street attendance" for the defloration-curettage that had saved a royal line from mongrelization. "And I hadn't thruppence to my name," she said. "I couldn't very well get a loan from Jerry, as he was terribly angry with me at just this point for what he called my treachery— though what I owed him after keeping him a year while he read every day in the British Museum, I can't say—and besides he hadn't thruppence either, poor dear, for Mavis Burke-Lancaster had just put him on the street as well. I had to sell my cello. Nasty instrument anyhow. I had never cared to play in public. The big, bulgy thing seemed somehow like personal ostentation. I might have had the creature, as Vive Roye-Cutter had and no one was the wiser until her Gran came on her in Charing Cross Road looking as if she'd swallowed a football. Poor thing, it died and Gerald buried it on the Embankment. None of that for me, especially as I was frightfully *off* Tex for what he'd done. He *had* played the part of a cad, don't you think? Quite deliberately?"

I said it looked that way, but I wondered if she had made the mistake of confiding in Tex her misadventure with the dark prince. She answered reflectively, "I might have done. I had no secrets from him and why should I, since I had every reason to believe we would marry?"

Sweet Thames, flow gently 'til I end my song. With the twenty-five pounds she got for the cello, she went to a midwife living in the country beyond Hampton Court. "I wasn't keen on it, but the time had come for decision." The midwife was most kind and sympathetic "considering the sort of person with whom she ordinarily came in contact," and a great deal of her excellence appeared to Mesmé in her not "preaching" as the Harley Street physician had done. "Defend me from those who know what's right and wrong," Mesmé said. "I once knew an older man who said he'd be justified in turning me over to the police. I've never in my life used that word *justified*."

The midwife gave her pain killers and told her to go home and wait. Home, at that time, was a gaunt, cold, and enormous flat she shared with six other girls and a medley of masculine names—"journalists, artists, writers, producers, all really quite

sedate except for Donald and Esther, though quite without a
penny. A school friend of Aunt Cecile's called one time and reported home that I was living in a brothel. Not a bit fair to say, of
course."

In this menage Mesmé had a room of her own, "not grand,
but adequate now that Jerry had left and had taken his books
and Tex never stayed overnight even before his incarceration.
He hated a single bed, and I must say that I got tired of it too in
the thirteen months Jerry stayed."

Alone in her room Mesmé waited until the pains "quite like
labor pains as I've been told of them" came. Then, in a borrowed
dish pan, and for the second time, in pain and travail she gave
back to nature what nature had so blithely entrusted to her. "I
didn't know what to do with it," she said. "The kitchen was at
the far end of the apartment, and I'd had to wait so long I heard
Rosemary and Roberta come home and some men talking. I covered it with a newspaper and went through, explaining that I'd
been sick. All very well, but it clogged the sink, and I stood there
poking, poking, you know, wondering if I should faint. The girls
were frightfully worried about me, though I don't think they
knew—thought I'd gone a bit off, I dare say. They were most
gracious about bringing me biscuits while I was confined to my
room later. There's a special sort of hard, dry, I think quite tasteless, little biscuit called Grugg's Delight that I'd become keen on
during the war. Rosemary brought me I can't think how many
tins of them in this trying period."

I said I could certainly see why she wanted to go to America, and she said that while she'd been eager to see New York
and the West for some time, it had actually been Tex who had
fixed her determination. "He had such stories to tell. Life over
there seems so much more exhilarating. Perhaps it's your open
spaces." I could only concede that maybe they *were* the key to
our basic American natures.

From a climax, even if it's only to a goddam story you hear in
a bar on a boat wallowing westward through a gray snowstorm,
there's nowhere much to look except back. And you know what
follows is going to be more upbeat just because it really, once
upon a time, preceded instead of following. What followed—
running backward in Mesmé's tale—was poor Jerry kicked out,
if you'll remember, of his cozy berth with Mesmé by the appear-

ance on the scene of the overwhelmingly frank and candid
Texan. Right now, on this day that we braved the Atlantic chill,
old Jerry was established on some *guru* in the Midi, living high
on the *guru*'s hog, eating wheat germ and blackstrap molasses.
The *guru* was giving Jerry some final pointers on how to shape
up the mystical book he'd been working on for so many years,
and had put him in touch with an international set of Zen fags
who thought his book might "go" if it was pushed right. In London, where everyone knew everyone, there were those who
blamed Mesmé for making Jerry homeless. "But after all, it was
summer," she said. "Jerry loved to cycle and he had a sleeping
bag that the Persian had given us. There's always somewhere to
sleep in the country, and from there it's only an hour and a half
ride in to the museum."

I said she must have been getting more or less deformed sleeping two in a single bed for all that time. She brightened at my
interest, said, Oh yes, there was that aspect, but actually she had
always rather looked forward to coming home late from work and
finding him there, sacked in and warmer than a hot-water bottle.
They read a great deal together during the nights. All his friends
were publishing in *Horizon* and the *New Statesman* and they read
these new things as well as Nietzsche, Dostoevsky, Madame
Blavatsky, Lawrence, Kierkegaard, Henry Miller, and Yeats' and
William Blake's prophetic works. "I shouldn't like to say we
merely read," Mesmé emphasized. "Indeed, Jerry was very
good for me, very tender. We did seem to get rather bored with
orgasms after all the trouble we'd been to getting adjusted, but
at second hand I got it from Alex DuVerde that they'd lunched
and while comparing notes on me, Jerry said that my —— always reminded him, rather, of the sporting club at Monte Carlo.
Edwardian in its amplitude and elegance. Poor Alex simply hec-
tored the wits out of Jerry trying to get the secret of how he
made me come, when for all those months with *him* I hadn't. He
said Jerry didn't understand it either, and I assured him I did
not, unless it was that Jerry was less aggressive. Alex used to
read me all the pertinent medical literature and send me out for
nights with someone else. And with them I always did, and
when I reported so, he was *furious*. I told him the watched pot
never boils, and that made him no happier. Do you suppose I
refused just *so* he would be wretched about it? He used to bully
me so with that dirty old Freud and an American volume that

I understand is found in every middle-class home; naturally I should seek some method of vengeance."

I said that seemed natural to me.

"I suppose Alex was fond of me, in his own way, though," she said dreamily. "When I saw him two weeks ago he said, 'Mes, you should know me now that I have money.' You see, I was supporting him, too, and he felt badly at the recollection. He was a sort of literary critic and I understand that he's doing very well these days. Cyril Connolly has mentioned him. He had to have at me one more time before embarkation to see if he couldn't bring it off, but it was no go."

I said it was nice they had parted friends anyhow, and she said they didn't really, for once again Alex had been unable to resist quoting Freud, probably only because he knew the great man's grandson, and she was certain (as I was, too) that Freud could not explain her.

"Only John Keats could," I said. "Your hair is long, your eye is wild."

She blinked her goddam gratitude at me for being intellectual enough to offer such grist for free association. She said, "I was once one's mistress, though never child, but I shan't say a word about him, for to talk about them is to talk against them, somehow, and he was most pitiful. *His* father had been shot down, too, over Tripoli. He taught in a boy's day school and it made him quite frantic. Of course Alex was always dabbling, you know, but that was rather different. He had such a lively curiosity. No doubt that's what gave me an attraction for him."

"Your privates, we."

"One may feel oneself basically a simple wretch who merely wants to get married and raise numerous children. And yet things happen."

Before Alex had moved in to peep and botanize there had been a doctor and a dentist who, between them, had put her in excellent health, remedying certain defects which she supposed were the result of wartime austerity, and supplying her with dentifrice and vaginal jelly enough to last a normal lifetime. Before them (or coincidental with them, since they were professional men who required neither food nor lodging from her and thus left her with a certain freedom of movement) there was the fashion designer.

"He liked my figger since no one else in the shop could wear his furs quite as I could. I appeared before the Queen Mother in a sable stole that rather drowned Priss and Con. Our Meg was there. Did you know she was practically a midget, poor thing? Comes only to one's armpit."

The designer's wife was also fond of Mesmé, but made neither advances nor protests in spite of knowing all, and to this menage a fourth member was added, a Greek nephew. "Rather like a golden, glowing fruit," Mesmé described him. "One seldom sees a tighter skin on a man—or boy, as the case may be better put. He had absolutely no mind at all. He smiled continuously, in the blandest way."

Before—I mean, if we didn't have to use that word and could just let it stand that my symbolic time piece hadn't been running all this while, I suppose I could convey better both the way I heard all this from Mesmé and the way it must have happened. I mean, anybody who's read *The Magic Mountain* knows how time is on a boat (just like in a TB sanitarium, tricky and ductile) and might very well find their intelligence insulted if I pretended we just sat on that long couch in the bar, like sitting at a multiple feature movie running backward, while I heard all her tales in sequence. I mean, even if Dexter and Billy almost never left *my* cabin, Mesmé shared hers with only an old lady, who was just mad about horse racing, bingo, and the dining-room steward.

I could go on plenty about how going furtively through the passages of our ship and into her cabin was like going through a time construction, through transitional or durational periods until I found where linear dimensions became spatial and something between us could *hap*pen. But all that's been done *before*. And yet I don't want to just throw out all the befores, because there was *a* time that all Mesmé's *temps retrouvés* were heading back for in just the same way—or rather in just the opposite way—that the ship was going on a compass track toward New York.

So, *before* serving time in the world of fashion, before the remedial work on her physical person and the broader outlook on sex given her by the professional men, before her subsidies of literary criticism and mystic thought, she had gone to France once with a "nasty little dilettante," presumably on their way to a Casals festival. They got only as far as Paris and the Hotel des Étrangers. "Nor did I get to see the Louvre," Mesmé told me. "Underneath all his pretenses, Edmund was mean to the core.

He didn't even like French cookery and we ate most often in the bistros near Pigalle that specialized in hamburgers for American servicemen."

She paid Edmund off for his meanness by deserting him one night in the Flore in favor of a Swede touring Europe in an ancient Buick with two Afghan hounds. That adventure ended in Geneva when "I realized my flight was mere escapism. It's not my nature to fly reality, and that is exactly what I had done. You understand?"

With drugs?

She shook her lovely head. "I never needed those."

But before escape, in the idyllic period of her first London months, she had slept lightheartedly around "amost like a deb, but there are certain men in London whose specialty is to sleep with everyone and I was careful to avoid such. I know many stories came back to me at secondhand from someone's saying, 'After all, everyone else sleeps with me. Why not Mesmé?'"

I said it was a good thing to regard oneself as an orchid and not as one of the common daisies of the field. She said, "Exactly!"

"Nevertheless," she said with a slanting, giddy grin, "one has a certain sense of control when one is able to sleep with as many as three friends in a day without one's emotions being shredded. I never thought of getting married in those days and generally I came with glorious ease."

She sat bolt upright in her berth one night and hugged her torso as if in a gesture of love quite beyond anything she had felt in my arms. Her ash-blond skin was goose-pimpled. Her splay fingertips sunk in smoothly ridged dimples of flesh, and she dragged her muscles so hard that her ribs looked like the phony gill lines scored on some kind of antediluvian reptile.

"Hurry up, please, it's time," I said. Mrs. Brindleman, her cabin mate, usually came down from Bingo at ten-thirty, and we tried to allow her at least a half hour variable to be on what Mesmé called the safe side, understanding so little of either safety or its value.

"I don't mind its being *time*," she said awfully. "It's a nasty paradox. I could come with so many others I don't love. Why can't I come with you? Can you figger it?"

I didn't say anything. I don't have a faculty for taking on because someone loves me.

"It's most unfair. It's always been unfair. The night they chose to tell me about my father was when George spilled everything to aunty. They shouldn't have done."

I said they certainly shouldn't.

"The wretched beast had put me up to it, too. I could hardly have got much fun from tossing *him* off. And yet, such fun as it was—they didn't have to punish it *so*. What are you thinking, darling?"

"Get dressed," I said. "Hurry."

"Don't you think it's unfair?"

I thought it would be further unfair if Mrs. Brindleman caught us as we were. She was not a lady who would understand why we had to undress and go through all these motions just so Mesmé could tell me how she felt when her father was killed.

When we were safely dressed and out of there, she dragged hard at my arm, as if blaming me for bringing her out just when she was on the edge of finding what was *wrong*. I think she would have gone back then and there and Mrs. Brindleman be damned, to try once more to get the secret.

"You know more about me than anyone in terms of brute detail," she said. "Can't you explain it to me without allusion to Freud?" Old Beardy was not going to have her as long as that roving hand could reach beneath the sheets of her new-found land for what had been taken away that night in the summer house. But I wasn't going to let on to her what I knew. I mean, when you're on public transportation you don't crouch in the corridors to clutch your belly and howl. I wasn't going to discredit my countrymen and Tex's by any disparaging predictions, either.

"About your daddy," I said. "It was the krauts that killed him, you know."

"Yes." She sounded like she was glad to have that straight again.

"*You* didn't do it."

"They shot him under the ear. He had parachuted safely, you know. It wasn't the worst time in the war for them, either. They might have taken him prisoner. They shouldn't have done. . . ."

Well, as Corporal Y never tired of repeating, it's taken a long time to get the *real* dope on the scourge of the swastika. That same night after I'd got tanked up enough to stop saying the Jesus prayer (which I pronounce with a high, whistling sibilant) and had taken Mesmé back properly to her cabin where she would sleep above Mrs. Brindleman, I ran into coarse, crude Y and we had our talk.

"You know something about that girl of yours?" Y said.

"She's not my girl. She's being met at the dock. There's a man who's been after her for years. He's flown over to Hollywood and will be back in New York."

Corporal Y gave me one of those gross, shocked but insensitive looks with which he is so prodigal. "Oh," he said. "Anyway, you know something? That girl is sad."

"It only hurts when she laughs."

"I mean, her story is *moving*."

"She tell you all the gore, too? About the drain stopping up?"

He nodded. "She tells everybody. She's compulsive, and I mean that's what's so goddam sad. I should think you'd be full of lousy tics and twitches if you cared anything about her at all."

I held out my hand to show him. My knuckles were snapping all by themselves with a noise like celery being snapped. I hoisted a drink to my lips by using my necktie as a sling to elevate my right hand, but my lower lip kept jerking so fast that I spilled part of it anyway.

"That's better," Y said approvingly. "You know Mesmé wouldn't be such a de*praved* orphan if it wasn't for what happened to England and her during the goddam war. Did you ever think of what her life might have been like if she'd kept on in school and practiced her cello and her father was maybe an air marshal now? You know he was a brigadier when the krauts murdered him. I mean, did you ever *think* about that?"

I said I hadn't given it as much study as it probably deserved, but once I got safely back on dry land I would sit down to think about it lots.

"If you think about it you'll see that why she's a nympho is her goddam aunt caught her practically in bed with the cousin and gave her a hell of a guilt feeling by telling her right on the spot that her old man is dead. So she keeps trying to repeat that night—that one lousy night—trying to make it come out different, so that after she's been had someone will, like, whisper in her ear that her daddy's safe. I mean, he parachuted down and according to the rules of the Geneva convention they got him in a PW camp with his gallant buddies planning how they're gonna fool the slow-witted Bavarian guards and escape, see?"

I said even if I could see it I didn't know what it was I saw.

"Don't know *what?* What part of it? Whether I'm right or not? Listen, my ex-wife taught psychology at Western *Reserve*. I did plenty of reading trying to keep up with that girl. Mesmé's fixated on that one moment out of all time, when, for every English girl, it is still beddy-bye time on September sixth, 1939, or whatever day the war hadn't started, and Daddy's up there in his unsinkable Beaufighter and the smuggled copies of *Lady Chatterley's Lover* have made the simultaneous orgasm practically a national goddam institution. And whatever it may have been for the lower orders, for people of Mesmé's class, England was still merry. Why shouldn't she want that back again?"

"I don't know," I said. "I just don't think she wants it any more. And I'm sleepy, and we have probably passed the Nantucket Light. I've got to go to bed."

Well, we know what intellectuals go to bed for. It's to think. That's what we get drunk for, too, and as I came into my cabin that night, bouncing off the walls, I could see I was really ready for the old skull practice.

It was awfully late, but as I entered I heard *The King and I* going full blast, and there was little Billy with the machine in his lap and Dexter in his top berth practically covered with plates, cups, and saucers. They said that since this was our last night on board they had decided to celebrate and probably wouldn't sleep a wink. Dexter belched and said, "Laddie, m'scouts tell me you've been knocking off 'er lidyship. Har, har."

I reeled into my bunk and said word certainly got around, didn't it?

"The stewards keep their eyes peeled, they do. Laddie, let me give you a bit of advice. English girls wot's traveling third class, they ain't often no better'n tarts, whatever they talk like. There ain't no bleedin' morality left in our time. So don't let her hook you, lad. Tike your bit of pleasure and go your way."

I said that certainly *was* sensible advice and I rolled into my berth and covered my head. Even though I had so much I could have thought about, I decided it had better wait until it didn't have to compete with "the chill-duh-run, the chill-duh-run." For his celebration, Billy was playing it louder than ever.

It was Sunday morning when we came into the harbor, and *you* know what New York looks like on a cold, crisp *Sun*day morning. It looks like something abandoned on a dead planet— all that stone and no movement. It was so still. When Mesmé and I walked out on deck to have a look, we had just about passed Canal Street; then they shut off the screws and we coasted slower and slower into the Hudson current. It really was ghastly quiet then. There weren't even any gulls that morning.

"It's very un*like* London," Mesmé said uncertainly. She had made herself up gaudily to face her new home—bright-green eyeshadow, black penciling in the corners of her eyes, and a real paste of lipstick for her unchaste mouth. "In London they shouldn't be allowed to build so recklessly. I must say it looks a bit forbidding."

"Just tell yourself there are many warm, kind, friendly people dwelling in those cliffs," I said, already anticipating Nathan, I suppose. I mean, with all my pent-up thoughts and with my increased sensibility that could detect (hell! could hear, like the slam-bang from the village smithy) the ticking of my symbolic wrist watch, I knew the numinous moment was practically on me, so why shouldn't I speak from second sight?

I said, "Somewhere in that forest of glamorous stone, perhaps snoozing at this very moment, while visions from Masoch and Sade dance through the glades of his dreams, is the man you've been unconsciously looking for ever since that night in the summer house."

"One has to trust to fate," she said, with an ever so tiny smirk.

"And one dare not learn from experience," I said loyally. "I hope with all my heart I'll see you again often. But we'll never know as much about each other as we know just now."

She put her gloved hand fondly on my bare wrist.

"I don't have any more faith in Freud than you have," I said, hearing the crazy bang of that old timepiece under her fingertips. "But he can sometimes help us make up fables about ourselves. For kicks, I mean. I myself pass much time in Village bars and at home in Freudian speculation. It would be most valuable to me, *when* I think about you, if I knew the answer to one elusive question. Now if Tex and I—each in our characteristic American way—represent some facet of the ideal man you're seeking, may I infer that you want, not your father, but the man who killed your father?"

Projected against the rosy and buff towers of our island, motionless as goddam stalagmites, there was nothing less than a vision of beautiful orphans running to present themselves with servile curtsies to some two-gun, hypocritical intellectual. Their clear voices sang, "Daddy's dead and you are now king of the wood."

So much for retaining the faculty of seeing visions. They just generally upset you and make you say silly things like "Mesmé, take the next boat back" to a girl who's just arrived.

And you take a girl who knows what she wants, and she shakes off such advice like a duck shaking water off its back. For instance, Mesmé kept staring at the Sunday-morning shark's teeth of the Manhattan skyline, and pretty soon I knew she was rolling over in her mind my encouraging comment about the man who might be there waiting for her. The not literally impossible he who was morally prepared to match and mate the circumstantial devastation of her life.

Her eyes rolled back to follow the dream. Her lips rounded in a gloating smile. "I'm just a poor wretch who wants to get married and have lots of children," she said.

I said, "Kiss me, Hardy," and she reminded me that she already *had*, quite enough.

When Old Age
Shall This Generation
Waste

"She looks like you," David Swift said to his hostess about the eager-eyed blond girl Ed Maroon had brought to her party. Because his mind was lean and limber, as it habitually was on the second drink of an evening's program, he registered this resemblance less as a fact inherently significant than as a fact on which playful and imaginative significance might be built up—as in a child's game a coincidence of sounds or numbers can begin the invention of fabulous lives and relationships. "Like one of the first times I ever saw you. At that party in Mick's room."

"She's Midwestern and exophthalmic," Joy agreed. "In what other way?"

"You both intend to have the world."

"Stop promoting me," Joy said. "'Grant me an asylum for my affections.'" Absently she surveyed the menagerie of her single oversized room with its clumps of standing, sitting, and reclining figures composed uncertainly in silhouette against the fireplace glow or in the goldfish bowls of light from half a dozen wall and floor lamps. "Sweet narcosis is more my line, David. And she shows a good fifteen years younger than I—look at that skin. What makes you talk so funny, sweet man?"

He smiled fondly and patted her bare shoulder. "I was cuing you in on the origins of my lust after her. So you won't take it as disloyalty if I back her into the kitchen."

"Do," Joy said. "But gently. Ed's been making noises about marrying someone. Maybe this one."

"'I don't hear no golden bands—'"

"'—settling on them soft dumb hands'? Maybe not," Joy said. "Make what you can of it. I want you to be happy. What a dull party this is going to be. Will it go?" Again she looked hungrily, like a witch tainted with scientific heresy, at the still-civilized behavior of the others in the room. Then with her trademark giggle of a girl catching herself in unbecoming solemnity she added, "You can still hear the piano and it's going for eleven-thirty, waaaaaaaaaaat?"

"It will go. You've got the quartet here. For fragmentation."

"Oh, those boys."

"If you want to draw blood just keep having them around."

"They're kicks," Joy said. She patted his sleeve and, as though he had reminded her of a mingled duty and temptation, found a path toward the piano where the boys of the quartet were playing. They were a unit here because they ordinarily showed up at parties in the Village together (though they cruised separate bars), because they had once been employed together carrying spears at the Metropolitan, and because each of them found in sympathizers like Joy a diffusing medium that permitted them to be socially together without falling on each other with either lust or jealousy.

Now in their fortress corner of the room one of them hammered softly on a martini pitcher with the mixing rod. Another accompanied him on the piano, picking out with one finger the melodies of old show tunes. The other two leaned in, waiting for the moment to sing or make funnies that would draw into the square of their loneliness at least a few stragglers from the dialectic around them.

As Joy came to them they turned to welcome her, David

thought, like naked squabs greeting a parent. As so many have for so long, he thought. But what loaves, fishes, or worms has she really delivered?

For the next hour he moved from one group to another around the room with selective detachment. It was understood—by the waspish self-consciousness that had long ago fought the censor in his mind to an armistice—that he was a pilgrim on his way to Ed Maroon's girl, but it was a part of the terms that he must come at her indirectly.

He left a group discussing Indochina with a restatement of his warning, made twenty years ago, that the Communists were pretty Red. "And their children dance," he added, swept by a momentary shock of compulsion to expound on this text, but rejecting that in favor of leaving Job to be enjoyed by them as nonsense. He said to Gail Hunter and her new husband that it appeared to him modern artists took a lot of liberties with nature. That had to be categorized as a vice, he said, and if vicious were horses no one would ride. But they honestly did want to make a point, between themselves, about Motherwell, so he went to a far, secluded alcove off the room to confide in Mimi Hawk that even before he had read Kafka he had suspected people were not what they pretended to be. Mimi's escort, an instructor from Columbia, challenged him to explain this or get off the pot, but he would only leer and say that Kafka was deep. Terribly. Could anyone deny that and still pretend to intellectual responsibility?

Then, sick with himself for having only a mustache and an equivocal reputation as a wit to show how far he had come in thirty-eight years, he turned directly to the search for Ed's girl. He was fairly sure that now or presently she would be drifting unclaimed, since Ed's young and pretty girls were chosen to signify a pre-eminent manliness in him, and he did not really require them to be attentive once he had found his subject and begun to talk.

She was sitting by a tree floor lamp that cast one beam to the right and one to the left, spotting her and Joy equally, and again David was struck by their resemblance. The girl would pass for Joy's daughter, he thought, if it were not for some felt, intenser likeness which persuaded one that something stricter than a blood kinship had meant them to appear the same. The two of them sat in awning-striped chairs and naturally neither of them paid any attention to the other. From twin postures of relaxation their blue eyes watched the party with the same rapacity and the same need; and, at this moment, from each leaped a terse, female derision against the men who were foolish enough, for the moment, to ignore them.

But much as they look alike, David thought, the girl doesn't look the way Joy *did* fifteen years ago, and out of loyalty to Joy he could have added that she had looked then like the believer she was. She had believed in politics (a synonym for Roosevelt), in art (that is, Gustin, Kollwitz, and Picasso), and in the supremacy of personal relationships (or her first husband and David himself, the important single weekend when she had dragooned him into going to Boston with her "to find out what we really have").

Now she seemed to believe in very little except parties like this one, in the expense of spirit, alimony, and the trivial surpluses of her pay from a trade magazine to gather this team whose very presence in one apartment was like a ceremony to the failures of promises. Once he had suggested to her that she ought to paste a partyful of her friends onto a collage and call it "The Death of FDR," and when she had simply nodded, said, "Fair enough," he was sure she knew as well as he how deeply she had chosen to commit herself to the impossibilities her collections represented.

There had been a time when he wished this could be a sufficient reason for breaking with her once and for all, for never coming back to one of her parties. What prevented him was knowing too well what she had wanted and what she had looked like, with her eyes so bugged out and blue, at twenty.

When he "hummmmmed" beside the girl's chair, both she and Joy glanced at him. Then Joy looked back toward the quartet's noise, more desperately strident now.

"We need refills, don't we?" David asked.

The girl swished the contents of her glass experimentally. "I really oughtn't. I really ought to get Ed out of here." She studied his face and found him sympathetic enough to permit her adding confidentially, "I guess you know how hard it is to break him off when he's enjoying himself. I could get *loaded* if he decides to stay too long."

Together then they looked across at Ed, saw him lean into his conversation, hitching at his belt as though he could earn money that way. In full voice he was saying, "She hadn't even read it well enough to know what I was talking about and she sits there telling me to search my soul. And I said, 'I've searched my soul and now I know what I want to be. I want to be an earnest, liberal, voted-for-Stevenson career woman who don't know from owl turds about fiction, so I can get a keen editorial job and throw the blocks to writers.' She gave me the whole Smith class then, two hundred and sixty-nine of them, all being superior to a hick that writes what she for Christ sake is supposed to have sense enough to know how to buy, pulp fiction. Anyway, she was bigger than me and when I saw that old left shoulder go up over her chin, I died. Man, I died."

"A cube of ice would *freshen* it," she said. "OK. I'll join you."

In the white illumination of the kitchen that reflected in the same wavelengths from cupboards, stove, sink, walls, and refrigerator, some of the girl's prettiness came apart like ribbons peeled down from a gift. He saw the excess of fat that blurred the definition of her nose and brows. Both her eyebrow penciling and lipstick looked more humorous than witching, and seeing this he felt something like gratitude to her. He promptly kissed her, but the contact was lukewarm as a daily thanksgiving.

Gently she disengaged herself and said earnestly, "After all, David, I came with Ed."

"Yes, Pat."

"Well, that's the way it is."

"Are you going to leave with him? What if he never finishes kicking down the—uh—enemies of light?"

Pat shrugged her full, childish shoulders. "Don't say that. I like him to find someone he can discuss with. I worry that I'm not much companionship since my mind doesn't work like his. You know. On abstract things."

"Like money? Like contracts? Isn't that what he was so impassioned about?"

"He talks about everything. I'm willing to wait through what I can't understand."

"It's love?"

Pat seemed embarrassed by the naive word and lowered her

head. With a fiery, short fingernail she bobbed the new ice cubes in her glass. "I respect him a great deal, his being a writer and all, and what he stands for, his sense of fair play."

The ribbons are really unloosed now, David thought, and this little package wrapped a touching decency. Once more he could not help a comparison of her with Joy, who used to say the same about Ed, but who now was apt to call him "the fellow-traveling bore" or a hack, clutching him probably for that reason in her circle of misfired painters, musicians, and heterosexuals.

"Don't you think his writing is fine?" the girl said. "The way it shows all this sympathy with the underdog?"

Her blue eyes demanded that he help her keep faith, and tolerantly enough he said, "Yes."

Then some trick sprung by the earlier identification of her with Joy, which he had considered purely intellectual and therefore under control, surprised him into saying, "Yes, but . . ." And the fat was in the fire. The very strictness of her honesty (which had been Joy's once) demanded that he try to be honest too.

"It's fine, but it's only a pocketbook formula. Ed himself would tell you that about his books. I can't believe that every thug and hoodlum rapist who gets caught is Christ crucified. Neither does Ed believe it."

"What do you mean?"

"I like Ed. Ed's my friend." His hands flew wide in a testimony of good will, a gesture that might convey the absolution which he was giving Ed's *soul*. It annoyed him that he had made such a gesture and he tucked his empty hand under the arm with which he held his drink. "Ed's one of my oldest friends, so I can say this. Taking him seriously isn't the same thing as taking him seriously as a writer. You know—hasn't he told you—why only two of the novels he's written since the war got published?"

"People are reactionary," Pat said. "They don't like his message."

"It's not exactly that, dear."

"What is it, exactly?" He saw that she was disturbed, perhaps angry now by what she must think of as a disloyal attack on Ed. And he wanted to tell her, I'm only explaining this because you're more precious than Ed, younger, better than any of us, so you have to know where we all went wrong.

"It's *exactly*"—a humorously self-deprecatory inflection there which she would have to take as a promissory note, the token of inner humility—"it's exactly that Ed is half a step off each time he sets his foot inside a publisher's door. Look, dear, he's written eight novels since the war. I've read them all. Like I say, I'm his friend."

"What do you do?" Pat said suspiciously.

"Photographer's agent. I scoot around town and find jobs for them with magazines. But this is no qualification here or there. I'm Ed's *friend*. We were in college together. I always wanted him to do the great good thing. More and longer than you."

This last appeal seemed to work on her. She nodded humbly and licked her lips. "I guess probably. Go on."

"He wrote one about Hiroshima. It came a little bit late, just before the Korean war. He wrote one about the Commie general in Paris but left out the part where he behaves sadistically with the boys in *La Reine Blanche*. One about a veteran on the trail of killers but couldn't think of anything for him to do for kicks except shoot naked blondes with his forty-five. He wrote one about a homosexual who wanted to get well. Another about a cripple who masturbated on the pad of his crutch, but everyone told him it was too dirty to print. Then he did a summary of the life of King Saul for the Bible Sex trade, but he couldn't patiently dig a gimmick on it because he can't stand to read the Bible. All that work and . . ."

She had suspended listening some way back to corner a thought, holding it in a passionate suspension, waiting for him to be through so she could lave him with its overwhelming sweetness.

She said enthusiastically, "All right. He doesn't think all his characters are Jesus, but don't you yourself think there's a lot that needs saying for people who never had a chance?"

"Lots."

"Yes." She glowed with her triumph, forgiving him, it appeared, for anything he might have said, since clearly he too was pure at heart in spite of all his talk. "That's why I love Eddie's position. I know I may be talking like a schoolgirl, but that's not the awfulest thing in the world, is it?"

"By no means," he said, believing. He drank on that, feeling both purged and, now, forgiven.

A flush of heat had spread upward from her throat like a further and this time conscious sacrifice of prettiness for a higher cause. She shook her close-cropped head. "Besides his books, Ed and I have discussed things enough so I know how he feels about life. He's helped me *so much* with my own thinking." Earnestness half-choked her voice. Prettily she coughed and smiled at this fault. She said waifishly, "You may know him better than I. But I know he *means right*. I guess you can put some more stuff in my drink. Then we'd better go back. Ed doesn't like me to wander off."

He lost track of her for a while then, except by some inward contact with the sustenance of that healthy error she had offered him as an antidote for the rest of the party. To be as wrong as she was, as innocent of complications, was tonic, he thought, and justified a faith in the eternal renewal, which in turn justified him in taking more drinks than he had meant to allow himself.

He heard the tall Welshman to whom Ed was talking cry out, "Let them call me before a committee, and believe me, fellow, I'd stand up to them. I can't understand you chaps. Is it your country or isn't it? Isn't it, after all?" He knew Ed's answer down to its last polished evasion, and he felt with quick wonder that the polish didn't matter. Those who don't know what it's about will save it, he thought.

They come on, he thought, the innocent and ruthless young, gathering us up with them as they sweep over our mistakes and cowardice with each other. The image of Pat (and the others, this shouting Welshman with the twist of ears hardly emerging from his curls, all the others) sweeping on in an undamaged tide, unspoiled, moved him almost to tears. He almost wept then for the young man who, somewhere, might be for him the fresh counterpart that Pat was for Joy. David Swift without the holes in his head or life.

" 'You think I'll weep,' " he said to Gail Hunter, apropos of nothing but his own thoughts and the fast metabolism of alcohol. " 'No, I'll not weep. This heart shall crack into a hundred thousand flaws or e'er I'll weep.' "

"Why weep?" she said to this nonsense. "Look."

She was pointing to the quartet, on the floor now, more or less under the piano, which a while before they had been on top of. One of them, kneeling by the piano's side, was pantomiming two people kissing goodnight. He had wrapped his long arms around his back and was fingering his spine while his three friends tinkled and screamed with laughter, shilling for a more attentive audience.

Pat tucked her skirts primly and sat on the floor with them. Her round face shone willingness to be delighted, and David, watching, envied and blessed her once more.

It was much later, a little past two, while he was climbing the stairs back to Joy's apartment, that he encountered Pat again. At this hour he was content that the party's peak was over. He saw the rest of the night diminish away like a drooping plateau down which he could roll comfortably and effortlessly as a rubber ball. Already some of the guests were gone. He had walked down as far as the corner with Gail Hunter and Matthew. They had said a few things indicating that this might be the last of Joy's parties they would come to. Not that they were revolted or indignant— no, it was hard to describe, but there didn't seem to be any *use* in her parties. They didn't *mean* anything. Matthew had seemed like a good fellow. Maybe old Gail knew what she was doing this time, after three grueling and patently doomed efforts to stay married. He hoped so. She deserved a replacement on the scene, too. She'd done her stint.

Above the first landing of the stair, Pat bore down on him like a furious stranger. The brindle light of the hall reshaped again the personality she wore in his eyes, and seeing her in such expressive motion he thought, not displeased at all, she's told Ed Maroon off. She's leaving the sunken ship, too. A young fate on her way. Then he realized that she was going without her coat.

Clearly she was angry, and though she stopped to speak to him, her pause had some quality of illusion, the camera's arrest of a body in flight, a static lie without influence on the real forces that shaped trajectories in the physical world.

"Where on earth?" he questioned.

"It's *those fellows*." It was almost comic how precisely her emphasis identified the quartet.

"Don't let them grind you down."

"I'm mad. They really got my Irish up. Let me go. I'm going to wait at the front door for Meredith Stark. We'll see about this."

"Stark?"

"You know. The movie star."

Suddenly alerted to the grotesqueness of what she was saying, feeling an initial compassion, David put his hand on the duckling plumpness of her shoulder. He turned her toward the stair light to examine her, believing that she was out of her mind from drinking.

"I've just spoken to Mr. Stark," she said. "When I explained the situation to him he agreed to come over." She was very close to crying, but except for the peculiarity of what she was saying, she did not seem to be drunk.

"Do you know Stark? Mr. Stark?" David asked cautiously.

"Of course I don't, but I think he has the same rights as anyone else. As you or me."

"Sure. But who—"

"Those *fellows*. One of them is even his agent, but when they began to say those ugly things about him I saw red. Honestly red. That's a dirty thing when he's not here to defend himself."

"Said—"

"Said he wasn't *normal*." The last word came as from a dutiful child who is reporting a forbidden term strictly in the line of duty but who feels nonetheless the imminence of punishment.

"Oh." The reason and the method of her duping became clearer than why or how she had impressed herself enough on the quartet to make them choose her as a victim. As he began to shape a soothing explanation for her, though, a sound like the breaking of phonograph records, glasses, and the toppling of table lamps came down the stairs from Joy's apartment to remind him that Joy set up her parties to cause such improbable chances for involvement.

"You shouldn't mind what the lads say," he told her. "You don't care what they think. Besides, Stark is a public personality, and don't you think everyone in such a position *will* be smeared, now and then? It can't hurt him because he'll never know."

"He *knows* already," she said in a martyr's whisper, pulling herself free, without a show of anger toward David, but with the air of one who has heard the whisper of treason. "I told him what they were accusing him of. Naturally he resented it. Can't you see? I merely want him to be able to come into that room up there and defend himself like *people*. I don't know anything about him being a public personality. I think he's got a right to state his case."

David sighed. "Well, dear. You believe all this? Well, if he's coming over—and of course he wouldn't—he can ring. You don't have to wait for him at the street door."

"He's going to get his break," she stormed. "He's going to be *heard* if I have to smack them all down to do it."

David persisted. "I doubt that you really talked to Mr. Stark. None of these boys is his agent. They're hooked up with a theater crowd, but what probably happened is that they called one of their pals for you and he pretended to be Stark. Isn't that likely? Did you dial yourself?"

"You're very persuasive," she said in bitterness. "Telling me all that stuff about Ed and now about Mr. Stark. So were *those fellows*, and I gave him my word I'd meet him at the door."

With a quick lunge she was past him, fatal and certain and unamused as she went to keep her word. She gave no sign of hearing when he called after her, "Don't wander off."

But she must have been drunk, he said to himself, even before his concern made him report the incident to Ed. She wouldn't have taken those four clowns seriously if she hadn't been.

Ed confirmed it. "Certainly. There're two things about Pat. She drinks like Hemingway and she can't hold it. God, she's not quite so bird-brained as to think Stark would come across the street to answer a charge like *that*. I hope." Joy approached, led by the amused roar of his voice, and he flung his arms around her. "Joy, this will tickle you. My chickadee has come through with the best comedy of the evening. Hear this." When he had sketched in the story he was gasping and the tears coursed down his leathery face as he said, "Imagine, only imagine, what Stark would say if he did come. She'd ask him, 'Mr. Stark, are you normal?' and he'd answer like Mistress Quickly, 'No one ever accused me of *that*.' God, I wish it could really happen."

"You don't know anything about Stark except gossip," David said, amazed that he could feel reasonably pure anger as he spoke, could feel himself share Pat's pure anger.

"Whaaaaaaat?" Joy said, delighted to see him exposed like that.

"We don't really know that Booth shot Lincoln," Ed said loudly. He reached under his jacket to scratch his back defiantly. "Tell me, Davey, did Booth shoot Lincoln? No, I'll tell you. It was theatrical jealousy that fingered Booth. Gossip."

"Aren't you ever wrong about anything?" David asked, and

through the pounding of pulse in his ears he heard Joy's admonishing and surprised voice—"David"—and he knew he was being in their eyes foolishly, childishly emotional. Very well. He accepted their judgment with pleasure. Their very contempt intoxicated him enough to swell on in righteous indignation. "Are we always to be so sure that there's a dirty story about everyone? Oh yes. Oh yes, dear ones, we're always sure, and the reason for it gets pretty hideously plain finally, doesn't it? We can't afford to believe there's anyone better than we or anyone who might, for his talent or even for his luck, deserve more than we've got in the way of recognition."

"Big. You're being big," Ed said. "*We*. The generous soul includes himself with us, Joy."

"Quit it," Joy said. "Come watch the boys."

But David couldn't stop. A wide anger and a sense that he had been too long their creditor drove him on. "What have you got to be so snotty about that girl you brought tonight, Ed? And you are being. You are. If she has a decent impulse you've got to snicker and feel superior. Why, Eddie? Feel a little insecure about the prospect of bedding with her? Think you might not be up to it? So you've got to beat her down before you get her there, is that it?"

"Not before," Ed said. "She has nothing to complain about there." His face was flushed, but he was staring fixedly into his glass so that there was something fortlike and rigid about his exterior, as if thought and even anger had retired to a redoubt deep inside.

"Why fight?" Joy said. "Come on, Davey, let's go read *The Magic Mountain*. I do love you both, and if you either hit each other something might break. David!"

He turned to her, mastering the pitch of his voice but feeling the clear blade of his anger swing as if in open air above him. "Now you've heard the gentlemanly boast," he said to her. "A while ago I happened to—in a disinterested way—happened to ask Miss Pat if she loved our friend. She blushed over the word *love*. For which in return she gets from him public statements on the course of their sexual congresses." Again he turned toward Ed to ask, "How was she, Ed? You won't mind telling us. How was she?"

He had put Ed to flight. At least, with a grimace like a tic in his right cheek, Ed turned, shrugged, and walked to the kitchen.

"Proved your point?" Joy said acidly.

He took a deep breath before he could meet her eyes. He felt a kind of nausea, as he had once when he had been in a real fist fight—very long ago, certainly close to twenty-five years ago—and had won, by the sheer expense of adrenalin. He was not a person who could easily or often take the loneliness of victory.

"I was offensive," he said. "I offended you, but that doesn't mean I was wrong, Joy."

"Oh, you'll weigh it out on your little silver scales," she said. "With charity and justice for all."

"Don't *you* fight me, Joy."

"I never fight. I read *The Magic Mountain.*" Their eyes met in a long contention. She dared him to name her and her party as he had named Ed—and at the same time pled with him not to.

Then one of the quartet screamed ticklishly. His friends were lifting him by arms and legs. Half of Joy's remaining guests followed them as they carried him to the bathroom. When they pulled the shower curtain closed in front of him and turned on the hot-water tap, one of his friends explained to Joy in the polite tones of a grade school boy justifying a game to some stuffy aunt, "He was awfully drunk. He had begun to say things that he'd be ashamed of and he'd've thrown up in a little bit. He *always* does, y'know." Smiling, he wrinkled his nose to underline the cuteness of this circumstance.

Through the shower curtain the errant one thrust his head. His eyes under his plastered-down hair were pink and certain of their woe. "I loved her," he squealed.

"Who, Kevin?" the spokesman said.

"I was only teasing her about Stark."

"He means that deevine little girl," the spokesman explained.

"She was the only girl I ever loved except my mother," the boy said, and everyone who heard him tittered uneasily. "I wanted to marry her and settle down."

"Don't be *boring,*" the spokesman warned him, like a ventriloquist pretending anger at his puppet. "He always talks like that," he explained at large. "And it's so basic it's *boring.*"

But the boy with his head through the curtain had twisted his face into a real wad of agony, and all at once he bellowed gutturally, hopelessly, with such genuine horror of himself and the world that it seemed to David only cruelty to him even to listen.

"Now, Kevin," the quartet spokesman said, "you were unnecessarily rude to your friend on the subject of Stark, besides getting Maurice to impersonate him, and no one is surprised that she left you. No one."

Another of them tried to put a drink in Kevin's dripping hand, but the glass slipped through his bony fingers and smashed inside the tub. "I want that girl," he howled. "Want her to know I love her even if—"

"Don't say it," his friend warned him. "Do you want me to be ill?"

The boy clambered out onto the bath mat and began toweling off his face and his clothing.

"Revolting, isn't it?" Joy asked David with a thousand-times distilled and qualified enthusiasm. Her blue eyes twinkled with the self-punishing smile of Circe grieving.

He nodded with an honest agreement that she could hardly have guessed, as though he knew some final, stubborn suitor in his heart had said goodbye to her, as though the impulse which had made him quarrel, for the first time openly, with Ed had gone on now to its natural consequences. Sadly he knew it didn't matter any more that Joy had her reasons for being and for staying where she was.

Free now, he would go down to find Pat by the door or on the nearby Village streets. He would find her chilly and lonely now, he thought—probably at last convinced that she had been tricked by her own generosity of spirit, but maybe too proud to come back and be laughed at until she had lost that generosity in the vortex of denial that Joy presided over.

He would take her arm and they would walk away from it like two Chaplins—the old Charlie, that is. Maybe they would go no further tonight than to some coffee shop where they could sit and talk while he explained his claim and right to be with her rather than with *them*. And the explanation, now structuring itself like a law in his mind, would be the bridge on which the two of them, recognizing a mutual need, could cross. *When we came out of exile, we were as those who have dreamed,* he would say to her. Nothing could matter less than her failure to spot the source of the quotation.

He would explain how he had felt after the quarrel with Ed—not that he would quote Ed's painful remarks to her, of course—and quickly divert this explanation to the episode it reminded him of. I had a fist fight once, he would say. Only one in my whole life; for better and for worse I've not been the physical type; rather an egghead—and that was before you were born. I was fighting for a girl at a dance—she was one of my eighth-grade classmates who had danced all evening with one of her cousins I despised—and afterward on the stairs down from the American Legion hall I hit him with the heel of my hand and called him "a rotter" and told him "to keep a civil tongue in his head" when he answered in the lovely and wholesome vulgate that I was a bastard. Then I beat him up and ran twenty blocks home through the moonlight, thinking I could do anything, since I'd won my fight; I could go everywhere. I think I've got that confidence back now. Some interior season has changed. I can do anything. Can't I? Can't I?

But when he had sneaked Pat's coat from the hanger, folding it inside his own so no one would suspect what he intended, he found it hard to assemble the right words for saying goodbye to Joy—since it would be dishonest not to hint at the finality of his going.

"Don't go yet, lamb," she said when he approached her with the coats on his arm. "Tomorrow's Saturday, you know. Well then, you have to." She leaned against him tiredly when she kissed him, and he understood that she had counted on his staying to the end of the party. It was in the later hours that she needed him to help sort out the living souvenirs, so to speak, of the smashed bric-a-brac left around her then—he the knowledge-able audience for her loyalties and the one who remembered as well as she the true Eden, those days when all their painter friends were on the Project, those train trips down to Washington where the war was, Sally's play, Mick's affair with a two-star general, the major called Snow White, and Ed's first book.

She needed him to watch with her, in the New Testament sense, while she played out her caricature of the Passion.

Well, he was tempted to stay with her, even then. But while he fingered her shoulders fondly he heard Ed, again in his argument with the Welshman, pleading the Fifth Amendment for his being at such a party among alcoholics and perverts, for his lack of reputation, and for the quality of his prose. Mimi Hawk was necking on the sofa with the instructor. The one of the quartet who cared had turned on TV for the Late Late Show. The wet one sat huddled in one of Joy's dressing gowns, explaining in an awed voice that he was a clown because his male parent was a brute.

"It's been a big evening," David said, dragging the coats between himself and Joy and turning. "Spiritually enriching."

Pat was not inside the street door as he had expected, and when he did not see her he was momentarily chilled by the idea that she had gone without him.

The street door was still open in his hand and he was peering timorously, molelike, out of the shelter of the building when he saw her a few feet to the right of the steps. With her, soldiers.

So afterward he had this to bear on his conscience: That if he had merely had the physical courage to let the door slam behind him so the spring lock could snap fast, no one would have been hurt except perhaps himself.

He held the door open, though, because his first glimpse of her among the soldiers set his heart pounding and choked his breath. He thought of jumping back inside until he could understand what she was doing with this uniformed crowd, two of whom were holding her in their arms as if to keep her warm that way. He wondered if he would have to save her from them and instinctively rebelled. He looked beyond them for a policeman but saw only empty streets. It was as if the soldiers had been sent here, as a unit, on purpose; but of course it was Pat who had stopped them or attracted them to this door.

"Hiya," Pat called to him in a not unfriendly voice.

He heard one of the soldiers ask her, "Is that one of them?"

She shook her head. "Not exactly. David," she called, "I've found these boys that are all of them from the anti-aircraft or anti-something."

"Aircraft," one of them announced in angry pride. He drove his fist into his palm and bounced on his toes.

Pat shook the soldiers' arms from around her and stepped toward him. The soldiers followed her in a crowding phalanx, not noisy, just attentive and ready.

"They're ready to help," Pat said. "When Mr. Stark comes they're going with me to make sure he gets a chance to defend himself."

"No," David said hopelessly. He slid back a little farther into the open door, thinking that Pat was having her joke too, but that she had gone too strangely far with it. "You know Stark isn't coming," he said. "Don't you know that yet, Pat?"

"I don't care," Pat said.

"Then how could he defend himself if—"

"We all like him," Pat said.

"Of course you do," David said. "I like him too, but that isn't the point, since he's not coming."

Pat climbed half of the four steps. The soldiers didn't follow her, though two of those in the lead put their feet on the lowest step. "Do you want me to go up there and listen to *those fellows* rub him in the dirt?"

"We'd better go back up," David said, clearing his throat. "Ed's worried about you and you'll get cold down here without your coat." We can straighten it out later, he thought. When the soldiers are gone. He wondered whether the soldiers might be drunk, but that did not seem to make much difference.

"Ed . . ." Her lips curled in an unmistakable, knowing grimace of distaste. "I don't care what Ed worries about. I'll go back, though, if you want me to."

There was a kind of querulous muttering among the soldiers, but they still made no move. Pat climbed another step, her eyes square on David's. He lifted the arm with which he held the door to let her pass under it.

The first blow came from her shoulder hurled against his ribs as she thrust him aside. The next several blows were light, merely the passing stiffarms of the leading soldiers as they swarmed in toward where Pat was screeching for them. David glimpsed her mouth open in a red zero and heard her shrill instructions melt into a high, quavering, vindictive scream before one of the raiding soldiers paused long enough to knock him down.

From the sidewalk he watched the running tide of them go in and begin to climb toward a door that would not be locked against them. For some reason he tried to count them as they went, but he could only be sure that there were enough of them to get a hearing for Mr. Stark.

The Invention
of the Airplane

I

While Todd Galen taught here at Tabor University, no one in
our department became close friends with him and his wife,
though some choose to remember that before Sue Anne's death
they went out of their way to make her and Todd feel they belonged among us. These are the people, I find, who are most
conspicuously anxious to find a complete and unified pattern of
explanations for what the Galens did. Some minds cannot rest
until they have attached a rag of explanation to all events—particularly to those that are most bewildering and to all appearances most unreasonable. And I must not fail to say that Todd
Galen himself was one of the most insistent manufacturers of
explanations I have met in my academic career. Mysteries of any
sort were a hair shirt for him. They made him itch unbearably,
and as a young man he did not mind scratching in public.

Perhaps that passion for revelations and exposure estranged him from the well-meaning faculty families at Tabor. Of course we are all professionally committed to extending the borders of all sorts of knowledge. The mottos over the library doors and our own eyes in our shaving mirrors pledge our enmity to the dark places of existence. And yet I perceive that few who have stayed with the institution as long as I can thrive without a decent veil of shadows around them, from which they emerge only in a chosen direction and on occasions sanctified by convention.

Todd itched for explanations. He gave and took them with an evident indifference to the sort of embarrassment they might sooner or later cause. For instance, there were his memorable explanations of their wealth. In the autumn they first came to Tabor it was evident they had a great deal more money than most faculty colleagues. They bought the Kanfer House, which had been first of all the home of a territorial governor before it was enlarged and elaborated by a Civil War profiteer. The city had been talking of converting it, with its gardens and meadows behind, into a public park. The Galens bought it only a few weeks before an election to decide on a bond issue for its purchase. For this coup they had a certain notoriety in advance of their arrival in town—nothing malignant, of course, merely a neutral prominence in the anticipations of socially-minded matrons among the university family. There was a little period of excited speculation and jockeying for position among those who had helpful ideas of how the Kanfer House might be refurbished with authentic antiques from our territorial days.

Sue Anne submitted meekly enough to this interference, and while the house was being thus co-operatively given its tone, she and her husband began to entertain on a scale that suggested, after all, the place was to be devoted to public recreation.

All in a rush of lights, good food, dancing, boozy breakfasts, and marathon lunches in their gardens while the weather held good, they began their first school year at Tabor as if they were inaugurating a country club. Their generosity should have established them on a footing of ease with their associates, but Todd was uncomfortable about the whole thing until occasions came for him to explain it. And they came whenever one or another of us tried to express gratitude for his hospitality.

Todd would not accept this for himself. He wanted it known that Sue Anne came from a prominent California family, their money from her family's wholesale grocery company. If we had enjoyed ourselves at Kanfer House, we ought rather to thank John Dale & Co. than Todd. He had been a self-supporting student at Illinois when he met the granddaughter of good old John Dale. Todd considered himself still, in a manner of speaking, self-supporting. The gracious living of which we had partaken was his to dispense in the role of custodian. At least I understood this to be the implication of what he was determined to express, though he wound these feelings with considerable ribbons of liberal political commentary.

And Sue Anne, who never liked any of us, seemed at least to concur with Todd's views on his custodial role, a role that included mere custodianship of her as well as her inherited money. She had about her some quality of an heirloom, a priceless and useless fragility that suggested how she had been treasured from childhood on. When I first saw her, she struck me as one of the most beautiful girls I had ever been close to. She had a lovely, small figure, a complexion of the sort that is enriched one way by daylight and another way by lamps and candles. Her hair was an incredible auburn. A sunset color.

I first saw her in profile and took my impression of perfection before I saw what everyone best remembers her by—the great spider of a scar that covered the better part of her left cheek and gave to her left eye its peculiar witch-like slant. I hope I was no worse than others in suppressing my shock when I glimpsed the scar.

Whether I was or not didn't matter. A gasp and a gawk would not have mattered. It hurt one to look at it, like a gouge in the bowels, and by some process of sympathy and shame which I would not like to analyze too closely, it hurt her to be looked at. As if her blight were the overt reflection of something denaturalized and ugly hidden in each of us. I realized later it was no accident that I had seen her first in profile. Nearly everyone did. She had had the scar for over fifteen years and she would never be used to it. The way she turned to expose it—the hardest gesture required of a human being, I should think—led to my surest insight into her marriage.

Todd would have said to her—it was absolutely in his nature to say this—"Show it and get it over with. Don't try to hide it. Then people will forget it is there." That is what her mother would have told her, too, in the years of her growing up, but I'm afraid that Todd may have overstressed this tactic—in his anxiety to be a good custodian—so she never had even the minimal chance of forgetting it. Even with people who saw her often the exposure of her flawed side was always a deliberate act of will, a voluntary submission to the impossibility of hiding it unless she hid herself entirely, a submission she always charged to a secret account that would one day be collected. No one else ever got used to her scar because she never did.

Her self-consciousness seemed less in crowds than with individuals, and even there most people carried away from her small talk some sense of her waspishness. I remember one time when I was telling her a harmless anecdote about the Chancellor of Tabor, and she burst out at the finish to say, "What a despicable man!" I read this excessive interpretation as a key to the distance that separated her emotional life from those more normal ones around her.

There was sweetness in her, too. Heavens, that was just the disturbing thing. One heard it, one strained to bring it out more fully, and it eluded one like a nostalgic face disappearing in the crowd she was determined to keep around her.

And she had her secret accomplishments of a considerable sort. At length, after her death, in fact, a literary quarterly published an unusually large selection of her poems. Todd thought of reprinting these and some others in a memorial volume. "They're not just faculty wife stuff," he wanted us to know.

Finally he explained that the reason the memorial volume would not appear was in deference to Sue Anne's wishes. "She didn't intend it for anyone else. For her friends? What friends? Didn't she make it clear enough that she never really had any?"

Oh my. Yes, she had. But that clarity was just what those who would have to remember her could hardly tolerate as an ingredient of memory. I suggested that her poetry might still accomplish a revelation of that remote, real self that was never entirely accessible in social contacts.

"You saw that? You felt you knew her?" he asked in a painful tone of disbelief. Poor man. He lived in the rut of conviction that only he had been appointed to vouch for the shy undamaged soul behind his wife's appearance. He tried and failed to believe that others might sufficiently want to love the hidden person he had loved so much.

In the meantime he had, as a matter of course to him, explained the origin of the physical scar which was so fatal a part of his life and Sue Anne's. He could hardly overstress its absurdity. She had been taking part in a Christmas pageant at church, a perfectly normal and pretty girl of seven in circumstances as safe as our culture can provide. Sometime in the course of the evening an electrical connection near the roof of the church had begun to burn invisibly above the plaster ceiling. Burning matter had fallen, still undetected, through the hollow walls to burst out in a basement room where twelve little girls were getting into costume. Still a major disaster was improbable. Eleven of the little girls with two grown ladies assisting them had run squawking and squealing up three or four different stairways to safety. Only Sue Anne had taken the wrong turn, had found herself at the head of a stairway closed by a locked door. Within moments that locked door was battered down by hefty members of the congregation.

But Sue Anne had not waited, had gone down again into the room where litter and costumes were flaming up. Her angel wings of crepe paper had caught as she ran through the blazing room to another stairway. *Still* she might have escaped with minor injuries if she had not lost her footing on the stairs and collapsed backward into her flaming wings.

It was the linked chain of events that had marked Todd's mind in a way analogous to the visible scar on his wife. He was abashed by his inability as an intellectual to either deny or affirm that this tight chain of improbabilities meant anything. It had the smell of punishment, a supernatural intent, about it, and the more rigid religious mentality of another time would have accepted it so. But it was just Todd's role—he being one of us— that he had to deny it meaning.

"It *didn't have to happen* just as it did," he said when he told me. "Things didn't *have to* be this way." I remember the peculiar note of awed rebellion in his voice—as if he thought it was his duty, simply, to retrace the way back through time and eradicate that one frightful knot of coincidences from Sue Anne's life.

He never literally expressed so impossible a thought. Rather say that I imagined I heard it in the prayerful distraction of his voice. I was troubled, at the same time, that he had talked at such length about Sue Anne's disfigurement. To know its origin made her scar more distinctly visible.

I was bothered, too, that I was far from being the only one at

Tabor who heard this story from Todd. He told it compulsively. He told it as much in defiance of our generous sympathies as in an appeal for them. Yet this explanation, like the scar itself, might have faded back from the spotlight of consciousness if Sue Anne had not, herself, found so gruesome a fashion of reviving it—of bringing it, in a manner of speaking, to show a meaning that had not been visible to anyone in the original coincidence of her misfortune.

The Galens had lived as our neighbors in a tolerant and undemanding community for almost six years. If they had never become exactly intimate with anyone, we had come to count on them. They remained childless, but our children played in the gardens at Kanfer House or flew model airplanes in the meadows out behind. Many of us used their tennis court. The Galens continued to entertain on a scale we would lack without them—they entertained for holidays, for visiting firemen. That at least we counted on.

One spring morning while Todd was teaching a class in Victorian History, Sue Anne went to their basement, poured gasoline over herself, and burnt herself to death.

After that, as I said, a certain type of the timorous busybodies among us found it possible to guess, invent, or otherwise fabricate reasons why she had done such a dreadful thing. I never had the heart to try.

II

Some blamed Todd. Their accusations were never very openly voiced and were, of course, without any material substance whatever. In his own way he had tried to take care of her. One might as well blame her for the savagery with which she had repaid his intents. Either way one comes to bewilderment. Why not leave it alone?

Undoubtedly Todd blamed himself, too. At any rate, he took off, as if in flight from guilt, without announcement to anyone, a short time after her death. Even the head of his department did not know for years whether he meant to return.

Rumor and then solid report placed him in Europe. The Schoenemans encountered him in Munich, looking fat and tranquil, they said. Paul and Paulene Dufy saw him later at Antibes with a peroxided English girl. He seemed to be taking good advantage of the money that had come to him through his marriage. The crudest sort of gossip found in this some evidence of his private conduct with Sue Anne.

It was possible to reason—if one wanted to—that he had all along accepted her for her money's sake, that he had not kept from her this last, intolerable insult added to her injury. With such an explanation one might close the Galens' account and forget them.

But there was still the possibility that he might, after all, return to Tabor. He still owned Kanfer House, though it was now rented year after year to a Colonel Beach, head of our ROTC program. The Beach family was already numerous and was increasing with a biennial pregnancy. They nevertheless affected an impermanence of a military sort, letting it be known that they were ever ready to move should the country need them, parents and swarming progeny, elsewhere on the globe.

My own guess was that Todd would return sometime. I suppose I thought he could not rest without giving to us some final explanation of himself. I knew I would see him again. Yet it was a great shock for me when I ran into him unexpectedly in New York five years after his departure from Tabor. We met in the Public Library. We had both entered the elevator near the 42nd St. entrance and had taken our places on opposite sides of it when our eyes met. And then I might not have known him except for the wincing squint of his recognition of me. He was tanned, lean and leathery; not with a playboy tan but with the look of a middle-aged farmer or cowboy. In that palefaced crowd he seemed taller than I remembered. At the moment of our mutual recognition I felt a strong sense that unless he spoke to me I *ought not* to speak to him. He seemed like someone surprised in a completely illicit enterprise—he could not have looked more distressed if I had caught him, like the Dufys, with his English tart.

Strangely we rode all the way up in that big antique elevator and then rode back down again. In silent agreement, altogether eerie, we got off together and went out on the steps. All this while Todd was deciding whether he wanted to and then whether he needed to speak to someone who might understand his actual purpose. His first words were questions about my wife and children, what research project had brought me to New York, and whether, indeed, I was still on the staff at Tabor University.

Assured that I was still rooted there, he said, "Come!" in a kind of croaking imperative.

He had decided I was to hear everything—though his story would be in terms so alienated from common sense that I would be hard put ever to report its central meaning.

He led me to a bar on 40th St. While we were waiting for our first drink he explained his winter tan by saying he had been until recently on the North Carolina beaches. "At Kitty Hawk," he said, giving the name a confessional emphasis.

"You're doing a book on the Wright brothers," I guessed.

He shook his head with that obsessive, tortured impatience I was to see persisting through the years to come. Yet he laughed a bit, too, as if he as well as I or any sane man could appreciate the absurdity of what he had next to say. "I'm trying to invent the airplane," he said.

Just that once I thought he was joking. I relaxed, saluted with a cocky finger and said, "Good luck, chum." This was more innocent and ingratiating than other hobbies of the rich he might have fallen into.

He was stubborn in reaction to my misinterpretation. "No, no. I think I really can. I came near it this fall. We've been gliding very successfully from the dunes. My crew and I are ahead of Lilienthal, though what we owe him . . . I think we're ahead of the Wrights. This winter, if I can solve the problem of a power plant . . . I was at the library to get some notes on Langley's steam aerodrome. I doubt if a steam engine will do it. Then I also want to check out the Manly five cylinder rotary . . . I need a place to set up shop before I go back to the dunes again next summer."

Where he wanted to work through the winter was in the converted stable behind Kanfer House. "But if I came there . . . Would people let me alone?"

I thought he was asking whether old acquaintances would bring up memories of Sue Anne or her death. "I think the past can be confidently left alone," I said. "Tabor people won't press you more than you want to be pressed."

"Because it's all important that no one get ahold of my plans until I've made this next crucial step. Gliding is one thing. I'm learning to fly. But can I fly under power before someone else does?"

Gently I pointed out that our town was now served by a

feeder airline. Every morning at 11:15 a lumbering DC-3 appeared over the river bluffs, landed, and took off several minutes later for St. Louis. Very often we saw the contrails of B-52s flying east from Omaha on training missions. Would these evidences that someone already *had* invented the airplane disturb his project?

"I've shut all that out," he said. "I've learned to look at the sky without seeing them." As he had learned, once, to look at Sue Anne without seeing her scar? But had he? He had never taught anyone else how to do it, or taught her to believe it could be done.

Anyway, his suggestive comment had put me on the track of what he was up to. I had caught his note, so to speak, and in the close atmosphere of the bar, at least, I found my disbelief relaxed by the very intensity of his compulsion.

"I've had to shut out so much," he said. So much. Oh yes. He might have been lucky to go insane, to lose all memory, on the spot when the smell led him to his wife's body in the basement of Kanfer House. Then all the evil we must witness under the sun—and somehow must come to terms with—would have been shut out at once. No more wars, no more death, no more unintentional cruelty or torture, no more frustration of the unspeakable words of love. But the merciful natural protection of insanity had been denied him.

So—how can I put this?—he had, step by step, over the years, in the full possession of his reason, invented a substitute for insanity. He made me see his invention as analogous to those artificial organs—heart, gut, or hearing aid—which we so much applaud as achievements of the art of physical medicine. Or perhaps it was analogous to Proust's achievement in the literary art, culminating in what Proust called his last volume, "The Past Recaptured."

Clumsily, experimentally at first, Todd Galen had gone about the task of reconstructing not only his own personality but the world—even the world of personal history—in which it had its existence. In Europe at first he had tried merely to live in different styles. True, the Schoenemans had seen him living the life of a bachelor scholar in Munich—with music, beer, and philosophical companions. This had not "worked"—the word is his—but he had learned then some concepts of philosophic time that had been "useful" later. What is more, he had met a fellow-historian who was working on a scientific biography of Otto Lilienthal, the great German pioneer of manned flight. Through talk with this man Todd had glimpsed how the invention of heavier than air machines had ended one epoch and begun ours.

But the first attempt at reshaping his life had been, on the whole, a failure. Then he had embarked on the hallucinating drugs and the life of debauchery in which the Dufys had observed him. There were women, gambling, and an elaborate sort of costume play with him in the role of an Edwardian dandy.

This didn't work either. Only, somewhere—in what extremity of hallucination or despair you can guess as well as I— the intuited possibility of another life which *might have been* his appeared clearly enough to determine him to go on.

The first clumsy attempts at transformation failed him. He was still, afterward, the man whose disfigured wife had found so distressing a manner of pronouncing him a mortal failure.

"Things didn't have to be this way." I had heard him say that once before. He didn't repeat the words during our afternoon in the bar. He didn't have to. They whispered around us, around the whole weird, untenable suggestiveness of the confession he made to me.

"You're trying to invent a time machine, then," I said at one point. "You want to go back to a happier time."

He stared at me with a kind of impatience, as if I and not he were the dabbler in the frail concepts of romantic daydream. "I'll know what I've invented when I've done it," he said. "I'm trying to invent the airplane. If I can do that, maybe I can get back to the point before things started to go wrong. I want to *see.*"

Philosophy or madness, he wanted to see by experimental methods whether the actual, historical consequences of the invention of the airplane were fatefully necessary or mere chance. I am not saying that the nature and objectives of his "experiment" would have any scientific validity whatever. He was trying to break away, to break beyond, the scientific fashion of knowledge. And in a scientific culture that is no more and no less than derangement.

Yet something in me was persuaded that afternoon. Call it some unfortunate strain of primitive susceptibility to magic or astrological utterances and dismiss it as you will. I can only testify that the readiness to respond—to try to follow him—was there.

Maybe it was only my wish. He had his own reasons for settling on the airplane as a symbolic focus of the times we live in.

Mine, as I received his story, were no doubt different. I thought of the frightful wars of our century, the excesses of extermination associated with aerial bombardment. He gave me a vision of the millions burned, blasted, obliterated from the earth. Did he see something even worse?

Against his share of the universal dread of our times, Todd had proposed a mere wishful fantasy. One part of my mind skeptically refused to go beyond a notation that Todd could afford his elaborate hobby—but envied him for his evident absorption. The other part listened as one listens to the persuasions of romance or music. It strained toward belief like an animal on a leash. It struggled toward a different world. It echoed back Todd's question in all sincerity. "The airplane did not have to be a weapon, did it?"

Yet you must understand that I was purely the listener that day. I was reserved, even to the point of academic stiffness. I went no further with Todd than to reassure him that his home at Kanfer House would be a possible retreat where he could carry on his work. If I restrained my skepticism out of respect for his suffering, by the same token I withheld my impulse to assent.

I remember, though, that as we walked out of that bar into the dusk of 40th St. and I looked up beyond the towering walls around us, I saw a sky without threat in it. Rosy, violet, and gray, and at peace. Maybe that was the first time since Hiroshima that I had glanced upward without some shadow of apprehension that in my lifetime the worst would come down on us from above.

III

Like the Wright brothers sixty years ago, Todd was zealous to keep the news of his success a secret from the general public. I have a telegram from him, sent from Kitty Hawk in the following summer: ACHIEVED POWERED FLIGHT THIS AM STOP FOUR HUNDRED AND TWENTY FEET STOP ALTITUDE UP TO TWENTY FEET STOP AIRCRAFT DESTROYED ON LANDING STOP RETURNING TOMORROW TO KANFER STOP GALEN.

The newspapers of the same day were full of the exploits of two Russian cosmonauts. Any notice given to the accomplishment by Todd and his helpers Grant and Maxwell would, of course, have been in the realm of a feature story about some cranks. Yet that is just what local papers love to set on, and it is altogether mystifying to me how Todd managed for the next two years to keep his efforts so well veiled. There were some besides myself in the community who knew what his hobby was. There was some stir of gossip after he displaced the Colonel Beach family and secluded himself with his helpers in the stable behind Kanfer House. Motorists driving near the stable had occasionally pulled to the curb to see what was wrong with their cars—only to realize that the uneven roar and clank of an engine and chain drive was coming from inside the thick hedge—from the Manly rotary he was installing on his improved craft.

Some of us had been invited to see the new ship taking shape. Besides me, Vernal and Charcot of the Tabor Art Department, Milburn of Physics, and Butcher from English had been invited separately and as a group to see it.

Bob Vernal was especially fascinated by it. He thought it was a form of Pop Art altogether more witty and "significant" than the constructions of old sofa springs, automobile bumpers, and soap cartons one saw these days in New York galleries.

"If it isn't art, what is it?" he used to demand of Todd. I trembled to think that Todd might try on him the explanation he had once given me. Thank God, he did not. In these days he was straining everything from his feeling and thought into the success of the new machine. If it worked—and if he learned from its success what he had conceived he might—then there would be time enough for explanations. So he seemed to believe, at last.

"I suppose it should rather be considered a sport," Doc Butcher said. "That's the way Chanute and some of the other old boys conceived it. They had a rather more gentlemanly view of their contraptions, some of them, than the Wright brothers, who meant from the beginning to sell it to the army that would bid highest."

Todd looked pained. "It shouldn't be—altogether—for sport," he said. Ah, for him, as I was theorizing by this time, it was an effort to lead his camel through a needle's eye. It was a preparation to explore the unknown land between religion and art.

But, mystical theorizing aside, my story properly takes up again on the May morning when Todd invited the few friends I have mentioned to see him attempt flight from the meadow behind his house. By the time we had arrived he and Grant and

Maxwell had trundled it on its bicycle wheels down the gentle slope from the stable.

There it sat on the soft grass in the early morning light. The long blue shadows of poplars lay on its white wings. The slender spruce members of its frame gleamed like the spars of a clipper ship catching the light of an Atlantic morning on her maiden voyage. As I patted its flexing lower wing, my hand came away moistened with dew.

I don't know how to explain the premonitory excitement I felt—only to say that it was extreme, out of all proportion to the actual occasion. My heart was thumping, my breath coming quick, and I kept wanting to laugh out of pure eagerness. I watched the topmost leaves on the poplars in anxiety that they might show a rising wind that would make the flight impossible. A little black and white dog came at a furious gallop from the far end of the meadow, straight to the plane. He slowly sniffed its glue and varnish until the hammer and clank of the engine— when they started it—made him scamper fifty yards away.

I could feel the current of wind from the propellor. The smell of fish oil from the exhausts reminded me of the dirt-track racing that had so excited me in boyhood. The craft was trembling up and down on its shiny wheels so it seemed that Grant and Maxwell, at the wingtips, were more trying to hold it down than hold it back.

Todd took his place on the seat in front of the motor. He turned the wheel a time or two to warp the wings. He pulled the bill of his cap down tight on his neck and tugged at the strap of his goggles. Then he must have signalled to Grant and Maxwell to let her go.

How delicately it went bounding off across the meadow grass! At first it seemed it could hardly outdistance Grant and Maxwell, running beside it. Then, as if it had hit a mole hill, it sprung two or three feet off the ground, so gently thrusting forward that it looked like a puff of steam moving on the wind.

The air received it then. There was an instant of mental transformation in which I realized for the first time what flight was—I who had traveled so many thousands of miles on modern airliners, who first saw planes over my hometown forty years ago. I had never before intuited what it might have been like to witness the Creation, to see the chaos of matter merging into lawful forms. I was crying and shouting when Todd, at an altitude not much higher than my head, began his first turn. Beside me Vernal shouted, "I'll be damned, it flies!"

A quarter of a mile from us the meadow bordered a field of corn. Flying parallel to the fence, Todd's machine cleared the black horizon of the plowed earth. Just short of some maples at the farthest corner he warped the wings again and gained some altitude in spite of moving down the light breeze.

Then he went over us. I suppose he may have been thirty feet up on this pass. Nothing clears your eyes like elation, and I could see the quiver of spruce in all the wing ribs and the long spars of the fusilage like a tremble of fine flame. The exhaust ports fired their blue-brown smoke exactly like a Gatling gun.

Doc Butcher came over beside me and gripped my arm. "Look it. The big fool's going clear out of the ball park this time," he said. There was no doubt about it. Todd was in control of his machine, confident, really *flying it*. He almost went past our horizon on this circuit. To finish off the morning, he made a wobbly figure-eight.

I had been so absorbed, straining so hard with breath and muscle to keep Todd aloft, I did not notice that someone else had joined us while he flew.

Col. Beach and his two oldest boys had come down through the gardens from the street. They had been driving past and had seen Todd taking off.

One of the impressive coincidences of the morning was that Col. Beach was in full-dress uniform with a chest full of ribbons. He must have been on his way to some ceremonial function of the ROTC when he came to the house he had occupied for so long.

I remember that Col. Beach was the first of us to rush forward when Todd had landed. He was holding Todd's hands in his and his military blue eyes were shining as if Todd had given him an utterly astounding Christmas present. "I never thought I'd live to see it," he boomed. "The boys and I used to fly our models down here. Well. Well, I never. Yes sir. You've really done it this time."

His boys were examining the structure of the machine with the envious eyes of the semi-professional. They touched with experienced fingertips. They stroked, they pinched, they fondled. They had so many tumbling technical questions that those of us who had merely enjoyed the spectacle or undergone an emotional experience were quite excluded from expressing our feelings to the inventor.

Presently I heard Todd explaining to Col. Beach that, no, he had not built it according to anyone's ancient plans. He had figured it out for himself.

Then I thought the Colonel might rise off the ground. His splendid chest heaved with the thrill of understanding. Yes, by George and by God. Of *course*. Who should grasp Todd's essential passion if not the Colonel? Was he not also one of those born too late? He, who might have commanded one wing of the encircling movement at Cannae, who might have commanded Napoleon's artillery at Wagram, who might, like Sheridan, have turned defeat into victory at Cedar Creek in a famous ride—he, who was in fact the bored, fattening clothes horse at Governor's Day parades and lecturer on logistics and supply at a tame Midwestern University.

That morning when he saw Todd's white wings wobbling a little above the hedgetops, a little lower than the trees, the Colonel found his dream.

"You're a great one. Oh, aren't you something?" he boomed with his arm around Todd's shoulders as Todd walked away from his drooping biplane. "Look, those boys of mine will do just anything you ask if you'll take them on as helpers. So will I. I tell you, *I will too*."

"We'll see. We'll see," Todd laughed, bewildered and flattered by this volcanic attention. My study of his face convinced me, too, that the very experience of flight had worked on him incalculably. He was still up there in that peculiar region where all human objectives are clouded. I had the panicky feeling that in his triumph he was already forgetting why he had set out on his eccentric quest.

IV

What can ever be said of a mental aberration? Only this, I suppose: that sooner or later it must end its course in a collision with reality. It is born of the wish to escape intolerable memories or present pain. The groundless hopes it generates in its first escape from the normal go sour and contribute to the inevitable ultimate disappointment.

What became of our heroic Todd Galen after he had, in his

own aberrant, bullheaded fashion, conquered the air? For one thing, now that his story began to get around, he became an entertainer, if not an outright clown.

Now there were human interest stories about him and his machine in the Midwestern papers and the hobby magazines. The photographs of him with his cap on backward and his goggles pushed up on his forehead made him look like the player of a zany game.

Traffic began to pile up on Sundays when he was expected to fly either from the meadow behind his house, from a sward in the State Park fifteen miles down the river, or from the local airport. Hundreds of people, I am told, wanted to go as his passenger, but since the CAB would not license his plane, he was kept from that risk and folly. Still it was common knowledge that he had taken the Beach boys and Col. Beach himself as passengers at one time or another.

In the summer following his success he made exhibition flights here and there at a Fourth of July celebration and various county fairs. He was a flash celebrity and among other incongruities was the fact that one could now watch his "pioneer flights"—for they really were that, after all, since he had never had any instruction in flying—on television. Or, when one went to the field where he was to take off, one would see a television truck with all its cameras and equipment spread out to report his venture.

He was "Airman Galen" for a season or two. Then everyone was pretty well bored with him. The friends he had thrilled on that first morning flight behind his house had lost their enthusiasm for seeing it repeated. On an action instigated by the CAB the courts had enjoined him from flying anywhere except over his own property and in no case in the presence of a crowd at a public gathering.

It is roughly true to say that only Col. Beach and his boys remained loyal to him at this time, though, in a more remote way, I was too.

The Beaches had practically moved into Kanfer House again. They were helping Grant and Maxwell with a new plane. It was going to resemble a Bleriot monoplane to about the extent that Todd's first effort had resembled a Wright biplane—there being, it seemed, a certain physical rationale about aircraft design that would keep the descendants of Todd's first ship within the bounds of family resemblance to those that had succeeded the Wrights' constructions.

And by now I had the feeling that Todd himself was bored and restless with his developments. The rut of reality was taking him in again. Increasingly, when he spoke to me, I heard complaints against his great good friend, the Colonel.

"You know what he's suggesting now?" Todd said finally. "He wants to practice *bombing*. He's figured out the *principle* of a bombsight."

"Figured out?"

"All by himself," Todd said with a self-mocking grimace. "He's *invented* it." Where Todd really, by now, found himself was in the position of having invented a new hobby of reinvention, nothing more.

"Throw the Colonel out," I recommended.

Todd looked dismayed, almost offended, like a husband who wants to complain about his wife but is insulted by a suggestion of divorce. "He's more enthusiastic about it than I, by now."

"You didn't begin this for him."

"No." He remembered, at least, the mood of our talk in the bar in New York. "I was going through a bad time. I've seen it through. That's all I can say. I may start teaching again in the fall. I've talked to the head of the department. . . ."

"And leave your invention to the Beaches?"

"Maybe."

"No. You mustn't. No."

But I couldn't shake him. Perhaps I would have felt foolish now to try as hard as I could have now that Todd had been reclaimed from his black despair. Nevertheless I felt a great sadness when I learned that he and the Colonel had begun to practice bombing over the meadow. They dropped paper bags of flour at canvas targets on the ground. It took little imagination to guess that the Colonel was busy at home inventing a recipe for something he would call dynamite.

And so the future was going to repeat itself like the past. If Todd had proved anything, he had merely confirmed the inevitability of the historic process in which we gasp for hope.

Yet—he got out of it. He flew away.

Grant and Maxwell told the story, as much of it as they knew, as much of it as anyone would ever know.

Todd roused them out of their quarters one morning before daylight. It was their impression that he had not slept at all. Grant had heard him in the basement sometime after midnight. His face was strained with fatigue. He kept bumping into things that morning as if his sight was failing, though they described his eyes as abnormally wide open.

They helped him fuel up the biplane and move it into place for a takeoff. Then the three of them trundled out the advanced model the Beach boys had been working on. Todd scratched a match on the seat of his pants and set it afire.

The flames of its burning were still rising straight up into the windless dawn when Todd lifted the big, soft wings of the biplane onto the supporting air. He went straight down the meadow and over the sprouting corn in the adjacent field. The last they saw him, in dark silhouette against the coming light, he was some hundred feet over a farmhouse on the next hilltop.

Then no one ever saw him again. He vanished totally. He had left the meadow with fuel enough for a flight of not more than thirty miles. The search for him and his plane—or the wreckage of it—found no trace within a radius of fifty. Through his connections in the Air National Guard, the Colonel had the whole state photographed from the air, and none of the photos showed that splotch of tattered white to indicate where Todd might have gone down.

No doubt he staged this disappearance to look as if he had flown clear away from us, to go on and on like some Flying Dutchman beyond our hideous times. It was the last token he had to give us of his mental derangement—a derangement sufficiently confirmed for his friend the Colonel by the destruction of the advanced monoplane.

Todd couldn't be still flying. Even if he had stashed supplies of fuel on his escape route, reports of the plane would surely have come back to us sooner or later. They never did.

Of course his vanishing was only an act, a staged performance that might, indeed, have left us all marveling and curious—but which never could have convinced even those who wished him well that he had achieved an abrogation of natural laws. We have found no proof of how he contrived the illusion of disappearance. But we will go on convinced that there *must* be a simple explanation, if we only knew. . . . Among the literal explanations rumored among his friends and former friends at

Tabor, I am most inclined to accept the notion that he flew the plane to a waiting van or truck, dismantled it or smashed it, and hauled the wreckage away to be burned or buried.

Yes, he faked his going. He tricked us at last in a cheap and desperate attempt to make us believe in a miracle. He wanted some of us—one of us at least; maybe me—to believe that his invention meant all he wanted it to mean. But now. . . . Well, it is just pity for him on my part that forbids me to say all he hoped it would signify. I will not expose the full grandeur of his insanity. Let it go. Let it go that still—once again and forever—he meant to affirm the possibility of making the worst disaster, error, or mischance come out right.

Fracture

"I won't have him in the house any more," she said. "I know that sounds like I'm getting old and mean and middle class and all that. But I simply don't want him here again. Is that unreasonable, hon?"

And the odd, characteristic thing about Margaret's ultimatum was that it didn't climax a discussion with her husband, who sat among the papers he had brought from the office, quiet as a well-fed Buddha. They didn't argue. Had they ever argued seriously? He couldn't remember a time. The ultimatum came at the end of an interior discussion so detailed that one suspected a regular little courtroom inside her head, where the advocates of conflicting views were allowed to confront, scowl, and grimace at each other.

So Worth thought. He had mentioned Harold at dinner. "Don

Carpenter had a time with Harold yesterday," he said. "Seems Harold was coming over to his place for something. Well, Harold called to say that he'd got stuck in a bar on 83rd and wondered if Don would pick him up. When Don got there Harold was out in front heckling a parade of school children. I guess he was in wild shape—not shaved and you know how he looks with a beard on that green depraved face of his. Everytime a bunch of kids in costume would pass him he'd say loudly, 'Ain't that gawd dam cute?' Don says that there was a big circle around him, an empty place where women had pulled back away from him with their babies, kind of watching him uneasily out of the corners of their eyes."

"Oh good Lord," Margaret said.

"Then—this is the rich part—Don took him home and it seems that Don's uncle had just dropped in, too. Don went out to the kitchen to mix a drink. Harold followed him out and said in a very loud voice, 'Where'd you get that ugly ball-headed sonofabitch? Uncle huh? Uncle Shmunkle.' Don's mother came tearing out and made Don get Harold out of the house."

"I admit," Margaret said, "that I don't see what's funny about it. Harold's just pathological. He ought to be locked up. There's nothing funny about a sick man. Harold is disgusting."

"Oh well," Worth said. The matter seemed to drop, but he knew it was being argued further in her mind. Since they had left the table and come to the living room, sitting with Margaret had been like sitting in a theater where the curtain for some reason is not yet raised. The action has evidently begun and sometimes the curtain is bulged or fretted by the movement of the actors. There is suspense but no sound until suddenly the stage manager resolves the conflict, says "I won't have him in the house," banishes the contentious pleader so that when the curtain does go up the stage is vacant—but very orderly. Reason has swept it clean. The closed session has found results which may be published. Margaret has made up her mind.

"Whatever you want," Worth said. "I can take Harold—usually I can take him—or leave him alone. If you don't want him here . . ." He shifted in his chair to settle back in contentment with her and the life they worked out together. She makes up her mind, he thought, just the way she set about fixing up this apartment, considering each of the rather drab possibilities and finally imposing sweet reason on what had been a hodgepodge of dowdiness when they moved in. Two years ago when they came to the city they had no choice but to take this fantastically old-fashioned apartment in a gone-to-seed neighborhood. And now look at it. The brown and purple drapes were gone. The lighting was rearranged. Painting the walls in the best modern way, working their furniture into place so it seemed to fit not only the dimensions of the room but the very habits of their living together had transformed the grotesqueness that seemed, God knows, to have been built into these rooms to a gray, white, and ivory order in which their large Braque reproduction fit as smoothly as the parts of a gyro compass. When he came home in the evening there was a kind of soothing each time he passed from the battered street to the precision of their apartment. This orderliness was Margaret's way with all things. His comfort was all her doing.

Of course it was all her doing, and yet it was an important part of her orderliness that she should ask, when the question had really been tied up and disposed of, "Is that unreasonable?" Her arrangements would be incomplete without his approval. And of course he gave it.

"It isn't at all, darling. There is no point in injuring ourselves trying to be courteous to Harold. He doesn't live in a mental world where courtesy makes any difference anyhow." Worth yawned. "You're the one to say. It's your home. He's your family friend."

"Well," she said, and obviously this was a point she had dispatched far back in her silent debate. "I don't think his coming from the same town makes an obligation at all. No . . . there are so many things about him that I can't stand. Like the change he picked up in the bar the other day. I don't think he was so drunk he didn't know whose it was. I would have called him to book for that."

"I should have," Worth said. "My fault, dear. I could have pointed out to him quietly that it was ours. It didn't seem worth mentioning at the time."

"How much was it?"

"Seven or eight dollars. I should have. . . ."

"I won't have you blame yourself," Margaret said. "It simply isn't your fault. You always act in a good sane way. But there goes Harold with our seven or eight dollars. So . . . then his harping at the Courtneys. 'The Courtneys are sonsofbitches, the

Courtneys are sonsofbitches.' I think I told him rather stiffly that
the Courtneys are friends of ours. He didn't pay any attention to
me. That's too much. He says the same things about us to other
people, for no reason. Did we ever give him any reason? I admit
nobody believes him, but it scares me to know he's talking like
that about us."

"I doubt if he talks about us," Worth said.

"How can you be sure?"

"I think he likes us. Poor Harold."

"OK, Worth. There's no way to be sure. Let's drop that point.
But about a month ago—I didn't tell you this—I caught him
stealing a bottle out of the closet right there. He looked like a
mean little kid. I thought he was going to hit me when I caught
him. I was truly scared. You were in the kitchen and I almost
screamed."

"Oh not Harold. Harold wouldn't hurt a fly."

She came over and sat on the arm of the chair. Her plaid wool
skirt rubbed his arm. He smelled the briskly clean smell of the
wool. "Is it really all right with you if we don't have Harold here
again? I mean not let him in if he comes? He'll be here knocking
at our door sometime and we'll have to tell him he can't come in.
I'll do it. I wouldn't expect you to because you're so softhearted.
But is it really OK if I tell him *NO* he can't come in?"

"Sure." He smiled, pulled her down to him so he could rub
her forehead with his nose. "After all, our marriage would be a
poor partnership if we couldn't talk and arrange things like this.
Let Harold go."

"You're so good," Margaret said. "You're good to everyone
and I'm not like that. I'm just not made that way," she said in a
childlike voice. He pecked happily at her cheek.

Presently when she had gone to the kitchen he had a pleasant
vision of her in this part of her self-created setting, her blade-
slender figure among the gray and white planes of the kitchen
furniture. The warm brown gray of the walls was one of the colors that Margaret had mixed herself. A real triumph of taste.

Thinking of her in her simple and spotless kitchen and thinking how much the simplicity and severity of it pleased her, he
wondered what had got into him that evening when he had
thought of buying her the bracelet. Her thirtieth birthday was
not very far off. This year he had not known what to get her.
Since he'd come back from the ETO, birthday presents had been

quite simple for her. Clothes that she had halfway picked for herself—pausing just far enough short of actual selection so he'd have an area of choice to make it his gift—or something for the apartment. They were settled now and her wardrobe was well rounded. It would have to be something different this year. Still the bracelet had been a wild impulse, clear off the track.

The jewelry she liked was the sort which had the plain beauty of a microscope or a camera or some other instrument of precision. Her jewel box looked like an instrument case. Silver went with her clothes. He supposed the cool color of silver was really meant for her.

The bracelet fitted none of these conditions. He had noticed it in the window of a shop just at the edge of their neighborhood. The shop window was stuck full of junk, bracelets and rings and necklaces that were completely tasteless. At first glance this bracelet was the same kind of thing. There were spars of gold angling out of the band like the grains in a head of barley. It was oddly made. There were three coils of gold wire ending in the spars and the clasp fastened by wrapping these coils together like a spring. When his eye had stopped on it among the other junky pieces it had occurred to him that it had a quality of its own. It looked genuinely like a savage ornament, and it seemed to him Margaret might like it for its outright contrast to the other jewelry she owned.

Now that seemed a bad idea. Still he would not make up his mind. A bit of contrast quite unexpectedly given might please Margaret more than he knew.

Later that evening they talked more about Harold. She had passed judgment and even the specter of him should have been banished out of the apartment. It hadn't gone yet. She was restless. She might have been feeling that in her efforts at justice something had been overlooked. At last she said, "About Harold. Do you really agree with me? I can't be sure of myself. I knew Harold when he was a little boy, and I used to remember that I thought—after I left home, I mean—that he wasn't like the rest of the Parsons, not so stuck up. Maybe now that I have the chance to be nasty to him I'm paying back the Parsons family for the way they used to be. And if he's the only good one in the lot. . . . He is awfully poor, don't you suppose?"

"I suppose."

"And he is an artist."

"Not really. I don't think he works at all. He talks big about a book he's writing. Nobody has ever seen a page of it."

"I don't want to hurt him because there's something malicious in me," she said. "I want to be right."

"Now, darling, you gave your reasons like a little lawyer. They seem adequate. You could probably find more if you thought longer."

"Only, am I sure?" she said.

"Hon, it's all settled. Good-bye to Harold."

She sighed her contentment, twisted down in the couch so the breeze from the window would not touch her head any more.

"Thank you for keeping me straight, friend. I couldn't stand to have him come here any more," she said.

Thursday evening on their way home from the movies they stopped in the neighborhood bar and found Harold there. He had been waiting for them, it turned out, after he had called their apartment and got no answer.

They had not noticed him when they came in; they had taken their usual table back by the empty dance floor and had been served their drinks. They sipped and then there was a moment of silence. Worth was wondering if he ought to give his wife the bracelet which he had, after all, bought for her birthday. That odd gold bracelet was right now in his inside coat pocket, wrapped in a tissue-paper parcel. There were only two more days until her birthday and they had never made much of waiting to show the presents they had for each other. Now he was feeling that he might be able to explain well his reasons for buying something so out of character—so garish—for her. He might make a few amusing observations on the subject which she would remember and which would associate themselves ever after with the gift.

Then all at once Harold was standing over them. His shocking face peered down at them woefully. "Hello. I know I made a big ass out of myself the last time I saw you," he said. "Gawd. I can't drink decently and I know it. What's that got to do with it? No excuse. I made an ass out of myself. Period. See? I don't even know how to apologize decently. Oh forget it. Jesus." His face in the bar lights looked decayed and his clothes smelled with a combination of wet wool, urine, and tobacco smells. "Can I sit down?" he asked. "Or do you want me to get to hell away from you?"

Worth threw a smile to his wife and said, "Sit down, please. What will you drink?"

"Listen," Harold said doggedly, like a child who drives himself to say something which is not only painful but which seems to him to verge on nonsense as well. "May I sit down, Margy? I know what I did, too. I know I got some of your money the other night. God. I don't know how I did it. Did I . . . ? I guess not. Forget it. I know I didn't have any and then the next morning right in my breast pocket I found six dollars. How much was it now? I want you to tell the truth." He pushed a handful of dollar bills across the table, fifteen or twenty of them, wrinkled so much the pile stood an inch thick. "Please now, tell me."

"Never mind," Margaret said sharply. "We've forgotten about it."

"No, no, please tell me."

He's going to cry, Worth thought, and that isn't necessary.

"Here's the whiskey. Drink up, everybody. It was change from a ten, Harold, about eight and a quarter," he said.

After he took the money they drank in silence. A boy and girl left their stools at the bar and came back to the dance floor. The boy put a quarter in the jukebox, turned to the girl with an almost imperceptible shrug of invitation. Her body rose to meet him as the music began. She went on tiptoe against him. The music had been chosen for the season—to say it was April, to make blatantly clear what the wind on the streets was all for.

"Jesus," Harold said. "Too much noise. We can't talk here. I hate to ask. . . . Forget it. Can we go up to your place for a nightcap? Here's the pitch. I've got to talk to you people tonight. That's not a joke."

"Well . . ." Margaret seemed to be deliberating.

"I know what you must think of me," Harold said.

"We'll do it this way," Worth said. "Margaret's tired, but you and I will run down to your place for a while. For one drink. I've got to be at the office tomorrow and that's no joke either."

The street, when they went out with Harold, seemed by accident or miracle to have changed from what it was twenty minutes before. Perhaps because the bar was so dark, there seemed to be a luminosity in the air that they had not noticed, as if the air were full of a million sequins. When they had come from the theater the street was empty. Now a whole parade of boys and girls moved up the block—not exactly conjured by magic, because it was time for intermission at the Y dance, but magically making the night big and disquieting.

"I'll be home by twelve," Worth said; and at that moment as he looked around he was startled by his wife's face, her look of frightened determination.

"If it's only for that long"—she laughed—"I'll come too. If I may, Harold?"

Why? It was too silly, Worth thought, to believe that she was afraid Harold would lead him astray. He could not account for it.

"Please," Harold said. "I'm glad you're coming. The two of you together is what I need to get me out of my rut. I mean you people are such a team. Nuts. I mean I like you sooo." Delighted now, he made them hold the cab while he went back inside to get an extra pint.

They had been fooled and taken in, there was no doubt of that. In their moment of compassion in the bar Harold had made a demand on them they could not refuse. Who could tell what desperate thing he might do if they would not help him? He had looked so terribly wasted and shaky. Now, climbing the stairs to his apartment, his drunken unbearable arrogance was loose again. The taxi ride had given him time to drink half the pint like a happy child drinking pop.

"You might know them sonofabitching Courtneys," he said to Margaret. "You know what that bitch Alice Courtney said to me the other day? 'Harold, you're malodious,' she said. I ought to let her have it right in the mouth. So she thinks I'm a bum, so what? Forget it." He had grabbed Margaret's arm—his black fingernails pinching into the cloth of her coat—and was dragging her up the stairs at his own headlong pace, thrusting his ugly happy face toward her, ignoring her anger. "Yeah. That bitch. You know who she's playing around with while that fag husband of hers goes out with his fag pals? I'll tell you. . . ."

"Oh!"—the convulsive, revolted sigh of Margaret's breath.

It seemed to Worth that his wife would turn at any moment and march righteously toward home; and he thought later that she might have done so if they had not come then to Harold's door and into what he had always referred to as his apartment.

The shock of seeing it—the immediate acid shock—must have restored anyone from the notion that Harold was more to be blamed than pitied. There was a studio couch unfolded in the room with a brown blanket rumpled across it, crumbs and grease spots on the blue couch upholstery, and no sign of any linens. In front of the couch was a long coffee table crowded with beer cans from which the roaches poured as the light went on. Among the cans were crusts and slivers of meat. There was a chair in the room. There were three skillets and some dirty plates in the opposite corner on the floor. Something that looked like an egg had been trampled into the linoleum.

"It's lovely, Harold, lovely," Margaret exclaimed. Her voice rang with triumph. After all, her excursion over here was not in vain. To see this den of corruption was revenge for the embarrassments he had caused her. "Maid's day off?"

He stood blinking in the harsh light from the ceiling fixture. He had not counted on the room's being this way. His befuddled face suggested that gnomes must have come in while he was gone and lived the hell out of his room. "It's kind of messy," he said in a diminished voice. "Glasses. We've got to have glasses. You see any?"

"I'll look under the couch," Margaret said. While he went out to get some she asked Worth, "Are you going to sit *down* here?" She pulled her wool skirt against her hips as if it were iron that she was fitting close for protection. She moved away from the couch. It might have jumping bugs.

Worth said, "Kilroy was here. Before that Raskolnikov had this suite, I suppose. What the hell? Let's sit down and have a drink anyway. Maybe he does have something on his mind he needs to talk about. You take the chair. I'll sit on the couch."

"He doesn't need us."

"We'll see."

"Worth, doesn't this bother you? I don't understand you."

"I wouldn't want to live here. It's interesting."

"If you could tell me why. . . . It's just filthy."

Down the hall they heard Harold speaking and heard a woman's voice—a bawdy, bubbling, fat-woman's voice—answer him with a joke.

"Don't needle him about it," Worth said.

The glasses Harold brought were greasy. Beads of cold water

huddled on their surfaces. He divided the whiskey and took an armful of the beer cans from the table so they would have a place to set their drinks.

"It's a mess," Harold said. "But let me explain something— it's always this way." When he laughed very heartily at his joke the laughter turned into prolonged coughing. He rubbed his lips with his fist after he coughed and rubbed his fist on the cover of the studio couch. Margaret set her glass down hard. After seeing the slime on his lips she had no intention of drinking from any of his glasses.

"Have you been doing any work, Harold?" Worth asked. "We hardly know what you're doing these days. The novel you were . . ."

"I haven't committed it yet," Harold said. "I been thinking about it. I may make it oral." His eyes were swinging to cover every detail of the room, as though some arrangement of the papers piled on the floor, the cans, the skillets, and the milk cartons behind the door might hold a pattern which he did not yet know. "Needs a woman's touch, don't it? But nothing like I do. Pretty Sarah is the girl. That's what I have to talk to you Joes about." Again he coughed and rubbed his mouth. "Women, shmimmen. I had a babe and now she's gone."

"Sounds like a blues number," Worth said.

"Don't it? Listen I wrote some song lyrics yesterday. Tell me what you think of this." He began humming the tune of *Night and Day.* "Hell, I don't remember. It was about a guy whose girl left him and it's spring, see?"

"Never mind," Worth said. "Tell your story. You had a girl and she's left you."

Margaret's face tightened even more. She had never looked colder, more like a disapproving schoolteacher. She was carried by the intensity of her disapproval to a foolish question. "Here?"

"Here, shmere," Harold said. He was jolly drunk enough to ignore what Margaret might think of him. "You know her, Worth, old boy. You ought to know her. Found her when I came to hunt you one day. Never did find you. Found her. She works at your office. Out in the pen in front where you got this acre of pretty girls. Pounds a typewriter. Pretty Sarah LeRoy is the one I mean."

"You're joking," Worth said. "LeRoy's a kid. She can't be more than . . ."

"Well, she's seventeen."

"Good God, Harold."

"Now wait. I ain't so old myself. Relative matter of course. I'm only twenty-seven and the baby of the family. Right, Margaret? Margaret knew me when I was a baby at the breast."

He kept on talking, a harsh croon intended obviously for himself, but pointless and perhaps impossible to him unless he had them there to sit as though he were telling them something. Worth did not listen. He was thinking about Sarah LeRoy. Such a pretty little kid. The starched white of her blouses every morning, the skin that kept fluctuating in color whenever he talked to her, her pleasant eagerness to get work done just right for him, "Yes, Mr. Hough. Yes," the hands that looked so clean and creamy but not yet shaped like a grown woman's hands, the smooth fall of her hair brushed neat for school, he thought, a pretty little maid from school. His idea of her had been so fixed that what he was hearing from Harold stabbed at him like the discovery of a betrayal.

". . . Damn near three months," Harold was saying. "Through the winter when it was cold. Happy as little old puppies. Bang, Slam, one day she hits me right in the mouth. 'Only reason you want to marry me is you think you ought to.' 'Right,' I said. I was real smart. Whatta quick comeback that was. So bang, slam, she let me have it while I was lying flat on my back in bed. Out the door she goes without even waiting to pack her douche bag. I shouldn't have said that to her because this weather is so nice. I sure need her because . . ."

"Please," Margaret said. "You have no right to tell us things like that. Oh come on, Worth. I can't stand any more of this."

"Sure wish I could coax her back," Harold said. "She was so pretty, so beautiful, so lovely." He lay over against the arm of the studio couch, breathing heavily through his mouth. His tongue lay for a second against his ugly lips. "Listen, Worth, old boy, she won't even let me come near to her. I chased her on the street one day, and she ran up to a big fat mean-looking cop. That's a fact. You hear me, Worth? Here's what I want you to do. . . ."

Margaret was at the door, her gloved hand resting on the frame and her whole body inclined for immediate exit. "Worth . . . ," she said.

"Coming."

Harold said, "What I want you to do is talk to her for me."

"I'm sorry, Harold."

"Now listen, Worth, I know what I'm talking about. She thinks you're brains from the belly up. That's a fact. She told me. You're her boss. Now listen, you talk to her. Tell her old Harold's cleaned up and quit drinking. If you get a rise out of her, I will, too. Anyway talk to her sensible. Tell her . . . I mean she's an adult. Don't give her any Sunny School guff. Just tell her old Harold . . ." Then gently his voice stopped. His hand with the fingers spread and cupped moved caressingly over the arm of the couch. His face in their last glimpse looked sick and moldy as the room, but young, like a debauched-child's face.

Their taxi moved for what seemed a very long time through streets of velvety darkness. Over and over Worth thought, Not Sarah LeRoy. It seemed impossible to him and then impossible that he should have been so wrong about her. He had been thinking of her as he would have thought of a daughter, and she was living with a man almost his own age.

Once when they stopped at a traffic light and the cab was lit from the store windows on the corner he noticed Margaret watching him distantly. "You're not going to, are you?" she said.

"Going to what?"

"Going to talk to this tramp about Harold?"

"No. Of course not, darling. She's not a tramp, though. We mustn't jump to any judgments."

"Living with *Harold* in that sty? Oh no." He could not see her face, but he felt her shudder.

He smiled to himself. He had the melancholy and lonely notion that he was assailed from all sides by the grotesque emotions of other people. "Now, darling," he said, "love and cleanliness are not necessarily mutually dependent, whatever the soap ads say." As he spoke it seemed that the cab might as well be the basket of a balloon carrying him miles above the earth while down below the earth was twinkling with the thousand garrulous lights of April. How comic and melancholy to ride at that height saying reasonable things to the empty air.

"Love!" Margaret said. "I've heard everything now."

She went to bed as soon as they got home. "Don't stay up too late," she said.

When he saw the light go out in the bedroom he got a small glass of whiskey from the cupboard. Something soft that the wind carried beat twice against the window. He went to the window and looked down. It was too late now for anyone to be on the street. The upreaching branches of the trees below him swayed as though they were a scaffold that might sometime—soon—collapse all at once to show him the secret and filthy processes of spring among the roots. In the meantime it seemed that this fragile scaffold was supporting him at a lonely height. If the wind rose more, he might hear the snap of branches giving way, letting him drop.

"Margaret," he called. "Margaret? Tonight *was* good-bye to Harold. Never again." He called this out jovially. He went to the bedroom door, wanting to talk to her. If the two of them could really agree and think together they might keep their lofty and precarious perch above the mess that the Harolds and LeRoys made of their lives. He peered toward the dark bed. "Margaret?"

"All right," she said. "I heard you. Please. I'm too tired to talk about it tonight any more."

But I have to talk about it, dear Margaret, he thought. Tonight all this has jarred me loose. He went back toward the window and this time, as he approached it, was sharply aware of his own reflection emerging on it—the reflection of his white shirt; his head, hands and trousers being darker hardly registered on the transparent pane. The white animate shape jiggled on the glass. Then in a trick of vision it seemed to be moving against the cover on Harold's couch, an immaculate substance on the dirty blanket. As though it were one of Sarah LeRoy's white blouses he was staring at.

Sarah LeRoy—how wrong could he be about someone? For a long time he thought he had her figured out perfectly, and he was quite wrong. From his height in the air he had never seen her as a woman at all. He had missed the simplest fact in the world. A surge of self-pity struck him, the realization that his cleverness had someway cheated him.

He drank and then without thinking lifted his hand to the pocket where the bracelet lay wrapped in its soft paper. His fingers tightened on it and he felt its spring give under the pressure. Margaret's bracelet for her thirtieth birthday. No. He saw now why he had bought this gaudy bit of jewelry. It was not for Margaret.

He was pinching the bracelet together as though he were already fitting it to someone's wrist.

"Sarah LeRoy," he whispered in amazement. "I'll be damned."

Harold seemed to him, just then, very lucky. He envied Harold everything—his enemies, his dirty room, his mammoth drunks, his cough, his Sarah. He saw now why Margaret had wanted so much to get Harold cleanly out of their way. She had been afraid sometime he might envy Harold. She had known what that envy would mean to him; she had known what he was just beginning to grasp—that envy would never lead him to imitate Harold, nor even actually give the bracelet to Sarah, but that it would swing a cold light on his own incompleteness. He saw—or thought he saw—how every limitation in Margaret's life had been placed carefully, like a spar to shore over and hide from him his own matching frailty, and his heart was stung with a treacherous wish to wake her and tell her he understood. At the same time he knew that the time itself for such communication had been spent as ransom against his terrible need.

He opened the window a little as if the stable air of the room were choking him. A flat tongue of wind came in, sliding its secret dampness and urgency against him with a tremor, and on its motion he heard the crackle of branches breaking.

The Inland
Years

"Lake Arthur—round as the world" it said in the publicity
folder we received from the Arthur Chamber of Commerce, and
the folder contained a map which truly showed the lake like a
blue globe in a green surrounding atmosphere of Midwestern
prairie. The town of Arthur sat on top of it like an exaggerated
polar cap, and it was ringed with the traces of highways and the
indication of beaches where summer cabins clustered like sham
cities. But Ellen said in amusement, as she had ever since I first
met her, "It's square as a bear."

Before her family dispersed when she was fifteen she had
spent several summers at Lake Arthur with them, and of course
from the time she and I began talking of the possibility, one of
her motives for vacationing there was to make a nonsentimental
pilgrimage—like going back armed and disinterested to see
something you have loved and been deceived by.

In the time when we were first married, nine years ago, and were trying to give each other our childhoods for sympathy and safekeeping, she had told me a lot of stories of Lake Arthur's summer society, and her mother's adventures and preoccupations with it. From Ellen's insistent presentation Lake Arthur had come to stand for a bogey of the past that we were fleeing together—a world without more roots than were required to make it viciously rigid, not particularly rich except on a Midwestern scale but still wealthy enough to base its behavior and tastes on distinctions of ownership, outrageously provincial in its belief in its own cosmopolitanism, and as capable of dictating the path of error to those who fascinated themselves with it as the bigger Society that Edith Wharton wrote about. This last was classically demonstrated by the nonsensical marriage and divorce of Ellen's parents. So Lake Arthur, as Ellen used to speak of it, was a well-understood point of reference from which we could orient the departure of our lives.

Of course I had not the same personal recollections of it that Ellen had. When I was a child I saw pictures in the Sunday paper of people boating on Lake Arthur, the governor holding a pike and embracing a UP official from Omaha on the amusement pier at Arthur, this or that family breakfasting by the lakeside with their guests from Minneapolis. It hadn't made a great impression on me until I heard Ellen talk of it. Then I took over, perhaps with some sentiments of gratified snobbery, Ellen's resentments toward it.

I felt, though, that I knew Lake Arthur well enough so that for me as well as for Ellen going there would be a sort of return, however partial and qualified. She and I were much too poor to take better than a cabin on one of the newly built-up beaches where there were only marsh and forest the last time Ellen had seen it. That would be close enough to spy, from a removal of years and circumstances, on a landscape and a way of life which were reminiscent of "some baggage we checked somewhere."

Of course there were more definable reasons for choosing to go there. In anticipation we spoke of the coming week at the lake as our "bourgeois vacation" because it was to be the first in our nine years together when we were going to give up ambitious plans for trips and lie back resting in a lakeshore cottage. Some years when we had no money or I was in the army there'd been no vacation at all, and again we'd made hectic and too extravagant trips to Mexico, Canada, and California in unreliable cars. This was our year to rest, and be damned to all that might be interesting and far off. Also we had no car to go junketing in. We were both thirty-one that year, and in the spring we'd put all the money we could raise into a down payment on a house. I had a job on a home-furnishing magazine which looked as though it would be the one to last unexcitingly forever, so buying a house had at least seemed justifiable.

For my part I was wonderfully content with our plan. I couldn't have faced the idea of traveling, which always manages to concentrate my interest in myself. For me it was a great thing to lapse entirely, so that what I saw could become more important than I, even if that was no more than the banal perimeter of the lake and the static weather of early August.

For the first couple of sunny days there I had an orgy of dissolving myself in favor of whatever I could see without rolling too energetically from a prone position on the beach or the pier. Such effort as I made was like taking a bit of plain bread and concentrating fully on how it tastes. I would squint over the lake and think, How round it is, and, because I wasn't in any competition to prove myself smart, could be pleased with such a perception. I got the same kick out of the straightness of the light rays that made the chiaroscuro of the diving tower at the end of the pier. With the little girls who went out to dive I could enjoy either the color of their legs and suits against the blue sky or their adolescent shapes without feeling the slightest interest in them as people. I watched the boats tick and sway against the pier and sometimes fixed in a dumb way on the pink house directly across from us on what was currently the "best" beach.

Built as it was down close to the water it looked like a tunnel mouth or a bomb shelter except for its vivid color. Really it was impossible not to look at it. It would seem to be in my eye, just as it was in the natural colors of the lake and woods, like a metallic grain, an annoyance, however beautifully modern it might be. Sometimes in utter childishness I would hold up my little finger to blot it out. It was an irritant that made me think—about bomb shelters and modern architecture and home furnishings and what they each cost—and my sun-softened body protested against thinking.

I made some querulous jokes about it to Ellen—this was her lake, how did she account for this monstrous piece of candy cluttering up the shoreline? All she knew about it was that it had been built since her time, as any jerk ought to know. "At least it's better than they used to build," she said. "We'll go across to Arthur one time and I'll show you the Swiss chalets and English half-timbered houses they threw up in the twenties." I began to argue that sometimes irrational structures like those fitted ideologically into a landscape—I may have said "timescape"—even though aesthetically they were grossly out of place.

"I don't know what you mean," she said shortly. I admitted I didn't either and said I certainly didn't intend to argue about it.

Ellen laughed. "Then the vacation is paying off already. Let's row over and see the pink house. Want to?"

The rowing put me in an odd state, seeming about to wake me up but never fully succeeding, as though I had been deeper immersed in sleepiness for the last few days—or maybe much longer—than I had realized. The afternoon wind on my chest and bare arms and the slap of waves on the boat bottom were so insidiously insistent on my relaxing into sleep that I had a period of silly panic in which I would keep glancing over my shoulder at Ellen to be reassured that she was actually there.

"You're huffing and puffing, old boy," she called. "We don't have to go this fast."

"Pretty big waves," I said. "I want to get in closer to shore." Frightened by something I couldn't name I was trying to cover it over with a more ordinary fear.

Ellen said, "Relax. If we swamp I'll hold you up. But this is nothing."

Idling to a stop forty yards out from the pink house, dropping the oars and turning to look squarely at it for the first time, I saw why it might have made me think of a tunnel entrance. The lower story was all open to the lake, an austere concrete cave overhung by a deck and the rooms of the second floor. I had not been able to make out these details of construction from my view on our beach, but I suppose they had registered and called up that particular comparison.

Everything about the house looked groomed, polished, stripped for action. A beautifully varnished speedboat hung on davits at the house corner which thrust a little way into the lake—it could have been the lifeboat hanging at a ship's side. There was no sign of any inhabitants. I assumed—projecting my own state, I suppose—that they were sleeping through this hot part of the afternoon.

I asked Ellen how she liked the house and she shook her head. "It's a machine for living. I'm not for it, are you?"

"It's very Walt Disney," I said. "I personally believe that the people who live here are all enchanted. Look, not a creature stirring. Want to land and look in?"

"Oh no. But let's drift here a minute. You tuckered yourself out with that speed coming over."

We bobbed there for a while without saying anything. After a while a dumb-looking boy in a sweatshirt with the legend "Athletic Dept. U of Minn." appeared on the second-story deck and leaned on the rail, peering at us in the same dull way we peered at him. He had a drink in his hand from which he gulped occasionally, but he made no sign of recognizing us as human beings. It was like being with someone in a dream and feeling as though you knew him well and being at the same time unhappily doubtful that you would know him if you saw him again. The few yards of water that separated us from him might as well have been an ocean.

"Screech at him," I said to Ellen in a low voice. "See if he's real."

The boy up-ended his glass, worked for a while to get an ice cube into his mouth and pointed the glass at us. "Oo. Dayox oh eh."

Ellen said, "That's right, I remember now. He says there's rocks over there. Swing us with your left oar and then pull out farther. I thought I knew this place."

Once I had turned I kept going. We had seen the house and I felt enough anxiety, however unwarranted, about the crossing back to want to get it over with.

"You know about those rocks?" Ellen said. "There used to be three frame cottages up above them on the hill and that's the way I had them located. Well—those rocks were where the eighteen high school kids drowned once."

"Shipwreck?" I said brightly.

She began moving in the most oblique ways toward her story. It was perfectly simple in essence, but in her memory it was confused with a lot of recollections of the way the shoreline had looked to her when she had first heard of the disaster, what her father had said to her about it, and how, year after year when she returned to the lake, she had felt when she looked at or passed near that point. For her, clearly, this personal recall was of the same material as the incident itself.

"It was the whole senior class from Rhinebeck," she said finally. "Rhinebeck's a little town about fifty miles from here. There were eighteen in the class. I think it was eight girls and ten boys. They'd come up here and rented a couple of cottages for their senior sneak day. As far as anyone knows they must have gone wading out on those rocks. Then one of them fell into deep water or got panicked and the others tried to help and the consequence was that every one of them got drowned."

I can't say what it was I didn't like about her telling that story. Perhaps part of it was a lack of satisfaction with its realism. As she told it, it didn't seem quite true. "Couldn't any of them swim?" I asked. "Surely one or two of them could have got out."

"I didn't know them personally. Maybe they couldn't swim," she said. "I think I'd seen some of the boys because Rhinebeck had a whiz of a basketball team and they used to come down to the state tournament nearly every year."

"Who saw all this to tell about it if everyone was drowned?" I demanded.

"I don't know," Ellen said doggedly. "That's the way it happened and there were people who knew."

The reason for my resentment of the story began to clear. In her tone I had heard something of her love for the lake, a new revelation of an attitude that seemed incongruous with the person I had felt sure of knowing, a revelation of something she had never wished to share with me, pretending to share everything. And yet, it was too silly to argue straightforwardly over her repetition of a story she once heard.

"Wasn't there a chaperone with them maybe?" I asked.

"I suppose so. Either they'd stayed overnight or were planning to stay overnight, so there must have been a chaperone."

"No chaperone," I said. "That explains it all to me. Whew. These eighteen kids had the greatest orgy Rhinebeck ever produced, so they made a suicide pact and drowned themselves for shame the next day. Kids then weren't as nice and well brought up as they are now."

Our rowboat grounded gently just about this time, and that seemed to me a lucky termination for such a pointless argument.

I hopped out briskly and tied up the boat. Ellen was looking back over the three miles of water to where the pink house squatted at the shore, frowning toward it as though it might be the memorial of those drowned kids she was remembering or imagining.

She said, "It was an accident and one of them wouldn't desert the others."

"Be realistic. Maybe some of them tried to get away and the others dragged them down."

"I don't know why you have to have it that way."

"I merely happen to think it could have happened that way."

"I suppose so," she answered somberly.

Later that night we were wakened in our cabin by a rainstorm that beat loudly on the roof and blew in chilly drops at a couple of windows. I closed the windows and lay comfortably, feeling protected against the wide, noisy attack of the rain. I could smell our wet bathing suits in a far corner. The smell of drying wool and of dust enclosed me peacefully enough. I knew Ellen was awake but we did not speak for a long time. I thought she must have fallen asleep again when all at once she said, "There was a pair of twins on the Rhinebeck team. I remember them as plain. They were tall and shy and everybody that saw them play said they were the greatest ever. I guess that must have been the year I had my little red coat with the rabbit muff. I thought how fine it would be if one of the twins noticed me. I was so little then that of course they wouldn't have. They seemed like real grown-ups to me, though they were probably only sixteen or seventeen."

"Were they in that bunch that drowned?"

"I think so."

'I never heard of an orgy involving twins. Must have been quite a gathering."

"Oh, funny," she said. "Go to sleep."

"Are you going to sleep?"

"I will pretty soon. You go ahead."

In the morning, well rested, I went with cane pole and sunglasses to fish from the pier. Arthur was the kind of lake where any dope or child could catch perch by dropping in a baited hook and where good fishermen, given luck and patience, could bring up some pretty fancy pike and lake trout. I only wanted to be idle and perhaps get enough perch for dinner.

The beach's population of adolescent girls was out in force by the time I took my station. I ought to mention that from the time of our arrival Ellen and I had been aware that there was no one else our age renting at this beach. There was one generation ranging up from about ten years older and another one ranging from sixteen down. This latter included an unaccountably large number of daughters fifteen or sixteen, probably spending the last vacation they would ever have in the bosom of their family. These girls were addicted to gum, fluty cries, fancy sunglasses, and to giving sultry glances to every passing male except their respective fathers. Impatiently they lay tanning, and sometimes, rolling over to expose another slope or muscle to the sun, they stared out with fierce virility at our little lake as though it should have been a thousand-mile stretch of sea. It was these teen-age girls who gave our beach its one quality beyond comfort and quiet and made it seem worthy of looking out on something broader than the 1950s and the mediocre tremor of inland waves.

Pretty frequently, in late morning or late afternoon, boys came in speedboats from other beaches to raid our beach for these girls. You'd hear sooner than see the speedboats. They would blast a high note out beyond the pier end and settle to a halt almost within the waves of their own wake while four or five boys in sweatshirts and trunks studied the display of girls. The boat would creep in to be tied up at the pier with flourishes and self-conscious horseplay.

In the morning while I was fishing the boat came from the pink house. I recognized first the boy with the U of Minn. shirt. There were three others, and after tying up they strutted with more than the ordinary raiding party's arrogance among the blankets where the girls—and a few parents and wee ones— were whiling the morning away. While they went up the beach like a party of slavers a sort of hush ran along parallel with them the way it will when a visiting general passes groups of soldiers not yet at attention. It occurred to me that the mothers, fathers, and tots as well as the daughters were holding their breath and waiting for the choice to be made. There was a twitching of little tan thighs and shoulders and, I hope, a clenching of little jaws on the chewing gum.

I missed the actual selection because Ellen had come down from her housework in the cabin "to see what I was catching," and I turned my attention to chatting with her. Presently I heard the speedboat start and looked over her shoulder to see the boys.

When the aristocratic blatting of the motor died, the beach sounds dropped to normal, though they seemed clarified, as though the addition of an intense chemical precipitated out a certain former murkiness. A little kid was yelling, "Daddy, float over to me, over to me." The little boys playing shuffleboard on a floor among the trees resumed their clatter. I tried to communicate to Ellen the total impression this raid for girls had made on me. She snorted and accused me of exaggeration.

"You make it sound like Pluto coming up to steal that girl, whatever her name was," she said.

"That's it," I said. "We won't have summer again until he brings her back."

She scratched my belly with her knuckles. "You big fake. Here you are broiling in the sun and still pretending it's not summer enough for you. Look"—I heard the motor noise grow as she pointed—"they're bringing them back already. It's just an innocent young people's way of getting together here. It's always been done that way, my lad. When we used to come up here there were motorboats too, and the boys bummed from one beach to another in them to get acquainted with the girls."

"I wouldn't let a daughter of mine go out in one of those hell boats. I'd sooner see her dead at my feet."

"It's probably just as well you haven't any daughters."

"All right," I said. "I'd let them go. They could do what they pleased."

"Look, there are your little girls back safe on dry land. Not hurt a bit and they've had fun."

"And the boys line them up for hanky-panky later when it's dark."

Ellen was sitting with her knees folded up to her chin and her arms locked around her knees. Above her knees she gave me a secretive, happy smile that clung a long time on her mouth. "You caught on. The girls will take the steamer over to the amusement pier tonight and the boys will meet them at the dock there and they'll go up for a dance at Roseland. At intermission they'll bum down the Midway and eat cotton candy or something else awful, pick up a kewpie doll, and get kissed a time or two on one of the benches at the dock while they're waiting for the last steamer to bring them home."

"Well, happy memories," I said. "After all these years I get confessions. Who was the man—boy?"

"Mmmm—no one. None in particular. A kid named Charlie Fox one time. Someone—I can't remember his name—that I thought was the smoothest dancer."

"Did he have a speedboat?"

"I don't know. Listen, let's take the steamer over tonight. Will you?"

"It would be fun."

"Lots." She stood up suddenly and prepared to leave. "Catch fish," she said.

The steamer was the grandest relic left at Lake Arthur. I suppose it must have been about sixty feet in length, and, put-putting solemnly around the shoreline as it did five times a day, it appeared to be almost as high as it was long. I'm not sure whether there was a lot of grillwork and gingerbread around the upper decks or if it merely gave that impression. It was completely white, and against the color of the lake it always struck me as being phony and nice—the white and blue were just as starkly innocent as something you'd see on a postcard. For all its height the steamer had an absurdly shallow draught and could pull into water you would not think deep enough to float one of the speedboats. It stopped at any pier where someone hailed it, chuffling and whistling and being a great delight to the children as Ellen said it had been for as long as she could remember.

It was as much fun to ride as to watch. Our trip around to the amusement pier at Arthur was probably the nicest hour of our vacation. Ellen had dressed for the occasion in a fresh and billowy print—one she'd debated bringing, since we'd been dead set on the principle that this trip was to be as uncomplicated as possible—and she seemed to feel how pretty she looked. In the dusk she seemed suddenly shy and withdrawn from me, yet happier to be with me than on any occasion I could remember of the recent past.

Mounting the steamer we leaned into the half-enclosed engine room set slightly below the main deck to see the old machinery hiss and slide like a dinosaur breathing. We read the 1897 in raised letters on the steam cylinder and suddenly looked at each other as though we'd shared an insight, but also as though neither of us could say what it was.

We climbed to the top deck to sit alone while the steamer backed away from our pier, and we remained alone up there until it had made two more stops. Then a family of five came up and took benches ahead of us.

I was surprised by how few lights seemed to border the lake as we went around. Those few appeared weak and almost desperately isolated. It was then, I suppose, that transitional hour when most of the vacationers were hanging on to the last of the day's outdoor pleasures before going in to light their cottages and begin the evening.

Underneath us—it seemed very far down—the lake was a steady and yielding blackness. Now and then a solid wave would collide with the bow and split away hissing. I remembered being frightened the day I had rowed Ellen across to see the pink house and I was ashamed that I had permitted myself that fear.

Ellen touched me and said, "You know, I'm happy," and I answered that I was glad of that. For the time of the trip we seemed equal to the cold neutrality of the lake, balanced, and owing it neither fear nor gratitude for what it might be.

When we landed it was still not time to go dancing, so we turned along the Midway, trying with a little too much eagerness to be excited by the music from the merry-go-round, the smells of popcorn, and the thin crowd. After I'd tried the shooting gallery and Ellen had thrown hoops at a peg floating in a water barrel our good judgment suggested that we not spoil the evening by trying to eat either cotton candy or any of the other confections available and there was nothing else to do. Ellen was sure that there were some bars up in the town, and we left the pier to find them.

The one we picked at random—choosing it with no special reason—was called the Orchid Room. It was small, which we could tell from outside, and expensively furnished, which we discovered with some uneasiness once we had entered. I was afraid the price of drinks would not suit us.

At that time we were the only customers, though there was a green-faced fat man on a raised platform between a piano and a Hammond organ and a middle-aged woman behind the bar. It was fairly dim in the room, but not so dim that we missed being impressed by the white orchids painted on all the walls.

As we sat down the fat man played a run on the Hammond

and asked if there was anything we wanted specially to hear. Ellen said "These Foolish Things" would be fine. He shook his head comically and answered, "That one was before my time." Then he began slowly picking it out on the Hammond and presently was playing it confidently.

"How about the piano?" Ellen asked. "I'd rather hear it on the piano."

Obediently he swung half around to face the other instrument. "The old songs are corniest, aren't they?" he said. He played marvelously well. We relaxed to listen while the little place began to fill with customers. Presently those who came in were moist with rain, and Ellen, noticing this, said, "Anyway we can't go to the dance until the rain's over. How about that old 'Running between the Raindrops,' Zach?"

"Zach"—because by now she had discovered who the piano player was, and in the general fondness she was feeling for anything that echoed from her past she was insistently overusing his nickname. Sixteen years ago Zach Winthrop and his Rhythm Boys had been very popular in this part of the state, she explained to me. She thought it probable that once when she was at Roseland his boys had been playing there, and she meant to ask him in some break between numbers if this might not be so.

But presently when she went to the toilet she found Mrs. Shaw, and Mrs. Shaw kept us busy for the rest of the evening. Mrs. Shaw—who had been Rita Chase before she married and had spent summers in the cottage next to the one occupied by Ellen's family—struck me as being drunk as a pig when she wobbled to our table with Ellen. However, she went by waves, apparently ready to pass out for a period, then, recovering herself, was remarkably, bitterly, and suspiciously sober, while we went more steadily downward.

"Well, murder, kid," Mrs. Shaw would say to Ellen, "we've certainly got to do something about this. You know I had no idea that you or any of that silly family of yours was in this part of the country any more. I really hadn't thought of you for years and then"—turning to lay her round, moist little hand on the back of mine—"I go in to daintily powder my nose and who says 'Hello, Rita' over the partition to me but silly little Ellen Park."

"This isn't home country any more," Ellen said. "Harvey and I are only—"

"What do you know about that?" Mrs. Shaw marveled. "That

is, what do you *know*? Hey, Sally." She was calling to the woman behind the bar and beckoning her over. "Sally, guess what the rain druv in. It's stupid little Ellen Park that used to live next door here at the lake when I was fresh and young." She put her arm around Sally's hips and hugged her with an immoderate shiver. "You kids know who Sally *is*, I'll bet, don't you? Why, you're sitting in her *intime* establishment. Sally, they never heard of Sally Racine."

"Of course we have. Hello, Sally," Ellen said. I rose and shook hands.

"Hi," Sally said. "Everybody having a good time?"

Mrs. Shaw wiggled her finger at me. "Who is Sally?" She tightened her hold on Sally and leaned in my direction. "You don't know, you silly ass. Well, you can just go over there and look." She flung her free hand toward a glassed display panel on the opposite wall. "Go on and learn something."

"Don't pay any attention to her," Sally said, breaking free.

Ellen prompted me nervously, "Miss Racine was a *Scandals* star."

"She was the goddam White Orchid of 1921," Mrs. Shaw said. "Get over there and look at that picture." I did as I was told and found that the glass covered a two-page spread, in color, from a 1921 magazine. On one page was a picture of Sir Harry Lauder looking rosy-cheeked as a Boy Scout. The other page carried a full-length photo of Miss Sally Racine, the White Orchid. She too looked healthy and plump and, in her weird costume, about eleven feet tall. I stood for some time studying the pictures, trying to assemble an appropriate comment to carry back to the table.

Fortunately Sally had gone—to mix us drinks, as it turned out—and Mrs. Shaw was on another line by then. She was talking about Ellen's grandfather and then about Ellen's brother, who was killed on Saipan. She remembered his building a tree house down the bluff from the cottage and calling it the Park Hotel. She rubbed some tears away. "Then the silly little jerk got himself shot boom, boom in their silly war. Isn't that the way it goes, Elly? Tell me, isn't it?"

She went on, "I remember The Champ—I call my husband The Champ and God knows why—used to play catch or toss a football with him sometimes when he'd come around to pick me up for a date. Thought he was the swellest little guy in the world. He really did, Elly. When he heard about him getting shot he really took on. I can't remember all the things he said."

"What's your husband doing now?" Ellen said. "I remember him very well."

"He's doing all right," Mrs. Shaw said. She yelled for Sally. "Give us another round, Sally, and God bless us every one."

I protested against any more drinks, not very vigorously, I suppose. At any rate they paid no attention to me.

"What's become of that insane grandfather of yours that had the fish farm?" Mrs. Shaw demanded. "He must be dead."

"He wasn't insane," Ellen said laughing. "He was the smartest one of the Parks, anyway. You know there's a bronze plaque for him in the town hall here for what he did in conservation." Her glance flickered in my direction and she said, "I'll show you sometime if you're interested."

"Why sure," I said.

"He was really a professor, wasn't he?" Mrs. Shaw asked.

"Yeah. He taught at Creighton for just dozens of years before he started the laboratory here. How I loved that old man, Rita. You remember the way he and Grandma were with each other? It was always 'my love this' and 'my love that' with them." She coughed suddenly with laughter. "You know that old Hupmobile he drove for so long. He'd get it out to drive into town here, then the two of them would be standing by it and Grandma would say, 'Darling, hadn't you better, if you want to, change your shoes before we go?' 'Well, honey,' he'd say and balk like a ten-year-old and sulk till she made him go neat up. They were so great. And I remember . . ."

I felt chilly and cheated and again commenced to argue that if Ellen and I were going to the dance at all we would have to leave soon or risk missing the last boat back to our beach. My argument wasn't solid. Then there was still plenty of time, of course. I became further irritated that the two of them could so easily refute me. "It wasn't entirely my idea to come to the dance," I pointed out.

"Relax, then," Ellen said. "We'll finish this drink and by then you may be in a better mood for the dance."

Mrs. Shaw said grimly, "You're not going anywhere while we're having fun. If the boat's gone I'll drive you home. Where you staying, Elly?"

"Gorsky's Beach," I answered. "It's a long way around by road. We won't trouble you."

"Drink up and be quiet." She pinched the skin on the back of my hand with her red, dirty nails. "What are you doing around at Gorsky's? It's no fun clear over there."

"We can afford Gorsky's," I said. "We can't afford to have fun." In my agitation I had gulped my drink and was waving at Sally to bring us another one. I still didn't mean to get drunk that evening, but in some irrational way that felt like a revenge for the mesh of weakness and accident that had involved us with Mrs. Shaw I wanted to get just a little higher. There seemed to be something waiting to be said that would solve her—I remember thinking in those terms.

Ellen said, "We have fun in our own way, Rita. We enjoy quiet things. I read a lot and Harvey fishes. We row in the afternoons."

"Huh," Mrs. Shaw said, "that sounds dull as hell. What do you read? You mean he *fishes?*" She crawled half across the table to peer at me.

"He watches the little girls, too," Ellen said.

"Like your papa did."

"I don't either," I said. "I'm interested in people, that's all."

The two of them laughed absurdly, as though they shared a vision of my motives so secret that I could never hope to guess it.

"He is interested in people," Ellen said. "He's gathering material for a play. He wrote a play once, right after the war, about his experiences on a Liberty ship."

Mrs. Shaw studied me with a momentarily sober and perfectly hard amusement. "I know that one. *Mr. Roberts.*"

"You've got it," I said.

"Well, he almost sold it," Ellen said. "I told him he should go on and revise it or write another one. That's been four or five years now."

"I didn't almost sell it."

"Anyway the people he showed it to thought it was very good. Of course *Mr. Roberts* had come out by then," Ellen said. I could see she was wobbling in her chair. I thought perhaps I ought to grab her arm and drag her out of the place—even give her a swift punch and carry her out, the way you do in rescuing someone from drowning. I let the moment of good intention pass and dissolve in sulkiness and resentment.

That my quiet Ellen was drunk is true, and that fact explains exactly nothing. Of course the alcohol and our encounter with Mrs. Shaw were necessary to start her talking, but they merely released something which had a dynamic of its own and was in motion below a level that the alcohol could reach. For a little while longer it was not apparent that Ellen was pouring out a monologue. Mrs. Shaw interrupted with questions or irrelevant attempts to change the subject or turned frankly and drunkenly to start a separate conversation with me, and from time to time I made my own bitter additions.

But as an hour passed and another after that, Ellen kept talking, piling up more and more of the whole story of her life. She kept smiling apologetically and abstractedly, and while she appeared to be watching Mrs. Shaw—she certainly wasn't telling it to me—perhaps she was looking past Mrs. Shaw too. It was, I suppose, like listening to a medium, though here it was Ellen talking through herself.

There was a long part of it which was given over to an account of her life with me. At some point she mentioned the way we'd married in haste in 1943 when I was being drafted into the army and how that hectic time had been brightened by the promise of the life we'd begin when I got back. Then there was the leave spent together in San Francisco. She'd just heard of her brother's death, but we'd been able then to keep a good heart because the war's end was at least visible. Then came the year in the trailer while I was finishing college, the year I'd written my play and we'd talked of how great it would be to get out with jobs of our own and our own apartment. Then how I'd got involved with Larris in promoting his cartoon books and how we'd traveled all over the country on that scheme. How we'd saved money on different occasions to buy a house, had spent the money and started saving all over again.

She said at one point that now we were really about to begin some of the living that we'd postponed so long, but this observation was given in passing. There was no end. Her story kept lapping back over itself as though a while before she had passed over too quickly—or missed—a key episode on which all the rest could hang.

I don't know what the ugliest point of her monologue was, whether it was her pathetic eagerness to get it all spilled out, or Mrs. Shaw's drunken, uneven attention, or my own resentment of what the story implied. The details of the story were ordinary enough, yet among the three of us we managed to qualify them so it seemed to be an endless record of failure. The same incidents might have sounded different somewhere else. Yet I hated

Ellen because I thought she was using an unbearably strict measure to account for our lives, a measure strict as the edge of a knife—and then offering this knife edge to Mrs. Shaw to use against us in whatever capricious, drunken way she wanted. I thought it was as though Ellen refused to judge Mrs. Shaw in some desperation to submit us two to judgment.

I remembered, without wanting to go there any more, the dance at Roseland. I imagined that the dumb-looking boy from the pink house would be there with one of the girls he had found that morning on our beach. Later they might go to the steamboat dock and kiss while they waited for the last boat. I was afraid that even if we went now, I couldn't stand seeing those kids.

I shook the table and said, "Let's get out of here." To Mrs. Shaw, "Come on, you said you'd drive us."

"Lay off, Harvey. We're having a good time, aren't we? There'll be a lot more interesting people in here before it closes. A lot more interesting than you two, I might add." She put the back of her hand beside her mouth and stage-whispered to me, "What's your wife telling me all this crap for?"

"So we've bored you," I said. "OK. Take us home."

"Christ, if you've gotta go, call a taxi. What's the matter, can't you even afford a taxi?"

As a matter of fact and among other things, I was not sure that I could. After the first round I had paid for everything, including a pack of cigarettes for Mrs. Shaw. The drinks hadn't been cheap, and here I was left with less than two dollars.

"Never mind," Ellen said dreamily. "We'll take a taxi."

I said, "I'm not sure we have taxi fare. Get this old bag in motion. She's your friend, remember?"

"Sally," Mrs. Shaw yelled. "Sally." The music from the organ stopped and everyone was watching us. When Sally arrived Mrs. Shaw said, "What class of people you catering to these days? These two latched onto me and now they want me to drive them home. I'm afraid of them. Tell them to get out and leave me alone."

Sally winked at me to show she was not taking this quite seriously. She beckoned me to come with her to the bar. "Look, Rita's drunk," she said.

I heard Mrs. Shaw wailing, "They get me off on a dark road and God knows what would happen to me."

"You don't want to ride with her anyway," Sally said. "I'll

have a taxi here in a jiffy. You have money? Never mind, I'll fix it with the driver and get it from her tomorrow when she's cooled off."

"But she's a friend of my wife's," I said.

Sally, not bothering to try to understand that one, grinned wisely. "Rita's nobody's friend. You and your wife can wait in the entry if you want to."

While Ellen and I waited Mrs. Shaw came out to us. "You know how it is," she said. "If I left here now I'd be all sobered up before I got back, and my whole evening would be shot. Besides, I'm afraid to drive that far by myself. I've only got this silly little Pontiac and I don't like the way it drives. You see how it is, Elly?"

"Sure, honey," Ellen said. "Stay and have a good time."

"Oka-a-ay," Mrs. Shaw said reluctantly, as though we were forcing her to an action she would undertake only because we wanted her to so badly.

"It was nice running into you," Ellen said. She was swaying and looking pale. I could not tell how sober she was.

I said to her, "You might at least get your fat buddy to kick in for cab fare. Or for one round of drinks, just as a sign of affection."

"You bet I will," Mrs. Shaw said uncertainly. "Wait, don't move. I must have left my purse at the table, or I can borrow something from Sally. Don't go away. Wait. Wait now."

Who knows whether she came back with the money? The cab honked in a little while and Ellen and I went to it quickly, agreeing on that without having to speak to each other.

We sat on opposite sides of the seat. It was raining a little again, and the windshield wipers seemed to be cutting even pink slices of the neon lights from the bars bordering the road.

"You had nothing to gain by that last byplay," Ellen said.

"It did me good. Why take all that guff without answering?"

"You couldn't make allowances, could you?" She hiccuped gently. "Rita used to be such a quick, wonderful girl, I thought."

"You wanted to be like her when you grew up. I know."

"Yes, I did. Yes. To hell with you."

"That's a good reason for telling her what a crumby life you've had with me."

"I didn't tell her that. I told her where we'd been and what we'd done, like—Don't quarrel with me any more, just for tonight, please. I'm too tired of it, and I don't know how much longer I can take it."

"So I'm always at you," I said. "I never give you a minute's peace. If you'd just realize sometimes that it hasn't been all roses for me either. Then, while I didn't spend my childhood in this paradise, I have my feelings about it, too. Why am I excluded? Why do you have to talk to a drunken pig like that instead of me?"

"Yes, why?"

"I give up," I said. "I merely thought we were going over to dance at Roseland. Just like old times. Was it my fault we never got there?"

"No. It wasn't your fault. You win the argument."

"At least you admit—"

"You always win your argument."

"Then what—"

She interrupted me by turning abruptly against the side of the cab and crying, knowing that I knew my own answer, knew that she knew, knowing that neither of us could ever hide from the other again the commitment to betrayal that time had forced on us by the subtlest and most kindly-seeming frauds. I knew that it was nothing so easy as a particular or personal sin that she was accusing, and in the dark cab the longer I thought this over in silence the more it began to seem to me that she was weeping really for those children from Rhinebeck who had drowned once in the lake, holding each other's hand in a faithful line and never letting go.

This Hand,
These Talons

There was a thick mist through town and the roads were icy
when they came back from hunting. They put the shotguns in
the hall closet and took off their boots on the carpet by the door.
Martha ran across the kitchen in her stocking feet, holding the
pheasants up high in front of her and holding her hand under
their necks to catch any blood that might begin to flow in the
warmer air of the house. The pheasants had not bled very much
when Willy pulled off their heads, holding their necks under his
foot in the snow. The afternoon had been cold enough so there
was not time for much blood to flow before it started to congeal.

"Willy," she called back to him, "you go and look at the clock.
Could be that we're late."

As he went obediently, it seemed to him all at once, and in a mixture of sensations, very luxurious to walk in stocking feet across the warm hardwood of the floors, through two gray rooms whose windows bloomed with the dead light of the fog. The smoothness underfoot was like the rice-straw mats in a Japanese home, a luxury of touch that was one of the good things he remembered from his time overseas. And now it was just a little more than a year since the evening he and Kitz and the Australian F.O. took off their boots and went into the house in Sasebo to meet Mr. Hagawa, Hagawa who grinned and hissed like Fu Manchu himself and said, "Weh-oh-come frins," and later put them wise to a clean, exclusive geisha house.

The clock with the bronze griffins around its face had stopped; nevertheless he called, "Eleven-thirty."

"Oh, come on now." Martha said, a touch impatiently. "It must have been running backwards then. It was running when we went out. I was sure. Never mind, anyway. My watch must be in the bathroom."

He half skated, half walked, like a child discovering some novel pleasure in the matter of fact of adult utilitarianism, across to the coffee table, where the design of a Ronson concentrated most of the light there was in the room and showed it off against the dark wood. The cigarette tasted like the first one in the morning, harsh and fine. He unbuttoned his jacket, and as he sat on the davenport the shells in his pocket rattled around his thighs. The weight of his hunting clothes, the weight of his body, disappeared in the gentleness with which the furniture received him.

It was very good to come back from hunting to a house as comfortable as his father-in-law's. Such a return was the real reason for hunting, he thought, for a lot of people like himself.

The fog even, cold and distorting the shapes of the houses across the street like some malignance of decay that killed angles and straight lines, was a part of the general luxury as long as the windows kept it out where it belonged.

In his and Martha's apartment they had a reproduction of Breughel's picture of the hunters, and the good, satisfying thing about that, too, was that the hunters were almost home. Out of the spooky woods that weren't actually in the picture they had come back to the edge of their own town.

"Willy?"

"All right," he said. He went to the kitchen where his wife, already changed out of her snowsuit, was filling a kettle with water and had turned on the knobs of the electric stove.

"Willy," she said, "we do have time if we hurry. If you'll help me clean the pheasants we'll have time to get them roasted before Daddy and Mother get here. Or would you rather have them fried?"

"Either way."

"Daddy likes them roasted, then."

She stood poised briefly, with a thoughtful frown on her face, staring at him, and he thought she would probably ask him presently if he knew where she had put the roaster on Sunday. But she said, "Wasn't it a thrill? You're a good shot, Willy. I didn't know you were so good." Her smile trembled with perplexity. She put her hand in his armpit, and he could feel her fingernails punch his side.

He swung away from her, "So let's have a drink, then," he said. He reached for the bottle on the high shelf, the shelf above those where Mrs. Norton's Spode sat covered with felt.

"Isn't there any of ours left?" his wife asked, and he drew back. "Well, go ahead," she told him. "Only, my gosh, I thought there should be almost a full bottle of ours left."

"I won't take any if you don't think I should," he said.

"Don't pout like a baby. It's only that Daddy will be upset if he finds too much of his whiskey gone."

"So to hell with it."

"No," she said, "go on and pour yourself a little."

He collided with her when he went to the refrigerator for ice. With a purposeful and direct movement she seemed to come around him as he approached, and when he put out his hand, hers was already there, opening the door. "Scusee. Let me see what we have for salad," she said. "OK. You may have to drive to the little store. I'll see."

The old man kept good whiskey, sure enough. A little more now, he thought, for the sake of coming home from hunting. It was too late now for him to say any longer for the sake of getting home from the war. That slogan had lost its humor months ago, even if the feeling had not gone. He filled the tumbler around the ice a good half full. Martha had time to watch that.

"Too much?"

She pursed her lips, her fine, plump lips. "Don't pour any for me," she said.

"Then have some of mine."

"I don't want any. I really don't," she said.

"Oh, screw. It's only whiskey."

He sat down by the cupboard, waiting for the water to be hot enough to start scalding and cleaning the birds. He tasted the very good whiskey that her Daddy portioned out so very carefully.

"It's simply that they were good enough to let us have the house for a week," she said. "That's all. I think we should respect their things."

"Sure, I know," he said. The mouthful of whiskey solaced him, and he told himself that he did respect the Nortons' things. He'd kept the old man's shotgun cleaned, used coasters when he took his drinks into the front room. He respected the Nortons' bedroom where he and Martha had been sleeping. It was as though they were somehow not absent from their room, and he had respected them and their white-legged child who lay there beside him. It had seemed prohibitively wrong to touch her in that bed except for goodnight kisses, and in the absolute quiet of twelve, one, and two o'clock he had lain there wondering why nothing belonged to him any more.

On Mrs. Norton's dressing table in that bedroom was a little collection of her souvenirs. The collection included three things pertaining to himself and Martha. There was a silver-painted doll's chair, like a little throne just two inches high. There was a photo of himself wearing dress uniform and all his ribbons. He had sent it to them from Japan last year. And there was a model, gilded like the doll's chair and mounted on a stick, of the P-51 he had flown during the war.

The street light shining through the window showed him the silhouette of the plane sitting fixed like a dead shadow or a trophy amid the junk that Mrs. Norton had collected, and he had lain stiff in the bed on those nights thinking, She's welcome to it.

The two pheasants he had killed this afternoon were lying in a dishpan under the sink. The bodies merged in a disordered rust-colored shape—the color of new rust—in the dishpan, and their feet stuck out. The feet were black. The points of the nails were bent in on one foot as if it were clutching hard at something.

"Yeah," he said, "it was good out there hunting today." He looked at the back of his wife's head. "For some reason you're prettier in a cornfield. With the stubble. Gloomy sky. For a background, you know." She turned from the sink and gave him the teeth in a single, efficient motion before she resumed her work. (Who was it used to say that—McElroy? Kitz? Give us the teeth, boy, the Old Man really loves you, he just don't know any better way to show it.) Those suitable, matching teeth, just what the dressmaker or the jeweler or whoever it was ordered for little Martha, the prettiest little girl they ever fixed up in Bloomsdale and sent down to be the prettiest little Pi Phi at State. Quite a credit to her, those teeth, even counting all the rest. But he really wasn't worrying about her looks so much any more or letting them bother him the way they had. During the tough week before he had gone to Student Health and begun his treatment her good looks had been a torment of accusation to him, like a ring he might have hacked from a dead man's hand, or the gold Jap molar that Kitz had carried.

He was over that part of it. He knew that Martha was all right. The trouble was not with her.

"It did me good to kill those birds," he said. "They're big enough so it means something, not like the quail. Then the place we were had a lot to do with it. Gee, it is funny the way I remember it right now. It hasn't been but an hour or so, and I guess naturally I'd remember it all right for longer than that. But it's like it was still happening, it wasn't over yet. Like you have dreams. Do you have dreams, honey, where you think all day afterward that you're still having them?" He stopped at this because he knew it annoyed and scared her to hear him talking about his dreams or the way they affected him. It reminded her of the bad week. But this was another matter, after all—he was getting well now—and he went on stubbornly.

"The main thing is the way the birds look when they're hit. You don't think they are heavy at all until they are hit and when you can watch them hang there a minute before they start to fall." He put his hand up with the fingers slightly spread, watching it, trying to make it imitate in falling to his side the plunge of the dead bird. It would not work the same way.

But without his hand obscuring the image, he could see it

quite clearly against a gray like the sky that the impressed nerves of his eyes retained. That moment of suspension was the main thing. The bird all at once scattering feathers, losing what had been an almost visible course strung like a wire through the air. (Hell, but how could he explain it to her? Martha ought to turn and help him a bit. He thought there had been a time when at the crisis she pulled his ideas out of him, like the evening in '43 when the Cadets had beaten the University Freshmen at baseball and afterward in Martha's car, parked in front of the Pi Phi house, there had been a kind of glory from it to explain, something he had got from helping win the game, something solid and certain in him on that spring evening that would make whatever he was going to do soon much easier; when he had told her that he was going to act bravely through the rest of the war, she had helped him. She had not laughed or got coy when that sounded like cheap flag waving. He had put his thumb up against the side of her throat and felt the even, heavy beating of her pulse while he said it and while she had looked at him in that wonderful way that made him able to talk. . . .) That moment he had watched the bird was like the moment the Zeke had started going to pieces. The immense *slap slap* of the wing guns that made him want to yell or come, the fast silver plane that had no weight at all, suddenly getting very heavy there ahead with pieces flying out of the wing and the cockpit cowling, seeming to hang without moving while the junk came out of it, getting heavier until it seemed that he was going to run into it before it started to fall. It had looked that way then. The film from his camera had shown it just that way. It had looked like that this afternoon.

Falling after that second of suspension while the wing feathers broke and seemed to blow upward while the body dropped, the first bird had struck behind a row of corn stubble. By the time he got to it, it had propped itself upright. The neck he reached to grasp was pulled back like a snake's head, the eye a black spot on the blue feathers like a snake's eye, not frightened at all but full of hate for him. Just as he had ahold of it, everything left in the bird's body struck at him—the broken wings, talons, body itself fighting his hold until he swung it around a couple of times.

"You know," he said, wondering, "killing is a serious thing. You understand that when you do it."

With the bird hanging limp in his hand he had turned to see Martha coming across the stubble behind him. She was out of breath from running and her lips were apart. Against the slate sky her white face and almost-white hair looked like a photograph—and a particular photograph, he realized, the one he had tacked to the beer cooler at the head of his cot while they were on Okinawa, identified as the one that Kitz made the joke and the gesture about everytime he looked at it. Kitz made him mad with that at first, but later it was pleasing in a natural enough way to have someone else confirm the meaning of those expectantly narrowed eyes and the parting of the lips. There had been times later when it was reassuring to have Kitz see this thing in the photograph. There were times when he would lie there on the cot, reading the damn poor letters that Martha sent, telling about the Pi Phi dances and what her daddy thought of Roosevelt and the war, listening to the radio play jazz in the next tent, hearing the jungle insects thump against the screen—times when he would stare at the white and gray picture and see only something smooth, toothy, and cold. Kitz, finding him like that, would sit on the cot and say, "What an expensive-looking beast," while he looked at the picture and wiped his chin. They would have a drink on that, and afterward in his imagination the picture would become a living thing again.

"Killing can be a good or bad thing. Like these birds . . ." he said eagerly and once more attempted to imitate their significant death with the dropping of his hand.

"The water's hot," Martha said. "Roll up your sleeves."

He turned red and gulped the rest of the whiskey swiftly. He said, "I bitched that, didn't I?"

"Why—what?" Then she understood and came to put her arms around him. "I heard every word you said. It was a lot of fun. I think it did you a world of good. I think you're sleeping better these nights than you have since last year. You feel lots better than when we came, don't you? You'll be ready to go back to school next week, I'll bet."

"Sure." He began to make a fuss over scalding and plucking the birds.

"We'll have to hurry," Martha said. "Mother and Daddy will be cold after their long drive. They said they'd be here tonight by dinnertime. It would be nice if we could have dinner all ready for them when they get here, wouldn't it?"

"You bet," he said. We have to make a good showing for Daddy and Mother, he thought.

"Say, here," Martha's father said jovially, at the same time with an assertive, manly deprecation, "what kind of a book is this?"

To Willy the question seemed a continuing of the friendly measurement to which they had been subjecting him since they got home. He wished he did not need to answer. This was not the time when he could talk to Mr. Norton, because he felt, after the hunting and then the whiskey, more tired and exposed, more likely to give himself away to them than he had even on the last visit. He wished he could push himself simply a little farther back onto the expensive softness of the davenport and pass strangely out of the room where he sat having to talk while the women finished getting dinner.

At the door itself, on the minute of their arrival, he had felt their eyes checking him at once as though their main interest was to find the flaw in his tall enough, athletic enough body or in his face, the flaw that had justified a university doctor's having told him to rest a week in the middle of the semester. Then, as though to hide or camouflage her curiosity, Mrs. Norton had tugged at him with her plump arms stretched over his shoulders, trying to kiss him, make everything quite ordinary enough, while he pulled away from her in shamed awkwardness.

They were after him in their kindhearted way like horse-traders who have bought some handsome horseflesh, led it innocently and proudly enough home to their stables, and then with the beginning of wonder and suspicion that they have been cheated, sense some flaw in the blood which spoils their bargain, which will make the beast worthless and in time will make them laughingstocks of the community for having been taken in by it. They had been measuring him like an animal, he thought, or going on with the idea, maybe like parents who suspect their kid has swallowed a pin or stuck a bean up his nose and are trying the means of kindness to get him to confess this so they can take common sense and practical action to remove it.

"'Only one death to a customer, you understand,'" Mr. Norton read from the book. "I'll be damned. Is that supposed to be a joke or something? Why is it printed lengthwise like that?" He turned the face of the page toward Willy and held the book out at arm's length. "I notice the printing is queer in this book. I never saw anything like it. You have to read this book for one of your courses?"

"No. A friend of ours lent it to me."

"You like to read this kind of stuff?" He could see Mr. Norton stiffen like a pointer that has caught a red-hot scent.

"I don't know," he said. "I don't really understand it. It's a kind of poetry, I guess." And Mr. Norton relaxed with a sort of visible reassurance, still puzzled though.

"Some of those 'friends' you had when you and Martha lived in that rathole apartment house? This is the kind of book I'd expect them to read." His thin-lipped mouth fell into a smile. "God, I had a time with Momma after we'd been there to visit you. She thought she'd got the bedbugs. Myself, I wouldn't have minded that. Kids just get married, housing the way it is, won't hurt you to rough it a little. Those people, though, bedbugs and lice. Four-Fs and Jews running all over the place. You still see them since you moved?"

Willy said, "Yes, once in a while. Weiss's wife loaned me that book."

"Weiss's wife, huh? I think you introduced us to this fellow Weiss." Mr. Norton took a cigarette from his case and put it in the short black hard-rubber holder he always used at home. He seemed to be examining the implications of the fact that Weiss had a wife whom he had not seen and who, of course, might be seductive in some Levantine way. "Do you think Martha likes these people?" he asked abruptly. Then he shook his head in a hard, uncompromising gesture. "As a matter of fact, I'm sure she doesn't. Not from anything she has said to us. Martha is not the kind to complain. You know that. No, but she let little things slip out. That was part of what was behind it when we got so— ah, you know, Willy—when we got on your tail about moving to a better apartment last summer."

Mr. Norton slumped a little bit in his chair and let a tall unwavering streamer of smoke rise from his cigarette while he thought again. He said gently, "I was seven kinds of a small-town fool the way I handled that, Willy. I don't blame you for getting sore and saying the things you had to say about it. But Momma was upset about Martha living in such a place, and women are. . . . You said a lot of true things then, Willy. Momma and I were talking on the way home and I told her what I thought. I said, 'Look here what we did. We jumped into the

kids' affair and got Willy to make a financial move he couldn't
see his way clear to taking right then and then by God I had the
gall to make him sign a note for the money it would take to get
this other apartment for a year.' I thought no wonder with that
hanging over you when you've still got two years to go that
you've been"— Mr. Norton looked as hard as he could for the
kindest, most reassuring word here—"*worried sick.* So—" he
fumbled in his inner coat pocket and from several papers selected one. His hard honest face turned pink in self-consciousness. "I'm going to tear that note up. Christmas present from
Momma and me."

Willy said sharply, as the paper was already coming apart between Mr. Norton's fingers, "Don't do that."

"Christmas present," Mr. Norton said. Martha came into the
room and sat on the arm of her father's chair while he explained
the gift to her. Willy watched her beautiful silk-clad leg swinging
back and forth.

Sure, he thought, that apartment house where we lived and
where the Weisses live was no place for her. They had come to it
in the kind of thoughtless desperation which the news that
there was any apartment at all vacant in the university town
seemed to stir up in otherwise sensible people. It was pure accident that he and Martha got into that building.

Right after he came home from Japan and they were married
they'd got a trailer. Handsome little trailer acquired by the university for housing just such as he and Martha; but the things
which had happened between him and Martha in its regimented
space were not exactly what either of them had been hoping for
while he was overseas. They both felt cramped in the trailer and
thought they had to have an apartment soon if they weren't
going to get so irritated that they would be forced to quarrel with
each other.

Willy had been more afraid of a quarrel with Martha than of
anything else. He had not by any means forgotten the years
when he wanted her so much and couldn't have her, and a quarrel was impossible after all that waiting.

So they had held their noses and moved into the buggy apartment house. They thought they could fix their place up some.
They could paint the walls and build in bookcases and have
space to use the really nice wedding presents they had got from
Martha's family and friends. Some crumby-looking people lived

in the house with them. Graduate students and art majors. There was no law they had to associate with them, though, just because they lived in the same building.

How they got mixed up with the Weisses and their parties and friends he did not yet know, but by now he had come full circle to the point of wondering why all these people should like him. He really didn't know what they talked about. He hadn't read the books they shouted and quarreled about while everyone got drunk. After Martha would go home to the apartment down the hall he would sit crosslegged on the floor among them, like a big innocent puppy, while the hot angry dispute went on around him. Sometimes, when they talked about the war or the desperate things they would do in case of another one, they appealed to him—the halfway hero in their midst, the fighter pilot—as a judge, thrusting their sick, bearded, myopic, pimpled faces close to his own. Or they demanded at other times that he side with them in their interpretation of Marx, Freud, or James, and he went home and tried to read the books they yelled about.

Even after he and Martha moved, they kept asking him back to the parties, and this fall he went to most of them—once a week or so—and Martha had never gone or objected to his going—"If you have fun."

It was not fun, and he knew these people were not any happier than he was, but the late drunken hours of their parties had more attraction for him than just the noise or the whiskey.

He would be sitting there maybe, among the 4-Fs and Jews, the graduate students, bedbugs, and cockroaches, looking at the sea-green Kemtone (the sea far below him as it had been beyond his wingtips in the Oriental dawn) on the wall, hearing a fanatic insistence in the voice which was saying ". . . this thing of Jeffer's where the soldier has his mother put her hand in the rotten hole in his side . . ." The voice sounded like the speaker was being killed himself and wanted very much to live, like the wish to live was sickening him.

In those climactic flashes he got from them the feeling he had this afternoon when the pheasant struck its broken bones against his wrist. He did not really understand the books they loaned him; he wanted desperately to do so.

He had the book in his hands now, though in front of Mr. Norton he didn't wish to read it. He was leafing through it slowly and carefully toward the passage which had so amused and outraged his father-in-law. It had sounded familiar, and he thought he remembered seeing it somewhere among the scattered fragments of slogan and typographical fancies that made up what the publishers called a novel.

Martha's mother beside him was holding her hands up in a pudgy triangle, describing to Martha a faille dress she had seen in Nieman-Marcus. "We had such a good time in Dallas, Daddy and I. They can say what they want to about California, but I think Texas is the coming place. Why, it was the best part of the trip, and the people there are so friendly. I wish we could move there for our 'old days' when Daddy sells the store . . . or when you and Willy take it over." She turned smiling to Willy, not wishing to leave him out of the conversation which she had kept up since dinner. "You were in Dallas or thereabouts when you were in training, weren't you? Didn't you find the people nice, Willy?"

"I liked them," he said.

"Such an exciting place," Mrs. Norton said. "So many nice eating places, and the stores—my!—and theaters and nice houses, not mansions but just nice. Such sunny-looking people. My, I've never seen so many pretty young girls walking along the streets. They all seemed so well dressed."

"Were there pretty girls in Dallas when you were a cadet?" Martha asked. She looked at him cutely, flirting, lowering her lashes over her blue eyes; she arched her back slowly and ran the fingers of both hands through her hair, watching him watch her.

He nodded, thinking crazily, God, she's asking for it, and she didn't dare ask until they came home to be her reinforcements; worked it out, and thinking, I owe it to her, I owe it to them.

"Then we can't move down there," Martha said to her mother. Her voice was husky and suggestive. "I'd never be able to bring Willy down on a visit."

Mr. Norton, on the other side of the room, in his own chair and under his lamp again, rattled his newspaper and cleared his throat.

"I don't think you have to worry about Willy looking at any 'other' pretty girls," her mother said and patted Martha's knee, smiling. "Willy, you wait until you see Martha's new negligee that we got her. It's—well, not for an unmarried girl, but it's pretty."

"Don't make Willy blush, Mother," Martha said. The red line of her lips was fixed in a stubborn smile. Her eyes were uncertain.

"I'll try to stand it," Willy said, and the sarcasm in his voice shamed and surprised him.

"You can, all right," Martha said.

He thought, She's already talked to her mother about me. While they were washing dishes they were talking about me, and Mrs. Norton is trying to encourage me because she still thinks I can be all right if I want to. He shrugged and said, "I'm tired," as though he meant "Leave me alone."

Something in the tension of their speech, something that had not been present before the Nortons arrived home, was heavy enough to break the conversation for a little while.

In the silence Mr. Norton snapped the paper he was reading. "Here's a story will amuse you, Willy. As a veteran. 'Sentenced for Refusing to Register. Judge Albert Minor today sentenced Orlin Johnson of Kahokia to two years imprisonment for refusing to register for the draft. Johnson pleaded not guilty, declaring that he had seen a vision'—get it, seen a vision—'which made him unable to comply with draft requirements. Johnson, the father of three children, described a series of sleepless nights preceding his decision not to register. On one occasion, he declared, he had seen a vision in which he was swimming in a sea of vomit, and after seeing this he felt himself unable to enter the armed services. Other defendants pleaded guilty and were given suspended sentences.'"

When the word "vomit" was read by her husband, Mrs. Norton waved her hand and said "Oh Charlie" in protest against her husband's teasing her by reading this dirty word.

"What do you think of that?" Mr. Norton said to Willy, folding the paper together and resting it on his knee.

In his back, just above the hips, Willy felt a surge of muscle and a tightening so intense that he thought for a minute he was going to lose his water. "They ought to beat his head between two stones," he said.

"Ha," Mr. Norton chuckled.

"The judge," Willy said.

The family group of four sat there in a sudden immobility, like the fabled people caught in the attitudes of pleasant sociability in a familiar room by an instantaneous fall of lava. As though the secret which threatened Willy's mind should have been brought to light—as they had wanted, of course—with a mad inversion of the proprieties through which they wished to see it.

First Mr. Norton said, "I've talked to plenty of veterans. . . ." Then it took him several minutes of alternate rage and calming before he said, "Everybody to his own opinion. I couldn't stay in business a minute in Bloomsdale if I talked like that."

Willy shook his head miserably, "I don't have an opinion. It's the . . ." They waited for him to finish. He could see Martha getting terribly ashamed for him. He saw Mrs. Norton moving her lips as though she were trying to help him with the word, but he did not know what it was.

He heard Martha say, "Daddy!" and he felt as though he could strike her for interrupting, because he had to say this thing as soon as he could. Then miraculously it seemed that she had guessed close to what he meant, because she began gaily talking about the afternoon. "In back of Lotterman's grove," she said, "and Willy killed one before I knew what was happening. Before he knew what was happening, I guess." She laughed and her parents laughed a little, politely, still watching him.

"It's the . . ." He sat there strangling over the obscene word *death* which he wanted to say to them, so just once they would understand what his world and his war were about.

"What, Willy?" Mrs. Norton asked, softly as she would coax a child.

"Oh, Willy," Martha said sadly, disappointed in him that he would not let her smooth his way.

He walked to the stairway and then felt his way up by hanging on the banister. He did not hear them talking behind him, or Mrs. Norton's sympathetic exclamation, but he knew they would have things to say to each other in which he could take no part.

Then he was in the Nortons' bedroom, standing in the center of it like a prisoner who could not answer the accusation of its witnessing furniture. He looked at the picture of himself and the model plane on the dressing table, and now he was frightened stiff by the Nortons having kept them there so long after the war was over and it was time to replace them. He picked up the toy chair—like a diminutive throne—that had belonged to Martha.

In a little while he reached for the model plane and was surprised to see it break from its mount, thinking he had touched it lightly. But then he picked it up and squeezed it. The wood crumpled in his hand. One by one the splinters slid off his palm. He set his thumb on the toy chair and smashed that too.

Only that wasn't mine to break, he thought in an immediate reflex of emotion. They kept that and the plane too because they loved us. He looked at the scraps on the table top and thought stupidly, They can glue them back together if they want to and keep them forever. Only to hell with it, because they would never forget that the things had to be mended.

He carried the fragments to his suitcase and, opening it, hid them under some dirty underclothes in the side of the bag where he kept things for the laundry. From the side in which his clean clothes remained he took his Japanese pistol and stuck it in the waistband of his trousers.

Martha stopped him at the back door as he was going out. "What's the matter, Willy? Don't be unhappy tonight, hon. Oh, what a silly mess, damn it."

He stepped past her into the cold night, and she followed him. "Go on back," he said coaxingly. "Shoo. I'm all right. I just want to walk by myself awhile." He saw the wind moving the beautiful tips of her hair against her cheek. "I don't feel so very well. I guess those fine birds we got didn't agree with me as well as they did with your folks. The air will fix me."

"Are you sure?" she said. "Let me come along."

He took three steps down the walk and paused as though he were going to explain something further to her.

"Please," she said.

"Naa," he said. "You're not wrapped up. Run back now. Quick." She looked as beautiful in the porch light as he ever remembered seeing her—in the photo on the beer cooler, on the campus before the war, anywhere, anytime. "You're nice," he said. "I wish. . . ."

She shivered and left him with one more admonition not to stay out too long. He walked toward the edge of town, in the direction of the viaduct. When he reached it, he stepped over the guard cables of the approach and slid down the dirt embankment. He edged around the embankment until he felt his way into a clump of weeds that seemed to shelter him from the nagging cold of the air. He took out the pistol and set the muzzle against his neck. Because he was a nice boy, he felt a pang of conscience about causing the Nortons all this trouble and all they were going to have afterward, but in a way they had brought it on themselves.

The Crime of
Mary Lynn Yager

I

The yellow school bus bearing the name of Barstle Consolidated was parked at the edge of the picnic grounds on the hilltop. It contained empty thermos jugs, baskets with leftover
buns and bananas the second graders from Barstle had been unwilling or unable to eat, two neat little bags of garbage collected
before Miss Carlson would let her charges go for their hike on
the wooded lakeshore, and the sweaters that had turned out to
be unnecessary on this early May day. It sat square and clumsy
in the sun, casting a dingy black shadow on the gravel. Nevertheless, seen from below through the branches of beech and elm
on the slope, it looked like something alive. Like a great yellow
burst of flowers, or like a giant golden animal crouched in the
branches watching the second graders and their teacher.

Clarissa Carlson had noticed this before she turned her back on it. With the sun on her eyelids, the warmth of it striking through her skirt and toasting the limestone outcrop on which she sat, she forgot the bus and nearly everything else except the immediate joy of their outing.

Clarissa had taken off her shoes and dangled her feet in the water. It was already quite warm in the sandy shallows of the cove. She had brought her pupils back to it on purpose because she was satisfied it was safe for them to wade here. Bobbie Tenman and Ronnie Cole, Frieda Smith, Nickie Pelligrini, and June Moore were splashing more water than they should be, perhaps, as they skipped in front of her. It was apparent that their pleasure and the extravagance of its expression were doubled by Clarissa's watching. Those who had chosen not to wade were hunting the underbrush for fossils or flowers, ducking spiderwebs. These were in orbit around her, too. Though they might edge away in brief absorption, they quickly swung back toward her when their diversions paled, knowing that where Miss Carlson was the fun would be. She felt herself holding the group together by some natural authority quite distinct from her authority as their teacher.

Frieda and June pranced toward her in a decorative shower of splashes. Too gently to have any effect, she cautioned them not to get their dresses wet. All knew that didn't matter. The sun would take care of that. It took care of everything for them today.

"What's . . ." Frieda said in an explosive giggle of breath. "No! I mean what's black and white and red all over?"

"Newspaper. She means a newspaper," Bobbie Tenman yelled. He had launched himself forward to twist between the girls and spoil their riddle—rather, to win again the competition for Miss Carlson's attention.

"Shame on you, Bobbie," she said. He was not rebuked. His loving teacher no more shamed him than the sunlight did or the mellow air that softened all squabbles. He knew from her look she felt like kissing him.

"Now tell me, Frieda," Clarissa said formally. "What is black and white and read all over? I can't guess."

Behind her was the rustling of small shoes on the carpet of the forest floor. The other children were edging in to hear how Miss Carlson made everything all right once again, how deftly she corrected rambunctious boys and lifted shy girls to a comradeship of interest. She felt them coming to her and the breath swelled in her throat with happiness. "Tell me, Frieda."

"A . . . a . . . a *motorcycle!*" Frieda squealed.

"How could a . . ."

"Motorcycle!"

". . . be . . ."

"Haw!"

"Black and white?"

"Red?"

"Read?"

"Must be black and white on one side and red . . ."

"All over!" Frieda shouted. Her eyebrows lifted as if she had a vision of this improbable object. She nodded a frantic affirmative.

"Must look . . ."

". . . couldn't."

"Funny!"

"Children, children. Hush, you children dear," Clarissa said, not even bothering to raise her voice into their din. In a minute she was going to be swept into laughter so tender it might almost go over into tears. She had never loved anything as she loved this moment with all of them together, ringed around her on the stone, counting on her.

And it would be over so soon! The long-planned picnic was an end-of-year event. And this was her second and last year of teaching. She would be married in August when Joe Meadow got his MA in chemistry and took her off "to the Seattle area." (People didn't plan to live in *places* any more, her father had grumbled sweetly. They meant to live in *areas,* as if—six years after VJ day now—they were still in service.) Joe had an offer from Boeing contingent on his degree. He was flatteringly impatient to get her out to the coast where they could enjoy water-skiing and other marital pleasures together.

In fact she had been at least as impatient as he for these last two years. She had taken the teaching job at Barstle solely because it would keep her within twenty miles of Joe at the University in Iowa City. The location of her job had let her spend most of her weekends with him as they had done when both were undergraduates, dancing at the Hawk Ball Room, drinking beer with the Pi Phi's, watching television in the sorority lounge. It was only at the end that she could say her teaching had been rewarding to her.

The frustration of waiting was gone with the winter. In these last few minutes before she herded her fourteen little ones into the bus and drove them back to Barstle she was ready to admit how much she had liked her work. Sitting on the warm stone she felt an almost dangerous maternal passion for these kids, strangers still, almost nameless creatures of air and light, figures in a painting with her portrayed enthroned at its center. She sat with her eyes nearly closed. On her plain, pleasant face was the motionless smile of an idol. She had never felt so pretty before, had never felt so intensely what it meant to be a woman. She felt this moment to be a premonition of a time when she would sit with her own children around her on the shores of the huge Pacific, in the Seattle area.

Then, in the very instant of her dream's intensity, as if she had done something wrong, she felt the children's attention lift from her. It seemed the day had quickly chilled. Had they seen before she did that yellow shape among the trees—which was really only the aged bus that every day carried them to and from school—begin to crawl toward them, flicking a powerful tail? Before she looked where they were looking she noticed that the breeze had stopped altogether. She had not been aware of its cessation.

With them she saw a fat old man running in their direction on the path twenty yards across the cove. He was older than her father. His breath-stretched mouth was red as fresh hamburger, and there was a great tuft of gray hair protruding from the collar of his shirt. He stopped once as if intending to yell, seemed unable to muster enough breath, trotted a few steps farther to a point where the path was less screened by underbrush. He put his hands around his mouth and shouted.

"They's one in the water. Must be yours."

Her sun-drugged mind batted the horrid notion back like a ball. He had come from the direction of the dam and they hadn't even hiked down that way. Plainly the old fellow had some dreadful news, but she knew how to shelter her children from it. She would stay calm, though now it was time to marshal all fourteen of them for the climb to the bus. She would still get them home in their holiday mood, subdued but clucking from their day in the sun.

It was only on her count of thirteen that she was on her feet and running.

II

Clarissa would never be excused from the moment of relief when she understood that it was Mary Lynn Yager she had lost. As she ran weeping and panting across the long dam to the cluster of fishermen near the spillway and recognized the soaked little body at their feet, Clarissa's first ghastly emotion was thanksgiving. All her good ones were safe.

Months ago she had identified Mary Lynn to Joe Meadow as "the kid I can't abide." Mary Lynn had been, beyond all question of a biased judgment, a tattle tale, always trying to get one of the others in trouble. In schoolyard games it was her tactic— Clarissa was long convinced this was on purpose—to bump herself or fall down and then pretend to be hurt worse than she was so that again and again a recess that had begun with pleasure had ended in confusion, anxiety, and an irritation on Clarissa's part that had to be suppressed because you could not make accusations against a seven-year-old girl whose knee or elbow was often actually bleeding. In the classroom when the others thrilled or laughed together at a problem or story, Mary Lynn's mouth habitually puckered as though she had bit something sour. She used to squint her close-set eyes and nod over her desk as though she had caught them at something illicit. Sometimes she would break into furtive laughter in the midst of a quiet period and then slyly refuse to admit what she found so funny.

"I know the type," Joe had affirmed. "Accident prone. But more than that. I knew a nut like that in high school. He was a drop-out finally. He was a wrong guy."

Up until now it had been all right to think of Mary Lynn as "a wrong little girl,' one problem at least that could be left behind when Clarissa quit teaching. But now Mary Lynn was dead. That was something else again.

Clarissa dropped prone beside the limp child and opened her mouth over Mary Lynn's in the way she had been taught. It was as if a part of her terror lay in the conviction that Mary Lynn was getting away with something that mustn't be allowed.

Two of the fishermen lifted Clarissa and set her on her feet. "We tried that," one of them said from far away. She strained to listen. "Me'n Roscoe took turns. We done the right things. She been in too long."

As the coroner would declare later, Mary Lynn had been in the water for probably half an hour. It would seem certain she had simply not stopped with the others at the cove below the parking lot but had slipped on through the budding undergrowth to the dam. At its far end she had crossed on a catwalk plainly labeled "No Admittance" to the concrete intake tower of the spillway. Leaning over its edge she had fallen and remained unnoticed until the old man, coming near to fish with his wife and sister, had seen her at the tower's base partly supported by a pile of underwater stones. Beyond any question that could be decently or reasonably asked, it was an accidental death. "Foul play was definitely ruled out," the coroner said.

And so was negligence, said Mr. Tobra, the principal at Barstle Consolidated, who never dreamed of denying he had given Clarissa permission to take her grade to the lake for their picnic. Only Clarissa Carlson would never be sure of either verdict.

At least she had mastered herself enough to keep the rest of her children from going hysterical. They had followed her part way out on the dam. It seemed to her that her legs had to provide all the strength required to walk them in a huddling cluster up to the bus. Fortunately one of the fishermen came along to drive it back to town.

A mile out of Barstle Clarissa became aware that cars were falling in behind them. These were the parents of the survivors. Word of the drowning had gone into town ahead of them. The schoolyard when they swung into it was full of other cars and a humming crowd. It throbbed with the passion of the event, and a new dynamic of excitement rose with the shrieks of Clarissa's children tumbling from the bus into the arms of mothers and fathers, trying instantly to answer what had happened.

It was this babble that began Clarissa's hysteria. It seemed to be her fault that she could not make out a single line of meaning from the babble of grief around her. She saw that great purple thunder clouds were piling up above the maples of the schoolyard and obscuring the sun. These towering heights of darkness, edged with smoky scarlet and gold, seemed to mean something, too. But though she tried very hard she could no more decipher their message to her than she could grasp the anxious, gentle questions being put to her by Mr. Tobra and by Mr. Hearst, the mayor of Barstle who was also the chairman of the schoolboard.

Seeing her condition, these good men led her into the school-

house and up the oil-smelling stairs to Mr. Tobra's office. They
urged her into the swivel chair in front of his desk. There was a
phone immediately in front of her and the first intelligible words
she heard came from it.

"You hang on. Hang on, Clarissa," Joe Meadow was saying to
her. "I'll start from Iowa City in ten minutes. Have you called
your father?"

She said, "I tried to give her mouth-to-mouth in the proper
way."

"There was nothing else you could do."

"It wasn't my fault," she said eagerly. "Mary Lynn was being
naughty. . . ." She put down the phone reluctantly. It was like
tearing a sprained muscle to turn from it and face Mr. Hearst
and Mr. Tobra. "I'd rather have lost my hand," she wept to
them. "I'd rather have lost a . . . a . . . a *leg*."

"Surely. Surely," Mr. Hearst said.

"Mary Lynn's parents . . . Everyone will assume it was my
fault."

"Oh no. No!" Mr. Tobra cried in the bewilderment of his responsibilities. He might not be much else, the principal of Barstle, but he was fair. If he could not be fair in this crisis, it would
break him. "Only you mustn't . . . You mustn't say to anyone
that Mary Lynn was being . . ."

Still he couldn't force himself to repeat the word and Mr.
Hearst had to finish for him. "Being 'naughty.' Don't say that. It
was a pure accident, such as happens." Mr. Hearst closed his
eyes and held his breath for a minute as if it had become more
precious to him now.

Joe Meadow arrived on the scene convinced that his one duty
was to take care of Clarissa's interests. His young, clean jaw was
set. From the minute he walked into the office his manner declared him on Clarissa's side, though Mr. Tobra and Mr. Hearst
kept humbly evading the idea that there was cause for taking
sides.

"This Yager girl," Joe wanted to know, "didn't she have a
record of being accident prone?" It sounded as if he were asking
about a police record.

"Record?" Mr. Tobra stared at him. Shook his head in re-
proof. Mary Lynn had no record, of course, except a report card,
on which the letters Clarissa had entered had no pertinence
whatever now.

It wasn't in Joe to be overbearing. He too knew there was a

painful mystery to be respected. Only he was more persistent than their good will warranted. Perhaps Clarissa's words on the phone had set him off on a risky tack. "Well, what can we expect from the child's parents?" he asked. His tone was very businesslike. "I mean, have you heard from them yet? Does anyone know what they think? What sort of people are they?"

"Why I don't know much about them," Mr. Hearst said. "No one else in Barstle does either." This seemed a favorable point to Joe, just a pity to Mr. Hearst. He went on as if all such explanations were bitter now, "I hear they are renting on the Whittaker farm. Been there since a year ago March. They have several children don't they, Tobra?"

"Five others in school," Mr. Tobra said.

"Joe," Clarissa said, rising abruptly and moving toward the door and the stairway, "take me out to their place right now. I want to tell them." If others got there ahead of her, Mary Lynn's parents might get the wrong idea. . . .

"Miss Carlson, you don't have to," Mr. Tobra said. "Your father will be coming down. Talk to him first."

She kept on going without even shaking her head. When Joe and she were in his car and searching down the country roads for the farm where the Yagers lived, it seemed to her she was moving through a dark tunnel at the end of which glowed a blue, underwater light, gradually but constantly diminishing. The sky had gone completely gray now, without the angry fringes of red and gold that had heralded her return to town in the bus.

"I never let her know," Clarissa said, "that I disliked her."

"Of course not, sweetheart," Joe said smoothly.

"It couldn't have been that that made her do it," she said. "If I showed it a little, it still isn't enough to make her do that."

"Make her . . . ? Make her do what?" Carefully Joe's brown hands managed the shift and steering wheel to bring his car to a halt at the edge of the gravel. They stopped in dark green weeds at the roadside, and they could smell the rain advancing over a nearby field of young alfalfa. "Now sweetheart," he said. He turned toward her like a doctor preparing stern instructions for a child. "Sweetheart, we can't go out there while you have ideas like that. Mr. Tobra was right. Talk to your father. Made her do *what?*"

She saw the horror in his eyes as if he thought she had enticed him in deeper than he wanted to go. She saw him fight a horror no one had any right to inflict on the survivors. She wanted to tell him that it was Mary Lynn who inflicted it, not her, but she bit her lip to keep silent.

"She didn't intend to. For God's sake," he said. He began to rub the edge of his hand against the sleeve of his jacket. His voice softened to normal. "Come on. Let's scoot into Iowa City and wait for your father there."

The light at the end of her imaginary tunnel was almost out. She said—calmly, she thought, understandably, she thought— "We were all so happy there wading until she did it." Then the rebuke of his expression was too much to bear alone. She threw herself on him, her mouth on his, bearing him back against the side of the car, fighting him for the reassurance she absolutely needed to save herself.

She tasted on his lips the taste of lake water. She knew he was tasting the same thing. Then she began to sob without restraint.

"Darling," she heard him say. "I have to get you to a doctor." It seemed to her the car was constantly accelerating as they went from gravel to paved highway and on to the University Hospital in Iowa City. Joe took her straight to the emergency room where she was given a drug that quieted her. Mercifully she forgot what she had been about to say to the Yagers about their trouble-making child.

III

By the time she called on the Yagers the next evening her thoughts were "all squared up,' as her father phrased it. Of course it was he who had done most to give her perspective. He and her mother had driven down from Dubuque, and during the night while she slept under the cloudy influence of the drug, he and Joe had "made inquiries." They had talked to nearly everyone who might be officially concerned with the tragedy. They had the word from the coroner and a deputy sheriff who had questioned such witnesses as there were to the discovery of the body. They even spoke to the parents of some of Clarissa's pupils, the Tenmans and the Pellegrinis.

In the late morning when Clarissa woke rested and had eaten a good breakfast with Joe and her parents, her father drove her out to the dam to look at it again in daylight. "A thing like this," he said, "it will bother you worse if you just remember the place from the time something . . . you know, real *tough* was happening than if you look at it again and see the old world is still what she was in spite of people's losses." He had been in the Normandy invasion and she remembered how he still meant to go back sometime and see the hedgerows and a seacoast town near Caen.

In a gray drizzle they walked across the dam and he held her hand while they looked down into the calm water where Mary Lynn had fallen. She stared timidly toward the parking lot where she had seen the yellow bus in ominous distortion. There was nothing to see now except sopping trees against a sky smeared like a blackboard. She squeezed her father's hand in gratitude for his comforting demonstration.

"I *want* you to go out and see the parents," he said. "You wouldn't be my little girl if you didn't show them you shared their sorrow. But remember this, will you? Don't go into detail about your feelings. All right?"

"Did Joe say what I told him last night?"

"Honey, Joe knows and you and I know you went over the edge last night. No. He didn't go into details. I just meant there is good reason to be kind of . . . kind of *formal* in such a situation. The Yagers are good people from what I hear. Fine people, I imagine. They maybe aren't just like you is all I mean."

She frowned her bewilderment.

"I mean they're not educated like you. You might confuse them if you weren't . . . sort of formal. Not cold or anything. You know what I mean."

She thought she did. Part of the requirement seemed to be to dress as carefully as, on Easter mornings in her sorority house, she had dressed for church. That was very different from dressing carefully for a special date. It was not vanity but respect. It was part of her code that the Yagers would sense her attitude if she deeply believed it.

Sloshing into the waterfilled ruts of the Yagers' drive, she was not so sure. There were ragged walls of maples on either side, but their gloom didn't hide the shabbiness of the house. She had not believed there were such ramshackle places in Iowa any more. The hulls of old cars shone phosphorescently near the barn amid a forest of junked machinery. A runty yellow dog with eyes that reminded her of Mary Lynn's barked ceaselessly at the dripping sides of her car. She was not so much afraid that he would nip her when she got out as that he would jump on her and muddy her nylons or her skirt.

At the side of the slanting and unpainted porch, at least four small faces watched her predicament from the bottom of a lighted window. Surely they would let it be known she was here, surely someone would come to call off the dog.

As she waited minute after minute for that, she became aware of another sound as a kind of background for the dog's intermittent fits of barking. She thought it might be cattle lowing in the fields beyond the house, but it went on and on without any real breaks. She realized the sound was coming from a human throat.

"Jiggs!"

This was a woman's hard voice, sounded from an angle of the porch where a flimsy screen door opened. The dog quieted at once. The woman, who must be Mary Lynn's mother, edged farther into sight and stood watching Clarissa approach across the mud with an expression neither inviting nor menacing nor curious, but merely steadfast.

Mrs. Yager was huge. Inside the yellow-lighted dining room among her seven surviving children she looked like a full grown turkey hen incongruously mothering a brood of bantam chickens. They all shared with their dead sister a ferret-like evasiveness, as if it were the human characteristic this family was born to perpetuate.

"I'm so sorry. I want you to know . . . ," Clarissa began with brave formality. As if to drown her words on purpose the lowing of grief from the adjoining room rose in pitch. Her startled glance through the door showed a man, who must be Mr. Yager, lying on his back on a bed. He was fully clothed, but his shirt tails were out and hiked up so she could see the surge of his ribs as his breath moaned in and out.

"It's the bad luck of it," Mrs. Yager said as she closed the bedroom door. "I think the Mister's taken on so because we lost one over to Remsen year before last. The little boy."

"Boy?" Clarissa was already rocking into bewilderment at the contrast between the total abandonment of the moaning and this woman's apparent complacency.

"A horse kicked him. He was jabbing it in the withers with a branch. That's what they said. You can't tell. It was bad luck and two in a year, that's what's hard on him."

Clarissa raised her voice and began all over again, "I want you to know how much we will miss her."

The woman smiled as if at the recognition of a lie she needn't even bother to contest. "Yas'm," she would agree as Clarissa went on with her prepared sentiments. "Oh?" she would ask when Clarissa said something nice about Mary Lynn. "Well!" she would exclaim. But her eyes, as she rocked slowly back and forth demanded, What do you know about death or life either, you with your sorority clothes and something nice to say about everything? It seemed the woman knew she had been coached, had been coddled with a numbing drug, had only come here to shed quickly the burden of death, leaving it on the hands of those who had been chosen to bear it.

Then Mrs. Yager said, "Mary Lynn thought so highly of you." The fraudulence of this sentiment seemed all the worse for sounding like an imitation of what Clarissa had to say. "She wished to give you something. Something as a tribute," the big woman cooed. "Something she was working on and making herself for the last day of school. Course she never finished it. Luanne, you go fetch it so Miss Carlson can *see* anyhow."

The eleven-year-old lounging by the door looked stupefied for a minute. She was going to ask, What are you talking about? Then she seemed to understand what was expected of her and disappeared.

"I've gathered up all her books and exercises and the pictures she colored," Clarissa said. She opened the bag she had prepared, offering it like a salesman showing unwanted samples.

"We'll be glad to have them." Mrs. Yager lofted her great bulk and went to the door to shout, "Luanne, Luanne, can't you find the tribute?" And then—quite careless of whether Clarissa really believed her lie about the present or not—gave up and said, "I *do* have this that you may keep to remember Mary Lynn." In a ladder of shelves along the wall she rummaged for a minute and brought out a two-by-three inch photograph mounted in a paper easel. It was the picture of herself Mary Lynn had brought from school after the class was photographed by a traveling photographer in March. It had not even—not even tonight—found a place to be displayed in her own home. But now, as part of the

weird bargain being completed, it was to belong to Clarissa forever, that dreaded little face to be hidden or displayed as she
chose.

"She would want you to have it more than anyone," Mrs.
Yager said with nameless triumph.

Clarissa fled with the picture in her hand. She did not actually *run* from the bad luck of the house. She had her manners
and, still, the remains of confidence that since her father had
said so, formality would see her through. She made some further small talk about the funeral. But she realized she had come
before a jury that had rejected her plea. If she had come last
night, surely there would have been an armistice better than this.

Outside, a breeze was tearing away the cover of clouds. Irregular points of starlight glinted watchfully among the maples.
The dog did not bark at her as she slunk to her car. It needn't
bother now.

IV

Clarissa didn't marry Joe Meadow in August of that year. She
never married him, and she was never quite sure that their plans
collapsed because Mary Lynn Yager had died in the lake, though
this thought occurred to her again and again in times of bad luck
or grief. She could neither hold onto this as the reason nor get it
permanently out of her mind. Of this much she became fairly
certain: If Mary Lynn had not drowned when she did, the *proba-
bilities* were that the marriage would have taken place. She
would probably have gone to Seattle with Joe, improved her
water skiing, and given him the family he wanted.

It was not that they talked much about the accident after the
child was buried. She was in Dubuque with her parents that
summer. He was bearing down on his studies. They had few occasions to talk at all. When they did she noticed a growing impatience with her on his part.

"What's the trouble?" She asked it often.

"The trouble is your asking 'what's the trouble?'" he said
once with a brutal burr of anger in his voice. He apologized
promptly, but something had been exposed that might be hidden again far more easily than forgotten. The thought formed in
her mind: This is no way to begin a marriage.

They quarreled because she would not go to St. Louis with

him over the Fourth of July. He meant, of course, to stay with her in a motel. And she might have—she had no objection to it on principle—but the *way* he asked her now convinced her that he held her cheaper than before.

"I need your support in these last tough weeks," he said angrily. It seemed to her a cheap thing to say, degrading her to the level of pep pills or a diverting session on water skis.

"If we care about each other we can show it by waiting until August," she said. But she thought they were really quarreling about something else. Something they were afraid to put a name to.

One night she dreamed that she had lost one of her hands and one of her legs in an accident. Because of her disfigurement Joe didn't want her any more. Waking, she remembered that she had told Mr. Tobra and Mr. Hearst she would *rather* have lost her limbs than have lost Mary Lynn in the lake. All through the depressed day that followed she had the feeling that she had been taken at her word.

By whom? By what? It might not make sense, but that was how she felt. Still in the grip of her feeling, she wrote Joe a sharp letter saying that maybe they should put off the wedding.

He drove up to Dubuque when he got the letter and actually talked with her father and mother as well as with her about the pros and cons of waiting until he was "established" in his new job. His air of judicious disinterest made her so furious that she settled the discussion peremptorily. She was *going* to teach school one more year. If *he* wanted to wait for *her*, that was up to him.

Actually the wish to teach some more had been growing since she left Barstle. She wanted to go back there and prove something that had been left in question. Her father heard her out, but reasoned that Barstle was not the place if she meant to go on teaching. Mr. Tobra, when she called him, disconcertedly agreed. He knew of a job in Parkins, over in the western part of the state. Parkins was a somewhat bigger town than Barstle. He knew the principal over there and would certainly give her the finest recommendations. His very enthusiasm for helping her be happy *somewhere else* contributed to her itchy feeling that something menacing to her still lurked there, something that had not been buried with Mary Lynn's body.

Before she left for her year of teaching in Parkins, Clarissa said to her father, "Joe can't help thinking that I was careless in letting the Yager girl go. He *must* have the notion 'What if it had been one of our kids?'"

She stopped writing to Joe by Christmas. Instead of one year, she taught three in Parkins. At the end of her third year she married LeRoy Peterson, who owned the town lumberyard and speculated on feeder cattle. Her father said she was lucky. Though LeRoy was a divorced man he was a fine man, old enough to have learned his lesson and settled down. Clarissa thought he *could* be fine and the marriage could ripen and thrive even if it got off to an unlucky start. LeRoy was an enthusiastic bowler and had got her started bowling. He took her with him to a bowling tournament in Sioux City. She was six weeks pregnant when they hastily married.

She was moving her things into his ranch-style house at the edge of Parkins when she came across the picture of Mary Lynn that Mrs. Yager had wished on her. Clarissa shuddered when she saw the pinched little face staring up at her from among the souvenirs of her college days. She burned the picture and then had bad dreams of fire that burned without consuming.

While they lived in Parkins she bore two children to LeRoy Peterson. The first Mrs. Peterson, who would not move out of town and leave them in peace, took both children as an affront. She had been separated from LeRoy before he ever took up with Clarissa, but the suspect circumstances of his second marriage offered material for vengeful gossip. Jane Peterson gossiped about them in church circles and even began to build the legend that it was Clarissa who had broken up her home. If it wasn't Clarissa, it was "someone like her," the gossips said, and then forgot the distinction.

So, in spite of the fact that his lumberyard was making money, Clarissa persuaded her husband to sell out in Parkins. Before their little girl was a year old he moved Clarissa and the children to Rapid City, South Dakota. There he meant to concentrate entirely on his profession as a cattle trader. Two seasons of falling beef prices wiped him out. He had to take a job as lumber salesman for a Dakota chain of lumberyards.

In his disappointment he blamed Clarissa for all their bad luck. "Even my damn bowling game is shot," he raged once, in the intoxication of self pity. "You haven't left me anything."

"I've always tried to do what you wanted."

If *one* time she *hadn't* done what he wanted—that is, spend the night with him in a motel in Sioux City—then they might never have fallen into the trap of marriage. He didn't even have to say it, it was so clear to both.

"I've given you the children," she argued in retreat. He exploded. He'd *had enough* children by the first Mrs. Peterson. If that was what he wanted out of his dwindling life. . . .

The truth was that neither of them liked their children, LeRoy, Jr., and Penny. He blamed them as dependents who kept him from the flamboyant spending which used to sustain his vanity. She disliked them for their physical resemblance to him. His heavy masculine features became for the first time repulsive to her when she saw them reproduced in the faces of the growing children. And in spite of her quiet manner and what she had learned about child management from her days of teaching, they quickly showed patterns of their father's emotional extravagance. That had overpowered her once; in marriage it had become an affliction. Was it inevitable that both children should take after him?

She brooded increasingly on the riddle of heredity as she watched them grow yearly more alien from her. In the mornings when she washed dishes she stared over the suds at row beyond row of cheap suburban houses spread to the stark Dakota horizon. When the children were old enough to be in school, she wasted afternoons by sitting in her front room staring at the unlighted television screen or the thin, depthless imitation fireplace, wondering what was to blame for the decay of her life. She accepted LeRoy's view that they were running in bad luck. She also began to agree with him that it was she who had brought it on them—and this guilt made her quicker to oppose him in their protracted hostility.

All her concentration on the troubles of her marriage had one positive value: it left neither time nor room in her mind to recollect the tragedy of the strange little Yager girl.

During their fifth year in Dakota she found out that LeRoy was giving money to a high school girl. Perhaps on purpose Clarissa chose a bad moment to confront him with this discovery. He roared back at her, "You know it, Lady! And you want to know something else? She's pregnant just like you were. and you know something else? This time I'm too smart to get saddled with it."

In two days it became apparent that his smart move had been

to take their station wagon and every penny he could borrow or draw out of their savings account and disappear. Clarissa had to call her father and ask him to drive from Iowa to pick up the children and herself. When she saw his exhausted face at the end of his hurried trip, she was convinced that he was dying. The shame of having to be carried home this way made her believe that she was killing him.

As they rode eastward under a relentless sun, father and daughter kept up a pretense of deciding—or just discussing—what Clarissa "would like" to do next with herself. In the back of the car young LeRoy pounded his sister or yelled that he was thirsty. Penny took advantage of the elders' demoralization to demand incessant cokes as bribes to be quiet. Then she got sick and vomited into the front seat. Later she was clammy and feverish, as if something worse than an upset stomach had overtaken her.

They crossed back into Iowa that evening under vast, ornate temples of cloud that looked more familiar to Clarissa than any of the landscape around her. The traffic ground past them like a mechanized army intent on extermination. The wheels of passing semi-trailers whined their intent to murder. Headlights coming on in the twilight were searching for innocents to mangle. Clarissa felt the ripples of disaster spreading as if they meant to engulf the horizons. She was alone at their exact center. She could not touch any life without poisoning it.

Passing through a small town, she saw the sundown glitter on the windows of a consolidated school closed for vacation, a lifeless, pale glitter like watchful eyes. She said suddenly, "I'm not going back to teaching school. That's one thing I mustn't do, whatever happens."

Her father turned a worn smile and patted her knee. "Surely not, honey. Surely not. You can do whatever you want. After you get rested, that is. When you have time to think your situation out."

V

Her father was not dying—at least not in the sense she had feared at the bottom of her bad luck and depression. True, he had had a heart attack some months before, but not a severe one. He was supposed to take things easy. His anxious trip to rescue Clarissa and the children wore him down so he had to spend a couple of weeks loafing in bed or on the front porch glider before he was ready to go to the office.

As the weeks passed, though, he carried her with him in his recovery. His unshakeable confidence gave her a line to follow in the time that unavoidably stretched ahead of her. "You have the children," he kept insisting in the face of her collapse. "You have the children. That's what most of us live for honey. They are what has always kept this old world going." In his view—and he forced her to accept it as often as her fears denied it—her responsibility for the children was a foundation on which a good life could still be built. "You'll see . . ." That was his watchword. "You'll see. . . ."

"You'll see in a year that this depression of yours didn't square with realities at all." She wondered what *he* would see if he went back to Normandy now, sixteen years after the invasion. There would be pleasant vineyards there. Happy, hard-working people in the fields he remembered under the wrath of shellfire. She saw that he no longer needed to make the actual trip back to believe that goodness had returned.

It was her father who thought of sending her to Iowa City to apply for the job of housemother at a sorority. For a few days it seemed the Pi Phis might need her. That didn't work out, and she had the feeling that her still unsettled relationship with LeRoy might have weighed in the decision. But through her sorority connections, renewed by interviewing for the housemother job, she got a decent kind of work in the bindery section of the University library.

"See?" her father jollied her. "See how things link up? See how they are connected? Now you're on the track again, Sis. Hold onto it and you'll see. Might even be that down there at the University you'll meet a fine man again."

"I'm old and plain," she said. She had never been really pretty, though it was probably fair to say she had been attractive. She had not been really popular with the sorority crowd, but she had made friends. She might have had more if Joe Meadow had not monopolized her time.

"You're not *old*," her father said.

"I'm getting old and was never pretty," she insisted again. If he would accept this bitter pill, she would accept the optimism he was trying to force on her.

"Some fellow will come along and you'll think again that you're pretty. You'll see."

Though she admitted it reluctantly, her work in the University library made her gradually feel more human again. She rather liked the girls she worked with. By mid-year she was having some of them to her apartment for drinks or tea, depending on their age and taste. She went to plays with them at the University theater, to the foreign films they were so enthusiastic about, to lectures and concerts occasionally. A few times she dated a tall, balding man in Cataloguing. There was not much interest on either part, but he was definitely cultured and she was starting to hope that culture might open up for her some of the things her life had denied.

Her children were fitting in to the school and nursery school here rather better than she had expected. Sometimes, even in her first year, she had glimpses of an almost static future for herself in her job, with the children going through college right here. It was not a prospect to dismay her, though nothing to delight her, either.

Then, on a flashing spring day one of the gray-haired library girls brought to her attention a newspaper story containing a name she had neither heard of or thought of for many years: Bobbie Tenman. Robert Tenman. He and six other boys from Barstle and vicinity had been arrested and charged with vandalism in Iowa City. "I think it's just terrifying how these country boys drive into town in their jalopies and run like mad dogs," Clarissa's friend said. "They slashed tires all over the student housing area. They're worse than city delinquents."

"It's certainly a problem," Clarissa agreed. "I used to teach at Barstle, you know. Eleven years ago. I don't recognize most of the names but I remember this one boy . . . fellow . . . young man. . . ."

"Mad dogs!"

"Yes, but he was a sweet little guy," Clarissa said. She blinked and wiped her eyes. "It's ghastly to think how a lovely child can turn out." Then she bent her head and pretended to be studying the newspaper—for an involuntary, a really shameful smile of pleasure played on her lips. "Bobbie Tenman! Well!" She could sound shocked if she had to, but something fresh and delightful was stirring at the fringe of her mind.

She went to the hearing of the case in the county court house.

Rather surprisingly she had no trouble recognizing Bobbie. Of course he had changed astonishingly in eleven years. He was tall and strong, and if she had chosen to stare squarely at him she would have seen some of the arrogant coarseness that had so unluckily attracted her to LeRoy. But if she merely glanced at him from the corner of her eye, it seemed to her she saw something left of the lovely child he had been. She remembered his hands cupped around a yellow Easter duckling he had brought to school one time and the serenity of his blue eyes as he raised them to her above this treasure. She would have given anything if her boy could look the way Bobbie used to.

Her pulse raced in excited relief when the judge suspended sentence on Bobbie and his accomplices. As she walked back to the library from the court house under the lilting, tossing clouds of April she was breathless with pleasure in thinking: *He got away with it!*

Of course she shouldn't think that way. The judge hadn't intended his clemency as anything but a chance for Bobbie to reform. What did she really care about judicial intent? In the maimed frustration of her loneliness any evasion of just punishment shone as a sign of hope. It was like a premonition that, at last, something good might come into her life to stay. She might get away with something, too. "I see!" she whispered as if her father were there to hear her. She was like a blind child touching its eyes.

After that she meant to have a genuine heart to heart talk with her father. At last she was ready for the kind of talk one can only have with a parent after one has lived through mistakes that have seemed to finish off one's chances. She meant also to drive out to Barstle some time and look for Bobbie Tenman. She might or might not chat with him. Maybe she would merely catch sight of him and drive away. That would be like touching a good luck charm.

She didn't act on either intention, but her new line of confidence sustained her when the police caught LeRoy on the coast in June. He hadn't got away with as much as he thought he would, and his trouble was still hers. There would have to be a prosecution and a divorce, not to mention some kind of settlement with the wronged high school girl, a long, humiliating, weary mess.

She didn't dread the prospect as she might have even weeks

before. From mysterious origins had come the strength to face nearly anything. After the trouble was over, she could believe there were still good times to come in her life. She was just thirty-five. She was better with her children lately. She liked them more. She regretted the empty days in Dakota when she had sat staring at the walls. She might have been doing constructive things with LeRoy, Jr., and Penny all that while. She might have been improving herself for challenges still to come.

She met Bobbie Tenman face to face at an ice cream drive-in near the dam and power plant in Iowa City. She was walking home late from the library and meant to pick up a treat for the children. When she left the counter with a cold sack in her hand, she saw a ten-year-old convertible parked on the gravel apron with its motor running. Almost instantly she recognized the driver. "Bobbie," she called, but he didn't hear until she came to the side of the car and repeated his name.

He looked up from the radio dial, snapping his fingers twice to the music before he said, "Yeah?"

She smiled her delight, "I'm Miss Carlson. Remember?"

"Miss Carlson? Yeah?"

"I was your teacher. . . ."

"Oh, Miss Carlson, Gee. Miss *Carlson*. Gee, What a surprise."

"Bobbie, how are you getting along?"

He scowled until he concluded she wasn't asking if he had broken his parole. Then he said, "Well, just fine, Miss Carlson. Just fine." His nervous foot twitched down on the accelerator twice and the motor growled.

In the sultry night she could feel a warmth like sunlight on her skin. She knew her eyes were glowing like a young girl's. The floodlights of the drive-in were unfolding like flowers. "Do you remember?" she breathed. Suddenly—so vividly that it blotted out everything but his brash blue eyes watching her— she remembered the way the children had looked to her, dancing in the bright arbors of water just before Mary Lynn's death. Bobbie Tenman, Ronnie Cole, Freida Smith, Nickie Pelligrini, and the rest. She hadn't forgotten a single one of them. They were still hers, dancing in their beauty, their unmarred happiness. She had kept them all alive in her heart from that day to this. "Oh, don't you remember, Bobbie?"

She kissed him then. She did not know what kind of kiss she had intended—something fond, nostalgic, motherly perhaps, for the sake of an occasion he should remember as she did. Whatever she had intended, it was a lover's kiss, so large and long delayed that all the smothered passion of her life was in it.

"Jeez Christ!"

"Hey!"

The voices exploded simultaneously in her ears. Bobbie was shoving her away with his hand on her throat. His eyes were round with panic as if he had been attacked by a rabid dog.

And there beside her, clawing at her sleeve, was Bobbie's girl, a small, crumby country girl wearing a blouse and bermuda shorts, a girl Clarissa had not seen since she sat in the Yager's dining room one night long ago, one of Mary Lynn's sisters. "Who the hell you think this is you're kissing?" the girl said, either to Clarissa or Bobbie or both. "Who the hell . . . ?"

Then, incredibly, without deliberation the girl tossed a paper sack into the convertible and in the same swirling motion knocked Clarissa down. Falling, Clarissa saw a thin wedding ring on the hand that had dropped her. "Let's roll, jerk," the girl said to Bobbie.

They were out of the parking lot before Clarissa got to her feet. It's all right, she told herself. She brushed the gravel from her skirt. It's all right. I only kissed him for old times' sake. The wife misunderstood. Sometimes there is a misunderstanding. The Yagers had always misunderstood her.

She looked for her ice cream. It had been knocked from her hand—no, she must have dropped it when she leaned in to kiss Bobbie—and both the sack and carton it contained were broken. One corner was moist when she picked it up. Why had he married so young? Why couldn't they wait?

She must hurry. She must get home with the ice cream before the broken container began to leak all over her. She walked faster. *She must get home while the children were still there.* Within a block she began to run. She heard, without quite recognizing it, the thunder of water going over the dam by the power plant.

Her apartment was on a slanting side street that rose from a slanting thoroughfare. It was something of a climb at best. It always took her breath. Now she ran at the slope as she had run only once before in her life. Again a yellow shape of fantasy pursued her, again there seemed to be a man older than her father insisting that she go faster. Again there seemed to be a corpse at the end of her running. She was not sure whose it was.

She would not go on to face a death and the fishy tasting mouth again. She would hide somewhere. Teetering for balance she stopped and stood with her feet apart on the steep sidewalk. She knew, as clearly as if she had been riding with them, what Bobbie and his little wife were saying about her. "I just seen this crazy old dame and it was *her*." To them she was only the woman who let a child drown. That was the way she had to be identified, all there was for her to be identified by. That was the identification that had patterned her life and her soul.

Trembling, she started down the hill again toward the voice of the water by the dam and power plant. She crossed the street against a red light, just vaguely aware that cars were veering to miss her and honking some ultimate contempt. Everyone knew she had lost in her last try. They had seen her knocked down by the little witch who had got Bobbie too.

She came to the railing by the spillway and leaned over to look for a body that might or might not show itself. Her father had taught her to look at things again in the rational daylight. Didn't he know that night would come again and the dreams with it?

From the roil of white water Mary Lynn was taunting her. The eyes in the photograph Clarissa had burned stared at her from a sanctuary where nothing could ever make them close. Mary Lynn was there just beyond the reach of fair punishment. All these years the evil child had been waiting for her schemes to ripen. She had never had to run in panic and desperation as Clarissa had. Mary Lynn's play with her teacher's life had been foul play, and she had got away with it.

No use trying to answer the jeering of those eyes or that voice in the water. No use expecting that the bad luck of living would be remitted. Clarissa was not one of those whose sentence could be suspended. At best it could be borne, but while she bore it she would know that Mary Lynn could never be brought to an equal justice.

Believing this fully at last, holding on to the concrete railing, wanting to let go, holding onto her tongue, wanting to scream with rage, Clarissa waited.

The Suicide's Cat

Someone had to take the cat in. That was all there was to it.
After LeMoyne went to the basement and shot himself with a
small calibre revolver, his relatives, social workers, and leery
neighbors moved in to take care of his inanimate remains. Le-
Moyne's married daughter and his nephew from the Seattle region arranged for an auction of the furniture and arranged with
a local realtor for the sale of the house. The woman who was
said to have been LeMoyne's mistress fifteen years ago reappeared to squabble with his daughter about certain letters she
thought might still be in LeMoyne's possession. The woman left
without any letters that might have been kept, but carried with
her some photos taken when the dead man was in his prime and
his well-worn copy of *This Is My Beloved*, the poems with which
he had courted her.

That left the cat—whom he had called MacDuff in his alcoholic exaltations and called Smoky in his daily routines.

None of the close-in neighbors liked the cat. It was a secretive, overweight tom given to mauling smaller cats that came within his territory. Some of the neighbors also resented Smoky's habit of peering into their first-floor windows from a porch rail, fence, or the lower branch of a tree.

So finally when the last of the furniture that no one had bought at the auction was being hauled off by the Salvation Army and the house was to be locked up pending occupancy by the new owners, Vernon Reiss did the decent, necessary thing about the cat. He took it home and into his keeping.

Vernon lived with his wife and three children two blocks away on Almond St. He had seen Smoky prowling the streets and dodging traffic, but he had never been subject to the cat's window-peeping. His motive for adopting the animal was simple but double-edged: he sympathized with the fat and aging cat; he had a hollow, disturbing sense that LeMoyne had forgotten Smoky at the instant of pulling the trigger and was trying to reach back from the beyond to make up for his oversight.

"It's the kind of thing I wouldn't rest easy about," Vernon told his wife.

She said all right, since they already had one cat, one more mouth to feed wouldn't make all that much difference. Smoky was getting old and couldn't last that much longer in case the price of cat food went out of sight in the inflation. Smoky seemed to be satisfied with dry cat food, morning and evening, and the dry was cheaper than the canned tuna they usually provided for their little striped female Ginger. Evidently Smoky had got used to inexpensive diet while he was with LeMoyne.

The Reiss children neither liked nor disliked Smoky. They didn't pay much attention to him after the first few days he was in their house. All three of them were in school or kindergarten by this time, and their lives did not have room for another pet with so little charm. The younger two still cuddled Ginger on long evenings in front of the television and on cold Sundays when they could not go to the playground or onto the streets or down to Benson St. where the shops were. The oldest, a girl, was beginning to have dates and no longer cared about either cat.

There was no sign that Smoky minded the lack of affectionate attention. As long as he was fed his dry food and could come and go through a patented plexiglass door set into one of the basement windows, he was placid and content. Often in the mornings he would be out early, stationed on a branch outside the kitchen window, peering in at Mrs. Reiss while she got the children's lunches ready to take to school and fixed breakfast for the whole family. She said this did *not* give her the willies, as some of LeMoyne's next-door neighbors had complained in earlier times. She did not much care whether the cat was inside or out. The stare of his scummy, yellow eyes was barely interested in her movements around the kitchen.

Near the end of the first year the Reisses kept him, Smoky got in a fight with another animal, probably another cat about his own size as near as anyone could figure out. No one saw the fight. Smoky's left jowl began to swell and for a couple of days he was extremely lethargic. "I think he's been bitten by a snake or something rabid," Mildred Reiss said to Vernon. She had grown up on a farm in Dexter County and had always been afraid of snakes. "We don't know whether he's ever had any rabies shots."

"Well, keep an eye on him," Vernon said with some unease, but nothing approaching panic.

"I'll keep him locked in the basement away from the kids," she said.

By Thursday Smoky's swollen jowl was dripping a milky pink fluid and all the hair on that side of his face was gone.

"Jesus," Vernon said. "Have we got any of that antibiotic left we got for Ginger?"

Mildred found two capsules left in an envelope with illegible markings. She thought they were the antibiotic the vet had given them for the other cat a couple of years before. The two of them managed to force these down Smoky's throat. In the process Vernon was scratched lightly on his left breast, Smoky's claws penetrating his work shirt and leaving three punctures that itched like hell. "I think you may be the one who needs an antibiotic," Mildred said.

"No, no. Hell no. I'll squeeze some blood out and put on Bactine."

On Friday Smoky's face looked even more revolting. He kept rubbing it with the back of his paw and licking what he rubbed away. On Saturday, when Vernon did not have to go to work at the body repair shop, he and Mildred drove the cat to the pet hospital.

"He's been in a fight," Dr. Armbruster told them. He showed them the four puncture wounds on the cat's face, wounds they never made out distinctly in the bloodied tissue. "Probably another cat, though I can't be sure." He gave the cat a shot of penicillin and his receptionist assistant gave the Reisses a new envelope full of tablets. On the bill she listed the cat's name as "MacDuff Reiss," since Vernon had given the name "MacDuff" when they entered the waiting room.

With the medication Smoky healed promptly. His laceration, resulting from the bite and the scratching he had done to rid himself of the itching infection, healed faster than the puncture wounds on Vernon's chest. In a week Smoky seemed to be himself again. The hair was beginning to grow again on his face. The little punctures Vernon had sustained were neither better nor remarkably worse. They looked like mosquito bites and itched comparably. Mildred still worried about them, but Vernon refused to see a doctor unless they swelled more or got more painful.

By July, when the family drove north for a vacation in Canada, the punctures were finally healing. Parents and children had some time on the beach of a lake in Ontario. Vernon's chest tanned and the sun seemed to finish off whatever infection had lightly penetrated his skin.

"I told you not to worry," he said to Mildred.

"I wasn't worried that much, but you never know."

"You never know," he agreed.

His skin was healed, but there, lying on the beach where the sun hit the blue-brown water with summer force and his children swam out farther than he or Mildred thought was safe, he found himself for the first time truly regretting that they had taken the dead man's cat into their family. He hoped that when they drove back home something would have happened to it. A car in the street, a falling branch, poison, shards of broken glass, a heat-maddened police dog, boys with slingshots. . . . He hoped they would return home to find that Smoky was dead or gone.

Smoky was waiting for them unchanged. Ginger gave some signs of having missed them. She wanted to be petted by the kids. She followed one member of the family or another upstairs and downstairs even after she had been well fed. She arched her back for their caresses and made sounds of relief that nothing had happened to them on the highway or at the Canadian lake.

Smoky, no. It seemed he couldn't care less whether they were in the house or not. He had his days to linger out. It didn't matter to him who fed him or whether anyone noticed him. He stared with fixed, unblinking eyes at anything that passed, then closed them drowsily.

In October they had a scare about their daughter Margaret, the eldest of the children. First Mildred caught her with Tim Keefe in the back seat of Tim's father's car. The car was parked by night in the alley behind the Reisses' house. Margaret claimed nothing had happened but some heavy making out, and Mildred did not even mention this to Vernon. Then, because she kept track of Margaret's periods, she was terribly frightened that Margaret might be pregnant.

"What on earth will we do?" she demanded of Vernon. "Every time I try to talk to her she either screams or cries. She's three weeks overdue. I know that."

"The little fool!" Vernon said.

"I mean, an abortion or what? She's only fifteen."

"It's not time to talk about that yet. Until we know."

"She's doing so well in school. She was until this came up."

"Do you want me to talk to her?"

"I don't think you could. I don't know what you would say."

"I would say . . . I would just inquire gently. I think Margaret's always trusted me." He thought Margaret had *never* trusted him. Nor Mildred. Nor the other children. Why should they? "We'll wait a few more days," he said.

He was working on an old Chevy Impala when something went wrong with the jack. Maybe he had been careless in placing it before he raised the front end of the car to get at the welding of the front right fender. He had time to scoot most of his body out from under before the brake drum hit the greasy concrete of the garage floor, but his wrist was broken and his left hand was a mess. He had to be in the hospital for the better part of a week while surgery was done to straighten up the bones that could be saved in his hand.

While he was in the hospital he got the good news about Margaret. "She's come around," Mildred said, sitting beside his bed in a smell of roses and iodoform. "At least you don't have to worry about that, Papa. She's come around and it's getting so she and I can talk to each other again. At least we've got that to be thankful for."

He thought he was happy to get this information, but he couldn't think what to say about it.

Mildred said, "Dr. French is *very* optimistic about your hand. He took another X-ray yesterday, didn't he?"

"Yes."

"Well, it looks just fine. And you tell me there isn't much pain or anything."

"I can hardly feel it. It feels all right. When they take the cast off, we'll see."

"I know it's going to be all right. We'll have compensation until you can go back to work. I thought we might drive over to Olmstead to see the autumn leaves. There are still some pretty ones up. We can drive over next week. Margaret can feed the little kids and put them to bed."

"And the cats," he said.

He and Mildred drove to Olmstead where his parents were buried and where he still had friends from high school days. They went on a bright, crisp day. Just as Mildred had promised, there were still a lot of pretty leaves on the elms and the maples. The leaves would last a long time yet on the oaks. He had a cast on his right arm up to the elbow. The arm had to be carried in a sling.

Mildred enjoyed the drive a good deal. She had brought chrysanthemums for the graves. She had always liked Art Henderson and Glenn Michaels. They had dinner in a Ramada Inn with Art and his wife and Glenn and his nephew, who was home from college at the state university. Very cheery, with lots of jokes about Vernon's accident and what he could do without a left hand.

By the time they got home that night, the children were all asleep. There was no sign of either cat. Vernon was feeling a little tipsy still from the drinks they had in the Ramada bar.

"You go on to bed, honey. I think I'll sit up a while."

"And have a nightcap?"

"Why not? I don't have anywhere to go tomorrow. It seems funny not to be going to the shop."

"Don't sit up too late," she said.

He was sitting on an old aluminum and plastic lawn chair in front of the furnace when he heard Smoky come in through the patented door in the basement window. The sound of fur and bending plastic.

"Howya?" he asked, saluting the cat with his glass of bourbon and water. "Howya, Buddy?"

The cat wandered around on the basement floor a while before finding a soft spot on a pile of laundry in the corner opposite him. From there it watched him with a steady gaze.

The furnace kicked on and he heard the steady purr of gas burning inside it. It was a peaceful sound, a summoning, slow hiss.

He was thinking about his mother on whose grave he had laid the bronze chrysanthemums earlier today in Olmstead. She hadn't had a bad life, all things considered. Maybe it was the old man who had taken the shit, though he was not one to complain about it. A tough life, anyway, and his death pretty messy. All that argument with the Union at the end about whether he was or was not entitled to a pension. The anger at the union officials and the goddamn bureaucrats who were trying to slicker him out of what he had worked so long to have in his old age. The "little stroke" that spoiled the old man's face and made his speech sound like he was an imbecile. The Ford piled up off an easy curve near Caseyville when the old guy probably shouldn't have been driving at all.

"I guess he knew what he was doing," Vernon said to the cat.

It seemed to him that no one knew how many old people took their own lives. No one could know. How would you get statistics on that? For all he would ever know his father had killed himself just as LeMoyne had when the going was too tough.

It came back to him that when Mildred had first talked about the possibility of an abortion to head off Margaret's trouble what had been in his mind as another alternative was . . . well, other girls he had heard of had killed themselves when they were in trouble and there seemed to be no other way out. That had been in his mind while he was talking to Mildred and it had been in his mind while he was lying in the hospital ward in the late hours of the night, when he couldn't get out of bed to come and comfort his daughter in her agony. When he simply didn't have the strength to pull himself upright and get dressed and come home.

"I thought about it all right," he told the cat. "But I never let it pass my lips. By God, I didn't say a *word*."

The thought of his helplessness and his silence undid him

and he began to cry. To get hold of himself he drank off the rest of the glass of whiskey and water and went up to the kitchen to refill it.

When he came back down to sit in front of the purring furnace, the cat whose name was MacDoolie, or MacDiddle, or MacDuff, if you goddamned preferred that name, was asleep.

It certainly looked asleep. "All right, take it easy," he said to the cat, but it didn't even open its eyes at the sound of his voice. "You can afford to take it easy," he said.

As he went on drinking the good bourbon and water he tried to steady himself by reviewing the figures on the money he would get from workmen's compensation and insurance coverage on his accident. He thought about what jobs he could do at the body shop if he went back before his hand was entirely healed. To the extent it would ever heal. Dr. French had not promised him complete mobility of the hand. There were too many nerves and muscles involved besides the bones for anyone to be sure that he could ever again work as he was used to working.

But the money that would be coming in was not bad. It wasn't bad at all until he thought that it was nowhere near enough, and he would have to think about ways to expand his income while inflation was getting worse every day.

He had so much wanted Margaret to be able to go to college. Damn it, she was brighter and prettier than most of the kids she ran around with. If she had made a mistake with that Keefe boy, you couldn't say he was exactly a rotten kid, either. He was a good boy and if it had all happened at the right time, they might have had the kid and gone on to have a good marriage. After college and after she had a chance to look around and find herself and decide freely what she wanted to make of her life.

College for the other kids, too. But somehow her trouble had made Margaret even more special to him than she had always been, being the first and being his little girl and all that shit.

"She's going to college," he told the sleeping cat. "You goddamn sonofabitch try to keep her from it and I'll kill you. I'll kill you. I'll kill you."

He heard Mildred's feet on the basement stairs behind him. He did not turn around to meet her eyes.

"I went right to sleep as soon as I lay down," she said. "I don't know what woke me. But you weren't there."

"I haven't finished my drink," he said. "I'm thinking."

"I know you are. Bad thoughts?"

"Just thinking," he said.

"Would it be all right if I got a drink and came down and sat with you for a while? Today was such a good day for us, driving in the nice weather and all. It seemed easier for us to talk to each other than it's been for a long time. So there *is* a silver lining."

"There always is," he said.

"Shall I . . . ? OK," she said. "Just don't sit up too late, even if you can loaf around tomorrow and for a while yet."

"Don't you lie up there thinking."

"I won't. Ginger's up there with me. I found her asleep when I went into our room. I see Smoky's come in."

"MacDuff," he said. "Why would anyone name an ugly, fat cat MacDuff?"

"I don't know."

He chuckled to show he thought it was only funny. She kissed him and went upstairs to bed again.

When Margaret went to college there would be some other young bastard—lots of them—trying to get into her pants and spoil her life. How could any woman stand up against it? You think because you've got some brains and are young that you've got a little margin. You think it won't hurt to try anything once and maybe you'll get by with it.

You won't get by with it, because that goddamn cat is always there, pretending to be asleep. But not asleep. The goddamn cat has got all the time in the world to wait and let you use up your time and get nothing for it.

Unfair. But really, Jesus, he had always known it was going to be unfair before anything started to happen. Before he knew his mother was a whiner and she was going to wear the old man down with it. Before those three kids had caught him in front of the pool hall and roughed him up and stolen the money he had for the movie that night. The old man had given him money to make up for what had been stolen, but it was too late to get back to the movie that night, even if he had not dragged home crying and messed up his face so he was ashamed to go back down on the street by the theater where he could be seen.

"So what?" he said.

You lived a long time, really, and there were silver linings always. If Margaret didn't make it, either, she would still learn from the experience, and her kids would make it where she

hadn't, and it would keep on going on like that. Or her kids'
kids . . .

"Some day!" he said.

But in the far corner of the basement the cat had opened its
eyes and was looking at him.

The Pursuit
of Happiness

That November evening as Ruth and I came home past the neighborhood theater we found Warren Gamaliel Spence standing there in the snow studying the ads for a Rock Hudson movie.

"Never saw anyone who looked more the part of an art student," Ruth said. "Do you suppose he hasn't got an overcoat?"

"He's never confided," I told her. Warren was hugging an armful of books against his pigeon breast, and as we came up to him I could see the snowflakes lodging in the rough kinks of his hair. He was too engrossed in the billboard to notice our approach—as if by pure concentration he was trying to will himself into the scene where uniformed Rock waved a pistol against the background of palms and a coral beach.

"I want to give him your extra overcoat," Ruth muttered and I muttered back, "Ha ha ha." Ha ha ha, we sang together in chagrin, because I was a poor art student, even if it was Warren Gamaliel who looked the part. He went to the School of Commerce.

Ruth ran her glove across his sand-blond hair to brush the snow away. "Hi kids," he said, looking at us as though we had not only violated his privacy but had suddenly made the snow real and him and Rock Hudson cardboard.

'You're not going to see *that thing*, Warren? Not all by yourself?" Ruth asked, jerking her head toward the theater door.

"Well . . ." When Warren grinned you thought of a puppy cringing toward the boot that kicked it.

"You come home with us for some spaghetti," Ruth commanded.

He showed no sign of pleasure at the invitation. "Don't bully him," I said to Ruth.

"I'm not bullying anybody. We've got half a jug of lovely wine," she coaxed him.

He still held out until she grabbed the sleeve of his jacket and said, "It would make us happy and you can see the movie later." Then he grinned again and let her take him with us.

In our building Warren stopped briefly in his second-floor room—to leave his books and, it turned out, to put on a clean shirt and tie, instructed to such a nicety by the native impulse that had brought him to the School of Commerce in the first place—while Ruth and I climbed to our apartment on the fifth floor.

Ruth asked, "Are you mad at me for inviting him? You are."

"No," I said with all the insincerity I could muster. Our place was dark and dank as we came in, and through the dark she moved to clutch me against her. I could smell the snow on her coat and in her hair and could feel the demanding thrust of her body against mine from the knees up. "I couldn't bear to think of anybody going to that movie alone at dinner time. Not on a night like this," she said.

"If the Lisbon earthquake or Hiroshima or the Black Death were to show up in human form I'd sooner or later have to sit across the spaghetti from them," I said. It was true enough. Show her a disaster and she would try to mother it. She did not read tabloids for her sentimentality, weep over the abuse of animals, or encourage unknown drunks to pour out their tales, but she often saddled us with horrid company.

"Warren Spence is a Shetland pony's ass," I said, pushing her off me.

"Hush."

"The one man Lonely Crowd."

"Please," she said. "Can't you hear him coming?"

Besides Ruth and me, Warren was the only student living in that sad house on 54th Street. The other tenants whom we knew at all were surfaceline employees, stockroom help at Spiegel's, and a Hadacol distributor. Up until now our acquaintance with Warren had been held down to a decent one in which we exchanged the time of day at the Halstead car stop or on the stairway. I understood from Ruth that she had ridden downtown on the streetcar with him a time or two, but she could not remember what they had talked about or that they had talked about anything. Only once, much earlier in the fall, when we were playing penny ante with two friends from the Art Institute, we had had the bright idea of inviting Warren up to sit in. The result was grim. He would sit there endlessly trying to decide whether or not to meet a two-cent bet. He would not let anyone look at his cards to advise him, but when this was offered he would commence to shake and grin as though he had heard of sharpers like us—and presently would seem to forget that it was his turn to bet and that we were waiting for him. When we told our friends later that he was a Commerce major at Northwestern, they said with hard skepticism, "Some Mr. Jay Gould you've got there folks. He's going to really sweep the marts." Ruth, I assumed, had agreed with me that he was not to come across our doorsill again.

But here he was, in a clean shirt and tie, exuding a kind of surly resentment that kept him from talking much. I figured that he was sore about being pulled away from the movie, and this made me mad. I hardly spoke to him. So Ruth kept a unilateral conversation going while she cooked. Warren and I merely waited for food, drinking wine faster than we should have.

In the middle of our glum meal we heard the superintendent calling for him from downstairs. He was gone a long time then, answering the telephone. Ruth and I dallied, got more depressed by the cooling of the spaghetti, and finally finished our helpings before he came back.

If I had thought him mentally capable of even such a simple acrobatic, I would have said that he had gone into a trance. He sat down as if he didn't see us there, took a couple of ineffective bites, belched lightly—then, literally, sat staring. Through the smoke from my cigarette I could see that he was sweating.

"All right Warren," I said. "If you want to go to the movie so badly, you are excused."

He was not offended—probably even at another time he would not have noticed my deliberate expression of annoyance, but now it was as if he only heard a human sound and welcomed it for his own vapid purposes.

"It was that girl, you know," he said, like a medium, maybe a medium through whom his own departed spirit was trying to communicate to us.

"What girl?" Ruth said encouragingly after a while.

Warren G. filled his glass from the wine jug, nodded confidentially as he drank from it, and said. "It was the girl who calls me." Then, without looking at either of us, he began to talk. We were so used to thinking of him as little better than a mute that the sheer flow of words was stunning at first.

Sometime—he was not sure of any dates, the whole fall seemed kaleidoscopic to him—sometime since September he had begun to get regular phone calls from a girl whom he had never seen and whose name he had not been able to get.

At the time of the first call he had been lying on his bed reading "elementary bizz practices." He said that he had known "but not really known either" that the call was for him before he heard the superintendent's voice summoning him. When he got to the foot of the stairs, the super was there holding the phone out to him with one hand and pulling a bologna rind from between her lips with the other. (He snickered about these details, but they came out stressed as if they were important.)

"Warren," a girl's voice had said. "Can you help me? Can you tell me? I . . ." Her voice faded away so that he believed the wire had gone dead. He was ready to hang up before she said, "That wasn't the way I planned to start. I want everything to be perfect between us. Always. I meant to say something to you that would make you say something nice to me. Why don't you say something to me?"

"Who is this?"

"I didn't mean for you to say *that*. There isn't any use talking about who I am. Don't ever ask again because I won't tell you. I know you, though. I've seen you around school a lot of times. I guess you know I have or I wouldn't be calling."

"I guess you've got the wrong number."

"Not if you're Warren Spence."

"I'm not going to tell you whether I am or not."

"You don't have to tell me, because I know you even if you don't know me. But you mustn't get any ideas because I thought it was time to get acquainted and didn't know any other way. I'm not a bad girl, and you're not mad at me are you?"

It occurred to him for the first time when she said this that perhaps he should be angry, and he reasoned back from this theoretical anger to a motive for it. If he was angry, then it was because someone was playing a trick on him, one of the bitch sorority girls that the fellows in his class had put up to calling him.

"Sorry, wrong number," he said frostily. "This isn't Warner Spender or whoever you want." He hung up. But before he had climbed the stairs the phone was ringing again and the superintendent was answering it. "You," she called to Warren. "Oughta finish talking before you hang up on your lady friends."

This time the girl was saying breathlessly, "Please, oh please you mustn't ever do that to me again. I need you so much. You have to listen."

"Lay off me. You better lay off calling me. I won't let you make a joke out of me," he shouted to her. He held the phone away from his ear and thought he heard her laughter. Then he realized it might have been crying just as well, but he hung up anyway.

The next evening at exactly the same time the girl called again. This time she didn't say anything, Warren explained to us. How did he know it was she? He could tell. She just breathed, he said. She breathed into the phone and after he had listened to this for several minutes he knew darn good and well who it was.

The third evening she said, "Be patient with me, Warren. If you're patient I'll explain. I want to tell you things. Please? Like about the gray gloves I bought this afternoon. They're like pussy willows. So soft. Can you feel them, Warren? And when I was driving home I swung the caddy out on the Outer Drive. Don't you know how I felt? I was going faster and faster and there was a haze coming in from the lake, so it was like I was flying away into it. I was passing a few cars and they all began to honk at me. I thought they must be chasing me because I was going so fast, and then I outran them all and then I had to call you and tell you about it."

"What's your name?"

"And something happened then. Something happened, Warren. I must have been going too fast. But I'm all right if I can talk to you about it, am'n't I?"

"Who are you?"

"Oh . . . I'm not so happy. Isn't that enough for you to know now? That's why I talk to you. Please, always listen to me, Warren."

He had promised her that he always would.

I had not expected ever to hear so much talk from Warren; and I had not expected that I could listen to so long a story from him. Ordinarily he was just too dull. But as he kept talking now I got the notion that the wire—some kind of a wire—was hooked directly to him and not simply to the phone in the hall downstairs. I said that he seemed like a medium, and in an eerie way I seemed to hear the girl's voice coming from his lips, no more distorted by Warren's reproduction of it than it would be by the mechanical distortions of the telephone. I remember thinking, as I closed my eyes and listened, *Warren is a girl, is that girl*.

And so I anticipated that after he had brought us up to date on the telephone calls the wire in him would go dead and he would become again the bumbling and dumb Warren of our acquaintance. It didn't work that way. When he was through telling what the girl had said, another wire cut in; and the voice speaking now to our seance was of a shadow Warren Spence, a kind of bastard knight errant, a grail-follower, a boy who had seen a vision, one of the last of the Americans who could ever give himself completely to the Horatio Alger dream.

As he told it, he had never wanted much nor expected much out of life until he had been drafted and sent to Korea. It was out there, on some clay hillside, by night, while he guarded a supply warehouse from the starving gooks, that the vision had come to him. It had not come in a single burst of light, but more slowly, week after week as he became impressed by the trucks rolling into the warehouse yard and the trucks rolling out—all of them glutted with a waste of goods that the natives would and did risk their lives to grab. The substance on which his vision grew, the absolute, unarguable bedrock of it, was the observation that the United States of America had "so much."

Merely that—a fact that any GI or even any reader of the newspapers would not even consider worth noting because he knew it so well already. But Warren had noticed, as if he were a traveler from another, less jaded, planet, and not merely a boy from Garrison, Nebraska—where they had trucks loaded with the fat of the land, too. He had a vision of "so much" and there were voices in the night that told him what to do about it. He listened to the men in his outfit. And granted that their talk was ordinary enough—the cars they had left behind them, the money they could be making instead of GI pay, and the girls they had dropped—what Warren made of this talk during his bleak hours on guard was something frenzied and new. They might be talking to pass the time. From their boredom, eroticism, and envy he made a plan for his life. And what he came home to conquer, in 1954, was a land more lurid and mysterious than anything the old conquistadors had dreamed of, a land spangled with sex and gold, where the people, citizens, denizens, were no more fellows to him than the Indians had been to Cortez's bullies. In his own mind Warren was a pirate and a titan, here for looting. His purposes were as ruthlessly clear to him as his inability to carry them out was to me.

He told us finally that he meant to "play along" with the girl who had been phoning him, but when the time came he would drop her with no more compunction than he would have against stepping on a bug. Marriage was out of the question, whatever she expected. "You may think that I'm pretty immoral," he said defiantly.

Ruth knew better, but she said, laughing, "Well, she's asking for it."

"Warren, this is just some loony who's calling," I said.

He refused to let me shred his faith. "You never can tell," he said, with a cunning curl of his lip—as if he had the solemn word of his whole platoon that it was doubters like me who always missed the good stuff.

"If she's crazy enough to call, she may be crazy enough to do a lot of other things," Ruth said. "You *can't* tell."

And after Warren had left us, when I reproached her with encouraging his fantasies, she said bitterly, "You don't know everything. You don't know who this girl is. If it makes him happy to get what he can—or thinks he can—out of her, why does it bother you?"

"Warren scared me," I told her. "Now you're scaring me. If you can't tell the difference between daydreams and reality I may have to put you away, too."

"Daydreams . . . ," she scoffed, "but the phone *really* rings."

"He's still psycho. He uses magic to make the phone ring."

"Hurray for common sense."

"So what would you do for him?"

"At least listen to him," she said. "He needs someone to unload all that crap on."

"Little mother."

"Little father."

"Not if I can help it," I said. "My only interest in Warren is one of legitimate self-defense."

There were a lot of times in the next few weeks when I believed that Warren was sane—at least sane enough so my conscience didn't require me to finger him to the Dean of Students at Northwestern or locate and write to his family in Nebraska, asking them to come for him. Anyway, when you've known students a long time, you get used to believing that craziness is common, that maybe they pay for a share of it when they pay their tuition, and anyone who doesn't pick up his share is missing a really liberal education. Furthermore, there's always a lurking suspicion that when you call the paddy wagon for a fellow student, he's apt to turn on you and say convincingly enough to the men with the net, "Not me. *He's* the one you want."

We saw Warren—Ruth and he between them contrived this— very frequently for a few weeks, and now that he'd found his opening, like any persistent salesman he continued a tidal wave of autobiography and schemes, returning always to the central theme of his telephone romance. I heard a large part of this at first hand and more of it from Ruth. Two or three times I arrived home to find him in our room, straddling a chair and babbling to my entranced wife as she worked on a meal. Then, in the nights I would listen to her retell the latest installment of his adventure.

How much she added or changed or dressed up in retelling, I don't know. I was by then afraid to know, for it seemed that Warren and the Telephone Girl were already too much in our lives—a legend that we had acquired by a sort of contagion.

Once I almost came to the point of insisting that we break with Warren. That was when I found stuck under our door the cover of a magazine with the almost life-size picture of a twelve-year-old girl smiling sexily. It was there when we got up one morning.

"That dumb sonofabitch," I said. I had a sense of shock as

though something physically unpleasant were happening to me, and there was a kind of fear that came ahead of the anger. Then I was all right, thinking, *the sonofabitch knows what he's doing, he's a salesman and he's selling her to us.* I was watching the stiff paper twinkle with reflections as I held it.

"What's the trouble?" Ruth called from the bed. When I showed her she grew very thoughtful. "But I don't see why you're *angry*," she said.

"Because he thinks we're enjoying this instead of humoring him," I said. "Because he takes it for granted I'm as interested in little girls as he is." I rattled the picture and then wadded it up and threw it away.

When she had fixed us coffee and we both had the comfortable jolt of it on our nerves to get us out of dreamland, Ruth said thoughtfully, "I admit this stunt is childish, and I think he went too far."

"So, let's stop encouraging him."

"We don't," she said. "He needs it, this playing. I know you're right about him and it is rather disgusting, but aren't you, darling, your brother's keeper?"

I said, "There are two words I don't like in that. One is brother and the other is keeper."

But that night Warren came up, touchingly, I thought, to show us the new alarm clock he had bought—bringing it proudly and naturally, as though he no longer had any restraints about considering us his family. He told us he'd paid eight dollars and a half for it, and I said, "Jesus Christ, you paid *that* for an alarm clock?" and he hung his head and claimed it had an "all steel" frame, and my anger, stored up from the morning, evaporated in amusement with him. I went to sleep that night thinking, *It's only that he isn't as old as he ought to be, as we expect him to be.*

Then, in a few days, Warren told us that he had quarreled with the Telephone Girl. I took this news as a good sign, a sign that we were at least good for him. I figured that it might have been my needling that brought him to the point of questioning her.

He said, "I wondered if she wasn't like they say about pen pals. I thought maybe she was crippled or something nasty like that, was the reason she wouldn't let me see her."

He reported that he had asked her, "Are you ugly or something?"

To which she answered, "My friends think I'm quite pretty.

My hair is a kind of blonde. Pinkish blonde. Some people like my fat little face. My husband likes it well enough. Some people think I have a pretty figure."

The mention of a husband seems to have triggered all his frustration into jealous rage. "You're lying," he shouted. "You never had a husband because you're some kind of a freak. What do you think of that?" Then he slammed the receiver down like a little man.

When he finished telling us about this, he looked at me instead of at Ruth—appealing naively for my approval.

I said, "That's fine. That ought to shut her up."

Ruth said, "If she wasn't scarred or crippled before—I suppose she is now. After what you said to her, Warren. You didn't have to be cruel."

"Ruth!" I said.

She smiled uneasily. "I liked to think of our little friend as being perfect, that's all. Silly, wasn't it?" She flipped her hands in a gesture of resignation.

Then we saw almost nothing of Warren for a period of weeks. He didn't move away. He was there on the floor below us. Again, as it had been in the early fall, our contacts with him were the accidental ones of meeting at the carstop or on the stairs. We learned later that the girl had stopped calling him during this period, and it was as if he knew as well as we that it was only her calls that had made him interesting. We learned this on a Sunday night when he shoved the door of our room open and walked in with a scared, happy look on his face.

"She called just now," he shouted. He looked defiantly at me, collapsed in our big chair, and began crying. "It was a hell of a day. Sundays are such a hell of a day."

"Sure it was," I said, and I knew I was speaking for myself as well as to console him. It had been a grim, leaden day outside and I had been working on a drawing of three heads since noon, and while the drawing had gone further and further wrong I had got the black depression that he had come up to express.

Ruth picked him up, mothering him, coaxing, and even dabbing at his tears with a handkerchief until he had relaxed. She supplied the little persuasion necessary to get him talking, and when he started, the wire seemed to be hooked into him again as it had been the first evening he told us about the girl.

He claimed that all morning—while the snow was beating at our windows and his—he had been afraid he would have to kill himself today. He went out about eleven to get the funny papers to take his mind off suicide. When he'd read them he rolled up in a comfort on his bed and tried to sleep, consoling himself now by thinking "how nice" it would be if he were dead. About four he went out again. He had walked east toward the lake and then turned south to the Loop. Before he had gone very far, the buildings on one side and the lake on the other had "got too big." I saw what he meant.

"Something ripped" in his mind and he remembered, not serially but simultaneously, all the fears of the dark or of being alone he'd had as a child. When he drove them off by thinking he was "too old for that," he remembered how afraid of the dark he had been on the nights when he pulled guard by the warehouses in Korea.

He was not sure how much of the distance home he had covered at a run. But, "It was lucky I ran like I did, because she called just two minutes after I got here. I was still out of breath."

She was sorry, she told him, that she had not called for so long. But *now* (it was fascinating to guess whether the *now* was hers or his) whatever misunderstandings they had had were passed over. Now, knowing each other better, they could be truly friends.

That's what she had told him, and out of pity we encouraged him now to believe her.

A routine began after that in which she called Warren every evening, as reliably as his all steel alarm clock called him from sleep in the mornings. He explained this punctuality by an increasingly elaborate fiction. Because of her social position she had, he thought, only a few minutes free each day from her routine of rising (from a perfumed bed in a velvet curtained room), of breakfasting (on gold-rimmed dishes in a room open to the south), of lunching in the Pump Room or the Drake Hotel, of driving her Thunderbird out to visit friends in Hinsdale or Winnetka, of dining with her family in a paneled, vast room decorated with the loot of Europe and paintings of their English ancestors. He was pleased to think that she fooled her friends—and she had lots of them, nearly all rich—into thinking that she was one of them, that she was perfectly satisfied with the life she was living among them. But she was not satisfied at all. Her life would have been complete and utter trash without the calls she made to Warren every evening.

I am ashamed to think how much of this more-elaborate fantasy we appreciated. It was no longer a question of believing or not believing. It entertained us; it gave us something to value in a peculiar, abstract way. It pointed up to us that we did not need to own what the rich owned in order to be pleasurably corrupted by it.

The girl had begun telling him not only of the things she saw so vividly during her social day, but of the recollections of her wealthy childhood—of the twelve-room cabin in Nevada with the bearskins in front of the fireplaces and the big windows that opened on the valley where the frost and mist sparkled, of winters spent sailing or fishing in the waters off Acapulco or Florida, of flights to Paris and London for Christmas with her mother's people, of her eccentric uncle who had a complete, working model of the Panama Canal built in his basement. There were dozens of descriptions of the interiors of houses and hotels in which she had been a guest. They were like the ads in a snobbish magazine—and we made that comparison, Ruth and I— but with an authority that impersonal ads could never have. I would not say that anybody attained a sense of participating in the Telephone Girl's life. Her experiences were not ours. But they came to exist in some area of our minds just southwest of memory. They were *almost* ours.

I suppose it was our attention to this glamorous biography that drove Warren on and worked him up to demanding a meeting. He came to the point (he told us) of replying to whatever she said with a single question: "Where are you?"

She told him, at last. At least told him that she was calling from her own room and described it with voluptuous evocation—a room in which a woman is alone with herself and the unguents, smells, and cloth of her private luxury. Then, as if his wooing her this close to the present had made her melancholy, she asked, "Why can't all this talking be real? Why can't you *do something* to make it real?"

Of course this plea was as cloudy and, under the circumstances which she had set up, beyond practical interpretation as her original motives in beginning the calls. But he responded with a certain pitiful valor. "Tell me what," he said.

"Oh no. Things can't happen for us. You couldn't go with me to the places I've been, could you? I don't know how to explain, darling, but it couldn't work. There was someone I used to talk to on the phone—don't be jealous, he was an old, fine, silver-haired man, older than Daddy—and he promised to take me back every-where. But I found out he was lying to make me feel good, and I had to quit talking to him. We can't make our lives what we want. There's something funny about me. Darling, you've al-ways known that. You accused me of it once upon a time."

"Don't you say that. Let me see you."

"I want to," she said. "I guess you know. Maybe someday I will. I'll be waiting for you some evening when you come home."

Maybe she did come for him. Anyway, a few days after this I was walking home from Halstead Street with Warren when we saw a big car with a uniformed chauffeur parked across from the door of our rooming house. (I know it was really there because a little boy on roller skates lost his balance beside it and put his hand on it to recover himself.) Warren started running as soon as he saw it—as if it had never once occurred to him to doubt whose it was. But the car pulled away just before he reached it.

"Did you see who was in it?" he asked as I came up.

"Nobody but the driver."

He looked at me angrily. He must have wanted me to confirm what his own eyes would not—that she had been there in the car. "Maybe she sent a note," he said grudgingly.

I went with him to his room, after he had looked in the mail-box, but there was nothing there, either.

But within an hour she had called and Warren was at our door to report this in triumph, and to ask our advice. This time the girl had said, "Something awful has happened. I need you. I don't know what to do at all, at all. I can't even tell you about it over the phone. Can you come to see me in about three hours?" She gave him the name of the most famous of the lakeshore hotels and the number of the room to which he was to come.

"You're not going, are you?" Ruth asked him worriedly. "You know it could be just a trick."

Warren glared at her and turned to me.

"Double or nothing," I said. "Give it a try. Maybe you'll crack her, laddy."

His eyes lit up with mean viciousness. "If I do," he said, "if I do she doesn't need to expect that it puts any obligation on me. Not after all the trouble she's given me."

"That's the spirit," I said.

"If she's not there, to hell with her," Ruth said. "It's a test. If she doesn't do her part, forget about her."

"She might be ready. She might feel tonight's the night," I said encouragingly.

"If you're going, let me press your suit," Ruth said. "You go bathe and change your shirt."

When we had sent him off—like bad parents sending their child on an errand where he will certainly meet a wolf, I thought—I felt a tremendous relief. I wanted to laugh or hit something. I suggested to Ruth that the two of us go on the town and get very drunk. I felt like spending our little savings. "At last I've figured out why she's been calling him," I said. "Nobody else would appreciate her the way Warren does. She probably seems ordinary to other people, but for him she's the Taj Mahal or the Statue of Liberty. You know Emerson says if the rich were rich the way the poor imagine riches they'd be richer than. . . . Nobody, but nobody, is poorer than Warren."

"I know," Ruth said. "And you had to send him out on a cold night like this."

"I? I sent him out? Let's take it easy, baby." Then with a bad conscience I muttered. "What the hell? Maybe this freak will be there. I'm jealous. I should be so lucky."

I remember that Ruth was standing by the window as we had this talk. With her fingernail she was cutting little streamers of frost from the glass. Where her fingernail had scraped there was an odd interweaving of loops that might have been a face. Through what might have been its eyes the black and terrible coldness of the Chicago night looked in at us.

"So you're afraid of what she might do to him if she's real?" I asked.

"Keep laughing, smart boy."

I said, "Maybe he'll come back a man, Mama."

He didn't come back at all. The next evening the landlady told us that he was in County Hospital, and the morning after that Ruth and I went there to find out about him.

The psychiatrist to whom we talked eventually told us that Warren had been undressing in front of one of the hotel room doors when the house detectives caught up with him.

"Quite devoutly," the psychiatrist said with a nervous giggle, "like King David disrobing before the Ark of the Lord." He was a small insecure type with a brown mustache like a mouse under his nose. "Your disturbed friend put up quite a resistance when they tried to get him away from that door. He believed it was his duty to be there."

"Did they check on the person inside the room?" I asked. "He'd been asked there by her."

The psychiatrist leafed through the notes on the clipboard that held Warren's chart. He found an entry worth reading and then said, "Yes. It was occupied by a perfectly explicable couple who didn't know the patient at all. A couple who'd just arrived that day from St. Louis. Respectable people."

"Maybe he went to the wrong door," Ruth said. This was her last effort to sustain some truth in Warren's illusion, and after she had made it, something vital and hopeful collapsed almost visibly within her. "*Someone* told him to go to that hotel."

"We don't know that," I said sharply. "We only have Warren's word for that. He may have invented it all."

"She could have been waiting for him there, and she was in trouble, too," Ruth said.

The psychiatrist peered at her and then turned on me. I didn't like his looks. "Come on," I ordered Ruth, and I took her arm to lead her away—to wherever it is we go and face those guilts for which there is no rational remedy.

The Black Horse

Between the boys, like some trestle of startling fragility, the balsa framework of the wing lay across the card table. A scrap of red tissue paper rising from the kit box ticked back and forth under Keith's careful breathing as he worked. There was a tube of cement open at the center of the table, and a clear drop formed as the cement oozed from the tube.

All afternoon the storm window of Paul's bedroom had been tapping in its frame like the sound of a telegraph receiver, and now, as though the code of this sound had finally taken on meaning, Keith clicked his tongue and muttered, "I wouldn't want to take her out on a day like this. I wouldn't try to fly her in this wind." With his little finger he hooked the drop of cement from the end of the tube before it could fall on the table top.

Paul Brown looked at the window which showed only the gray

blank of the sky. His room was on the third floor of the house, and on this side there were not even treetops that reached this high. "I wouldn't give a damn," he said.

"She'd break up like kindling wood," Keith said. "Even if it didn't hit the house or a fence the wind would blow her wings right off."

"I'd like to take her up on top of the house and wind her up and head her into it and just see," Paul said. He put down the spar he was sanding and sat idle for some seconds with a private grin twitching his mouth. "If we had her finished I would, too."

Keith was cutting notches in a rib. He pushed the razor blade into the flesh-colored soft wood on either side of the notch, broke out the waste, and touched the new edges with sandpaper. "Look here," he said. "There's just one thing I wish you'd promise me and that is you won't try to fly her when I'm not here."

Paul said nothing.

"I know it's your Christmas present," Keith said, "and that your mother brought it to you."

"Stepmother," Paul said. "She bought it in Hollywood."

"I know she did," Keith said, "but even if it is, I've done at least half—more than half—the work on it, and I don't want it all busted up before we even have a chance to find out how well it flies."

"You don't want," Paul said. "*You* don't want."

"Please," Keith said. He stopped working on the rib, holding it, as though with clumsy respect, between his thumb and forefinger. Its clear curve and its whiteness looked alien in his grimy hand. He was frequently ashamed that his hands seemed to get dirtier and always stay dirtier than Paul's even if he could do many things with them that Paul bungled.

"*Please*," Paul mimicked. "OK. I don't want to wreck her either. Anyway Faye wouldn't be happy if I wrecked it." Faye was the professional name of his stepmother, and although his father, who had known her since she was a child, still called her Garnet, Paul insisted on the other name. He had also, since his father had brought her back to this house, picked up mannerisms of her speech—"be happy about" instead of "like" something.

After a while Paul said, "Hey, don't you think Faye's beautiful?"

By this time Keith was cementing the rib in place on the main spar of the wing. Getting it aligned took a good deal of care, so he answered offhand, "Yeah. I guess everybody thinks their mother is beautiful sort of."

Paul whooped with laughter and jumped out of his chair so quickly that he bumped the card table. He danced to the bed and threw himself face down on it. He began laughing so hard that Keith was sure he was forcing the laughter.

He was afraid of Paul when Paul was like this, and because Paul always demanded some servility, he was afraid enough now—as though afraid that Paul might not let him work on the airplane model any more—to go sit beside him on the bed. He looked back rather sadly at the rattling window and at the white wingframe on the card table, waiting for Paul to finish his uneasy laughing and be placated.

All at once Paul whipped an arm around his neck and dragged him flat on the bed, pushing his face into the coverlet and hissing amid his laughter, "Look, I don't mean beautiful like your mother. Don't you know anything?"

He could feel the moisture and warmth of Paul's breath on his ear.

He struggled to free his face from the coverlet, but Paul increased the pressure and kept whispering, "Don't you know anything? Don't you want to know how I saw her the other afternoon when I was coming down the hall? Don't you even want to see the pictures of her that my father's got?" Gradually, gradually the pressure of Paul's arm slackened and Keith could have got away if he had really wanted to. Instead, now, he lay fixed. His eyes were open and he was staring at the khaki coverlet half an inch beneath them. The coverlet was a blur of shadow and color with no distinction of texture focused.

"What pictures?" he asked.

Paul sat up and began brushing the wrinkles out of the sleeve of his sport shirt.

"What are they pictures of?" Keith asked.

"I asked if you wanted to see them."

"Can I?" Keith asked, pleading.

"Well, the pictures are in their room and they're gone," Paul said. "Come on."

At the door of his room, Paul took off his shoes and motioned Keith to do the same. The hall down which they moved was floored with slick oak. A graylighted window stood at the end of the hall. They passed the stairwell, skating quietly and hardly breathing.

Down those two flights of oak, Paul's grandmother would be sitting in front of the fireplace, and now, feeling the springs of wisdom coil in his belly, Keith guessed some of the quality of her vigil—she sat there like a white-haired queen, with senses of hearing and sight that missed no one's guilt.

II

He knew she sat there plump and soft and aged, and that she would be smoking a cigarette in a long holder while she brooded on the fire. Sometimes that fall, when he had seen her sitting in apparent utter relaxation, he had felt *She's doing something, I can't tell what it is, something is shaping in her like in an egg, something has been shaped, she's bigger than she looks.* It was a quality, not detail, that he sensed in her, and the detail of her concerns this afternoon was no more to be guessed than he could have guessed six months ago that there was a family like the Browns anywhere.

Before he and his folks had moved to Chesterfield he had certainly never known anyone like them, nor seen around any of the little Iowa towns in which he lived his twelve years anything like the scale and grandeur of the way they lived. Their house— down whose upper hallway he was now sneaking—was the big measure on that scale. He had seen it first during the previous summer, white and immense, a full quarter of a mile from the country road and a mile and a quarter from Chesterfield, fronted by a lawn that by itself looked to him big enough for a farm and waving with unmowed bluegrass among the elms and catalpas.

"The Browns," his father had said as he herded the Chevvie past that lawn that first time—getting the lay of the land around Chesterfield on the Sunday after their arrival. "I hear there is an old lady and her son Garris Brown. I hear they own four sections of land running back to the river, and more than that up toward Barrett."

"Why look at those barns," his mother said. "One, two . . . four of them. Four barns, Keith, look."

"One for the money, two for the show," his father said. "Three for the show, four for the showoff."

"Look at all those flower beds, Keith."

And (they were not yet past the frontage of lawn) his father's lips stuck out rudely when he said, "Like some damned English lord with his country seat. His seat, hah. But I reckon if we can get Roosevelt in this fall it will take the wind out of the sails of people like that." Then they were past the elms that bounded the lawn and passing the row of little houses that Keith would learn later were tenant houses and that he would hear his father call "the slave quarters" when his mother, glancing back, said, "Keith, look, there's an airplane landed out behind those barns."

His father said, "Sure, sure. I hear that Garris Brown is going to buy an airplane. When some of us can't get a new tire for our cars. And I suppose he's gone and bought it." It did not occur to Keith to doubt his father's implication that the owning of an airplane was a corruption, any more than it occurred to him to pay much attention to his father's judgment of the rights in the matter. Staring from the car window, glimpsing the plane for only a second between trees and shed, he saw it shine illicit, delicately malign, and yellowfleshed, and he stored the memory of it permanently among his lecherous thoughts.

His father had lapsed into a heavy silence then, no doubt thinking that after November, Roosevelt would clip the wings of them as tried to fly too high above their fellowmen. It was after he had turned the corner toward Chesterfield that he said, "I hear that Garris Brown has got a boy about Keith's age, but he's probably too spoiled and rich to look at Keith." Keith looked self-consciously at his hands, feeling himself blush, feeling like an ugly daughter.

Spoiled and *rich*—he remembered those terms, too, and they remained part of his image of Paul Brown even after he knew that Paul came to school in Chesterfield just as he did, and after he became Paul's friend. Paul wore leather sports jackets and had lace-up leather boots which he said had been imported from Canada. He looked expensive and a little foreign when he sat in the schoolroom among the town boys in their wool clothes and the country boys in overalls—*spoiled*. During the fall he rode a big Morgan horse into town. When the weather turned sharply colder his grandmother brought him in from their country house in a green Lincoln. The word *spoil* returned to Keith sometimes with the smell of peaches fermenting in the dim coolness of the fruit cellar.

The first time he had gone to Paul's house he had ridden his bicycle beside the Morgan horse and they had giggled along, talking about their teacher. Her name was Miss Roberts; Paul was calling her "Miss Rabbits." On the quarter-mile lane to the house Paul suddenly broke off the conversation, rose in his stirrups, and thrust the big horse into a gallop. Keith pedaled as hard as he could, feeling the raw creep of air burn his lungs with his speeded breathing, but there was no hope of keeping up. By the time he arrived at the house Paul had dismounted under the porte-cochère and was talking to a man in overalls who held the reins of the sweating horse.

It was right after that when he met the grandmother, believing at once with absolute and mystic certainty of belief *she is the meaning of Paul.* When she smiled and reached out her hand to take his it was as though she might be giving him not money but the significance of it, and promising him that its sacraments could be familiar to him. From the instant of meeting and the first smile it was also as though she had said *We will take care of Paul. We know and we must.* But Keith knew nothing except that there was a promise in her.

His father watched him form this friendship with dry skepticism. A time came when he could tell his father that the Browns—especially Garris Brown, who was on a long visit "in the West"—were Roosevelt people. His father had grimaced and said, "Sure. You bet. But let me tell you it's only on the Prohibition question they're with him. Not for what he'll do for the common people."

One night when Keith was running across his back yard to the privy he saw the distant lights of the Brown house and realized that the leaves of the trees between were gone with the changing season. It was October then, the wind picking at the corners of his clothes and chilling him. He watched the lights a mile away and thought of the grandmother and the way she had hoarded a secret from the old times like a hoard of big coins. *Like some damned English lord* (smell of English bitter walnuts) *like the taste of the times before Prohibition. Prohibition* sounded like the wind blowing around him, over the bare stars and the cottonwood tree by the privy. He felt a great cold hope that Paul would lead him to the old lady's secret.

But it was soon after this that a little twist—surely a twist of his own feelings—blunted and postponed the promise. He and Paul had come into the big house together on a Thursday evening not long before Christmas. Old Mrs. Brown met them with a gray letter in her hand. "Your father," she said to Paul, waving the letter. "*Guess* what he's up to now." It was as though she might have been talking about a character in an adventure story that she and Paul were reading serially and that could not be interpreted to Keith.

"Well, he's getting married," she said. She put the gray, masculine stationery into Paul's hands. While he read she turned to Keith. Her eyes were remote as though she were looking at a stranger. "Paul's father is getting married in Hollywood," she said.

He nodded.

"You met Paul's father before he left, didn't you?"

"Yes I did."

"Of course. I'd forgotten. It's hard to keep track of time." She hummed a little to herself.

"How are your parents?" she asked Keith politely. Before he could answer she said to her grandson, "Isn't this the *nicest* thing?"

It seemed to Keith that a hard, defensive circle had closed while he was two steps outside.

III

She knows what we're doing, Keith thought, feeling the crisp slickness of the floor move under his feet and imagining the old woman down there in front of the fireplace. She knows and meant it to be like this. The belief that she was somehow permitting this search, that even the ritual of secrecy was merely an obedience she required, added a sharpness to the search that Keith could hardly stand. He could have thrown up easily.

Paul passed in ahead of him onto the blue carpet of the room. "Now be quiet," Paul whispered unnecessarily. He crossed with intent, savage absorption to a chest of drawers by the windows.

There was a thick smell, almost palpable, that enveloped them, a smell of perfume, of the wallpaper, of leather, with a discreet underlay of the smell of sweat and human presences— so discreet that it, too, might have been the product of some glamorous catering.

"What's that?" Keith whispered and then he could feel, not hear, the thud of silent giggling transmitted from Paul through the dense air.

"One of her mules, you sap."

The black-furred thing—it might be a mule but Keith still didn't know what it was—lay at the very edge of the bed's shadow as though it were alive and might waken anytime and skitter away. He wanted to touch it but was afraid to while Paul was watching. He trembled, sensing the snowy air that rubbed the walls outside.

"Hey," Paul said. He was lifting a revolver from one of the drawers. It had a polished walnut handle. The barrel was almost black, but splinters of light moved on it when Paul swung it around and pointed it at him. "Did I ever show you this?" Paul asked.

"Don't point it at me."

"Well, then, don't talk so loud," Paul said. "You want to lift it? It's heavy."

"Yeah," Keith breathed. "Ye-e-eah."

Paul's clean and long-fingered hands slid through the contents of the drawer, lifting handkerchiefs and leather boxes. Presently he took a leather-covered flask from the drawer, unscrewed the top and thrust it out for Keith to smell. "It's had whiskey in it," he said.

"Where are the pictures?" Keith asked.

"They were in here before." Paul looked annoyed, closed the drawer and opened the one beneath it and said, "But look at this." The drawer was full of Faye's underwear. It shone in pale colors, some lavenders, and whites, and greens. On top was a piece embroidered with the word *Toujours*. "That means *always*," Paul said.

"Always what?"

"You're dumb," Paul said.

"I don't see why."

"It means always love. You get it? Hey, let's take this. Put it inside your shirt," Paul said. He unbuttoned Keith's shirt and thrust the silk inside.

"But where are the pictures?" Keith asked. It seemed to him that the multitudinous odors of the room, the sight and danger of the gun, the flask that smelled the way he thought a battle must smell, and the sensation of the undergarment against his side were sensations that rose in a series of waves that flipped him around. The idea of the pictures beckoned through his mind like some sourceless light.

He was moving impatiently to get into another drawer when

they heard the car come up the frozen drive, crunching snow and gravel as it stopped under the porte-cochère.

"It's Pop and his gang," Paul said. "Let's go down and see them."

"Maybe we better go back and work on the plane," Keith said weakly.

"Don't you want to see Faye?"

Keith looked at his grimy hands and wished that they would shrivel off as he started to follow Paul.

IV

And it was only when he was shaking hands with Faye, trying to meet her eyes but not managing to look above her round red mouth that he remembered what it was that was bulging inside his shirt, and remembering he almost decided to faint, collapse like rubbish right on her shoes.

Two other couples had come home with the Browns and when the boys came down they were still hanging up coats and finding chairs, and Garris Brown was heading for the kitchen, asking what everyone would have. Keith heard a flurry of names. Paul's grandmother introduced him to all of them, but after the introduction he could remember only Mr. Rimmey's name—a fat man who sat on the edge of an overstuffed chair rubbing his hands together. Rimmey's cheeks were smooth shaved but nevertheless had the bluish-black color of his beard.

"Which one of you's the oldest one?" Rimmey asked and then when it was explained to him that Paul and Keith were not brothers, he said, "Ah, buddies uhh?"

"Now, they don't look alike," Faye said.

"Well, they got the same look in their eye," Rimmey insisted. When everyone laughed at this, as though it had some clever meaning, Rimmey rubbed his hands together very fast and bounced in his chair.

Keith backed off to a chair behind the circle the others made around the fireplace and sat watching Faye talk to Paul and Rimmey. Mostly he watched Faye. Her straw-yellow hair looked like fire in the dark luxury of the room. She remained standing and from time to time swung her head or gestured with her arm and shoulder in an extravagant way. Her mouth was an agile, scarlet pouch, never immobile.

Through the trance of his embarrassment, Keith became aware

that they were talking about him, and once Faye flung her hand in his direction as though she were, by the gesture, creating him. He heard Paul's voice and noticed the way it caught the inflections of Faye's. Paul was praising him, but still Paul seemed to have accepted the spirit of the grownups where the words of praise were just a way of mocking.

"Well, well, well, well," Rimmey said. "So pal Keith has got an ROG that could undoubtedly fly rings around a Camel. How about that? How ABOUT that?" He rubbed his hands together, hitched at his trouser legs, and yipped three or four times like a kicked dog, but it was laughter.

"The ROG stayed up four minutes when we flew it off the roof," Paul said. Keith wished to God Paul wouldn't talk about certain things in front of these people. It was like selling out these good things they had done together just so they would think he was cute.

"Four MINUTES!" Rimmey said.

"That's lovely," Faye said. "Will the one I gave you stay up that long?" Keith could see her smile glitter in the firelight while she waited for an answer.

"It's a heavier machine," Paul said, frowning as he considered the question.

He don't know anything about it, Keith thought. He wished they would ask him. He wished he had not sat so far back from their circle.

Even while he was wishing this, Rimmey said, "Maybe we ought to ask pal Keith. He seems to be the engineer. How about it Keithie? What would you think?"

The wise, assured, and uninterested eyes of the adults swung to him and he mumbled furiously, "I don't know."

Paul's father brought in a tray of drinks in which the ice was tinkling delicately. After he put the tray down he said, "Hey you boys, why don't you skip along? We've got some serious work here."

"Serious," Rimmey said. "How ABOUT that?"

"I'll bet," Paul said.

His grandmother called softly across to them, "Hunting. Couldn't you boys go hunting?"

"We could," Paul said.

His father cuffed him affectionately and said, "There's snow enough for rabbits. Why don't you and Keith go track some out behind the horse barn?"

"Can I have the Winchester?" Paul asked.

"Use your own gun," his father said.

"I thought if I could have the Winchester, Keith could use my Stevens."

"Oh." Garris Brown's eyes rested briefly on Keith with a look of utter weariness. "OK," he said. "Don't shoot toward the horse barn."

V

"Grandma is the reason we couldn't stay," Paul said. His boots plowed a steady furrow through the snow of the pasture and broke the splintery tops of weeds. He carried the pump gun in the crook of his arm loosely. "I could have stayed but they couldn't have you there."

Because they're afraid I would've told, Keith thought. Because they're going to do something that. . . . He was aware of the large warmth of the house behind him like a hive of mysterious lusts. Against the gray shapes of snow and the desolated trees at the pasture's edge he saw projected, with visionary sharpness, the image of the black thing under the bed—the "mule." And he wanted to say, I would not have told, whatever they did, are doing. He wiped his nose on the back of his mitten.

"Grandma drinks too," Paul said. "She doesn't want anyone in Chesterfield to know it. You're not going to tell your folks, are you?"

Keith shook his head. They walked on through the heavy cold, and now they had begun to descend toward the woods that bordered the pasture. They had been here before when they hunted rabbits, and this border had always been the edge of real excitement for Keith, the woods beyond somehow peopled. Along the fenceline now they found a maze of rabbit tracks, but the tracks were eroded by the wind and melting. Obviously they had been made days before. The boys stood by the fence looking into the corridors of the timber.

"Is Mr. Rimmey from Hollywood, too?" Keith asked. The steam of his breath whipped down the fenceline. He rested his mittened hand on the barbed wire.

Paul said, "He's a bootlegger from Granite City, and I guess he used to be a pilot in the war. Don't you tell that he's a bootlegger. I'd be scared to tell anyone myself because he's got gang connections."

"Oh," Keith said. The awareness of the secret house behind him expanded again with this information. His hand twitched on the wire, in the immense cold, and it seemed to him that the secret beating of his heart was impossible to contain. He lifted his rifle and fired it at random into the woods ahead of him.

"What you shooting at?" Paul asked.

"The cops. Let 'em have it." Keith guiltily watched the spot where his bullet had kicked up snow. He groped for another cartridge. Maybe he was playing silly now and maybe Paul would laugh, but he intended to shoot again anyway. Before he got his gun reloaded he heard Paul firing the pump gun beside him, the steady small crashes of .22 shells. He clenched his teeth as though in this way he could prolong the excitement of the moment. But it died as soon as Paul's gun was empty and he had to pause to reload.

The wide sky seemed to be listening to them, awfully, as though it were contemplating punishment.

"Well," Paul said, giggling, "if there were any rabbits we've scared them now. So we might as well go back."

"Maybe I ought to go home," Keith said.

"Well, if you want to."

"Or we could attack the barn," Keith said.

"It's too cold."

"We wouldn't have to crawl this time. We could rush it."

"We'll give them the grenades when we get close enough," Paul said. He scooped a chunk of snow and lobbed it like a grenade at Keith. "Come on." He raced away, doubled over to present a low silhouette, and then, still ahead when they had recrossed the field, he began to zigzag. Finally they rushed in through a small halfdoor of the horse barn and flopped against a pile of feedsacks.

"Wow," Paul gasped. "That was a good run. Only they'd have got us. We weren't zigzagging enough."

Keith could not answer for a while, but he was angry at Paul for saying that. He had done his very best, and it seemed unjust to think that an enemy bullet would have struck him in such a case. He felt the sweat soaking his underwear, and he lay there smelling the feedsacks that smelled something like the disinfectant in the school toilet. He could hear the wind outside again, sounding just as it had outside the room where they had searched for the pictures. Up in the top of the barn he could hear pigeons.

Some of the horses moved and stamped: there was a clinking of chains.

It seemed to him that in storming this barn he had stormed the house and won it. The barn was a secret version of the house, like a dream would be. He felt the bunched shape of Faye's underwear against his stomach. He sprang up and shouted shrilly, as though the game had completely possessed him, "Come on. Let's get 'em."

VI

They stood on a two-by-four leaning over the box stall where the stallion was kept. They had made their way in stages that were half the pretense of military game in which they sought Huns in the grain bins and the back corners of the mow and half a purposeful search for something nameless—had made their way to where the big black horse stood in a kind of sullen, self-contemplative might.

Paul threw a handful of oats down on the stallion's shoulder and the skin twinkled when the horse shuddered them off. There were blue lights, menacing as sparks of electricity, that danced on the skin.

"Do you know how much he cost?" Paul said. "Thirty-five hundred dollars." He tossed some more oats. "Boy, I'd hate to fall in there. He'd kill you as quick as look at you. He's mean as a snake."

"Then maybe you better not rile him by throwing things."

"He doesn't mind that," Paul said. "Because do you know what he's thinking about?"

"No."

"You'd know if you'd seen those pictures we were looking for."

Keith hesitated for a little while. When he spoke there was a note in his voice so odd that even he could not tell whether he was asking a question or stating something. "I don't believe there ever were any pictures," he said. "Of what?"

"The old horse knows," Paul said. "But you couldn't understand that either because this is the first time you've ever seen him."

Keith said, "Give me some of those oats." He threw half a dozen grains at the horse. Then he whinnied. He did not know exactly why or how he had come to think of this, but the effect was immediate. The stallion, which had paid them no attention, lifted his head, big as a suitcase, and began pawing with his front feet. Keith whinnied again and this time the stallion replied.

"My word," Paul said. He whinnied too. The stallion reared and struck at them with both front feet. The wood partition shivered beneath them. The horse was watching them, and before his gaze they retreated and climbed higher, standing on a beam at the edge of the mow.

Now both of them whinnied at the animal in complete abandonment. Aching, wild, Keith tore the scrap of silk underwear from inside his shirt and threw it. He laughed crazily as he watched the garment flutter down to the dunged floor of the stall and he seemed in a flash to have seen the pure white shape he had imagined the photographs would reveal.

Paul was shaking his arm. Paul grabbed his ear and jerked it painfully. "You've done it now," Paul said. In Paul's eyes he saw the danger that he had exposed himself to.

"There's no way to get them out," Paul said. "You fool, you fool. Now somebody will find them there and it will be terrible." He slapped the side of Keith's face.

"Cut it out," Keith said wearily. He could feel his legs sag with a cold weariness. "Maybe we could lead him out or . . ." Paul slapped him again.

"Cut it out."

"I didn't know you were going to be such a baby fool," Paul said.

"All right," Keith said. He walked to the mow ladder and descended to the floor of the barn.

VII

He could not tell if the stallion heard him open the door of the stall. The square flanks were motionless ahead of him. The black skin twitched as it had when they threw the oats down.

He felt the smooth, old wood of the stall side meet his hand. He glanced down to make sure of his next step. Something stung his face sharply. The stallion had flicked its tail. The great black body was motionless.

When he had lifted the bar from the stall door, Paul had called down to him, "Don't let him know you're afraid," and he had nodded back. There was no need to answer. There was nothing left of him but fear. The horse knew it. The horse was the black image of his fear, not really there an arm's length away, but inside ready to explode him.

He knelt at the side of the stall, put one hand on the floor, and leaned forward. The silk garment lay beside the front hooves. He could read the embroidered letters. He could not force his free hand to cross the last few inches to take hold of it. In the moment that he wrestled with the hand, trying to move it, he could hear the pigeons somewhere over his head. It's my hand, he thought, in an agony of rebellion. He began to withdraw it as slowly as he had thrust it out, and just beyond it he saw the black hooves begin to rise from the floor.

He heard the halter rope snap before he was hit and heard the bones crackle in his cheek when he was thrown against the side of the stall.

The next thing he heard was the tinkle of several voices around him. Presently he knew he was in the house and lying on a sofa. When he breathed he could feel the hitching of his broken guts. Now his eyelids were as stony as his hand had been when he tried to reach for the silk piece that said *Toujours*. The eyelids felt cold, and he imagined them to be very thick.

"Jaysuss, Jaysuss"—this was Rimmey's voice—"look at his damn face. What do you think, Garris?"

Keith did not hear what Garris thought. After a while he heard Paul's grandmother say, "He's on his way now. That's the best we can do." Her voice went on but it became something besides words. After a while the voice was like ice sliding on ice, and it seemed to be getting bigger. Then against his immovable eyelids he saw the old lady quite clearly and after that he understood what it was that she had always been urging him on to hunt for.

A Journey
of the Magi

Dang Wuk John huddled under the Dean's armpit when the Dean introduced him to Mr. Collins, the art teacher at Mount Tabor College. Then, acknowledging Mr. Collins' welcome, he thrust out a toy-sized hand on which a big diamond glittered. "I am an exchange stoo-*dent*," he said in an alarmingly bass voice, though the Dean had just explained the whole circumstance of his late enrollment.

Then, as if his big voice were a trick to confound Mr. Collins' expectations of him, Dang jiggled and pranced with amusement. He said, "Have come to study your art." He pronounced *art* with such lack of self-consciousness that he contrived to make it sound like an hermetic art—one shaman come to learn the craft of another, Mr. Collins thought. He felt momentarily that he should apologize for the day-lit, academic barrenness of this studio, where seven of his students were painting a still life of wax fruit, brass samovar, and an antelope skull.

"Dang speaks English very well," the Dean said hopefully.

"Yas. Speak English," Dang rumbled.

"It doesn't matter. It wouldn't matter," Mr. Collins said. "We don't need much language here in the Art Department, except the universal language of forms." He was as surprised by his own deepened voice and this uncommonly elegant statement as he had been by Dang's voice. He did not like to think that it might seem a toadying to the Dean. He had tried to be worthy of whatever expectations had brought Dang halfway around the world to this little college in northern Iowa. But, whatever his justifications, he had gone out of his way to match the Dean's fulsome benevolence, knowing very well that exchange students were dearer to the administration than he or art were. It was Mount Tabor's religious and missionary affiliations that had piped Dang up from one of those jungle states bordering on the Indian Ocean, and it was by the religious and the missionary that Mount Tabor defined its widest purpose.

"I'll leave him in your capable hands," the Dean said to Mr. Collins. "When the period is over I'll have someone here to pick him up and take him to the student cafeteria."

"Cafeteria is eat," Dang said with an explosion of purest glee.

"At twelve o'clock. When the bell rings. Mr. Collins will tell you when," the Dean said and sidled away.

"Is eat, is eat, is eat," Dang said.

"The first thing is to give you a list of the supplies you'll need here," Mr. Collins said. "Come on in the office with me."

But Dang had taken an observer's stance in face of the class— most of whom were watching him in return—and seemed not to hear.

"Come on," Mr. Collins urged. "I'll introduce you later." He moved toward his office, and suddenly Dang had skipped around him to block his way. Dang shook his head importantly. "Love of life," he said—or at least that was as close to an interpretation of his breathy cry as Mr. Collins could come.

"That's a very good philosophy," Mr. Collins said. He tried to twist Dang by the shoulders and point him at the office door.

"Tomorrow. Tomorrow tell me," Dang said. "Today no. Love of life. America the Beautiful." The radiance of his eyes rebuked

Mr. Collins and then forgave him. Jauntily Dang walked out of the studio.

From his office window Mr. Collins watched Dang sprint across the autumn-dappled campus, climb in a Buick convertible parked behind the chapel, and, with a wave that flashed his diamond like a signal, drive away in the direction of town.

The next day Mr. Collins commissioned one of his students named Kirby to go downtown with Dang for art supplies. Neither of them came back during the class period, and at the following session Kirby appeared but Dang did not.

"The last I saw of him yesterday afternoon," Kirby explained, "he was in the bar at the Homesteader Hotel."

"The Homesteader?"

"He was drinking orange pop. He was among friends."

"That may be. Maybe. You might have taken him to a place that was a little easier for a foreigner to grasp." The Homesteader in these later years had become a crossroads for farmers, high school adventurers, packinghouse workers, salesmen, truckers, and B girls. "Anyway, you shouldn't have left him there alone," Mr. Collins said, worrying inhumanely about the boy's diamond and the school's reputation, rather ashamed of himself that he should automatically focus his thought on such things.

Kirby smiled cautiously. "Well, but that's where he lives. I suppose, sure, that he'll be in a dormitory like all the rest of us, but I mean they haven't got him in one *yet*. And he didn't seem to be not at home in the bar."

"Well," Mr. Collins said. "Well." Love of life, indeed. And some of his secret pleasure at this information must have shown on his face, for Kirby warmed up and said, "That boy's a regular Jimmy Dean. I didn't know they grew them over there. The way he drives that car, human life must be cheap over there, you know."

"The college won't let him keep his car, either. Too bad," Mr. Collins said. A justifiable but usually suppressed malice reminded him that life might not be quite so cheap here at Mount Tabor if, say, tricky young Dang managed to establish a third-floor joss house at the Homesteader—almost within the college's orbit of sanctity. He felt the artist's predilection for rebellion warm him. He forgave Dang his absences and for the rest of the week believed himself fond of the newcomer.

But this was an illusion based on much too scanty an acquaintance. Once Dang began attending sessions of the painting class with some regularity, he became a sheer nuisance. He knew nothing at all about how to paint the still life which Mr. Collins had prepared for the class. He seemed to get pleasure in squeezing the paint out of the tubes—but neither pleasure nor edification in mixing it to match the wax and brass for value and color. The task to which he set himself while Mr. Collins was occupied with other students was the seduction of Juanita Grisby.

Next to Dang himself Juanita was far and away the poorest student of them all. She was a town girl, a Junior whose insistence on majoring in art puzzled Mr. Collins almost to the point of fury. Against his counsel that she turn her efforts to Home Economics, she insisted doggedly that art was to be her life work—and yet her efforts hardly ever went beyond a sullen compliance with instruction or the disciplines that the material itself imposed. She went at a still life as if it were just too much that wax apples should be red, while lemons were yellow and grapes purple. She listened to criticism with the patient outrage of a Christian martyr tolerating the heresies of her persecutor. She had no interest in the jokes or enthusiasms of the majority of the students. During the previous spring the other students had organized a pale but jolly Beaux Arts ball in the college gymnasium. Juanita had said it was all nonsense and merely an excuse for some whose names she could have mentioned to risk the college reputation. She had not attended.

Completely banal in appearance, she was also twice as big as Dang. She was a bad substitute, according to Mr. Collins' way of thinking, for the depraved girls of the Homesteader whom he had briefly imagined as the natural targets of Oriental taste. In the spectacle of Dang's courtship there was only a collapsing interest, like discovering a book in a foreign language to be a gardening manual instead of a treatise on the art of love.

In his wooing Dang gave over language as probably too difficult or perhaps too compromising. He laid siege to Juanita by getting in her eye. It was his strategy to place himself frequently between her and the still life. Then he would flutter his arms and skip back and forth while he threw her smiles over his tiny shoulder. He made his diamond twinkle at her. Now and then he made soft clucking noises.

Experience seldom interrupted Juanita. At first she simply stared at her wooer with the heavy acceptance she accorded all phenomena except those that might have promised bodily harm. Mr. Collins believed she was not even, for a while, curious about Dang's objective—though the rest of the class were, and their paintings advanced unevenly through that week. Her small blue eyes remained imperturbable. Finally her tight mouth relaxed. She was amused. She had been won.

The next thing Mr. Collins knew of the rake's progress was that Dang had got her to play ping pong with him. On his way back to the studio after the mid-morning coffee break Mr. Collins saw them in the rec room—Juanita solid and determined as she beat back the little fellow's rallies, Dang whirling like a dervish, seeming to multiply the number of balls in play by sheer agility, pinwheeling, slashing, leaping as if the air over the table were full of white celluloid galaxies.

As Mr. Collins passed nearby, Dang paused just long enough to shout "Joy of heart," before he smashed a ball at Juanita's torso.

The nuisance of this innocent pastime came when the couple began to stretch the mid-morning break for as much as an hour of ping pong. Their palettes sat messily by their unfinished paintings like an incitement to idleness for the other students. Mr. Collins' minimum discipline was slipping. Also, Dang was supposedly an art major and Juanita would be hard put, at best, to improve the D she had got in the spring semester. The prospect of flunking her consoled Mr. Collins a bit, but Dang's problem filled him with foreboding. Already when the Dean had asked about the boy's progress and Mr. Collins had told the truth, the Dean had had this to say, pointedly: "Spend more time with him." There was just no question about it. Dang's career at Mount Tabor had to be successful.

But how spend more time with him? Mr. Collins hated to police his students as if he were still teaching in high school. All his predilections in favor of liberty were revolted when he had to shanghai Dang back to class after the coffee breaks. It was not easy, even so, to make sure that Dang returned. When the humor for ping pong was on him, he was apt to utter a slogan like "Vision of eternity" as Mr. Collins interrupted his game, and then escape surveillance by going to the men's room and ducking away through the corridors.

Mr. Collins tried to put on pressure through Juanita. She replied, "What can I do? He's no friend of mine, particularly."

"You see quite a bit of him."

"I see a lot of boys," she said grandly. The lie was so hopeless that Mr. Collins lacked the heart to puncture it. He wished she had not made him pity Dang by her denial. That only complicated the situation from which, by now, he hoped for nothing more than deliverance.

After a humiliating number of wasted warnings, Mr. Collins laid down the law—either Dang was going to be punctual henceforward or the two of them were going to the Dean for a showdown. Dang went visibly dim at this threat. Some evil spirit must have possessed the heart of his friend Mr. Collins, he implied by his grieving silence. To fight this evil and suspicious spirit—which must be the enemy of both of them—Dang developed the habit, trick, or excuse of panting. Thereafter when he came in an hour late in the morning or forty minutes late from the coffee break, he panted as if he had run all the way. In sublime confidence that panting worked—though Mr. Collins gave no indication that he was much impressed—Dang began to use it also whenever Mr. Collins approached his easel to check on the progress of his work. Pant, pant, pant. The little torso heaved like an exhausted steam engine every time Mr. Collins stood over the boy. And the worst of this was that the whole class—except, perhaps, Juanita—had caught on to the play by this time and could only be contemptuous of any failure to manage it.

One Tuesday morning in November Mr. Collins ended the foolishness by bursting into rage. He had come up silently behind Dang while Dang was pretending to highlight the horns of the antelope in his painting and was actually simpering disgustingly across the room at Juanita. Delicately and sensitively as an animal he registered Mr. Collins' approach. The whole room filled with the sound of his heavy breathing.

"Stop that," Mr. Collins commanded.

"Stop *that?*"

"Stop panting."

In a sham of obedience—it must have been a sham, Mr. Collins reasoned later; it could not have been stupidity or an innocent failure of communication—Dang drew back from his canvas and put down his brushes.

The onlooking class caught the pun and howled with laughter. Glancing shyly around Dang began to laugh, too—recklessly, with an absolute abandonment to mirth that was inhuman in its completeness. He giggled and trembled like an insane child.

"Stop panting! I said 'Stop panting,'" Mr. Collins insisted. He grabbed Dang by the collar of his shirt and hoisted him into the air. For a minute he held the boy dangling—and his anger vanished in the purely sensational shock of feeling no weight at all. It was as if he were waving a tissue paper figure. Nevertheless, he managed to round out the scene in ordinary terms by saying, "If you ever try that panting trick again, I'm going to drop you right out that window, Dang." Then he put the boy down and walked into his office.

He told himself that it must have been his anger, and the increased strength it had given him, that accounted for his inability to feel any weight when he had lifted Dang into the air. No doubt. But at the same time nothing affected his attitude toward Dang more than that uncanny sensation that had come to him while anger made him vulnerable. After this he found himself thinking often, *Something's got to be done about him.* It was folly to let matters drag on. There was absolutely no sense in hoping that Dang would change into a reasonable student. For everyone's sake in the name of the minimum academic proprieties, something should be done.

Mr. Collins had his chance to do something a week or so later. He was summoned to the Dean's office one morning and as he entered saw a dark, tall man in a black suit and a turban seated beside the Dean's desk. This was Mr. Wuk, the Dean explained, an uncle of Dang's. Mr. Wuk was in the midwest on a business trip and had stopped at the college to inquire about the progress of his nephew. Mr. Wuk closed his eyes and bowed slightly. His smile had the composed sadness of a Khmer deity.

"We've talked to Dang's other instructors," the Dean said, "and to his adviser. I think Mr. Wuk would appreciate a frank and candid appraisal of Dang's work with you." There was something urgent, admonitory in the Dean's tone—but what he was urging was indicated by nothing. He studied the yellow shaft of a pencil and squinted earnestly at Mr. Collins.

"Yes," Mr. Collins said. "Yes. Let's see if I can summarize.

Uh. Maybe you'd like to come out to the studio and see what he's been doing, Mr. Wuk."

"No," Mr. Wuk said.

"That won't be necessary," the Dean echoed. "You can summarize it for us."

"Well, to put it in perspective, there's the language problem," Mr. Collins said. "Dang's English—"

"Hasn't improved remarkably," Mr. Wuk said.

Mr. Collins nodded and turned toward Mr. Wuk. The patient, luxurious sadness of Wuk's face invited him to deliver the truth like an honorable blow. Across Mr. Collins' mind flashed the all too exact recollection of Dang's wretched still life, the spiritless daubing and the lazy unconcern with the shapes lit so pitilessly by the studio skylight. As he saw this, the actual materials of the still life appeared—the antelope skull, the wax fruit, and the greening brass—all of it so real and so banal, the appearance of nature itself a tedious exercise. For a moment of irresolution nature and discipline, all that his class represented, seemed tawdry in comparison with the dreams of laziness, and in that moment he really thought, Dang is right and we're wrong. I'm wrong.

Of course such a thought was too far out to be given credit. Common sense wouldn't tolerate it. But nevertheless Mr. Collins seemed to have been dragged into compromise and he said, "Dang is doing very well at the things that interest him."

"Very well?" Mr. Wuk asked with polite intentness.

"Very well. Yes," Mr. Collins said.

"You tell me that grading art students is very subjective," the Dean rumbled. "Mr. Wuk is interested in our young man's grades, so he can report to the father. Is it too early in the semester to consult your subjectivity and—?"

The hint, it seemed to Mr. Collins, was broad. What the Dean meant was that art students here were graded by whim, and whim had better favor Mount Tabor's interests. "Dang doesn't need to worry about his grade in art." Mr. Collins said.

The Dean and Mr. Wuk both thanked him for this reassurance.

And then, almost within the space of hours, Mr. Collins learned that it was his testimony and his alone which had kept Dang on at Mount Tabor. Dang's other instructors and his adviser had also been summoned for their moments of truth in the

Dean's office. Without exception they had agreed—Dang was failing all his courses. Except for art, where subjectivity, whim, caprice, or sheer dishonesty provided him with shelter, Dang could not expect to win a single credit point for the semester.

This fact, when it emerged, struck Mr. Collins with all the nasty venomous keenness of poetic justice. It paid him back for his carefully cherished isolation from the rest of the Mount Tabor faculty, for avoiding membership on faculty committees, for insisting on his agnosticism to avoid the sociability of religious jollifications, for preferring to build up and enjoy a record collection in his bachelor apartment rather than exchange Sunday evening dinners with his married colleagues. Until he went inquiring, he simply did not know what the common gossip of the school could have told him about Dang. The boy had worn out tolerance weeks ago. Far from being pet and pride of the school—like the other two dark-skinned exchange students, with whom Dang had refused to associate, anyway—he was a hazard, a liability, a blot that even the Dean was ready to erase from the Mount Tabor record. It was no accident that his uncle had visited the school. Mr. Wuk had flown out from New York because the Dean had asked him to come. Only Mr. Collins' ignorant intervention had prevented a reasonable settlement of the Dang problem.

"He may have some special gifts in art," Miss Henderson of English said. (Mr. Collins winced.) "And after all that's his principal excuse for being with us. But the suspicion will not down in my mind that Dang *lacks something* that we won't be able to instill."

"Yes," Mr. Collins said hoarsely.

"But if you see promise in him, I suppose it's up to the rest of us to keep trying," Miss Henderson said.

To cap the mortification of having toadied to his own detriment—and Mr. Collins was merciless in accusing himself of this—he had to endure accusations of dishonesty from Dang himself.

The day after Mr. Wuk's visit Dang skipped silently into Mr. Collins' office and stood by his desk without the usual benison of a smile. Today Dang was not loving life.

"Why did you tell my oncle I do well?" Dang asked.

"If you'd make a real effort, Dang—"

"Am not doing well."

"Well, that's true, but—"

"Am disgrace to my father. Joke to stoo-*dents*. Misfitting."

Something that could have been light broke for Mr. Collins. "Are you trying to flunk out? Do you want to get away from here?" He recalled the Buick, now immobilized at a downtown garage because of college rules, the secondhand picture of Dang living it up among the folk at the Homesteader Hotel before the college cooped him in a dormitory, and all that a rich boy far from home might envision when he said "life," even if that rich boy might be a midget with dark skin. "Because if you want loose, I'll go complain to the Dean about you right now. Write your ticket. I've doubtless been on the wrong track."

"Wish to make father proud of me," Dang said, swelling his chest like a toy soldier. "Wish to learn ideals of Christian man-hoo-ood. For my people."

"Oh," Mr. Collins said thoughtfully. "Oh." The notion occurred to him that if he were not an agnostic, *something* might offer him guidance at this moment. "All right, Dang. I've set up a new still life this morning. Throw away that canvas you've been working on and make a brand new start. I mean, cut it up in pieces and throw it away."

Following the visit of his uncle it was apparent to Dang that he had reformed. It was apparent to Mr. Collins only that Dang had found a more devious form of the panting trick—a form that could not possibly be dealt with by an action as crude as throwing Dang out of the studio window.

When Dang came late to his work in the studio there was something heroic in his satisfaction with himself. His bearing and the trig reassurance of his smile said plainly, "See? I am no longer *forty* minutes late from the coffee break, because ideals of art and Christian manhood have penetrated bosom." After some lazy daubing at the new still life—now a cactus plant, drift-wood, a fishnet, opera-length gloves, a lorgnette, and the front page of the Des Moines *Register*—he welcomed Mr. Collins' approaches to his easel with a pleasure that said, "Now have disciplined love of life with love of serious labor."

He expected now to be praised for his efforts, and with desperate whimsy—since no other approach worked, anyway—Mr. Collins praised. The new still life was exactly as bad as the one Dang had abandoned. And as he stood in front of the painting and said, "That's good" of the botched perspective, or "Nice color, Dang" of the acid viridian which represented the shaft of the cactus, Mr. Collins knew that the reasons for failure were exactly the same as before the reform. The same superhuman unpunctuality, the same vast boredom with everything but motion, the same vain courtship of the fat Juanita—a ritual now so well established that the other students no longer seemed to notice it.

"You're making progress, Dang," Mr. Collins said recklessly, feeling his own established values slide away like sand into the aboriginal pit. He had liked to think that at least in his teaching he was honest. Dang lured him on into more and more pointless lies. Hatred for Dang scorched his narrow life from side to side, and when Dang said reverently, "You, Mr. Collins, have made me see joy of obedience," Mr. Collins answered with unholy duplicity, "I hope I've been some help."

As far as he could tell, the other instructors and administrators concerned had accommodated the boy on his—*his?*—recommendation. For convenience, perhaps, they took Dang's reformation at face value. "At least he comes to class now," Miss Henderson said. MacDougal of biology reported that Dang had suspended his religious scruples against dissecting creatures with a face, though what the boy was finding in the jeweled entrails of a frog was not perhaps what the science predicted.

A week or so before the Christmas holidays Mr. Collins attended a pageant in the college chapel. The pageant was an annual affair, presented jointly by the college and the local church of the same denomination, and for Mr. Collins to have absented himself from this occasion would have displayed not merely his agnosticism but downright lack of loyalty to his employers.

The college orchestra and glee club supplied an ornament of music. Dr. Welker, the president, spoke of the season's joys and solemnities. To the small, thrilled piping of the glee club the pageant of the Nativity began.

"Look who it is this year," said old Dr. Ranney, nudging Mr. Collins. Above the manger bed, in spotlight glory, shone the face of Juanita Grisby, blessed among women and no doubt selected for this role because of some politics involving the local church, since Juanita had grown up in it—certainly neither for beauty, popularity, scholarship, nor the other attributes to be considered in casting this part. "This year I believe it," Dr. Ranney whispered through a phlegmy chuckle. "Last year they erred with that Hodges girl."

Mr. Collins was annoyed. Agnostic he might be (while Dr. Ranney prayed with the stoutest publicans) but he was fastidious, and in this season of redemption any sensitive man could take joy in the illusions of the myth and the stage, even if the stage was that of the college chapel and the myth beaten thin by the hypocrisy of lukewarm worshippers. Juanita was not the Virgin, but how stale a joke to point this out, how insensitive not to recognize that beyond this awkward obeisance glimmered the transcendent mystery of The Virginity. It was the duty and privilege of art to abstract as much of the pure mystery as possible from the earthly circumstance that embodied it, Mr. Collins reflected, and for a proud moment of piety he felt himself the champion of faith in this host of infidels.

Then Dang Wuk John came onstage in Eastern trappings, flanked on either side by the other exchange students (though one was female and thus, by Dr. Ranney's profane calculation, a silly choice for a Wise Man). Dang's presence did funny things to the theatrical illusion. When he raised his hand to offer frankincense and myrrh, his own diamond took the overhead light like a star. Even from a distance Mr. Collins recognized the familiar, idiotic instability of Dang's expression. He remembered—if he could not quite see—the tricky and perhaps malign evasiveness in the very depths of Dang's brown eyes, and though he should have been able to sift this out as extraneous to the meaning of the pageant, he could not. He found himself thinking that they should have picked someone else, more certifiably average in intelligence, at least, for this part. Then he thought, his mind drawing large circles around the smaller ones, I picked Dang for them. If it were not for his blundering tolerance, Dang would not be on the stage now, complicating the simplicity of the ritual with a perverse ambiguity. What disguised monster had he set loose among them to rip the web of their innocence? Mr. Collins recognized, for the remaining minutes of the tableau, a guilt that was half responsibility, half anticipation. When the lights went up, the guilt submerged. Evidently it was as impermanent as his agnostic, aesthetic faith.

Nevertheless, his conscience throbbed mysteriously all that night, and when his ringing phone woke him at eight he had a well-developed premonition that he was being summoned to judgment. The call was, indeed, from the police station.

"We got a boy down here we can release to you," the officer on duty said.

"You can?" Mr. Collins' left ear seemed to go deaf and he transferred the phone to the other side.

"He's one of your students up there, and he says that you personally are in charge of him."

"I am?" Mr. Collins asked fearfully.

As soon as he could dress and bundle himself against the cold, he drove downtown to get Dang. He had not taken time to shave, and this neglect seemed a serious mark against him, as though the forces of the law might take him to be an accomplice of Dang's, as though they might be right.

While Dang was being fetched down from the bullpen, the officer on duty explained, "The reason we called you instead of the Dean's office is why get the students in more trouble than they're already in? I mean, if they've got drunk or stole a sign or tore up a lawn. And you being his adviser, as well—"

"Thanks for calling me," Mr. Collins said.

"He swore up and down you were his only friend, so I thought, Why not? But this time it won't do him any good because of how serious it is."

"Yes," Mr. Collins said, already braced to accept his moral complicity in the worst of crimes, only waiting to hear what Dang had done.

"He took this girl Grisby up to the Homesteader Hotel and into a room. Well, between you and me, I don't know what he tried to do then, but she got scared and called her mother."

In spite of his attempt to keep a tight hold on reality, Mr. Collins could not suppress a vision of Juanita as she had appeared on the stage last night (*only* last night, he thought, and only a couple of hours before her fat, still virginal hand had lifted the material phone to call for temporal help) with a light that seemed to fall with the radiance of eternity on her unawakened face. His mind was still too scrambled from sleep for him to dissociate her conveniently from her role or to say, "For just so long she was the Virgin; after such and such a moment she was only the virginal Grisby." He had been tempted down into the dream in which the pillars of the rational universe go soft as noodles, and it was strangely against his will that he must abandon that dream now.

"The old lady I guess was a riot when she come," the policeman went on relentlessly. "Though it isn't as if I blame her. Got little girls myself. But anyhow she and the girl too was claiming he'd hypnotized her. Well, if one of my girls told me that, I'd take a strap to her and unhypnotize her pretty fast. They think you'll swallow anything. I suppose he probably gave her a drink and she wasn't scared till she got to the room. Who knows? Who cares? And I'm telling you this because, see, it isn't going to make any difference we didn't call the Dean. The old lady's so wild he's gonna hear about it in any event. Here's your boy."

Tears as fresh as water streamed on Dang's face. As he received his diamond, his wallet, and a small address book from the policeman at the desk, he took them back like a dispirited child whose toys have been devalued by adult intrusion into his dreaming games. Now they were only diamond, wallet, and book.

Dang turned to Mr. Collins—fortunately he did not run to the older man and throw himself into his arms—and said with a woeful grin, "Love of life. Resignation of spirit."

"Sure. Let's get some coffee and I'll drive you up to the college."

They sat together in a lunch wagon near the railroad. Steam from their coffee rose between them while Mr. Collins waited for Dang to compose his thoughts to speak. The waitress called, "O.J. on one." A passing train shook the lunch wagon like a dragon giving warning.

"Will have to leave Mount Tabor?" Dang asked.

"I'm afraid you will. You went a little too far. Someone should have advised you about Grisby."

"Advice," Dang said with expectant faith, as if even after the event advice might prepare him against its failure. "Kirby's advice: 'Show her an etching.' I bought. She looked. Then said, 'Take me to my home.' I do not know what to do."

Simple disappointment blocked the sympathy that Mr. Collins was prepared to feel. Only the administration of Mount Tabor would think that Dang had gone too far. "You should have hypnotized her," Mr. Collins sighed. He closed his eyes against the rattling morning light, as if to visualize the thousand

and one glamorous iniquities to which the gross Juanita might have been subjected. Now that the scare given him by the call from the police was fizzling out, his cornered heart complained that Dang had failed him in the moment of trial, had denied him the chance to side with real wickedness.

"Well, you *did* hypnotize her," Mr. Collins said. "Only, it didn't last long enough." And that was the trouble with all magicians, he realized, accepting his unacceptable lot—not that their magic was evil or against nature, but that there was too little of it. It could not prevail.

The train passed the lunch wagon again, shunting on the spurs. For a suspended instant the locomotive blacked the window beside them. It hissed expressive jets of steam—as if, Mr. Collins thought, it meant something, as if its artificial heat meant to overcome the sparkling frozen midwestern morning. He watched it with utter disillusion, finally with loathing and dread.

The Hot Girl

Byron was lying on the porch glider reading *The Big Money* when the preacher and his wife arrived. He heard their feet on the concrete steps and before he turned over to face them he thought with lazy resentment, They've found us. They couldn't wait.

The small town afternoon was brutally hot, and for a couple of hours the edge of sunshine had moved toward him across the porch floor until finally when he rocked to the left, it lit up the corner of the glider. On that corner the glider frame had become too hot to touch. He saw from this that he would have to move soon, but he hated the preacher and his wife for disturbing him ahead of what he considered the natural time to leave his reading and speculating.

This was only the second day he had been in this town, coming home from his Freshman year at college after his parents had moved, and it struck him as pretty nice to be where you didn't know the neighbors and they didn't know you. The two days had been a mediocre idyl, as innocent and vacuous as the scratching of the vine leaves when they moved against the splinters of glass embedded in the kellystone wall.

"Afternoon, afternoon," the preacher said. His wife stood behind him grinning.

She was ugly enough to fit as a preacher's wife, Byron thought.

"Is the father home?"

What father? *Our* father?

"Dad," Byron yelled. He sat upright and pulled his T-shirt down to cover his stomach. "Won't you folks go right in? Dad and Mother must be in the front room."

"It's almost too hot," the preacher's wife said, and then jerked her head nervously as though she felt she shouldn't be the one to say such a thing.

Byron stared at her with mute hostility and then, as his father came to the door, rolled and squirmed back to the most comfortable position he could find for reading, back to the drugged, imaginative mood that was composed more of the licking heat and wind-sounds than of the book he was reading. But he read this weather into the pilgrimage of poor Charlie Anderson, tumble-weeding back and forth over the American spiritual desert.

He heard the preacher and his father talking inside and the subdued obbligato of the women's voices. Every awareness floated in the great washtub-pudding of what he called his *thinking about things*—Charlie Anderson, the red and blue glints on the kellystone wall and the pocks like navels where the glass bits had fallen out, Margo Dowling, the preacher's voice, Rodney Cathcart, the burned pasture down the hillslope, the stringy twitching of his belly.

"It's all there," he thought luxuriously. If he wanted to grab one thing out of the pudding for study or to play with, all he had to do was fish down. To play with the preacher, for instance, could spin out in a realistic drama that was kind of funny to think about now. He would bet the preacher was around drumming up trade for his church, and he had swooped on them because they were new in town. His father would fall for it, and about supper time his father would say to him with a phony innocence, "About time to get cleaned up a little, isn't it, boy?"

He would come back with just a little more innocence, "What for, Dad?"

"Why, why, didn't I tell you? The Christian minister specially invited us to come to services tonight."

Then his mother would say tightly, "Ralph, I don't think it's fair to force Byron to go. Maybe he doesn't think that way any more. Maybe he feels different."

"Force him? I only said . . ."

"I know. *I* think it would be all right if only you and I and Sarah Jean went. Then people couldn't say anything. They wouldn't think anything about it if Byron didn't come. Maybe it's against his *principles* to go to church."

By this time his father would be turning purple (and he couldn't say he blamed him much). *"Principles? Force him?* Oh *gracious* no! Is he too pure to step inside a church? I never heard of anyone else too pure to go to church. What is he? An *atheist?* A Robert Ingersoll? My God, I'm only suggesting this because we're new here in town and we want to do unto others and we ought to act a little *friendly.* . . ."

His mother would smile and nod ironically. "Friendly doesn't mean you can let other people tell you 'Oh, you have to think this; oh, you have to think that; oh, you have to come to my church and fold your hands and pray just like me.'" Her falsetto imitation would mock the Pharisees around about.

"I don't give a goddamn what friendly means! I'm only saying will he go to church tonight if he's not too PURE?"

That's just the way it would go, if he let it. Now that he had foreseen it all, why bother? Be big, he told himself cynically, Go to the Christian Endeavor meeting. You're not too pure. Go scare up some quiff.

He flicked over a number of pages so he could read the part about Margo Dowling while the urgent heat snuck onto the glider.

II

There were fourteen young people at Christian Endeavor, and they sat centered in the hot, wood-rot-smelling gloom of the church on the two benches directly in front of the pulpit. Now, in the late dusk, one of the diamonds of red glass still burned in the west window, and the island of girls in light dresses and of boys straining their throats to sing or nudging each other hung compact as a group of pagan votaries celebrating the omnipotence of the blood. A basket of gladiolus, brought for the morning service, drooped softly in the heat around the yellow shaft of the podium.

Sniffing at her sweated powder, Byron decided his pitch was for the girl with the black hair and white dress. While they all sang "Though Your Sins Be as Scarlet" the girl, as though the song might be a curtain that hid her, kept peeping at him. Her eyes were dark, tapering to points at the outer corners. Her mouth caressed the song with little kissing pouts.

"God bless you and keep you. Amen," the preacher said. "Don't forget the ice-cream social Friday night. Like to have you all stay for the sermon now."

But they all left—either to go home or to wait in the cooler air outside until they would be joined by a handful of older folks for the second part of evening services.

Passing through the vestibule the black-haired girl rubbed Byron's arm and said "Whee-ew" enthusiastically. She touched her sweating forehead with dark-red fingertips and filled her lungs with the even air that met them at the outside door.

"Yeah," he said. "Yeah."

A car with a cutout passed on the main street, a block away. Its red taillights flew among the trees like scattering sparks. He could hear children shouting at an after-dark game.

"Say." He faced the girl squarely and watched her queerly squeeze her eyeballs with her lids and smile disdainfully at him. "May I take you home?"

"Mmmmm," she ran her tongue slowly across inside her lower lip. "I'm not going home *now*."

"Whenever you go, I mean." He prepared himself to sit through the coming sermon if necessary.

"I have to go to the UB church and play for my mother. She's gonna sing. You can walk up there with me but don't if you don't want to. It wouldn't be any skin off me."

"Sure I want to."

"Really? Oooooo!"

As they walked along a dark sidewalk in a part of the little town he didn't yet know she said, "You don't know my name but I know yours. You're Byron Schwartz and you go to college. I knew a college boy once. Wowee! Well, I'm Ginger." She giggled for reasons of her own, and while he was trying to think of a reply he suddenly and surprisingly felt her fingers slip up to his armpit.

"Well, I'm ticklish," he said.

"Goody."

"Ginger Rogers?" he asked.

"No. I wish I was half as pretty as her. I'm just Virginia Burke. Ginger Burke."

Ahead of them the arched lights of church windows appeared and they heard the singing of the United Brethren like the lowing of goaded animals.

"I love nights. Any kind of nights," Ginger said. "I wish I didn't have to go in that hot hole. We won't stay long."

"Fine. Where do you live?"

"A long way," she said archly. "Clear past the edge of town. Out where the grass grows tall."

The church to which they had come was much smaller than the other one, but so crowded with the seated congregation that they had trouble finding seats. Exposed to the crowd-stares Byron had the first of his regrets that he had ever seen Ginger, but she seemed to joy in dragging him up and down the aisles and whispering loudly. She found them seats, finally, near the back. They sat beside a scowling old woman, whose eyes in a sagged face had the mean, agate look of a hawk's.

The sound of the preacher's voice now squealed and prayed through the packed room and Byron felt both excited and disturbed by it. It upset him that anyone should do such unnatural things with his voice, but that someone was doing it seemed to hint at licenses he had never been permitted or even told of. Ginger's shoulder and thigh were jammed tight against him and the skin of their forearms touched. He felt something rub the back of his leg and when he realized that it was the arch of her foot, a tough, pleased, dazzled assurance that he was going to get her settled like a crown on his brows.

Slyly she had reached her hand beneath both their adjacent arms to take his. In his damp palm her hand was dry, grainy, rubbery. She began to squeeze rhythmically, her hand performing that learned imitation of peristalsis that farmers use in milking. He submitted happily, passively, but after a little while she whispered, "Whassa matter with you? Squeeze back. Squeeze *back!*" He started to giggle nervously, but the stare of the old woman beside them quieted him.

"I've got to go now," Ginger said. "That's my mother. She's going to sing." As she slipped past him the gilded, crazy feeling collapsed, and for a moment he considered getting away before she came back—away into the cool of the night. The old woman kept staring hatefully at him.

He made an effort to listen to her accompany her mother's song. He told himself, as if that mattered, that neither Ginger nor her mother ought to be allowed to perform in public. They were dismal. But he wanted her back beside him.

The song concluded the service. In the rising crowd he dodged swiftly away from the old woman, gauging his course so as to catch Ginger at the door. He watched her come toward him, but she was looking past him; her eyes, round with alarm, were fixed on something or someone outside on the church steps.

She did not pause at all when she came even with him, only turned her head down enough to hide the movement of her lips as she whispered, "M' boyfriend's out there. He'd kill us both. See you later." As if she were actually a creation of his overheated thoughts—or some nightmare that sprang from his being in a strange town—she disappeared. When he got up nerve to sidle out on the steps he saw no sign of her.

All the way home he kept wondering if she were real, and it had all been upsetting enough to scare him some with the thought that she might not be.

III

The ringing of the telephone the next morning penetrated his dream like a summons to rise and account for his guilty lusts of the night before.

While he lay there listening to his mother answer in the next room he knew—he told himself later that he had known—the call was for him and knew who was calling.

His mother smirked as he walked to take the phone from her hand, but he scarcely looked back at her.

"I have to see you," Ginger said.

"Never mind," he croaked nervously. "Just forget it."

"No, no. I *have* to. I'm down at the Post Office. You come *down*. You've got to."

"I've got to eat breakfast."

"No, no, no, no. *Now!*"

He looked once across the sun-white dining room and into the kitchen where his mother was already laying strips of bacon in the skillet for his breakfast. He groaned and ran out of the house, hearing his mother's voice diminish behind him, "Byron, boy, are you pretty hungry this morning?"

It was her skin that fascinated him as he stood beside Ginger at the Post Office. She was even better-looking in the daylight than he had thought when he first saw her the night before. Her arms, legs, neck, and, so far as he could tell, her breasts had a tight, swollen look. Her long, black hair hung on her shoulders alive as snakes. Her skin was odd, rather olive-colored, though just now its tight-drawn surface was misted with sweat so it had the acid-gold appearance of flypaper.

For the benefit of the people who were picking up mail she pretended surprise at seeing him—another gambit he could not understand, for of course she had used the phone inside the post-master's wicket and everyone in the room must have heard her call. She was hard at work addressing a postcard, and he leaned on the desk beside her. When he asked, as casually as he could, what was going on, she whispered dramatically, "Not here. Wait a sec." In a little while she took his hand and led him to a side street which, in the syrupy heat of the morning, was empty.

"I told him last night," she said. She turned to face Byron, so close that her breasts almost touched him. "I told him about *us*. I broke with him. He said he would kill himself, then he said he'd kill me. My boyfriend. Tell me I did right, Byron."

"What is there to tell him about us?"

"The way we feel, silly."

"Oh."

A truck with two farmboys riding in the bed swung around the corner and sprayed gravel into the dusty weeds in the ditch. The delicate, separate puffs of dust raised by the falling gravel went up separately into the barred light.

"OK," Byron said. "You told him."

"I love you, Byron. I honestly told him last night that since I'd met you I couldn't stand him any more. I wouldn't even let him touch me." She giggled. "He was so mad, because usually I do." Then her face, quick and easy as winking, took on an expression of wonder and suffering. "I can't stand it until you tell me that you love me too."

He shifted uneasily from one foot to the other, looked in her eyes, as brown and cloudy as an animal's. He looked at the shadow her dress strap threw on the skin of her shoulder. "What is love?" he said uneasily.

"You know."

"OK," he said. "I do." She swayed toward him, recovered, and led him a few steps further before she turned.

"That's fine," she said. "Then I want you to come out this afternoon. Can you dance? I'll teach you. Come about one. Only Bryon, if he—I mean if he should come to your house looking for you, don't even go out. He might kill you."

When he agreed to come to her place, he was making a surrender to a state of fantasy that would last through the week, and yet it was not pure lunacy for him to yield—he still knew, in a reserved corner of his mind, what was going on. Lying on the porch glider an hour after he had met her in the Post Office—his eyes not quite focusing on the maple leaves in front of them, he remembered the declarations of love with cynical amusement. Whatever weird things this dummy might think of next he would go along with, but without believing them quite real. He began to see that this unbelief was even a part of the pleasure she tempted him toward, an unreality that would give him a freedom he had never experienced except in dreams.

From here, looking back, it was almost as if, when he had changed buses at Des Moines on his way home from college, he had stepped through a wrong door and had been carried into a world that looked real enough and familiar enough at first, but which was actually shifted a quarter of an inch from reality so no chain of consequences seemed to work. His own thoughts took off now from this quarter inch of deviation, making him a spectator of whatever he might do. "I'll be damned," he whispered to himself. " 'Don't go out if he comes looking for you. He might ki-i-i-ill-ll-l you.'" The word kill seemed particularly ridiculous and tickling—as though in this atmosphere of strangeness it referred to nothing that could possibly happen to him.

"What are you chuckling about?" his mother asked. She had brought her sprinkling can to water the ferns ranked at the edge of the porch, but this work was only her excuse to be where she could talk to him. He knew she thought he had been avoiding her, that he hadn't shared with her as many of his thoughts as formerly.

"Ah, the world's a big farce," he said. "A big farce. People never know what they're up to themselves. You know—how they get involved in what they do. It's all a mystery, so why try to understand it?"

His mother shook her head. "Oh, I don't think that's necessarily so. I think if we approach things right and honestly try to do our best then we can work our problems out."

"Naa," he said. "It's hopeless, that's why it's all right. We're just puppets. 'Chemisms' like Dreiser says."

"I don't think he says *that*, does he?" his mother asked anxiously. "'The world is within you,'" she quoted. "That means you can be just as fine a person as you want to."

"Hogwash," he said. "We're nothing but blind worms."

"Now where did you learn to be such a pessimist? That isn't learning. Our biggest men, like Einstein and John Dewey, think there's, perhaps, some hope for the world. If only we're patient with our fellowmen and don't throw ourselves away foolishly, why I think there's hope for a better world. I know there are bad men who think we're going to have a war, but we don't have to pay any attention to them."

"Naa. It's all crazy and that's all right. I'm not complaining."

"I know you're not," she said. She looked down at him rocking on the glider with such an overflow of love that it seemed it might suddenly rush down, entangle him, hold him safe and forever, horribly motionless. He wished that she would go away and let him think about this hot dolly Ginger. That seemed a dirty way of putting it, but he did not want his mother persuading him out of anything that might be coming his way.

"You mustn't just pessimistically throw yourself out of life's race," she said. "I don't know who that young lady was that called you up so early this morning. I guess it must have been someone you met just last night, and I expect she's a nice girl, but I do think it's a little funny she should be calling you up so soon. My goodness. I wouldn't want you to throw yourself away, I mean. Why don't you drive back to Davisburg and see Francine? I'll ask Daddy if you can have the car. You could stay with one of your friends, and . . ."

"I don't want to see Francine." She had been his girl in high school, and she was fine in her way, but she didn't seem worth the effort of going to Davisburg and there was no hope of getting anywhere with her unless she'd changed plenty since he saw her last.

"Well, I thought you always got along so nicely with Francine." His mother reached to stroke his hair and he squirmed at her touch. "Francine is a pretty girl," she said.

"So I know she's pretty. Have I got to go see her just because she's not a crow?"

His mother's lips trembled. "I can't always follow your *reasoning*," she said. Then she began her most devastating line. "I know we haven't given you as much *stability* as we should. It does seem that we're always moving from one town to another just when you've made friends one place. But it isn't fair not to stick to old friends. Francine . . ."

"Don't worry about it. You seem to think whatever I do is bad."

"Oh no. You're *good*. It's simply that I don't want you to throw yourself away on this girl when you're too young to know about life."

"But Mama, I'm *not*. I'm not throwing myself anywhere. Don't you understand?"

She would not be consoled. "There're a lot of worldly tricks you don't know about. Some women are tricky."

"I won't even be here long enough to get mixed up with her. You know that."

"That's another thing," his mother said. "I wish you'd give up this idea of hitchhiking clear out to California. You could stay around here, or if we bore you too much you could go back and get your job in Davisburg. Then you'd have time to read and think. You always tell us you want to be alone so you can read and think. You're too young to be tearing breakneck all the time. If you'd just stay here we'd try not to get on your nerves too much."

"I want to go to California," he said in exasperation, closing his eyes, hoping she'd leave him alone soon.

"I don't know why. Don't you think we worry when we know you're wandering around like some tramp?"

"I feel like I need to," was all he would reply to this. Then he simply refused to answer at all and she went away. Lying there, he shut his eyes and had such a spicy vision of Ginger as he had not yet allowed himself—to make up for the worry of being in a world where everyone wanted to nag at him.

But he managed no vision of her quite so troubling, withholding, promising, yielding as Ginger herself. That afternoon at her house first she took him into the parlor to dance. Her mother was busy in the kitchen and the baby sister was pretending to help her. They were only a step out of sight around the edge of the parlor door, and the way Ginger rubbed herself against him kept him nervous and afraid that her mother might step back and see them. Instead of holding Ginger—instead of having to hold her—he leaned back in her strong arms and let her whirl him around. Whirling, getting dizzy in the heat, he saw the windows spin slowly, as though he were in a cistern and the windows were the far-off top through which he saw the sky.

"You aren't trying," Ginger said crossly.

"Yes I am."

"Well, give," she said, and grabbed him again. He imagined then, not quite sure yet what it was she wanted him to try, that he might be an explorer at the world's edge, caught by a woman-shaped beetle that clutched him while he still dispassionately tried to study it. He felt that maybe he had become tiny enough so a common beetle could whirl him around as it pleased.

"You better try," she threatened again.

"What?" he asked desperately.

"Yeah," she said, grinding against him and letting him go. "Come in here. I want to show you some graduation presents." The next room was her bedroom and after she had led him there she began piling his arms full of boxes. Tissue paper rustled out of some of them, and from some came the smell of powder and perfumed things.

"Here," Ginger said, "isn't this darling?" A comb and brush. "This is sweet." A blue robe. "How do you like this?" She held a pair of panties to her body and seemed daring him to look down at them. She began to hum and wiggle. "Like it?" she said.

A small cardboard box fell from the top of the stack he was holding. He got very red and squatted to pick it up.

"Vir—JINNya," her mother called. "You come take Marilyn a while. She's in my way too much and you're not doing anything."

Ginger ran out of the bedroom, throwing something at his face as she ran. He carefully set down the boxes and got his shaking hands on what she had thrown. He had to hold it quite close to his eyes before it was clear to him that this was another pair of panties, yellow, with a green, embroidery script that said *Forget me not.*

The room had become a solid dream where he was lost and from which he would have to be led.

IV

"Do you want to go on, for gosh sakes, and play in the barn, Marilyn?" Ginger asked nastily. The little girl, who sat between them on the front steps, refused to answer. She only turned her face to her sister with a grave, hurt stare.

"I said DO YOU WANT TO GO PLAY IN THE BARN MARILYN?" Ginger shook the child. "Well, you do whether you know it or not. We'll all go."

Since they lived a little past the edge of town, the Burke's place was something like a farm. There was an orchard of some size along the highway, a fenced lot where the cow pastured, and a barn much too big for any present use they had for it. Mr. Burke wasn't a farmer; he ran the lumberyard, Ginger said.

The big, cathedral-like barn had been put up before the farmland behind their place had been separated and sold. It was a tall, gray building full of rooms of corridors with ladders here and there going to the upper floors.

"Here's the oat bin," Ginger said. She led the two of them inside, knelt, and picked up a handful of grains and let them go sliding through her plump fingers. "Wouldn't you just love to play here in the oats, Marilyn?"

"No-ooooh," Marilyn said.

"Now look here, sweetie, Byron and I are going to play upstairs and you'd be afraid to climb up there. YOU PLAY HERE NOW, MARILYN."

"Don't want to."

"PLAY!"

Deftly she got Byron outside and locked the door of the bin on her little sister. They listened a minute to see if the child would cry, and when she didn't—she only seemed to be scratching at the door with her fingernails and crooning—Ginger kissed him and said, "Let's go."

Their progress through the barn was this: In each room she would throw herself on him, whining, muttering, dodging, and squeezing him breathless while they kissed. Intermittently she would peel her mouth from his to say, "I know you love me," or "I want to be yours, Byron—*Byron*, what a silly name," or "I didn't know love could be like this." In each room he attempted to wrestle her to the floor, but she was too strong and when he tried she would lead him to another room. Finally, they climbed into the high-roofed, empty haymow.

Pigeons flew out through the haymow door when they appeared. In this big space a kind of hush came over their feelings. It was simply too big to be appropriate for the kind of mush they had been talking; they were too insignificant under the broad arch of the roof to keep any intensity mustered.

Somewhere Ginger had walked through a cobweb and there was a smudge of dirt on the sweatslick of her forehead. She looked like a farm girl just come in from hoeing in the corn.

She stood leaning against the frame of the door, sulky, and after a while asked, "Was I dreaming? Or did you ask me to marry you?"

He put his arm around her and began to fondle her once more. "You weren't dreaming," he said tentatively.

"Can it be that I've only known you since last night? It seems forever. Don't do that, they can see."

"There isn't anyone out there to see."

"We've got to go let Marilyn out. She could smother in the oats or something."

"Will you come out with me tonight then?"

"I know what you mean," she said thoughtfully. "No."

"Why?"

"Oh Byron, I want to wait until we get married."

"To hell with it then."

"You mean—getting married?"

"I don't remember saying anything about that. I just went along with the gag."

Her lips pouted. She looked at him—not like a jilted girl, but like a very small one who has been cheated in a game by a rule-breaker.

"I'll bet you think I'm in love with love," she said.

This was too much for him and he burst out in a satisfying laugh. He sat in the door and swung his legs against the side of the barn. He watched the pigeons circle back toward the barn and veer off with swift, jerking wings. "Why don't you forget it? You've seen too many bad movies."

When she sat beside him her skirt came up well above her knee to where the skin was not gold-colored but white with the blue mark of veins in it. She watched him look at the leg.

"I know how we could manage," she said. "I don't think my folks would let me if I told them I want to marry you, but you say you're going to California, and I'll go too. They'll buy me a ticket and you can meet my train in Kansas City and we'll get my ticket changed so we can ride out in a compartment. I've got lots of money. Will you, Byron?"

He lit a cigarette and watched the match fall to the ground below them, spinning like a maple seed.

"I wouldn't do that," he said.

"I bet you want to go back to college instead of getting married. I bet you have a lot of fun with the college girls, huh?"

"Sure." He laughed bitterly, thinking that if he had, he wouldn't be making such a fool of himself now.

"I know what," she said. "You get your father's car tomorrow night."

"He won't let me have it."

"Get it. We'll go out and see what kind of man you are."

That struck in his mind, not as ideas are supposed to strike, but surprisingly like an actual blow at the top of his spinal cord, with a blinding, hurting flash, and he saw her momentarily, swinging her white legs toward him, then gathering her feet under her to stand, through a haze fretted with red.

She ran then and kept running for the rest of the afternoon. She kept just out of reach as if daring him to grab her. When he went home at five he felt as though he had done a day's work.

Supper with his family was an ordeal, though he felt better afterward. About eight o'clock, when it was beginning to get dark, he called Ginger. He couldn't help it. After a hot, wrenching moment of hope while the phone rang, her mother answered and told him she had gone out riding. After he figured on that one a while both his anger and his sense of the ridiculous told him with whom she had gone.

V

It was late, probably two or three o'clock, and he had been lying on the porch roof a good long time with his arm thrown across his eyes to shut out the yellowed moonlight. After the crisis moment of the phone call he had gone to the edge of town and had run for a while—partly on his own silly initiative and partly because he remembered a lecture in which a minister had said that such exercise drove away the torment of impure thoughts. When his thoughts seemed funnier if not purer he returned to the house and tried writing a letter to Perry Klein, who was still back in Iowa City going to summer school.

"No sooner do I get home than I meet the most ridiculous quail," he had written. "In a church, no less. She acts hotter than a firecracker but I can't quite make her out or, I mean, make out with her . . . YET ! ! !" But he couldn't hold to the letter. A really bright plan lured him and he fancied it up.

He would keep on with Ginger, long enough to take her in the conventional fashion, and just before he did it he would give her some gum to chew—a gesture of his contempt, a sort of prophylactic measure that would keep her from becoming any serious responsibility of his. Really, that would protect him from any of the consequences that a guy could imagine. If the rubber should break, and he guessed such things happened, he wouldn't have to feel sorry for a stupe who would chew gum while she screwed. He could leave her laughing.

He went to bed with this thought, hoping it was good enough to put him to sleep. But it wasn't, quite. He tossed a great deal and thought of dying, as he too frequently did when sleep wouldn't come. He felt his pulse. Then he pushed open the window screen, looked both ways to make sure the maples would hide him from any neighbor or passer-by, and crawled out to lie naked in the clean wash of the moonlight.

With his arm across his eyes, taking the moonlight only on his goose-pimpling skin, he began to see the car, the heavy car, in which Ginger was riding with the killer boyfriend.

He saw them driving on a dirt road that swung through a shadowed valley and then, liberated, upon the wide bulge of a hill, rise to the very top—then sinking, pointing, falling in an immense glide into another valley whose cleft was furry with willows growing along a creek.

He was wholly with them—first above them like an eye from which they could not escape, next, becoming the killer himself, watching Ginger shrink from him at the far side of the seat.

The car was stopped among the willows. His shadow moved across the seat toward her. Moved closer until she lost the separate curves of feminine articulation and overfilled his sight the way a yellowed wall of ice might confront him when he got to the mountains. There was no real flesh to stop him, to thrust back and impede his desire with its counterlunges, and so his desire swept on through her to a brief, terrible vision of understanding, and he saw himself nakedly encountering the king, fear, and the glacier, wall, the infinity beyond his desire, in which he would be lost, nothing. He had in imagination passed through her as old pagans might have passed a natural gateway of stones to face and scream at the unknown landscape beyond and carry from that the strength to endure afterward. All of a sudden it seemed to him that he had to have her, and that from this challenge he dare not flee or allow himself to be driven. Either he must take her yielding for an armor or vulnerable go on from here.

At the end of his knowledge—as insight drained away like lust itself—he found himself trembling in frightened impatience to see her again. To see her and shape from her body the magic that would save his life.

VI

"I thought I told you to get your old man's car," Ginger said. "Whatsa matter? Wouldn't he let you have it? Then I won't either."

She was not at all in a good humor. She had gone to a lot of trouble to look nice for him when he came for her. Her hair was tied with a virginal bow; her mouth was spread with a rich paste of lipstick. And after all that he had appeared without a car. She snorted but agreed to go the drugstore for a coke.

On the way he fumbled an explanation, "The clutch isn't in very good shape."

She didn't believe this at all. "Whaaat? Ha! Can't you drive, either?"

"I can drive. What do you mean, *either?*"

"You sure can't dance. It's no *fun* to dance with you. I don't know what else you can do."

"You said you'd see. You will."

"Oh don't talk fresh."

"As a matter of fact Dad had to have the car tonight. That doesn't make any difference does it?"

"I'm certainly not going to walk out in the country with you,"
Ginger said.

At the drugstore they had their coke in hostile silence. A
couple of boys Byron had seen on the street came in and began
teasing Ginger by flipping water on her with the tips of their fingers. She seemed to get so much fun out of this, writhing and
bouncing, that Byron was worried about how to get her away.

One of them put a piece of ice down her dress and she twisted
so much in trying to get it out that the white-haired druggist
yelled "Wheeee" in a tone that made all of them catch their
breaths.

"Give me a pack of gum," Byron said to the druggist.

"Where's Carl tonight?" one of the boys asked Ginger.

"Never you mind where Carl is. Carl gets along all right without your help," Ginger said.

"He'll be around looking for you pretty soon," the other boy
said. "Shall we tell him we seen you?"

"You tell him NOTHING," Ginger said. "You NEVER MIND."
But the mention of Carl seemed to make her proud and excited.
She gulped her coke, took Byron by the arm and led him out.

"You still afraid of Carl? That's your boyfriend, isn't it?"
Byron asked.

"I'm not afraid of anything."

"Have some gum." She peeled the tin foil luxuriously from
the stick, put the gum flat in her mouth, tipped it so the front
end went up against the roof of her mouth, and quickly bent it
double with a fierce thrust of tongue muscles.

"Well?" she said.

"Come on."

"Where?"

"Where we can be alone."

She didn't answer, but she took his hand and shortly he became aware that she was guiding him, or maybe even leading
him, and a little later on he understood that they were going to
the UB church.

The grass in the churchyard had been newly mowed, and because it was so dry it felt stubbly under their feet as they sneaked
around the building. At the back a stairway went down three
feet to the basement, and it was to the well of the stairway that
she led him. They sat on the third step.

"Let me throw my gum away," she said. She did not actually

discard it, though, but wrapped it in its tin foil and put it in her dress pocket. "OK," she said.

So that part of it had not worked out exactly as he had seen it in imagination, and he began to feel, even as she relaxed toward him, victimized and angry. Even the rising, answering, budding thunder of his body that began readily enough had something mechanical and hateful about it. When he put his hand on her breast, he felt both an elation and that he was being cheated. Why was it such a mean slut who was offering him something so nice?

The first time he pulled at her skirt she fought him off. "These steps would hurt my back," she whispered. "Why didn't you get the car?"

"Let's go up in the grass."

"I will not. What do you think I am?"

She rolled against him, her body within the dress straining against the angles made by his upraised knees. This time he got under the skirt and surprisingly found her hand following his, restraining sometimes, often seeming to guide, controlling him powerfully, but not fighting him away.

Now the action, and even his consciousness itself, limited as that was, centered in the caprice of the two hands under her skirt, the drama moving with a certain order of attempt, resistance, yielding. He withdrew his hand a minute. "No," her breath roared through the whisper. "Don't stop now you fool!" She dragged his hand back.

She gasped and lay beautifully still. Her face left his and turned to the stars, the beautiful, beautiful stars, so far away.

She said—talking aloud now, not whispering, as though whispering were no longer necessary—"We aren't going to keep God out of this union, are we?"

"It's not a union," he said in a pitiful, angry whisper.

He didn't know why it was time to give up, but he did so, lighting a cigarette while something inside prompted him to say in spite of shame, "I need you."

"Ginger," he whispered.

"That's enough now," she said. She was not speaking coldly. There was even a kind of fond chiding in her tone. It was the remonstrance of the completed and all-knowing female to a foolish child. His humiliation was complete.

He imagined for a second that the stairwell was surrounded by antagonistic figures—her boyfriend Carl, the woman who had watched with hawk eyes while Ginger worked him up in the church, his mother. Ginger could have saved him from their scorn.

"Let me have it, Ginger," he said in an artificially bass voice.

She slapped at him playfully, not actually touching his face. While her arm was uplifted he caught it. The cigarette dropped from his mouth. He slammed her against the concrete stairwell.

"No rough stuff," she said commandingly, but she was down and he had his knee on her belly, ripping the clothes from around her neck. He saw the coal of his cigarette lying on the step and pushed her bare arm onto it. She was fighting back hard, but even when her arm snuffed the coal she didn't cry out.

She hit him in the throat with her fist, so hard he thought something was broken. His head was ringing. Then he struck back with his fist. He hit her right temple and she lay still.

He stood up panting and loosening his belt. Then all at once the air was coming easier, easy and big, into his lungs. Before he could censor the thought it came clearly—*I whipped her.* He let go his belt buckle.

Ginger stirred and crawled toward his feet so that he could stoop almost without shifting his weight and grab the scant silk from around her thighs—the garment catching once on the heel of her shoe, then hanging weightless in his hands. He ripped it across twice and dropped the pieces on her. "Forget me not," he said.

"You hurt me."

"Get home," he said. "Git."

"I'll tell," she said.

He laughed at her. He knew that he could kill her now, but happily he didn't have to. *I whipped her. In a fair fight.* The evil figure she had been, menacing him in his dream, wasn't even there to be thought of now. He had killed that, not just as he'd expected to, but killed it.

"You hurt me. I'll tell. I'll tell your mother."

By God, you got nothing if you waited for what they seemed to promise you. He lifted his foot and gently shoved her away. *Women,* he thought in his restored innocence, and hazily identified them with all the double-cross promises of the world, *they don't even put up a good fight when it comes right down to it.*

He slapped his fist into his palm resoundingly and walked up the steps to the grass. He felt clean as a whistle, free, ready to go wherever he had to.

My Brother, Wilbur

On that day in 1930 when Speed Holman died in his Laird biplane at the Omaha air races, I was sitting on top of the fruit cellar at home thinking about him. The day before, my father and brother and I had watched from the bleachers while the black plane came in upside down across the field and then held level for a mile with Holman's head hanging maybe twenty feet above the ground.

My father stood up and called out, "Jesus, he'll kill himself," but my brother Wilbur said, "No, Dad, the plane's built special for stunts like this." I sat between them with a Milky Way melting in my hand, certain that both of them were big fools.

At the edge of the airport Holman rolled his ship right side up to climb above the willows and shoot her like a dart into the haze over the Missouri River. I said to Wilbur, "There's no dihedral in the wings and the angle of attack is almost zero, but that doesn't mean it's safe to bring her across the ground like that."

"He does it for a living," Wilbur said patiently. "He must think it's safe."

"Some people have more of what it takes than others," my father said. "I'll salute that man up there." Since the War my father had nursed the shame of having saluted a number of officers not worth beans, and I was glad to see he was taking this favorable attitude toward Holman.

I made a noise in my throat like twin Spandau machine guns and had some more of the Milky Way while Holman swung it from the North and prepared to land. Made it this time, I thought. A little while longer . . . Tonight wine and the mamselles, Speed Holman. But tomorrow . . . !

From the top of the fruit cellar I could usually get a little more distance from my ROG. It had a fourteen-inch wingspan and the rubber band motor could be wound nearly two hundred turns. I had paced off the distance of its longest flight at just over eighty-five yards, counting the length it bounced when its right wing hit a mullen stalk. When the wind came in from south of our barn and crossed my mother's vegetable garden, the ROG could attain a surprising altitude above the tomato vines if launched from the very peak of the cellar's dirt covering.

With a hundred and ninety-one turns, the motor stick about to buckle and the wings vibrating from an unfortunate breeze, I let her go slightly south of West, meaning to take advantage of the lee afforded by the barn and any thermal currents that might be rising from the pile of manure my father was saving for next year's garden.

She went straight up and backward. The truth of the matter is that the wind was carrying it like a piece of newspaper, but for an instant or two the blurred propellor seemed to have some influence on its direction of flight. The stabilizer disappeared as she grazed our mulberry tree, and wing over wing, she went rolling into the woven wire fence by the tank. The propellor was still turning when she hit the wire, and I suppose that extra force contributed to the damage.

I didn't have the heart to go down and examine what was left of her. So I was still crouched on one knee several minutes later when Wilbur came out of the house looking for me.

"Speed Holman is dead!" he yelled in my ear. The motor stick might be saved, but I'd have to rebuild the wings and tail from scratch. Perhaps I could glue the propellor, although glue joints in straight-across breaks were never really satisfactory on a moving part.

"He ran it right into the ground!" Wilbur yelled. "They said dee-bree was scattered over an area of half a mile. A parked car was struck by one of the wheels from his famous black Laird biplane."

As you can see he had been plopped down in front of the radio while I was testing.

"Speed Holman is dead!" he yelled again.

"Yes, I know."

"You little fathead. You don't even care! Yesterday you sat there eating a candy bar and now you won't even listen. What's that?" He pointed accusingly at the wreck of ROG.

Limping from having knelt so long, my head erect, I walked down the slope of the cellar to retrieve what I could from the crash.

Wilbur lacked the single-mindedness required to get the most out of model airplane building. He was a craftsman. Admittedly he was better than I at bending piano wire fixtures and aligning glue joints. He was never vexed by the ambiguities of the instructions accompanying American Boy blueprints—"attach hanger H to 3/16" × 3/8" with white common thread in glue bead" and such.

Even so, from the beginning, from the time Doc Whittaker's kid brought his ninety-cent Comet kit to us for help in assembling and thus got us started in the field, Wilbur saw modeling as a means to an end rather than as an end in itself.

Example: When his twin pusher with Clark Y airfoil went down like a stone in the Chisman's yard, he allowed himself to be flattered by Grandpa Chisman and Otho Becker who were out sunning themselves near the point of impact. Mr. Becker said, "Lots of young boys hanging around the pool hall or breaking out street lights."

Grandpa Chisman said, grinning his four teeth at Wilbur and me, "Not these Carpenter lads." As a matter of fact I had broken five replacement bulbs in the streetlight near Jean Stacy's house. That was the only safe way to approach when I went to watch her and Boyd Baker in the hammock. The old fool Chisman said, "These boys are studying for the future. The future is in the air."

This made Wilbur arch his chest and lower his eyes. "I hope to go to air school upon graduation," he said.

"The day will come when they are no more motor cars," old Chisman said. "Regular airships just gliding into our back yards like this here toy."

"I beg your pardon," I said coldly. They didn't seem to notice I had spoken. "An airfoil of this thickness is unsuited for gliding after the power is exhausted." The damn thing had climbed pretty well from where Wilbur launched it behind the Baptist church. For a few seconds I had hoped it would glide into the Larimer's yard and thus give a chance to hook some pliers and a file from Fats Larimer's tool shelf in the garage. "Referring to an experimental model as a toy is dumb ignorance."

This made the old boys cackle. "Anyway you want to call it," old Chisman said, "it's a darn good preparation for the future." He actually patted Wilbur on the head. "I'll be expecting to read about you in the newspapers someday, son. Or see you landing a real airship here in my back yard."

How that Wilbur puffed up! He grabbed the model and trotted away with it, lifting his feet like a show horse and otherwise behaving like a fully accredited air cadet instead of a serious modeler. It was up to me to build a new, thin wing for that pusher and to get what we needed of Larimer's tools the hard way, by digging under the wall of his garage by night.

Nor did Wilbur have the courage to stand up to taunts from the ruffian element among the older boys in grade school. At the peak of interest there were only five youths, including Wilbur and me, giving our time to modeling. When we began to use the ball diamond outside of town for testing our more advanced craft, the jealous element passed word around that we were doing funny things to each other out there. Our vulnerability to such rumor must have come from accepting Pughie Whittaker into our group; it was known that he had indulged in unnatural practices with his Shetland pony. Be that as it may, Pughie was the only one of us who had the money for supplies we needed, and—perhaps because of his shame—he was always willing to run errands for us or hold the broken pieces of a model together while glue was drying.

One day we were at the diamond with a new Cessna scale that Wilbur and I had spent a lot of time on. It was not flying well and Pughie had begun to make maddening suggestions for trimming it. "Put some BBs in the nose. Put some more rubber on her." Worthless measures growing from pure impatience.

Between his distractions and the inherent problem, we did not notice the approach of the boys who had come out to use the field for its intended purpose. I had been kneeling over the Cessna and looked up to see them confronting us at close range, or rather enveloping us in a semi-circle of grinning faces. They might almost have sprung out of the earth, their appearance was so startling.

Wilbur and Pughie said "Hi" to them nervously. Not I. I finished scraping the nose block to give 2° right thrust, then stood up and began to wind, ordering the intruders to stand clear until we were through.

This made them all giggle. Marion Cloyd, the worst of them, said, "You little fruiters might just as well hurry right down in the willows by the creek, because we mean to *play ball.*" The tee-heeing among them became general.

I handed the Cessna to Wilbur, indicating that it was ready to wind and launch. To Marion Cloyd I said, "We have the permission of Rev. Abernathy and Mayor Carter to use this field when it is not being used by one of the organized teams of Boda." This was all nonsense of course, though Rev. Abernathy was known to have made some effort to systematize a summer athletic program, putting a lot of things on paper and appointing Baptist committees to attend to details.

The ball players all haw-hawed at me. Then Wilbur launched. The Cessna went down instantly, like a June bug with a broken wing, and began flopping around on the ground on its back. Too much right thrust. This spectacular failure drove the louts into an absolute hysteria of laughter. They hopped up and down, slapped each other on the back, screeched and whinnied. I could see by Wilbur's stricken eyes that he had been counting on a successful flight to awe them into silence if not respect.

"Oooh, if Wevvund Abbohnathy could see me now," Bill Brach said. He began to prance in an effeminate manner. He threw himself on his back on the ground and began to beat his elbows as he thrashed. His idea of imitating the poor, stricken plane.

Marion Cloyd said, "Skeedaddle. Go on downa the willows and play with yourselves." He threw out his pelvis and aimed an obscene gesture from his crotch at Pughie.

There was no use going further with such an exchange. Marion was holding a ball bat negligently. Quick as a wink I snatched it from him, rolled back on my heels, and let him have it across his upper lip.

The intruders couldn't believe their eyes. Suddenly their champion loudmouth lay on the ground, spitting blood and pieces of teeth. After I stepped back and rested both hands on top of the bat, spread feet and elbows, daring them to come on, the silence of the afternoon was enormous. The mellow sunlight seemed to have robbed us of the power of movement. I thought that if I should look up I would see birds fixed motionless in the air. It was all so strange.

"Jesus," Bill Brach said, "Why'd you do that? He was only kidding you a little."

Pretty soon he said, "We ought to nut you for a mean trick like that." Nobody made a move.

It may have been five minutes, it may have been ten, when Pughie suddenly bolted past me, yelling that he would bring his father, and a lot of others ran to fetch help for Marion Cloyd, who seemed to have passed out.

Needless to say, my defensive action caused an unholy rumpus, not only at home but throughout Boda. We were a marked family. The Mayor came. Marion Cloyd's father came and swore and stomped on our porch. Rev. Abernathy came and boohooed with my mother in the parlor.

It might have been easier all around if my father had let them take me away, as the Mayor suggested and as old Cloyd insisted. He was going to sue for ten thousand dollars, charging permanent disfigurement of Marion's ugly puss, unless I was put in custody of "the proper authorities" at the county seat. My father roared back that there had been a threat to use a knife on me—as indeed there had, though my father tampered with the order of events to make it seem I had been threatened first. As well as I could understand it, I was "paroled" to Rev. Abernathy, though paroled from what sentence or judgment was never clarified. That authoritative word seemed to satisfy the public conscience of Boda.

Anyway, people began to avoid not only me, but the family and even the house. Even the kid who delivered the afternoon paper got to standing back and throwing it folded onto the porch instead of bringing it to put inside the screen door as he used to. My father quit stopping by the pool hall for his after-work beer because he got in disastrous arguments about me with the crew that was established there.

This isolation was satisfactory to me. Wilbur accepted it. We had the new tools that I had stolen from Larimer and kept hidden under the floorboards of the barn. We were learning to make ribs for a full-scale glider, patterned after one that Otto Lilienthal had flown, as illustrated in *Boy Mechanic*. It wasn't a bad summer, though pitiably strenuous for my parents, who worried about what they could not understand.

Then that beautiful day in August. Late August. The color of the sky modulating toward autumn and the gentle piles of cumulus clouds cleaner than fresh washed bed sheets in the North and East. The smell of dusty alfalfa—a green smell, but delicately muted with the dust of a fading season. The sober nodding of maple leaves at the very peak of the trees in our yard. The soundless steps of a half-grown kitten in the powder of dust outside of the barn where Wilbur and I were working.

That day—and out of its sky came the Waco biplane. The beginning thunder of its motor was simply incredible. I thought something was wrong with me until the sound grew and shook me and seemed to lift me off the box I was sitting on and drag me to the door.

The Waco went over not thirty feet above the maples. They shuddered like me in its passage and then hid from my sight what it was now useless to hide. I had seen the mammoth wings and the flickering shield of the propellor.

"Do you suppose he's out of gas?" Wilbur asked. Now it was certain that the plane was landing in the alfalfa field beyond the ball diamond.

I could have laughed. Of course it wasn't out of gas. It had come for me.

Useless to attempt a rationalization of that thought—then or now. As I went at a dead run across our pasture, climbed the fence, and showered gravel with my Keds on the road out of town, I simply knew what I knew. It had come to take me away from a place where my true abilities were hardly guessed.

Wilbur never caught up with me, though he was close, and we were the first of the kids from town to reach the silent Waco, somnolent, resting, its wheels almost hidden by the alfalfa, like something floating in a green bay.

Beside the plane, cross-legged in the alfalfa, sat a man who said his name was Jack. He was pleasant enough in our first exchange of conversation, but not very communicative. He just wouldn't declare whether they were low on gas or not. His smile was unmistakably tired when Wilbur and I showed off our knowledge of Waco Series 2 biplanes.

His partner Joe rested his buttocks lightly on the edge of the lower wing, squinted happily at the sky from which they had come and emphatically declared that with any luck they would get home to St. Joseph that night. We learned later that they had been barnstorming up through the Dakotas and in Wyoming for most of the summer. They were following the Missouri River homeward now, picking up a little money by landing near towns as dull as ours to sell rides for two dollars apiece.

Before we learned that, the human tide had followed Wilbur and me out from town, kids afoot and on bicycles, Sam Warner's pick-up truck swaying and bouncing across the field to the plane, jostling the men and boys and the two big girls riding in the bed. Doc Whittaker brought Pughie out in his Essex, though they parked on the road with four or five other cars instead of following the pickup into the field.

Then, with an audience worth working on, Jack the pilot climbed onto the metal step attached to the wing and announced the price of rides.

Doc and his son Pughie were the first takers, and I will never forget the look of unworthy happiness Pughie turned on me as the slipstream began to whip his pompadour. He knew I should have been the first to go up.

Again Wilbur and I were off at a dead run, this time to wheedle money from my mother. She wasn't *sure.* Not sure whether we could afford the price and not sure whether it was safe for us to go up. After all, we ought to remember what happened to that fellow Speed Holman, she reminded us.

That's what I did remember! That plane black as death with its wheels pointing to the sky as it zipped level across the level ground at Omaha. It was to re-create that moment of rapturous identification that I had to go now.

"You'll have to ask your father," she said.

We were awfully close to sunstroke when we tottered into his office at the feed store—and found he was gone. Like most of the rest of the town he had gone to the alfalfa field where the

Waco was landing and taking off at five and six minute intervals. We didn't know that then. All I knew was that he wasn't to be found when I needed him most.

Surely my brother was as disappointed as I, was sweating just as much—his face was just as red from running. But he was ready to give up and leave that office; I put my hand on his sleeve. "Wilbur . . ." The way I said his name made him understand what I meant to do.

But he wouldn't watch me do it. He stood at the open door and he surely heard the click when I unlocked my father's cash box and took out the bills. He even kept his eyes averted when I pushed two of them into his overall pocket. Then, he ran as fast as I did to get back to the alfalfa field.

Of course we spotted my father almost as soon as we got back out there. The crowd was so big by then he didn't notice us for a while, and when he did he made no special sign of recognition.

The helmeted man named Joe was taking money for the flights and keeping order in the small line of those waiting their turns to go. There were only five ahead of us. When the plane came bouncing perkily up to the head of the line and swished its tail around in the alfalfa, two people moved up alongside to take their place in the front cockpit. That left only three in line and it seemed as good a time as any. "Come on," I said to Wilbur.

Joe already had our money before my father left the group around the pickup truck and approached us. He didn't seem overly concerned at first. Just dutiful.

"Yes," I said truthfully.

"And she said you could?" He had long been used to my logic-chopping answers.

"She said to ask you," Wilbur told him.

"Well, I guess it's all right. Everybody's doing it," my father said. Almost absently, turning to watch the takeoff, he asked, "She give you the money?"

"Yes," I said. "No," Wilbur said.

My father turned to us frowning. "Well now, which is it?"

"I've been saving money," I said. This quibble didn't even slow him up. "Where'd you get it?" he said.

The inspiration was on me. It was burning hot, the knowledge and the passion that had brought me this far.

"Wilbur . . . ," I began. I saw Wilbur's face go suddenly dead white. He understood that I was going to finger him for the robbery. I was going to put the blame on him so I could fly.

And he was going to let me!

The devil! "Wilbur and I ran all the way down to your office," I said, hearing my voice lose its insistent power of conviction. "Aw, tell him the truth, Wilbur," I said brokenly.

Wilbur shook his head, still with that awful look on his face, as if he knew what was in store for me and was going to stand by and let it happen.

He scared me into decency. I said, "I took the money out of your cash box. I knew you'd let us have it if . . ."

My father seemed to crouch down when I admitted this. If he'd been wearing a winter coat, he would have thrown it around me and smuggled me off that field so none of his friends and neighbors would see the monster he had fathered. What he said, from a stricken mouth, was, "At least you didn't lie about it. I'll salute you for that much."

A salute is a salute. It is pure and simple and makes no qualifications. It is never given for "that much." It is given for the thing done, the thing seen through to its natural end, for Speed Holman in the debris of his black plane. Not for me. I had faltered, and the justification for my lies, my thievery, and the cowardly attack on Marion Cloyd was gone.

I didn't wait to see how my father cleaned up this latest mess I had handed him. I learned later that he'd let Wilbur fly, and—so the money I'd already paid over wouldn't be wasted—let Pughie Whittaker have a second ride with him. Wilbur was even inclined to think my father would have let me go "after all" if I'd just stuck around until he got over the first shock of my confession.

Maybe. It wouldn't have mattered. The possibility was spoiled. Going and not going were the same. In some crucial and ghastly way I had learned my lesson without once actually getting airborne.

I remember going back to sit on the fruit cellar while practically all the rest of the town, except females, were still out in the alfalfa field watching the plane go up and come down in its safe, dull cycle.

Thinking—as I did—that Wilbur was probably on one of those flights and that he would come home after a while to tell me what I had missed, it seemed to me that I understood and accepted and was already forgetting. I couldn't feel the faintest envy of him. He was a good brother. He had done the right thing and always would. I wished him all the success in the world.

Frost and Sun

I

She has no one to blame but herself, Harry thought. He dragged himself down the ditch bottom, closer to the Everling house and to the lighted window behind which he supposed his girl Con Everling was getting ready for bed.

He clutched his bakelite field glasses in his left hand and gritted his teeth in his frenzy of determination. He was here to pay Con back for her refusal to walk home with him from Luther League. Only three blocks, he thought. I only asked for three blocks' walk with her. He believed, without the faintest whisper of skepticism to ease him, that she had let Roy McCune feel her breasts and let Sidney Beerman put a hickey on her neck. And she would not even walk three blocks through the dark with the man who loved her.

Behind him in the tickling weeds his friend Mark grunted and tugged at his pants leg. "Near enough," Mark said.

Harry stopped. In the manner prescribed by the *Boy Scout Handbook* he eased his head up alongside a mound on the ditch bank. He set his field glasses to his eyes and reconnoitered the porch of the Everling house. By the front door he could see the pulsing glow of the cigar Con's father was smoking as he rocked. Through the bay window Con's mother appeared, folding laundry on the dining-room table.

Harry tipped the glasses upward, fingered the nickel lever that was supposed to adjust the focus. I'm going to magnify her, he thought vengefully, and it didn't have to happen this way if she'd only let me walk three blocks with her.

"She's not there," Mark breathed close to his cheek.

"I can see that."

"Even with them dollar binoculars?"

"Wait," Harry said. "Look at that shadow moving on the ceiling. Look. It's her *shoulder.*"

"Whoo-ee," Marks said, "a shoulder shadow! Just don't get so excited. Give me a look."

Harry passed the glasses and gripped the weeds around him with both hands. He began to worry that he would sneeze. The weeds were thick with August dust and the smell of pollen tickled his nose. He would sneeze and Con's father would come baying down from the porch and catch them there. Let him, then, only not until I see her enlarged, Harry prayed, not until she passes that window squarely.

"You smashed a bug on the glass," Mark whispered. "I can't see anything but that bug." He started to polish one of the lenses with his shirt tail.

"There she *goes,*" Harry said as Con passed the window. He grabbed wildly for the field glasses.

Mark wrestled them out of his reach. "She'll come back. Don't run amok on me."

"She's down to her slip and you had to be wiping bugs off my glasses."

"Take them," Mark said. "Jesus Christ, doesn't friendship mean anything to you?"

"All right. Keep them."

"Hell with them. I can see better without. Hey, there she is again, but she's got more than a slip on. Aaaaah. That's the dress she had on at League."

For a dozen heartbeats Con stood at her bedroom window with the light behind her showing her in gray silhouette. Pearl gray, Harry thought, like the inside of a clam shell, laced with iridescence through its dappled paleness. If she was beautiful or not, if she was the prettiest of the sophomores or not, if she was not even so pretty as her married sister, didn't matter at all, any more than, probably, her being female did, or the decent dress from Penney's that hid that roundness Roy McCune described. What mattered was that through the field glasses, got by fraud and selling a few *Collier's* subscriptions, she was there on the moon-round field of his vision like the goddess stamped on a coin, the Diana of his despair with the common world.

Con turned from the window and put out her light.

"Whoo—eee," Harry whispered, trying now to perpetuate the awe of what he had glimpsed, feeling it elude, sift out through the hugeness of the night.

"Does that moron sleep with her clothes on?" Mark asked in disgust.

"I'd've given you the glasses in another minute," Harry said. "I didn't mean to be selfish, but my hands got paralyzed when I saw."

"Don't snow me, you didn't see a thing."

"Nipples," Harry said. "The shadow of them. You couldn't see because you didn't have the glasses. Her belly button. It looked like an eye socket. No kidding."

"They ought to lock you up, with an imagination like that," Mark said. "They ought to have you in a padded cell."

"'How da-dum like I see thee stand, with an agate lamp within thy hand,'" Harry whispered reverently, lifting his face toward the moon, naming its profaned whiteness with the virginal name of his love. Ahead of them the Everlings' terrier began to bark.

"An eye socket," Mark laughed. "What'll that boy think of next?"

To their left another dog barked. Above the lip of the ditch there was a sudden pattering of feet as the terrier, reinforced, made a pass toward them. They've got me now, Harry thought. He was on his feet and with a deer leap had plunged across the garden toward the railroad embankment, tumbling to all fours and bounding up again before he even heard Mark yell, "Split up," thinking, It won't be so bad if they catch Mark, since I'm the one who used the glasses on her.

Between the garden and the embankment a swale of brown

grass gave him a surer footing. Veering on it, because his one talent was for speed and he thought the dogs would have him if he tried the embankment, he raced down parallel with the tracks toward the stockyard, meaning to lose himself among the pens.

He was thirty yards from the loading chute when he saw the black shape of a car parked just beyond it along the tracks, fifteen yards when its headlights whipped him squarely in the face, and too exhausted to run any longer when a head leaned out and a man's voice commanded, "Come here, you."

Slowly, with his head bent heavily forward, Harry moved to the side of the car. A hand swept out to grab the leather bootlace from which the glasses hung around his neck, jerked it and let it go slack. "Caught you, didn't we?" Then he recognized Tony Wilson's voice, and as his eyes grew accustomed to the dark again he saw Lucille Zachary on the other side of the front seat. In the back was another couple, visible only in silhouette.

"The way you were galloping, you must have done something pretty mean," Tony Wilson said. His big hand, blond-glittering in the moonlight, lifted the cheap glasses. "What you got these for, Harry? Not much to see out at night is there?"

"Looking at the stars," Harry said. "Orion, Cornucopia." He wanted to strike the big hand away from his glasses. Yet to be held this way with a leather thong around his neck seemed a curiously natural and acceptable punishment for what he had done.

"Not much to see but people's windows," the man in the back seat said. It was Sid Beerman's brother Lloyd.

"Oh ho, oh ho," Tom Wilson said. "So you been out window peeping, Harry? Who was it up that way? Nancy Mosebach? I'll bet it was that little Everling girl. Now, you're not old enough for that, Harry."

"Let him alone, Tony," Lucille commanded. She leaned over to look up into Harry's sweating face. "Let him go. It's no fun to be stag on a night like this. Is it, Tony? Is it, huh?" She pulled the hair curling from the neck of his polo shirt. "How would you feel if I walked off with Harry now and left you alone?"

The illustration was too far-fetched. It only brought a grunt of contempt from Tony.

"Let him go, you dumb farmer," she commanded. "Pick on someone your own size."

Tony's hand opened from the leather cord and, with a movement almost swift enough to be a blow, he put it on Lucille's face, pinching so that her mouth (black in the moonlight) was higher than it was wide. "You about my size, honey? You about my size?"

The last thing Harry saw before he started to run again—on down the tracks and out of town before he circled toward home—was Tony leaning to kiss that distorted mouth.

II

Two days after that Lucille detoured through the Harrisburg square to speak to him. He and Mark had parked their bicycles against the bandstand and were waiting for the afternoon bus to bring Harry's papers from the city. They were using their time to perfect one more plan for hitchhiking to California after robbing the grain-and-feed company, for defrauding Crowell-Collier's of another premium for junior salesmanship, or for filing out a skeleton key that would let them into any house in town.

Lucille not only interrupted them, but stood there as if she wanted something, as if they were supposed to be interested enough in her to try to figure out what it was. She was five years older than they, and had graduated from high school the year before they started. It was hard for either of them to get the idea that she might have come over to them because they were boys.

"You want us to do something for you?" Mark asked warily.

"I thought maybe one of you would pump me home on your bike," she said, beaming the request at Harry.

"I've got a low tire," Mark said. "Anyway I make it a practice not to give people rides. Nothing personal. I like to stick to principle."

"I could ride on the handlebars," she said to Harry. "I've done that lots of times. When my brother had a bike he took me everywhere."

"I guess I could do it," Harry said. "I've got to deliver my papers, but . . ."

"They'll be here any minute," Mark said.

Lucille was already hoisting herself onto the bike. Her haunches bulged like white sails, entirely filling the space between the grips of his handlebars. As Harry shoved off and began to pedal, Mark called once more in a tone of self-righteous admonition, "You want me to deliver your papers then?"

"Yes, deliver his papers," Lucille shouted back.

"Get up some steam," she said to Harry, "or we're going to end up in a flower bed." Under her weight the bike was wobbling crazily. He rose on the pedals and with his cheek against her shoulder, blind and obedient, he straightened on his course.

When he caught up with Mark again that evening—two hours after the last paper had been tossed onto porch roofs or lawns—and tried to make his peace, he found Mark still more in grief than anger. "I thought you had some standards," Mark said. "You talk so big. I thought I could count on you not to go any lower than Con Everling. So you go pumping away out to the Grove with that cow. She might at least have the decency to wear a corset."

"We didn't go to the Grove," Harry said.

"Wherever you went."

"We went to her place and sat in the yard talking."

"All this time? Yeah? What were you talking about? What old Tony Wilson does with her three nights a week, not to mention that bald-headed Farm Bureau agent, and Lloyd Beerman, and the whole softball team from Elder?"

"That's all lies," Harry said. On the lawn of the Zachary house where Lucille had spread a quilt for them to rest on while they drank their lemonade, he had sat in a swarm of feelings so new to him that he could not yet defend them, even to himself. He was not even sure what all their talk had been about as the sun went lower and threw the geometric shadow of the grain elevator and then the fringy shadow of dark elm trees over the Zachary lawn.

He had heard a refrain of longing. Lucille felt she had been getting farther from all she wanted in the two years since she had graduated from high school. She hardly ever played the cornet any more and she felt *out* of things when her younger brothers and sisters came home with stories of school picnics and parties, or "just what they're learning—I've forgotten lots of things."

She wanted to go to college and her older brothers in the army had promised to help, but somehow each year that had got put off. Her father had had a bad time with his back so that he couldn't work at the garage as many hours as he needed. Her mother had had an operation for goiter. "And there's nothing in Harrisburg except to get married," she told him. "I don't want to marry Tony. What does he ever think about besides playing ball or tanking up on three-two beer on Saturday nights?" Harry had nodded sympathetically, flattered to think himself the ideal male with a treasure house of thoughts on all subjects that he could pour out for her if he chose.

"What's more," Mark was saying, "you hadn't been gone more than two minutes when old Tony came out of the pool hall right across there and stood with a beer bottle in his hand looking up and down the street. I about crapped. I thought he'd seen you pedal off with her, and boy, he's not letting *anyone* else get at her while she's his girl. You saw him beat the devil out of Larry Michaels for even telling that story about her and the softball team."

"Was that what it was for?" Harry asked, weakening. He *had* seen Tony whip Larry in the school yard. He and Mark and Roy McCune sat up on the fire escape that day and watched Tony run poor myopic Larry Michaels down three blocks from the cream station, catch him among the swings and teeterboards, and hold the boy on his knees while he alternately slapped him, lectured him, and hit him in the forehead with his fist. In spite of himself, Harry had enjoyed the display of dominance. He despised Larry Michaels and believed that everyone else in town shared his own admiration for Tony as an athlete. He had laughed when Larry kept trying to put his glasses back on for protection, and he had trembled to the thrill of watching Tony's blond arm lifted to strike. (When someone asked Larry how he got Tony to stop when he did, he grinned foolishly and said, "I kept telling him what a swell right-hand punch he had"—duplicity which lowered him even further in Harry's eyes.) But now those chickens were coming home to roost and Harry said, "Good Lord, Tony must know I wouldn't try anything with her. I'm not the kind that would take another man's girl."

III

He had no intention of going back, ever, to repeat the intimacy he had shared that afternoon when he and Lucille drank lemonade on the quilt. Con Everling was his girl, and if she didn't know it yet, she was *going* to know it.

He plotted a calendar of the weeks ahead and found a dozen occasions when, with luck, he might hope to walk home through the autumn nights with her. Soon after school began the town's annual Corn Festival would be held. He made up his mind to lie in wait until then, giving her time to get good and sick of Sid Beerman's moron jokes and Roy McCune's oversexed personality. His private superstitions fixed the date of the Festival as the occasion when all his forces and charms would be stacked like a mound of boulders ready to avalanche down upon the vulnerable girl. In the meantime he would concentrate on his cornet and orchestra practice.

The first thing that went awry in these mystic calculations was that when school opened in mid-September Lucille resumed practicing with the high school orchestra. She was looking for something to occupy her time—or maybe it had occurred to her that since she, too, played the cornet she and Harry would be sitting together during practice sessions.

When she first appeared at practice, he made up his mind to treat her with merely professional crispness. If she had questions about difficult musical passages or about Miss Fleming's instructions, he would answer her courteously, but he was not going to take the slightest risk of encouraging her. That would be hardly fair to Tony Wilson—or to her, for that matter.

As a cornet player, Lucille was five times as able as he. She showed him how to play the staccato passages in "Oenone's Plaint" that he had always slurred and lost the beat on, and she soothed his pride once when he played right through a rest and got, "Well, Harry, *really*. . . ." from the disgusted Miss Fleming. Further, she broke into warm, contagious laughter when he tried to be crisp with her, and thought it was an act he was putting on to amuse her. She always got his wisecracks, where a lot of people fumbled.

So when the orchestra began practicing at night in preparation for the Corn Festival it seemed natural enough (and no harm) that he should walk her home afterward. Tony Wilson, she told him, thought she was nuts to waste her time going to orchestra practice.

"He's right," Harry said. They were walking down the dark block past Will the druggist's house, their cornet cases clacking decently together between them. He did not mean to walk close enough to touch her. "I wouldn't come if my folks hadn't bought me this horn. I tried to tell them not to, but they had a big tizzy, so here I am."

"He's wrong," Lucille said. "*Now* it may not mean much to you. When you're as old as I am you'll be sorry you didn't practice more. You could be a good trumpeter."

Owlishily he weighed her comment. "How good?" he demanded.

"You wouldn't make a Harry James," she said. (Then where was the point of it? he thought.) "But good enough so it would be some satisfaction. Look, I could teach you a lot of things. Tonguing. You don't know anything about that."

"I do too."

"Show me." She laughed oddly (a little crazily, he thought) and put her free arm around him. For a minute she held her lips waiting for him, then kissed his mouth. The cornet cases knocked hollowly. "Well?" she said. Then to his disgust and before he could prevent it, her tongue slipped past his lips.

"Please *don't*," he said, wondering how a Wodehouse character would have squelched her in such a circumstance. He could remember reading nothing similar to this in Wodehouse.

"You little bugger," she said. "All right for you. You can bring the horse to water but you can't make him drink."

"What, exactly, might that mean?" *There* was the upper-class British frostiness he wanted.

"If you don't know, little Lucille isn't going to tell you."

Slowly, slowly the street lights parabolaed over their heads as they walked the remaining blocks to her house, and slowly as the stars swung their drunken circles through the blue night, the vastness and the enormity of what she meant circled and came home to him. She had offered him her body and he had refused.

When they went up the sidewalk to her porch, she was chattering about nothing—about some car that had been brought in smashed to the garage where her father worked. She opened the screen door, leaned bosomy against it, and said, "Good night."

He did not answer, but stood there with no sign of turning to go.

"Did I forget something? What is it?" she asked.

"Please," he said.

"What? Oh, Harry, don't be silly. Run home like a good little boy."

IV

He ran from her house that night, just as she told him to do. He did not believe he ran because she had commanded it. In those days he was always running.

He would run part of the distance of his newspaper route. He ran the seven blocks uptown and back when his mother wanted something from the store. Sometimes he ran out to the grove at the intersection a half mile north of town. He ran because it seemed to him that he could only think straight while his legs were pumping under him and his heart was thundering in his chest. When he slowed down his thoughts knotted with the absurd conflict that had come into his life.

He still hoped to take Con home from the Corn Festival. At last he worked up his nerve to waylay her at school one day between Assembly and the Ancient History classroom. Might he count on the pleasure of her company after the Festival?

"Yah," she said.

He put aside a dollar and a half to take her out for hamburgers on their homeward walk. Hamburgers probably meant sundaes and soft drinks as well, since she was said by the other boys to be a spender.

On the other hand wasn't he now committed—involved, sworn, pledged beyond the possibility of retreat—with Lucille? These nights after orchestra practice they were kissing so much he thought he might be ruining his lip for the cornet. In the black corner of Chader's hedge she had let him pet her a little. Now he knew what a nipple felt like through cloth, unless it had just been the stitching of her brassiere. Solemnly he recognized her claim on him. He would have felt like a dog if he refused to walk home from the Corn Festival with her—provided that could be arranged so Tony wouldn't see them.

Two days before the crisis smote him, Lucille announced she wouldn't play with the orchestra on the big night. "I'd feel silly sitting up there with you when all the rest of you are still in high school," she said. "Miss Fleming was nice enough to say it would be all right for me to sit in, but I said I'd rather not. So I'll stay home by my lonesome."

"I can see how you'd feel," Harry said, so moved by relief that his compassion felt genuine.

He was not sure that he was fooling her. She grinned slyly and said, "You could come and visit me after the doings. I really will be all alone except for the little kids. Dad's going into the hospital again tomorrow. Mother and Willis and Jane are driving him in to the city and they plan to stay aw-uh-ull night."

"That's too bad about your father," Harry said.

"Will you come?"

Twisting and writhing with embarrassment—sure that even his silence would not hide the compromising truth—Harry avoided an answer.

"I wish you would," she coaxed.

He had to run at top speed for half an hour after he left her to burn the same impure wish from his treacherous limbs.

Was he really sure that he had a date with Con? Her "Yah" echoed faithfully in his mind, but he also recalled that he had kind of caught her by surprise when he uttered his invitation, coming up fast behind her in his tennis shoes and beginning to speak before she had turned to recognize him. She couldn't have thought he was asking for after Luther League next Sunday . . . ? She might have, damn her. She might have.

On the night of the Corn Festival he arrived at the Opera House early, convinced that he should have fixed some definite point of rendezvous there and a specific time when he would meet her. He found that in spite of the rain that had persisted all day there were already more than three hundred farmers and townspeople in the building. They were milling around the church booths, clotting the displays of corn, vegetables, baking, and handicrafts like damp clusters of flies after the goodies. He could not find Con among them.

He lingered by the entrance as long as he dared, hoping that she would arrive before he had to take his place with the orchestra on stage. At five past eight when Reverend Olsen rose to open the program with a prayer, she had not yet appeared.

He played through the first number without bothering to tongue a single passage, though it was, according to Miss Fleming, a "sprightly air." He watched the crowd more than he watched the music on his rack.

The Mayor made a speech of welcome to the former residents of Harrisburg who had come back for the night. Miss Fleming announced the orchestra would play a march—"El Capitan."

Con came in then. With her raincoat belted, her tam perched on the side of her curls, and her green umbrella still haloing her, she looked to him like Spring come to see what had grown from her sharecroppers' planting. He thought that she nodded an affirmation when she glanced up at him. His tongue vibrated in the nickel mouthpiece and his soul marched as he blasted the glory of "El Capitan."

Then, as the school superintendent began his long rigmarole

preparatory to awarding the "yield" and "best ear" prizes for the corn, Harry noticed that Con had found a seat by Roy McCune.

Well, that didn't mean anything. Well, the crowd was large and seats were scarce, and naturally that dirty sneaking bastard Roy, too stupid to play an instrument in the orchestra (alas, too wise), had beckoned her over to a seat that in his sneaky way he had been saving for her. That still didn't mean she had forgotten her solemn promise . . . that inconsidered "Yah". . . .

Harry felt the sweat start on his face. How could he get down from the stage in time to save the evening? Well, he might puke in Larry Michaels' French horn to signal that bad health would not permit him to continue in the position of second cornetist. That was a brilliant scheme, all right!

He had to sit up there and endure everything, every word his stupid elders could think of to say about corn and home-town loyalty. How much banality does it take to kill a man? he wondered, not daring to look down and see Con and Roy snickering together as they watched his discomfort.

He tried to bolt the stage ahead of the speakers and corn judges when they were finally done. Miss Fleming pinched his arm and thrust him back with the whisper, "But we're the *orchestra*, Harry."

With her interference and the slowness of old Mrs. Gorley on the steps ahead of him, he did not get to the front door of the Opera House until Con had gone out. When he stampeded through the umbrellas and bodies clogging the doorway, she was already walking away into the rain. And Roy McCune was close beside her.

"Con." Harry's shout sounded even to him like a cry for help. He was furious with himself for being unable to control his voice. But at least the shriek had stopped her.

She and Roy turned and waited for him to come up. Roy shrugged his raincoat collar high, averted his face, and began to whistle.

"Hello, Harry," Con said. "Isn't this rain awful?"

He was afraid to try his voice for a minute, almost frenzied that he couldn't answer such a simple question. "Thought we had a date," he growled.

Roy whistled. Con looked blank. "Now? It's so rainy tonight. It's awful. Roy . . . "

"Yah?"

"Roy, I did say something to Harry the other day about going home with him."

Roy started to whistle again.

Harry said, "I suppose I speak the English language sufficiently that persons of ordinary intelligence can grasp my meaning when I ask them a simple question."

"My, my," Roy said.

"I don't know what that means," Con said.

"I asked you in so many well-chosen words of the English language if could you would me take home tonight." The words sounded screwy to him, but he heard only their betraying falsetto that rose in spite of everything. The rain seemed to sizzle on his face like grease in a frying pan.

Con shook her head in puzzlement and something like contrition. She lifted her hand to pull Harry's jacket tighter against his neck and let her palm lie fondly against his cheek. "I'm sorry if there was a misunderstanding," she said. "Couldn't we all three of us go down to the Hamburger Heaven and talk it over out of this cold rain? Brrr."

"Brrrrr," Roy said.

Fondly, falsely her hand lay on Harry's chest. He slapped it away. "I'm not going no goddamn where and talk anything over. You promised and now, you big whore, you're ratting out of it."

"Now listen," Roy said. He took his hands out of his raincoat pockets.

Harry put both hands against Roy's chest and shoved. The fury and surprise of the onslaught worked. Roy went sprawling out among the parked cars.

"I spit on you," Harry shouted at Con. "I spit on you." He meant to do it, too, but in all the moisture of that night, his mouth was like Sahara in August. Before he burst into tears, he cut ignominiously through the parked cars and began to run.

V

In that October rain which matted his pompadour and soaked the jacket his mother had pressed for Con Everling's sake, he knew for the first time, surely, that he had no home. When he took shelter on the unlighted porch of the Baptist Church and huddled against its kellystone wall to think, it was as if the shrouding rain itself had orphaned him. He felt it strike the brown grass and ooze downward into the loam where all his people were buried. Eyeless they lay beneath its insulting fall. Nothing watched him. In the Halloween of rain the church was his to despoil, and he felt he could not go home until he had committed some avenging sacrilege.

Con's family had been Baptists until the pinch came and this church had failed two years ago, overcome like the town's second bank by the depression. Now the Everlings claimed to be Lutherans, which showed how good their word was. Anyway it was in this building that he had first seen Con, not so long after she had moved to Harrisburg. She was wearing a green-and-white dress that day, he remembered, and her hair was cut in a Dutch bob then. He could even have described the shoes and socks she had been wearing if anyone had asked him. That there was no one to ask him filled him again with sentimental rage, and he hissed at the dark bulk of the church, "I spit on you."

He began trying the basement windows. On the side that faced an alley he found one unlocked. He pushed it open and dropped to the invisible concrete floor inside. Around him was a smell of dankness from the damp concrete, of unpainted wood from the floor beams, and—after all this time—an undefinable essence of cookery from all the chicken fried here in the epoch of Coolidge prosperity.

He found the stairway and mounted, coming out in the Sunday school rooms behind the pulpit. He heard mice skitter back to their hymnbook nests as the floor creaked under his weight. "Fly, mice," he said in the tone of Fu Manchu.

In the wide, vaulted space before the pulpit he felt a pang of uncertainty from the mere sensation of standing alone in so much emptiness. He fought it down with a reckless commitment to blasphemy. "Boo," he shouted. God did not answer the insult.

He heard the rain gust against the imitation stained-glass windows and thought, Even the building won't last long against that. The Chinese water torture. Even Inspector Nayland Smith couldn't hold out against that when old Fu Manchu put it on him. Nayland Smith and the burden of empire indeed. If he had old Nayland Smith here he'd put him on that altar and cut his gizzard out. Him and his smelly pipe. If Smith got the better of Fu Manchu so often it was only because Smith had all the sneaky, McCuney cruds on his side. At least Fu was a man. Fu always came back, with his whips and his tortures and his admirable contempt for the cringing weakness of the whites. . . .

Then Harry's thoughts seemed so ludicrous to him that he tried to laugh. It was no good any more to go around hissing contempt like Fu Manchu and thinking that meant anything in the real world. Father Fu was under the rain like the other fathers, and with him had gone all the comforting nonsense of childhood.

The oleographed pageantry of a thousand Sunday school cards swam around Harry in the dark of the church. He could still sense what he had intuited before—the tang of the Orient and its vices mingled with an austere Midwestern piety—Joseph's tricky coat of many colors, the female, dagger-hiding robes of the biblical hordes, the saw teeth of palm trees, the insidious faces of the camels that brought Wise Men out of the East. But even these intimations had lost their power to awe him. The sacrilege he needed could not be found here.

On the instant he realized this he remembered where he must go to find it. He would wallow with Lucille. Now neither loyalty to Con nor respect for his own athletic nature would restrain him. At the very moment Lucille soiled his flesh he would laugh his contempt for the treacherous Everlings.

He was drenched to the skin and cold when he slipped through the mulberry bushes at the corner of the Zachary lawn. He saw no light in the house and debated whether to knock at the front door or go around in back. The back door seemed the logical choice, even if it might be closer to the room where the little kids were asleep and he might wake them. It would be Lucille's problem to get them back to sleep. On the other hand, there should be still some heat from the kitchen range and he needed to be close to warmth when he shucked out of his wet clothes.

He had come to her with faith—as he had never, really, had faith that Con would keep her promises to him. The faith had been as sustaining as certainty, and yet, this time, he was not really surprised when he saw Tony's car parked in among the bushes near the back door. On the contrary, he was almost glad. For one thing, it confirmed his cynicism about the world—there wasn't a bitch of them you could trust. For another, his excess of emotion had worn him out. And finally—why not admit this, since he had already admitted there was no God, no laws, no responsibility?—he liked the idea of Tony's being with her more than the idea of his own success.

In the shelter of the eaves, he stood outside the back door listening. Presently he heard cinders fall softly in the range. He tugged at the tar-papered screen door and found it unlocked. With infinite slowness he turned the knob of the inner door and thrust it open an inch. Now he could hear something definite—the creak of springs and two voices. Tony's was dark and low. There was no making out what he said. But, listening painfully hard, he heard Lucille saying, "I've told you so many times, Tony, I just don't want to any more." Ha, he thought cynically. If she means that, why aren't there lights and why are the springs squeeching?

A bright flash of lightning threw Harry's shadow inward onto the kitchen floor. After the following thunder he heard Lucille demand, "What was that?"

Then he heard one intelligible word from Tony—"Nothing."

The springs banged devilishly as she seemed to be trying to fight her way from the couch. Perhaps she meant to come investigate whatever she thought she'd heard; maybe she was only trying to get away from Tony. In either case, Harry thought, he won't let her go. And he exulted, Tony's too strong.

The idea of Tony's strength emboldened him, as if it were his strength, too, as if Tony really meant to do this for him. He stopped to pull off his squishy shoes and then entered the kitchen. The coals in the stove glared like jack-o'-lanterns' eyes and it was hard to see past them, but he made out that the door between rooms was open. He asked for lightning from the window beyond them to define the couple to his straining eyes.

The struggle on the couch was more violent now. An elbow crashed against the plaster of the wall. The sounds described a body turning and Lucille said, "Don't make me hate you, Tony."

"Stop your goddamn tricks. Roll back." Another flurry of struggle and Tony said, "All right, bitch. One way or another you're going to take it."

"No." There was a sound like a boot hitting a pumpkin and Lucille moaned, "Don't." A thousand devils in Harry's mind howled "Do."

And now with the stallion thrash of a table being kicked over, lightning blasted the rectangles of window and door, and in the patterning of white against white, black against black, Harry saw one crescent thigh repeat the crescent beneath, as if while he were watching a half moon he had taken a blow on the head that made two exact and overlapping images profiled together against the flat infinite line of the couch's blackness, saw her knee on the floor beside the couch and thought, Not just for me. To me. The aftermath of thunder growled that it would not be mocked. Harriet crouched while Harry panted, felt the double blossom and remorse of sin.

"That's quicker'n other way," Tony said in a tone so shabbily apologetic that Harry hated him. Too quickly lost. No lightning came a second time to create the scene again.

From the second floor came the sound of a door opening and a child's voice calling, "Lucille? Lucille?"

"You had to kick that end table over to wake them up," Lucille said crossly. "It's nothing," she shouted. "I bumped something. Go back to sleep."

"Why isn't there any light, Lucille?"

"I'm trying to sleep down here. Please get back in bed."

"Can I come down to the kitchen for a drink of water?"

"There isn't any water. You're not thirsty. Go back to bed."

"There is too water."

"There's the rain. That's all there is. Go back to bed."

"Come up here, Lucille, we're afraid of the dark."

"I can't come up. Don't you think it's dark down here too? I'm not afraid."

"Good night, Lucille."

"Good night," and then a long, frail silence before the springs creaked again and Lucille said, "Well, you did it, didn't you? And I've got to start all over again."

"There's no use talking like that," Tony said. "You got what you bargained for. How come you had no pants on?"

"I wasn't going out on a night like this. Why get dressed up?"

"Maybe you were expecting someone else."

"I wasn't expecting *you*. I truly wanted to go to sleep early."

"Maybe little old Harry. I hear you've been walking home with him from orchestry practice."

"Who told you that?"

"The birds. I may have to whack him around a little."

"Don't be silly. Harry hasn't got anything."

"If I promise to be nice and not whack Harry around will you be nicer to me?"

"I don't care about Harry."

"You better answer me nice and straight when I ask you something."

"You can do what you want with Harry."

"That's not my answer. You gonna be nice to me?"

"Yes."

"Whenever I want?"

"Yes."

"Whatever I want?"

Yes, Harry thought in the silence.

VI

In the following golden days of November a worse restlessness than he had ever known settled fast on Harry. Nothing that he could think of, or usually counted on, would satisfy him. He went on long hunts through the woods with Mark and sometimes Jimmy Store. The crisp fall weather and the satisfaction of physical fatigue afterward could not touch the core of change he felt swelling within him. Killing squirrels and rabbits with his Stevens "Crackshot" was good as always. It was simply not enough.

When the basketball season started, he went into the first game as forward and scored fifteen points against Bremerton. He was something of a hero around town after the game. Doc Store stopped him on the street to say, "Don't let them tell you because you're light that you aren't damn good athletic timber. You've got a fighting heart . . . and . . . and, a tricky little dribble. Keep going and we'll get the County Championship." That *should* have been all the reward he needed. It wasn't necessary to poke fun at Store for having got drunk and smashed his Buick, or to tell Jimmy Store that his father was known to be messing with a married woman in the city—this spitefulness because Doc's praise hadn't been enough.

The great thaw took place when his twelve points helped the team nudge out Oxley 31–30 and Con Everling *arranged* to ride back to Harrisburg with him in the school superintendent's car.

"Frailty, thy name is women!" he said to Mark later. "Here, it hasn't been two months since I called her a whore in the public street and spat in her face, and I climb into the car with her and Beuleen Chisholm and find her actually *smiling* at me."

"So?" Mark said.

"So I made the most of it."

"Whatever that might mean."

"I copped my feels."

True, he had got one avid finger past her garter on the victorious trip home. But nothing Con was likely to permit would be enough to pacify him. "You take over," he said to Mark. "I'm through with her and I've spoiled her for jerks like Roy McCune and Sid Beerman."

Because nothing would salve the itching dissatisfaction—except dates with Lucille, he thought, and she would not date him now—he led Mark and Jimmy Store into trouble that they would have never touched without his daring them. One night they went into the building of the defunct State Bank of Harrisburg and carried off a gunnysack full of old business papers from the files. They hid them in the furnace of the Baptist Church. On Sunday mornings they would go to read through them for the scant bit of dirty light they might shed on the lives of Harrisburg people. Mark found a letter from Con Everling's father promising "immediate restitution" of the eleven hundred dollars he had evidently embezzled to use on the Grain Market back in '27. It was fixed with a notarial seal applied by an out-of-town notary and the fussy language "sounded like a Jew lawyer," Mark thought. It made Hubert Everling's reputation as "the one honest man" in the failing bank look pretty bad, and the boys talked of using it to blackmail Con into meeting them there in the abandoned church basement. The scheme petered out from sheer impossibility, of course, but also from Harry's lack of enthusiasm.

He dared Jimmy Store to swipe his uncle's .32 pistol from the glove compartment of the car. The theft was staged during a basketball game so the uncle would think the boys from Oxley had done it. They kept the pistol, too, in the Baptist Church furnace between their hunting excursions. The only thing they ever killed with it was a rabbit that they had driven into a culvert. Mark held the pistol inside the culvert and shot blind, automatic fire and when they pulled the rabbit out with a stick, its head and front feet were a pulp of brown hair, blood, and white bone splinters.

He and Mark hitchhiked to the nearby city one day and ran into Lucille on the street there. Harry thought that her face looked worn and older than he was used to thinking it. The scarf tied round her head was pulled so tight that she looked like the pictures of European peasant women.

"Mark and I are going to see 'I Am a Fugitive from a Chain Gang,'" Harry said. "Come on and go with us."

"That ought to be a pretty good movie. But I can't," she said.

"We can go back on the evening bus," Harry said.

"No, I couldn't do that."

"Paul Muni's terrific," Mark said. "It's a better film than 'Scarface.'"

"Oh," she said. "How do you know? You haven't seen it. Little boys have such big imaginations."

"Little boys, hell," Mark said. He pinched her breast hard with his left hand, smiling. "Any time you want to find out, Grandma. . . ."

"That hurts, you dope."

"Then don't call us little boys."

"Oh," she said. "I guess that hurts, too, doesn't it? I'm sorry." She made a mock curtsy of apology to both of them. "I wouldn't think being a boy was the worst thing in the world."

"Walk on a minute," Harry said to Mark. "I want to talk to Grandma. Why can't I ever see you any more?" he asked her.

"I've quit the cornet," she said. Then said, "I guess you know why."

"Tony?"

"Him."

"You told me you'd thrown him over."

"I lied. I tell a lot of lies, Harry. So do you and you ought to stop it."

"I don't know what that means," he said. He felt the hot cud of danger cutting down his breath. Did she *know* he had been in the kitchen that night? She couldn't know. But if she knew, how more desirable then. . . . "It's the truth that I love you."

"Oh, please," she said, jolted into laughter again by the sheer surprise of his declaration. "Run on and see Paul Muni in the chain gang. I've got to meet Tony down at the tavern by the bridge. I'm already late."

"When?" he called after her retreating back.

"When what?" was all she answered.

As they were coming out of the movie Mark said (in imitation of Helen Vinson as she had appeared five minutes before) "'What do you do for a living, Harry?'" And he, as Muni, vanishing into the night, said, "'I steal.' The end. Listen, did you ever tell a girl you loved her?"

"Were you sitting in that movie thinking about *yourself?*" Mark asked incredulously. "Haven't you got any soul at all? Here's this poor sonofabitch gets trapped onto the chain gang for what he didn't do, and you sit there with your little personal problems. Kay-rist."

"I mean it seriously and I expect a civil answer. Did you ever tell a girl. . . ."

"I tell them all that. You've got to. You mean did I ever use those words? Naturally not. I'd feel like a hypocrite if I did and maybe laugh. What you have to do is make them think you said it when you really said something like, 'It's not hard to think of loving you.' That's my line and I'm giggling inside whenever I use it."

"Does that work?"

"Of course not," Mark said. "We've still got an hour before the bus. Let's go down to the dime store and steal something. 'What d'you do for a living, darling?'"

"'I steal.'"

Among other objects that Harry lifted from the dime store that afternoon—a stocking cap, a palm-sized flashlight, and a screwdriver set—he took a little blue-covered book of poetry on sale for twenty-five cents. It was the most feverish tour he had ever made of the counters. Usually he rationed himself to only one pair of socks, women's garters, or a single piece of fishing tackle.

When the loot had been deposited in the Baptist Church furnace with the other junk they had stolen that fall, Mark was going through it one day when he paused to read the book.

"What did you take this for?" Mark asked.

"Present for a girl," Harry said. "I told you I was in love."

"With who? Don't pull that stinky line on me. With Con? With Lucille? Don't give this to that cow. There's some good stuff in it. There's one by John Crowe Ransom about the Blue Girls and there's something else by a Joyce that I really like. 'Wind whines and whines the shingle. The crazy pier-stakes groan. . . .'"

"Do you have to whine when you read it?"

"'. . . and in my heart how deep, unending, ache of love,'" Mark finished. "Why not whine? It's onomatopoetic that way."

"I'm going to give it to Lucille," Harry said grimly.

"You'll end up marrying that cow and living your whole goddamned life in Harrisburg," Mark said. "And you'll get your head beat off besides."

"I don't give a damn for Tony Wilson," Harry said, against the hot knocking of his heart. "He's a goddamned bully. If he tries anything with me, I've always got the pistol."

"Hey," Mark said. "Take it easy."

"I mean it," Harry said. "Things can't go on this way."

Lucille was more pleased than he had expected by his gift. It had seemed only like an excuse for talking to her again, for however short a time. But when he had knocked at her front door and whipped the blue book from under his leather coat, tears actually came to her stupid eyes.

"You bought it—for me?"

"There's some good stuff in it," he said. "James Joyce and Johncrow Ransom."

"Well," she said, "I'll read it. Do you want to come in for some coffee or something? Isn't it starting to snow?"

He saw her father hoist his spectacles up his nose and peer at them from the living-room couch. Her two younger sisters crept down the stairs like big-eyed mice. Her mother's face shuttled across the kitchen door and returned to hang stationary, like a pot suspended from the lintel. His courage failed. He couldn't go in and make like a boyfriend with a girl as old as she.

"When can I see you alone?" he whispered hoarsely.

"Oh"—she closed the door behind her and stepped out with him onto the wind-whipped porch. Her arms were bare and she hugged them with her hands. "I don't know, Harry. You know how I feel about you. I never could hide anything."

"Tomorrow night there's a movie at the Opera House."

She shook her head. Flakes of snow were beginning to lodge in her hair. "Tony'd see us. He's always hanging around downtown."

"All right. Meet me by the stockyards. Where you were that night. . . ."

"I know," she said hurriedly. "OK. Eight o'clock, and I'll tell them I'm going to the movie."

"Good-bye now."

"Can't you come in even for a minute?"

"I got to run and get my papers," he said.

She left a track in the new whiteness of the snow as she turned from the sidewalk to walk toward him. From the boxcar where he watched her approach, Harry thought, That's bad. The snow was a bit of bad luck he hadn't counted on. Anyone might come along and see the tracks where they had no business being and investigate.

"My feet," Lucille said, as he helped her climb into the car. "Ooooo, they're frozen. I had to wear decent shoes if I was going to a movie. I couldn't very well come out in Dad's four-buckles."

"I'll warm them," Harry said crisply. He rolled the boxcar door shut with little noise. One good thing about the snow was the way it muffled sounds. "Take your shoes off."

"Right," she said obediently. She sat on the gunny sacks he had brought and let him take off her shoes. Silently he chafed her feet. He tried to put his hand straight up under her dress.

"Hey," she said, laughing and putting her forehead against his cheek as she grasped and forced back his arm. She smelled of powder and a recent bath. Her cheek seemed to smell of the snow. She seemed very glad to be with him, strangely gentle in spite of the power of her grip. But she said, "Hey," and twisted him into a seat beside her.

"I might as well face it . . . I love you," he said. (None of Mark's ineffectual compromise *now*.)

"You don't love me any more than I love you," she said gaily. "We like each other quite a lot, though, don't we?"

"It's not hard to think of loving you," he said. (Maybe the tricky approach did work better, after all.)

"Hey," she said, rejecting his hand once more. "I read your book and I liked just what you did. 'Blue girls, under the towers of your seminary . . .' I like it better than Shakespeare. Well, not really, but I like it *so much*."

"It's not bad," he conceded owlishly. He had not read the Ransom poem, but since there were Mark's coal-smudged fingerprints in the book he had to keep up the pretense that if anyone read it, it was he.

"I lay in my bedroom upstairs all afternoon reading them," she said, "and watching the snow come down over Halvorsen's pasture. It was wonderful, and I think I know some of them by heart. All of them are beautiful, but I like some of them better than others." She began to recite random lines, asking him to share her admiration.

No doubt the lines were beautiful. No doubt in their proper place the labors of Ransom and Joyce were deserving of praise.

But Jesus God, why did it have to be here and now? This boxcar should have been consecrated to some other brightness than that of verse.

The evening that began with poetry ended with her tongue in his mouth and the feel of her mounded coat tingling against his fingers. When he had finally silenced her quotations, she had taught him with a mute, tormenting medley of promise and denial that seemed to change him like a change in the chemistry of his body. He might have been, at least, grateful if he had not wanted so much more.

His next move was an attempt to spy on her with Tony again. He was nearly caught by one of the Zacharys' neighbors, and his narrow escape set him worrying again about what might happen if Tony caught him. His talk about the pistol, which lay among the papers, candy, and socks in the Baptist Church furnace, did not seem so easy any more. But if Tony caught him he would have to use the pistol, for it was not the stolen gun that frightened him most at the threshold of dreams. With recurrent terror he relived that moment when he had seen the double curve of buttocks and had thought, Mine is like hers. Oh, he had wanted to be in her place. And what did that make him? A lousy maphrodite who went around pretending to be a clean, earnest athlete? No! If Tony ever so much as touched him he would kill . . . somebody.

The hidden evening rendezvous with Lucille went on past Christmas and gradually he forced down and destroyed the gay lightness he had felt that first night in the boxcar. She wanted to *talk* to him. It made her feel his age again, not already old and spoiled. He knew this and grimly made the barter that both of them at length accepted. He would talk and she would endure the wrestling that he wanted in exchange. Maybe she even liked the hours of kissing that they found together.

She would say sometimes. "Oh, I want to, but it would ruin things for us. Let's not ruin you and me, Harry."

"But you've done it."

"Yes, I've done it."

"You're still doing it with Tony."

"He makes me, and you can't. I didn't mean that. I love you and not him."

So it was love now, he thought, sarcastically. Love was so

cheap. What he wanted was so desperately beyond even imagination, except by that one act where the union would take place
that must never take place otherwise, the lightning-illuminated
identification of his father-mothering flesh known once with
such damning briefness.

VII

Their stalemate ended with the exhausting of her need for a
compensating illusion of Virginity Recaptured. It ended, in any
case, with her decision and to Harry's surprise.

One thawing Saturday in late January, she met him on the
street as he was going about town making the weekly collection
for the papers he delivered. It seemed she had come looking for
him. It was clear enough that something bleak and painful had
risen up to worry her. "I want to be with you tonight," she said,
with a failing attempt at light-hearted coquetry. Whatever her
misery might come from, the fact of its existence was as clear to
the eye as the wisping cloud of her breath in the winter air.

Moved a little by pity—but annoyed, too, by the impulse that
muted the pure savagery with which he wanted her—he said
only, "Yes. What about Tony?" Thus far all Saturday nights had
been Tony's, with what other times he might demand.

"Don't be afraid of Tony," she said with a small, wry twist of
mockery in her voice.

He jingled the small change in his canvas collecting sack and
asked, "Where?"

"I don't know," she said. "Can't you even think of a place?
Oh, Harry, I can't count on you for anything. You can't even
drive a car so we could go out in the country. Harry, what have I
got myself into with you?"

"At the Baptist Church," he directed. "As soon as it gets
dark. Go around the corner by the alley. Push the second basement window."

"Harry! We can't go in there."

"There isn't any place else."

She looked away for a long time—up the ice-bright ruts of the
street toward the central square. A farmer's wagon mounted on
runners for the winter went past them. The steel-shod runners
shrieked in gravel exposed by the thaw. "All right," she said,
"but not until after supper."

"Not after eight," he said. "What's eating you? You act so funny today. You had another fight with Tony?"

"Oh no," she said. "I haven't seen Tony all week." She stared him down in his effort to read her secret in some betraying waver of her eyes.

He went hunting, alone, that afternoon, driven on and on under the clearest of winter skies by some imminence that seemed to hover always behind the back of his head. As he slopped through decaying snowbanks five miles from town, premonitions told him that the long equilibrium in which he had spun with Tony and Lucille was about to be broken. But as if he were only partly himself any more and already partly his own insatiable nemesis, he could foresee already that he was going to be both the victim and perpetrator of the change. It had been as if he were already delivering himself to sacrifice when he blurted out his suggestion of a meeting place. At the same instant a cruel lucidity had reminded him that the pistol was hidden there, and that with the pistol he could force her to what she had refused thus far.

He was desperate enough to threaten her with the pistol. Sure. She had made him desperate by letting him go so far before she stopped him. And yet he could not bear the thought of menacing her plump and lovable body with the gun. He remembered how Mark had chopped up the rabbit with the gun, and the image suddenly overlapped his recollection of Lucille's good-natured face.

To blot this terrible confusion from his mind he ran at a dead run up the drift-covered slope of a long hill. At full gallop he held the Crackshot in front of his breast with both hands, the way the marines charge in the movies. For his country, home, and beauty he put the last painful ounce of his energy into the daredevil attack. He ran in the purity of mindless heroism.

When he stood on the crest of the empty hill and looked down into the blue, snow-shadowed valley beyond, the filthy determination to use the pistol if he had to crept back like his returning breath.

I won't really shoot, he told himself. I'll be careful. I'll make sure the safety is on and just put it behind her ear and tell her coolly what she's got to do. But—damn her—she had acted so unhappy about something this morning that she just might say, "Go ahead and shoot, Harry."

What if she said that, Little Harry, Lighthorse Harry?

He charged down the hill, falling where the run-off from the snow had begun to freeze, snarling and catapulting to his feet again. In the willow-furred ravine at the valley's bottom he pulled up staring at a stone girdled with a frilling lace of ice, thinking, It can't go on this way. It's got to end. I've got to make it end.

At six that evening he entered the Baptist Church basement. Huddled into a ball for warmth, he ate some of the candy bars that he and Mark and Jimmy Store had cached there. ("It would be wrong to steal them if we weren't going to eat them," Mark had said in their first gorging after the theft. "It would be un-Indian. The Red Man never steals more than he needs.") But the bars were stale to begin with and most of them had lain too long with the other junk of the magpie's nest.

When he had finished eating, he took the pistol from the furnace and went upstairs. Selecting a bench near the center of the main room, he put the pistol into the hymnbook rack and lay down to wait. He did not particularly feel cold any more. He did not feel anything. He heard a few cars pass outside as the farmers began coming in to town for their Saturday night, and he thought of what they might soon be doing with a weary, detached amusement. The women would be going to Finley's store to sell their eggs, shop for groceries, and finger the dry goods while they waited for the men to come back for them. The men would stop by the cream station for a little gossip. Some would go to the pool hall, and some of the younger ones might go up to the dance. They would stomp around to the hill-billy music, and . . . and finally everyone would go home. Out there was the world of people who went home. He was alone in the vigil of those who could not.

His watch said seven-thirty when he pulled it from his pocket. He dangled it by its chain from the hymnbook rack near his head. He watched each of its luminous hands move (he was sure that his filed senses caught the movement of the hour hand, too) and thought that they were closing a final lock, turning the way a key turns in the door of a death cell.

At a quarter of eight he went back down to the basement window. When Lucille knelt to push it open, his face was so close to hers that she ducked back in fright.

"Harry?"

"Sure. Come in."

She giggled as she dropped to the concrete floor beside him. "I never thought I'd be breaking in *here*," she said. She kissed him wetly and said, "I never thought I'd be making love in church. But if you get married here, why not?"

"I never believed in marriage," Harry said. "The way I see it, if two people *feel* they're married that's a lot more important than having a dumb old preacher say some words over you." He did not know what he believed or, just then, what he was saying. The words were a gambit to divert her attention from where he was leading her—up the stairs and back to the selected worshipers' bench.

She let him seat her on the bench and then she laughed again. "Well, start the sermon," she commanded into the dark. "What he's saying now is, 'Those highfalutin scientists will tell you they can look at some bones and tell you how old the world is. They think they can prove there's evolution that way. I want to ask you, could those scientists go out in your pasture, look at the old cow's bones, and tell you when the old cow died?' Oh, Harry, preachers are all so silly, just like you say." Her gloominess of the morning was being swept away on the tide of her amusement with their adventure.

He heard her gaiety rise far away. He put his hand out to touch the pistol butt and wondered, *Now, or shall I give her a chance?* The touch of cold metal sickened him. He felt the hard ball of candy thrust out against the walls of his stomach and he realized he had broken the athlete's rule of eating light before a game. He had better give her a chance. He kissed her and began to unbutton her coat.

"It's so cold in here," she said. "Brrr. Wait a minute. You and I think a lot alike, Harry. What difference *does* it make whether some stupid preacher mumbles a marriage ceremony? That doesn't change . . . what's happened."

"Or what's going to happen," Harry said.

"Or what's going to happen," she agreed philosophically.

"Marriage is strictly immaterial to a *thinking* person," she said. "Guess who just got married."

"Dunno."

"Tony."

"Who?" A strange, wild singing had begun in Harry's ears.

"That idiot Tony Wilson. He married some slut from Oxley, whose family hasn't got a *nickel* and so now the lazy bum is going to have to go to work. I think her father's a miner and they may have him down shoveling coal, which would serve him right. They're Catholics too and I'll bet a dollar that the reason he married her was she wouldn't give in to him otherwise, though Tony takes what he wants, so I don't know how it happened. But I heard about it and didn't even cry. I'm a thinking person and was glad enough to be rid of him if he's as stupid as he seems. But my family—oh lord. They're disgusting. You'd think I'd brought some terrible disgrace upon them instead of keeping them from having a moron for a son-in-law. You see, some of the times I've been meeting you I've told them I was with him and Mother notices things . . . spots and tears . . . when there's straw from a box car or stuff. . . . The old biddy will probably find a hymnbook page in my pocket tomorrow, but I don't care, after what they said to me since they found out he's married. My own damn parents."

He's gone, Harry thought. We've lost Tony and she can only think about what her silly folks said to her. "I didn't think he'd get married. A guy like that."

Lucille clutched the sheepskin collar of his coat and then buried her face in it, next to his. He felt her tears sliding against his cheek. "They've been so devilish with me I haven't had any time for myself," she whimpered. "Don't they think a person has any private thoughts on a thing like this? Maybe I loved him, but all they can think about is, Why didn't I hook him?" Her strong shoulders trembled. "Harry, you didn't hate Tony, did you?"

"No." He felt cleaner, purged, now that he had been able to come this close to a declaration—not of love, maybe, but of the lightning-colored desire that had flickered so long now in the cave of his dreams.

"I know I double-crossed you with him. But you didn't hate him?"

"I thought he was a pretty swell guy."

"Harry . . . this is why I can talk to you. You don't see just your own side like everyone else in the world does. You're . . . decent."

On the sweep of this praise Harry said his love words incautiously, "He was good-looking. Strong. I can see how you loved him."

"I guess I did," she said. "No, I didn't either. I'm not much good, Harry. Would you hate me if I told you a secret? The only thing I loved about him was . . . what we did. He was such a dog otherwise. Do you hate me for saying that?"

"No."

"Harry, I've been so bad to you, and you're so decent. You are, you are. You're better than Tony. We're going to forget all about him. I'm going to be better to you. Really, really. I'm too tired to fight any more. I don't want to fight you, Harry. Harry, I can't fight you too."

He lay on the straps of her garter belt like a dead fly on a white web and she said, "Never mind. It's all right. You'll do better next time."

"It's not," he said, choking with a failure she could never help him now to understand. "It wasn't like with Tony, was it?" he said with plummeting bitterness, expecting no answer since it was himself who would have had to answer if either of them did. He had expected the instant of contact to recover for him the total vision that had branded him in the lightning glare; he had tensed waiting for it like a child fishing over mossy water who sees the bright scales and then the form itself for an instant clear in the depths, rising, swimming toward his hand; had grasped for it in the total physical convulsion that sent the bright spray geysering around him, all gasp and rainbows; and had driven both scales and form forever out of sight, himself on shore again and, for his pains, merely wet.

The two of them lay there, both doubly bereaved of each other and the faithless Tony. Because they had to get up, both go out from the sacrilegious encounter on which they had counted so much, each had to invent a way to go.

She said, "I never knew I loved you this much. You'll do better next time."

He thought, She only wants me because she can't have him. Con Everling wouldn't have done this unless she really loved me and probably after we were married.

Covering her against the vicious cold to which he had exposed her, he said with a pretense of solicitude, "I'm sorry your folks are giving you a bad time. It's a tragedy all around that you and Tony didn't get married."

"It isn't. I'm so glad it worked out this way. I'm going to make you happy."

"Oh, I'm happy enough," he said. "Brrrrr."

Silenty they retraced their steps to the basement window. Before she let him open it she said, "You don't have to marry me, you know. If that's what's worrying you."

"I'm not worried. You go on ahead. It will be better if we don't go out together and I've got to go back upstairs to get something I left."

"Oh," she said. "My word. Yes you'd better. People would really hit the ceiling if they came in and found something like that left lying around a church."

He thought she, too, meant the gun, and he was quite a little shaken to think that she had noticed it. But he comforted himself by believing she thought he had put it there for their protection in case they were caught.

VIII

The initiation, which robbed him of the hope that he could reach Tony Wilson through her, delivered him as well from the twisted obsession of his desire.

He went home from the church that night with hardly a thought of Tony, as if by marriage to the miner's daughter the bright lawless figure had been condemned again to work those tunnels of darkness from which he had risen. "They may have him down in the mine, shoveling coal," Lucille had said. Let him stay there, Harry thought.

He had other worries now. Time, which had narrowed to the black wedge described by the hands of his watch, was unfurled in the whiteness of snow that seemed to loop outward from the town over all the hills to the world's end. In the reprieve of time he could think soberly. He had *better* think soberly if he didn't want to be stuck down in the mine, so to speak, himself. She had said he didn't have to marry her. OK. In the past months she had said a lot of things and then had changed her mind. It seemed to him that she had a powerful claim on him now, or could have if this went on. He did not mean to spend the rest of his life in Harrisburg, working for her. Out and over the icy slopes of time his imagination skied. He had far to go, and if a woman went with him, it would be Con Everling, who knew how to wait.

He was in full rebound toward Con in the days that followed. He dated her for the county basketball tournament and *bought* her for Valentine's Day a vast heart-shaped box of candy at

Will's drugstore, though he knew where he could have stolen one almost as good. He shared a hymnbook with her each Sunday night at Luther League. Her parents and her married sister began to tease him suggestively, and one night old man Everling got him in a long discussion about going to college. Though Harry argued that he was going to be a world traveler like Floyd Gibbons as soon as high school was over, Mr. Everling was good-humoredly sure that he would go to college and make something of himself.

"So you finally got burned on that cow Lucille?" Mark asked, observing the change with unaltered cynicism.

"I play the field," Harry said. "I'm not a one-woman man."

"You will be when that Everling gets through with you. She's the kind that knows how to put a price on her cherry. When you make out with her they're going to be singing hymns over you and throwing rice. Gaaa, it makes me sick. Oh, she'll pet a little, but let me tell you the truth. You aren't going to get paid for the time you put in, let alone the money you sink on her."

"I don't care about that. You can't seem to understand decent feelings."

"From you," Mark said, "no. I figure you spend more time worrying where to get in than anybody I ever heard of. You'd take on a snake if someone would hold its head."

"I get all of that I want. Anyway, it's not what it's cracked up to be."

"You're lying."

"I'm not lying. I get it once a week—if I want it."

"Not from Con."

"Not Con. I told you I play the field. I've got my stock lined up."

"Boy, you better watch out," Mark said. He was envious, all right—but, beyond this, disapproving and honestly worried for Harry's sake. "I hope you're using a good brand of protection."

"Na," Harry said, feeling fear and guilt and a more generalized remorse shake him, trying to cover it with a stupid veneer of acting tough. "I don't use anything. It's the babe's worry. She wants it. Let her look out."

"Here's my jackknife," Mark said. "Since you want to cut your throat, go do it the easy way."

He laughed at Mark's warnings—to Mark's face. He could hardly laugh at the continuing situation that he dragged along with him. For if he had rebounded again, it was not with the simple billiard-ball ricochet that had sent him from Con to Lucille in the first place. He had not broken with Lucille, not even emotionally as he had once broken with Con; and if he talked like Tony Wilson about her (and sometimes thought of her, too, *I spit on you*) it was no longer because of adulation of Tony's ways. Rather, this brutal talk was a fashion of punishing himself, a self-degradation performed in contriteness for what he felt her to be suffering. He pitied her now. Was it pity that her loins had been unable to bear him the total, perverse pleasure he had once demanded? Was there still at least a taint from that impossible expectation? It did not matter. He pitied her that she, too, had wanted so much—her expectations no less impossible than his—and got nothing for her pains except to be tossed from one pair of faithless hands to another. Now, in the unleashing of time and the growth it had forced on him, pity was no longer antipathetic to desire. He could see her now as doomed and hurt by the female condition from which he had once dreamed so fiercely of liberating his mother—and in the sweeping current of his pity would feel desire waking once again. He would arrange meetings with Lucille then in spite of his resolutions. On the couch of her living room and—when the weather was milder in the advance of spring—in haymows and finally in her back lawn (always in the dark and always with a panicking haste) he tried to appease them both with what both knew was an inept sin.

"I told you it would ruin us," she used to say quietly afterward.

If you knew what I didn't, he thought, mournfully, then why did you let it happen? "We're not ruined," he said doggedly—so many times. And she would think about this awhile as if he had delivered a careful opinion, and agree, "No, I guess it's just fun as long as we're careful. You are careful every time, aren't you?"

"Yes," he said, because in the mire of his own guilt and the conscientiousness of his pity for her he could bear neither to admit his trickery nor to make her worry.

"You're getting better at it," she said. "Maybe we'll turn out all right together."

We'd be all right . . . if we could just quit doing it altogether, he thought. If I was man enough to stop.

Then, in May, she avoided him for several days when she first believed herself pregnant. He took her willful absence as a sign that she had finally seen they had made a mistake. In the exultation of the fine weather and some heart-to-heart talks with his real girl, Con, he convinced himself that Lucille's own good sense had told her what he had never dared voice—or maybe, conveniently, that she had found a new boyfriend. He had tried seriously to interest Mark in her once, hoping to get her off his hands. Mark was too smart. But there were plenty of young men in town constantly looking for what she had too much of. It even seemed possible that Tony Wilson, three months married now, might have resumed his office. Well, if Tony had returned to satisfy her, that was just fine.

Harry still tried to hold on to these fantasies when Lucille met him on the street and told him the truth. "You're not going to have a baby," he said stupidly, avoiding the calm, pained, steadiness of her gaze. "You're not *either*." He laughed loudly as if she had told a really good joke. She would not laugh with him, and the sound froze in his throat.

But because she had given him the news so calmly—and was remaining so calm—he clung wildly to the temptation of thinking. She's not sure. She hasn't been to a doctor yet. She doesn't know.

In a pitiable, nasty imitation of her calm, he asked, "What are we going to do?"

"Wait another two weeks to make really sure," she said. "Can you think of anything better?"

"Do you want to get married?"

It was some relief that she laughed in his face.

"You lied to me, didn't you, Harry?" she asked gently. "Were you ever careful?"

"All but once."

"Oh no," she said. "No, you weren't. But it's my fault, too, because I knew you were a liar. I should have known this would happen. I wanted to help you. Ah well. At least a man would have been too scared to . . ."

"OK. I'm not a man."

"You're my bargain, Harry. Don't worry. We'll wait."

That very night, after the dance at the Opera House, he walked Con Everling up to the highway viaduct that passed over the railroad tracks and under the benign stars asked her to marry him. This seemed to him the ultimate of recklessness and now he felt himself committed to recklessness. In the simple justice of retribution he had to take all the chances there were.

Con laughed mournfully. "I wish you'd waited a *little* longer before you asked me, Harry."

"I can't wait much longer." The luminous constellations moved like watch hands, narrowing his time again to the black wedge where all sin is done and where it must be paid for.

"Silly. You could wait two more years at least. *No one* gets married any younger than that." Two years—enough time for dinosaurs to hatch and glacial icecaps to creep down from the poles to chase them away. Time enough for Lucille's child to recognize its daddy.

"I can't wait that long. You don't know what goes on in my mind."

"I know you have a busy mind," she said. "Buzz, buzz, buzz. It's running all the time. But that doesn't change anything."

"I think about my uncle," he said. "Maybe he was right to take the old rope. I don't think it's the coward's way at all. It may be the bravest way."

"Harry!"

"Look down at those rails," he said. "You stand here until the engine is twenty feet away. Then alley oop." He feinted a vault on the viaduct rail, thinking, as the sweat crept in his armpits, But I'm not *really* kidding this time.

"If you talk like that I'm going home. Don't spoil it, Harry. Tonight started out so *perfect*."

"Oh deary dear, I'd hate to *spoil* a perfect night."

"Harry, what have I done that makes you this way?"

"I asked you to marry me and you say I'm not a man yet."

"I didn't say that." Her soft small fingers moved cajolingly on his neck. "Harry, look at the stars. It always helps to look *up* when you're feeling low. Harry, I know what you *mean* about getting married. Don't you think I have my dreams, too? It isn't so hard to think of loving you."

"What?" He jerked away as if a bee had stung him.

"Harry! You're crazy tonight. If you're not nicer to me I might *as well* go home. That's better," she said as he kissed her and put his hands around her waist, "ever so much better. When you're good, you're very, very good and when you're bad you're . . . Harry."

"There's so many things you don't count on in this life, Con. You've got to believe me. It's all *fun* to sit around and talk about maybe we'll go to the same college. It can't happen. It can't."

"I see it in the stars."

"You've got to realize I'm serious. Just do one thing for me, give me an answer. Will you marry me?"

She looked very solemnly at him. He could see the whites of her eyes enlarge. She said caressingly, "Yes, Harry, I will."

"All right. There's just one thing. You know how I think. I'm a lone wolf and I don't have a lot of use for formalities and ministers saying a lot of blah over you and there isn't time. . . . Did you hear this radio program where the girl died of appendicitis before she could marry her sweetheart and afterwards it comes out that they'd spent a week together at a cabin camp when her folks thought she was visiting her aunt. . . ."

"What on earth are you talking about?"

". . . and the point of the whole thing is her father's *glad* when he finds out about her lying, because even if she's dead nothing can ever take away from the sweethearts what they'd had together."

"Harry, I'm afraid of you when you talk the way you have tonight. You've spoiled everything."

"Yes. I spoil everything," he said. "It's nice tonight and the stars are fine and I spoil it all."

"Oh, don't think you're so important," she said. "It's late. Walk me home."

He woke at 5:15 that morning when he heard the milk train rush under the viaduct. The first streaks of dawn were in the sky. The smell of greenery was in the breeze. Intermittently a rain crow called from the direction of the railroad embankment. Now the light came in to touch the red feathers of his hunting arrows and the whitish crescent of his bow, hung above his worktable with the pictures of Jimmy Doolittle, Frank Luke, and Cotton Warburton. A little spider dangled from the filament it had spun down from the window curtain. It swayed with a joyous ease back and forth. Like a hanged man in the antic of death. "I spoil everything," he said.

The streets of the town seemed swollen with Lucille's presence. He did not know as the deadline ending the two-week wait approached whether he was avoiding her or looking for her as he rode his bike around or went delivering his papers or ran home from school. He did know that she was hinted everywhere in the green fecundity of the season. The lilac buds swelled. The neighbor's cat bore a stunning number of kittens.

Hap McDougall's wife went around looking like she had a basketball under her dress. Tony Wilson announced to his cronies
at the pool hall—and Harry heard it secondhand from Mark—
that his wife was going to show how good a Catholic she was in
September. Hens seemed to cackle all day long in everyone's
back yard. Two dogs were led to couple one Saturday night in
the cream station and then scampered, wild with terror and still
linked back to back with a horrible ligature, from one side of the
room to another while Don Alpen sprayed them from a hose
and the crowd of men roared their amusement.

The human heart could not stand two weeks of this waiting.
But two weeks was very short. He had not actually seen Lucille
for half of that time when she sent him word through Mark that
he was to meet her one afternoon by the bandstand. He was to
ride his bike up and go ahead with the delivery of his papers if
she didn't show up.

"What's going on?" Mark asked in honest grief. "I never
heard of anything so spooky. Is she trying to blackmail you?"

"That's nobody's business."

"Look. We can use Plan A and hit for Colorado now. I won't
even go home for clean clothes if it's that bad."

"Let's cut out the kid talk," Harry said.

"All right. It's your funeral."

The ultimatum was ready for him and he could not face it. He
sat from eleven in the morning until four-thirty in the basement
of the Baptist Church with the pistol at his feet. He watched
the shadows of branches and low-growing shrubs move on the
frosted glass of the windows so he would not have to look at the
sun until the last minute. He tried not to remember the coupled
dogs shivering under the onslaught of water, but it was all he
could do to keep from barking his terror as they had barked.

He picked up the pistol and looked down the barrel. It was
like everything he had seen before rather than like a gun. Like
the reflection of the day moon in a cistern he could see the
copper-tipped end of the bullet when he held the pistol in a certain light. Moon in the cistern, fish in the moss-dark pool, it was
what he had wanted. All he had ever truly wanted.

He felt very sleepy as he watched the fish (or the moon) seem
to enlarge as if now it were truly coming to his hand. Sleep now,
dream now, find it now. He put the gun back on the floor.

With a jolt he shook himself awake. There was no use rushing it. It would be there when he wanted it, and in the meantime he had to examine every wonderful flaw in the cement of the floor, every wave in the uneven surface of the window glass through which he saw the shadows, every splintery miracle of the raw lumber in the floor over his head. Between sleep and full consciousness he begged, *Let me stay here,* and now the church, which had seemed so empty of everything except the phantoms with which his eroticism had populated it, seemed full of Gracious Ones who could stoop to save him if they chose. Even if it's dull as a sermon, he begged them, let me stick around and hear it all. The leaden minutes filed up through the hollow handle of his world, gleamed, and pierced his egg-shell skull. They all hurt, but what hurt most was that one of them would be the last.

No, he said.

The silence in which No One came said *Yes.*

Let there be some mice at least, he prayed, anything at all for company. But it was broad daylight and the mice God might have sent him by night stayed hidden in the walls.

No, he said. *I* won't do it. The silence said, No one else is going to and it has to be done. Thy will be done, Harry. Thy will be done.

His watch said four-thirty. He was already late. By now if he had not been a coward he would have been at the bandstand to hear the news. Or he would have been dead.

He took off his shoes and began running silently from side to side of the basement, returning always past the stuffed belly of the furnace and the one black item that counted from all his pilfering. I won't do it until I've worn myself out, he thought. There's no use wasting all this energy that I can use.

His breath grew short from the running and then he wanted to sing. With the first gasping note he got out, he heard someone tap or kick against one of the windows. They've come to stop me even from this, he thought. He quit the song and walked dutifully to where the pistol lay on the concrete. Before they interrupted he had to finish the business that was private, between No God and himself. He thumbed the safety off and stared right down the barrel. The angle of light was wrong this time, and he saw no moon-shaped curve of the bullet's nose. It would come out of the dark.

"Harry," Lucille said. "Harry, be careful."

"How did you get in?" he said. Sluggishly he recognized her, though she was dressed in Sunday clothes and seemed so unlike anyone he had ever been in the basement with before.

"Harry," she said cajolingly, coming like his mother to take something dangerous out of his infant grip. He let her take the pistol. She laid it on the floor before she took him in her arms to cradle his head on her breast. "Harry, Mark said you might be here. It's all right, Harry. Everything's all right."

"I spoil it all," he said from a dry mouth.

"Harry, why I wanted to see you was to tell you not to worry."

"Did you see them laugh at those goddamn dogs?"

She shook him roughly and said, "Harry, Harry, wake up. There aren't any dogs."

"What are you doing here?"

"I came to tell you, is all. I'm not going to have a baby."

"Why'd you tell me you were?" He began to blubber awfully.

"Because I was," she said. "Now I'm not. It's all right now. That's what I wanted to tell you, Harry. Now you can go out and celebrate with Connie."

"I don't want Con. I don't want anyone."

"Hush," she said. "There's no use crying. Hush."

"But I did such *terrible* things."

"I guess we both did. Maybe some old preacher would think we ought to go to hell for it. I never had a lot of faith in what they said. We lived through it all right. What else do we have to say?"

Now laughing, crying, he hung with his arms around her neck, against that good, sturdy body dressed in its best clothes. "But I was so goddamn *dumb*," he said, not loudly, but with his breath roaring it, cascading it out of the full treasury of his relief.

"Well, I wouldn't argue about *that*," she said.

Gently, firmly she thrust him back from her. "Now stand up by yourself," she commanded.

It was over, but the cleaning up remained to be done. "Old Mrs. Chisholm was out in her back yard and saw me come in here," she said. "We can't hang around much longer. She'll call someone and they'll be down to investigate."

"You didn't have to come," he said in stupid gratitude.

"Mark said you looked scared to death." She made no refer-

ence then or ever later to the gun she had found in his hand—
only to his fear.

They dropped the gun down between a wooden wall and the
stone foundations. Quickly he went to the furnace and set a
match to all the loot they had been accumulating there through
the winter. This was the emergency plan he had worked out
with Mark and Jimmy Store.

"Someone will see the smoke," Lucille protested, but when
she glanced inside at the bank correspondence, the stocking
caps, the fishing tackle, and the old candy boxes, she fell silent
in agreement. Only she said, "I'm getting out now. I'll walk
right out the basement door, since it's only bolted. And if anyone sees you go out . . . I might just go to your folks and tell
them everything."

"Good-bye," he said. "I'm sorry."

"Good-bye was all you had to say."

An hour later he sat on a hill just outside town watching Mr.
Everling, Tim Carey, and Waldo Smith arrive separately, but
within five minutes of each other, to enter the church and see
why a plume of dun-colored smoke came from its chimney on
this mild May evening.

They won't find anything, he told himself. We were careful
about that at least and all there is left to show is the smoke.

The Squeaky Wheel

Beyond the door of the penthouse lay the unreconstructed tarpaper roof. In the dusk a two-foot railing of brick was visible between this building and the next one in the row. Where the tarpaper ended in front there was nothing. A hundred feet of glooming space separated it from the blank, arched windows of the lofts across the street.

Satellites of the densely packed party inside, a few couples had come out to lounge on brick buttresses or the deck chairs that their host had scattered on the roof. A Princeton type and a girl silhouetted like a white butterfly were leaning over the front edge to peer six stories down into the street.

"We have to go look, too," Eilis Harper said. "It must be the feature out here." She spoke in slight disappointment with the crudeness of the roof after the glib sleekness of the penthouse.

A friend of hers was renting this place for the summer, and this was her first visit of inspection. She took Howard Seabright's hand and with a counterfeit of bravery—or perhaps only of that recklessness which simultaneously damned and protected her—led him forward. The boy and girl who had been there backed away from the edge at their approach, as if afraid of being pushed.

Eilis said, "Not too close, hon. I have it, the fear of high places, whatever the technical name for that is. I told Marian about it"—Marian was her analyst—"and do you know her response? 'All right, don't go to high places,' she said. I really get full value and my money's worth from that woman." While Eilis spoke her white pumps crept forward on the last eighteen·inches of tarpaper like two forefingers tugging back the edge of a cloth. Finally the toe of one of them came just even with the end of the roof. She clutched hard at Howard's sleeve and he could feel her balance go awry as she stiffened.

She lurched back and said, "Wheew, I did it. It makes me feel better when I can force myself to do it. I've got to be master of *something*, so why not of myself? I told *that* to Marian, too, and she said, 'Then do it if it makes you feel better.' Should I quit going to her? Why should I pay for banalities that I don't say to myself only because I don't bother any more to think of them?"

"There ought to be a rail there," Howard said. As he led Eilis back toward a more central part of the roof he felt them sucking the danger of the edge with them, as if it were some chill, sticky fluid that they had touched and which was now clinging to their flesh.

But at least it was comforting that there were other guests out there with them. Most of the others did not look as if they would attract danger nor tolerate it if it came. They were younger and handsomer than he and Eilis. The dull rose of evening wrapped them kindly like a medium in which they could simply float if necessity required it. But in spite of the reassurance Howard got from looking around him, stone, steel, and tarpaper quivered under his soles, quivering all the way down to the granite base of the island. He said, "This roof may be safe enough for adults and when they're sober, but it's downright foolish to have a party here."

"Bernie is foolish," she agreed peaceably, though on the taxi-

ride to the party she had been childishly enthusiastic about
their host and the chance to see the penthouse he had lucked
into for the hot months. "If someone falls off he'll cry tomorrow." She found a vacant deck chair and sank into it to get her
breath back. "Bernie wouldn't even see it was dangerous until
there was a body down there, oozing life. I see it because I'm
timid as a cobra in the face of a mongoose. *You* see it because
you're such a sensible man among us."

Now some outside lights went on, illuminating the roof and
changing what had been light in the sky above them into a darkness that swallowed nighthawks and small gray bulges of cloud.
In this change the tarpaper seemed like a long, festive raft anchored over submarine streets.

"You even divorce sensibly," Eilis said. "I've never done it the
way you're doing it. With me it's either the man hates me or I
hate him and then we go jump off a high place. You and Betty
are still negotiating like sensible people. Like, I ask myself why
you even need lawyers. And you go have a little affair with me
like you were taking it for your stomach instead of what in mah
childhood was called the heart. And you carry on."

Howard laughed. "We're not much like lawyers."

"You told me Betty cries a lot, but I mean tears aren't everything. It's what's behind them. I cried a lot every time in spite of
it being different reasons. But I don't have good manners and
you and Betty do."

"I'm trying to improve them," he said, half-gravely. "They're
about all that help much."

"That's what Marian tries to tell me. We have enormous arguments and I suppose it wastes my money to argue, but I can't
make myself believe in manners. Nothing really counts except
the honest, genuine, bed-rock way you feel," she said. "I never
am myself unless I'm so much in love I could kill myself and
paying the penalty. It's like some women who have to be pregnant all the time. I'm in love now." She jerked her black and
white Irish head toward the penthouse through which they had
passed a little while before, "He's in there."

"What?"

"It's not *Bernie*. Ha ha ha. It's certainly not Bernie. And I'm
out here fighting not to go in and speak to him in front of that
bitch he's with. You noticed I resisted speaking to him when we
came in."

Howard shook his head in puzzlement. He had noted only the smart reconditioning of the penthouse, surprising in this part of the East Side and atop such a drab old building—that and the faintly troublesome youthfulness of the mass of guests whom Bernie had assembled. "For heaven's sake," he said. "I gather that I'm part of a conspiracy." He spoke with a certain relief. When Eilis had been so insistent that he bring her to this party he had been a little afraid of it, afraid of what she expected of him, afraid of taking her home afterward.

He had felt that the nearly dispassionate, almost impersonal affair in which he had lingered with Eilis through the past spring while his divorce was being concluded was over. In the season of high school and college graduations it had seemed to him that they had both graduated from the brief, practical need they had for each other.

Two months before Eilis had said to him, "When you're making love to me, I wish you'd say you love me. It's all right. When I'll think about it afterwards I'll know it didn't mean anything. It just makes things *nicer.*" That arrangement—a matter of manners only—had been the *bona fide* of their relationship. Their responsibility and affection for each other had been established so it would remain as conditional as a caress—subject to total discount when its occasion had passed. They did not talk about the future or much about the past. Howard had learned a good deal about her, but much of what he knew was the product of second-thought and analysis rather than from any probing attempt to possess by knowledge the detail of her life.

For a considerable time after he had met her in December (in the San Remo bar, as a matter of fact, though he was seldom there) he had been attracted by her apparently endless acquaintance with people around town. She mentioned hosts of actors, technicians, ad people, writers, and fast-buck specialists who had promised to help her organize her own TV company. Then, when these people turned up, here or there, it proved true that she knew them, and they were evidently fond of her. An impressive number of them kissed her when they met on the street, even if none of them showed any serious intention of getting involved with her in business. *Delcor,* her projected TV enterprise, had remained for two years no more than a forty-pound pile of tan letterheads stacked in a corner of her apartment, but it gave her a kind of status in her own eyes and gave her something to talk about with a host of colorful people.

Watching her with them and gathering scraps of biographical data on her, Howard had thought once that she had done everything a woman can do by thirty. (He meant everything the emotions are capable of seeing one through.) She had been married three times, divorced twice and widowed once, had tried religion, hard work, and Lesbianism.

But then his insight had sharpened and before they drifted out of their affair with the same haphazard carelessness that had brought them into it, he came to believe that she had never known anyone, had never done anything, and had never had anything of her own. He sensed in her an isolation so prophylactic that not even her diseases were her own, even they to be experienced as through the glass screen of a hospital amphitheatre, so that her real suffering was totally separated from her voluble expression of it. She was the true Lady of Shalott, though the shiny webs in which she dealt were the actual involvements with fleshly people like himself and the mirror in which she watched the world was whatever glistened at the back of her own optic nerves.

At the end of their affair he felt only a certain respect for her that she should have gone on so bravely for so long a time when there was so little to sustain her, and a generalized pity. Both pity and respect had worked on him when she called and asked him to bring her to this party tonight. But only so much can be asked of such emotions, and he was glad, now, that she had used him only to bring her to her love.

"If you didn't see me flustering and blushing with my back pointed at him you probably saw the viper with bangs he was with," Eilis said. "She was leaning forward for all to see, and he likes that. He's not mature at all. He's always buying himself new clothes and getting himself new girls, and I suppose that's natural. I'm six years older than he is and should accept the laws of nature."

"Yes," Howard mocked tolerantly.

"Well, *no one* can. Don't tell me they can if they want to or about manners, which don't count though they're nice. I'd literally push her off the roof here if it was the right tactic to get him."

"Obviously . . ."

"Don't lecture me. I know. I know. He wouldn't take it in good part and thereafter would find it hard to be at ease with me. But we *have* used up the daylight out here and I *do* need a drink badly even if it's punch. So why shouldn't I speak up to him when we go in for it?"

Howard nodded. "I'm on your side. Wouldn't it be better . . ."

"Of course," she said with sarcasm. "Of course it would be better to make him hunt me out. I know how his mind works. He wouldn't. I don't expect to accomplish anything except to let him see I know how his mind works."

Howard followed her into the crowd inside (seeming now to grow steadily younger in the artificial light and to be more alien in their youth because of what Eilis had told him) with the definite sense of being wagged. Years ago in college he had cured himself of the habit of collapsing his left shoulder at social events, but he felt it dropping now. He realized there was no way to hold her back except by physical restraint and he still lacked the sufficient excuse for that.

And yet, watching her track her love through the undulant color, the unfused potency, and the familiar unfamiliar gesture of the party, he knew the beginnings of terror like that which some new watcher of the skies knows when he sees a hot missile quarter and home to the drone it has been sent up to kill.

The boy, on the other hand, seemed remarkably unterrified by her approach. He sat with his elbows behind him, resting on the edge of a wide oak table. He did not move his knee from its light contact with the girl's thigh as Eilis stopped in front of him. He merely said, "I thought maybe you'd gone to the Cape this week, Eilis. Eilis, I'd like to present Miss Curtis." He was a handsome boy with high color in his cheeks and eyes exactly the color of a chocolate slab.

The girl with bangs twinkled at Eilis and Howard. "Nancy," she said.

"Nancy," Howard acknowledged her, and then to disengage her from the imminent combat asked, "Didn't you work at that sweater shop on Eighth?"

"Oh, I did. For about a year," she said, flattered that he should remember her. And then to mitigate at least her reception of this

flattery, wobbled her whole sweet body to indicate girlish confusion. "I work uptown now at NBC. I'm sorry I don't remember you."

"You knew I wasn't going until at least August," Eilis said
furiously to the boy. She caught herself a little and turned to
Nancy. "I think it's remarkable that Howard would remember
you. Isn't that remarkable? Bob, don't tell me you couldn't at
least have phoned to see if I had gone."

"I was in the shop with my wife a time or two last Christmas," Howard went on dutifully. His whole left side, exposed
and sensitized to the radiations of fury that Eilis was sending
off, had begun to tingle. "You were wearing your hair in a pony
tail then," he said, not taking his eyes from Nancy's face.

"I *was*," Nancy crowed. "I'm *awfully* sorry I can't remember
your face, but I don't remember faces very well. I'm more a
name person, which I hardly ever forget." Now she had achieved
an expression of honest regret, and Howard settled on the couch
beside her to exploit this for more than it could possibly be
worth. He meant at least to cover the flank loyally for Eilis' vain
aggression on Bob.

He discussed with Nancy the girlish motives involved in the
decision to cut her hair and to move out of the Village to a job
uptown—and all the problems that ensued, like a lot of people
not recognizing her without the pony tail and she had to spend
so much more for clothes now that her better pay was hardly
worth it, all things weighed together. And he believed that she
was doing exactly what he was, as consciously as he giving Eilis
the chance to speak her piece. He approved the cunning justice
of the girl's manners when she led him from the couch to pick
up drinks. They were working together as smoothly as they
might have begun a familiar dance step.

They came back with the drinks to find Eilis compounding
her original blunder. She was saying to Bob in an uncontrolled
voice, "Well, you better."

They heard his almost amused answer: "You can't get blood
out of a turnip."

"The last letter is different. You're no turnip."

"Some other time, Eilis," Bob said, turning to smile at Nancy
and to take from her hand the moist glass she offered him.

Eilis stood taut, with no dignity except that of pathos. Her
face was chalky under the black sleekness of her hair and her

eyes were frank with hatred for all three of them as she smiled. "Excuse us a minute, Howard. Bob and I have a couple of personal things to say yet. We'll be just outside on the roof." She bent to grab Bob's arm.

"Of course," Nancy said. "We'll stay here, Bob."

Then the boy shrugged sulkily and followed Eilis out through the French doors onto the roof.

After a little silent and reflective sadness Nancy said, "That wasn't very pretty was it. I told Bob we should have left the party when you came in. I mean she came in. That is, I knew who she was because Bob had told me about her and when he pointed her out, I thought . . . Bob isn't very considerate. He's like children that don't believe anything hurts anyone else though he can be hurt. I don't blame her for her . . . act. He's treated her very callously and he'll treat me the same way if . . ."

"If?"

"You know, when he's made it." There may have been some brooding of anticipation in her eyes as she said this, but there was no inflection of doubt that he *would* make it. She saw fate and she was still young enough to love it.

She loved what must happen, but Howard did not. He was shaken strangely by her fatalism and sat without a word.

She put a hand on his shoulder and said like a sister, "I didn't mean to imply anything wrong between them. I only know that he saw her a lot last month and with the way he is it's not hard for a woman to think he's interested." Her young eyes begged Howard to put the kindest interpretation on anything that any-one of the four of them might have done. The temptation to be-lieve with her that only a kind interpretation was necessary to save them all beguiled him like drink. He wanted to float with Nancy in this rosy twilight of illusion. Yes, we were all mistaken *before*, but now we have *learned* from our mistakes. We have made it with so many and so many have made it with us, but that's only the *past* her youth whispered to him. And yet, to have accepted her kind insistence was almost like believing that out there on the roof Eilis was listening to reason and growing calm, like believing that there was no real point at which unwary feet could go off the roof.

With a groaning grunt Howard heaved himself to his feet. "I've got to see if they're all right," he told Nancy, averting his eyes in some subtle shame.

"Don't worry about them," she commanded.

"That roof isn't very safe."

"They're both sober."

"It isn't that," he said rigidly, feeling himself unable to listen to the girl's reasonableness, feeling himself moved as compulsively as Eilis was, drawn fatally into the wake of her passion by his dread.

"All right. Go," Nancy said with an unwilling and unmistakable contempt. She had tried to warn him against butting in—as he had tried to warn Eilis a while before.

He found them where he had not quite dared to imagine them. Eilis was standing at the perimeter of the lights at the extreme edge of the unrailed roof, flicking ashes from her cigarette down into the street below. Bob was a foot or two farther from the drop. Between them, like the spark of an arc-lamp between electrodes, was the almost visible snap of their hatred. It seemed to Howard that he could feel it burn him (the pain was in some neural center at the back of his head, as if his hand had been anaesthetized by its intensity) when he panted up to them and took Eilis' arm to pull her back for the second time that evening.

"But I've *tried* everyone else," Eilis howled to Bob, even while Howard was dragging her away. "You're the best."

Bob seemed glad enough to have found help. He said formally to Howard, "I'm sorry we were rude. Didn't mean to be gone so long. I'll think about what you've said, Eilis."

"You rotten," she yelled at his retreating back, squirming to get away, to follow him and strike with her fists. "He is, Howard. He's a worthless, rotten, arrogant punk."

"Sit down a minute," Howard crooned, feeling his legs tic and soften. He tried to laugh it off. "If he's all that, why are us gentry worried about him at all? Can't we sit down calmly even if he is?"

As he was pushing her softly into a deck chair, their host Bernie came hurrying out with a towel slung over his left shoulder. He peered owlishly up and around into the night. To no one in particular he said, "They told me somebody was out here too near the edge and the way things are going tonight I'd get blamed if they fell off and it isn't my place." Manfully he advanced to the precipice and, with one hand on a knee and the other braced at his waist, he leaned to look down. "No one *yet*," he croaked. "The irony of it is if it would be me fell, who's merely trying to see that everyone has a ball for Jesus H. Christ's sake." Then, at less than a trot he went inside, waving the towel like a soiled flag.

As her breath slowed to normal and her pulse slackened under Howard's fingers, Eilis mourned, "I comprehend that he's a stinker, and what I try to do with him isn't what I tried to do to hold onto Nelson." (Nelson was her first husband.) "I didn't have any taste left for Nelson, but the reason I used to threaten him with suicide was to make him do the right thing. Sometimes it's your sense of justice that is hurt. I was just as lonely with Nelson as without him, so it's clear I wasn't trying to keep him. See? I know *all* about myself in spite of what Marian says. I know that justice is as important as bed, even if she has taboos against discussing justice with patients. Anyway, she couldn't tell me it was justice I want from Bob. But then it isn't physical either, you know that? It's just *wanting*. You don't understand that. You don't want anything."

"I want you to suffer less."

She kissed his hand for this, but when she went on it was as if she hadn't heard him. "Who knows why anyone would want a pearl for example? It's shiny and has lots of colors in the gray. So you want it and nothing on earth can help except having it. Why not try for it and threaten as loud as you can? It's the squeaky wheel that gets the grease."

"Did you?"

"Get grease? I, ha ha . . ."

"Threaten to jump?" He knew she had. He knew as well as Bob must have known that there was no other point in their having gone so perilously close to the edge. There was no use putting her through an inquisition, though. That could only demonstrate the misguided futility of her move, and she must have understood that before she made it.

She was a compulsive. She was not like others, but now she was crying as anyone else would have done. "I was so close to going on over," she said. "I could feel there wasn't even an inch—in my mind, I mean—between doing it and not doing it. The only thing was, right then the *arguments* for and against it began to go back and forth so fast I lost track of them. That made me mad."

"I know."

"It made me so mad I nearly did it," she said with a bellow of despair. She writhed like a pig scratching its back on a post. "I'm going home. Don't come with me, please. I'm too tired and I'd be awful company. It's hard work to be a neurotic, whether it looks like it or not."

"I know," he said in contrition. He kissed her cheek, tasting it like a poisoned wafer offered to him in a communion that he had not chosen and still could not choose.

It was three hours later when he took a cab across town with Nancy and Bob. They were all a little bit high now, and they were more candid than old acquaintances could have been. Their vulnerability to Eilis had drawn the blood in which they had scrawled the oath of this quick intimacy. This far her assault had succeeded: she had driven them back past the civilizing paths of childhood to the common earlier recognition by which children are leagued against the black woman who is the other aspect of the mother. They knew this and they drank and chattered together while the party swayed around them. As victims they were forming a society against Eilis, and all their analyses of her performance were tied with the cord of a common need of defense. Only what they had individually learned of manners seemed to shape their differing opinions on "what could be done for her."

"Out there on the roof I made sure of my footing and got ready for a judo hold I know and then I said to her, 'Go ahead and jump,'" Bob said.

"You might have gone with her," Nancy said, shuddering.

"Would you have?" Howard asked. In the taxi he was slumped shoulder to shoulder with Nancy. He felt her shudder and took it personally. With every mechanical jolt of the taxi he felt the plumpness of her upper arm and sometimes felt the refined articulation of her knee bumping his. He didn't blame his new friend Bob for preferring her to Eilis. He would have liked to know a judo hold with which he could have thrown Bob out of the cab so he could have her for himself. It would be nice to have her for himself alone, as a protection against Eilis and her skull.

Nice indeed. But every motion of the taxi seemed like the terminal operations of a machine that had long ago ground out his capacity for any such direct or panicky clutch at salvation.

"Would you have gone with her if it didn't work, your hold?" he demanded.

"The point is, she didn't mean it," Nancy said doggedly. "I know she was bluffing, even if it's cruel to talk about her like this when she's so obviously suffering."

"Of course she's suffering," Bob and Howard said simultaneously. "Of course it's cruel."

"Saying not to talk about her because she's suffering is talking about her too and saying this is talking about her too and repeating it . . ." Howard said. He felt as if the taxi were waggling his jaw, and, by that strange connection between mouth and mind, were waggling his thought toward its mechanical language. "It's making a judgment."

"I didn't mean to," Nancy protested innocently.

To mean and not to mean were both operations of the machine on whose treadmill they were running, he thought. Hatred or love. The back and forth of any dialectic they might be swept into or invent was only the flap flap of the arguments Eilis had heard ricocheting so fast at the roof's edge. Here in the taxi's enclosing body they might find words to temper or extenuate their hatred of Eilis—and the wheels ground on toward her death.

Howard shouted to the driver, "Turn left on Charles Street." In embarrassment he explained to Bob and Nancy, "I want to stop at Eilis' place after all and see how she is." Her living face greeting him at the door would veil over for a while longer the bloodless reality of the suicide that he knew to have been already committed. Or if, by chance, he should find her dead there he would have the refreshment of tears that the machine's tempo would not yet permit.

"Go straight ahead driver," Bob said. "Now really, Howard. We *know* Eilis is all right. You're as tired out by this as the rest of us. Why not go home and sleep it off?"

The driver pulled his cab to the curb to wait for a decision. (He's not waiting for it, Howard thought, by waiting he's making it.) Howard pulled at the door handle to get out. Bob grabbed his wrist.

"If you're trying to make me worry about her, you can't," Bob said bitterly. "There on the roof I called her bluff and that's that. She's not going to do anything. You'd only humiliate her more."

"I'm not trying to make anyone do anything," Howard said. "Let me out of this goddamn cab."

He had thought—or only wished; in his fatigue the fine distinction between the processes was breaking down—that when he put foot on the sidewalk he would be rid of his awareness of the machine. But this was not the way it worked. In the silence on Charles St. the machine simply seemed to be running more quietly again, as if some drying part had been doused with oil. BRRRR. BRRRR. BRRR. There it went racketing again when he rang Eilis' doorbell. Grind, squeak, gibber, like a human thing it went while he waited uselessly for her to answer.

She had left the party three hours ago and he knew that she had come home. Her failure to answer now could not be taken as a sign that she was luckily asleep. Even Bob knew that her performance on the roof was a further humiliation, one more reason to make good the next time she tried. She doted on sleeping pills—which Bob probably knew, too, though he would not have said so in front of Nancy.

Howard trotted around her apartment building to the fire escape. By standing on a garbage can he could jump to the bottom rungs of the fire escape ladder. As long as his muscles were straining to the climb he felt an odd release of happiness, the one respite he had enjoyed during the evening.

But then the chilly pane of her window blocked his way. The sound of his knuckles rapping on it was like the sound of a jack hammer. The reflections of streetlights trembled regularly under his mechanical blows.

No instant came at which he chose to break the window. He had known for a long while that she couldn't hear him before his hand went on through the glass. His searching fingers found the regular latch and then another patented bolt before he could raise the frame. Poor damn fool, he thought, panting with haste now, to be that much afraid of what meant to save her.

The light went on in her bedroom door as he stepped in through the window. Eilis called, "Who is it?" in a serenely sleepy voice. It took her several seconds to recognize him after he had come into the light.

"I took some sleepy pills," she said. "Why are you bleeding? Why are you here?"

"You didn't answer your bell."

"Bell?"

"I suppose I cut my hand on the window."

"You were worried," she stated groggily. "Dear Howard. Good Howard." She moved with zombie grace to kiss him on the mouth. "It's good that somebody loves me in my condition." She kissed him again. "Stay, Howard. It's late. Stay with me. Be a jewel."

"Your pearl," he said, returning the ice-cold kiss of her lips. "How could I leave now?" he asked, intending this as a joke.

Deep under the murk of sedative she was glad to have him with her, and for a while he was consoled to know this truly. But before he fell into a greasy sleep—with her comradely arm thrown over his neck as a drowned swimmer might hold a drowned lifeguard at the ocean's bottom—he thought, Tomorrow, when she sees the other side of it, she'll drag me one step farther. She knows what I still have to find out. I'll have to be one twist braver or more foolish to reach her in time, just as I'd have to be loosened one twist to be quite cowardly or wise enough to get away. He thought of their host Bernie, who said, "The irony of it is if it would be me fell." Then, though he had thus far saved some principles against self-pity, he began to pity himself more than he would ever be able to pity Eilis.

The Waiting
Room

It was a warm and promising rain that fell on the bus between Washington and the Marengo junction. By now it was eroding the last big snowbanks. It ran black in the ditches and among the soppy grasses of the fence rows that bordered the road. Little Mary Adams sat with her face close to the bus window admiring the way the rain worked outside and still savoring the way she could sit intact within the steel shelter of the bus, the shelter of her pleasant clothes, and the impalpable shelter of going back to college with an engagement ring from Joe Perry.

Ahead of her was a ten-minute wait at the Marengo junction, forty-five minutes more on a bus to the depot in Iowa City, six minutes in the taxi, one minute on the walk, two minutes on the stairs, and then she would come into her own room at the dorm. There she could lie warm through the night while she heard this snow-melting rain at work out past her window. She could sleep with the knowledge that the years of anxiety—her own and in some subtle way the anxiety of her parents—were quieting away behind her, like an ambiguous excitement that had simply never let her breathe. She could go to sleep feeling that it was not just Joe Perry she had engaged herself to this weekend, but also had engaged herself to "time to come"; that she was not only going to marry a nice boy who worked in the John Deere office but marry the solid years of the future as well.

Naturally—she knew this in spite of her dreaminess—her anticipated schedule wouldn't work out quite as she hoped now. Naturally she would run into Sarah, or Chris, or Elizabeth in the dormitory hall, or maybe meet someone in the john and she would tell them, naturally. The news would tinkle around the third floor and presently her room would be crowded with friends. She would have to get out her photos of Joe, show the ring around, explain about Joe's job, laugh and spar away some of the comments Elizabeth was sure to make right in front of them all—(Elizabeth's voice throaty and half masculine, "Manly chap, ain't he?" "Mmmmmm." "And those beeeg hands." "Oooo." "Well, I'll bet you're glad you've been a good girl haven't you?" "*Uh huh.*") But after all the gabble there would still come those minutes of falling asleep cuddling the intact assurance which had become clear for her as the bus rumbled on.

"Marengo Junction," the driver called. He half-turned his head to speak, and Mary noticed, as she had not before, that he was an old man, old for a bus driver anyway, she thought, and the style of his mustache was positively ancient, like those pictured in her mother's albums. He had turned on a small light and the windshield wipers flicked behind him like crazy sickles.

She buttoned her coat, took her bag from the overhead rack, and felt the corners of the seat for her purse. At first she could not locate it, and her banished anxiety was suddenly with her again, toppling the structure of her comfort. Her bus ticket and every penny she had were in the purse, though her mother had often warned her not to travel without some kind of reserve fund tucked in her brassiere or in her shoe.

The purse must have slipped to the aisle floor. Someone must have stepped on it there, because her fingers touched mud when she picked it up. She had it open and was checking hastily to see if anything might be broken in it when the bus swung off the pavement and stopped and the driver called again, "Marengo Junction."

"Bad night," he said to her as she stepped down.

"Oh, I think it's nice," she said. "And it's springy."

The old driver grinned. "Sure," he said. "Only eight or nine months to Christmas, too. Naa, this is no spring. The waiting room's right in there, lady."

Out of the lone building that was a combination of a filling station and other things, a man came shielding his head and shoulders under a raincoat. He began a shouted conversation with the driver while Mary trotted in out of the rain.

The waiting room was a dark green place and hardly lighted at all, though one end opened on short stairs to a sandwich bar, brightly lighted enough, and there were neon signs, MEN and WOMEN, at the other end that flickered a red bloom of light over the nearer benches. Some of the waiters' benches were occupied. Some odds and ends of luggage were stacked on one.

Mary chose a seat next to a woman holding a child, looked indifferently at the people around her—who sat with the kind of resignation that suggested they might have become natives, citizens, of the room—and then began flicking the drops of rain from her coat. They were icy to her touch, but as they flew from her fingertips they looked reddish black, and her ring too, when she watched it move with the gesture of her hand, was full of novel red tints.

Someone entered the sandwich bar through an outside door and she heard talk come loud from there, like the voices of a pair of announcers.

"Allo, Ace."

"Allo, Eugene."

"It's a bad night."

"It's snowing over West."

"It'll snow here before morning."

The child twisted beside her in its mother's arms. It muttered demandingly in its sleep. Its foot slipped from where it had lain hidden inside the mother's coat. Mary saw that the foot was covered only with a stocking, and the stocking looked like a small sack bulging full of hazelnuts.

She wanted to reach out and touch the grotesque little foot. It was as though she ought to make some obeisance to it in passing. The feeling was so strong that it nearly overcame her tact, but she knew that she would not reach out. Nevertheless, the impulse of sympathy made her lift her eyes to the mother, and she saw then that the mother's face was incomplete. The woman's eyes met hers out of a bland mask of skin that had no shape for a nose except a bulge with nostril holes and no ridges to define a brow.

"Seems like that darn bus won't never come," the woman whined. She grappled the child higher on her lap, pulling its foot inside her coat again.

"It's nearly time for it now," Mary said. She consulted her watch, shook it, and held it to her ear. "I guess I don't know exactly what time it is, but I'm sure the bus must be due in a minute."

"It should've been here before the Iowa City bus come," the woman said.

"Come? You mean came?" Mary asked. "But it hasn't come yet. It's due about this time."

"It come," the woman said.

"But when?"

"I dunno," the woman said. "We haven't got no watches."

"Before I got here?"

"Oh my yes."

Feeling that her confusion and dismay must be plain on her face, Mary believed that when the woman smiled now it was with malice, and at any rate the smile was horrible for her to watch. The woman's mouth opened to reveal a tiny rim of teeth, each one broad enough but hardly emerging from the gum— like the white tips of fingernails.

"Oh," Mary said, "I just assumed that you were going to Iowa City too, and . . . I didn't know there was another bus. Well, of course I knew there were others that went through the junction, but not . . . I'd better try to find out, hadn't I?" She nodded a confused appeasement and good-bye to the woman and walked rapidly up the steps to the sandwich bar.

"Please," she said to the man behind the counter, "has the Iowa City bus gone yet?"

"One of them has," he said. He was wiping glasses. His sleeves were half rolled up to expose arms slick with a reddish mat of hair. "What's the matter? Miss connections?"

"I don't know. When's the next one?"

"Couple of hours."

"If it don't get held up by the snow." The man sitting at the end of the counter was speaking. "You can't tell this time of year." His voice was extremely loud—too loud for the close range—but unsubstantial in a lardy way.

She sank on one of the stools near the center of the counter and said, "I don't understand. They told me in Ottumwa I'd only have a ten-minute wait." In her cascading disappointment it seemed to her that if she could only state her expectations coherently they would somehow be true in spite of time and the gap of distance widening between the place she sat and the physical bus, now an unknown number of miles to the East. Superstitiously she half-expected to hear the horn of the Eastbound bus sound while she proceeded to explain to the counter man the whole of her transactions at the ticket office and how the bus which brought her had driven briskly and on schedule, she supposed, in spite of the rain.

"No." The man behind the counter had stopped drying glasses to devote himself to the conversation. "You must've gone to sleep or dreamed or something if you thought you was on time. The driver told us there was a semi tipped over on the road by North English that you had to wait forty minutes for them to get it pulled away."

"I couldn't have," she said, appealing to him. "I remember the whole trip. I could not have gone to sleep."

"Kid, none of us can ever go to sleep. None of us can ever dream something. Certainly not. Only we do. How about that, Eugene?"

"That's right, Ace. You must have been asleep, kid, if you thought that bus got here on time."

"Well . . ." she straightened her back stubbornly and lifted her chin. "All right," she said, "only it's this, having to wait here I mean, that seems like a bad dream." She laughed to them in a friendly way, but neither even smiled in return.

"This place is no dream," Ace said. He picked up another glass and rubbed it with the towel.

She tried to explain, believing that perhaps the two men were simply not bright enough to catch the point of her joking comment, but they only watched her and listened noncommittally. Presently she realized that Ace was staring at her hands, and she wished they were gloved.

"If I have to wait," she said, "maybe you've got some magazines or Pocketbooks I could read. Two hours is a long time to wait."

"You're going to live a long time, kid," the man called Eugene said. "Get used to it." He began to laugh very hard.

Ace was shaking his head. "We've got nothing here but some food and a rest room. That's all we got. Maybe you could sleep some more. Like you did on the bus."

"Oh nuts," she said petulantly. She rose from the stool and went to the front door, looking out for a while at the encompassing rain and the blackness. There was traffic on the highways that converged here, still quite a lot. The shapes of headlights, like capricious nebulae, grew substantial out of the rainy distance, seeming without motion at first and gathering speed until they whipped by as comets might pass from dark to dark across the tiny illumined face of the earth. Watching them she had the fancy that it was just such a growing and vanishing light—not even having or needing the structure of the bus to move it or hold it to its course—that had brought her here to this place, and no light could ever carry her weight away.

But then she thought, how silly an idea. She reminded herself that it was mere good sense to settle comfortably for a bit—a couple of hours, that was all.

She turned to the room and the men and ordered a sandwich.

"You're burning it," she said impatiently. Ace had gone to the end of the counter to carry on a whispered conversation with Eugene while the ham for her sandwich fried. She had not heard what they whispered about—and had tried not to listen—but still it had come insistently down to her, especially the points at which Eugene would whisper loudly, "I can't," and then again with a hissing laughter, "I can't." While they were absorbed, the meat Ace had thrown on the griddle sizzled briskly and then began to smoke. The white-and-pink edges curled up from the heat and blackened. Then the pleasant odor of it turned to the smell of burning before she spoke.

Ace looked at her disdainfully. "Got to let it get done," he said. He did not move from where he half lay across the counter with his head close to Eugene's.

"Are you burning it on purpose?" she said. The pitch of her own voice startled her.

He ambled to the griddle, his reddish arms swinging slack by the sides of his apron. The expression on his face, she thought, was a baffling mixture of humility and contempt, and she could not understand what he saw in her that should have bred such feelings. At the same time she felt sure there was something about her, definite as the blue and white pattern of her suit, which he had noted, and which was making him behave this way.

He lifted the meat onto a slice of bread, covered it with another slice that he flipped from the stack beside the stove like a card dealt from a deck, and put it in front of her.

She leaned forward in anger. "What do you want me to do with that?" She half nodded down at the spoiled thing on her plate.

"Do with it?" he asked with the same mixture of abjection and arrogance she had seen in his walk. "Why, eat it."

"I will not," she said. She felt her hands begin trembling and knew she could not bear the onslaught of his hostility much longer without beginning to cry. She drew a little back and opened her purse for money. The sight of the yellow bus ticket still lying in it, not lost but still secure, was almost a surprise and in her state of mind a surprisingly firm reassurance. She put thirty cents on the counter and whirled to go back down the steps into the waiting room.

Behind her she heard Ace saying, "Got to have another penny. We got taxes in Iowa." And she heard Eugene laughing fatly from his corner.

Again she took her seat beside the woman with the crippled child, who seemed now to have sunk into sleep, huddled far over the child in her lap like a motionless and crude representation of grief. As soon as Mary was seated the woman said, "What made you ask if we was going to Iowa City, like you did."

"I wasn't thinking," Mary said. "I suppose I was thinking about the bus I wanted to take. That's all."

"Oh." The woman's head nodded, but after a small silence she insisted, "It's kind of funny you saying that because we have been once to the State's hospital. It was for the boy's foot. The old doctor the County has made us go up there, but they ain't going to do nothing for him. Hospitals ain't any good."

"They're handy sometimes," Mary said. She leaned her face back against the collar of her coat and wished the woman would stop talking to her.

The woman muttered incoherently, the sound like some mem-

ory of anger or disappointment. "I don't think they are at all,"
she said. "Nor them old doctors that won't leave you alone and
won't do a thing for you. It's only Christ and Him crucified that
will help you. My older boy he lost his arm one winter and they
took him and the County put some kind of a rig onto him that
they called an arm, but he couldn't no more use it than I can fly.
And the girls they're all the time bleeding and coughing and
they got them sores they can't get rid of so they can't hardly go
to school any time at all. Then there was my Ma, she had a tu-
mor on her that came out of her side. It was as big as a pumpkin.
Why I remember she couldn't even get a bathrobe on her, just sit
around in a blanket all the time at home, and the doctors didn't
know a thing they could do about it, just to thump her and
squeeze her around and make her cry . . ."

"Please," Mary said.

"And with all that pain it was only Christ and Him crucified
that give her relief."

"Please," Mary said.

"Oh," the woman said. "Maybe you want to go to sleep and I
won't talk to you if you want to sleep. Do you want me to be
quiet?"

"I would like to sleep," Mary said.

She really did manage to sleep, passing through graded stages
of semiconsciousness in the first of which she was still aware of
the glow of the rest room signs, the chuckle of voices from the
sandwich bar, and the sound of breathing from the waiting
people around the room. And when she woke she found herself
circled by all of them.

The woman with the child was still sitting on her left, but the
others stood close around her as though they were watching.
Ace was directly in front of her with fat Eugene beside him,
Eugene's body slanted massively toward her and his shoulders
stretched upward with crutches. Ace was staring at her hands in
her lap, and again she was queerly aware of the nakedness of
her hands.

"Is the bus here?" she asked, as though this simplest of questions might conjure them back away from her.

A sort of humming murmur ran around the circle, but she
heard one voice answer clearly, "Not yet."

"What is it then? What's the matter?" she asked. In her fear it seemed that the circle of people edged closer to her. She saw that a young man on her left had his arm in a white sling. A loose lock of hair fell attractively across his forehead. His mouth was partially open as he stared at her.

There were a man and woman behind Ace whose torsos were hidden from her, but when she saw that the other two on his left both had hooks glittering below their sleeves she thought crazily, I don't dare look down because there won't be enough feet for all of them.

"Why are you watching me?" she said. The circle hummed again and then edged back from her as she got up. She saw the neon sign WOMEN and put up her hands to fight her way to that door, but the circle opened to let her pass through.

Inside she slid the bolt and stood panting. She wanted not to believe the thing that had just happened, but then she realized she could neither believe nor disbelieve because she did not know what it was that had happened.

I can wait here, she thought, until the Iowa City bus honks outside and then run for it. Then with all the people on the bus, they wouldn't dare . . . Dare what? she thought. She did not know.

Possibly it was snowing by now and the bus was delayed. There was a tiny window in the room, but she could not bring herself to open it to check the weather. She listened against its frosted glass. She heard the sound of rain.

Naturally while she waited in there, trembling and gasping, she thought of Joe Perry's being there, of how splendid a dream it might still be if he should defend and rescue her, but quickly after she had thought of him she was glad he could not know the terrible and silly predicament she was in.

She let warm water run into the basin and put her hands in it. This was a trick she had learned to use when she felt faint. As she stood there soaking her hands she looked around the walls of the room, as though she were looking for a ladder to climb out with. A penciled inscription caught her eye. She leaned to read it. It seemed that it might have been put there on purpose to carry a message to her.

The neat script said, *"Ace Power is not a whole man."* Just above it there was a lipstick print of lips.

Mary thrust her hands in the water again. I can't pass out, she thought. The bus might go by while she was fainted and she would have to stay forever. The water refracted the image of her hands so they seemed no longer neat and useful things, but broken and uneven. It occurred to her that she could no longer hear the rain outside.

A craftiness that she had not known she possessed took over her mind. She lifted her hands out of the water, stared at them, put them back in, staring and staring. Her eyes went over the whole interior of the room until she saw what she wanted. There was a nail point protruding from the bottom of the window sill.

They'll let me out with them now, she said to herself, and in the moment of that wisdom jerked her palm across the nail.

"Aaaaah," she moaned, quite loudly enough for them to hear in the waiting room if they were listening. She put her torn hand in the basin of water and the blood boiled delicately up around her fingers. Like the ink a squid shoots out to hide itself, she thought, remembering some grade school lesson in natural history. With a handkerchief she wrapped the hand and went out.

All of them sat where they had been when she first came into the room. Ace Power was behind his counter and no one was paying the least bit of attention to her. She sat down for the third time that evening beside the woman with the crippled child. She left her wrapped hand lying on her lap as a kind of badge for them to see if they wanted to. And presently, when her bus had come in with a merry honking, she took her ticket from her purse and held it in the damaged hand until the driver collected it.

Now, when she got to the dormitory the girls would not ask first about her engagement, but ask, "What happened to you?" There would be no way in this world to explain it to them, but that was all right. It seemed to her that far away in the secret of their future lives they would come to understand it and then remember.

The Winchester Papers

In all humbleness and humility I believe that I have finally dredged to the bottom of the greatest or at least a human interest story devolving around an important literary man of our time.

If you know anything about his life at all—and you probably at least have read about him in Speed Mason's novel *The End of Our Day*—you probably think of F. Payne Winchester as a drunk, an undisputably former talent, but gone to seed and liquor.

Not so. He was on the verge of a real comeback and had found himself through the love of a good woman if he had not met with death at the wrong time. Not everyone knows that, and it is the story I have unearthed. People would see him at parties and what would he be doing? Drinking. But people would not see him in his secret life, at home, sitting hunched over his typewriter, about to finish the greatest novel of his career. No one knows how this girl helped him remake himself from the very depths.

They were life rafts to each other in the cross-currents of Hollywood and he helped her remake herself, too. That is their secret life together and how they saved each other is my story.

Of course, as things turned out, I had to use almost psychoanalytic methods to get it, but then even becoming another personality is not unfamiliar to me if I have to. You may know the books—or have seen the films—that I ghosted for Meredith Custer and Vivian Delmont. Totally dissimilar personalities, one a man and one a woman, but I managed to make myself each of them and to speak in their voice. Each of them was a drunk—like Payne—and though I am a quite moderate drinker myself and seldom have a cocktail before five o'clock, I was able to imagine the depraved and sordid depths in which they wallowed before they were able to find themselves and make a comeback.

Cecile Carmen is not a drunk, but in this case I had to make myself into two personalities—hers and Payne Winchester's—to be able to speak in their voice. How well I succeeded, of course, the public will have to judge. But whatever the verdict of the public, I tell you that this is great stuff: what they should see in each other—she a young, beautiful girl with everything to look forward to—Success—and he a broken down has-been hack overflowed by the times and forgotten by the public that had once adored him . . . how they met at a crazy party one Sunday evening and in a single glance knew they were for each other.

She was the embodiment of all his themes—Romance. Ah ha. That explains him. But he was twenty years older than she and he had such a bad reputation that people were almost afraid to ask him to their parties. He had arrested tuberculosis and a kidney condition and she'd had dates with big people such as Arch Orcup and everything to look forward to. He was like a little boy with his nose pressed to the window of a restaurant where people are eating though outwardly a nasty drunk. What could she possibly see in him?

She hadn't even read his great novels which had once been a household word almost before she got to the age of cognizance. Well, I know now that it was by some undefinable instinct or intuition that she pierced the shell through to him and saw the great, humble human qualities inside him. It was much the same thing as happened in the case of Vivian Delmont when she met Gorth Lee, her present husband and agent, at a cocktail party and he instantaneously perceived the nature of her tragedy and all that had happened to her.

Cecile gave of herself to this nobody who was Payne Winchester for four years and introduced him to Arch Orcup, who was incidentally going to be the central protagonist in Payne's greatest novel. But it was not as if she did not get something in return, for in learning the beauty of sacrifice and of steadfastness she transformed what had been a girl without direction—herself—into a mature and radiant woman who was able to have a mature marriage after Payne's death, raise lovely children, and nevertheless have a career for herself.

By his suffering he made her see what she had been before—selfish, thinking only of self, and it is in recognition of an unpayable debt to his genius that she has finally consented to confide the material for what we're going to call with great simplicity *Payne Winchester*. For years Cecile was toying with the idea of writing this material herself and publishing it under the title of *My Four Years with Payne Winchester*, but that would have been in bad taste, and on this count is where I enter into the picture. Arch Orcup, Jr., at Mogul Pictures found out that Stalk & Bywaters were considering Cecile's manuscript for publication, and because his father had always had a special place in his heart for Payne, Arch called me to do a possible screen treatment if I liked the book.

My instantaneous frank thought on the matter was that it would not be in good taste for Cecile, who is known to many Hollywood people and was a wife and mother for a good many years, to bring out such a book under her own name, and I think that Arch—who is every bit as keen as his father, though not of the same stature, perhaps—at once grasped my thought and suggested that I drop by Stalk & Bywaters to discuss my impression with them and have a look at what Cecile had written.

I had not read twenty pages of the manuscript when I saw that Cecile had missed the real significance of the experience she was attempting to recount. Whatever great benefits Payne Winchester had endowed to this girl he had not made her into a writer.

As you know, it is almost twenty years since Winchester's untimely death and for a part of that time he was in obscurity as well as many people dying who might have once had some importance in his life or got drunk with him at this or that party. Cecile had evidently made two immense mistakes. One, she had worked from a diary. Two, she had originally put her material together the year after Winchester's death with the thought in bad taste of selling it to Arch Orcup, Sr., and had not sufficiently updated her material to satisfy the present interest in Winchester. She used a lot of names that are no longer familiar to the present generation who would hardly remember Arch Orcup if it were not for the presence of Arch Jr.

Stalk agreed at once when I pointed out these flaws that a professional writer would not have committed and at once called Cecile in Hollywood to persuade her that she must talk to me before anything further was done. I was on the plane that night.

Flying out, I had a chance to peruse her document more thoroughly and to review my own recollections of Payne Winchester at more leisure. I remembered that Payne had been the idol of his generation before he embraced alcoholism and the quality of his work no longer found favor with the public and he regarded himself as a mere Hollywood hack trying to pay off the debts he had incurred on himself in the Roaring Twenties. Youth, bobbed hair, kisses, rebellion against parents who do not understand the younger generation—that had been the Payne Winchester whom we had taken into our hearts.

That was the Payne Winchester to whom Cecile Carmen had given her youth that he might recapture the laughing but matured vision he had lost at a thousand cocktail parties. But Cecile—of all people—had written of him as though she did not understand what made him drink, as though what he said in his blackest moods of *de profundis* represented his true view of the novel he was never to complete, and as if he continued to drink as heavily during the period of her aegis as he had before he met her.

She was aiming at two stools when she wrote and consequently failing to satisfy either one. She was evidently very much impressed by and under the cloud of Payne's literary friends who have been bleeding for twenty years about what Hollywood did to Payne without ever having the common decency to think that they might be wrong.

The other error Cecile had made was in trying to sex up her material. Evidently it was her impression that this might make it more saleable, but the opposite is often true and I have always found that with a mature audience you can count on them assuming that when a man and woman get together and there is no third party present the normal things happen. I fought a terrific battle to keep sex out of the Meredith Custer Story, and the public, which was tired of having his proclivities toward the sexual underlined, vindicated me. (I think the upshot has also been that Meredith is a better man since the movie appeared.)

Well, I had no more difficulty than I had anticipated in bringing Arch to see my point of view and in persuading him to make Cecile forthwith an option that would convince her of our seriousness and deep interest.

However, in that short span of no more than twenty-four hours since she had first been sounded, someone had been at her, and when I called her from Arch's office she began cursing Stalk & Bywaters, her agent, Arch, and me. She hung up cursing like a fish-wife and threatening to sue Stalk & Bywaters for breach of contract.

"Wait," I said to Arch. "We will give her time to talk this over with her agent. Stalk & Bywaters haven't signed any contract with her. She has a very poor basis for suit and will call back when she has had a chance to think."

"We'll see how the cookie crumbles," Arch said. "Personally it would be my view that we can do this thing very well without Cecile if she doesn't choose to play ball."

"No," I said quietly. "There's only one right way to manage this property and to do justice to F. Payne Winchester and that is to make full use of undisclosed facts that only Cecile knows, which she has not yet even written about but are probably buried in her subconscious. She is, after all, the same person who turned the tide for Payne and helped him see that he could get back on the track, and I'm convinced that we'll find the selfsame qualities in her today. I need her full cooperation."

He must have thought that I was a raging lunatic to insist upon perfection when it might have been superficially easy to work from the facts of the case which long ago were public knowledge or gossip. But he bore with me and I was vindicated when that evening Cecile called me at my hotel and asked me to come and see her.

Now, mind you, I did not know then what I know now about Cecile and that was the first time I had laid eyes on her, when I went to her apartment, but I will take credit for seeing through the exterior she presented as soon as she opened the door and in a single glance glimpsing the almost leprechaun quality in her that Payne had adored.

She was little more than an average housewife of forty-five as far as the average eye could see, though she had tried to get herself up with a certain overdone sophistication for the occasion.

Cecile introduced me to her husband and two children with an almost apologetic manner. She seemed to sense that they were, so to speak, obtrusive to what I had come for. I took an instant dislike to her husband, as if already adapting myself to the role of alter ego for Payne and he had come back to life and found somebody else married to his girl and the father of her children. He had wanted something better for her than this, and I was here to help her get it if she played her cards right.

Also in bad taste was her daughter Winnie, who very quickly forced the subject of conversation around to Payne before any of the amenities were wholly observed and while her father was still in the living room with us. In view of the extreme way she, so to speak, threw her mother's lover in his face I can sympathize partly with the way he stalked out of the room without even the courtesy of bidding me good night.

Winnie was full of half-baked romantic ideas about Payne, and she ran off at the mouth for twenty minutes about the way his relationship with her mother could be looked at. Finally I shut her up by asking, "What are you doing? Writing?"

She blushed and admitted that, No, she couldn't write but had thought about it a whole lot. She was in retreat and when her mother told her that we had some business to talk over, she left the room without being able to meet my eyes.

Cecile, who it is her nature to be honest and candid, at once wanted to know what kind of a deal I had to propose. And just as honestly I told her I wasn't sure yet until I saw what each of our contributions would be to the property that might emerge from our joint efforts.

She may not have liked this at the time but sensed with her instinct that I would be more than fair when the time came and there was nothing she could do but wait until I saw things more clearly.

And then she asked, without any prompting, the next vital question, which was how we were going to work together on so intangible a project as I appeared to have in mind. Now that was one I hadn't faced yet, but as happens with most of us creative people I trust in playing by ear and everything turns our mill once we have thrown our full creative force toward a goal.

So I answered without a pause that it might be most profitable if she would go around with me to the places where she had been with Payne—not so much for me to see her in those backgrounds as so she would be refreshed to live the past and dig up those fresh, vital memories that were so absent from her manuscript that I had seen.

She answered that she would have to talk this over fully with her husband before she agreed, and I answered with dignity that that was the natural thing for her to do.

For a week and in all good faith we worked like slaves. We drove all over the county to studios and night clubs and to see some of her former friends (who mostly tried to cooperate but did not have the feel of what I was after) and even to look at where the site was of the apartment building where she had lived with Payne, though it has been torn down long ago. I took reams of notes, as I have trained myself to do.

But both of us were sitting in a gloomy down-hearted silence late one evening in a bar not so distant from where Payne had his office when he worked for Arch, Sr., when she said abruptly, "You're not getting what you want, are you?"

Taken aback and startled as I was, I instantly acknowledged the truth of her perception. I told her that she had shown me many things and told me many facts but there was as if a cloud in my mind and I could not see clearly where and how it had all begun between Payne and her. I used the metaphor that it was as if there was one particular, important place that she was deliberately blocking and not taking me to.

"All right," she said. "You're a cunning old bastard. There is a cabin up in the mountains where—where it all began. Where we used to go when we got afraid for each other. I didn't want you or anyone else to ever see it. But I'll take you up there this weekend."

She seemed to have said this rather defiantly, and I said I would only go if she felt sincerely that it would help lubricate the flow of her memories to do so. And she said she was sure it would.

That weekend was the turning point toward Success. Partly it must be admitted that once the money-angle worries had been removed from Cecile's mind she was able to probe deeper without them. And by an unexplainable coincidence of things happening together I had become confident enough of what we had unearthed during that weekend to make her a substantial monetary offer that she could never have got dealing by herself as she tried to do with Stalk & Bywaters, not to mention Arch, Jr.

I have nothing but praise for the way she opened up subsequently and was able to divulge all sorts of intimate, significant details that she had not even suspected that she retained up to her present age. Not all of these details, naturally, proved to be usable in a book that will be intended for wide circulation, but as any writer can tell you, what is published is only one-tenth of the iceberg, the other nine-tenths being submerged but just as necessary to the final product.

She even went so far as to let me use what I am going to refer to in the introduction as the Winchester papers—that is, the letters, notes, bills, and whatnot that threw so much light on Payne's many-faceted personality.

I learned that it had been touch-and-go whether these would come into my hands or go astray and cause untold suffering to many innocent people. It seems that some graduate student from Berkeley had been courting Winnie—obviously for ulterior motives since he was so much older than she and could hardly have been interested in her for herself alone—and the Winchester papers actually belonged to Winnie. That is, Cecile had sentimentally and recklessly put them in a safe deposit box for which only Winnie had the key. This graduate student had been for some time trying to entice Winnie into letting him buy the papers and had even got up a small fund from his school for that purpose, and it was only after Cecile had a serious talk with Winnie that the decision was made to turn the papers over to me instead of to him.

That decision was like a miracle, for all the papers represented the part of the iceberg that should remain perpetually submerged. They were not in the true style or spirit of Payne

Winchester or his joyful view of life, but rather represented the dark forces from which Cecile had done so much to liberate him. I felt that it was carrying farther what she had begun when I took it on my own head to burn those papers rather than return them loose upon the world. All that was meaningful of them I digested and put under water—just as she had converted all that was still any good in him into something youthful in his middle age. He never came back so far but what his light side needed to be protected from his dark side. It was up to us who cared about him to do it for him.

It is best that the spiteful depressed things he wrote about even people like Arch Orcup who had been known to one and all as his friend should be kept from readers unequipped to understand. And furthermore, Cecile is never going to have to worry that anyone will come along with any material that throws doubt on our definite book. However, burning those papers was one of the things that, I believe, she has not yet forgiven me for, though I know enough of human nature to know that she will. We have got, jointly, a highly potential property in *Payne Winchester* and when the benefits begin to accrue in, she will see how right I was.

She had been cooperating so smoothly with me once we got in stride together that I was not aware she harbored any resentment against me at all until she drove me out to the airport to return to New York. When she would not let me kiss her goodbye, I could tell she was not in her sunniest humor and the leprechaun quality was not visible at all. Nevertheless, I played my part and said what I had been meaning to, which was: "I feel that I have got to the bottom of just what you did for Payne, since you have done the same thing for me."

"I guess I have at that," she said with an unwholesome look spoiling her pretty face.

"I am grateful, just as I believe he should have been," I said.

She was so unable to control the upset of her conflict of emotions she said, "I guess it was all lubrication wasn't it, so why should I call it whoring? You sonofabitch. We wiped him out at the cabin, didn't we? So there's no place I have to go back to any more. You know I only did this for Winnie's sake, don't you? I want that perfectly clear."

It would have been unfair and not in good taste to have tried at such a moment to make her see how wrong she was to speak like that to me, so I maintained a dignified silence.

Though I never liked Winnie, and though the girl never put herself out to get along with me as she could have so easily, I am quite willing to concur in this wish of Cecile's, if that is all she wants. Far be it from me to go back on any agreement I have signed my name to, and I will see to it that Winnie gets every penny she is entitled to. My own satisfaction will be of a different kind. I personally feel that hundreds of thousands of American readers are going to learn a lesson of hope from *Payne Winchester,* and I will derive my pride from that fact.

The First Day
of School

Thirteen bubbles floated in the milk. Their pearl transparent hemispheres gleamed like souvenirs of the summer days just past, rich with blue reflections of the sky and of shadowy greens. John Hawkins jabbed the bubble closest to him with his spoon, and it disappeared without a ripple. On the white surface there was no mark of where it had been.

"Stop tooling that oatmeal and eat it," his mother said. She glanced meaningfully at the clock on the varnished cupboard. She nodded a heavy, emphatic affirmation that now the clock was boss. Summer was over, when the gracious oncoming of morning light and the stir of early breezes promised that time was a luxury.

"Audrey's not even down yet," he said.

"Audrey'll be down."

"You think she's taking longer to dress because she wants to look nice today?"

"She likes to look *neat.*"

"What I was thinking," he said slowly, "was that maybe she didn't feel like going today. Didn't feel *exactly* like it."

"Of course she'll go."

"I meant she might not want to go until tomorrow, maybe. Until we see what happens."

"Nothing's going to happen," his mother said.

"I know there isn't. But what if it did?" Again John swirled the tip of his spoon in the milk. It was like writing on a surface that would keep no mark.

"Eat and be quiet. Audrey's coming, so let's stop this here kind of talk."

He heard the tap of heels on the stairs, and his sister came down into the kitchen. She looked fresh and cool in her white dress. Her lids looked heavy. She must have slept all right—and for this John felt both envy and a faint resentment. He had not really slept since midnight. The heavy traffic in town, the long wail of horns as somebody raced in on the U.S. highway holding the horn button down, and the restless murmur, like the sound of a celebration down in the courthouse square, had kept him awake after that. Each time a car had passed their house his breath had gone tight and sluggish. It was better to stay awake and ready, he had told himself, than to be caught asleep.

"Daddy gone?" Audrey asked softly as she took her place across the table from her brother.

"He's been gone an hour," their mother answered. *"You* know what time he has to be at the mine."

"She means, did he go to work today?" John said. His voice had risen impatiently. He met his mother's stout gaze in a staring contest, trying to make her admit by at least some flicker of expression that today was different from any other day. "I thought he might be down at Reverend Specker's," John said. "Cal's father and Vonnie's and some of the others are going to be there to wait and see."

Maybe his mother smiled then. If so, the smile was so faint that he could not be sure. "You know your father isn't much of a hand for waiting," she said. "Eat. It's a quarter past eight."

As he spooned the warm oatmeal into his mouth he heard the rain crow calling again from the trees beyond the railroad embankment. He had heard it since the first light came before dawn, and he had thought, Maybe the bird knows it's going to rain, after all. He hoped it would. *They won't come out in the rain,* he had thought. Not so many of them, at least. He could wear a raincoat. A raincoat might help him feel more protected on the walk to school. It would be a sort of disguise, at least.

But since dawn the sun had lain across the green Kentucky trees and the roofs of town like a clean, hard fire. The sky was as clear as fresh-washed window glass. The rain crow was wrong about the weather. And still, John thought, its lamenting, repeated call must mean something.

His mother and Audrey were talking about the groceries she was to bring when she came home from school at lunch time. A five-pound bag of sugar, a fresh pineapple, a pound of butter. . . .

"Listen!" John said. Downtown the sound of a siren had begun. A volley of automobile horns broke around it as if they meant to drown it out. "*Listen* to them."

"It's only the National Guard, I expect," his mother said calmly. "They came in early this morning before light. And it may be some foolish kids honking at them, the way they would. Audrey, if Henry doesn't have a good-looking roast, why then let it go, and I'll walk out to Weaver's this afternoon and get one there. I wanted to have something a little bit special for our dinner tonight."

So . . . John thought . . . she wasn't asleep last night either. Someone had come stealthily to the house to bring his parents word about the National Guard. That meant they knew about the others who had come into town, too. Maybe all through the night there had been a swift passage of messengers through the neighborhood and a whispering of information that his mother meant to keep from him. Your folks told you, he reflected bitterly, that nothing is better than knowing. Knowing whatever there is in this world to be known. That was why you had to be one of the half dozen kids out of some nine hundred colored of school age who were going today to start classes at Joseph P. Gilmore High instead of Webster. Knowing and learning the truth were worth so much they said—and then left it to the hooting rain crow to tell you that things were worse than everybody had hoped.

Something had gone wrong, bad enough wrong so the National Guard had to be called out.

"It's eight twenty-five," his mother said. "Did you get that snap sewed on right, Audrey?" As her experienced fingers examined the shoulder of Audrey's dress they lingered a moment in an involuntary, sheltering caress. "It's all arranged," she told her children, "how you'll walk down to the Baptist Church and meet the others there. You know there'll be Reverend Chader, Reverend Smith, and Mr. Hall to go with you. It may be that the white ministers will go with you, or they may be waiting at school. We don't know. But now you be sure, don't you go farther than the Baptist Church alone." Carefully she lifted her hand clear of Audrey's shoulder. John thought, Why doesn't she hug her if that's what she wants to do?

He pushed away from the table and went out on the front porch. The dazzling sunlight lay shadowless on the street that swept down toward the Baptist Church at the edge of the colored section. The street seemed awfully long this morning, the way it had looked when he was little. A chicken was clucking contentedly behind their neighbor's house, feeling the warmth, settling itself into the sun-warmed dust. Lucky chicken.

He blinked at the sun's glare on the concrete steps leading down from the porch. He remembered something else from the time he was little. Once he had kicked Audrey's doll buggy down these same steps. He had done it out of meanness—for some silly reason he had been mad at her. But as soon as the buggy had started to bump down, he had understood how terrible it was not to be able to run after it and stop it. It had gathered speed at each step and when it hit the sidewalk it had spilled over. Audrey's doll had smashed into sharp little pieces on the sidewalk below. His mother had come out of the house to find him crying harder than Audrey. "Now you know that when something gets out of your hands it is in the Devil's hands," his mother had explained to him. Did she expect him to forget—now—that that was always the way things went to smash when they got out of hand? Again he heard the siren and the hooting, mocking horns from the center of town. Didn't his mother think *they* could get out of hand?

He closed his eyes and seemed to see something like a doll buggy bump down long steps like those at Joseph P. Gilmore

High, and it seemed to him that it was not a doll that was riding down to be smashed.

He made up his mind then. He would go today, because he had said he would. Therefore he had to. But he wouldn't go unless Audrey stayed home. That was going to be his condition. His bargaining looked perfect. He would trade them one for one.

His mother and Audrey came together onto the porch. His mother said, "My stars, I forgot to give you the money for the groceries." She let the screen door bang as she went swiftly back into the house.

As soon as they were alone, he took Audrey's bare arm in his hand and pinched hard. "You gotta stay home," he whispered. "Don't you know there's thousands of people down there? Didn't you hear them coming in all night long? You slept, didn't you? All right. You can hear them now. Tell her you're sick. She won't expect you to go if you're sick. I'll knock you down, I'll smash you if you don't tell her that." He bared his teeth and twisted his nails into the skin of her arm. "Hear them horns," he hissed.

He forced her halfway to her knees with the strength of his fear and rage. They swayed there, locked for a minute. Her knee dropped to the porch floor. She lowered her eyes. He thought he had won.

But she was saying something and in spite of himself he listened to her almost whispered refusal. "Don't you know anything? Don't you know it's harder for them than us? Don't you know Daddy didn't go to the mine this morning? They laid him off on account of us. They told him not to come if we went to school."

Uncertainly he relaxed his grip. "How do you know all that?"

"I listen," she said. Her eyes lit with a sudden spark that seemed to come from their absolute brown depths. "But I don't let on all I know the way you do. I'm not a . . ." Her last word sunk so low that he could not exactly hear it. But if his ear missed it, his understanding caught it. He knew she had said "coward."

He let her get up then. She was standing beside him, serene and prim when their mother came out on the porch again.

"Here, child," their mother said to Audrey, counting the dollar bills into her hand. "There's six, and I guess it will be all right if you have some left if you and Brother get yourselves a cone to lick on the way home."

John was not looking at his sister then. He was already turning to face the shadowless street, but he heard the unmistakable poised amusement of her voice when she said, "Ma, don't you know we're a little too old for that?"

"Yes, you are," their mother said. "Seems I had forgotten that."

They were too old to take each other's hand, too, as they went down the steps of their home and into the street. As they turned to the right, facing the sun, they heard the chattering of a tank's tread on the pavement by the school. A voice too distant to be understood bawled a military command. There were horns again and a crescendo of boos.

Behind them they heard their mother call something. It was lost in the general racket.

"What?" John called back to her. "What?"

She had followed them out as far as the sidewalk, but not past the gate. As they hesitated to listen, she put her hands to either side of her mouth and called to them the words she had so often used when she let them go away from home.

"Behave yourselves," she said.

The Romanticizing of Dr. Fless

After his first year in college my friend Dick Samson came back to Chesterfield for the summer determined to be a writer. This was not a total surprise to me, his family, or the other few people he told about it. Dick had written the senior class prophecy in high school and the most sarcastic comments in the humor section of the high school annual. But, until that summer I had half believed he meant to be a big-time thief and was just using his attendance at college to establish a front.

He had once dragged me into plotting the robbery of the Chesterfield post office, and from a year ago I remembered sitting with him half the night in a ditch by Casey Meardon's house while he told me how we were going to steal Casey's Pontiac, how we'd take it to Kansas City where there were plenty of fences eager to handle it, and how we'd have a few royally debauched days and nights there before we drifted back to Chesterfield with perfect alibis. He said the only thing that prevented our snatching the car that night was my ignorance of how to work the ignition without a key—and he said with a note of injury that I should have known, since I worked part time in the Standard filling station. He convinced me that it was possible to start the Pontiac without a key, and he wouldn't let me say that anything counted in such matters except possibility. I suppose I should have known from this and from the lush detail of the alibis he worked out for us that he would end as a writer.

Well, in that year at college he had plunged through his English class into a creative writing club, like a diver going through a paper-covered hoop into the tank, and when he hung around the Standard station that summer, it was to talk to me about the career he was beginning. He was dead serious about the economic side of it as well as about the imaginative. His folks were after him to get a job that summer—"at least take some of your poems up to show Ed Taylor at the *Excelsior*," his father had said to him. "Maybe Ed will give you some work in your own line." But Dick had held out against this so he could have his mornings to work at home. He told his father that this would pay off in the long run.

But he wasn't quite so sure of himself as he made out to his father. One afternoon when he'd come back from the post office with a story rejected by *Esquire*, he stopped by the station to warn me that if he couldn't "make a living by his pen" in a couple of years he "would do worse than Hart Crane did."

I was checking an inner tube for leaks at the time, turning it in a tub of water, but his threat stopped me. "What did Crane do?"

"Jumped off a ship," Dick said. He slapped the water in the tub so that it splattered both of us. "Why the hell not? Nobody'd buy his stuff. 'Blue latitudes and levels of your eyes.' Isn't that wonderful? Only what the hell good does it do you to write that well if nobody wants it? You may write the best poetry in the world, but the damned pigs force you to write prose to make a living.

"It's the machine," he said cryptically. He told me about the fellow in his writing club who was conceded by all of them, including the professor who headed it, to be the best of the lot. This fellow, too, seemed destined to leap off the back of a ship with a huge splash. He had written, Dick said, "I would fling

my brain into the machine to stop it if that would do any good."
Free verse.

"But it wouldn't," Dick said. "The machine has got us all.
Look at you. Grunting and sweating on a piece of rubber tee-
oob"—he'd got that pronunciation from college, too—"for no
human purpose. Merely so you can satisfy a mechanical nuisance that's gradually depriving man of the use of his legs."

Now, of course, I had a pretty good deal in my job at the station. It was in the residential district of our little town, shaded,
almost lost under the dense elms and maples. On weekdays
hardly anyone did business there except a few farmers who lived
out the Lineville road, those who'd dash in quickly to fill their
tanks at the nearest station so they could get back to the fields.
Aside from pumping two or three hundred gallons of gas, sweeping out the station, hosing off the concrete apron in front, and
maybe patching a few tires, I was free to spend most of the day
lolling in the hammock my boss had rigged beside the station.

I could have pointed out to Dick that he enjoyed certain advantages from my situation, too. The station, as I ran it, was a
fairly clubby place for him to hang around. Since he despised
swimming and softball, wasn't working at a job, was generally
sore at his family, and since "no good writer works on his stuff
more than two hours a day," as he said, he needed the station
and me.

For amusement, he and I sometimes put strings on coins and
milked the peanut and candy vending machines in the station.
They were fairer game, you see, than the cash register, being the
property of an out-of-town salesman who filled them twice a
week. Quite a few friends would drop by to talk a while and
more girls went past the station than passed Dick's house.

Further, the station gave him a place to sit and watch characters he could use in his writing of fiction. What this mostly
amounted to was that he'd loll there in the hammock or between
the roots of a big elm and make up the most horrible libels about
Chesterfield people as they went by.

If the Methodist minister came up that street Dick was apt to
say he knew where he'd been, though really he had no idea at
all. "He's been visiting Maude Slater," Dick would say. "Do you
get the picture? Her husband is lying there paralyzed and can't

lift a finger to stop them while they carry on their rituals in front of his eyes."

"He'd tell on them."

"No he wouldn't," Dick silenced me. "He'd be ashamed. How do you like this for a final scene—they cut Slater's throat—they can't stand his eyes following them—and both dip their hands in his blood. Like that?"

When Stan Bailey, the town's softball star, drove along in his pickup truck, Dick would imagine what was happening between Stan and his girl, Doraline Everest. "Did you hear that screaming over in the east end of town last night? More of a keening, you might call it. Well, Stan has got Doraline with child and she's run mad. He'll desert her. Probably go to California. She could hang herself in a clothes closet."

After he'd worked out on the passers-by his stories would lead naturally into retelling some story or other that he'd recently read in *Esquire*. Usually it was one involving mutilation. He was trying, professionally, to harmonize Chesterfield with the *Esquire* market because, he said, as far as prose writing was concerned he couldn't imagine aiming beyond. He said that when he sold them something he'd quit. Then he'd be in the league with Hemingway and Fitzgerald and there was nowhere to go beyond that.

Dick and I had our one big argument of the summer—almost a fight—because he made up things about a girl I was feeling tender toward. Marilyn Frank played piano for the Christian Church choir that summer, and nearly every afternoon for a couple of weeks she'd go up the other side of the street, in front of Dr. Fless's house, on her way to practice for a program the church had planned for an August Sunday. She pretended not to notice us over at the station, but I could see from the way her arms stopped swinging as she came abreast of us, and by the way her hands bent stiffly back from the wrist, that she was aware of certain emotional signals I was beaming at her.

"I figure Marilyn for a guilty attachment to her father," Dick said.

"She and her father get along fine," I said angrily.

"Yeah. Sure." His eyes narrowed like a DA's and he picked at his teeth with a broom straw, spat. "The problem is how did they trick her mother? Maybe they pretended to go on a picnic out at the lake—see?—and then Marilyn says she doesn't feel very well. Maybe she *didn't* feel very well that day, because human character can't be all black and white. OK, her father says, he'll take her home. They leave the old lady out there by the lake munching sandwiches. Look at the irony. The story ends with the old lady munching away at a tuna sandwich, stupidly watching the sundown, without the faintest suspicion of what is going on. The last sentence could be, 'the tuna tasted good to her, she had bought a good brand.' That's the way Stephen Crane would end it. Ironically."

"It's too far-fetched," I said uneasily. "Who'd believe a story like that?"

I guess I'd trapped him into aggression there, so that to defend his fiction he had to insist that he could believe it as an actual fact in the Frank family. "Can you prove that it didn't happen just the way I told it?"

"Don't have to," I said. "We've got to draw the line somewhere so why don't you lay off that kind of imagining?"

"Innocent," he said contemptuously. "What do you know about psychology? Have you ever read Krafft-Ebing?"

As a matter of fact I had got an A in high school psychology—from which I had learned that it is impossible to identify a man's profession or social class from his photograph, that you'd rather have a Kallikak for a pal than a Jukes, and that dogs can be made to salivate on an audible signal—but Coach Davis, who taught the class, had never mentioned the great German.

"It isn't a question of psychology," I said. "I'm asking you to be decent or stay away from this station."

A stricken look spread over Dick's face. He gasped a couple of times, then stared at the concrete apron under his feet, nodding. It scared and impressed me to see what I'd done. Pretty quickly I felt I'd gone too far, and yet I didn't want to make a straight retreat.

So I said, "It's all right to think about such things theoretically, but not when it has to do with real people."

Without answering this he went to pick up his polo shirt from the hammock and walked ponderously toward home.

Only, at the edge of the concrete apron he stopped to fling back the epithet which, I suspect, has been used only once, to this date, in Chesterfield. "Caliban," he called me. It didn't sound vindictive except for the intonation he gave it.

Of course he came back a few days later—having nowhere else in Chesterfield that he particularly wanted to go—and of course he went on with his literary amusements and bawdy fictions about the innocents who went past.

Dr. Fless and his daughter, who lived directly across the street from the station, were at the same time the most inviting and most frustrating of his targets. They invited speculation of a morbid kind, while I don't think that most of the other people in Chesterfield did.

The Fless house, for example, had all the conventional properties of the haunted house in spite of being situated on such a humdrum block. It was a gaunt, square, three-story clapboard house, unpainted for so long that it had the silvery gray color of old barns you might find in the countryside around town, yawing down rottenly in abandonment. Green window shades were always drawn in the windows on the street side. Particularly on the upper story, where a row of close-set windows indicated some kind of a sun room, the drawn blinds suggested a purposeful and persistent secrecy.

A thick stand of fir trees hedged the Fless lawn—foreign colors, shapes, and duskiness in that block of familiar elms and maples. As each summer advanced the blue grass would grow unmowed, and by the end of July would have gone over into a greasy, shimmering surface that hid the pathways of Miss Fless's cats as thoroughly as the window blinds hid the secret ways of these two old people.

It is not quite true that everyone in a small town knows everything about everyone else. About all I really knew of the Flesses was that the doctor had a long time ago given up calling on patients, and now only a very few of them ever came to see him for professional services—mostly farm families, I think, from far out of town, those in whose family history the name of Dr. Fless was associated with some remote exploit of healing or of inspirational conduct when death came in spite of his efforts.

He was then nearly eighty and as far as I knew he never passed the doors of his house. It was very rarely that his daughter went farther than the front porch, where each morning she fed the cats that came swarming up silently from their grass-hidden pathways in the yard.

Miss Fless was a terribly ugly and terribly dirty woman. She would come out of the front door into those calm, sunny mornings as if already stooping to pour milk into the cats' bowls, as if before she would open the door she had composed the single posture in which she wanted to be seen. Scurrying to the end of the porch to meet the scurry and climb of the cats that had been waiting, she would pour the milk, then throw over her shoulder the shamed, defiant, white-eyed look of a zoo animal which doesn't quite trust the bars to keep off the human danger it smells.

It got to seem that this daily brief turning of the face was a turning toward me, since it wasn't often that anyone else was close enough to fall within the orbit of her fear. This made me uncomfortable and resentful. I was rather reassured by the frightful stories that Dick made up about these people.

He knew even less than I about them, I think. Once he and I and Waldo Herman had broken into the doctor's garage—we were looking for dope, on the inspiration of Dick's drive to adventure and his conviction that doctors frequently left morphine lying around in their cars—and all we saw before the barking of the neighbor's dog scared us away was a 1925 Ford touring car in factory-new condition. The paper wrappings above the running board had never even been taken off. But you couldn't make much of that, Dick thought.

I had been inside the Fless house once, or more exactly, down a short corridor to the doctor's office. When I went out for the freshman basketball team I had to get a doctor's certificate of fitness, and out of some devious adolescent uncertainty had been afraid to go to the doctor whom my family would have called if I were sick.

Old Fless will go easy on me, I had reasoned—if it is possible to speak of reason in connection with such a foolish shyness as I had felt then. And he had. There had been a minimum of frail tapping at my chest, a bit of listening with the stethoscope while the doctor's labored breathing had been the loudest sound in the office, and then a single question—"Do you smoke cigarettes?"

I had come out of the examination, up the narrow corridor to the front door and the wholesome street, with a tingle of silly triumph, as though in getting Fless's signature vouching that I was sound for basketball I had outwitted some hostile authority. It was as though the old, old man might be another kid who had helped me put something over on the grownups.

Dick had never been in the house and he was badly dissatisfied with what I could tell him about either the interior or the Flesses.

What did the office look like? I could only remember the qualities of choked light coming in through the venetian blind and the common iodoform smell of a doctor's office faintly tinged with another smell like cinnamon. I had no language for describing these sensations and no way of knowing that they were significant enough for mention anyhow.

What was Dr. Fless himself like? Was there anything suspicious about him? I had kept only an impression of the paper whiteness of his hands and of his wheezing as he moused around the office.

Miss Fless? Well, she had answered my phone call asking for an appointment, then met me at the front door, hiding her toothless mouth with her hand when she spoke, and pointed the way back to her father's office. Her words were on the order of, "The doctor is expecting you."

In fact, the two of them had seemed to me as dull as stones before Dick had set his imagination to work on them and had suggested there might be profit in dreaming up or discovering some dirt about them.

"They've got a secret," Dick would insist often, "a ready-made story." He suggested that we break into their house some night to look it over at least and see what we could find of use. "There must be old letters lying around," he said. "If I could get some old letters or diaries or albums I could get to work on them."

That seemed overdesperate, so I said, "Why don't you go knock on her door and see if she'll talk to you or let you see the old man? Tell her you're a writer."

I put this last in as a kind of dig to quiet him down. It wasn't fair, because I knew he was not the kind of writer who merely goes and asks people to tell him facts. But it seemed a useful sort of dig, and I brought it out several times after that to slow him down when his fantasies about the Flesses were running too free for even my taste.

One afternoon when he was comparing her to Miss Emily Grierson in a story of Faulkner's and saying that Miss Fless looked like "something long submerged" and that her eyes "were like pieces of coal in a lump of dough," I dared him again to cross the street and talk to her.

He took a deep breath and marched straight over there. I saw
Miss Fless answer the door. The two of them talked briefly, both
looked across to where I was pretending not to watch. Then they
went inside.

It was almost two hours before Dick came back and when he
came there seemed to be something strangely sick about him. I
didn't ever remember seeing him so muted or thoughtful.

"What did you find out?"

He sat in the hammock and began to gather pebbles from
around his feet. At last he said somberly, "She's a writer, too."

"Is that all you found out? Didn't she have her lover's skeleton
in her bed or anything like that for you to use?"

He ignored me. "She *sells* stories all the time to *Range War*
and *Holster Western*. She writes under the name of Tom McCoy
and has a New York agent and all that stuff. They write her
fan letters—I've been reading them. They ask this Tom McCoy
where he ever learned so much about what people were really
like. She's got a letter from the president of a railroad division
telling her what a great writer she is. God almighty." He threw
his handful of pebbles out across the apron. "It's disgusting
that someone who writes that kind of chuff can make a go of it
while people who try to tell about things as they are just can't
communicate."

He brooded some more. "She offered to put me in touch with
her agent or sign me up with the correspondence course where
she learned to write this."

"Are you going to?"

Briefly he came out of the daze to make his contempt emphatic. "Are you crazy? I'd *sooner* jump into the ocean than soil
my mind that way. I'm going to write about *her*. I'll find out
something yet."

"Anyway, you tried."

"It was the wrong approach," he said. "I let you talk me into
it against my better judgment. She paints, too." He was back in
his daze again. "We went in their parlor and the whole room is
full of this kind of painting you see them do in dime-store windows. It's sitting all over the furniture, against the walls, and on
the mantelpiece. Hundreds of them. Moonlight scenes and wa-
terfalls and Indian canoes. She doesn't even sell those. They're
her best hobby, she said, and she said they were probably a

nicer hobby for a person than writing. She said why didn't I try them? *Hobby!*" He was almost crying. "It's only a damned hobby for her and she sells her stories as often as she wants to turn them out."

I hated so much to see him suffering this way that I suggested a way in which he could use the dope angle on them. "Plenty of doctors *do* have the habit," I said. "Maybe all these years he's kept her in bondage by giving her opium. You could have a terrific climax where she finally kills him and staggers out of the house to freedom. Too late though. She's old and not beautiful any more. She would get about as far as the sidewalk there and crumple up, because she would see that even killing him was useless. Do you like that?" It was rather surprising to me that I had come out with all that and a little bit disturbing, because I didn't have Dick's professional license to keep the curse of lying off of it.

"That's crud," he said petulantly. "I'm going to write nothing but poetry from now on. What's the use of trying to compete when it's so clear that readers are morons? A railroad division president. . . . They like the kind of stuff she grinds out. Believe me, no one would ever like what I have to throw in their stupid faces."

To some extent he carried me along in his depression. It did seem unfair that someone like Miss Fless could succeed so easily while a bright person like Dick had to face so many setbacks. On the other hand, the discovery that Miss Fless was an author added an exciting new dimension to her, and for that matter, to the town. It seemed to me very good to know that Chesterfield had an author. I made up my mind to look for the name McCoy the next time I saw *Range War* and *Holster Western* on sale.

The house across the street looked different to me after that. It still looked haunted, but with more lively ghosts, ones that would not quite keep the easy formlessness of white foggy shapes. It was still only by an act of imagination that I could know the Flesses, but I could at least imagine Miss Fless in other postures than that of feeding her cats.

It was on a blazing hot August morning, quite early, that Miss Fless called me over. I saw her standing in the shadow of the porch, stooped a little, and hanging on the door frame as though she were afraid to let go of it and come farther. When she saw that I was looking at her she beckoned me with a wide clutching swing of her arm.

Then she shouted—or screeched, or keened, the sound was indescribable—"Come boy."

All the shocking possibilities that we had invented flashed into my mind. I thought, She's done it. I shook my head.

She started down the steps and toward the sidewalk, but instead of crumpling up she appeared to be dazed by the sun striking her white head. She stopped with a bewildered flutter of her arms. Once more she uttered a half-articulate squawk.

As I went over and approached her warily, she said, "I need you to help me. I don't know what to do."

"I could help," I said, "except that I can't leave the station."

"Come in and see if he's dead," she said from behind the fingers with which she covered her mouth. "I think the Doctor has died." Then she added absently, plaintively, "I expect Aunt Myra will blame me, too."

I started again to refuse on grounds that my work at the station didn't permit me to leave, but she had got hold of my bare arm and was drawing me with her toward the house. Her cold, moist touch was like an authoritative but puzzling message, some unarguable guarantee of her right to lead me with her to the first-floor bedroom where Dr. Fless slept. Just inside his door we paused like two children trying to be stealthy enough to avoid wakening their own fear.

Dr. Fless lay covered to the chin with sheets and an old-fashioned comforter that was completely unruffled by any movements made in sleep. He was so neatly and precisely laid out that he almost looked packaged. His pure white head was thrown back a little against the white pillow as though the one strength which had remained to him was in the muscles of his neck. His lips were open.

"Go feel him," Miss Fless whispered.

"No."

"Go on."

"No thanks."

"It's all right," she said. "I did. He felt cold to me."

Even so I wouldn't approach the bed. I made up my mind to plead faintness if she kept on insisting. "Hadn't we better call a doctor?" I asked.

"Oh," she said with a sigh that mingled disappointment and relief. She nodded and like children abdicating their game in favor of adult business we crept out of the room and silently closed the door behind us.

I called Dr. Buhie for her, and in spite of my rather frantic statement he didn't seem greatly concerned that Dr. Fless was probably dead. "You tell Miss Fless I'll be right down. Maybe you'd better call some of the neighbor women in to stay with her."

"But we don't know if he's dead," I protested. "You'd better hurry."

"That's right," Dr. Buhie admitted. "I'll tell you, I'll be down in a few minutes. He didn't appear to be suffering, did he?"

As soon as she knew Dr. Buhie was coming, old Miss Fless shed her signs of panic and seemed, for the time at least, to accept what had happened with some degree of tranquillity. She asked me to sit with her in the parlor to wait, and when I was seated, remarked on how hot the last few days had been. "But the Doctor liked hot weather better than cold. He dreaded another winter coming."

While I muttered back my own feelings about seasons I looked here and there at the dozens of small paintings hung, leaned, or stacked wherever there was room for one. Their tone was uniformly blue and whether they varied in detail—with Indians and their canoes in some and stiff-looking deer in others—a full moon and its stylized glitter on water appeared in all of them as far as I could tell, like a patiently stubborn insistence that things did not change. The front door beside us was open and some of the unstable currents of warm outside air came and played in the mustiness of the room, and it occurred to me that it was the doctor's death which permitted this carelessness about a door that was usually closed as snugly as an icebox door.

Miss Fless noted that I was looking at the paintings and said, "The Doctor favored the ones with Indians. He was always interested in Indian lore."

Partly for Dick Samson's sake, I ventured a single question, "Was he ever out among the Indians?"

"Oh no," she said, chuckling a little at the sheer absurdity of my question. "Why, he used to tell me it was too bad that even when he was a boy the Indians were all on reservations. He was just *interested*."

With Dr. Buhie's arrival some of her anxieties reappeared

and her first question to him was, "His sister can't blame me, can she?"

"Of course not," Dr. Buhie said. "It was time for him to go, Dora. Nobody can blame you."

It seemed to me quite wrong that he should say this before he even looked at the body, but I had to admit that in my glance at it I had seen nothing except the most natural appearance of frailty drawn to a fine edge and then abandoned.

It must have been the very absence of a shocking, anchoring point of detail in his death that began to make me uneasy. Death, which I supposed ought to lie on the far side of such warning signs as violence, shrieks, convulsions, or at least the anguish and surprise of the survivors—decently segregated from life— seemed that morning to have revealed itself like an undetectable taint in the air.

I felt my uneasiness about it come on for the rest of the morning while I worked alone at the station. I felt I couldn't trust even the things I saw, and my general state was like being hungry. Something in my mind was growling to be fed the way my stomach growled when a mealtime approached.

Against the evidence of my honest recollection, I tried pretending that Dr. Fless's lips had been open in a smile—that they had been making some kind of a sign to whom it might concern. To me. It wouldn't have mattered a whisker whether that sign was devilish or heavenly. What did count, in all the empty heat and dazzle of that August morning, was that the sign hadn't been there. He hadn't smiled. His mouth had been open. There was nothing else to say about it.

I swept the concrete apron good and hard, washed all the station windows, and looked around for other things to keep me busy. Finally I gave in to my need to talk things over and called Dick's house. His mother said that he'd gone to the post office to wait for the morning mail. "Some magazine has kept his poems a long time and he thinks maybe they've taken them," she explained. Then, on a more troubled note, she ended by saying, "I wish you'd come over some afternoon and chat with me about Dick. I'm afraid I don't understand him very well and maybe you can help."

I agreed that I would come soon. Because Dr. Fless was dead I

wanted to do anything I could to help anyone at all. I was in a
real mood of contriteness, and scared, too. I lay in the hammock
beside the station thinking that a few years ago, when I was
little, I'd been afraid of the dark and those toothy, slimy mon-
sters that hung around in it, but I hadn't ever expected to be
afraid of the light the way I was then. Up over my head the elm
branches flicked back and forth to give me glimpses of the emptiness of the sky and I figured that it would be good to live in a
jungle so thick you couldn't see out at all.

Pretty soon I saw Dick walking savagely down in my direction from the post office. I went part way up the block to meet
him. I pointed out Dr. Buhie's car still parked in front of the
Fless house and started to tell him what had happened from the
time I saw Miss Fless beckoning.

"Who gives a damn?" he said. "It's too bad he's dead, but he
was awfully old. So what?"

Lamely I said, "Well, I thought maybe I'd seen or heard something you could use. For instance, she told me the Doctor had
been living with the Indians when he was young."

"Use?" Dick said. "You mean *write*?" He laughed hollowly and
pulled a manila envelope from his back pocket. "I'm through,"
he said. "You know what these are? Poems. Everything I've
done this summer. They just came back from *Poetry*. Well. . . ."
He ripped the envelope and its contents into several pieces,
which he put back carefully in the pocket from which he had
taken them. "I'm through with all that. I may become a physicist
or a spy or a fight promoter. I'm not even going to think about
what I'll be until I get back to school. You know, the writer
hasn't got the chance of a yellow dog in an age like this. Let me
tell you what my own family did to me. They've got a reunion
coming up this month at Grandpa Fletcher's in Ottumwa. *So,*
my mother and Aunt Beth get the insane idea that it would be
cute for me to read the whole family some of my poems. Got
the picture? I read right after my cousin plays a trombone solo
and right before little cousin Nancy gives a humorous reading
about Uncle Bill and the Phonee-graph. They used *my* typewriter to write up the programs for the reunion, and they've already sent them to the rest of the family. I won't even go to their
damn reunion now."

He wouldn't stop with me at the station. He was on his way

home for a showdown with his mother. Probably he had saved the fragments of his poems so he could tear them up again in front of her.

I was too young then to realize that his renunciation was temporary, and I felt that it was too bad in more ways than one. Now I supposed the story he meant to write about the Flesses would never be written. We would never know even what *could* have gone on all those years in the closed-up house. All of it was lost.

I sat inside the station watching Dr. Buhie come down the steps and get in his car. After he had gone there was nothing more alive in the street than the wobbling pattern of shade.

Tearing the July sheet from the station calendar, I turned it over and began writing on the back:

FALL OF THE HOUSE OF FLESS
Among the gloomy pines that served as a windbreak, the unpainted and ghastly house . . .

That might have been all right, I thought, if someone else had written it. But it seemed awfully flat as I looked at it and compared it to what I had really felt when I was inside the house.

I tried again farther down the page:

Dr. Fless Carruthers lifted his eyes suspiciously as the new chief Yellow Dagger came into the tepee . . .

That was about as far as I pushed it. I couldn't convince myself of what ought to come next. I would stare at the paper and see nothing but a suggestion of the printing on the other side that numbered all the days of July in neat, uninteresting squares.

I wished Dick would come back to spin a horrid, exciting story about the Flesses. However fantastic his explanations were, they were a lot better than nothing.

The Martyr

Not many years after Professor Alleman began his teaching
career, he had a pretty and rambunctious nun as a student. She
told him nothing was worth aiming for except sainthood. When
he first heard this opinion, he scoffed gravely, arguing that this
might be her personal truth but that it had little merit as a cate-
gorical imperative. When she remained insistent, he understood
what she wanted from him but discreetly avoided the occasions
when it might have happened. She never made the move from
which he refrained but grew spiteful, distempered, and presently left the Church. Was he to blame?

After she was married and had gone to live in New Jersey, she
sent him annual postcards. These were subtly chosen to mock
him for what he had missed or to accuse him for what he had
defiled. At least, as he studied them one after the other, a year

apart, he believed he was deciphering a code of cruelly seductive and everlasting malice toward himself. She never signed her
name to these cards. She never had to. As soon as he got the
first one and knew what state it had come from he had a powerful intuition of what it was intended to say—and that he could
never expect to be let off. His continuing analysis of the religious
iconography that made the series of cards coherent confirmed
the theme she meant to drive home. The saints always appeared
in their hours of martyrdom, never in glory.

Perhaps Alleman's wife knew what to make of these cards
better than he. "Another missive from the woman scorned," she
would say as the years went on and the cards kept arriving with
no written message or signature. Usually they came with the ad-
vent of spring, in March or April. "You certainly left an indelible
imprint," his wife said. She noted the representations of writhing
saints with little snorts of approval.

In his mid-forties Alleman was having an affair with a student
named Lois. Lying in bed with her in her off-campus apartment
he told her all he remembered and all he thought about the nun
and her postcards. To his surprise, he burst into tears of remorse
during his recital, though he had begun jokingly with all the sardonic irony the situation deserved.

"I'll make it up to you," Lois promised. She hugged his quivering shoulders and rubbed against him until he began to smile.
"You never know what is the right thing to do until it's too late,"
she comforted.

"I still don't know what would have been the right way to
handle her." Now that Alleman had started to smile, his smile
became uncontrollable. Presently he was giggling while the
tears were still wet on his face.

His confession about the nun stirred depths of seriousness in
Lois that she had never exposed to him before. His laughter distressed her more than his weeping. She let go of him and furtively crept out of bed, as if she had wakened to find herself embracing some furry creature of a nightmare.

She went to examine an avocado plant which she kept on her
radiator. He saw her youthful figure swaying between the desire to order him out of her life and the desire to plunge with
him deep into the complicity of his guilt. She ran a fingertip
down the rib of an avocado leaf in a gesture of incredible delicacy. "Oh!" she cried with ghastly compassion. She scampered

back to Alleman, mounted him and pumped away as if her heart were breaking. Scalded, he rose into her in what he imagined to be the fashion of a soul ascending from its discarded body.

"Wasn't that *good?*" she asked afterward. "Wasn't that worth it?"

"Worth what?" His mind was already working professorially again, anxious for the guidance of certainty.

"I mean, if you had gone after your nun, wouldn't it have been worth your both going to hell?"

"You're a warm-hearted, well-meaning person," he told Lois, folding his arms under his head on the pillow and seeming to speak to her from the distance of years that separated them, though she was still sprawled over his left leg. "But the woman, whose name was Sister Agatha, has nothing to do with us. It was an indulgence for me to mention her. I don't think she wanted me to go to hell with her. Perhaps she wanted me to prove to her that hell is just a superstition."

"She wanted to marry you and have your babies."

"It might have come to that," he said, careful to qualify his remarks. He saw that mention of the nun might have given Lois a cue to speak for herself. He tousled her hair affectionately to remind her that what they had done together was all in fun.

Lois was listening to another level of dialogue. "I don't want you to marry me, because I know you're married and you can't," she said. "But I want it to be as serious as what you did to Sister Agatha."

"I didn't do anything to her."

"You did *something.*"

"I swear I didn't." He supposed he could laugh off what Lois was suggesting as he laughed at his wife's innuendoes about the nun, but Lois grabbed his balls with a painfully tight grip and hissed, "Give me a baby."

He was frightened by the delirium of her squeezing, so he said, "All right."

She went to the bathroom, where he heard water running. Through the half open door he saw the flash of a towel like a cockatoo's feathers as she dried herself. When she came back to him she was carrying her case of pills in the palm of her left hand.

"Here. You throw them in the wastebasket," she said. He took them from her, took his glasses from the bedside table, and scrutinized the pills attentively. They had an unwholesome

color, and he imagined he could see tiny grains of poison sparkling in the compound like mica in a rock.

After an effective interval, he returned the pills to her, commenting that, after all, they had to be sensible. He purposely
met Lois's eyes when he said this, though doing so was as brutal
as setting his thumbs to them and gouging back the wild tenderness that had surfaced.

She let her breath go in a sigh. "Ugh! I sure don't have any
use for a baby. I just wanted you to know we took you seriously."

"You and Sister Agatha?"

"All the women you're married to." She gripped him again,
unthreateningly, to show that the moment of challenge was past
and she could joke right along with him.

Yet, after that, through the spring he was often preoccupied
by what Lois wanted of him and what was the right thing to do
about her. She was a senior and would graduate with her class
in June. In his office they discussed how he could help her get
into graduate school at a university on the other side of the con-
tinent. She was not a girl who expected or thought much about a
career. Graduate school was someplace to go, since she was too
lazy and too well oriented to the academic routine to leave it
voluntarily.

She came to him bringing forms to be filled out and asking for
letters of recommendation. "You could tell them what an obedient lay I am," she said *sotto voce* from the chair beside his desk,
keeping her voice down so no one passing in the hall would
overhear, "On one of the forms you're supposed to rate me for
discipline."

"Top five per cent," he agreed, feeling his own discipline like
a scab about to peel off. While the edge of his attention was occupied with the papers in his hand, he was thinking that within
a few months she would probably be sleeping regularly with another professor—very likely of rank equivalent to his, since she
didn't like to play around. She liked one-on-one tutorial arrangements and she basked intellectually in the reassurance of a
faculty connection. On his desk sat a framed photo of his wife
and two children which, to Lois herself, he had once defined
as "the warning on my label. It's the test line. If a girl wants to
cross across it, I assume not only full consent but also informed
choice." Debonair from the beginning, Lois had disdained the

warning. It was on this very desk top, cushioned by her fur coat, knees supported by the crook of his elbows, that she welcomed his initial thrust with clucks of encouraging gladness—while the ignored photo escaped shattering by pure luck.

Now he checked and signed her recommendation forms with equal bravado and promised to deliberate on the contents of the letter that would accompany them. "If that's what you definitely want. If I can do you this slight service at the end."

"Not quite the end," she reminded him. "Since I've got me a part-time job in the controller's office for the summer, and I can keep my apartment." Until August he could help himself to her goodies. "What else do you want anyway? After that maybe I'll send you postcards once a year."

He was not ungrateful for her casual air. Surely it was best that way. August seemed still remote—but like something remotely in the past, not in the future. The intact photo of wife and children on his office desk was not a line that fenced him in, but a line that fenced him out.

"Got any other suggestions?" she asked in pity for his melancholy. Resolutely he shook his head.

"Then what do you want?"

"I want to be a saint," he said.

No doubt he wanted to be a saint because it was out of the question. Aside from his sexual record he was a decent—even an admirable?—man. The chances were that he always would be. Virtues and accomplishments could be listed on his tombstone without hypocrisy. That ought to be enough, but it wasn't. If he had done nothing to the nun, she had done something to him, it seemed. At least it was as if she had planted an itch in his fertile mind and then gone out of his life while it came to term. Had he cared to admit it, he could have truly declared that the itch for sainthood was not something he had ever quite disentangled from the restlessness that led to involvements like the one with Lois. For what he wanted with irresistible hunger, he needed the support of woman. The women in his life reversed the field so that he found himself carrying the ball toward his own goal line, so to speak.

He needed a woman to discuss with him the dilemma Lois presented as she prepared to leave. Once in May when he and his wife had taken their children to the lake for their first swim of the year, he suddenly sat upright in his coral-colored swimming trunks and, squinting at the sun, cried out, "I *want* to be a saint."

His wife did not even lift her cheek from the blanket on which they were sunning beside the water. "I *know*," she said. Her intonation was so larded with sinister mirth that he rose without another word and began swimming toward the float where his children were practicing their dives.

"Oh Daddy," they said when he hauled himself up panting, "you're getting out of condition."

For such impertinence he showered them with water shaken from his skin. He promised that by August he could beat either of them in any swimming race or anything else they might propose. August was his deadline for everything. In August Lois would be gone and the tug of contradictory desires would no longer cancel his good deeds, his good wishes for all his loved ones.

Since Lois was a treasure that could not be stored up, that summer he gorged himself on hours spent with her. She worked mornings in a University office, but two, three, or four afternoons a week when he was supposed to be in the library advancing his research, he was, instead, sweating in her untidy little apartment under the eaves of a clapboard house four blocks from the campus. His appetite raged in what seemed direct proportion to the shortening of the time before she would leave him forever. His appreciation of her body was keener day by day. Even when they talked now, the talk narrowed irreversibly into matters of sex and sensation. Mostly they put a stack of records on her hi-fi and as the records slid one by one down the spindle he tried sweatily to consume her. He wanted there to be nothing left unfinished, untried, when she went away.

It was not working. In her naked arms he knew he was swimming against a tide far greater than the muscular effort he could pump into it. At last, with profound humility, he brought himself to say, "I made a mistake. I want you to stay another year at least. I can't let you go now."

"I can't keep my job at the controller's," she said. "I suppose I might work at the book store again. Or tend bar, now that I have my degree."

"You could do your graduate study here. I could direct your thesis."

"But you told me to go."

When he thought it over, he realized that in spirit she was already gone. If not to Oregon, then someplace where he had even less chance of following her. All his lunges into her were a pursuit, not a meeting.

With great emotion he said, "We could do the big thing. I want to give you a baby. Take the big chance."

She was not unstirred by this offer, though she said, "Ho ho!" She was moved, though, by a kind of pity for him that neither had the courage to examine candidly.

One night in July as he was driving home from an errand to the milk store he saw her on the campus walks arm in arm with a bearded graduate student. Maneuvering ingeniously through side streets and alleys, he kept track of them just far enough to make sure that they were headed for her apartment. Then he gave up. His whole instinct told him he could not afford jealousy. It was the ultimate trap. If he fell into it he would be destroyed, finished. So he managed to turn the danger right around and use it as a warning. Her promiscuity was a solid excuse for letting her go. God knew he needed something solid to hang on to.

Lois made no secret of what had happened between her and the graduate student. "It's I've been faithful to you so long. I was timid about what it would be like from now on. Adlai was just right because he turned out so easy to manage. He was like a little boy playing in a sand box."

In fact her night with Adlai had provided her with a whole set of perceptions she could use in packing her experiences as she prepared for her move. She could now say, "You and I were Wagnerian. Adlai's still playing in the high school band." Or, "I'm built for the mile and a furlong. God didn't mean me to be a Shetland pony." Or, "It was the difference between Morse code and color TV."

Alleman was supposed to take comfort from these favorable comparisons. They certainly put him in a good light. The trouble was that they might convert to accusations with the sheer passage of time. He might have been dropped into eternal darkness by the rages of jealousy, but he did not want to be put in any light, either, unless it was the radiance that had first beckoned him into this folly.

Lois was not so far gone as to be insensitive to his feelings. She promised him one bang-up night before she shipped her baggage and got on the plane. "I don't want to leave owing you. I guess you know how much I've learned from you that I wouldn't have got just being in your classes. I learned what ecstasy and commitment were, even if they couldn't last. When it's all added up, you may turn out to be the most important man in my whole life. It shouldn't matter that we couldn't be married or how long or short the time was if we each got something we couldn't have got without each other. Boy, if I've got any secrets from you, one thing's for sure: nobody else is ever going to get to them."

She promised that their last long night together would be a sabbath of celebration. Nothing withheld. It was to be on a night early in August when his wife was out of town at a women's meeting.

Because of the heat some of the other students who had apartments in her building were out on the stone steps when he arrived carrying the huge art book he had bought her for a going away present. They had to move to make way for him to climb. On the second flight of stairs inside he had to make way for a fat, long-haired young man in purple swim trunks and an athletic department T-shirt, who narrowed his eyes disapprovingly but said nothing. It came home sharply to Alleman that his whole liaison with Lois had been under the tolerant but contemptuous scrutiny of strangers. Only the details and the essence of it were unknown to them. Unless the essence justified it, he had no plea against the common judgment that he was an adulterous fool.

But passing the door of her apartment gave him respite from the cosmic ridicule that seemed indistinguishable from the smothering weather of the street. Her stereo was playing Mahler's *Das Lied von der Erde*. The room was all ashimmer with candlelight from the candles set on her bookshelves, atop the refrigerator, and on the footlocker at the foot of her bed. Lois herself was naked when she answered his knock and let him in, and though that was customary through this summer, tonight it was less casual, more ceremonial. He took it to be part of the staging she had planned in advance. "Oh, you've brought me that book of Roman frescoes," she said, unwrapping his package. "Perfect! Listen," she said earnestly, holding him hard by the wrist, "I intend for everything to be perfect tonight to make up."

"Make up for what?"

"Dunno. You think it out. For what can't be, that's all I know. I thought about getting you up here and shooting you, but that wouldn't seem to fill the bill."

"It might be a kindness."

"We deserve more than kindness. Don't you know that?"

It seemed, while he listened to her music, that they did. Its lamentation and exultation seemed to go out into the night and return through her screens from the uttermost boundaries of the dark. Like a corn-fed geisha she hustled him out of his clothes, seated him on a small rug on the floor, and brought them both wine from her refrigerator.

"Nope. Not yet," she cautioned when he tried to acknowledge her thoughtful stagecraft by kissing one of her roseate nipples. "This is Madame Shibbaka's tent of illusions and you've got to be *ready*. Just listen a while and try to meditate."

She brought out her stash and rolled a cigarette skinny as a candle for a birthday cake. Marijuana seemed to him one of the more distressing student habits, and he had never shared it with her before. Tonight he motioned for her to share it with him. It was the taste of the smoke, he thought, more than any chemical effect that did the work for him. On his taste buds it prompted a deluge of memories so primitive he could not believe they were his own, however familiar. And then, when the music shifted to Brahms—as if his memories of taste and smell were somehow implicated with the sounds and became indistinguishable from them—he let himself go down an endless vortex. The feeling was purely pastoral. He knew what it was like to be a satyr in one of the Roman paintings in the book he had brought for her. It was innocent, it was good, said the music, and he believed it. As he had that first time on his office desk, he admired the bounteous foliation of her pubic hair, arcadian in its lushness. "I get the message," he said, reaching for her again. The message seemed to be that there was no such thing as guilt in nature, and no tomorrow.

"Not yet," she said, "but we're on our way."

She gave him more wine and rolled them another joint. Now no inhibition kept him from drawing heavily on the smoke. He felt his lungs expand like proud wings unfurling. When she rose up from where she had been sitting beside him, it seemed that a white temple was being erected, towering dizzily until it went out of sight. Fine. However high her walls were, tonight he felt the potency to scale them.

He had no sense of the interval in which she was absent from him. He did not even think she had left when she startled him by saying, "Look!"

She was standing in black silhouette in the bathroom door, a silhouette relieved only by the chaste white band across her forehead and the lesser white of her grin. "I'm your nun," she said. "Do with me what you will!"

At what precise point in real time had he then struck her?

That would not come clear to him in the days when he harrowed and harrowed his shattered recollections of the evening in an attempt to make them whole. He could only be sure that once upon a time he had been squatting like an undiapered boy child on her rug, gloating in his liberty, persuaded it had no limits. Then the walls rushed in. Before her trap closed he popped her in the mouth. When their speech became intelligible they were quarreling.

She dabbed at her lips with Kleenex, seemed incredulous that the blood was real.

Had he not understood that she meant it as a joke?

Had she not understood that there are limits, even to a joke?

Now he was exposed as the pussyfooting little fart he had always been.

Now he understood that her youthful liberty was simple sluttishness.

His knuckles might break her lip, but names could never hurt either of them again. He was up and struggling into his clothes. He had his pants on and was lacing his shoes when his eye caught the ludicrous shape of his flowered shorts lying between his feet and the refrigerator door. Unluckily she saw them at the same time and burst into unrestrained laughter.

"You silly man," she said now. "That about does it. Now get out."

Without retrieving his underwear, without giving her that satisfaction, he made for the door and the stairway. As he scampered down, again he passed the long-haired fat boy, climbing.

Whatever that night had been intended to do, it drew for him, at last, a clear line between reason and insanity. With the boundary defined, he could play both sides with confidence. No one would ever catch him again.

September would come. His classes would resume and deliberately, minute by minute, he would maintain before his students the invulnerable figure he now knew how to present. There would be, unquestionably, another Lois—why not two or three at once to forestall the chance that personal affection might again weaken him to the point of trusting any of them? Now that he had become insane he was safe.

He could manage now. Even if Lois—vengeful—should come up his front walk with his flowered shorts fluttering from disdainful fingers and fling them down before his wife and children in his presence he would be able to defuse the clamor with chilling laughter. Now he was one step ahead of his wife, as well as Lois. The one step that counted.

Before Lois took the Oregon Trail later that month, Alleman afforded himself one more spectacle at her expense. Again he saw her and Adlai headed by night for her apartment. With his renaissant vigor, Alleman outraced them. From an alley fence he leaped onto the fire escape of her building. He was stationed silent as a cat with his eye at the slit of her window blind when they came in.

He had the satisfaction of seeing her, somewhat later, emerge from the bathroom door in her nun's habit. He watched Adlai divest her of the cerements and scrabble like a boy digging in a sandbox for a treasure long ago lost or squandered.

The Knight
and the Hag

I am the type person who, when he has ten thousand in the
bank, will find five dollar bills in trash baskets or blowing down
the street—but when he's down to his last twenty will lose it.
When I'm making out with a girl who does me credit, I have
more live phone numbers than I can possibly use. When the
luck she runs bad . . . Oh.

It happens that I had ten thousand in the bank the last time
I crossed to France. And it happens that I made out with the
daughter of an air force colonel whom all the roisterers in Cabin
Class called Snow White. (Her hair was just that shade of white
that looked like it had been rubbed with gold leaf and her complexion was like translucent china, showing blue veins and a
pink, wholesome flush when she was excited.) Happens, too,
that when she got sick in the Channel there was a reinforcement

on hand, so I saw the foggy dawn and the harbor lights of Le Havre through the porthole of a singer who claimed she would be billed in Paris as the "white Bessie Smith." Big, strong girl with a lovely voice, I mean.

I had a good summer—in Paris, Vienna, Bandol, and Rome. It seemed that the girls had been told I was on my way and were waiting for me—like finding my feet wrapped in big mark, franc, and lira notes every time I set out on a windy street.

And even my money would have held out if I hadn't decided to break the bank in the Bandol Casino. The luck had been so good. It seemed as if it ought to go on forever. But I pushed it too far.

So I was coming home Third Class in October, dead broke, no deals in sight, and—as I found—with no appeal for any of the girls on board. I mean I was whipped down to size and I hadn't set my sights high. I might even have settled for companionship—a pretty little girl to play knees with, trade limericks, lure onto the windy decks for some high school type petting behind the lifeboats. But I absolutely couldn't connect. I bought a few drinks for the blowsy English wife of a midget who spent afternoons and nights playing nickel limit poker in the Winter Garden, and when I suggested that we go to my cabin for an after-dinner drink, she *told* him. Little devil threatened to cut me. Showed me his razor. Then there was a bunch of college girls, any one of whom might have soothed my lonely soul, but they all went mad for folk singing and a bucktoothed Princeton boy with a guitar. I mean they were a closed corporation and they couldn't have been colder if they'd believed I was married, and to a Communist with a social disease.

By the third day out of Genoa I was *contrite*. Pull down vanity and bow that head, I told myself. I'd had runs of bad luck before, but nothing this bad. I mean I looked myself over in a full length mirror. Everything was there. It didn't look so good to me when it didn't look good to them.

So I said to myself, Jamus, you've got to start back from somewhere. The old wheel's got to turn again, and if you start with the worst, everything after will be an improvement. But start. I made up my mind to have at the ugliest girl on board.

I already had my eye on her. It was hard to miss Annabelle; she was that repulsive. Hair that strung together in little bunches like the root system of a swamp-loving plant. Twice the ordinary number of teeth and none of them similar. I mean those teeth seemed to have a life of their own. Lips like what you see crawling on a sidewalk after a heavy rain. But if I went on I'd make a sonnet. Her figure ought to be mentioned, though, to give you an idea. The first time I saw her climbing a ladder ahead of me I thought I was watching a couple of shoats tied in a gunny sack, and down where the legs ought to be was more like the piling of a bridge. Tree trunks.

That is, the one emotion a girl like Annabelle ought to have when any man paid her attention is gratitude. She was not, technically speaking, deformed. Speaking aesthetically, she just wasn't formed at all.

In a spirit of utmost humility I accepted the challenge and approached her one afternoon when I spotted her sitting alone at a table in the bar. As I came up I noticed she was drinking lemon pop.

"Rough day," I said to her jovially. I grabbed a chair-back and did some stumbling antics near her table. "May I sit down? It's rolling pretty bad."

"It's *pitching*," she said. Her voice was that of a female condor contradicting a male condor on the next mountain. She stared at me as if she wanted me to fall on my can. *That* might have got a smile out of her. Nothing else in my repertoire could.

Right away I discovered there were handicaps to this make-out that I hadn't counted on. The flesh is weak, damn it, and though I'd made up my mind to stare fondly into her eyes, I couldn't for very long. Her pupils would bob when the boat rolled (or pitched) and they reminded me of something floating loose on the wild, wild waves. They were the color of lichens growing on a yellow stone.

As a positive accomplishment that afternoon, I got her talking—not exactly friendly, but at least without the chilling suspicion she'd displayed when I first sat down. She'd been to Southern France, she told me, to visit her uncle's family. Her uncle was a policeman, she claimed. (Police spy, I figured, maybe the guillotine mechanic on the local force. It would have taken a special family tree to produce one like Annabelle.) She had "just hated" French cooking, French wines, and "the way French girls are."

"How *are* the French girls?" I demanded eagerly, glancing at those adrift eyes, then glancing away before I got seasick.

"They don't care what they show off in those bathing suits," Annabelle said. "I was disgusted."

"They disgust me too," I said piously. "The kind of girl I like"—I looked over her clothes again—"is the kind that dresses for *warmth*."

"I don't like girls," she said. She set her empty glass down squarely on the table and leaned toward me for an announcement. "I don't like *humans*."

Turned out she was particularly fond of hares, many of which she raised as pets back home in New Jersey. Jocko, Thumper, Beetly, Herman, and Tootoo were practically the only living creatures on the planet that she really cared much about.

So I thought maybe the hares were my opening. "I've always been fascinated by the breeding habits of hares," I said.

"Not mine." Fiery breath came out of each nostril. "I've had them *fixed*."

On that cheerful note she hauled herself onto her gargantuan feet and padded away. Padded? She had on what the French call concierge's slippers, and they give you roughly the idea of winter footwear at Valley Forge.

You know, I sat there about three hours after she left me. The chair I was on would slide away from the table when the bow of the ship went down, would slide me tight against the table when the bow rose, and I was too depressed to try to fight the motion. Only I had several shots and my mind was all the time trying to catch hold of some straw that would float me. It seemed to me certain and pitiful that even Annabelle didn't like me. She liked . . . those *fixed* rabbits.

But I could make her like me, I thought when the whiskey warmed me. It seemed clear that she just wasn't used to male attention. Once the sunshine of my personality began to thaw away that twenty-seven-year-old chill she might become very fond of me indeed. I shuddered.

What the hell? I had started on a course. I would see it through. I had another whiskey and thought of something I read once in school. It was about a knight who runs into a "foul hag" in the forest. For some reason—maybe he's sworn some silly oath—he has to marry this one. So he does, and on the wedding night when he unwraps her, lo *and* behold, she's pink and white and as neat as a showgirl from *La Nouvelle Eve*. The moral to that story fascinated me. Maybe it would turn out that way for me when I unwrapped Annabelle. I walked out of that bar that afternoon in a daze, I'll tell you. My mind astonishes me, now and then.

I found her that night puffing up the main ladder from the dining room, headed for B Deck. At least she had put on flats instead of the concierge slippers, and it looked like she had wet down her hair for the occasion. But how do you add something to zero? I wouldn't claim she was anything but a mess.

"Mademoiselle," I called to her. "Will you do me the honor of joining me for a *digestif*. Perhaps mademoiselle would care to look in on *le dancing* later?"

"I'm going to play Bingo," she announced. But she gave me a sour little smile. I was becoming her friend!

"May I join you?"

"Got your own money?"

I had a little bit left. Enough so I could afford a few cards of Bingo at a quarter a throw. And I'll be damned if I didn't start winning. My second card paid off six dollars and fifty cents, and three times later I won again. By midnight I had won—believe it or not—more than fifty bucks. In a small way that's more of a triumph at Bingo than winning ten bets in a row at roulette.

Annabelle, who hadn't won a damn thing all evening, had been grumpy—almost angry—with me at first for winning when she didn't. But as I kept on I could feel her begin to warm up with something like comradely pride. It got so I was the center of interest for all the kids and old ladies playing in that salon, and each time I yelled Bingo there would be a tittering "Ooooo" sound from all over the room, and they would say, "It's *him* again." And the last two times I won Annabelle jabbed me sharply in the ribs with her elbow. I guessed, correctly, that it was her way of showing affection.

Afterward I again suggested a drink and Annabelle accepted. To my surprise she permitted me to order her a gimlet. She drank it down with no protest—maybe thinking it was just a fancy way to serve lemon juice. Her eyes seemed steadier and they were watching me with a kind of leering amusement.

"You know," she said, "when you sat down at my table this afternoon, I figured there was something wrong."

"Good Lord, why? How could you ever think that?"

"You seemed kind of . . . sneaky," she said. "I didn't know what you were after. But I guess you're all right."

"You're all right too," I said. "You bring me luck." As soon as I'd said it—meaning luck at Bingo—I thought again about the knight and the foul hag. A *very* interesting story. "Stick with me and bring me luck," I said. I took her muttony hand in mine and said, "I think we can be darn good friends."

"If you don't try nothin'!" she said. She gave me the kind of look she must have cast on Jocko and Thumper before she hauled them off to the veterinarian.

But I was going to try something. I was going to try to keep my luck running, and with every ounce of superstition I could muster I believed that making out with Annabelle had something to do with it.

I managed to kiss her the next night when I called at her cabin for her, and then she sat beside me while I won two hundred and thirty dollars in a pot limit game in the Winter Garden. That midget who'd threatened to cut me had graduated to this game on his nickel winnings, and I am happy to say that I took most of my winnings from him. Annabelle worked—as they say—like a charm.

Toward two o'clock that night I got a couple of drinks into her, got her out on deck, and put my hand inside of her warm jacket.

"What you doing?" she said with such genuine bewilderment and alarm that I thought no one—no *human*—had ever tried it before in all those twenty-seven years. "What you after, feller?"

She hit me a mean lick across the forehead with her arm and went stomping away. I let her go and then—just to prove something—went back to the game. I lost every penny I had, my wristwatch, and my high school ring.

That settled it. After that I really began to pay court to that woman. I've had some instructive experience about the way to a woman's heart, and believe me, with Annabelle I used it all. It isn't easy to go to the post with a woman who is just plain startled and surprised when you reach for her hem or her blouse buttons. I've made it a thousand times easier with starlets and models and even with molls. In a sense with Annabelle I had to supply—in a few short days—everything that most girls accumulate in the way of attitudes and familiarity toward men over a span of years.

I'd lure her into my cabin when I'd arranged with my cabin mate to stay away, and then, more patiently than I'd done on the first date in my life, I'd trick her onto the berth, get the lights out one by one, sit down beside her—and try to persuade her that since we were good friends now this was *all right*. And again and again she'd ask sincerely, "What you doing, feller?" Only once did I get my hand inside what I thought must be her brassiere.

There were two things about that memorable occasion. One, I cleaned up three hundred and eight dollars (on a twenty-dollar stake from my cabin mate) within three hours afterward. The other, I felt something . . . *funny.*

Don't ask me funny *how.* I don't know. I suppose it was a breast. I've tried to recapture the feeling by all sorts of psychological tricks—I mean, like visualizing, like trying to recall the temperature, the texture, the resistance . . . all that jive. I don't know. It was funny indeed, and I can't say that the touch was pleasant. I remember that's one of the times she didn't have to throw or shrug me away from her. I pulled back my hand like I'd been burned.

And the next day I couldn't find her anywhere. All afternoon I looked in the bars and salons and out on deck. I watched for her in the dining room at both sittings, and she didn't show. Finally I tried her cabin again, though I'd knocked there several times without getting an answer.

Who opened the door was one of the college girls who'd given me such a brisk brushoff the first day or two of the voyage. A cute kid with black bangs, a wide mouth, and what they call "roguish" eyes. Her eye lit cold on me. But then she said, "Oh, you're Annabelle's *friend*," and in recognizing me that way she seemed to thaw a little bit. I mean, we had a subject for discourse and I might have tried to carry on from there if I had trusted my luck. I liked that big mouth. But I put her down for later—maybe—and went on with the hunt.

I don't know where Annabelle vanished to for so long. I waited for her in the salon where the Bingo was until they folded up the game and she never showed. (I didn't win a card.) But then the next morning she was around again as usual and I picked her up soon after breakfast.

All that day I worked on her—all the tricks—and finally I pulled the most dangerous and the most reliable. I asked her to marry me.

Now this was one thing that Annabelle understood. What

woman doesn't? "Jim," she said, "now I know what you been up to."

"I'm going out of my mind wanting you," I said.

"I just wonder what would happen to Jocko and Thumper and the gang if I was to . . ."

"Never mind them," I said hoarsely. "They'll be taken care of. Think of me, Annabelle."

Well, asking her to marry me worked. I don't pretend I know exactly how her mind operated on the idea and put it together with the other things I was asking of her. I'm a more practical than a theoretical scientist in such matters. What I do know is I persuaded her to arrange for her cabin mate to stay away from the cabin that night so she'd be alone and waiting for me there.

"I don't know," Annabelle said. "LaVerne might think it was pretty funny. But I'll do it for you, Jim, if that's what you want."

"That's what I want," I said, thinking, So the girl with the fine big mouth is named LaVerne, is she? Well, it looked like my luck was going to change. Then, LaVerne . . . we had a date. We were still two nights out of New York. Time enough to touch base with Annabelle and head for the plate.

But then it seemed to me that my luck changed before I got to Annabelle. I was sitting in the bar that night (no pitch, no roll, the sea was like glass) having some Bourbon to nerve me up for the Big Test, when the sultriest voice in the world said, "Hello," right in my ear.

It was LaVerne. And she was smiling knowingly at me. And she was dressed to show things I hadn't seen before, like maybe something she was bringing home from Paris to show she'd been somewhere—a frou-frou dress with a neckline that plunged and plunged and plunged. When she sat down I knew what was to the right and left of that plunging neckline. If there was anything artificial, it was only those dabs of lipstick.

"I . . . have . . . a . . . message . . . for . . . *you*," she said.

I'd already registered a couple of messages, but I said, "You have?"

"Annabelle is waiting," she said. Her eyes were shining with malicious amusement. "Your lady waits. I loaned her my *Nuit d'Amour* perfume."

"Why are you laughing at me?"

"I'm not," she protested, trying to keep it deadpan. We sat there for several uneasy minutes. I couldn't make a move, but she made some. Little ones. Like she was a piece of bread that had just come upon a man starving to death in the mountains. "You've roused my curiosity," she said huskily.

I thought very deeply, had another Bourbon, and said, "There are two ways of satisfying that in this present situation."

"Why don't you," she asked, "take the easiest way?"

So I did. LaVerne had promised Annabelle she wouldn't be back to their cabin until four in the morning and she wasn't, because she was in mine until four-fifteen when my cabin mate knocked on the door and said for Christ sake he was dying of sleepiness and couldn't he come in to bed.

And during those first hours I thought I was riding in luck again, and in the intervals for respiration I congratulated myself that I'd bought my luck back at a lower price than I'd been willing to pay.

But you know, the funniest damn thing, along about two-thirty I discovered that, whatever else, my curiosity wasn't satisfied. You know, I began to *wonder* about Annabelle, and then damned if I didn't wonder whether I'd made a mistake.

I mean, LaVerne was fine. But, let's face it, there were no surprises. I won't say I got bored while she was there. Not quite, but my mind wasn't with it.

When she left she said, "See you tomorrow night, darling."

I said, "We'll see about that."

The next morning while LaVerne should have been still asleep I caught up with Annabelle on deck and tried to make my peace with her.

She wouldn't have any part of it. "You lied to me," she said.

"I drank too much," I said. "I was so nervous I drank too much and had to be carried from the bar down to my stateroom."

She put an end to this by saying, "LaVerne told me. You're no better than any other human." She turned away to look out over the sea, which was the color of lead, and her eyes were the same color—like greased bullets. "You missed your chance, buddy, with me." And she walked away.

I could have had LaVerne again that night. It was all arranged that way. She sent me a note by the steward to say she would be waiting for me to come to their cabin while Annabelle was up playing Bingo. But when the time came, I stayed flat on my back in my own berth, sucking up on a bottle that I'd managed to save for what should have been a happier occasion. The boozier

I got the more my curiosity got after me—like a bad toothache. I lay there in pain wondering what it would have been like with Annabelle. The terrible thing was just that I'd never know. I tried to recall the sensation I'd got that one time I touched inside her clothes, but the more I worked at catching it the fuzzier and vaguer it got until I lost it altogether.

So—I never saw Annabelle again. We docked the next day in New York and I suppose she hit straight for home, where she keeps those unlucky hares.

Like I'd meant to do, I stayed in New York, trying to live on my luck with women, cards, contacts, and the easy dollar. Let me tell you something about my luck since that trip—it stinks. The meanest part of my life these days—I get more mental as time goes on—is I keep thinking of that story about the knight and the hag. I mean, when you're trying to shape your luck, you've got to follow through.

Shadow
of a Magnitude

From her place in the second row Jody could see the shameful glitter, which almost certainly meant sentimental tears, in Professor Sloan's eyes as he lifted them from the page and let his voice sink to an even more doleful note.

"'By brooks too broad for leaping'," he sorrowed, "'The light-foot boys are laid'."

Once Mr. Sloan had showed select members of his Senior Lit class, including Jody, a photograph of himself as a bearded graduate student at Princeton, a photo in which the beard, the bushy hair, and the frailty of his nose bones had made him look very poetic, all right. He had sighed then for "lost youth" and the failure of his talent to ripen since. Perhaps now as he read Housman to his twelve second-year girls he was forgetting them in some vision of "golden friends" of another spring and of himself bushy headed and gamboling among them before he settled to the grind of teaching at Larchmoor.

Even so, tears during class time was going a little too far, Jody thought. There happened to be a semester test in Lit coming up and it was Sloan's job to see that they were prepared for it, Housman and all. Let him cry on his own time.

"'And rose-lipped girls are sleeping . . .'"

Indeed they are, she thought. At least rose-lipped Jody Foster is close to it. But not all her drowsiness was Sloan's or Housman's fault. The classroom window was open beside her chair, and in the corner of her eye sunlit dogwood blossoms trembled. Further, three o'clock in the afternoon was no hour for them to have scheduled seniors to study English Literature and Its Backgrounds. Further, Housman was clear in the back of the book. When she looked at the page number—866—it seemed to her that the weight of all those pages piling up since September and Beowulf was pressing her brain into a drowsy little pancake. Please don't cry, Mr. Sloan.

"I thought someone would have to go pat his cheek when he came to 'In fields where ro-o-o-oses fade,'" she said a while later to her roommate Nan. They were together in a booth at the Students' Rec Cabin, their favorite late afternoon spot on the campus during this fine weather of the semester's end.

"He really cried, huh?"

"Of course it is sad," Jody reflected. "Of course it's a lovely great poem, but I dislike to see anyone get over-emotional. A person can feel very deeply and still not show it." She was thinking how deeply she felt, for instance, about her friends here at school whom she would be with for such a little time more, and about the beauty of the old campus that seemed to pause and hush in respect for their imminent graduation and departure. "Even if poetry is supposed to carry you away you ought to keep it to yourself."

With a casual glance and nod Nan answered, and for this precisely right response all the warmth which the classroom had denied moved freely. It was as if the poetry which had been marks on paper and then sounds in the air were now around them like an atmosphere compounded of sympathies.

They're not to talk about, but there really are golden friends, Jody thought. With the abundance of them at Larchmoor she had grown from half-awareness and uncertainty into the estate of being a personality among others like herself. She had learned a subtle codified vocabulary with which to reach someone as outwardly different from her as Nan.

Her thoughts ran large. She felt a gratifying, inexplicable flight of confidence in her ability to get over to Nan the sentiments of these last days without saying sloppy things that would make Nan shut up in embarrassment.

"I don't think his carrying on proves it's good poetry," she intoned softly, forever fencing Mr. Sloan out of the charmed areas of rapport where she romped with the elect.

"It doesn't prove a thing." Nan's total agreement, in the moment of shared attitudes, covered much more than Mr. Sloan. It agreed to unspoken things and put a period on them. Enough had been said.

So Jody asked, "By the way, did you pick up my five from the dresser? My turn to pay this afternoon and I need cigarettes."

"It wasn't there," Nan said with an abrupt narrowing of her eyes, a tensing as she leaned forward on the table in the booth.

"It had to be. I remember distinctly how I left it . . . with my lipstick on it to keep it from blowing away. Well . . ."

"I looked," Nan protested again with such concern that Jody felt the trivial problem threaten to rip the contentment they had just achieved.

She was almost glad, therefore, to see Loreen Cory hovering close to their booth—*even* Loathesome Loreen—as though trying to make up her mind whether to show them what she was holding. Loreen with all her awkward demands that they accept her had pestered them unbearably for most of the winter. For the moment Jody welcomed her. "Come have something with us," she called. "What've you got? A letter from home?"

"I've already seen," Nan said. "Loreen is spoken for, betrothed, and engaged even. This is the incredibly lucky creature." With the side of her hand she pushed toward Jody the snapshots that Loreen eased onto the table between them. "Sit down, Loreen."

"Thank you," Loreen said. "How do you like him, Jody?"

"Wonderful man," Jody said. As a matter of fact, she was surprisingly well impressed. The boy in the photos was tall and rather handsome if you liked them with lean faces and strong noses like De Gaulle's—and she did. Her own boy, Larry Martin, was something like that. She felt, not quite pleasantly, compared to Loreen and linked in terms of others' estimation.

"He's got the swellest job," Loreen said. "He manages his father's oil wells."

"Loreen's marrying him for his money," Nan said. She kicked Jody's foot under the table—a signal warning her that here was sport to be had, a gag to be built up if she did not nip it by being too quickly skeptical. They had baited Loreen before, never very maliciously, but enough to pay for the boredom she tried to inflict on them.

Loreen stared at Nan for a moment as though she knew too that a game was beginning and as though she were calculating a witty reply that would enable her to score in it. But all she finally managed was an indignant, "Oh, I am not."

"He's very handsome. Really," Jody said. Somehow she couldn't just now see the sport of making fun of Loreen. She wanted to let her off gently from any cracks that Nan might be building toward. "Is he coming for graduation? Or the dance?"

"Oh no," Loreen said. "He's in Mexico."

"Among the oil wells," Nan said.

"Are you going to marry him and not come back to school for your second year?"

"To this cruddy place?" Loreen shook her head and tried to smile disdainfully. The smile emerged small and ugly enough to remind Jody of a bouquet of coarse flowers. "I wouldn't come back for anything."

Nan shredded the remnants of the soda straw with her thumbnail. "What Loreen is trying to tell us is that she is flunking History and Zo."

Her own position in this developing unpleasantness became more uncertain for Jody. It had started a real tremor of anger to hear Loreen, of all people, disparage Larchmoor, and yet she would be disgusted with herself if she let this anger reply.

"The grades aren't in," she said soothingly. "Nobody knows if anyone else is going to flunk anything. Not even the teachers themselves know yet."

"Besides which," Nan said to Loreen, "those aren't your pictures, are they? You borrowed them from Jackie Raeburn. Isn't that true, Loreen? That's Jackie Raeburn's brother, to be exact."

"Oh, you . . ." Loreen stood up fiercely. Even in this the dignity of indignation failed her, for in rising she knocked over her coke glass and the remnants of liquid and ice bounded across the table top into the front of Jody's dress. Loreen wavered above them, large, awkward, enraged, repentant, helpless. "I didn't mean to do that." With her handkerchief she dabbed at the spots while Jody shrank to withdraw them from her reach.

"All right," Jody said. "No damage."

"It was an accident," Loreen said. "I'll pay for cleaning it." The more she made herself abject the more something really vicious showed itself through her expression. Jody tried to wave her away.

"It's cotton and will wash," Nan said.

And when Loreen was dismissed at last they were left with a hangover of uneasiness, which now forbade between them the kind of relaxed intimacy the afternoon had permitted a while before. Who had spoiled it? Loreen? Or all three of them, each contributing some inadequacy that had mounted to an unstable pile and tumbled?

"I can understand Loreen pulling a stunt like that," Nan said, "but I can't swallow it."

"If she hadn't said such uncalled for things about Larchmoor."

"She's got to run it down below her own level and, boy, that's below sea level."

"I guess she means well."

"Don't we all?" Nan said. "Somebody ought to write a psychological study of Loreen. It could be done."

"But I feel sorry for her having to pretend she's got this handsome guy."

"Sure," Nan said moodily. "Let's go to the dorm, huh? Did you say you needed cigarettes?" She took a five dollar bill from her coin purse and held it with the check as they went to pay.

"My five?" Jody asked.

"No, really," Nan said. "It really wasn't where you thought." Her hard frown reappeared. "I just hope no one swiped it."

"Oh, no one *would*," Jody said.

"They would, all right," Nan said. "There's some that would."

"I'll look in the other places I might have left it," Jody said hopefully, beginning to see that if it were stolen that would be worse than any other thing that could have happened to it. "I might have even grabbed it up and then lost it. I was so foggy this afternoon. But I was so sure . . ."

The money had been stolen, Nan insisted, and throughout the evening Jody found all the other explanations she ventured, the more tolerable possibilities, dissolving against the rock of that probability.

"Betty, or Barbara Crosby or someone else from our floor needed money in a hurry," she suggested, after she had looked in pockets, drawers, and between the pages of her dictionary. "I can see them rushing in looking for us when we weren't there, and they just borrowed it. They'll tell us about it at dinner. Everybody's sending telegrams these days, and they needed it for a telegram or something like that."

But at dinner in Gillespie Dining Room she greeted most of the girls who were friendly enough to have taken the money without worrying and none of them mentioned it.

After they had eaten, Miss Drake, the Dean, rang the silver bell that stood on her table at the front of the room. Rising, waiting for silence to arrive and settle, Miss Drake said in her poised, cheery way, "Before long all of us will be rushed half to death with end of semester activities. There will be *tests* and *guests*— arriving next week. So this evening, while there's still only the Larchmoor family here, I thought we might happily sing some of our songs. If you'll light the candles, girls, I'll suggest that we begin with *Larchmoor Calm and Serene.*"

The overhead lights were extinguished and all over the room points of candlelight appeared quivering over the white tables. It was not yet wholly dark outside, but the shadowing elms of the West Campus made an intensification of twilight beyond the windows. The dimmed windows multiplied reflections of the flames.

The song began softly, rose in confidence and volume with the sweetness of reliable, familiar emotions. It came from Jody's mouth as it came to her ears. But in the trammeling interval of her mind there seemed added to it a sprinkle of malicious notes like a whinny of discord.

Singing, she thought for the first time *maybe the money was stolen.* Maybe someone here singing like a little angel had the five tucked in her brassiere. She stared appalled and felt her voice slip away until she was making no sound at all. It seemed that she would go on hearing the discord, though, until she knew for sure what had become of the money.

So later she and Nan went systematically to each of the other rooms on her floor of the dormitory to see what they could learn. Anne Billings, whose room was at the end of the hall, had been in it most of the afternoon with her door open. "A lot of the girls came and went," she said. "You think it was hooked between three and four? Gee, let me remember. Well, I saw Nan here, and Barbara, and Mary Lee, Penny, and Ginny. Loreen came around with some pictures of the guy she's going to marry, poor guy. Can you imagine Loreen getting such a heap of man? I mean there's something screwy about the situation. But that's all, kids. If you're sure somebody stole it, you'd better report it to Miss Drake."

Ginny Fredericks said, "You mean that? Somebody took it right off your dresser? That's dirty, really dirty." An odd embarrassed expression passed across her face. "You know what? Remember when I lost my watch? I thought it had fallen down the lavatory drain because there's no strainer in it, and I did lose a stocking down there once. Only maybe somebody stole my watch, too. They could have."

Barbara Crosby said, "How awful—because, gosh, we're all under suspicion sort of with that kind of thing going on."

"Oh no," Jody insisted, feeling miserable that she had to go around asking like this. "You're not at all."

"We're adding up information," Nan echoed.

Nevertheless, Barbara insisted that since she had been on the floor at the time of the theft she had to be considered a suspect. She brought out a hundred dollar check that her father had sent her from Tulsa, and then said glumly that of course that didn't prove anything except that she didn't need money and she might be a kleptomaniac for all they knew.

Four of the girls to whom they talked also insisted uneasily that they wouldn't blame Jody for wondering if they might have done it, so she just had to catch the thief for their sake. The rest were indignant and upset that such a thing had happened. By the time she and Nan had completed their circuit of the floor, Jody had the feeling that she had gone around planting malicious little seeds that were already vining up into a jungle around her.

The next morning, immediately after Sociology, she went to Miss Drake's office. After assuring Miss Drake that there couldn't have been any mistake about the money, and after Miss Drake had been sympathetic and non-reassuring about the prospects of getting the money back, Jody said, "We've nearly got to find out who did it. It's poisoned things on our floor."

Miss Drake smiled at so much intensity. "I know what you mean, Jody, and we must certainly try. I'll make inquiries. It's entirely possible the maids may know something."

"I don't think any of the maids took it," Jody said.

"Of course not," Miss Drake said with so much emphasis that Jody's faith in the maids rocked momentarily. "But one more thing, my dear. You must be careful, more careful, not to leave money lying around."

Jody smarted. There it was again, the slanting, unintentional accusation that she was involved with the theft's knot of guilt in spite of being its victim. "I know," she said meekly and then with a defiant afterthought asked, "Would you rather I hadn't said anything about it?"

"That isn't what I meant at all," Miss Drake said. "We ought to remember, however, that when we permit disorder to start it is apt to keep snowballing. That's what I meant. Responsible people must assume the responsibility for denying an opportunity for disorder. Tell Nan, too, what I said, won't you?"

Nan, who had known of her intention to go to Miss Drake, was waiting for her in the Gillespie lounging room. She motioned Jody to the canvas chair beside her. "Whatever she said didn't make you real happy."

"Yeah," Jody said bitterly. She slumped in the chair and gazed across the room at the columns of sunlight slanting in from the windows. The way they'd slant into some dungeon, she thought. "She practically insisted that I'm the criminal. I shouldn't have left it around to be stolen."

"She didn't," Nan said. "That's too much."

"She doesn't have the courage to face up to it, that's all. I accused her of trying to smooth things over, and I think all she wants is to pretend it didn't really happen. It might damage the fair name of Larchmoor."

"Let's not blame it on Larchmoor."

"All right, but at this point you don't expect me to stand up and exactly cheer do you? Miss Drake stands up in chapel and talks about respecting the truth and then she acts like she's afraid it would bite her."

Barbara Crosby perched momentarily on a nearby chair arm. "Find your money yet, Jody?" she asked.

"*Find* it? You mean I lost it? Well, I didn't."

"Don't grind your teeth at me, honey. I thought it might turn up in another purse or something." She smiled, a touch derisively, as she left.

Jody said, "Now that about creams it. I'm going to show them. I'm very well going to catch the thief and show them."

"Tremendous new idea," Nan said. "How?"

"Come along."

Amid the smells of the Chem Lab on the top floor of Thornton Hall they found Professor Harvey reading in his cubbyhole office. He sat totally relaxed at his desk, wearing a witchy-looking black apron, scratching his cheek gently with a pipestem as he read. His brown eyes rose to confront them with a cautious challenge, like a fencer coming on guard.

"We have troubles, Mr. Harvey," Jody said.

"That's not exactly my department, since neither of you is in my class any more. But I'm willing. You don't—uh—require poisons I suppose?"

"You told us once about a chemical that police use to stain the fingers of shoplifters and people like that. . . . They put it on things to catch thieves. It's a powder or an acid or something."

He said in the coquettish tone of a teasing old man, "My. You remembered that. Isn't it downright odd what trivial, unrelated details stick in our minds? We forget valences and atomic tables and laws and remember the least consequential anecdotes, don't we? I wonder why?"

Impatiently but politely Jody said, "Is there really such a powder, Mr. Harvey?"

Ignoring her directness, he went on, "It's as though there's a little vulgar gossipy person in our heads who hears a scrap come in the ear and says, 'I'll save that nonsense up. I'll want it sometime for mischief.' And he will, but who can tell why he'd grab this scrap and let that one go?" He looked owlishly at Jody as though he might expect to see the little person with purposes of its own watching him through her eyes. Then he snapped out of his clowning and answered. "Sure. There is such a thing."

"Can you give me some?"

He nodded. "So you want to catch a thief? Or is this some trick you're going to pull on a friend? Or"—he sucked noisily through his pipe, making a thick bubbly sound—"do you want to catch one of your friends?"

"I suppose someone who steals money from you isn't your friend," she said huffily.

"That sounds logical," he said. Mean laughter seemed to

struggle behind his teacherish irony of manner. It was almost like an accusation—or so she felt it—of one of her friends, almost as though he might mean that Nan could have taken her money, and it was just against such suspicions that she felt herself to be waging an honorable battle.

She explained the disappearance of the money to him, and when she finished he went without comment to the next room and returned with a pill-box full of powder.

Holding it out to her he said cutely, "Be careful. Don't get it on your own hands."

In their room while they set their trap they treated the powder as respectfully as if it were poison. Nan held four dollar bills with eyebrow tweezers over a newspaper while Jody dusted them with the powder. When they set them on top of the dresser and weighed them with coins, these also powdered, the little stack appeared malignant as a living rodent which might have crept up the walls among the vines, insinuating itself into their room, a green smear of mischief on the white cover of the dresser.

The weekend passed and from Monday through Wednesday final tests loomed threatening and then blew past with less lightning and disaster than they had seemed to hold.

A brief spell of uncertain weather lasted through Monday night. The next morning brought them into a June purer than a winter's dream of it. Everywhere on the damp hedges, tennis courts, grass, walls, and flowering bushes lay the abundant light. High over the girls' heads as they followed the campus walks the elm leaves moved lazily in a dream of wind. On the ground level around them, the heat seemed of itself to flower into a million yellow and orange-yellow blossoms.

Jody in this time came to think that in the center of the month's loveliness, like its negative core, was the pile of money on her dresser. On the first day she had left it—leaving the door carefully half-open, too—she had returned after three hours with a breathless panic tightening her as she saw it still there. She dropped her books to the bed and lay beside them, listening to the pounding of her heart and the loud pulse in her ear against the pillow.

One day she touched the money purposely with the edge of her little finger. A brown-black stain, too small for anyone else to notice, appeared on her skin. In the middle of her Lit test—she was stuck briefly trying to remember which poet had written "all experience is an arch wherethrough gleams that untraveled world"—she found herself chewing at the stain. That evening she sanded it off with a nail board.

Once as she woke in the morning she dreamed that she had a pet animal in her hand which suddenly twisted to bite her. She wondered if the dream were a memory of something that could have happened when she was very young. She could not be sure.

But perhaps these disturbances were a natural reaction to the tension she built up while tests were still in progress, for after them on Thursday she was inwardly as placid as the weather in which she walked, and if the knowledge of the money trap could not be quite excluded from her mind it had nevertheless become remote.

Her boyfriend Larry Martin arrived early Thursday afternoon. From the dormitory window she saw him swing his blue convertible into the parking lot and she was already racing for the stairs when Nan shrieked in contagious excitement, "Kiss him for me."

She did, after she had kissed him properly for herself. In the course of that good afternoon as she and Larry rambled the more remote paths of the campus she kissed him four or five times more. They circled the pond to the riding ring and the edge of the Larchmoor woods. It was like being a figure in a painting. She saw the shadows of pine boughs painted on his face and shoulders while his posture before her registered attention and love.

For an hour they languished like painted figures by the pond. Some little brown ducks sailed past them, rippling the reflection of clouds white as flowers. In an unbreaking wave of calm she listened to him plan their coming summer. He was going to work as a counselor in a boys' camp a hundred miles from her home. Every weekend he would drive to see her, and in her town they would swim at the Country Club, play tennis, dance, and he would teach her bait-casting. He insisted, "It's going to be *the* great summer, Jo. The most." She believed and took the promise for the reality, though just once she felt as if the summer he was talking about was one that had already passed, and in the moment of that error wanted to cry for its having evaded her. She clung to him then—not caring if the strollers on the far side of the pond saw—until she believed again that summer was truly ahead of them as he had described it.

At four he had to leave the campus briefly. He had taken a hotel room in Appleton and was going back there to shower and dress for dinner and the Senior Dance which would follow.

"This afternoon," he said. "Well, it's the way things are going to be."

"Promise?"

"Yup."

He backed the convertible past her, flicked his left hand up in a pilot's gesture, and the gravel whistled as he headed out the drive.

He's so good, she thought, and it seemed to her that the other boys she had known were only nice, or good-looking, or smart, or entertaining. Being *good* was very much more important.

She strolled weakly toward the dormitory. Approaching the point where two walks converged at the end of a hedge, she heard voices and speeded up, wanting to avoid people.

But it was her luck to encounter Loreen and a woman who was quickly introduced as Loreen's mother. The mother was a surprise, almost a shock, for she was so attractive and unlike her daughter. There was a gay grace about her walk and her gestures and speech which were so unlike the essential qualities of Loreen that Jody had a sense of imposture, as if this creature were an invention, too, like the invented boyfriend.

"Of course," Mrs. Cory said, "I feel you're an old buddy because Loreen has written and talked so much about you."

"That's nice," Jody said, feeling a clear guilt because of the many unkind things she had said and thought of Loreen.

"I'm sure I heard about you before I heard about anyone else at Larchmoor," Mrs. Cory tinkled, "because Loreen liked you so much right away last fall. Weren't you a speaker at the first Vespers last fall?"

"Yes." Jody blushed and ducked. She wished that this forgotten distinction were really beyond calling up again.

"And you were so nice to Loreen when she was finding her way around in the first days here."

Well, yes. That had been her duty. There had been nothing *personal* in her being nice to Loreen. She wanted to protest that it hadn't been really more than a matter of manners.

Mrs. Cory said, "Didn't we see you walking by the pond— *sitting* by the pond—with your young man? I'm sure we did, didn't we, Loreen? Well, you're one of the lucky girls tonight then. Poor Loreen"—she lifted a perfectly made eyebrow to suggest a nonserious sarcasm—"*poor* Loreen. Her man—her fiancé—Do you still use that old word?—can't be here tonight, and she's a one man girl it turns out. She *wouldn't* accept any of the other prospects . . ."

Excessively struck with the ugliness of this kind of talk, Jody wanted to stop her, even with rudeness. "I know there isn't any fiancé," she might have said just then. She had not quite the courage in spite of her pained resentment, her pity for Loreen.

". . . so I suppose she'll have to go alone. But I'm sure she'll have dances enough, don't you think?" Mrs. Cory babbled on.

Over Mrs. Cory's head Jody caught a look of dumb protest and anguish on Loreen's face, the most human communication that had ever passed between them. Mrs. Cory's exposing lie seemed to cut like a whip across Loreen's shoulders and the big girl took it like a horse clubbed by its venomous little rider. The same blow that wounded her warned her not to protest.

For a good-bye as they separated Mrs. Cory said, "We'll certainly see you at the dance, my dear. I intend to come and look on." To force unnaturally some effort to make Loreen as popular as she was not by nature, Jody thought.

Jody fled up the stairs to her room, pursued by some knowledge of how it was possible to use glad occasions for times of torment. Her throat ached with anger and she wished she could strike Mrs. Cory in the face.

That terrible, terrible little glittery woman, she thought. How can she be so insensitive to her own daughter? If I had a daughter and she looked eight times as homely as Loreen I'd love her too much to humiliate her that way. You'd think God's lightning would strike Mrs. Cory where she stands.

Calming down a little, she thought, at least I can get Larry to dance with Loreen a few times. He will—without any smart cracks about it or any smart-alec winking—because he's good, good.

But "that terrible woman" . . . The phrase pounded in her brain, made her almost lose her anticipation of the evening to come.

"But that terrible woman," she was saying to Nan at exactly three o'clock in the morning, after the anguish of the evening had been played out and it was time to gather up the fragments.

The two girls sat in their pajamas before the window of their room. They had long since put out the lights and dropped their voices. The moonless night was impenetrable as a door.

"I agree, and maybe the mother is responsible for what's wrong with Loreen," Nan said. "But there're other items to take into account. Like it's you that has to decide what to do about it before it gets too late tomorrow. Like if you want to prefer charges against Loreen."

The diffused menace that she had reckoned with for some time had come to a head during the dance. After a sweet beginning to the evening that had seemed to sweep away all concern with Loreen and her mother, the climax had come during intermission, when she left the dance to go to her room for an address that she had promised to Barbara Crosby's boyfriend.

She had found their floor of the dormitory nearly silent and, as far as she could see, deserted. The faroff music of the orchestra reached it faintly, and in a troublesome way seemed to obscure a presence that was like her own fear given a body and claws, lurking behind one of the familiar doors.

She stood in the center of her own room a minute trying to figure out what was strange there. It was like being in a room that was only *similar* to hers, stripped of the identity it had owned a few hours before—or it was like the same room in a world suddenly merely similar.

Then she saw there was no money on the cover of the dresser. That one detail removed was the agent of the change she had felt.

As if the thief were still there, still outrageously extending a hand to steal, still potent with danger if challenged, Jody tiptoed back out into the silent hall. She looked at the other room doors. Two of them stood open on dark rooms. Under Loreen's door a line of light showed, and Jody went toward it without yet knowing why—perhaps because even talking to Loreen might be consoling. She thought, No. Loreen already has enough trouble for one evening. I can't upset her by asking if she's seen anyone slip into my room.

She turned to the bathroom. When she thrust open the door she saw Loreen furiously scrubbing at her hands.

She spoke Loreen's name wearily and saw Loreen's mouth tremble open in fear and shame. She spun when she heard Jody and for an instant held out her hands, dripping with suds, in a gesture that might have been supplication or threat. The chemical had blacked all the fingers and the palm of her right hand.

"I spilled some ink," Loreen said. She waited for Jody to answer but then added, "No. You know what it is, don't you? What did you put on it?" She rushed past Jody and into her room. She was sobbing on the bed when Jody reached her.

"I don't know why you did it," Jody said. "That's all. I'm not mad, Loreen. Don't cry like that. Tell me why."

"Because I hate you. You have everything."

"Oh."

"I don't hate you. I liked you and I liked Nan so much and I thought you should like me."

"If you liked us that isn't any reason to take . . ." Jody shook her head.

"Go tell them," Loreen spat at her. "Get all those bitches up from the dance to look at me. Go tell my mother. But please get out of here. Get *out*."

Loreen flung herself upright; her smeared and ugly face jerked like a severed muscle. "If you don't get out of here I'll hit you. Get *out*." Her big fist flew up higher than the level of her shoulder.

"Yes," Jody said. "But please, you crawl in bed so no one will see your hands tonight. I won't tell anyone tonight. Honest. You try to sleep. It will be all right. Please."

She returned through the long corridors and the deserted reception rooms toward the dance, moving in a daze of special torment. The rose-lipped girls, she thought, the girls—let them sleep. In fields where roses fade, burn, blacken, stiffen, sting. Her pity for Loreen swelled through the romance of the night until it was a pity for herself, Nan, Larry, and Nan's boyfriend, all her friends. All of them danced in the shadow of Loreen's disaster.

Later she had only a small recollection of her behavior for the next hour, except at the end of the dance when Larry was saying, "Jo, I don't know what's happened or what I've done, you're so still. If I've made you sore . . ."

"It's nothing you've done. I've got moody. I'm sorry. I wanted you to have the best time."

"Was it something I said? I joked a lot, but I didn't mean to say anything you wouldn't like."

"It wasn't that, Larry. I'll write to you and I'll see you real soon. I'm glad you could come."

She walked with him to his car and let him kiss her a few times, but it was not the same—not as it had been, already existing, already finished, in anticipation.

"I'm so sorry the evening didn't end the way it began," he said.

She let a few tears come as she crossed the parking lot and went to her room. By the time Nan had come in, she was sufficiently in control of herself, but yet so in need of comfort, that she told Nan at once what had happened.

"The end of a perfect day," Nan said. "That's fine. We've caught her and this will quiet everything back to normal."

"I'm not going to tell," Jody said.

That began an argument that lasted for two hours. While they undressed Jody described her meeting with Loreen's mother, her dislike of the woman, and her conviction that Mrs. Cory's competitiveness was somehow to blame for Loreen's "trouble," and Nan said, "Well gee, maybe that's all the better reason for reporting it to Miss Drake. She's had a lot of experience, and she'd know what to do. *You* don't, do you?"

Jody shook her head in half-submissive stubbornness.

"We did our part," Nan said. "Miss Drake can take over from here. Don't you have faith in Miss Drake?"

"Miss Drake would have to punish her some way for the sake of the other girls. I don't know if that's exactly fair," Jody said. "Loreen isn't just another one of the girls. I mean she's after all different."

"What gets me," Nan said, "is that day at the Rec Cabin when she must have had your money in her pocket when she was showing us those phony pictures. What gall. Can you explain that? She's no good."

"I guess not," Jody admitted. They sat in their dark council peering at the night as though to watch its emptiness reflect the loaded secret of their hearts. "I can't explain anything. I feel something bad happened to Loreen or she wouldn't do bad things like this. If we'd been more kind to her . . ."

"How kind would we have had to be?"

"I don't know."

"OK, you win," Nan said. "Loreen will probably be leaving by noon tomorrow. She can wear gloves until she goes. You don't have to tell. Give her a break if you want to."

"Can I give her a break?"

"Oh now," Nan said, "you're arguing on both sides. I'm going to bed." She heard Nan move in the darkness and finally heard the springs yield softly in Nan's bed. Nan's voice came tranquilly, "You can decide easier after you've slept."

Morning only complicated the decision. A dozen other matters—some trivial, some important—demanded Jody's attention and pulled her here and there. Her parents were arriving in the afternoon. Books had to be taken to the book exchange. She had to pick up her cap and gown.

Toward eleven, holding her breath for a decision, she set out for Miss Drake's office. It seemed to her that all she could do now was keep walking toward Miss Drake's authority and it would be as if her feet had made the decision her mind was incapable of.

Perhaps they did, for she walked right past the hallway that would have taken her to Miss Drake and again climbed the stairs to the Chem Lab and the cubbyhole office where Mr. Harvey sat. It was exactly as if he had been sitting there among his elements and retorts for no other reason except to await her, knowing she would have to come back.

Nevertheless it took an effort to begin speaking to him. She started awkwardly, "You remember the powder you gave us— gave me? Is there some way you can use a chemical to get that stain off?"

He shook his head. "It wears off in time." His eyes questioned her further with harsh patience and she told him everything. She tried—harder than ever before in her life—to explain not merely the facts but the way the facts had made her feel and the way her feelings had become facts demanding adjustment.

"Jody Foster." He pronounced her name as though there might be a puzzle even in these syllables. "What's going on? Are you trying to squeeze an education out of Larchmoor at this late date?"

She responded half-angrily. She felt he must be taking her attempts at real honesty as subject matter for another of his irresponsible jokes. "All right. I'm not the smartest. It all boils down to we were going to catch whoever took the money. I didn't know there would be so much to it."

"Now you know."

"But that doesn't help anything."

"You talked about a thief and then went and caught a human being. At least you know now you're dealing with a person."

Presently Jody asked, "Is it a good thing to know that?" An unselfconscious frown marred the smoothness of her face. "Probably the more we know the better off we are. . . . Is it any *good* to know so much you don't know any more what's right to do?"

From across his desk he stared at her with a sympathy that erased the difference in their ages. He tapped his pipe and waited as though she must help him by discovering the answer to her own question. From outside the light streamed in across the sterile neatness of the room, wavering as the shadows of a hundred leaves entered it and waved out.

"Knowledge like that," he said. "No, it's something more or less than good. I don't know if it does any good to know that."

Once more she asked the childish question, realizing as she did so that she would never be able to ask it again any more than she would ever again love dolls or come as a freshman to Larch-moor, despairing as though something wonderful that had lain within her grasp were falling down time as she recognized and reached to seize it. "But is it good finally? I mean, in a *big* way?"

"You'll have to make your own answer to that," he said.

She left him to go try. From his office she walked out alone to the spot where yesterday Larry had spoken for her the dream of the coming unclouded summer. By the pond's edge she sank onto the stones where she had sat yesterday in a different world. The same brown ducks presently sailed in front of her in their tranquil, innocent parade.

She realized that knowledge had come like an armed angel forbidding her to report Loreen's theft, but in this omission—of course it was wrong not to report it, as Nan had argued—she felt a complex burden settling its novelty across her life. It seemed that from now on Loreen would go with her like her shadow or her reflection in the water, always to remind her of some irre-mediable distortion in herself, never to be utterly ignored. It might be, she felt, that the burden of this shadow sister would become intolerable some day. Who could tell if it might not make her falter on some slight obstacle that could never trip her while she ran in innocence? But there was a chance that it would make her strong, and in this tricky world, that was the chance she had to take.

The Father

This began many years ago. Since its origin was from an accident and since many of the consequences would never be duplicated, it may stand as a unique little history without much relation to the fated march of public events or the destinies of most people.

It began on a March morning when Cory Johnson was shelling corn in the crib on his farm. He had a rattletrap old sheller that he was rather proud of. Some of its parts—the gears and the rust-pitted flywheel bored for a hand crank—had come from a machine in use on this farm for longer than Cory had lived. But he had rebuilt the frame and replaced the shelling spikes inside. He had rigged an electric motor and a system of belts to run the apparatus after the REA brought the wires out on this mail route west of Boda.

The sheller worked well enough. When there was no load of corn hitting the spikes, the rising and falling hum of the motor and the sibilance of the belts on the pulley faces were reasonably quiet. Of course, when corn was actually being shelled, a deafening racket filled this solid-walled room in the corner of the slatted crib.

Cory thought he was alone on the farm at this hour. His wife had taken all three children with her in the Model A. The two older boys were in school and would not come home until late afternoon. His wife hoped to drive into Boda to see her parents if the roads had not thawed too badly. She meant to take Bobbie, the youngest boy, along with her. Probably those two would not be back much before noon.

Cory liked being alone on his place. The job he had laid out for himself this morning was not pressing. At mid-morning he would go to the house for coffee and cold pancakes with jelly. While he ate the snack he meant to listen to a science program broadcast daily from the station of the state university. He liked science. In his rural isolation he believed—then, early in the thirties, almost a full century after it began to dominate the life of the western world—that science was "the coming thing."

As he fell into the rhythm of it, he was enjoying his work as much as he ever had. The warming day, which would probably take the bottom out of the gravel roads between here and town before it was through, permitted him to take off his sheepskin coat. He was warm enough in a sweater as long as he kept busy, and for a good hour he worked without pause, bringing tin bushels full of corn from a pile in the slatted corncrib and feeding it into the machine.

While the ears ran down the trough to the hopper, Cory sometimes watched the throat of the outlet where the shelled grains poured into gunnysacks. Mostly the grains flowed out in a brisk, placid stream, but now and then above the main flow some single grains would leap like fast, yellow sparks from a grinding wheel. There was of course nothing extraordinary in the maverick behavior of these grains. They were the ones that had caught somehow between the cobs and the whirling spikes just long enough for elastic and centrifugal forces to build up, then hurl them like bullets ricocheting out the metal chute that filled the sacks. Still, their unpredictable flight suggested mysteries beyond the fringe of his experience. He had read in *Popu-*

lar Science Monthly where some Jap had invented a centrifugal machine gun. It pleased him mildly to think he was watching the principle of the gun being demonstrated by the apparatus he had put together. In another issue of the same magazine he had seen a photograph of electrons leaping through the dark of an experimental chamber, and though these pictures had shown no more than the scratch of a white line across a black rectangle, it pleased him to believe that electrons *really* looked like these hard-flung, zinging grains of corn.

Once that morning when Cory went out into the main storage bins of the crib to fill his bushels, he heard the electric motor change pitch. Its normal whine became a level, unpleasant hum. The slap and hiss of the driving belts had stopped. The motor was no longer turning over, and he had better shut down the current quickly before the armature burned out.

As he skipped for the door, the motor began to run again. A belt whistled on an immobilized pulley.

He saw his four-year-old son Bobbie standing beside the fly wheel with his gloved hand raised to the gear reduction. The boy's face was turned back over his sheepskin collar, and he was grinning the not quite honest grin he often showed when caught doing something destructive and forbidden—he grinned as if trying to minimize his offense.

Cory thought the boy had pushed a cob in the gears, experimentally, and thus had stopped the whole complex of machinery cold.

Then with a hawking scream that scalded his throat and the inside of his nose with bile, Cory called his wife's name. The boy's hand was in the gears. Down the fringed and starred cuff of his glove, blood was oozing briskly onto his sleeve and down the sleeve to the hem of his coat.

Cory had turned the power off and knelt with the boy in his arms by the time his wife ran from the car she had just parked.

As pain returned to the shocked nerves of the hand, the boy's grin merely enlarged until his mouth stood in a ridged O like the corolla of a white flower. He was now shrieking incessantly in fear and pain. He danced in his father's arms and jerked and jerked to free his hand. Urine bubbled through his overalls and mixed with the blood under his boots.

"Daddy'll get you out," Belle Johnson shouted in the boy's face.

"Daddy, Daddy, Daddy, Daddy," she moaned to Cory, depending like the child on his act to save them.

"Hold'm," Cory said. He vaulted the machine and knocked the belt from the drive shaft, vaulted back and set his shoulder to a spoke of the flywheel. When the gears moved, the boy shrieked louder and fainted.

"I'll take the sonofabitch apart," Cory said. He looked under the motor table for his toolbox. He remembered having put it in the trunk of the car. He was not sure whether he had left it there or had taken it out later in the barn.

"Daddy, he's swallowing his tongue," Belle said.

Cory put a finger and thumb in the boy's mouth. It was like putting them into an electric socket with the current on. The strength of the curling tongue seemed greater than any he could force into his own hand.

It took him five seconds to secure the tongue and press his wife's nails into it. He believed it had taken two or three minutes.

Sweat was blinding him. He thought the boy might die if he did not hurry, but he caught himself staring with revulsion at the machine, taking time to blame himself not only for the failure to enclose the gears in a safety box, but for making anything so ugly and rough—for presuming to do something that only factory technicians working for pay could do right.

He fished out his jackknife and cut away the blood-sopped glove from the jammed hand. He thought it possible that the jersey might have cushioned the bones at least. What he saw looked like boiled and shredded chicken in which a bad cook had left bits of gristle and bone.

"Daddy, his mouth is turning blue," Belle said.

"All right. Hold onto him. Hold him tight," Cory said.

He took a dark-bladed hatchet from its hanging place on the wall. There was not much room for it between the gears and the bottom of the hopper. With a three-inch blow he clipped the hand just above the wristbone.

"Get a tourniquet on him. I'll get the car," he told his wife.

The doctor in Boda, young Doctor Grant, said that Cory had done a pretty good job of amputation, all things considered.

"Bobbie probably never even felt what you did," Doctor Grant said, with his clean, pink-nailed fingers resting on Cory's sleeve.

"There was quite a little shock. Naturally. But if his hand was so badly mangled you couldn't get it free, you can be sure that's where the shock came from. Say, it didn't take you long to get him in here to me," he said with an encouraging gleam of admiration in his eyes.

"No," Cory said. "I just didn't pay any attention to the mudholes. I came through the bad stretch the other side of the bridge doing about sixty-five, I guess."

The doctor laughed quite loudly. "I'll bet you jumped that Model A right over the bad spots."

Now that he knew his boy was going to be all right—which at the moment meant that he was going to live—Cory felt an unaccountable but decent pride in his behavior after the accident. By God, he had held back nothing. He had ripped the guts out of his Model A, coming in from the farm in just seventeen minutes. By God, he had seen the mail carrier—the mail carrier, mind you—out beside his car studying the mire of gravel and standing water in the low spot beyond the creek and probably deciding it had thawed too bad for him to get the mail through. Now Cory could remind himself—what he wouldn't bend the doctor's ear with—that Belle had shouted from the back seat to go around the longer way by Hopewell Church when he took it on his own shoulders to give this way a try. He hated to think what might have happened if he had stuck the car in deep there, a mile and a quarter from town. And for a minute or two it had been touch-and-go with the mud geysering over his windshield and the car skidding always to the left against his pull on the steering wheel. He had seen the face of the mail carrier through a muddy window, puckered in disbelief, almost in awe, as he watched the Model A churn past him.

The car was still fishtailing uncontrollably when Cory took her up the bridge approach. The whipping rear end grazed half the girders of the span before he got her straightened. The rear bumper was gone and somewhere along the line he'd over-taxed the transmission so he couldn't get her shifted down from high when he had to wait for a truck to cross at the Boda stop sign. He killed the motor then and ran three blocks to the doctor's office with the boy in his arms and Belle unable to keep up with him. And made it in time.

In time. In time. In time. The thought quieted the thudding of his heart.

"I don't think there's enough loss of blood to worry us," Doctor Grant said. "The tourniquet worked very nicely." Doctor Grant was only concerned—just a little—about the effects of shock, he said. He wanted to drive the boy over to the hospital in the county seat as soon as he had seen two more patients. He wanted to make sure Bobbie had his strength built up "before I finish the job for you," as he put it to Cory, with a wink of complicity. The Johnsons could ride along in the doctor's car. Belle could hold the little fellow in her lap, and everything would be arranged so one of them could stay all night with him in the hospital.

In the meantime, while his parents waited, the boy was sleeping in one of the doctor's examination rooms. He had been given morphine. Everything seemed to be under control. The orderly flow of circumstance had resumed again.

Cory opened a magazine, there in the doctor's waiting room—not so much because he thought he could read anything just now as because he wanted some shield behind which to hide until he came to terms with himself. Most importantly, he had to choke down the boisterous, excessive pride that had come on the rebound of his relief. He kept wanting to grin when he thought of the mail carrier's face. But if he couldn't help grinning, no one ought to see him do it. Then, too, he might want to pray out some of this thanksgiving that the roads hadn't been too bad, that Doctor Grant knew his business, and so on. Cory was still religious in crisis, though in normal times he lived by the opinion that "a lot of people went too far" with the religious business.

"Cory?"

He heard Belle's whisper like something whispering to him out of the past—like his mother come to wake him for a fine day in summer after vacation from school had begun and he could enjoy himself helping *his* daddy around the farm.

He looked up from the magazine. Belle's face was so pale he was frightened for her. Her blue eyes looked black against her ghostly skin.

"Daddy," she said, "don't feel too bad. You had to do it."

Of course it would have occurred to him sooner or later, without any prompting from Belle, that he and he alone was guilty for the loss of Bobbie's hand.

Since Cory would rather—if wishes had anything to do with

the matter—have given his own hand, the way the guilt came to present itself was especially hard for him to master.

The point wasn't his negligence. As his father-in-law said, "There's a great many dangerous things around a farm, Cory. There always will be for kids."

"I know it," Cory said. "There's got to be machinery and animals and the pony that Joe and Gordon ride. You take the windmill tower for an example. I've caught Joe and Gordon up there I don't know how many times. They might any time fall and break their necks. Or the fan's going and they stick their heads up through the platform. Pfffttt!"

The older man extended the rhythm of agreement. "That's a fact, and you know Belle, when she was little, one time I nearly toppled a horse tank I was loading right onto her." He shuddered even now.

"Ah, but Dad, you held it," Belle recalled.

"I did," her father said. "And I paddled you for it when I saw you were safe. And I always remembered what a scare I had. But the point is that accidents just happen, Cory. After all, that's what the word *accident* means."

"Yeah, it does," Cory said.

The conversation was one of a great many that took place in the spring and summer after Bobbie lost his hand. They amounted to a kind of informal funeral, commemorating and at the same time draining away the immediate emotions of loss. It appeared, even to Cory, that it did him good to speak of the accident. He found no difficulty in saying man to man, man to wife, father to children—even to Bobbie—that an accident was something that just happened. Cory knew as well as any man that this was so.

Though he said many times that he could shoot himself for not having put a safety box around those gears on the sheller, this negligence was not the point that proved most crucial, either.

"You should have done that," his father-in-law said once when Cory lamented the absence of such a guard. "Well, we go on and try to make up for our past mistakes, and it does seem kind of sad to lock the door after the horse is gone, but that's what we do. I notice you took some rungs out of the ladder up the windmill."

"And Gordon climbed it the other night anyway," Belle said.

"Shinnied right up the frame and had to yell for Cory to come and get him off."

They laughed and Cory laughed with them. Yes. Just to go on living he had to accept the likelihood of accidents, particularly where boys were involved, and he could do that.

But it wasn't the accidental part of Bobbie's misfortune that settled permanently into Cory's mind, freezing it to a pattern of distress. What he could never face—could never understand— was that he was guilty in taking that hatchet down from its hanging place on the wall and cutting off his son's hand.

"You had to do it," Belle said. She was willing to repeat this assurance whenever she thought it would help.

It never helped. Cory knew he'd had to do it. But necessity was no excuse at all for the guilt that rode him. The more he rehearsed his motives, the less important they seemed in comparison with the immortal act. If it was only bad luck that had put him in a situation where he had no choice, still, that luck was *his*. The guilt seemed to reside in that simple fact.

"It's like if I'd been someone else, not any part of this awful thing would have happened," he said to Belle.

Now that her emotions had resumed their normal level, she was almost as much amused as concerned at this odd way of putting it. She probably thought he was fishing for sympathy, and though she didn't mind sympathizing with him all he wanted, she didn't know how to offer the right response to his fancy. She said, "Sure. Sure. If you were someone else you wouldn't have this farm. You wouldn't have your nice kids. You wouldn't be stuck with me. Well, that's all a pipe dream, old man. You're stuck with all of us, and we'll get along. You know we will. Bobbie's a brave little guy. We might just thank God he was always left-handed."

"I know we'll get along," Cory said.

"You shouldn't punish yourself this way, because there's nothing to punish yourself for."

"I know that too."

"Then don't get depressed like this."

He had not spoken from depression, but from guilt. He knew well enough what depression was. He was depressed in those years of the thirties when the drought took most of his corn crop two years in succession; when he let himself be cheated in buying a secondhand car that turned out to have a cracked block; when he had trouble with his gallstones and had to cripple around all one winter; when his oldest boy, Joe, had trouble with his high school studies and went off to join the navy; when Belle's father, a man who'd been so good to Cory and his family and so dear to Bobbie, died of cancer; when the war came and Joe was out there at Pearl Harbor, where the Japs dropped on them with their newfangled weapons, and so many didn't have a chance on the anchored ships.

Year by year there were things to depress him. Big things and little things. And through the same years there'd been good times and times of satisfaction when he *wasn't* depressed. Take the summer he'd put the family in the car and driven them out to Yellowstone Park. That trip was a pure satisfaction. He couldn't remember a thing wrong with it.

Easily he remembered the good winters when he and Gordon were teaching Bobbie to hunt with them. They would load the dogs in the back seat of the car and drive over to the creek bottom to look for rabbits, quail, or pheasants. Cory had his pump gun. Gordon and Bobbie "shared" the single-shot .410 that had been bought for Joe when he turned twelve. Off they'd mush through the snow and broken cornstalks, trying to keep up with the badly trained dogs, joking and trading insults like three men—or three boys, it didn't matter which. Once, Cory'd knocked down three cock pheasants from a rising covey. Bobbie clapped his mitten to the side of his head and howled in admiration and disbelief. "Purty good, for an old man," he yelled over the snow. "Purty good."

"Even if you did get more than the limit," Gordon put in. "You going to tell the game warden I shot one of them?"

What he'd seen in the boys' eyes that afternoon was unmistakable and worth treasuring—just standing there in the snow with the dead birds around them, the boys being proud of their old man. It was like the male satisfaction he'd felt the day he took Bobbie in through the mud to the doctor's. In time. Only now the boys were here to share and mirror back the lonely pride of his manhood.

There had also been the good times—not to mention *all* the blessings of the years—when Joe came home on boot leave; when prices picked up in thirty-nine and the same year Belle had another boy, Cory, Jr.; and when they got the first letter from Joe after Pearl Harbor saying he was all right.

The good things and the bad things of an ordinary farmer's life had happened to him. He had responded to them like an ordinary man, with satisfaction or depression.

But the guilt he endured was something else. It seemed to have a life of its own, to be almost a distinct life he lived when his ordinary life gave him the opportunity.

Weeks, months, years went by in which he forgot that he was guilty. During those periods he got quite used to Bobbie's disfigurement, as if it were a condition that had always existed, one intended by nature.

Fortunately, Bobbie wasn't the boy to feed on sympathy. He managed. As far as his parents could tell, he was a happier boy than Joe had been.

Cory watched without sentimentality as his maimed son grew up. But when the awareness of his guilt came back in one of its cyclic manifestations, he found that it had not diminished with time. After ten years it was as keen and lively as it had been that morning in Doctor Grant's office when Belle had unintentionally announced it to him.

An assortment of events served, through the years, to recall it, the way symptoms in the throat announce the approach of a general systemic infection.

For example, there was Bobbie's fight in the school yard when he was in the second grade.

Cory saw most of the mix-up. Driving homeward from an errand in Boda, he and Gordon stopped to pick up Bobbie from his play after school. From where the car was parked, they could see some boys darting back and forth beyond the schoolhouse, dodging, turning, skidding in the grass, swinging at each other in what seemed to be a game of tag. Then Glen Horstman chased Bobbie down into the corner by the well. Bobbie backed into the hedge separating the school yard from a cornfield. He sparred away the jabs and pokes the bigger boy aimed at him. It looked as if both boys were laughing breathlessly, having a lot of fun.

They saw Glen Horstman feint a kick and follow the feint with a blow of his fist that started Bobbie's nose bleeding. Bobbie signaled that he'd had enough: *Lay off. I surrender.*

Glen kept punching. He had knocked Bobbie to the ground

and was sitting on him when Gordon leaped the ditch and went running to the rescue.

Laggardly, Cory followed. He was only a few steps from the car when he saw Gordon chase Glen into the schoolhouse.

"Gordon!" he commanded.

Gordon stopped on the wooden stairs by the door and turned. His face was quizzical and angry. "Why, I'll just knock *him* around a little bit," he said.

"No you won't," Cory told him. "You and Bobbie come on and get in the car now. Bobbie'd better wash his face at the pump."

"But he's bigger than Bobbie," Gordon said. He blushed because he did not want to mention that Bobbie lacked one hand to use in self-defense.

"Get in the car!" Cory shouted.

All the way home from the schoolhouse, Gordon sat in incredulous, wounded silence. Bobbie, though, was talkative enough. He wasn't in any pain from his beating. He wasn't really mad at Glen Horstman. Now that it was over, the fight seemed to him a pure entertainment.

But that, as Gordon's silence implied, was not all that must be taken into account. On almost any other day he would have been there at school to protect his brother. At least, without his father's inexplicable attitude to reckon with, he would have known what he ought to do tomorrow.

After supper, Gordon went to his mother about what had happened. She, in turn, spoke furiously to Cory as soon as the boys were in bed.

"I think I'd just better get on the telephone and find out from his teacher if this has ever happened before—the kids picking on Bobbie. I won't have it. Just because he's crippled—"

"Aw, Belle, that wasn't why Glen done it. They was playing and he got carried away."

"Playing? Gordon said he hit Bobbie with his fist. He was sitting on him, pounding his head, and you didn't . . ." She didn't say what Cory should have done that he had omitted, but she shook her head bitterly. The more she thought, the more worked up she got.

"Well, you go ahead and call the teacher if you want to put your nose in it," Cory growled.

"I *will* put my nose in it," she said, "and you'd better go over to the Horstmans' place and have a little talk with Glen's dad, because I don't intend to have this kind of thing going on, whatever you intend."

"But Bobbie wouldn't want—"

"You can drive me over and sit in the car while I go in and have it out with them," she raged. "You can sit in the car if you're scared to tell Ralph Horstman we want this stopped."

The Horstman farm was less than a two-mile drive. Through the spring night and the murmur of a rainy wind, Cory drove slowly, telling himself that of course Belle was right. He sighed heavily and thought he'd want his friends who lived around him to come and tell him about it if one of his boys had done a wrong. But he seldom felt so uneasy about anything as he did walking in under the elms of the Horstman yard and knocking at the screen door of the back porch.

"He what? Glen done *what?*" Ralph Horstman bellowed. He grabbed Cory's shoulder and dragged him in from the back porch to the kitchen. "When'd he do that? This afternoon?" Horstman's throat began to swell rhythmically. He seemed to be growing taller and broader. "Mama, give Cory a cup of coffee or—or some *beer!*" he shouted to his wife. Then he fled the kitchen, pounding up the stairway from the living room like a plow horse frenzied in a burning building.

Cory and Mrs. Horstman heard the thump of a body dumped from its bed onto the floor and then a long, sleepy, uninterrupted wail, accompanied irregularly by the sound of slaps. In a minute Mrs. Horstman ran upstairs, too.

More slaps then. A more complicated sound of struggle began as the woman tried to mediate. Again and again, like the boom of outraged justice itself, Ralph Horstman's voice shouted, "He hit li'l Bobbie!"

After the condemnation, the smack of a hand on a rump, and then the woman's plea, seeming only to convince her husband that she had not understood the enormity of the offense. "But he hit li'l Bobbie!"

Downstairs Cory listened in what he could no longer doubt was envy. He knew well enough what he had no wish and no way of explaining to Gordon or Belle—that when he had seen Glen Horstman's fist bring blood from Bobbie's nose, he had felt a merciless identification with the aggressor. He had been unmanned by the recognition.

He had not wanted Bobbie hurt. No! He had never wanted

Bobbie hurt, but he had seen his own act reenacted and known himself as powerless to prevent the pain as before.

But Glen Horstman, because he was a little boy, could be punished for what was, after all, a small offense. Cory, for his immeasurably greater offense, could expect no such squaring of accounts.

Afterward, each time his guilt flared in his face, he had to endure it in the same way until, mysteriously, it faded in his mind again—not dead, not even eroded by the remorse he had paid for it, merely waiting to be wakened again and endured again like an operation submitted to without anesthetic because, though he was guilty, no one owed him punishment.

He was punished. In the last year of the war, Gordon had just been drafted and sent to Fort Bragg when Joe was killed near Okinawa. By that time Joe was a seaman first class serving on a destroyer escort. The DE was on picket duty about seventy miles east of Buckner Bay when it was attacked by a George fighter. The attack occurred near sundown. A broad highway of gold and choppy crimson opened away from the little ship toward the west. The fighter came down this road like an erratic spark of gallantry and panic, hurled without conscious aim. The big ring sights on Joe's 20-mm. cannon must have circumscribed the sun itself as he swung it over to defend the ship. The fighter struck just abaft and below the bridge. The ship lived for several hours more, time enough for the survivors to be transferred to a destroyer. None of Joe's shipmates saw him or his body after the attack.

When the news came to the Johnson farm, Cory wept like any father bereft. And his tears were partly tears of relief, for it seemed to him in the first debility of sorrow that this extravagant punishment might, at last, pay off his guilt. It was not even in his heart to protest that the payment was too great, though he saw no equivalence between the hand he had taken from one child and the life he must now yield helplessly back to darkness. If he was quits, he must be satisfied.

But when his grief diminished and his strength returned, Cory saw that whatever had happened to Joe had nothing to do with his old guilt, which was neither increased nor minimized by Joe's death. What little religion Cory had kept through the years melted with this discovery. Religion seemed foolish to him

now, a windy pretense at linking things that had no real connection. The issue was between himself and a chaos to which only a
fool would pray.

He had nothing with which to replace religion. His irregular
and shallow enthusiasm for science had long since vanished of
its own inanity. Besides, though science had once seemed to
him "the coming thing," he had never been notified that science
might pretend to explain what he thirsted terribly to know. It
had been fun to read about the novelties science discovered. He
had got bored. That was all.

In his whole life, as he could look back at it now, only one
condition had given meaning to his work and the depressions or
satisfactions that went with it. That condition was his fatherhood. Even if he had fathered his boys more or less accidentally,
in lust, in lukewarm fondness for his wife, his fatherhood had
come to be more than the sum of days and of forgotten wishes.
Before anything else, he was a father—and it was against this
definition of himself that he had been forced to strike that day in
the corncrib.

Belle died in 1950. Cory wept for her, too; envied her, too, for
he suspected she must have carried through life some secret,
like his, of undiminishable guilt for rebellion against the self that
time and accident had given her. But now she was free of it.

They said Cory's mind began to fail him after Belle's death.

His mind was working better than ever—and he understood
that was what his family and Doctor Grant *meant*, though they
had to express themselves by an exact inversion of the truth.

If they had said he was troublesome and a bit frightening to
live with, he could have agreed straightforwardly. But they
needed more than that. Like most people, they needed a shallow burrow of "reasons" and "explanations" because they dared
not deal with a sheer, objective fact. He could no longer live on
their sort of explanations, but he sympathized with them. So he
said, Yes, he reckoned his mind was going back on him. He
didn't want to be a trouble to them, and if he couldn't straighten
up by himself, he would certainly do what Doctor Grant recommended. He would go to the asylum "for a while." In the meantime, while they gave him a chance, he wanted to carry on his
share of the work on the farm.

In this period there were five of the family living together there. Cory, Bobbie and his wife Lucy, and their little boy Ed (after Lucy's father), and Cory, Jr. Between them, Bobbie and Cory, Jr., could just about take care of the farm work. Bobbie had been to Ag school at the state university and he was a fine manager, very good with bookwork and planning ahead about the crops and machinery and soil, and figuring how they could afford the new things they needed. Farm work was more and more a matter of business brains these days, and he was sure that Bobbie was all right in that department.

Bobbie had got himself a new device to use for a right hand, too, now that they could afford it. There had been so much more money coming in during and after the war! Now you take Joe, Cory would tell himself, we just couldn't have afforded to send him to the university, Mother and I, back when he might have wanted to go. Then, quicker than anyone else could have reminded him that Joe was not a great one for study or using his brain, Cory would throw in that very qualification and go on: Yes, but things are getting so well-organized that they can take a boy who's not so bright to begin with and kind of guide him over the hurdles and give him remedial work and guide him into the right niche and he does all right! This was the way Cory's mind went on and on in an endless series of examinations and connections. His mind was far from failing. It dealt with more all the time, and, insofar as the mind alone was concerned, it was dealing more effectively. The sickness was elsewhere.

What Bobbie had was too grand and clever to be called a hook, though he good-humoredly called it that on weekdays. On Sunday, for fun, he called it a prosthesis. It was really three hooks and a bar, all with a bright chromium finish that twinkled wonderfully in the May morning sun when the young man swung himself up onto the tractor seat and headed out to the fields, while Lucy held little Ed and waved to him from the back door.

It was so strange, sometimes, to Cory to see that shiny batch of levered claws on the baby's back when Bobbie was holding him—as at the homecoming picnic in Boda when there was a crowd and the Johnsons drove in to see all their old friends come back to this hick town. Gordon was with them, too, on that occasion, visiting a week from his job in Seattle, where he'd remained with an opportunity after the service.

That *thing* on the baby's back would look just as firm and tender as a human hand. Odd how Bobbie could use it to caress with sometimes, as if it were alive, though of course it had no sense of touch. It could express feeling though it had none. The only time the baby minded being touched with it was in cold weather. But Cory's thoughts were often busy on conjectures as to whether the baby *ought* to mind being touched by the lifeless thing. No end to considerations involved there.

With his prosthesis Bobbie could manage nearly any chore on the farm. No doubt if worst came to worst, everything could be handled without hired help if Cory went away. But Cory had made his place, now that the boys were taking over so much, by doing the dirty and menial jobs that their machinery still left undone. True, they had a milker, and even Cory, Jr., could handle the milking of their twelve cows without complaining he had been put upon. Someone still had to shovel up after the stock. The boys rented a corn picker from the elevator in Boda for the corn shucking. Someone had to drive the tractor into town through a November rain to get the picker and see that it got back on schedule. Cory always did jobs like that.

Doctor Grant didn't like it much that Cory should make himself into a nigger—that was his word—for the boys. As he saw it, this was another symptom of Cory's mental deterioration. But the doctor's opinion on this account was only one way of looking at it, and Cory was very well aware of this.

He realized that quite aside from any help he gave with the work or any hardship he imposed on Lucy by giving her another mouth to cook for, he *worried* his family.

He was sorry for this, but deliberately he went ahead with his alarming and aberrant courses. In the winter of 1952 he spent part of every day in the corncrib, where he was reconstructing the corn sheller that used to stand in the corner room. He scoured the neighborhood and the junk piles around Boda for old parts. He rebuilt the wooden frame where the electric motor had sat. He drilled bolt holes in the concrete floor he and Gordon had poured back in wartime when they junked the old sheller. He begged some secondhand lumber from the people who had moved onto the Horstman farm, not wanting to spend any more good money than he had to on his "foolishness."

It took Bobbie less than a week to figure out what his father was doing—a little longer to decide to intervene. Then one morning he made a point of sauntering down to the crib and entering the room where his father was hammering and sweating.

"What you up to?" Bobbie said. "I thought since I didn't have much to do this morning, maybe I could . . ."

The brightness and pretense—from both sides—faded quickly enough. A reckless pity shone from Bobbie's face. He wet his lips.

"Dad, you're making that sheller again, isn't that it?"

"Well, Bobbie, yeah, I thought I'd run her up again and see if maybe I could improve the design. Like you say, there's not too awful much work to be done these days, though maybe I ought to be down at the barn having a look at that loader Cory broke last summer." He started to leave the room.

Bobbie stopped him. "I didn't mean that, Dad. You don't have to work every minute. But—but, it seems kind of useless for you to be making a sheller."

"Yeah, it does."

"Then—"

"It kind of—"

"Dad, Lucy and I've been talking and we want you to, well, go out to Seattle and see Gordon awhile. You keep saying it would cost too much, and Seattle's a big place if you don't want to stay with Gordon. Look, I'm going to come right out with it. Lucy and I don't feel right for having called Doctor Grant in on you. Doctors don't know everything. But a family is different, and I know that Gordon would want you to come."

"—kind of helps me think things out," Cory said mildly, touching the homely machine he was building. "I'm not a hand like you are to put things down on paper or in words, either, and if I can build something to see, that helps with my brain work."

Bobbie gritted his teeth. "But you're thinking about things you ought to leave alone," he said. He held up his claw, glittering and lightly sweating in the cold room. "You're brooding about *this* again. For my sake, leave it alone. You think all my life I've blamed you somehow and I haven't. Can't you believe me when I say it? You *saved* my life and everyone knows that."

"I don't know," Cory said. "Maybe there was some other way to do it."

"*Was!*" The horror of that exploded syllable stood with them like the angel of death. What had been in time was not, any longer, in time. The past was unalterable, and yet they could not shake from their minds the illusion of free choice.

"I've had a good life," Bobbie said—as if that bore on the enigma that Cory wrestled. He might have had *another* life if his father had been the man to find another means of saving him. "What more could I want? I've been happy," Bobbie said.

"I know, son," Cory answered. "What I'll do, I'll get the pickup this afternoon and carry this junk down in the east forty and dump it. Guess I'd better save the lumber and use it for kindling."

Bobbie snarled in his frustration. "You don't have to do *that*, Dad. You don't have to do anything I tell you or anything for my sake. That's the point. Don't you get it?"

"Sure I see what you mean," Cory said. "I wasn't thinking about how you—and Lucy, I suppose—would feel about this contraption. Now let's just walk up to the house for some coffee and I'll tell Lucy I'm sorry I started it."

Bobbie said, "Maybe you'd better not mention it to her."

"All right," Cory said. "Whatever you think is best."

The next morning he was working on the sheller again. He had got to the point of installing the gears and covering them with a steel safety box.

Probably his queer behavior and his family's concern with it had been going on longer than he realized. Because they cared for him they would have taken what pains they could not to let him notice their precautions. Noting their few failures to be discreet was like seeing an advance guard of rats begin to invade the farm. Experience had convinced him that if you saw only the signs of depredation, that meant there were ten rats around your buildings. If you saw one rat, that meant a hundred. If you saw two together, a thousand, probably.

Now, to all his other considerations, he added the task of measuring the impressions he made each day on Lucy, Bobbie, and Cory, Jr. Like a stock-market gambler he read the daily quotations of his stock with them. Better this afternoon. Low and worried this week. Cautious. Desperate. Better. Better. The same.

They could not bring themselves to wound him by flat and final decisions in his behalf. If Bobbie had really insisted, Cory would have packed and gone to Seattle. Probably he would never have come back from that city.

At the same time, he realized that he confused their impressions by the very act of measuring them. And if their sanity

wavered to the magnetism of his craziness—as he saw it did—
then how could he trust them for reliable guidance, even in
what he ought to do?

He understood, sometime during 1953, that they had been
cautioned by Doctor Grant—or another authority they might
have consulted at Grant's recommendation—to be on the look-
out for a suicide attempt. He knew this first by subtle signs, as
he would have known about a family of rats in the corncrib before he saw the first darting black shape and prepared for a campaign of poison and traps. The subtle signs were followed by a
blunder so loving and crude it made him weep.

One morning he found that his straight razor had disappeared from the cabinet in the bathroom and had been replaced
with an electric shaver. The exchange had been made just one
week before Christmas, and he knew the electric gadget had
been bought as a present for him. In their anxiety they had been
unable to wait.

He picked up the shaver without hesitation. He accepted
whatever Lucy and Bobbie (or was it Lucy alone, weaker in her
fear, who had made the switch?) thought had to be done. He
put the plug into an outlet and set the humming head to his
cheek. He saw his cowed eyes under the windburnt sag of lids.
It seemed to him his courage was not adequate to his pity.

"Father," he said, as he used to pray in the time he had not
taken religion seriously enough to reject it. "Father." He heard
no distinct syllables, but a shapeless groan.

The futility of their gesture seemed unendurable. They had
taken his razor—didn't these children know that, on a farm, as
Belle's Dad had put it, the means to harm were never lacking?
He supposed they had hidden away the shells for his pump
gun, too, though he had not bothered to check for some time.
Odds and ends of rope had probably been gathered from the
barn and outbuildings (by Bobbie, careful not to let on to Cory,
Jr., why he was being so neat these days). They probably timed
his comings and goings, not to permit him to be too long alone.
And what good would all that do if he could claim the right to
kill himself?

To put their minds at ease he wanted to go to them now and
tell them how he had once determined to do away with himself
and why that was all past. The occasion had come soon after
Joe's death. The absence of the coffin from the funeral services

had served as a reminder of the absence of justice due from the empty heavens. That had been more than eight years ago. No one had worried then about gathering up ropes from the sheds, garage, or barn.

He had put a rope around his neck one morning before anyone else was out of bed, standing by the square opening in the floor of the haymow. There was enough light at that hour to show the churchlike vaulting of rafters in the empty mow. Nothing had ever tempted him more seductively than the black square in front of his toes.

But he had taken the rope off with the slow deliberation of a judge—not for a moment assuming that he was granting himself reprieve, but that in all solemnity he was refusing it. Self-execution was inappropriate to his guilt.

Well—of course he must not go to the children and tell them what he remembered of that morning. He was poor with words; he was more likely to scare them than to appease them. They weren't prepared to understand that what he had sentenced himself to that morning in the barn was *to think*. Under that sentence, he was obliged to respect all the problems raised whenever he was rash enough to solve one of them.

He had to think, though it was not easy for him. It was not easy to rid the farm of a pestilence of rats, either, but, again and again through his years on this place, he had set himself the task of poisoning and trapping creatures who had over him the advantages of number, secrecy, and natures that recognized no obligation except to exist. He supposed there had never been a day when the farm was free of rats. Yet, by unwavering persistence he had thinned the rat population again and again to the point at which it was tolerable.

It wasn't easy for him to get ahead of the problem he now presented to his anxious children, but he set himself to find how to make it easier for them.

Through that spring and much of the following summer he appeared to be succeeding. The cycles of compulsive thought that had made him careless of his behavior since Belle's death sped faster—of necessity—as they seemed to settle down into the tranquillity of age. Once upon a time he would have refused to believe himself capable of the nimble calculations that now became a commonplace.

He gave up working on the sheller in the corncrib—because

he had now got the whole material apparatus in his mind, from the grain of old wood to the bolts that fastened the electric motor to its bench, the pulleys and flywheel and their weight, strength, appearance, sound, and speed—all of this so completely transposed into an image that he could set the machine going in his imagination whenever he wanted. While he helped his youngest son with homework, or went over the accounts with Bobbie, or listened attentively to Lucy's frets about her new pregnancy, another part of his mind could repeat the crucial morning of his life.

So his family thought him better. They said he was "more himself" than he had been for years. They noticed how he gave up a share of the meanest work to each of his boys. Sometimes now he talked voluntarily of going to visit Gordon.

They were glad, again, to invert the truth. He saw that this second inversion did not cancel out the first—when they had believed him mad—but only made it incalculably more difficult to encompass, as if an already insoluble labyrinth should suddenly open out into its duplicate.

World without end, the world of thought that seemed bent on returning to some safe, lost starting point; but the prospect of its difficulty neither cheered nor daunted him. While he had strength of mind, he would go on as best he could, pretending that he was a juggler, an explorer, an acrobat, though he was only a big-footed farmer. At least he had learned to pace himself in his pursuit of multiplying complications. He had learned not to try too much at once. He was glad to think this adjusted pace—whether it meant success or failure to him—comforted his family.

One night in late summer he reached the end of thought. He had not foreseen (as a man with greater original gifts might have) that there could be an end of it. But there it was, confronting him. What had been a constantly accelerating series of wheels within wheels, wheels begetting wheels, a spinning and a spiraling that multiplied and exploded toward the ultimate horizons—all that was frozen in an instant into what seemed to him an immense sphere of light, motionless, achieved.

On the night it happened he was alone on the farm except for his grandson, who was sleeping upstairs. At suppertime Lucy had said with unusual petulance that she probably wouldn't get to go anywhere again for months or see any of their friends. The new baby was due soon. She would be tied down permanently after its arrival, so why didn't Bobbie take her anyplace any more?

Since he had been working hard in the hayfield all day, Bobbie might have snapped back at her. But Cory smoothed things over. He suggested that they drive through Boda to the county seat and find a place to dance or go to a movie. He was kind of tired himself, but would be glad to bathe Ed and read him a story and let him watch TV awhile before he went to bed.

Then Cory, Jr., had popped up and said he wanted to go along, too, and again there had been the threat of friction that Cory had to deflate judiciously. Why didn't young Cory ride just as far as Boda, he suggested, and drop off there to see some of his buddies? He could stay all night with Mickey Carnahan if he wanted, as a reward for working so well all day.

Cory had eased them away smoothly. The three young people left the farm after supper in a jolly mood. Young Ed had turned out to be no trouble at all. He nodded in front of the TV and went to bed early.

It was still not altogether dark when Cory took his cigar onto the screen porch to sit on the glider and do some thinking. On quiet evenings, left alone, he felt able to catch up on the arrears in his thought.

The night was faintly oppressive, though mild. He could hear the tree frogs dinning in the yard and the chug of the pump down by the barn. He heard the intermittent traffic of his neighbors going in late to Boda or the county seat, most of them traveling the new blacktop.

He thought about the highway and his neighbors and the way things had changed and the way things had been before. He thought, without emotion, of the difference between the blacktop and the muddy gravel he had charged through the day he cut off Bobbie's hand. Then he thought of the real sheller that had caused the accident and of the imaginary sheller that had duplicated it in his mind. And presently he was sure as could be that the sheller he imagined was run by the same principles that had run the sheller made of wood and steel. His creation and he were indistinguishable.

With that realization he reached the end of thought, knowing neither good nor evil but only guilt. The tree frogs, perhaps, continued their monotonous hysterical song in the dark leaves around him. There may have been a continuing traffic on the roads and the sound of the pump's piston beating back and forth in its imprisoning cylinder. He did not hear them. Whatever existed was silent and motionless. Eternal. As it had been and as it would be when time ended.

In that silence he rose from the soft glider and let himself out the screen door onto the grass of the yard. He walked, without needing a light, to the shed by the back gate. The motion of his body was fluent and easy, but he felt nothing. It seemed to him that he was constituted of the same material as Bobbie's well-wrought hook and had been able, like it, to express love without the ability of knowing it. (The proposition was the same if exactly reversed: to know love without the ability to express it.) The only passion remaining was for a justice that would bring a man in phase with the total equilibrium of the night.

From the shed he took a short ax and went upstairs to his grandson's bedroom. He came down a little later without it.

He sat in the glider and relit his cigar. After a while he found himself straining to hear the tree frogs. To hear anything. Because he was not dead he had to break the motionless, sound-less sphere of the thoughtless universe. He needed a noise to start him thinking again.

It was peaceful enough not to think—just to suck on the sweet cigar and let it all go up in a gentle exhalation. But he had to resume, if he could, the pain of thought so he could review what he had done in that silence when the sound of machinery stopped.

He had to plan the right way to present his act, or all those folks who relied on explanations would refuse to believe him sane. If they did not believe him sane, they would not punish him for this repetition of his guilt, and if he could not trick those who ought to love him into responsibility for a just punishment, then there was no hope for him in all this vast gleam of silence.

Where Saturn
Keeps the Years

You must see Helen Ward in her moment. It is that moment of blood and decision which makes her years of achievement intelligible, alas—which makes visible the ghastly halo she wears through her continuing service. She goes on, Helen, doing what she was trained to do. We are told she is one of the most respected pediatricians in Albany.

Helen was Amy Ward's daughter, and that in itself will have to explain why she was the first and only member of the Ward kin to become a doctor or, in fact, any sort of professional person. The Wards are good people, most of them, industrious, capable, and dependable, but they are essentially contented people. A couple of generations back they began to move into our little county seat town from the farms down toward the Missouri border and now they are installed here as proprietors of garages, dealers in farm implements and repair, beauty parlor operators, and rural mail carriers. Frank has the propane dealership for Hackett township, and two of his daughters are high school teachers. They have clung to the Methodist church, taught Sunday school, been fervid supporters of the high school athletic teams. Two of Helen's uncles went to Africa as missionaries in the thirties, and a cousin served a prison term for reviving the old crime of cattle rustling, stealing not only twenty-seven head of beef from feed lots across the state but the van in which he was hauling them to Kansas City for sale.

Deviants from a stock that has mostly bred true—bred true and married their kind, except Amy, who bore twin boys and Helen to Alvin Ward. Amy was a farm girl from one of those families that was not about to leave the home place until after the war when the banks and insurance companies bought up the worst land in the county, junked the houses and barns, and turned all the hopeless family farms into grazing land again. By then Amy had her children, but having come off the farm she was not as content as Wards are supposed to be to think that Chesterfield was the end of the migration. From that clay farm she'd brought a vision of the world and her responsibilities to see that it was run right. True, she taught in the Methodist Sunday school like her sisters-in-law—taught to eight- and ten-year-olds what most of their distressed parents would recognize as Communist doctrine about racial equality, the iniquity of the death penalty, and the treachery of Harry Truman in using the United Nations as a cover for imperialism in Korea.

"Amy *believes* these things," her husband defended her to his brothers, who thought that would have been all right if she just kept quiet about them at family dinners and didn't cause bad feelings in the church congregation "where, you know, Alvin, we got plenty of hard-shell old-timers that don't know they've come in from the farm, that still hanker for the old straight line gospel." Her in-laws might credit Amy for her "spunk"—but remembered that she herself had just come in from the farm. Amy had left high school to enlist for pilot training in the WACS during wartime and had failed at that. What made her so much smarter than the President of the United States and the editorial writers for the *Des Moines Register*? "You know, Alvin, it might make a little more sense, what Amy is crusading about, if there were any Negroes in Chesterfield, for an example," Floyd Ward thought. "Hell, there are not but three families of them in the whole county, I'm told. And I'm told nobody any more bothers them and they don't bother nobody."

Surely that was close to the way Alvin saw it, too, loyal husband though he might be. He was a troubled fellow when the Methodist minister had to arrange a showdown with Amy and relieve her of her duties as a Sunday school teacher. Alvin made the dignified compromise of ceasing his attendance at Methodist services, as of course Amy did too while the boys and Helen switched to the Congregational Sunday school, where they had as many friends as among the Methodists. And . . . is that all that's to be said about this almighty queer convulsion in which Amy Ward showed her colors—or not even her colors but something much more evanescent, the briefly twisting shadow of a banner on which there was surely more heraldry emblazoned than the trite old hammer and sickle some thought they recognized? From a perspective of thirty years that's all there is left to say.

And say it might have all faded, as so many inappropriate anguishes have faded into the anonymity of so many cross-grained circumstances in our town or in any town. The balance of most lives is close. Why shouldn't Amy have paid the price of being married to a good man like Alvin Ward and living her days with him in Chesterfield? There are compensations for submission as for rebellion, and fine women never lack an inkling this is so.

What got her out was an irrelevance. The year they were seventeen, her twin boys were killed in a car accident nine miles south of Chesterfield, just beyond where the gravel road on Swiss Ridge joins the blacktop. Tommy was driving. Tony was thrown clear as the loose gravel sent the car rolling down the hill toward the Rodney's barn, so at least he wasn't burned.

By the following spring Amy had decided she was going to college. In September she took Helen with her up to Iowa City and they never came back. Everyone, including probably Alvin, expected them back at least for the summer vacations, but he explained that first summer that Amy had found work in a bookstore near the campus and wanted to make the job permanent. By the next summer we knew she was living with another man up there and had quit her classes to support him and Helen. Doc Chader's son told that story, having his knowledge partly at secondhand from a poet he had roomed with before getting into the Medical School. "She is typing his thesis," Bob Chader said, with a tone of tolerant exasperation that may be obligatory in contemplating the fate of women at long range. "I don't know him but he's supposed to be some kind of radical Jew in the Writers' Workshop. And Amy is typing his novel besides working as a receptionist in this dentist's office."

As for Alvin, he moved to Seattle, where he got work with a utility company. Presently there was a divorce. To make things tidy, you might say.

I suppose some of the writers who have come and gone in Iowa City may have got Amy Ward into their published or unpublished works, since she went on as a character of some flamboyance for the next twenty years, involved perennially with "young people" in their moods and fashions of rebellion, achieving her greatest celebrity when the *Des Moines Register* ran a front page picture of her and some others stoning the car of the President of the University at the time of the Cambodian Incursion. "Same old Amy," Floyd Ward said when that photo lay before him on the kitchen table. His eyes twinkled mistily as he slurped his hot mid-morning coffee. You couldn't just say for sure he wasn't proud of having known her, having had her in the family. "Whatever you want to say about Amy, you can't say they beat her down, can you? Whatever you want to say about Amy, she's stuck it out, and she's put that girl through the Medical School. Can't everybody claim that kind of thing, you know."

They have strange, underground racial memories, these Wards. Loyalties much simpler than the crooked years that happen to us.

"First doctor there's ever been in the Ward family, by God," old Floyd said that morning. "That Amy! That Helen! I'd sure like to see that little girl again and shake her hand."

Helen came back when they brought her father home to bury him in the Methodist cemetery beside Floyd and their parents. Evidently she had not come expecting to be received as a member of the Ward family. At the funeral home where the relatives and old-time friends gathered on the night before the services to view the body, she seemed awkwardly startled that she had so many aunts, uncles, cousins, and shirt-tail relations who identified her in spite of her being unable to identify them. A tall, stocky young woman with rather sullen brown eyes beneath soft, untidy waves of brown hair, she stood uncomfortably with her arms folded across her chest while Floyd's daughter Marianne brought various kin to be recognized again after seventeen years. Stiffly Helen shook hands with them all and smiled at their greetings, but her eyes shifted furtively as if she had to keep track of the door through which she could escape if they turned on her as a pack. At least a dozen times she repeated that she had driven a rented car down from Des Moines after flying in from Albany.

"You do your practicing, then, in Albany?" they said respectfully.

"I'm a pediatrician, yes."

"Albany . . . isn't that where the Kasebiers moved to? I don't suppose you remember Vance Kasebier probably . . . or ever run into any of his family around Albany?"

"No."

"Well, there wouldn't have been any Kasebier kids in school in your time, but I'm pretty sure your daddy was friendly once with Vance."

"Yes," she said vaguely. She stayed well away from the open coffin where her father lay in gloomy profile against a satin pillow—as if she feared their curiosity about any emotion she might reveal, as if their curiosity about her father, mother, and herself could be kept in decent bounds only by her refusal to display any chink of emotion.

"I'm surely glad you could make it," her quavering Aunt Bess said, "what with being so busy and all. And you surely must be, in Albany, with so many little children needing you. I always thought you were your daddy's favorite, for I do remember when your brothers were lying there and Alvin hardly had the spirit to go on. And Alvin said, 'I'll go on for Helen, my little Helen.' And he would be—*was*—so proud of you for all you've accomplished. . . ."

"Yes," Helen said, her arms folded tight across her stocky chest.

But they got to her, of course, and the next morning in the dappled autumn light of the cemetery she and Marianne stood weeping with their arms around each other in front of the gleaming coffin and the rows of flowers. The wind made the minister's cheeks flush pink and teased a lock of his gray hair as he said, here again, "I am persuaded that neither life nor death, nor heights nor depths, nor powers and principalities can separate us from the love of Jesus Christ. . . ."

"I *am* persuaded," Helen said, letting go of Marianne's shoulders as they turned to walk hesitantly, confidently back up the slope to the undertaker's limousine. "Isn't it *funny?*" she said through her sloppy tears. She set her feet for a moment to look around among the shedding trees, to the yellow cornfields beyond, the lace of willows along the creek, and the silhouette of our town. At the Chevrolets, Fords, and Plymouths to which the Wards and their townsmen were slowly returning across the brittle grass. "Isn't it funny that it *does* persuade you?" She took Marianne's hand in a fumbling grip, smiling, holding her eyes.

"I know just what you mean," Marianne said huskily.

Later, after the luncheon served in the Methodist Church basement by the Ladies Aid, Marianne and her husband took Helen home with them for the hour she could spare before driving back to Des Moines. They gave her a Bloody Mary in the kitchen, and suddenly there was much too much for them all to talk about. The years were on them like mysterious baggage they had carried to this moment when it must all be opened, spilled out, rearranged and at last explained. The grade school and high school that Helen and Marianne and Marianne's husband Phil had attended, though in different years, the county fairs, the toys and bicycles and cars owned by everyone they had ever known, the Girl Scout troop and the bus trip to the Iowa-Minnesota game when Bud Schooper had puked his popcorn on the typing teacher. And beyond those ranks of easier memories, the ridiculous; grim memories of family anguish—even Amy's notorious Communist proselytizing of the tikes in Sunday school.

"I'd never say that Mom had a great life," Helen thought, her heavy brown eyes shining between reverence and joy and melancholy. "And Dad—oh, hell, of course she spoiled it all for him. But maybe you just *can't* spoil it. Last night before I went to sleep—and this morning with the silly coffin shut on him—I thought, well, there's just no way to spoil it all. I thought: He's had a great life, too."

"No way," Phil nodded, smiling to himself.

"I know just what you mean," Marianne said.

When they walked out into the chilly yard to put her in her rented car, Marianne said, "Don't make such a stranger of yourself, Helen. You've been away too long. You come back to see us now, you hear? I'm sorry the children are back in school this afternoon. You didn't get a chance, really, to get acquainted with them at all. So you just have to come back."

As she and Phil watched the Pontiac turn the corner of the block and disappear she said moodily, "I don't suppose we'll ever see her again, do you?"

"Ever's a long time," he said.

So Helen came back one more time, though it was four years later. She had taken a late September vacation at Aspen. She called Marianne from North Platte, Nebraska, to say she was driving home and would like to stop over for a night to say hello and to visit the cemetery.

"Why not a couple of nights? Three or four?" Marianne asked in the enthusiasm of her surprise.

"I *could*," Helen said. "I'm not expected in Albany before Monday."

This much concession permitted the momentum necessary for Marianne to arrange what she called a "big" family dinner (or a "big family" dinner) the evening after Helen drove in. "I sure didn't ask everyone who'd love to spend some time with you. But we're going to have to set up a couple of tables in the hall for the kids as it is," Marianne said. "I didn't ask Aunt Till and Bert because she's so set against booze and we've got some nice red wine in the ice box I just made up my mind I was going to serve. But Aunt Till was pretty excited to know you'd been in Aspen and you could stop by to see her in the morning. And though we'll have a houseful you can for sure ask Milly Glosser if you want. Wasn't she your big buddy in eighth grade and she was just sick she missed you when you came for your dad's funeral?"

"No," Helen thought. "Why not just family? I'm not good at talking to old friends." She was pleased, nevertheless, by the sheer, unshadowed vigor of the welcome, her usually taciturn face softened by amusement at Marianne's preparations.

"Well, you know, you're *somebody* for all of us," Marianne insisted. "Maybe you wouldn't call it famous, but . . . I wish I had the gumption to get out of Chesterfield."

"You've got a good life here."

"I serve wine with my dinner once a year? Oh, I know, I know, I know, Helen. But, you know, the universal complaint. . . ."

"I'm just a hard-working doctor. There's not much glamor to it. I don't know if it fulfills me. I used to ask questions like that in college. You have compensations and I have compensations for what we've missed. What else is there to say?"

But there was a lingering, hungry anxiety in Marianne's eyes for—for what wasn't *there* to be said. And her children were naturally pumping with less restraint for shreds of legend or romance. Nine-year-old Arlene nerved herself to ask if Cousin Helen had ever dee-livered a baby. ("I'll dee-liver you if you don't get that front room vacuumed," Marianne warned with a fond whack on the child's rump.)

"I *have*," Helen told the child gravely, "but mostly I give pills and injections and try to *think* what might be wrong with sick children."

"Was it . . . messy?" Arlene's face burned like fire.

"Oh! Out!" her mother said. "Please do your chores *now*."

"It was . . . kind of messy," Helen said. "Maybe nature is messy. Depends on how you look at it. But having a baby is natural, too. It's nothing to be afraid of." And with that tentative reassurance Arlene scampered to hook up the vacuum, while Billy and Brenda came in their turn to ask if Cousin Helen had seen John Denver while she was in Aspen.

"I thought I saw him one day coming out of the post office."

"Did he seem stuck up?" Brenda wondered.

"I'd be stuck up," Billy said. "I'd charge people a dime apiece for autographs."

"You've got such big ears, who'd want your autograph?" his mother teased. "Maybe you should study real hard and be a doctor like Cousin Helen."

His eyes narrowed slyly as if he saw to the very bottom of that trap. "Naa. I'd rather be John Denver and live in the mountains and fish for trout. D'you fish at *all* while you were at Aspen?"

Cousin Helen was sorry to disappoint him, but at least she could tell him about going on a jeep trail into the mountains, and the hawks circling so high, so high above the bright and dying leaves of the aspens. "And I bought some little Indian souvenirs I'll give you kids before I leave," she promised.

And what she promised, in so many words, seemed neither too little nor quite enough to the boy who stared guessingly into her face.

What did she have to tell any of them—the family from whom she had been removed so far—as she sat at the head of the table in Marianne's dining room? There were ten other adults at the same table and no less than fourteen youngsters at the two other tables Marianne had set in makeshift proximity where the dining room opened into the living room. The young folk of course were paying no attention now to anything she might say. Some one of them had even turned on the television beside the farthest table and they were listening to a game show that made a perfectly audible accompaniment to conversation at the adult's table. An undercadence of swift one-liners, yawps, and shrieks, not all of them from the instrument.

What had she brought them from the years, to be declared from her place of honor, sitting in a gray, mannish suit, sipping her chilled red wine and trying to respond to their warmth without too much reserve? "It was the best time of year for me to go to Aspen," she was saying. "The summer tourists were gone. The winter crowd that comes for the skiing hasn't showed up yet."

"I know just what you mean," said Marianne, who was never happier than in the midst of a crowd.

As if she had been caught in a confession and was being rebuked, Helen said to her—to them all—"It isn't that I don't like people. I'd better in my profession. For sure. But there I had it kind of all to myself, at least when I packed myself a little picnic lunch and hiked off the trail into the mountains. And, oh, I found my own little waterfall. That is, it wasn't mine, but I couldn't see a thing or hear a sound but the wind and the water rushing down. Do you know what I did? I sure stretched out on a rock in the sun. I didn't mean to sleep, but I fell asleep for hours and woke up not only not knowing where I was but who I was, can you believe it?"

Marianne was getting ready to say she knew exactly what this meant when her husband Phil lunged up from the table and almost upset the chair of his aunt, sitting next to him, as he galloped for the living room where now—above the idiot babble of the television—the idiot horror of children's shrieks, grunts, moans, beseeching roared through the house.

It was young Billy choking, startled into laughter by something said on the television just as he was beginning to chew a piece of beef. Now with his elbows flailing he was fighting away the other children while his head went arching back in a hopeless reach for air.

His father waded in to give a powerful whack on the shoulders, then shook him, pried his mouth open with one hand and reached in a forefinger of the other. "Ray!" Phil screeched for his brother, and Ray was there. To help.

To help! Between the two men they hoisted Billy, coiling and writhing in reptilian agony between them, holding him head down while his father hammered repeatedly on his back.

Then Helen was there, as she had to be. As if all this had been everlastingly appointed, and it was design, not luck, that in this moment of absolute need the Wards had someone trained to step between them and what must not befall.

She was there to—oh, to clarify the design their lives invisibly made, and as she moved decisively to take over, her big hands gave tugs to which the despairing men responded quickly enough. They let her take Billy, encircle him from behind with a fist in his stomach and her other hand grasping the wrist on which maximum and instant pressure must be exerted. When she jerked first, his head came back like a hammer, striking her in the mouth and drawing a faint squirt of blood from her lip.

She jerked again brutally. "Killing him," Arlene screamed, pissing on her legs.

"Knife! Knife! Knife from the kitchen!" Helen said in a harsh, clear voice to his father. To his uncle she commanded, "Get him *down!*"

She had straddled the boy's chest, pinning his shoulders with her knees when Phil came thundering back from the kitchen with six butcher and paring knives in his two hands. "Hold his head. Get your fingers in his mouth and hold him *hard*. Get his ears," she commanded father and uncle. "Someone sit on his legs. Quick!" She hiked back her skirt and again shuffled on the rearing body as the throat was exposed, curving upward as she made her poor selection from among the knives.

She closed her eyes while she took two steadying breaths.

And the years crowded to watch while she took everything on herself—her brothers burned and flung from the uncontrollable car, her father baffled and dismissed, her mother danced away by dreams of brotherhood and peace—and all the watching Wards who waited to see what it meant.

Her left hand did its business of placing the thorax and straining the skin. The knife point went in with savagery and restraint so delicately balanced that surely it was a miracle.

In that silence of abrogated time they all—all!—heard the blood-bubbling hiss of air sucked in. Air expelled. Something that was sacrament and air and slime sucked howling in.

"Love ya, boy. Love ya!" Billy's father cried encouragement at the purpling face that still fought his grip.

"Get my bag from the car," Helen yelled in a voice so brazen and impersonal that for a moment at least, the sense of what she meant was unintelligible to any of those crowding back, crowding forward in an intensity of animal sympathy for the enactment. "Run!" she bellowed. And now she must loosen her grip to twist and see if anyone was obeying. "Please run get my *black* bag from the car. Oh, call a doctor, ambulance. . . ."

Did she already know she had lost when the words formed just that way in her own breath and stricken mouth—when she, as any of them might have done, called for a *doctor?* If she did, she did not admit it then or later. She had a tube in her improvised tracheotomy and had Billy restrained on the kitchen table and mercifully freed from pain before Dr. Simms got there.

And did what he could to help. Not a lot. What was there for him to contribute, beyond admitting that Helen was a better doctor than he and assuring Marianne and Phil and all the Wards that never in his imaginable lifetime would he have found the courage to do what she had done. The only thing that could have been done.

They got the piece of meat out of Billy's throat before he died. Found or confirmed the obvious truth that it was too firmly insinuated to have been blown out by the standard maneuver Helen had tried first.

"Helen gave him a chance. That's all," Dr. Simms said. "We— *she*—held him a few hours at least. There was too much blood in his lungs finally. We couldn't stop it in time. You folks have to understand. Have to understand. She's a great woman."

"I know just what you mean," Marianne said, in a grief that had to be shaped somehow.

Words have their occasions, and surely Dr. Simms found the right occasion to label Helen a great woman. For the occasion the word helped, and for the eternity of that moment when Helen came home to define herself the word may be obligatory.

Whatever greatness she had put on did not see her through or give her strength enough to stay in town for Billy's funeral. Strength of some sort permitted her to drive out of town in her own car. She drove as far as Des Moines and there, as we learned later, put herself under a doctor's care. I believe no one of us ever learned or bothered to learn that doctor's name. What matters is that she submitted herself to the routine and discipline that permits continuation after such an ordeal as hers.

Presently she resumed her own proper place in that routine, after rationally administered drugs and other therapy had blocked and distanced the enormity that no one, perhaps, can bear in full consciousness.

It is good, surely, that she has continued her practice among those who are effectively strangers to us and who, as circumstances determine, are not so much strangers to her as her kin and townspeople are.

Here we are obliged to say we understand what happened. If we did not hold onto certain charitable words, we would understand nothing, nothing at all of what surely happened that evening on the bloody floor. Helen was great. She lost. We have no words to accommodate the event, unless those be enough.

R. V. Cassill was born in Cedar Falls, Iowa, in 1919. Author of twenty-two novels and four previous collections of short stories, Cassill has received Fulbright, Rockefeller, and Guggenheim fellowships. He has taught at the University of Iowa in Iowa City and at Brown University. Professor Emeritus at Brown University, Cassill edited both the *Norton Anthology of Short Fiction* and the *Norton Anthology of Contemporary Fiction*. He lives in Providence, Rhode Island.